13
SHORT
FANTASY
NOVELS

ABOUT THE EDITORS

ISAAC ASIMOV, one of America's great resources, recently celebrated the publication of his 300th book. No other writer in history has published so much on such a wide variety of subjects, which range from science fiction and murder novels to books on history, the physical sciences, and Shakespeare. Born in the Soviet Union and raised in Brooklyn, he lives in New York City with his wife, electric typewriter, and word processor. He recently achieved best-seller status with both *Foundation's Edge,* the 1982 Hugo Award winner for Best Novel, and *The Robots of Dawn.*

MARTIN H. GREENBERG, who has been called "the king of the anthologists," now has some 105 to his credit. He is also coeditor, with Bill Pronzini, of *Baker's Dozen: 13 Short Mystery Novels* (published by Greenwich House). Greenberg is professor of regional analysis and political science at the University of Wisconsin-Green Bay, where he also teaches a course in the history of science fiction.

CHARLES G. WAUGH, a professor of psychology and mass communications at the University of Maine at Augusta, is a leading authority on science fiction and fantasy who has collaborated on 75 anthologies and single-author collections with Isaac Asimov, Martin H. Greenberg, and assorted colleagues.

13 SHORT FANTASY NOVELS

PRESENTED BY ISAAC ASIMOV

Edited by
Isaac Asimov,
Martin H. Greenberg,
and Charles Waugh

With an Introduction by
Isaac Asimov

GREENWICH HOUSE
Distributed by Crown Publishers, Inc.
New York

Sleep Well of Nights by Avram Davidson originally appeared under the title
A Good Night's Sleep.
Storm in a Bottle by John Jakes originally appeared under the title
The Mirror of Wizardry.

This 1984 edition is published by Greenwich House, a division of Arlington House, Inc., distributed by Crown Publishers, Inc., by arrangement with Nightfall, Inc., Martin H. Greenberg and Charles G. Waugh.

Manufactured in the United States of America

Library of Congress Cataloging in Publication Data
Main entry under title:

Baker's dozen : thirteen short fantasy novels.

1. Fantastic fiction, American. 2. Fantastic fiction, English.
I. Asimov, Isaac, 1920–   . II. Greenberg, Martin Harry. III. Waugh, Charles.
PS648.F3B35 1984 813'.0876'08 84-6310
ISBN 0-517-44500X

h g f e d c b a

CONTENTS

INTRODUCTION

Larger Than Life
Isaac Asimov

How we love things that are larger than life! We insist upon them!
I don't know why that should be, but, after all, we each of us started life as infants, and that may contribute part of the explanation. Our baby universe was filled with mother and father, who were far, far stronger than we were and possessed powers of such vague magnitude that they were effectively infinite. It was to them we turned for satisfaction and protection and it may be that our first great disillusionment in life was the realization that they were not larger than life after all. As we get larger, and stronger, and, perhaps, wiser, we cannot avoid reaching that conclusion, however reluctantly.

No matter how we close our eyes to the truth, our parents *will* grow old and feeble and come to depend on us, and then, in ultimate betrayal, they will die, even if they avoid accident, and no matter how well we care for them.

We cannot replace them. Nothing else is quite like the mother and father we knew in childhood. But we cannot make do without them, either, so we fall back on our imagination.

I wonder to what extent the myriads of gods that humanity has invented owe their existence to the necessity of possessing fathers and mothers who are *forever* larger than life and who will *never* betray their role by falling into impotence and death as human fathers and mothers do.

Deities grow too perfect, though, and distance themselves from humanity to the point where they become etherealized into insubstantiality. For literary purposes, the demigod is more satisfactory. He is larger than life, yes, but not so much so that he cannot suffer pain and occasional defeat. He is larger than life but *remains one of us*. (At that, even gods were most popular when they were human enough to suffer death, at least temporarily—Baldur, Tammuz, Adonis, and so on. To be sure, they symbolized the winter-death of vegetation, but the touch of humanity implicit in their death endeared them to their worshippers, and their eventual resurrection gave hope that death might after all be defeated and that separation by death might not be permanent.)

The first great epic we know of is about 5000 years old and is of Sumerian origin. It is the tale of Gilgamesh, king of Uruk, who is mightier and more daring than a human can be and with whom we can vicariously share greater-than-human deeds, run greater-than-human risks, and suffer greater-than-human torment. Each culture creates its own superhero. The Greeks had Heracles, the Hebrews had Samson, the Persians had Rustem, the Irish had Cuchulain. Each carved his way through a hostile world by means of his mighty thews which more than made up for his usually less-than-subtle mind.

Oh, occasionally a superhero vanquished because of the subtlety of his mind; witness Odysseus. Generally, though, if wisdom that was larger than life was required, it made itself manifest through a knowledge of magic, such as was the case with the Welsh Merlin or the Finnish Vainamoinen.

And no matter how accomplished the tales might be of wizards and tricksters, nothing moved readers like the men with mighty muscles. It was the immediacy of the hewing sword that counted, or it was that the ordinary reader could more easily identify with a strong muscle and a subtle mind — he could perhaps develop something like the first, but he gave up on the second.

Throughout history, the larger-than-life muscular heroes continued to invade the literary field. In the Middle Ages, we had King Arthur and his knights, with the ever-victorious Lancelot as the acme of an artificial chivalry that never existed in real life. And there was King Charlemagne and his paladins, with Roland as exemplar. (The subtle trickster who was shrewder than life also existed, as in Reynard the fox, Till Eulenspiegel, and so on, but, again, never held quite the same appeal.)

Then came the sad day when gunpowder ruled the world and muscles and armor were no longer of use; when a cowardly, weak-muscled, low-born wretch, by taking aim, could clang Sir Lancelot to earth with a neat little hole drilled in his breastplate.

Alas for heroic fantasy. Had it not died?

Modern literature makes up for that death by giving us other varieties of magnification. We still retain the shrewder-than-life protagonists of mystery novels — the Sherlock Holmeses and the Hercule Poirots. We have the more-beautiful-than-life heroines and heroes of romances, and the more-dreadful-than-life menaces of the Gothics and the horror tales, and so on, indefinitely. We even make use of gunpowder for the purpose by inventing the faster-than-life Western hero, who punctures the villain even after allowing him to begin his draw first.

But nothing substitutes for the more direct form of violence. In every form of literature we end up with fistfights — a form of combat that is met with surprisingly seldom in real life. Detectives fight, Western heroes flail away, romantic lovers indulge in pugilistic displays. This is especially true in movies and television where they leave no bruises and muss no hair, though the sound of bone on bone is deafening.

But even that is not enough. We still want the old pregunpowder days, when mighty biceps were needed to raise mighty swords and when the hero had to find a way of defeating sorcery with nothing but brute muscle at his disposal.

So why not write the story? It doesn't have to be in the present world, does it? It can be in the past. In fact, it doesn't even have to be in the real past where it will be bound (however faintly) by known historical facts. Create a world of medieval civilization immersed in a sea of barbarism, and bring forth Heracles anew. You have "sword and sorcery." You have "heroic fantasy." You have all the dreams back.

Or you can add a little spice and variety to the mix. You can add a touch of advanced science, a soupçon of deliberate anachronism, a sprinkle of wry humor. The variations are endless and the opportunities for the freewheeling imagination are infinite.

Here, in this fat book, we have thirteen short fantasy novels long enough to give their authors scope to invent intricate societies in which to display larger-than-life heroes and heroines, facing larger-than-life evils and cruelties, suffering larger-than-life defeats, and winning larger-than-life triumphs.

You, caught amid it all, will live it all with them, and enjoy larger-than-life pleasures.

Remember, it's the oldest form of literature in the world, as old as Gilgamesh; and older, too, for heroes and heroics were probably celebrated by bards about campfires through the thousands of years before writing was invented and probably ever since Homo sapiens has existed.

After all, from the very beginning of human history parents died—and had to be replaced.

POUL ANDERSON
The Gate of the Flying Knives

AGAIN PENNILESS, houseless, and ladyless, Capen Varra made a brave sight just the same as he wove his way amidst the bazaar throng. After all, until today he had for some weeks been in, if not quite of, the household of Molin Torchholder, as much as he could contrive. Besides the dear presence of ancilla Danlis, he had received generous reward from the priest-engineer whenever he sang a song or composed a poem. That situation had changed with suddenness and terror, but he still wore a bright green tunic, scarlet cloak, canary hose, soft half-boots trimmed in silver, and plumed beret. Though naturally heartsick at what had happened, full of dread for his darling, he saw no reason to sell the garb yet. He could raise enough money in various ways to live on while he searched for her. If need be, as often before, he could pawn the harp that a goldsmith was presently redecorating.

If his quest had not succeeded by the time he was reduced to rags, then he would have to suppose Danlis and the Lady Rosanda were forever lost. But he had never been one to grieve over future sorrows.

Beneath a westering sun, the bazaar surged and clamored. Merchants, artisans, porters, servants, slaves, wives, nomads, courtesans, entertainers, beggars, thieves, gamblers, magicians, acolytes, soldiers, and who knew what else mingled, chattered, chaffered, quarreled, plotted, sang, played games, drank, ate, and who knew what else. Horsemen, cameldrivers, wagoners pushed through, raising waves of curses. Music tinkled and tweedled from wineships. Vendors proclaimed the wonders of their wares from booths, neighbors shouted at each other, and devotees chanted from flat rooftops. Smells thickened the air, of flesh, sweat, roast meat and nuts, aromatic drinks, leather, wool, dung, smoke, oils, cheap perfume.

5

Ordinarily, Cappen Varra enjoyed this shabby-colorful spectacle. Now he single-mindedly hunted through it. He kept full awareness, of course, as everybody must in Sanctuary. When light fingers brushed him, he knew. But whereas aforetime he would have chuckled and told the pickpurse, "I'm sorry, friend; I was hoping I might lift somewhat off you," at this hour he clapped his sword in such forbidding wise that the fellow recoiled against a fat woman and made her drop a brass tray full of flowers. She screamed and started beating him over the head with it.

Cappen didn't stay to watch.

On the eastern edge of the marketplace he found what he wanted. Once more Illyra was in the bad graces of her colleagues and had moved her trade to a stall available elsewhere. Black curtains framed it, against a mud-brick wall. Reek from a nearby tannery well-nigh drowned the incense she burned in a curious holder, and would surely overwhelm any of her herbs. She herself also lacked awesomeness, such as most seeresses, mages, conjurers, scryers, and the like affected. She was too young; she would have looked almost wistful in her flowing, gaudy S'danzo garments, had she not been so beautiful.

Cappen gave her a bow in the manner of Caronne. "Good day, Illyra the lovely," he said.

She smiled from the cushion whereon she sat. "Good day to you, Cappen Varra." They had had a number of talks, usually in jest, and he had sung for her entertainment. He had hankered to do more than that, but she seemed to keep all men at a certain distance, and a hulk of a blacksmith who evidently adored her saw to it that they respected her wish.

"Nobody in these parts has met you for a fair while" she remarked. "What fortune was great enough to make you forget old friends?"

"My fortune was mingled, inasmuch as it left me without time to come down here and behold you, my sweet," he answered out of habit.

Lightness departed from Illyra. In the olive countenance, under the chestnut mane, large eyes focused hard on her visitor. "You find time when you need help in disaster," she said.

He had not patronized her before, or indeed any fortune-teller of thaumaturge in Sanctuary. In Caronne, where he grew up, most folk had no use for magic. In his later wanderings he had encountered sufficient strangeness to temper his native skepticism. As shaken as he already was, he felt a chill go along his spine. "Do you read my fate without even casting a spell?"

She smiled afresh, but bleakly. "Oh, no. It's simple reason. Word did filter back to the Maze that you were residing in the Jewelers' Quarter and a frequent guest at the mansion of Molin Torchholder. When you appear on the heels of a new word—that last night his wife was reaved from him—plain to see is that you've been affected yourself."

He nodded. "Yes, and sore afflicted. I have lost—" He hesitated, unsure whether it would be quite wise to say, "—my love" to this girl whose charms he had rather extravagantly praised.

"—your position and income," Illyra snapped. "The high priest cannot be in any mood for minstrelsy. I'd guess his wife favored you most, anyhow. I need not guess you spent your earnings as fast as they fell to you, or faster, were behind in your rent, and were accordingly kicked out of your choice apartment as soon as rumor reached the landlord. You've returned to the Maze because you've no place else to go, and to me in hopes you can wheedle me into giving you a clue—for if you're instrumental in recovering the lady, you'll likewise recover your fortune, and more."

"No, no, no," he protested. "You wrong me."

"The high priest will appeal only to his Rankan gods," Illyra said, her tone changing from exasperated to thoughtful. She stroked her chin. "He, kinsman of the Emperor, here to direct the building of a temple which will overtop that of Ils, can hardly beg aid from the old gods of Sanctuary, let alone from our wizards, witches, and seers. But you, who belong to no part of the empire, who drifted hither from a kingdom far in the West . . . you may seek anywhere. The idea is your own; else he would furtively have slipped you some gold, and you have engaged a diviner with more reputation than is mine."

Cappen spread his hands. "You reason eerily well, dear lass," he conceded. "Only about the motives are you mistaken. Oh, yes, I'd be glad to stand high in Molin's esteem, be richly rewarded, and so forth. Yet I feel for him; beneath that sternness of his, he's not a bad sort, and he bleeds. Still more do I feel for his lady, who was indeed kind to me and who's been snatched away to an unknown place. But before all else—" He grew quite earnest. "The Lady Rosanda was not seized by herself. Her ancilla has also vanished, Danlis. And—Danlis is she whom I love, Illyra, she whom I meant to wed."

The maiden's look probed him further. She saw a young man of medium height, slender but tough and agile. (That was due to the life he had had to lead; by nature he was indolent, except in bed.) His features were thin and regular on a long skull, clean-shaven, eyes bright blue, black hair banged and falling to the shoulders. His voice gave the language a melodious accent, as if to bespeak white cities, green fields and woods, quicksilver lakes, blue sea, of the homeland he left in search of his fortune.

"Well, you have charm, Cappen Varra," she murmured, "and how you do know it." Alert: "But coin you lack. How do you propose to pay me?"

"I fear you must work on speculation, as I do myself," he said. "If our joint efforts lead to a rescue, why, then we'll share whatever material reward may come. Your part might buy you a home on the Path of Money." She frowned. "True," he went on, "I'll get more than my share of the immediate bounty that Molin bestows. I will have my beloved back. I'll also regain the priest's favor, which is moderately lucrative. Yet consider. You need but practice your art. Thereafter any effort and risk will be mine."

"What makes you suppose a humble fortune-teller can learn more than the Prince Governant's investigator guardsmen?" she demanded.

"The matter does not seem to lie within their jurisdiction," he replied.

She leaned forward, tense beneath the layers of clothing. Cappen bent toward her. It was as if the babble of the marketplace receded, leaving these two alone with their wariness.

"I was not there," he said low, "but I arrived early this morning after the thing had happened. What's gone through the city has been rumor, leakage that cannot be calked, household servants blabbing to friends outside and they blabbing onward. Molin's locked away most of the facts till he can discover what they mean, if ever he can. I, however, I came on the scene while chaos still prevailed. Nobody kept me from talking to folk, before the lord himself saw me and told me to begone. Thus I know about as much as anyone, little though that be."

"And—?" she prompted.

"And it doesn't seem to have been a worldly sort of capture, for a worldly end like ransom. See you, the mansion's well guarded, and neither Molin nor his wife have ever gone from it without escort. His mission here is less than popular, you recall. Those troopers are from Ranke and not subornable. The house stands in a garden, inside a high wall whose top is patrolled. Three leopards run loose on the grounds after dark.

"Molin had business with his kinsman the Prince, and spent the night at the palace. His wife, the Lady Rosanda, stayed home, retired, later came out and complained she could not sleep. She therefore had Danlis wakened. Danlis is no chambermaid; there are plenty of those. She's amanuensis, adviser, confidante, collector of information, ofttimes guide or interpreter—oh, she earns her pay, does my Danlis. Despite she and I having a dawntide engagement, which is why I arrived then, she must now out of bed at Rosanda's whim, to hold milady's hand or take dictation of milady's letters or read to milady from a soothing book—but I'm a spendthrift of words. Suffice to say that they two sought an upper chamber which is furnished as both solarium and office. A single staircase leads thither, and it is the single room at the top. There is a balcony, yes; and, the night being warm, the door to it stood open, as well as the windows. But I inspected the façade beneath. That's sheer marble, undecorated save for varying colors, devoid of ivy or of anything that any climber might cling to, save he were a fly.

"Nevertheless . . . just before the east grew pale, shrieks were heard, the watch pelted to the stair and up it. They must break down the inner door, which was bolted. I suppose that was merely against chance interruptions, for nobody had felt threatened. The solarium was in disarray; vases and things were broken; shreds torn off a robe and slight traces of blood lay about. Aye, Danlis, at least, would have resisted. But she and her mistress were gone.

"A couple of sentries on the garden wall reported hearing a loud sound as of wings. The night was cloudy-dark and they saw nothing for certain. Perhaps they imagined the noise. Suggestive is that the leopards were found cowering in a corner and welcomed their keeper when he would take them back to their cages.

"And this is the whole of anyone's knowledge, Illyra," Cappen ended. "Help me, I pray you, help me get back my love!"

She was long quiet. Finally she said, in a near whisper, "It could be a worse matter than I'd care to peer into, let alone enter."

"Or it could not," Cappen urged.

She gave him a quasi-defiant stare. "My mother's people reckon it unlucky to do any service for a Shavakh—a person not of their tribe—without recompense. Pledges don't count."

Cappen scowled. "Well, I could go to a pawnshop and—But no, time may be worth more than rubies." From the depths of unhappiness, his grin broke forth. "Poems also are valuable, right? You S'danzo have your ballads and love ditties. Let me indite a poem, Illyra, that shall be yours alone."

Her expression quickened. "Truly?"

"Truly. Let me think. . . . Aye, we'll begin thus." And, venturing to take her hands in his, Cappen murmured:

My lady comes to me like break of day.

I dream in darkness if it chance she tarries,
Until the banner of her brightness harries
The hosts of Shadowland from off the way—

She jerked free and cried, "No! You scoundrel, that has to be something you did for Danlis—or for some earlier woman you wanted in your bed—"

"But it isn't finished," he argued. "I'll complete it for you, Illyra."

Anger left her. She shook her head, clicked her tongue, and sighed. "No matter. You're incurably yourself. And I . . . am only half S'danzo. I'll attempt your spell."

"By every love goddess I ever heard of," he promised unsteadily, "you shall indeed have your own poem after this is over."

"Be still," she ordered. "Fend off anybody who comes near."

He faced about and drew his sword. The slim, straight blade was hardly needed, for no other enterprise had site within several yards of hers, and as wide a stretch of paving lay between him and the fringes of the crowd. Still, to grasp the hilt gave him a sense of finally making progress. He had felt helpless for the first hours, hopeless, as if his dear had actually died instead of—of what? Behind him he heard cards riffled, dice cast, words softly wailed.

All at once Illyra strangled a shriek. He whirled about and saw how the blood had left her olive countenance, turning it grey. She hugged herself and shuddered.

"What's wrong?" he blurted in fresh terror.

She did not look at him. "Go away," she said in a thin voice. "Forget you ever knew that woman."

"But—but what—"

"Go away, I told you! Leave me alone!"

Then somehow she relented enough to let forth: "I don't know. I dare not know. I'm just a little half-breed girl who has a few cantrips and a tricksy second sight, and—and I saw that this business goes outside of space and time, and a power beyond any magic is there—Enas Yorl could tell more, but he himself—" Her courage broke. "Go away!" she screamed. "Before I shout for Dubro and his hammer!"

"I beg your pardon," Cappen Varra said, and made haste to obey.

He retreated into the twisting streets of the Maze. They were narrow; most of the mean buildings around him were high; gloom already filled the quarter. It was as if he had stumbled into the same night where Danlis had gone . . . Danlis, creature of sun and horizons. . . . If she lived, did she remember their last time together as he remembered it, a dream dreamed centuries ago?

Having the day free, she had wanted to explore the countryside north of town. Cappen had objected on three counts. The first he did not mention; that it would require a good deal of effort, and he would get dusty and sweaty and saddle-sore. She despised men who were not at least as vigorous as she was, unless they compensated by being venerable and learned.

The second he hinted at. Sleazy though most of Sanctuary was, he knew places within it where a man and a woman could enjoy themselves, comfortably, privately—his apartment, for instance. She smiled her negation. Her family belonged to the old aristocracy of Ranke, not the newly rich, and she had been raised in its austere tradition. Albeit her father had fallen on evil times and she had been forced to take service, she kept her pride, and proudly would she yield her maidenhead to her bridegroom. Thus far she had answered Cappen's ardent declarations with the admission that she liked him and enjoyed his company and wished he would change the subject. (Buxom Lady Rosanda seemed as if she might be more approachable, but there he was careful to maintain a cheerful correctness.) He did believe she was getting beyond simple enjoyment, for her patrician reserve seemed less each time they saw each other. Yet she could not altogether have forgotten that he was merely the bastard of a minor nobleman in a remote country, himself disinherited and a footloose minstrel.

His third objection he dared say forth. While the hinterland was comparatively safe, Molin Torchholder would be furious did he learn that a woman of his household had gone escorted by a single armed man, and he no professional fighter. Molin would probably have been justified, too. Danlis smiled again and said, "I could ask a guardsman off duty to come along. But you have interesting friends, Cappen. Perhaps a warrior is among them?"

As a matter of fact, he knew any number, but doubted she would care to meet them—with a single exception. Luckily, Jamie the Red had no prior commitment, and agreed to join the party. Cappen told the kitchen staff to pack a picnic hamper for four.

Jamie's girls stayed behind; this was not their sort of outing, and the sun might harm their complexions. Cappen thought it a bit ungracious of the Northerner never to share them. That put him, Cappen, to considerable expense in the Street of Red Lanterns, since he could scarcely keep a paramour of his own while wooing Danlis. Otherwise he was fond of Jamie. They had met after Rosanda, chancing to hear the minstrel sing, had invited him to perform at the mansion, and then invited him back, and presently Cappen was living in the Jeweler's Quarter. Jamie had an apartment nearby.

Three horses and a pack mule clopped out of Sanctuary in the new-born morning, to a jingle of harness bells. That merriment found no echo in Cappen's head; he had been drinking past midnight, and in no case enjoyed rising before noon. Passive, he listened to Jamie:

"—Aye, milady, they're mountaineers where I hail from, poor folk but free folk. Some might call us barbarians, but that might be unwise in our hearing. For we've tales, songs, laws, ways, gods as old as any in the world, and as good. We lack much of your Southorn lore, but how much of ours do you ken? Not that I boast, please understand. I've seen wonders in my wanderings. But I do say we've a few wonders of our own at home."

"I'd like to hear of them," Danlis responded. "We know almost nothing about your country in the Empire—hardly more than mentions in the chronicles of Venafer and Mattathan, or the *Natural History* of Kahayavesh. How do you happen to come here?"

"Oh-ah, I'm a younger son of our king, and I thought I'd see a bit of the world before settling down. Not that I packed any wealth along to speak of. But what with one thing and another, hiring out hither and yon for this or that, I get by." Jamie paused. "You, uh, you've far more to tell, milady. You're from the crown city of the Empire, and you've got book learning, and at the same time you come out to see for yourself what land and rocks and plants and animals are like."

Cappen decided he had better get into the conversation. Not that Jamie would undercut a friend, nor Danlis be unduly attracted by a wild highlander. Nevertheless—

Jamie wasn't bad-looking in his fashion. He was huge, topping Cappen by a head and disproportionately wide in the shoulders. His loose-jointed appearance was deceptive, as the bard had learned when they sported in a public gymnasium; those were heavy bones and oak-hard muscles. A spectacular red mane drew attention from boyish face, mild blue eyes, and slightly diffident manner. Today he was plainly clad, in tunic and cross-gaitered breeks; but the knife at his belt and the ax at his saddlebow stood out.

As for Danlis, well, what could a poet do but struggle for words which might embody a ghost of her glory? She was tall and slender, her features almost cold in their straight-lined perfection and alabaster hue—till you observed the big grey eyes, golden hair piled on high, curve of lips whence came that husky voice. (How often he had lain awake yearning for her lips! He would console himself by remembering the strong, delicately blue-veined hand that she did let him kiss.) Despite waxing warmth and dust puffed up from the horses' hoofs, her cowled riding habit remained immaculate and no least dew of sweat was on her skin.

By the time Cappen got his wits out of the blankets wherein they had still been snoring, talk had turned to gods. Danlis was curious about those of Jamie's country, as she was about most things. (She did shun a few subjects as being unwholesome.) Jamie in his turn was eager to have her explain what was going on in Sanctuary. "I've heard but the one side of the matter, and Cappen's indifferent to it," he said. "Folk grumble about your master—Molin, is that his name—?"

"He is not my master," Danlis made clear. "I am a free woman who assists his wife. He himself is a high priest in Ranke, also an engineer."

"Why is the Emperor angering Sanctuary? Most places I've been, colonial governments know better. They leave the local gods be."

Danlis grew pensive. "Where shall I start? Doubtless you know that Sanctuary was originally a city of the kingdom of Ilsig. Hence it has built temples to the gods of Ilsig—notably Ils, Lord of Lords, and his queen Shipri the All-Mother, but likewise others—Anen of the Harvests, Thufir the tutelary of pilgrims—"

"But none to Shalpa, patron of thieves," Cappen put in, "though these days he has the most devotees of any."

Danlis ignored his jape. "Ranke was quite a different country, under quite different gods," she continued. "Chief of these are Savankala the Thunderer, his consort Sabellia, Lady of Stars, their son Vashanka the Tenslayer, and his sister and consort Azyuna—gods of storm and war. According to Venafer, it was they who made Ranke supreme at last. Mattathan is more prosaic and opines that the martial spirit they inculcated was responsible for the Rankan Empire finally taking Ilsig into itself."

"Yes, milady, yes, I've heard this," Jamie said, while Cappen reflected that if his beloved had a fault, it was her tendency to lecture.

"Sanctuary has changed from of yore," she proceeded. "It has become polyglot, turbulent, corrupt, a canker on the body politic. Among its most vicious elements are the proliferating alien cults, not to speak of necromancers, witches, charlatans, and similar predators on the people. The time is overpast to restore law here. Nothing less than the Imperium can do that. A necessary preliminary is the establishment of the Imperial deities, the gods of Ranke, for everyone to see: symbol, rallying point, and actual presence."

"But they *have* their temples," Jamie argued.

"Small, dingy, to accommodate Rankans, few of whom stay in the city for long," Danlis retorted. "What reverence does that inspire, for the pantheon and the state? No, the Emperor has decided that Savankala and Sabellia must have the greatest fane, the most richly endowed, in this entire province. Molin Torchholder will build and consecrate it. Then can the degenerates and warlocks be scourged out of Sanctuary. Afterward the Prince Government can handle common felons."

Cappen didn't expect matters would be that simple. He got no chance to say so, for Jamie asked at once, "Is this wise, milady? True, many a soul hereabouts worships foreign gods, or none. But many still adore the old gods of Ilsig. They look on your, uh, Savankala as an intruder. I intend no offense, but they do. They're outraged that he's to have a bigger and grander house than Ils of the Thousand Eyes. Some fear what Ils may do about it."

"I know," Danlis said. "I regret any distress caused, and I'm sure Lord Molin does too. Still, we must overcome the agents of darkness, before the disease that they are spreads throughout the Empire."

"Oh, no," Cappen managed to insert, "I've lived here awhile, mostly down in the Maze. I've had to do with a good many so-called magicians, of either sex or in between. They aren't that bad. Most I'd call pitiful. They just use their little deceptions to scrabble out what living they can, in this crumbly town where life has trapped them."

Danlis gave him a sharp glance. "You've told me people think ill of sorcery in Caronne," she said.

"They do," he admitted. "But that's because we incline to be rationalists, who consider nearly all magic a bag of tricks. Which is true. Why, I've learned a few sleights myself."

"You have?" Jamie rumbled in surprise.

"For amusement," Cappen said hastily, before Danlis could disapprove. "Some are quite elegant, virtual exercises in three-dimensional geometry." Seeing interest kindle in her, he added, "I studied mathematics in boyhood; my father, before he died, wanted me to have a gentleman's education. The main part has rusted away in me, but I remember useful or picturesque details."

"Well, give us a show, come luncheon time," Jamie proposed.

Cappen did, when they halted. That was on a hillside above the White Foal River. It wound gleaming through farmlands whose intense green denied that desert lurked on the rim of sight. The noonday sun baked strong odors out of the earth: humus, resin, juice of wild plants. A solitary plane tree graciously gave shade. Bees hummed.

After the meal, and after Danlis had scrambled off to get a closer look at a kind of lizard new to her, Cappen demonstrated his skill. She was especially taken—enchanted—by his geometric artifices. Like any Rankan lady, she carried a sewing kit in her gear; and being herself, she had writing materials along. Thus he could apply scissors and thread to paper. He showed how a single ring may be cut to produce two that are interlocked, and how a strip may be twisted to have but one surface and one edge, and whatever else he knew. Jamie watched with pleasure, if with less enthusiasm.

Observing how delight made her glow, Cappen was inspired to carry on the latest poem he was composing for her. It had been slower work than usual. He had the conceit, the motif, a comparison of her to the dawn, but hitherto only the first few lines had emerged, and no proper structure. In this moment—

> —the banner of her brightness harries
> The hosts of Shadowland from off the way
> That she now wills to tread—for what can stay
> The triumph of that radiance she carries?

Yes, it was clearly going to be a rondel. Therefore the next two lines were:

> My lady comes to me like break of day.
> I dream in darkness if it chance she tarries.

He had gotten that far when abruptly she said: "Cappen, this is such a fine excursion, such splendid scenery. I'd like to watch sunrise over the river tomorrow. Will you escort me?"

Sunrise? But she was telling Jamie, "We need not trouble you about that. I had in mind a walk out of town to the bridge. If we choose the proper route, it's well guarded everywhere, perfectly safe."

And scant traffic moved at that hour; besides, the monumental statues along the bridge stood in front of bays which they screened from passersby—"Oh, yes, indeed, Danlis, I'd love to," Cappen said. For such an opportunity, he could get up before cockcrow.

—When he reached the mansion, she had not been there.

Exhausted after his encounter with Illyra, Cappen hied him to the

Vulgar Unicorn and related his woes to One-Thumb. The big man had come on shift at the inn early, for a fellow boniface had not yet recovered from the effects of a dispute with a patron. (Shortly thereafter, the patron was found floating face down under a pier. Nobody questioned One-Thumb about this; his regulars knew that he preferred the establishment safe, if not always orderly.) He offered taciturn sympathy and the loan of a bed upstairs. Cappen scarcely noticed the insects that shared it.

Waking about sunset, he found water and a washcloth, and felt much refreshed—hungry and thirsty, too. He made his way to the taproom below. Dusk was blue in windows and open door, black under the rafters. Candles smeared weak light along counter and main board and on lesser tables at the walls. The air had grown cool, which allayed the stenches of the Maze. Thus Cappen was acutely aware of the smells of beer—old in the rushes underfoot, fresh where a trio of men had settled down to guzzle—and of spitted meat, wafting from the kitchen.

One-Thumb approached, a shadowy hulk save for highlights on his bald pate. "Sit," he grunted. "Eat. Drink." He carried a great tankard and a plate bearing a slab of roast beef on bread. These he put on a corner table, and himself on a chair.

Cappen sat also and attacked the meal. "You're very kind," he said between bites and draughts.

"You'll pay when you get coin, or if you don't, then in songs and magic stunts. They're good for trade." One-Thumb fell silent and peered at his guest.

When Cappen was done, the innkeeper said, "While you slept, I sent out a couple of fellows to ask around. Maybe somebody saw something that might be helpful. Don't worry—I didn't mention you, and it's natural I'd be interested to know what really happened."

The minstrel stared. "You've gone to a deal of trouble on my account."

"I told you, I want to know for my own sake. If deviltry's afoot, where could it strike next?" One-Thumb rubbed a finger across the toothless part of his gums. "Of course, if you should luck out—I don't expect it, but in case you do—remember who gave you a boost." A figure appeared in the door and he went to render service.

After a bit of muttered talk, he led the newcomer to Cappen's place. When the minstrel recognized the lean youth, his pulse leaped. One-Thumb would not have brought him and Hanse together without cause; bard and thief found each other insufferable. They nodded coldly but did not speak until the tapster returned with a round of ale.

When the three were seated, One-Thumb said, "Well spit it out, boy. You claim you've got news."

"For him?" Hanse flared, gesturing at Cappen.

"Never mind who. Just talk."

Hanse scowled. "I don't talk for a single lousy mugful."

"You do if you want to keep on coming in here."

Hanse bit his lip. The Vulgar Unicorn was a rendezvous virtually indispensable to one in his trade.

Cappen thought best to sweeten the pill: "I'm known to Molin Torchholder. If I can serve him in this matter, he won't be stingy. Nor will I. Shall we say—hm—ten gold royals to you?"

The sum was not princely, but on that account plausible. "Awright, awright," Hanse replied. "I'd been casing a job I might do in the Jewelers' Quarter. A squad of the watch came by toward morning and I figured I'd better go home, not by the way I came, either. So I went along the Avenue of Temples, as I might be wanting to stop in and pay my respects to some god or other. It was a dark night, overcast, the reason I'd been out where I was. But you know how several of the temples keep lights going. There was enough to see by, even upward a ways. Nobody else was in sight. Suddenly I heard a kind of whistling, flapping noise aloft. I looked and—"

He broke off.

"And what?" Cappen blurted. One-Thumb sat impassive.

Hanse swallowed. "I don't swear to this," he said. "It was still dim, you realize. I've wondered since if I didn't see wrong."

"What was it?" Cappen gripped the table edge till his fingernails whitened.

Hanse wet his throat and said in a rush: "What it *seemed* like was a huge black thing, almost like a snake, but bat-winged. It came streaking from, oh, more or less the direction of Molin's, I'd guess now that I think back. And it was aimed more or less toward the temple of Ils. There was something that dangled below, as it might be a human body or two. I didn't stay to watch, I ducked into the nearest alley and waited. When I came out, it was gone."

He knocked back his ale and rose. "That's all," he snapped. "I don't want to remember the sight any longer, and if anybody ever asks, I was never here tonight."

"Your story's worth a couple more drinks," One-Thumb invited.

"Another evening," Hanse demurred. "Right now I need a whore. Don't forget those ten royals, singer." He left, stiff-legged.

"Well," said the innkeeper after a silence, "what do you make of this latest?"

Cappen suppressed a shiver. His palms were cold. "I don't know, save that what we confront is not of our kind."

"You told me once you've got a charm against magic."

Cappen fingered the little silver amulet, in the form of a coiled snake, he wore around his neck. "I'm not sure. A wizard I'd done a favor for gave me this, years ago. He claimed it'd protect me against spells and supernatural beings of less than godly rank. But to make it work, I have to utter three truths about the spellcaster or the creature. I've done that in two or three scrapes, and come out of them intact, but I can't prove the talisman was responsible."

More customers entered, and One-Thumb must go to serve them. Cappen nursed his ale. He yearned to get drunk and belike the landlord would stand him what was needful, but he didn't dare. He had already learned more than he thought the opposition would approve of—whoever or whatever the opposition was. They might have means of discovering this.

His candle flickered. He glanced up and saw a beardless fat man in an ornate formal robe, scarcely normal dress for a visit to the Vulgar Unicorn. "Greeting," the person said. His voice was like a child's.

Cappen squinted through the gloom. "I don't believe I know you," he replied.

"No, but you will come to believe it, oh, yes, you will." The fat man sat down. One-Thumb came over and took an order for red wine—"a decent wine, mine host, a Zhanuvend or Baladach." Coin gleamed forth.

Cappen's heart thumped. "Enas Yorl?" he breathed.

The other nodded. "In the flesh, the all too mutable flesh. I do hope my curse strikes again soon. Almost any shape would be better than this. I hate being overweight. I'm a eunuch, too. The times I've been a woman were better than this."

"I'm sorry, sir," Cappen took care to say. Though he could not rid himself of the spell laid on him, Enas Yorl was a powerful thaumaturge, no mere prestidigitator.

"At least I've not been arbitrarily displaced. You can't imagine how annoying it is, suddenly to find oneself elsewhere, perhaps miles away. I was able to come here in proper wise, in my litter. Faugh, how can anyone voluntarily set shoes to these open sewers they call streets in the Maze?" The wine arrived. "Best we speak fast and to the point, young man, that we may finish and I get home before the next contretemps."

Enas Yorl sipped and made a face. "I've been swindled," he whined. "This is barely drinkable, if that."

"Maybe your present palate is at fault, sir," Cappen suggested. He did not add that the tongue definitely had a bad case of logorrhea. It was an almost physical torture to sit stalled, but he had better humor the mage.

"Yes, quite probably. Nothing has tasted good since—Well. To business. On hearing that One-Thumb was inquiring about last night's incident, I sent forth certain investigators of my own. You will understand that I've been trying to find out as much as I can." Enas Yorl drew a sign in the air. "Purely precautionary. I have no desire whatsoever to cross the Powers concerned in this."

A wintry tingle went through Cappen. "You know who they are, what it's about?" His tone wavered.

Enas Yorl wagged a finger. "Not so hasty, boy, not so hasty. My latest information was of a seemingly unsuccessful interview you had with Illyra the seeress. I also learned you were now in this hostel and close to its landlord. Obviously you are involved. I must know why, how, how much—everything."

"Then you'll help—sir?"

A headshake made chin and jowls wobble. "Absolutely not. I told you I want no part of this. But in exchange for whatever data you possess, I am willing to explicate as far as I am able, and to advise you. Be warned: my advice will doubtless be that you drop the matter and perhaps leave town."

And doubtless he would be right, Cappen thought. It simply happened to be counsel that was impossible for a lover to follow . . . unless—O kindly gods of Caronne, no, no!—unless Danlis was dead.

The whole story spilled out of him, quickened and deepened by keen questions. At the end, he sat breathless while Enas Yorl nodded.

"Yes, that appears to confirm what I suspected," the mage said most softly. He stared past the minstrel, into shadows that loomed and flickered. Buzz of talk, clink of drinking ware, occasional gust of laughter among customers seemed remoter than the moon.

"What was it?" broke from Cappen.

"A sikkintair, a Flying Knife. It can have been nothing else."

"A—what?"

Enas focused on his companion. "The monster that took the women," he explained. "Sikkintairs are an attribute of Ils. A pair of sculptures on the grand stairway of his temple represent them."

"Oh, yes, I've seen those, but never thought—"

"No, you're not a votary of any gods they have here. Myself, when I got word of the abduction, I sent my familiars scuttling about and cast spells of inquiry. I received indications. . . . I can't describe them to you, who lack arcane lore. I established that the very fabric of space had been troubled. Vibrations had not quite damped out as yet, and were centered on the temple of Ils. You may, if you wish a crude analogy, visualize a water surface and the waves, fading to ripples and finally to naught, when a diver has passed through."

Enas Yorl drank more in a gulp than was his wont. "Civilization was old in Ilsig when Ranke was still a barbarian village," he said, as though to himself; his gaze had drifted away again, toward darkness. "Its myths depicted the home of the gods as being outside the world—not above, not below, but outside. Philosophers of a later, more rationalistic era elaborated this into a theory of parallel universes. My own researches—you will understand that my condition has made me especially interested in the theory of dimensions, the subtler aspects of geometry—my own researches have demonstrated the possibility of transference between these different spaces.

"As another analogy, consider a pack of cards. One is inhabited by a king, one by a knight, one by a deuce, et cetera. Ordinarily none of the figures can leave the plane on which it exists. If, however, a very thin piece of absorbent material soaked in a unique kind of solvent were laid between two cards, the dyes that form them could pass through: retaining their configuration, I trust. Actually, of course, this is a less than ideal comparison, for the transference is accomplished through a particular contortion of the continuum—"

Cappen could endure no more pedantry. He crashed his tankard down on the table and shouted, "By all the hells of all the cults, will you get to the point?"

Men stared from adjacent seats, decided no fight was about to erupt, and went back to their interests. These included negotiations with streetwalkers who, lanterns in hand, had come in looking for trade.

Enas Yorl smiled. "I forgive your outburst, under the circumstances," he said. "I too am occasionally young.

"Very well. Given the foregoing data, including yours, the infrastructure of events seems reasonably evident. You are aware of the conflict over a proposed new temple, which is to outdo that of Ils and Shipri. I do not maintain that the god has taken a direct hand. I certainly hope he feels that would be beneath his dignity; a theomachy would not be good for us, to understate the case a trifle. But he may have inspired a few of his more fanatical priests to action. He may have revealed to

them, in dreams or vision, the means whereby they could cross to the next world and there make the sikkintairs do their bidding. I hypothesize that the Lady Rosanda—and, to be sure, her coadjutrix, your inamorata—are incarcerated in that world. The temple is too full of priests, deacons, acolytes, and lay people for hiding the wife of a magnate. However, the gate need not be recognizable as such."

Cappen controlled himself with an inward shudder and made his trained voice casual: "What might it look like, sir?"

"Oh, probably a scroll, taken from a coffer where it had long lain forgotten, and now unrolled—yes, I should think in the sanctum, to draw power from the sacred objects and to be seen by as few persons as possible who are not in the conspiracy—" Enas Yorl came out of his abstraction. "Beware! I deduce your thought. Choke it before it kills you."

Cappen ran sandy tongue over leathery lips. "What . . . should we . . . expect to happen, sir?"

"That is an interesting question," Enas Yorl said. "I can but conjecture. Yet I am well acquainted with the temple hierarchy and—I don't think the Archpriest is privy to the matter. He's too aged and weak. On the other hand, this is quite in the style of Hazroah, the High Flamen. Moreover, of late he has in effect taken over the governance of the temple from his nominal superior. He's bold, ruthless—should have been a soldier—Well, putting myself in his skin, I'll predict that he'll let Molin stew a while, then cautiously open negotiations—a hint at first, and always a claim that this is the will of Ils.

"None but the Emperor can cancel an undertaking for the Imperial deities. Persuading him will take much time and pressure. Molin is a Rankan aristocrat of the old school; he will be torn between his duty to his gods, his state, and his wife. But I suspect that eventually he can be worn down to the point where he agrees that it is, in truth, bad policy to exalt Savankala and Sabellia in a city whose tutelaries they have never been. He in his turn can influence the Emperor as desired."

"How long would this take, do you think?" Cappen whispered. "Till the women are released?"

Enas Yorl shrugged. "Years, possibly. Hazroah may try to hasten the process by demonstrating that the Lady Rosanda is subject to punishment. Yes, I should imagine that the remains of an ancilla who had been tortured to death, delivered on Molin's doorstep, would be a rather strong argument."

His look grew intense on the appalled countenance across from him. "I know," he said. "You're breeding fever-dreams of a heroic rescue.

It cannot be done. Even supposing that somehow you won through the gate and brought her back, the gate would remain. I doubt Ils would personally seek revenge; besides being petty, that could provoke open strife with Savankala and his retinue, who're formidable characters themselves. But Ils would not stay the hand of the Flamen Hazroah, who is a most vengeful sort. If you escaped his assassins, a sikkintair would come after you, and nowhere in the world could you and she hide. Your talisman would be of no avail. The sikkintair is not super-natural, unless you give that designation to the force which enables so huge a mass to fly; and *it* is from no magician, but from the god.

"So forget the girl. The town is full of them." He fished in his purse and spilled a handful of coins on the table. "Go to a good whorehouse, enjoy yourself, and raise one for poor old Enas Yorl."

He got up and waddled off. Cappen sat staring at the coins. They made a generous sum, he realized vaguely: silver lunars, to the number of thirty.

One-Thumb came over. "What'd he say?" the taverner asked.

"I should abandon hope," Cappen muttered. His eyes stung; his vision blurred. Angrily, he wiped them.

"I've a notion I might not be smart to hear more." One-Thumb laid his mutilated hand on Cappen's shoulder. "Care to get drunk? On the house. I'll have to take your money or the rest will want free booze too, but I'll return it tomorrow."

"No, I—I thank you, but—but you're busy, and I need someone I can talk to. Just lend me a lantern, if you will."

"That might attract a robber, fellow, what with those fine clothes of yours."

Cappen gripped swordhilt. "He'd be very welcome, the short while he lasted," he said in bitterness.

He climbed to his feet. His fingers remembered to gather the coins.

Jamie let him in. The Northerner had hastily thrown a robe over his massive frame; he carried the stone lamp that was a night light. "Sh," he said. "The lassies are asleep." He nodded toward a closed door at the far end of this main room. Bringing the lamp higher, he got a clear view of Cappen's face. His own registered shock. "Hey-o, lad, what ails you? I've seen men poleaxed who looked happier."

Cappen stumbled across the threshold and collapsed in an armchair. Jamie barred the outer door, touched a stick of punk to the lamp flame and lit candles, filled wine goblets. Drawing a seat opposite, he sat

down, laid red-furred right shank across left knee, and said gently, "Tell me."

When it had spilled from Cappen, he was a long span quiet. On the walls shimmered his weapons, among pretty pictures that his housemates had selected. At last he asked low, "Have you quit?"

"I don't know, I don't know," Cappen groaned.

"I think you can go on a ways, whether or no things are as the witchmaster supposes. We hold where I come from that no man can flee his weird, so he may as well meet it in a way that'll leave a good story. Besides, this may not be our deathday; and I doubt yon dragons are unkillable, but it could be fun finding out; and chiefly, I was much taken with your girl. Not many like her, my friend. They also say in my homeland, 'Waste not, want not.' "

Cappen lifted his glance, astounded. "You mean I should try to free her?" he exclaimed.

"No, I mean *we* should." Jamie chuckled. "Life's gotten a wee bit dull for me of late—aside from Butterfly and Light-of-Pearl, of course. Besides, I could use a share of reward money."

"I . . . I want to," Cappen stammered. "How I want to! But the odds against us—"

"She's your girl, and it's your decision. I'll not blame you if you hold back. Belike, then, in your country, they don't believe a man's first troth is to his woman and kids. Anyway, for you that was no more than a hope."

A surge went through the minstrel. He sprang up and paced, back and forth, back and forth. "But what could we do?"

"Well, we could scout the temple and see what's what," Jamie proposed. "I've been there once in a while, reckoning 'twould do no hurt to give those gods their honor. Maybe we'll find that indeed naught can be done in aid. Or maybe we won't, and go ahead and do it."

Danlis—

Fire blossomed in Cappen Varra. He was young. He drew his sword and swung it whistling on high. "Yes! We will!"

A small grammarian part of him noted the confusion of tenses and moods in the conversation.

The sole traffic on the Avenue of Temples was a night breeze, cold and sibilant. Stars, as icy to behold, looked down on its broad emptiness, on darkened buildings and weather-worn idols and rustling gardens. Here and there flames cast restless light, from porticoes or gables or ledges, out of glass lanterns or iron pots or pierced stone jars. At the

foot of the grand staircase leading to the fane of Ils and Shipri, fire formed halos on the enormous figures, male and female in robes of antiquity, that flanked it.

Beyond, the god-house itself loomed, porticoed front, great bronze doors, granite walls rising sheer above to a gilt dome from which light also gleamed; the highest point in Sanctuary.

Cappen started up. "Halt" said Jamie, and plucked at his cloak. "We can't walk straight in. They keep guards in the vestibule, you know."

"I want a close view of those sikkintairs," the bard explained.

"Um, well, maybe not a bad idea, but let's be quick. If a squad of the watch comes by, we're in trouble." They could not claim they simply wished to perform their devotions, for a civilian was not allowed to bear more arms in this district than a knife. Cappen and Jamie each had that, but no illuminant like honest men. In addition, Cappen carried his rapier, Jamie a claymore, a visored conical helmet, and a knee-length byrnie. He had, moreover, furnished spears for both.

Cappen nodded and bounded aloft. Halfway, he stopped and gazed. The statue was a daunting sight. Of obsidian polished glassy smooth, it might have measured thirty feet were the tail not coiled under the narrow body. The two legs which supported the front ended in talons the length of Jamie's dirk. An upreared, serpentine neck bore a wickedly lanceolate head, jaws parted to show fangs that the sculptor had rendered in diamond. From the back sprang wings, batlike save for their sharp-pointed curvatures, which if unfolded might well have covered another ten yards.

"Aye," Jamie murmured, "such a brute could bear off two women like an eagle a brace of leverets. Must take a lot of food to power it. I wonder what quarry they hunt at home."

"We may find out," Cappen said, and wished he hadn't.

"Come." Jamie led the way back, and around to the left side of the temple. It occupied almost its entire ground, leaving but a narrow strip of flagstones. Next to that, a wall enclosed the flower-fragrant sanctum of Eshi, the love goddess. Thus the space between was gratifyingly dark; the intruders could not now be spied from the avenue. Yet enough light filtered in that they saw what they were doing. Cappen wondered if this meant she smiled on their venture. After all, it was for love, mainly. Besides, he had always been an enthusiastic worshiper of hers, or at any rate of her counterparts in foreign pantheons; oftener than most men had he rendered her favorite sacrifice.

Jamie had pointed out that the building must have lesser doors for utilitarian purposes. He soon found one, bolted for the night and be-

tween windows that were hardly more than slits, impossible to crawl through. He could have hewn the wood panels asunder, but the noise might be heard. Cappen had a better idea. He got his partner down on hands and knees. Standing on the broad back, he poked his spear through a window and worked it along the inside of the door. After some fumbling and whispered obscenities, he caught the latch with the head and drew the bolt.

"Hoosh, you missed your trade, I'm thinking," said the Northerner as he rose and opened the way.

"No, burglary's too risky for my taste," Cappen replied in feeble jest. The fact was that he had never stolen or cheated unless somebody deserved such treatment.

"Even burgling the house of a god?" Jamie's grin was wider than necessary.

Cappen shivered. "Don't remind me."

They entered a storeroom, shut the door, and groped through murk to the exit. Beyond was a hall. Widely spaced lamps gave bare visibility. Otherwise the intruders saw emptiness and heard silence. The vestibule and nave of the temple were never closed; the guards watched over a priest always prepared to accept offerings. But elsewhere hierarchy and staff were asleep. Or so the two hoped.

Jamie had known that the holy of holies was in the dome, Ils being a sky god. Now he let Cappen take the lead, as having more familiarity with interiors and ability to reason out a route. The minstrel used half his mind for that and scarcely noticed the splendors through which he passed. The second half was busy recollecting legends of heroes who incurred the anger of a god, especially a major god, but won to happiness in the end because they had the blessing of another. He decided that future attempts to propitiate Ils would only draw the attention of that august personage; however, Savankala would be pleased, and, yes, as for native deities, he would by all means fervently cultivate Eshi.

A few times, which felt ghastly long, he took a wrong turning and must retrace his steps after he had discovered that. Presently, though, he found a staircase which seemed to zigzag over the inside of an exterior wall. Landing after landing passed by—

The last was enclosed in a very small room, a booth, albeit richly ornamented—

He opened the door and stepped out—

Wind searched between the pillars that upheld the dome, through his clothes and in toward his bones. He saw stars. They were the brightest in heaven, for the entry booth was the pedestal of a gigantic lantern.

Across a floor tiled in symbols unknown to him, he observed something large at each cardinal point—an altar, two statues, and the famous Thunderstone, he guessed; they were shrouded in cloth of gold. Before the eastern object was stretched a band, the far side of which seemed to be aglow.

He gathered his courage and approached. The thing was a parchment, about eight feet long and four wide, hung by cords from the upper corners to a supporting member of the dome. The cords appeared to be glued fast, as if to avoid making holes in the surface. The lower edge of the scroll, two feet above the floor, was likewise secured; but to a pair of anvils surely brought here for the purpose. Nevertheless the parchment flapped and rattled a bit in the wind. It was covered with cabalistic signs.

Cappen stepped around to the other side, and whistled low. That held a picture, within a narrow border. Past the edge of what might be a pergola, the scene went to a meadowland made stately by oak trees standing at random intervals. About a mile away—the perspective was marvelously executed—stood a building of manorial size in a style he had never seen before, twistily colonnaded, extravagantly sweeping of roof and eaves, blood-red. A formal garden surrounded it, whose paths and topiaries were of equally alien outline; fountains sprang in intricate patterns. Beyond the house, terrain rolled higher, and snowpeaks thrust above the horizon. The sky was deep blue.

"What the pox!" exploded from Jamie. "Sunshine's coming out of that painting. I *feel* it."

Cappen rallied his wits and paid heed. Yes, warmth as well as light, and . . . and odors? And were those fountains not actually at play?

An eerie thrilling took him. "I . . . believe . . . we've . . . found the gate," he said.

He poked his spear cautiously at the scroll. The point met no resistance; it simply moved on. Jamie went behind. "You've not pierced it," he reported. "Nothing sticks out on this side—which, by the way, is quite solid."

"No," Cappen answered faintly, "the spearhead's in the next world."

He drew the weapon back. He and Jamie stared at each other.

"Well?" said the Northerner.

"We'll never get a better chance," Cappen's throat responded for him. "It'd be blind foolishness to retreat now, unless we decide to give up the whole venture."

"We, uh, we could go tell Molin, no, the Prince what we've found."

"And be cast into a madhouse? If the Prince *did* send investigators

anyway, the plotters need merely take this thing down and hide it till the squad has left. No." Cappen squared his shoulders. "Do what you like, Jamie, but I am going through."

Underneath, he heartily wished he had less self-respect, or at least that he weren't in love with Danlis.

Jamie scowled and sighed. "Aye, right you are, I suppose. I'd not looked for matters to take so headlong a course. I awaited that we'd simply scout around. Had I foreseen this, I'd have roused the lassies to bid them, well, goodnight." He hefted his spear and drew his sword. Abruptly he laughed. "Whatever comes, 'twill not be dull!"

Stepping high over the threshold, Cappen went forward.

It felt like walking through any door, save that he entered a mild summer's day. After Jamie had followed, he saw that the vista in the parchment was that on which he had just turned his back: a veiled mass, a pillar, stars above a nighted city. He checked the opposite side of the strip, and met the same designs as had been painted on its mate.

No, he thought, not its mate. If he had understood Enas Yorl aright, and rightly remembered what his tutor in mathematics had told him about esoteric geometry, there could be but a single scroll. One side of it gave on this universe, the other side on his, and a spell had twisted dimensions until matter could pass straight between.

Here too the parchment was suspended by cords, though in a pergola of yellow marble, whose circular stairs led down to the meadow. He imagined a sikkintair would find the passage tricky, especially if it was burdened with two women in its claws. The monster had probably hugged them close to it, come in at high speed, folded its wings, and glided between the pillars of the dome and the margins of the gate. On the outbound trip, it must have crawled through into Sanctuary.

All this Cappen did and thought in a half a dozen heartbeats. A shout yanked his attention back. Three men who had been idling on the stairs had noticed the advent and were on their way up. Large and hard-featured, they bore the shaven visages, high-crested morions, gilt cuirasses, black tunics and boots, shortswords, and halberds of temple guards. "Who in the Unholy's name are you?" called the first. "What're you doing here?"

Jamie's qualms vanished under a tide of boyish glee. "I doubt they'll believe any words of ours," he said. "We'll have to convince them a different way. If you can handle him on our left, I'll take his feres."

Cappen felt less confident. But he lacked time to be afraid; shuddering would have to be done in a more convenient hour. Besides, he was quite a good fencer. He dashed across the floor and down the stair.

The trouble was, he had no experience with spears. He jabbed. The halberdier held his weapon, both hands close together, near the middle of the shaft. He snapped it against Cappen's, deflected the thrust, and nearly tore the minstrel's out of his grasp. The watchman's return would have skewered his enemy, had the minstrel not flopped straight to the marble.

The guard guffawed, braced his legs wide, swung the halberd back for an axhead blow. As it descended, his hands shifted toward the end of the helve.

Chips flew. Cappen had rolled downstairs. He twirled the whole way to the ground and sprang erect. He still clutched his spear, which had bruised him whenever he crossed above it. The sentry bellowed and hopped in pursuit. Cappen ran.

Behind them, a second guard sprawled and flopped, diminuendo, in what seemed an impossibly copious and bright amount of blood. Jamie had hurled his own spear as he charged and taken the man in the neck. The third was giving the Northerner a brisk fight, halberd against claymore. He had longer reach, but the redhead had more brawn. Thump and clatter rang across the daises.

Cappen's adversary was bigger than he was. This had the drawback that the former could not change speed or direction as readily. When the guard was pounding along at his best clip, ten or twelve feet in the rear, Cappen stopped within a coin's breadth, whirled about, and threw his shaft. He did not do that as his comrade had done. He pitched it between the guard's legs. The man crashed to the grass. Cappen plunged in. He didn't risk trying for a stab. That would let the armored combatant grapple him. He wrenched the halberd loose and skipped off.

The sentinel rose. Cappen reached an oak and tossed the halberd. It lodged among boughs. He drew blade. His foe did the same.

Shortsword versus rapier—much better, though Cappen must have a care. The torso opposing him was protected. Still, the human anatomy has more vulnerable points than that. "Shall we dance?" Cappen asked.

As he and Jamie approached the house, a shadow slid across them. They glanced aloft and saw the gaunt black form of a sikkintair. For an instant, they nerved themselves for the worst. However, the Flying Knife simply caught an updraft, planed high, and hovered in sinister magnificence. "Belike they don't hunt men unless commanded to," the Northerner speculated. "Bear and buffalo are meatier."

Cappen frowned at the scarlet walls before him. "The next question," he said, "is why nobody has come out against us."

"Um, I'd deem those wights we left scattered around were the only fighting men here. What task was theirs? Why, to keep the ladies from escaping, if those are allowed to walk outdoors by day. As for yon manse, while it's plenty big, I suspect it's on loan from its owner. Naught but a few servants need be on hand—and the women, let's hope. I don't suppose anybody happened to see our little brawl."

The thought that they might effect the rescue—soon, safely, easily—went through Cappen in a wave of dizziness. Afterward—he and Jamie had discussed that. If the temple hierophants, from Hazroah on down, were put under immediate arrest, that ought to dispose of the vengeance problem.

Gravel scrunched underfoot. Rose, jasmine, honeysuckle sweetened the air. Fountains leaped and chimed. The partners reached the main door. It was oaken, with many glass eyes inset; the knocker had the shape of a sikkintair.

Jamie leaned his spear, unsheathed his sword, turned the knob left-handed, and swung the door open. A maroon sumptuousness of carpet, hangings, upholstery brooded beyond. He and Cappen entered. Inside were quietness and an odor like that just before a thunderstorm.

A man in a deacon's black robe came through an archway, his tonsure agleam in the dimness. "Did I hear—Oh!" he gasped, and scuttled backward.

Jamie made a long arm and collared him. "Not so fast, friend," the warrior said genially. "We've a request, and if you oblige, we won't get stains on this pretty rug. Where are your guests?"

"What, what, what," the deacon gobbled.

Jamie shook him, in leisured wise lest he quite dislocate the shoulder. "Lady Rosanda, wife to Molin Torchholder, and her assistant Danlis. Take us to them. Oh, and we'd liefer not meet folk along the way. It might get messy if we did."

The deacon fainted.

"Ah, well," Jamie said. "I hate the idea of cutting down unarmed men, but chances are they won't be foolhardy." He filled his lungs. *"Rosanda!"* he bawled. *"Danlis! Jamie and Cappen Varra are here! Come on home!"*

The volume almost bowled his companion over. "Are you mad?" the minstrel exclaimed. "You'll warn the whole staff—" A flash lit his mind: if they had seen no further guards, surely there were none, and nothing corporeal remained to fear. Yet every minute's delay heightened the danger of something else going wrong. Somebody might find signs of invasion back in the temple; the gods alone knew what lurked

in this realm. . . . Yes, Jamie's judgment might prove mistaken, but it was the best he could have made.

Servitors appeared, and recoiled from naked steel. And then, and then—

Through a doorway strode Danlis. She led by the hand, or dragged, a half-hysterical Rosanda. Both were decently attired and neither looked abused, but pallor in cheeks and smudges under eyes bespoke what they must have suffered.

Cappen came nigh dropping his spear. "Beloved!" he cried. "Are you hale?"

"We've not been ill-treated in the flesh, aside from the snatching itself," she answered efficiently. "The threats, should Hazroah not get his way, have been cruel. Can we leave now?"

"Aye, the soonest, the best," Jamie growled. "Lead them on ahead, Cappen." His sword covered the rear. On his way out, he retrieved the spear he had left.

They started back over the garden paths. Danlis and Cappen between them must help Rosanda along. That woman's plump prettiness was lost in tears, moans, whimpers, and occasional screams. He paid scant attention. His gaze kept seeking the clear profile of his darling. When her grey eyes turned toward him, his heart became a lyre.

She parted her lips. He waited for her to ask in dazzlement, "How did you ever do this, you unbelievable, wonderful men?"

"What have we ahead of us?" she wanted to know.

Well, it was an intelligent query. Cappen swallowed disappointment and sketched the immediate past. Now, he said, they'd return via the gate to the dome and make their stealthy way from the temple, thence to Molin's dwelling for a joyous reunion. But then they must act promptly—yes, roust the Prince out of bed for authorization—and occupy the temple and arrest everybody in sight before new trouble got fetched from this world.

Rosanda gained some self-control as he talked.

"Oh, my, oh, my," she wheezed, "you unbelievable, wonderful men."

An ear-piercing trill slashed across her voice. The escapers looked behind them. At the entrance to the house stood a thickset middle-aged person in the scarlet robe of a ranking priest of Ils. He held a pipe to his mouth and blew.

"Hazroah!" Rosanda shrilled. "The ringleader!"

"The High Flamen—" Danlis began.

A rush in the air interrupted. Cappen flung his vision skyward and

knew the nightmare was true. The sikkintair was descending. Hazroah had summoned it.

"Why, you son of a bitch!" Jamie roared. Still well behind the rest, he lifted his spear, brought it back, flung it with his whole strength and weight. The point went home in Hazroah's breast. Ribs did not stop it. He spouted blood, crumpled, and spouted no more. The shaft quivered above his body.

But the sikkintair's vast wings eclipsed the sun. Jamie rejoined his band and plucked the second spear from Cappen's fingers. "Hurry on, lad," he ordered. "Get them to safety."

"Leave you? No!" protested his comrade.

Jamie spat an oath. "Do you want the whole faring to've gone for naught? Hurry, I said!"

Danlis tugged at Cappen's sleeve. "He's right. The state requires our testimony."

Cappen stumbled onward. From time to time he glanced back.

In the shadow of the wings, Jamie's hair blazed. He stood foursquare, spear grasped as a huntsman does. Agape, the Flying Knife rushed down upon him. Jamie thrust straight between those jaws, and twisted.

The monster let out a sawtoothed shriek. Its wings threshed, made thundercrack, it swooped by, a foot raked. Jamie had his claymore out. He parried the blow.

The sikkintair rose. The shaft waggled from its throat. It spread great ebon membranes, looped, and came back earthward. Its claws were before it. Air whirred behind.

Jamie stood his ground, sword in right hand, knife in left. As the talons smote, he fended them off with the dirk. Blood sprang from his thigh, but his byrnie took most of the edged sweep. And his sword hewed.

The sikkintair ululated again. It tried to ascend, and couldn't. Jamie had crippled its left wing. It landed—Cappen felt the impact through soles and bones—and hitched itself toward him. From around the spear came a geyser hiss.

Jamie held fast where he was. As fangs struck at him, he sidestepped, sprang back, and threw his shoulders against the shaft. Leverage swung jaws aside. He glided by the neck toward the forequarters. Both of his blades attacked the spine.

Cappen and the women hastened on.

They were almost at the pergola when footfalls drew his eyes rearward. Jamie loped at an overtaking pace. Behind him, the sikkintair lay in a heap.

The redhead pulled alongside. "Hai, what a fight!" he panted. "Thanks for this journey, friend! A drinking bout's worth of thanks!"

They mounted the death-defiled stairs. Cappen peered across miles. Wings beat in heaven, from the direction of the mountains. Horror stabbed his guts. "Look!" He could barely croak.

Jamie squinted. "More of them," he said. "A score, maybe. We can't cope with so many. An army couldn't."

"That whistle was heard farther away than mortals would hear," Danlis added starkly.

"What do we linger for?" Rosanda wailed. "Come, take us home!"

"And the sikkintairs follow?" Jamie retorted. "No. I've my lassies, and kinfolk, and—" He moved to stand before the parchment. Edged metal dripped in his hands; red lay splashed across helm, ringmail, clothing, face. His grin broke forth, wry. "A spaewife once told me I'd die on the far side of strangeness. I'll wager she didn't know her own strength."

"You assume that the mission of the beasts is to destroy us, and when that is done they will return to their lairs." The tone Danlis used might have served for a remark about the weather.

"Aye, what else? The harm they'd wreak would be in a hunt for us. But put to such trouble, they could grow furious and harry our whole world. That's the more likely when Hazroah lies skewered. Who else can control them?"

"None that I know of, and he talked quite frankly to us." She nodded. "Yes, it behooves us to die where we are." Rosanda sank down and blubbered. Danlis showed irritation. "Up!" she commanded her mistress. "Up and meet your fate like a Rankan matron!"

Cappen goggled hopelessly at her. She gave him a smile. "Have no regrets, dear," she said. "You did well. The conspiracy against the state has been checked."

*The far side of strangeness—check—chessboard—that version of chess where you pretend the right and left sides of the board are identical on a cylinder—*tumbled through Cappen. The Flying Knives drew closer fast. *Curious aspects of geometry—*

Lightning-smitten, he knew . . . or guessed he did . . . "No, Jamie, we go!" he yelled.

"To no avail save reaping of innocents?" The big man hunched his shoulders. "Never."

"Jamie, let us by! I can close the gate. I swear I can—I swear by—by Eshi—"

The Northerner locked eyes with Cappen for a span that grew. At last: "You are my brother in arms." He stood aside. "Go on."

The sikkintairs were so near that the noise of their speed reached Cappen. He urged Danlis toward the scroll. She lifted her skirt a trifle, revealing a dainty ankle, and stepped through. He hauled on Rosanda's wrist. The woman wavered to her feet but seemed unable to find her direction. Cappen took an arm and passed it into the next world for Danlis to pull. Himself, he gave a mighty shove on milady's buttocks. She crossed over.

He did. And Jamie.

Beneath the temple dome, Cappen's rapier reached high and slashed. Louder came the racket of cloven air. Cappen severed the upper cords. The parchment fell, wrinkling, crackling. He dropped his weapon, a-clang, squatted, and stretched his arms wide. The free corners he seized. He pulled them to the corners that were still secured, to make a closed band of the scroll.

From it sounded monstrous thumps and scrapes. The sikkintairs were crawling into the pergola. For them the portal must hang unchanged, open for their hunting.

Cappen gave that which he held a half-twist and brought the edges back together.

Thus he created a surface which had but a single side and a single edge. Thus he obliterated the gate.

He had not been sure what would follow. He had fleetingly supposed he would smuggle the scroll out, held in its paradoxical form, and eventually glue it—unless he could burn it. But upon the instant that he completed the twist and juncture, the parchment was gone. Enas Yorl told him afterward that he had made it impossible for the thing to exist.

Air rushed in where the gate had been, crack and hiss. Cappen heard that sound as it were an alien word of incantation: *"Möbius-s-s."*

Having stolen out of the temple and some distance thence, the party stopped for a few minutes of recovery before they proceeded to Molin's house.

This was in a blind alley off the avenue, a brick-paved recess where flowers grew in planters, shared by the fanes of two small and gentle gods. Wind had died away, stars glimmered bright, a half moon stood above easterly roofs and cast wan argence. Afar, a tomcat serenaded his intended.

Rosanda had gotten back a measure of equilibrium. She cast herself

against Jamie's breast. "Oh, hero, hero," she crooned, "you shall have reward, yes, treasure, ennoblement, everything!" She snuggled. "But nothing greater than my unbounded thanks. . . .

The Northerner cocked an eyebrow at Cappen. The bard shook his head a little. Jamie nodded in understanding, and disengaged. "Uh, have a care, milady," he said. "Pressing against ringmail, all bloody and sweaty too, can't be good for a complexion."

Even if one rescues them, it is not wise to trifle with the wives of magnates.

Cappen had been busy himself. For the first time, he kissed Danlis on her lovely mouth; then for the second time; then for the third. She responded decorously.

Thereafter she likewise withdrew. Moonlight made a mystery out of her classic beauty. "Cappen," she said, "before we go on, we had better have a talk."

He gaped. "What?"

She bridged her fingers. "Urgent matters first," she continued crisply. "Once we get to the mansion and wake the high priest, it will be chaos at first, conference later, and I—as a woman—excluded from serious discussion. Therefore best I give my counsel now, for you to relay. Not that Molin or the Prince are fools; the measures to take are for the most part obvious. However, swift action is desirable, and they will have been caught by surprise."

She ticked her points off. "First, as you have indicated, the Hell Hounds"—her nostrils pinched in distaste at the nickname—"the Imperial elite guard should mount an immediate raid on the temple of Ils and arrest all personnel for interrogation, except the Archpriest. He's probably innocent, and in any event it would be inept politics. Hazroah's death may have removed the danger, but this should not be taken for granted. Even if it has, his co-conspirators ought to be identified and made examples of.

"Yet, second, wisdom should temper justice. No lasting harm was done, unless we count those persons who are trapped in the parallel universe; and they doubtless deserve to be."

They seemed entirely males, Cappen recalled. He grimaced in compassion. Of course, the sikkintairs might eat them.

Danlis was talking on: "—humane governance and the art of compromise. A grand temple dedicated to the Rankan gods is certainly required, but it need be no larger than that of Ils. Your counsel will have much weight, dear. Give it wisely. I will advise you."

"Uh?" Cappen said.

Danlis smiled and laid her hands over his. "Why, you can have unlimited preferment, after what you did," she told him. "I'll show you how to apply for it."

"But—but I'm no blooming statesman!" Cappen stuttered.

She stepped back and considered him. "True," she agreed. "You're valiant, yes, but you're also flighty and lazy and—Well, don't despair. I will mold you."

Cappen gulped and shuffled aside. "Jamie," he said, "uh, Jamie, I feel wrung dry, dead on my feet. I'd be worse than no use—I'd be a drogue on things just when they have to move fast. Better I find me a doss, and you take the ladies home. Come over here and I'll tell you how to convey the story in fewest words. Excuse us, ladies. Some of those words you oughtn't to hear."

A week thence, Cappen Varra sat drinking in the Vulgar Unicorn. It was mid-afternoon and none else were present but the associate tapster, his wound knitted.

A man filled the doorway and came in, to Cappen's table. "Been casting about everywhere for you," the Northerner grumbled. "Where've you been?"

"Lying low," Cappen replied. "I've taken a place here in the Maze which'll do till I've dropped back into obscurity, or decide to drift elsewhere altogether." He sipped his wine. Sunbeams slanted through windows; dustmotes danced golden in their warmth; a cat lay on a sill and purred. "Trouble is, my purse is flat."

"We're free of such woes for a goodly while." Jamie flung his length into a chair and signaled the attendant. "Beer!" he thundered.

"You collected a reward, then?" the minstrel asked eagerly.

Jamie nodded. "Aye. In the way you whispered I should, before you left us. I'm baffled why and it went sore against the grain. But I did give Molin the notion that the rescue was my idea and you naught but a hanger-on whom I'd slip a few royals. He filled a box with gold and silver money, and said he wished he could afford ten times that. He offered to get me Rankan citizenship and a title as well, and make a bureaucrat of me, but I said no, thanks. We share, you and I, half and half. But right this now, drinks are on me."

"What about the plotters?" Cappen inquired.

"Ah, those. The matter's been kept quiet, as you'd await. Still, while the temple of Ils can't be abolished, seemingly it's been tamed." Jamie's regard sought across the table and sharpened. "After you disappeared, Danlis agreed to let me claim the whole honor. She knew better—

Rosanda never noticed—but Danlis wanted a man of the hour to carry her redes to the prince, and none remained save me. She supposed you were simply worn out. When last I saw her, though, she . . . um-m . . . she 'expressed disappointment.' " He cocked his ruddy head. "Yon's quite a girl. I thought you loved her."

Cappen Varra took a fresh draught of wine. Old summers glowed along his tongue. "I did," he confessed. "I do. My heart is broken, and in part I drink to numb the pain."

Jamie raised his brows. "What? Makes no sense."

"Oh, it makes very basic sense," Cappen answered. "Broken hearts tend to heal rather soon. Meanwhile, if I may recite from a rondel I completed before you found me—

> "*Each sword of sorrow that would maim or slay,*
> *My lady of the morning deftly parries.*
> *Yet gods forbid I be the one she marries!*
> *I rise from bed the latest hour I may.*
> *My lady comes to me like break of day;*
> *I dream in darkness if it chance she tarries.*"

SUZY McKEE CHARNAS
Unicorn Tapestry

"HOLD ON," Floria said. "I know what you're going to say: I agreed not to take any new clients for a while. But wait till I tell you—you're not going to believe this—first phone call, setting up an initial appointment, he comes out with what his problem is: 'I seem to have fallen victim to a delusion of being a vampire.' "

"Christ H. God!" cried Lucille delightedly. "Just like that, over the phone?"

"When I recovered my aplomb, so to speak, I told him that I prefer to wait with the details until our first meeting. I was a little late though."

They were sitting on the tiny terrace outside the staff room of the clinic, a converted town house on the Upper West Side. Floria spent three days a week here and the remaining two in her office on Central Park South seeing private clients like this new one. Lucille, always gratifyingly responsive, was Floria's most valued professional friend. Clearly enchanted with Floria's news, she sat eagerly forward in her creaky old lawn chair, eyes wide behind Coke-bottle glasses.

She said, "Do you suppose he thinks he's a revivified corpse?"

Below, down at the end of the street, Floria could see two kids skidding their skateboards near a man who wore a woolen cap and heavy coat despite the May warmth. He was leaning against a wall like a monolith. If corpses walked, some, not nearly revivified enough, stood in plain view in New York.

"I'll have to think of a delicate way to ask," she said.

"How did he come to you?"

"He was working in an upstate college, teaching and doing research, and all of a sudden he just disappeared—vanished, literally, without a

trace. A month later he turned up here in the city. The faculty dean at the school knows me and sent him to see me."

Lucille gave her a sly look. "So you thought, Ah-hah, do a little favor for a friend, this looks classic and easy to transfer if need be: repressed intellectual blows stack and runs off with spacy chick or something like that—only a little more interesting, looks like."

"You know me too well," Floria said.

"Huh," grunted Lucille. She sipped ginger ale from a chipped white mug. "I don't take panicky middle-aged guys anymore—they're too depressing. And you shouldn't be taking this one, intriguing as he sounds."

Here comes the lecture, Floria told herself.

Lucille got up. She was short, heavy, prone to wearing caftans that swung about her like ceremonial robes. As she paced, her hem brushed at the flowers starting up in the planting boxes that rimmed the little terrace. "You know damn well this is just more overwork you're loading on. Don't take this man; refer him."

Floria sighed. "I know, I know. I promised everybody I'd slow down for a while. But you said it yourself just a minute ago—it looked like a simple favor. So what do I get? Count Dracula, for God's sake! Would you give that up?"

Fishing around in one capacious pocket, Lucille brought out a dented package of cigarets and lit up, scowling. "You know, when you give me advice I try to take it seriously. Joking aside, Floria, what am I supposed to say? I've listened to you moaning for months now, and I thought we'd figured out that what you need is to shed some pressure, to start saying *no*—and here you are insisting on a new case. You know what I think: you're hiding in other people's problems from a lot of your own stuff you should be working on.

"Okay, okay, don't glare at me. Be pig-headed. Have you gotten rid of Chubs, at least?" This was Floria's code name for a troublesome client named Kenny she'd been trying to unload for some time.

Floria shook her head.

"What gives with you? It's weeks since you swore you'd dump him! Trying to do everything for everybody is wearing you out. I bet you're still dropping weight. Judging by the very unbecoming circles under your eyes, sleeping isn't going too well either. Still no dreams you can remember?"

"Lucille, don't nag. I don't want to talk about my health."

"Well, what about his health—Dracula's? Did you suggest that he

have a physical before seeing you? There might be something physiological—"

"You're not going to be able to whisk him off to an M.D. and out of my hands," Floria said wryly. "He says he won't consider either medication or hospitalization."

Involuntarily, she glanced down at the end of the street. The woolen-capped man had curled up on the sidewalk at the foot of the building, sleeping or passed-out or dead. The city was tottering with sickness. Compared with that wreck down there and the others like him, how sick could this "vampire" be, with his cultured baritone voice, his self-possessed approach?

"And you won't consider handing him off to somebody else," Lucille said.

"Well, not until I know a little more. Come on, Luce—wouldn't you want at least to know what he looks like?"

Lucille stubbed out her cigaret against the low parapet. Down below a policeman strolled along the street ticketing the parked cars. He didn't even look at the man lying at the corner of the building. They watched his progress without comment. Finally, Lucille said, "Well, if you won't drop Dracula, keep me posted on him, will you?"

He entered the office on the dot of the hour, a gaunt but graceful figure. His name, typed in caps on the initial information sheet that she proceeded to fill out with him, was Edward Lewis Weyland. He was impressive: wiry gray hair, worn short, emphasized the massiveness of his face with its long jaw, high cheekbones, and stony cheeks grooved as if by winters of hard weather. He told her about the background of the vampire incident, incisively describing his life at Cayslin College: the pressures of collegial competition, interdepartmental squabbles, student indifference, administrative bungling. History has limited use, she knew, since memory distorts. Still, if he felt most comfortable establishing the setting for his illness, let him.

At length his energy faltered. His angular body sank into a slump, his voice became flat and tired as he haltingly worked up to the crucial event: night work at the sleep-lab, fantasies of blood-drinking as he watched the youthful subjects of his dream research slumbering, finally an attempt to act out the fantasy with a staff member at the college. He had been repulsed. Then—panic. Word would get out, he'd be fired, blacklisted forever. He'd bolted. A nightmare period had followed—he offered no details. When he had come to his senses he'd seen that just

what he feared, the ruin of his career, would come from his running away. So he'd phoned the dean, and here he was.

Throughout this recital she watched him diminish from the dignified academic who had entered her office to a shamed and frightened man hunched in his chair, his hands pulling fitfully at each other.

"What are your hands doing?" she said gently. He looked blank. She repeated the question.

He looked down at his hands. "Struggling," he said.

"With what?"

"The worst," he muttered. "I haven't told you the worst." She had never grown hardened to this sort of transformation. His long fingers busied themselves fiddling with a button on his jacket while he explained painfully that the object of his "attack" at Cayslin had been a woman. Not young but handsome and vital, she had first caught his attention earlier in the year during a "festschrift"—an honorary seminar—for a retiring professor. A picture emerged of an awkward Weyland, lifelong bachelor, seeking this woman's warmth and suffering her refusal.

Floria knew she should bring him out of his past and into his here-and-now, but he was doing so beautifully on his own that she was loath to interrupt.

"Did I tell you there was a rapist active on the campus at this time?" he said bitterly. "I borrowed a leaf from his book: I tried to take from this woman, since she wouldn't give. I tried to take some of her blood." He stared at the floor. "What does that mean—to take someone's blood?"

"What do you think it means?"

The button, pulled and twisted by his fretful fingers, came off in his hand. He put it in his pocket, the impulse of a fastidious nature, she guessed. "Her energy," he whispered, "stolen to warm the walking corpse—the vampire—myself."

His silence, his downcast eyes, his bent shoulders, all signaled a man brought to bay by a life crisis. Perhaps he was going to be the kind of client therapists dream of and she needed so badly these days: a client intelligent and sensitive enough, given the companionship of a professional listener, to swiftly unravel his own mental tangles. Exhilarated by his promising start, Floria restrained herself from trying to build on it too soon. She made herself tolerate the silence, which lasted until he said suddenly, "I notice that you make no notes as we speak. Do you record these sessions on tape?"

A hint of paranoia, she thought, not unusual. "Not without your

knowledge and consent, just as I won't send for your personnel file from Cayslin without your knowledge and consent. I do, however, write notes after each session as a guide to myself and in order to have a record in case of any confusion later about anything we do or say here. I can promise you that I won't show my notes or speak of you by name to anyone—except Dean Sharpe at Cayslin, of course, and even then only as much as is strictly necessary—without your written permission. Does that satisfy you?"

"I apologize for my question," he said. "The—incident has left me— very nervous: a condition that I hope to get over with your help."

The time was up. When he had gone she stepped outside to check with Hilda, the receptionist she shared with four other therapists here at the Central Park South office. Hilda always sized up new clients in the waiting room.

Of this one she said, "Are you sure there's anything wrong with that guy? I think I'm in love."

Waiting at the office for a group of clients to assemble Wednesday evening, Floria dashed off some notes on the "vampire."

> Described incident, background. No history of mental illness, no previous experience of therapy. Personal history so ordinary you almost don't notice how bare it is: only child of German immi-grants, schooling normal, anthropology field work, academic posts leading to Cayslin College professorship. Health good, finances adequate, occupation satisfactory, housing pleasant (though pres-ently installed in a N.Y. hotel); never married, no kids, no family, no religion, social life strictly job-related, leisure—likes to drive. Reaction to question about drinking, but no signs of alcohol prob-lem. Physically very smooth-moving for his age (over fifty) and height; cat-like, alert. Some apparent stiffness in mid-section— slight protective stoop—tightening up of middle-age? Paranoic de-fensiveness? Voice pleasant, faint accent (German speaking child-hood at home). Entering therapy condition of consideration for return to job.

What a relief: now she could defend to Lucille her decision to do therapy with the "vampire." His situation looked workable with a minimum of strain on herself.

After all, Lucille was right. Floria did have problems of her own that needed attention, primarily her anxiety and exhaustion since her mother's death more than a year before. The break-up of Floria's

marriage had caused her misery, but not the endless depression now wearing her down. Intellectually the problem was clear: with both her parents dead she was left exposed. No one stood any longer between herself and the inevitability of her own death. Knowing the source of her feelings didn't help: she couldn't seem to mobilize the nerve to work on them.

The Wednesday group went badly again. Lisa lived once more her experiences in the European death camps and everyone cried. Floria wanted to stop Lisa, turn her, extinguish the droning misery of her voice in illumination and release, but she couldn't see how to do it. She found nothing in herself to offer except some clever ploy out of the professional bag of tricks—dance your anger, have a dialog with your young self of those days—useful techniques when they flowed organically as part of a living process in which the therapist participated. But thinking out responses that should have been intuitive wouldn't work. The group and its collective pain paralyzed her. She was a dancer without a choreographer, knowing all the moves but unable to match them to the music these people made.

Rather than act with mechanical clumsiness she held back, did nothing, and suffered guilt. Oh, God, the smart, experienced people in the group must know how useless she was here.

Going home on the bus she thought about calling up one of the therapists who shared the downtown office. He had expressed an interest in doing co-therapy with her under student observation. The Wednesday group might respond well to that. Suggest it to them next time? Having a partner might take pressure off Floria and revitalize the group, and if she felt she must withdraw, he would be available to take over. Of course, he might take over anyway and walk off with some of her clients.

Oh, boy, terrific, who's paranoid now? Wonderful way to think about a good colleague. God, she hadn't even known she was considering shucking the group.

Had the new client, running from his "vampirism," exposed her own impulse to retreat? This wouldn't be the first time that Floria had obtained help from a client while attempting to give help. Her old supervisor, Rigby, said that such mutual aid was the only true therapy, the rest was fraud. What a perfectionist, old Rigby, and what a bunch of young idealists he'd turned out, all eager to save the world.

Eager, but not necessarily able. Jane Fennerman had once lived in the world, and Floria had been incompetent to save her. Jane, an absent

member of tonight's group, was back in the safety of a locked ward, hazily gliding on whatever tranquilizers they used there.

Why still mull over Jane? she asked herself severely, bracing against the bus's lurching halt. Any client was entitled to drop out of therapy and commit herself. Nor was this the first time that sort of thing had happened in the course of Floria's career. Only this time she couldn't seem to shake free of the resulting depression and guilt.

But how could she have helped Jane more? How could you offer reassurance that life was not as dreadful as Jane felt it to be, that her fears were insubstantial, that each day was not a pit of pain and danger?

She was taking time during a client's canceled hour to work on notes for the new book. The writing, an analysis of the vicissitudes of salaried versus private practice, balked her at every turn. She longed for an interruption to distract her circling mind.

Hilda put a call through from Cayslin College. It was Doug Sharpe, who had sent Dr. Weyland to her.

"Now that he's in your capable hands, I can tell people plainly that he's on what they call 'compassionate leave' and make them swallow it." Doug's voice seemed thinned by the long-distance connection. "Can you give me a preliminary opinion?"

"I need time to find out more."

He said, "Try not to take too long. At the moment I'm holding off pressure to appoint someone in his place. Some of his enemies up here—and a sharp-tongued bastard like him acquires plenty of those—are trying to get a search committee authorized to find someone else for the Directorship of the Cayslin Center for the Study of Man."

"Of People," she corrected automatically, as she always did. "What do you mean, 'bastard'? I thought you liked him, Doug. 'Do you want me to have to throw a smart, courtly, old-school gent to Finney or MaGill?' Those were your very words." Finney was a Freudian with a mouth like a pursed-up little asshole and a mind to match, and MaGill was a primal yowler with a padded gym of an office.

She heard Doug tapping at his teeth with a pen or pencil. "Well," he said, "I have a lot of respect for him, and sometimes I could cheer him for mowing down some pompous moron up here. I can't deny, though, that he's earned a reputation for being an accomplished son-of-a-bitch and tough to work with. Too damn cold and self-sufficient, you know?"

"Mmm," she said. "I haven't seen that yet."

He said, "You will. How about yourself? How's the rest of your life?"

"Well, off-hand, what would you say if I told you I was thinking of going back to art school?"

"What would I say? I'd say bullshit, that's what I'd say. You've had fifteen years of doing something you're good at, and now you want to throw all that out and start over in an area you haven't touched since Studio 101 in college? If God had meant you to be a painter, she'd have sent you to art school in the first place."

"I did think about art school at the time."

"The point is that you're good at what you do. I've been at the receiving end of your work and I know what I'm talking about. By the way, did you see that piece in the paper about Annie Winslow, from the group I was in? That's a nice appointment; I always knew she'd wind up in Washington. What I'm trying to make clear to you is that your 'graduates' do too well for you to talk about quitting. What's Morton say about that idea, by the way?"

Mort, a pathologist, was Floria's lover. She hadn't discussed this with him, and she told Doug so.

"You're not on the outs with Morton, are you?"

"Come on, Douglas, cut it out. There's nothing wrong with my sex-life, believe me. It's everyplace else that's giving me trouble."

"Just sticking my nose into your business," he replied. "What are friends for?"

They turned to lighter matters, but when she hung up Floria didn't feel cheered. If her friends were moved to this sort of probing and kindly advice-giving, she must be inviting help more openly and more desperately than she'd realized.

The work on the book went no better. It was as if, afraid to expose her thoughts, she must disarm criticism by meeting all possible objections beforehand. The book was well and truly stalled—like everything else. She sat sweating over it, wondering what the devil was wrong with her that she was writing mush. She had two good books to her name already. What was this bottleneck with the third?

"But what do you think?" Kenny insisted, gnawing anxiously at the cuticle of his thumbnail. "Does it sound like any kind of job?"

"What do you feel about it?" she countered.

"I'm all confused, I told you."

"Try speaking for me. Give the advice I would give you."

He glowered. "That's a real cop-out, you know? One part of me talking like you, and then I have a dialog with myself like a tv show

about a split personality. It's all me that way, you're off the hook, you just sit there. I want something from *you*."

She looked for the twentieth time at the clock on the file cabinet. This time it freed her. "Kenny, the hour's over."

Kenny heaved his plump, sulky body up out of his chair. "You don't care. Oh, you pretend you do, but you don't really—"

"Next time, Kenny."

He stumped out of the office. She imagined him towing in his wake the raft of decisions he was trying to inveigle her into making for him. Sighing, she went to the window and looked out over the park, filling her eyes and her mind with the full, fresh green of late spring. She felt dismal. In two years of treatment the situation with Kenny had remained a stalemate. He wouldn't go to someone else who might be able to help him, and she couldn't bring herself to kick him out, though she knew she must eventually. His puny tyranny couldn't conceal how soft and vulnerable he was . . .

Dr. Weyland had the next appointment. Floria found herself pleased to see him. She could hardly have asked for a greater contrast to Kenny: tall, lean, a fine head that made her want to draw him, good clothes, nice big hands—altogether a distinguished-looking man. Though informally dressed in slacks, light jacket, and tieless shirt, the impression he conveyed was one of impeccable leisure and reserve. He took not the padded chair preferred by most clients but the wooden one with the cane seat.

"Good afternoon, Dr. Landauer," he said gravely. "May I ask your judgment of my case?"

"I don't think of myself as a judge," she said. She decided rapidly to enlist his intelligence by laying out her thoughts to him as to an equal, and to shift their discussion onto a first-name basis if possible. Calling this old-fashioned man by his first name so soon might seem artificial, but how could they get familiar enough to do therapy while addressing each other as "Dr. Landauer" and "Dr. Weyland" like two characters in vaudeville?

"This is what I think, Edward," she continued. "We need to find out about this vampire incident—how it tied into your feelings about yourself, good and bad, at the time, what it did for you that led you to try to 'be' a vampire even though that was bound to complicate your life terrifically. The more we know, the closer we can come to figuring out how to insure that this vampire construct won't be necessary to you again."

"Does this mean that you accept me formally as a client?" he said.

Comes right out and says what's on his mind, she noted; no problems there. "Yes."

"Good. I, too, have a treatment goal in mind. I will need at some point a testimonial from you that my mental health is sound enough for me to resume work at Cayslin."

Floria shook her head. "I can't guarantee that. I can commit myself to work toward it, of course, since your improved mental health is the aim of what we do here together."

"I suppose that answers the purpose for the time being," he said. "We can discuss it again later on. Frankly, I find myself eager to continue our work today. I've been feeling very much better since I spoke with you, and I thought last night about what I might tell you today."

"Edward, my own feeling is that we started out with a good deal of very useful verbal work, and that now is a time to try something a little different."

He said nothing. He watched her. When she asked whether he remembered his dreams he shook his head.

She said, "I'd like you to try to do a dream for me now, a waking dream. Close your eyes and daydream, and tell me about it."

He closed his eyes. Strangely, he now struck her as less vulnerable rather than more, as if strengthened by increased vigilance.

"How do you feel now?" she said.

"Uneasy." His eyelids fluttered. "I dislike closing my eyes. What I don't see can hurt me."

"Who wants to hurt you?"

"A vampire's enemies, of course—mobs of screaming peasants with torches."

Translating into what, she wondered—young Ph.D.'s pouring out of the graduate schools panting for the jobs of older men like Weyland? "Peasants, these days?"

"Whatever their daily work, there is still a majority of the stupid, the violent, and the credulous, putting their featherbrained faith in astrology, in this cult or that, in various branches of psychology."

His sneer at her was unmistakable. Considering her refusal to let him fill the hour his own way, this desire to take a swipe at her was healthy. But it required immediate and straightforward handling.

"Edward, open your eyes and tell me what you see."

He obeyed. "I see a woman in her early forties," he said, "clever-looking face, dark hair showing gray, flesh too thin for her bones, indicating either vanity or illness, wearing slacks and a rather creased

batik blouse—describable, I think, by the term 'peasant style'—with a food stain on the left side."

Damn! Don't blush. "Does anything besides my blouse suggest a peasant to you?"

"Nothing concrete, but with regard to me, my vampire-self, a peasant with a torch is what you could easily become."

"I hear you saying that my task is to help you get rid of your delusion, though this process may be painful and frightening for you."

Something flashed in his expression—surprise, perhaps alarm—something she wanted to get in touch with before it could sink away out of reach again. Quickly she said, "How do you experience your face at this moment?"

He frowned. "As being on the front of my head. Why?"

With a sick feeling she saw that she had chosen the wrong technique for reaching that hidden feeling and had provoked hostility instead. "Your face looked to me just now like a mask for concealing what you feel rather than an instrument of expression."

He moved restlessly in the chair, his whole physical attitude tense and guarded. "I don't know what you mean."

"Will you let me touch you?" she said, rising.

His hands tightened on the arms of his chair, which protested in a sharp creak. He snapped, "I thought this was a talking cure."

Strong resistance to body-work—ease up. "If you won't let me massage some of the tension out of your facial muscles, will you try to do it for yourself?"

"I don't enjoy being made ridiculous," he said, standing and heading for the door, which clapped smartly shut behind him.

She sagged back in her chair; she had mishandled him. Clearly her initial estimation of this as a relatively easy job had been wrong and had led her to move too quickly with him. Certainly it had been too early to try body-work. She should have developed a firmer level of trust first by letting him do more of what he did so easily and well—talk.

The door opened. Weyland came back in and shut it quietly. He did not sit again but paced about the room, coming to rest at the window.

"Please excuse my rather childish behavior just now," he said. "Playing these games of yours brought it on."

"It's frustrating, playing games that are unfamiliar and that you can't control," she said. As he made no reply, she went on in a conciliatory tone, "I'm not belittling you, Edward. I just need to get us off whatever track you were taking us down so briskly. My feeling is that you're trying hard to regain your old stability.

"But that's the goal, not the starting-point. The only way to reach your goal is through the process, and you don't drive the therapy process like a train. You can only help the process happen, as though you were helping a tree grow."

"These games are part of the process?"

"Yes."

"And neither you nor I control the games?"

"That's right."

He considered. "Suppose I agree to try this process of yours; what would you want of me?"

Observing him carefully, she no longer saw the anxious scholar bravely struggling back from madness. Here was a different sort of man, armored, calculating. She didn't know what the change signaled, but she felt her own excitement stirring, and that meant she was on the track of—something.

"I have a hunch," she said slowly, "that this vampirism extends further back into your past than you've told me and possibly right up into the present as well. I think it's still with you. My style of therapy stresses dealing with the 'now' at least as much as the 'then'; if the vampirism is part of the present, telling me about it is crucial."

Silence.

"Can you tell me about being a vampire—being one now?"

"You won't like knowing," he said.

"Edward, try to tell me."

"I hunt," he said.

"Where? How? What sort of—of victims?"

He folded his arms and leaned his back against the window frame. "Very well, since you insist. There are a number of possibilities here in the city in summer. Those too poor to own air-conditioners sleep out on rooftops and fire-escapes. But often their blood is sour with drugs or liquor. The same is true of prostitutes. Bars are full of people but also full of smoke and noise, and there too the blood is fouled. I must choose my hunting grounds carefully. Often I go to openings of galleries or evening museum shows or department stores on their late nights— places where women may be approached."

And take pleasure in it, she thought, if they're out hunting also—for acceptable male companionship. Yet he's never married. Explore where this is going. "Only women?"

He gave her a sardonic glance, as if she were a slightly brighter student than he had first assumed.

"Hunting women is liable to be time-consuming and expensive. The

best hunting is in the part of Central Park they call the Ramble, where homosexual men seek encounters with others of their kind. I walk there too at night."

She glanced at the clock. "I'm sorry, Edward, but our time seems to be—"

"Only a moment more," he said coldly. "You asked; permit me to finish my answer. In the Ramble I find someone who doesn't reek of alcohol or drugs, who seems healthy, and who is not inclined to 'hook up' right there among the bushes. I invite such a man to my room. He judges me safe, at least: older, weaker than he is, unlikely to turn into a dangerous maniac. So he comes to my hotel. I feed on his blood. Now, I think, our time is up."

She sat, after he'd left, torn between rejoicing at his admission of the delusion's persistence and pity that his condition was so much worse than she had first thought. Her hope of having an easy time with him vanished. His initial presentation had been just that—a performance, an act. Forced to abandon it, he had dumped on her this lump of material, too much—and too strange—to take in all at once.

Her next client liked the padded chair, not the wooden one that Weyland had sat in during the first part of the hour. Floria started to move the wooden one back. The armrests came away in her hands.

She remembered him starting up in protest against her proposal of touching him. The grip of his fingers had fractured the joints, and the shafts now lay in splinters on the floor.

Floria wandered into Lucille's room at the clinic after the staff meeting. Lucille was lying on the couch with a wet rag over her eyes.

"I thought you looked green around the gills today," Floria said. "What's wrong?"

"Big bash last night," said Lucille in sepulchral tones. "I think I feel about the way you do after a session with Chubs. You haven't gotten rid of him yet, have you?"

"No. I had him lined up to go see Marty instead of me last week, but damned if he didn't show up at my door at his usual time. It's a lost cause. What I wanted to talk to you about was Dracula."

"What about him?"

"He's smarter, tougher, and sicker than I thought, and maybe I'm even less competent than I thought too. He's already walked out on me once—I almost lost him. I never took a course in treating monsters."

Lucille groaned. "Some days they're all monsters." This from Lucille, who worked longer hours than anyone at the clinic, to the despair

of her husband. She lifted the rag, refolded it, and placed it carefully across her forehead. "And if I had ten dollars for every client who's walked out on me—tell you what: I'll trade you Madame X for him, how's that?

"Remember Madame X, with the jangling bracelets and the parakeet eye make-up and the phobia about dogs? Now she's phobic about things dropping out of the sky onto her head. It'll turn out that one day when she was three a dog trotted by and pissed on her leg just as an over-passing pigeon shat on her head. What are we doing in this business?"

"God knows." Floria laughed. "But am I in this business these days—I mean, in the sense of practicing my so-called art? Blocked with my group work, beating my brains out on a book that won't go, and doing something—I'm not sure it's therapy—with a vampire . . . You know, once I had this sort of natural choreographer inside myself that hardly let me put a foot wrong and always knew how to correct a mistake if I did. Now that's gone. I feel as if I'm just going through a lot of incoherent motions. Whatever I had once, I've lost it."

Ugh, she thought, hearing the descent of her voice into a tone of gloomy self-pity.

"Well, don't complain about Dracula," Lucille said. "You were the one who insisted on taking him on. At least he's got you concentrating on his therapy instead of just wringing your hands. As long as you've started, stay with it—illumination may come. And now I'd better change the ribbon in my typewriter and get back to reviewing Silberman's latest best-seller on self-shrinking while I'm feeling mean enough to do it justice." She got up gingerly. "Stick around in case I faint and fall into the wastebasket."

"Luce. This case is what I'd like to try to write about."

"Dracula?" Lucille pawed through a desk drawer full of paper clips, pens, rubber bands, and old lipsticks.

"Dracula. A monograph—"

"Oh, I know the game: you scribble down everything you can and then read what you wrote to find out what's going on with the client, and with luck you end up publishing. Great! But if you are going to publish, don't piddle this away on a dinky paper. Do a book. Here's your subject, instead of those statistics you've been killing yourself over. This one is really exciting—a case study to put on the shelf next to Freud's own wolf-man, have you thought of that?"

Floria liked it. "What a book that could be—fame if not fortune. Notoriety most likely. How in the world could I convince our colleagues that it's legit? There's a lot of vampire stuff around right now—

plays on Broadway and tv, books all over the place, movies—they'll say I'm just trying to ride the coattails of a fad."

"No, no, what you do is show how this guy's delusion is related to the fad. Fascinating." Lucille, having found a ribbon, prodded doubtfully at the exposed innards of her typewriter.

"Suppose I fictionalize it," Floria said, "under a pseudonym. Why not ride the popular wave and be free in what I can say?"

"Listen, you've never written a word of fiction in your life, have you?" Lucille fixed her with a bloodshot gaze. "There's no evidence that you could turn out a bestselling novel. On the other hand, by this time you have a trained memory for accurately reporting therapeutic transactions. That's a strength you'd be foolish to waste. A solid professional book would be terrific—and a feather in the cap of every woman in the field. Just make sure you get good legal advice on disguising Dracula's identity well enough to avoid libel."

The cane-seated chair wasn't worth repairing, so she got its twin out of the bedroom to put in the office in its place. Puzzling: by his history Weyland was fifty-two, and by his appearance no muscle-man. She should have asked Doug—but how, exactly? "By the way, Doug, was Weyland ever a circus strong-man or a blacksmith? Does he secretly pump iron?" Ask the client himself—but not yet.

She invited some of the younger staff from the clinic over for a small party with a few of her outside friends. It was a good evening; they were not a heavy-drinking crowd, which meant the conversation stayed intelligent. The guests drifted about the long living room or stood in twos and threes at the windows looking down on West End Avenue as they talked.

Mort came, warming the room. Fresh from a session with some amateur chamber-music friends, he still glowed with the pleasure of making his cello sing. His own voice was unexpectedly light for so large a man. Sometimes Floria thought that the deep throb of the cello was his true voice.

He stood beside her talking with some others. There was no need to lean against his comfortable bulk or to have him put his arm around her waist. Their intimacy was longstanding, an effortless pleasure in each other that required neither demonstration nor concealment.

He was easily diverted from music to his next-favorite topic, the strengths and skills of athletes.

"Here's a question for a paper I'm thinking of writing," Floria said.

"Could a tall, lean man be exceptionally strong? I mean a man with a runner's build, more sinewy than bulky."

Mort rambled on in his thoughtful way. His answer seemed to be no.

"But what about chimpanzees?" put in a young clinician. "I went with a guy once who was an animal handler for TV, and he said a three-month-old chimp could demolish a strong man."

"It's all physical conditioning," somebody else said. "Modern people are softies."

Mort nodded. "Human beings in general are weakly made compared to other animals. It's a question of muscle insertions—the angles of how the muscles are attached to the bones. Some angles give better leverage than others. That's how a leopard can bring down a much bigger animal than itself. It has a muscular structure that gives it tremendous strength for its streamlined build."

Floria said, "If a man were built with muscle insertions like a leopard's, he'd look pretty odd, wouldn't he?"

"Not to an untrained eye," Mort said, sounding bemused by an inner vision. "And, my God, what an athlete he'd make—can you imagine a guy in the decathlon who's as strong as a leopard?"

When everyone else had gone Mort stayed, as he often did. Jokes about insertions, muscular and otherwise, soon led to sounds more expressive and more animal, but afterwards Floria didn't feel like resting snuggled together with Mort and talking. When her body stopped racing, her mind turned to her new client. She didn't want to discuss him with Mort, so she ushered Mort out as gently as she could and sat down by herself at the kitchen table with a glass of orange juice.

How to approach the reintegration of Weyland, the eminent, gray-haired academic with the rebellious vampire-self that had smashed his life out of shape?

She thought of the broken chair, Weyland's big hands crushing the wood. Old wood and dried-out glue, of course, or he never could have done it. He was a man, after all, not a leopard.

The day before the third session Weyland phoned and left a message with Hilda: he would not be coming to the office tomorrow for his appointment, but if Dr. Landauer were agreeable she would find him at their usual hour at the Central Park Zoo.

Am I going to let him move me around from here to there? she thought. Shouldn't—but why fight it? Give him some leeway, see what opens up in a different setting. Besides, it was a beautiful day, probably the last of the sweet May weather before the summer stickiness de-

scended. She gladly cut Kenny short so that she would have time to walk to the zoo.

There was a fair crowd there for a weekday. Well-groomed young matrons pushed clean, floppy babies in strollers. Weyland she spotted at once.

He was leaning against the railing that enclosed the seals' shelter and their murky green pool. His jacket, slung over his shoulder, draped elegantly down his long back. Floria thought him rather dashing and faintly foreign-looking. Women who passed him, she noticed, tended to glance back.

He looked at everyone. She had the impression that he knew quite well that she was walking up behind him.

"Outdoors makes a nice change from the office, Edward," she said, coming to the rail beside him. "But there must be more to this than a longing for fresh air." A fat seal lay in sculptural grace on the concrete, eyes blissfully shut, fur drying in the sun to a translucent watercolor umber.

Weyland straightened from the rail. They walked. He did not look at the animals; his eyes moved continually over the crowd. He said, "Someone has been watching for me at your office building."

"Who?"

"There are several possibilities. Pah, what a stench—though humans caged in similar circumstances smell as bad." He sidestepped a couple of shrieking children who were fighting over a balloon and headed out of the zoo under the musical clock.

They walked the uphill path northward through the park. By extending her own stride a little Floria found that she could comfortably keep pace with him.

"Is it peasants with torches?" she said. "Following you?"

"What a childish idea," he said.

All right, try another tack then. "You were telling me last time about hunting in the Ramble. Can we return to that?"

"If you wish." He sounded bored—a defense? Surely—she was certain this must be the right reading—surely his problem was a transmutation into "vampire" fantasy of an unacceptable aspect of himself. For men of his generation the confrontation with homosexual drives could be devastating.

"When you pick up someone in the Ramble, is it a paid encounter?"

"Usually."

"How do you feel about having to pay?" She expected resentment. He gave a faint shrug. "Why not? Others work to earn their bread.

I work too, very hard in fact. Why shouldn't I use my earnings to pay for my sustenance?"

Why did he never play the expected card? Baffled, she paused to drink from a fountain. They walked on.

"Once you've got your quarry, how do you—" She fumbled for a word.

"Attack?" he supplied, unperturbed. "There's a place on the neck, here, where pressure can interrupt the blood flow to the brain and cause unconsciousness. To get close enough to apply that pressure isn't difficult."

"You do it before or after any sexual activity?"

"Before, if possible," he said dryly, "and instead of." He turned aside to stalk up a slope to a granite outcrop that overlooked the path they had been following. He settled on his haunches, looking back the way they had come. Floria, glad she'd worn slacks today, sat down near him.

He didn't seem devastated—anything but. Press him, don't let him get by on cool. "Do you often prey on men in preference to women?"

"Certainly. I take what is easiest. Men have always been more accessible because women have been walled away like prizes or so physically impoverished by repeated child-bearing as to be unhealthy prey for me. All this has been changing recently, but gay men are still the simplest quarry." While she was recovering from her surprise at his unforeseen and weirdly skewed awareness of female history, he added suavely, "How carefully you control your expression, Dr. Landauer—no frown, no disapproval."

She did disapprove, she realized. She would prefer him not to be committed sexually to men. Oh, hell.

He went on, "Yet no doubt you see me as one who victimizes the already victimized. This is the world's way. A wolf brings down the stragglers at the edges of the herd. Gay men are denied the full protection of the human herd and are at the same time emboldened to make themselves known and available.

"On the other hand, unlike the wolf I can feed without killing, and these particular victims pose no threat to me that would cause me to kill. Outcasts themselves, even if they comprehend my true purpose among them they will not accuse me."

God, how neatly, completely, and ruthlessly he distanced the homosexual community from himself! "And how do you feel, Edward, about their purposes—their sexual expectations of you?"

"The same as about the sexual expectations of women whom I choose

to pursue: they don't interest me. Besides, once my hunger is active, sexual arousal is impossible. My physical unresponsiveness seems to surprise no one. Apparently impotence is expected in a gray-haired man, which suits my intention."

A Frisbee sailed past them, pursued by a trio of shouting kids. Floria's eye followed the arc of the red plastic disc. She was thinking, astonished again, that she had never heard a man speak of his own impotence with such cool indifference. She had induced him to talk about his problem all right. He was speaking as freely as he had in the first session, only this time it was no act. He was drowning her in more than she had ever expected or for that matter wanted to know about vampirism. What the hell; she was listening, she thought she understood—what was it all good for? Time for some cold reality, she thought; see how far he can carry all this incredible detail. Give the whole structure a shove.

"You realize, I'm sure, that people of either sex who make themselves so easily available are also liable to be carriers of disease. When was your last medical check-up?"

"My dear Dr. Landauer, my first medical check-up will be my last. Fortunately, I have no great need of one. Most serious illnesses— hepatitis, for example—reveal themselves to me by an alteration in the odor of the victim's skin. Warned, I abstain. When I do fall ill, as occasionally happens, I withdraw to some place where I can heal undisturbed. A doctor's attentions would be more dangerous to me than any disease."

Eyes on the path below, he continued calmly, "You can see by looking at me that there are no obvious clues to my unique nature. But believe me, an examination of any depth by even a half-sleeping medical practitioner would reveal some alarming deviations from the norm. I take pains to stay healthy, and I seem to be gifted with an exceptionally hardy constitution."

Fantasies of being unique and beyond fear; take him to the other pole. "I'd like you to try something now. Will you put yourself into the mind of a man you contact in the Ramble and describe your encounter with him from his point of view?"

He turned toward her and for some moments regarded her without expression. Then he resumed his surveillance of the path. "I will not do that. Though I made a poor peasant-with-torch on another occasion, I do have enough empathy with my quarry to enable me to hunt efficiently. I must draw the line at erasing the necessary distance that keeps prey and predator distinct.

"And now I think our ways part for today." He stood up, descended the hillside, and walked beneath some low-canopied trees, his tall back stooped, toward the Seventy-second Street entrance to the park.

Floria arose more slowly, aware suddenly of her shallow breathing and the sweat on her face. Back to reality or what remained of it. She looked at her watch. She was late for her next client.

Floria couldn't sleep that night. Barefoot in her bathrobe, she paced the living room by lamplight. They had sat together on that hill as isolated as in her office—more so, because there was no Hilda and no phone. He was, she knew, very strong, and he had sat close enough to her to reach out for that paralyzing touch to the neck—

Just suppose for a minute that Weyland had been brazenly telling the truth all along, counting on her to treat it as a delusion because on the face of it the truth was inconceivable?

Jesus, she thought, if I'm thinking that way about him, this therapy is more out of control than I thought. What kind of therapist becomes an accomplice to the client's fantasy? A crazy therapist, that's what kind.

Frustrated and confused by the turmoil in her mind, she wandered into the workroom. By morning the floor was covered with sheets of newsprint, each broadly marked by her felt-tipped pen. Floria sat in the midst of them, gritty-eyed and hungry.

She often approached problems this way, harking back to art training: turn off the thinking, put hand to paper, and see what the deeper, less verbally sophisticated parts of the mind have to say. Now that her dreams had deserted her, this was her only access to those levels.

The newsprint sheets were covered with rough representations of Weyland's face and form. Across several of them were scrawled words: DEAR DOUG, YOUR VAMPIRE IS FINE, IT'S YOUR EX-THERAPIST WHO'S OFF THE RAILS. WARNING: THERAPY CAN BE DANGEROUS TO YOUR HEALTH. ESPECIALLY IF YOU ARE THE THERAPIST. BEAUTIFUL VAM-PIRE, AWAKEN TO ME. AM I REALLY READY TO TAKE ON A LEGEND-ARY MONSTER? GIVE UP—REFER THIS ONE OUT. DO YOUR JOB—WORK IS A GOOD DOCTOR.

That last sounded pretty good, except that doing her job was precise-ly what she was feeling so shaky about these days.

Here was another message: HOW COME THIS ATTRACTION TO SOME ONE SO SCARY? Oh ho, she thought, is that a real feeling or an aimless reaction out of the body's early-morning hormone peak? You don't want to confuse honest libido with mere biological clockwork.

* * *

Deborah called. Babies cried in the background over the Scotch Symphony. Nick, Deb's husband, was a musicologist with fervent opinions on music and nothing else.

"We'll be in town a little later in the summer," Deborah said, "just for a few days at the end of July. Nicky has this seminar-convention thing. Of course, it won't be easy with the babies . . . I wondered if you might sort of coordinate your vacation to spend a little time with them?"

Baby-sit, that meant. Damn. Cute as they were and all that, damn! Floria gritted her teeth. Visits from Deb were difficult. Floria had been so proud of her bright, hard-driving daughter, and then suddenly Deborah had dropped her studies and rushed to embrace all the dangers that Floria had warned her against: a romantic, too-young marriage, instant breeding, no preparation for self-support, the works. Well, to each her own, but it was so wearing to have Deb around playing the empty-headed hausfrau.

"Let me think, Deb. I'd love to see all of you, but I've been considering spending a couple of weeks in Maine with your Aunt Nonnie." God knows I need a real vacation, she thought, though the peace and quiet up there is hard for a city kid like me to take for long. Still, Nonnie, Floria's younger sister, was good company. "Maybe you could bring the kids up there for a couple of days. There's room in that barn of a place, and of course Nonnie'd be happy to have you."

"Oh, no, Mom, it's so dead up there, it drives Nick crazy—don't tell Nonnie I said that. Maybe Nonnie could come down to the city instead. You could cancel a date or two and we could all go to Coney Island together, things like that."

Kid things, which would drive Nonnie crazy and Floria too before long. "I doubt she could manage," Floria said. "But I'll ask. Look, hon, if I do go up there, you and Nick and the kids could stay here at the apartment and save some money."

"We have to be at the hotel for the seminar," Deb said rather shortly. No doubt she was feeling just as impatient as Floria was by now. "And the kids haven't seen you for a long time—it would be really nice if you could stay in the city just for a few days."

"We'll try to work something out." Always working something out. Concord never comes naturally—first we have to butt heads and get pissed off. Each time you call I hope it'll be different, Floria thought.

Somebody shrieked for "oly"—jelly that would be. Floria felt a sudden rush of warmth for them, her grandkids, for God's sake. Having

been a young mother herself, she was still young enough to really enjoy them (and to fight with Deb about how to bring them up).

Deb was starting an awkward good-bye. Floria replied, put the phone down, and sat with her head back against the flowered kitchen wallpaper, thinking, Why do I feel so rotten now? Deb and I aren't close, no comfort, seldom friends, though we were once. Have I said everything wrong, made her think I don't want to see her and don't care about her family? What does she want from me that I can't seem to give her? Approval? Maybe she thinks I still hold her marriage against her. Well, I do, sort of. What right do I have to be critical, me with my divorce? What terrible things would she say to me, would I say to her, that we take such care not to say anything important at all?

"I think today we might go into sex," she said.

Weyland responded dryly, "Might we indeed. Does it titillate you to wring confessions of solitary vice from men of mature years?"

Oh, no you don't, she thought. You can't sidestep so easily. "Under what circumstances do you find yourself sexually aroused?"

"Most usually upon waking from sleep," he said indifferently.

"What do you do about it?"

"The same as others do. I am not a cripple, I have hands."

"Do you have fantasies at these times?"

"No. Women, and men for that matter, appeal to me very little, either in fantasy or reality."

"Ah—what about female vampires?" she said, trying not to sound arch.

"I know of none."

Of course: the neatest out in the book. "They're not needed for reproduction, I suppose, because people who die of vampire bites become vampires themselves."

He said testily, "Nonsense. I am not a communicable disease."

So he had left an enormous hole in his construct. She headed straight for it: "Then how does your kind reproduce?"

"I have no kind, so far as I am aware," he said, "and I do not reproduce. Why should I, when I may live for centuries still, perhaps indefinitely? My sexual equipment is clearly only detailed biological mimicry, a form of protective coloration." How beautiful, how simple a solution, she thought, full of admiration in spite of herself. "Do I occasionally detect a note of prurient interest in your questions, Dr. Landauer? Something akin to stopping at the cage to watch the tigers mate in the zoo?"

"Probably," she said, feeling her cheeks grow hot. He had a great backhand return-shot there. "How do you feel about that?"

He shrugged.

"To return to the point: do I hear you saying that you have no urge whatever to engage in sexual intercourse with anyone?"

"Would you mate with your livestock?"

His matter-of-fact arrogance took her breath away. She said weakly, "Men have reportedly done so."

"Driven men. I am not driven in that way. My sex-urge is of low frequency and is easily dealt with unaided—although I have occasionally engaged in copulation out of the necessity to keep up appearances. I am capable, but not—like humans—obsessed."

Was he sinking into lunacy before her eyes? "I think I hear you saying," she said, striving to keep her voice neutral, "that you're not just a man with a unique way of life. I think I hear you saying that you're not human at all."

"I thought that this was already clear."

"And that there are no others like you."

"None that I know of."

"Then—you see yourself as what? Some sort of mutation?"

"Perhaps. Or perhaps your kind are the mutation."

She saw disdain in the curl of his lip. "How does your mouth feel now?"

"The corners are drawn down. The feeling is contempt."

"Can you let the contempt speak?"

He got up and went to stand at the window, positioning himself slightly to one side as if to stay hidden from the street below.

"Edward," she said.

He looked back at her. "Humans are my food. I draw the life out of their veins. Sometimes I kill them. I am greater than they are. Yet I must spend my time thinking about their habits and their drives, scheming to avoid the dangers they pose—I hate them."

She felt the hatred like a dry heat radiating from him. God, he really lived all this! She had tapped into a furnace of feeling. And now—? The sensation of triumph wavered, and she grabbed at a next move: hit him with reality now, while he's burning.

"What about blood banks?" she said. "Your food is commercially available, so why all the complication and danger of the hunt?"

"You mean turn my efforts to piling up a fortune and buying blood by the case? That would certainly make for an easier, less risky life in

the short run. I could fit quite comfortably into modern society if I became just another consumer.

"However, I prefer to keep the mechanics of my survival firmly in my own hands. After all, I can't afford to lose my hunting skills. In two hundred years there may be no blood banks, but I will still need my food."

Jesus, you set him a hurdle and he just flies over it. Are there no weaknesses in all this, has he no blind spots? Look at his tension—go back to that. "What do you feel now in your body?"

"Tightness." He pressed his spread fingers to his abdomen.

"What are you doing with your hands?"

"I put my hands to my stomach."

"Can you speak for your stomach?"

" 'Feed me or die,' " he snarled.

Elated again, she closed in. "And for yourself, in answer?"

" 'Will you never be satisfied?' " He glared at her. "You shouldn't seduce me into quarreling with the terms of my own existence!"

"Your stomach is your existence," she paraphrased.

"The gut determines," he said harshly. "That first, everything else after."

"Say, 'I resent—' "

He held to a tense silence.

" 'I resent the power of my gut over my life,' " she said for him.

He stood with an abrupt motion and glanced at his watch, an elegant flash of slim silver on his wrist. "Enough," he said.

That night at home she began a set of notes that would never enter his file at the office, notes toward the proposed book.

> Couldn't do it, couldn't get properly into the sex thing with him. Everything shoots off in all directions. His vampire concept so thoroughly worked out, find myself half-believing sometimes—my own childish fantasy-response to his powerful death-avoidance, contact-avoidance fantasy. Lose professional distance every time— is that what scares me about him? Don't really want to shatter his delusion (own life a mess, what right to tear down others' patterns?)—so see it as real? Wonder how much of "vampirism" he acts out, how far, how often. Something attractive in his purely selfish, predatory stance—the lure of the great outlaw.

> Told me today quite coolly about a man he killed once—inadvertently!—by drinking too much from him. *Is* it fantasy? Of

course—the victim, he thinks, was college student. Breathes there a professor who hasn't dreamed of murdering some representative youth, retaliation for years of classroom frustration? Speaks of teaching with caustic humor—amuses him to work at cultivating the minds of those he regards strictly as bodies, containers of his sustenance. He shows the alienness of full-blown psychopathology, poor bastard, plus clean-cut logic. Suggested he find another job (assuming his delusion at least in part related to pressures at Cayslin); his fantasy-persona, the vampire, more realistic about job-switching than I am:

"For a man of my apparent age it's not so easy to make such a change in these tight times. I might have to take a position lower on the ladder of 'success' as you people assess it." Status important to him? "Certainly. An eccentric professor is one thing; an eccentric pipe-fitter another. And I like good cars, which are expensive to own and run." (He refuses though to discuss other "jobs" from former lives.)

We are deep into the fantasy—where the hell going? Damn right I don't control the "games"—preplanned therapeutic strategies get whirled away as soon as we begin. Nerve-wracking.

Tried again to have him take the part of his enemy-victim, peasant with torch. Asked if he felt himself rejecting that point of view? Frosty reply: "Naturally. The peasant's point of view is in no way my own. I've been reading in your field, Dr. Landauer. You work from the Gestalt orientation—" Originally, yes, I corrected; eclectic these days. "But you do proceed from the theory that I am projecting some aspect of my own feelings outward onto others, whom I then treat as my victims? Your purpose then must be to maneuver me into accepting as my own the projected 'victim' aspect of myself. This integration is supposed to effect the freeing of energy previously locked into maintaining the projection. All this is an interesting insight into the nature of ordinary human confusion, but I am not an ordinary human, and I am not confused. I cannot afford confusion."

Felt sympathy for him—telling me he's afraid of having own internal confusions exposed in therapy, too threatening. Keep chipping away at delusion, though with what prospect—it's so complex, so deep-seated.

Returned to his phrase "my apparent age." He asserts he has lived many human lifetimes, all details forgotten however during periods of suspended animation between lives. Perhaps sensing my skepticism at such handy amnesia, grew cool and distant, claimed to know little about the hibernation process itself: "The essence of

this state is that I sleep through it—hardly an ideal condition for making scientific observations."

Edward thinks his body synthesizes vitamins, minerals (as all our bodies synthesize Vitamin D), even proteins. Describes unique design he deduces in himself: special intestinal microfauna plus super-efficient body chemistry that extracts enough energy to live on from blood. Damn good mileage per calorie, too. (Recall observable tension, first interview, at question about drinking—my note, possible alcohol problem!)

Speak for blood: " 'Lacking me, you have no life. I flow to the heart's soft drumbeat through lightless prisons of flesh. I am rich, I am nourishing, I am difficult to attain.' " Stunned to find him positively lyrical on subject of his "food," almost hated to move him on. Drew attention to whispering voice of blood.

" 'Yes, I am secret, hidden beneath the surface, patient, silent, steady, I work unnoticed, an unseen thread of vitality running from age to age—beautiful, efficient, self-renewing, self-cleansing, warm, filling—' " Could see him getting worked up. Finally stood: "My appetite is pressing. I must leave you." And he did.

Sat and trembled for five minutes after.

New development (or new perception?): he sometimes comes across very unsophisticated about own feelings—lets me pursue subjects of extreme intensity and delicacy to him.

Asked him to daydream—a hunt. (Hands—mine—shaking now as I write. God. What a session.) He told of picking up a woman at poetry reading, 92nd Street Y—has N.Y.C. all worked out, circulates to avoid too much notice any one spot. Spoke easily, eyes shut without observable strain: chooses from audience redhead in glasses, dress with drooping neckline (ease of access), no perfume (strong smells bother him). Approaches during intermission, encouraged to see her fanning away smoke of others' cigarets—meaning she doesn't smoke, health sign. Agreed in not enjoying the reading, they adjourn together to coffee shop.

"She asks whether I am a teacher," he says, eyes shut, mouth amused. "My clothes, glasses, manner all suggest this, and I emphasize the impression—it reassures. She is a copy editor for a publishing house. We talk about books. The waiter brings her a gummy-looking pastry. As a non-eater, I pay little attention to the quality of restaurants, so I must apologize to her. She waves this away—is engrossed, or pretending to be engrossed, in talk." A longish dialog between interested woman and Edward doing shy-lonesome-scholar act—dead wife, competitive young colleagues who don't understand him, quarrels in professional jour-

nals with big shots in his field—a version of what he first told me. She's attracted (of course—lanky, rough-cut elegance plus hints of vulnerability all very alluring, as intended). He offers to take her home.

Tension in his body at this point in narrative—spine clear of chair-back, hands braced on thighs. "She settles beside me in the back of the cab, talking about problems of her own career—illegible manuscripts of Biblical length, mulish editors, suicidal authors —and I make comforting comments, I lean nearer and put my arm along the back of the seat, behind her shoulders. Traffic is heavy, we move slowly. There is time to make my meal here in the taxi and avoid a tedious extension of the situation into her apartment— if I move soon."

How do you feel?

"Eager," he says, voice husky. "My hunger is so roused I can scarcely restrain myself. A powerful hunger, not like yours—mine compels. I embrace her shoulders lightly, make kindly-uncle remarks, treading that fine line between the game of seduction she perceives and the game of friendly interest I affect. My real purpose underlies all: what I say, how I look, every gesture is part of the stalk. There is an added excitement—and fear—because I am doing my hunting in the presence of a third person—behind the cabbie's head." Could scarcely breathe. Studied him—intent face, mask-like with closed eyes, nostrils slightly flared; legs tensed, hands clenched on knees. Whispering: "I press the place on her neck. She starts, sighs faintly, silently drops against me. In the stale stench of the cab's interior, with the ticking of the meter in my ears and the mutter of the radio—I take hold here, at the tenderest part of her throat. Sound subsides into the background—I feel the sweet blood beating under her skin, I taste salt at the moment before I—strike. My saliva thins her blood, it flows out, I draw it into my mouth swiftly, swiftly, before she can wake, before we can arrive . . ."

Trailed off, sat back loosely in the chair. Saw him swallow. "Ah, I feed." Heard him sigh. Managed to ask about physical sensation. "Warm. Heavy here"—touches his belly—"in a pleasant way. The good taste of blood, tart and rich, in my mouth . . ."

And then? A flicker of movement beneath his closed eyelids: "In time I am aware that the cabbie has glanced back once and has taken our—embrace for just that. I can feel the cab slowing, hear him move to turn off the meter. I withdraw, I quickly wipe my mouth on my handkerchief. I take her by the shoulders and shake her gently. Does she often have these attacks, I inquire, the soul of concern. She comes around, bewildered, weak, thinks she has

fainted. I give the driver extra money and ask him to wait. He looks
intrigued—'What was that all about?' I can see the question in his
face—but as a true New Yorker he will not expose his own ignorance by inquiring.

"I escort the woman to her front door, supporting her as she
staggers. Any suspicion of me that she may entertain, however
formless and hazy, is allayed by my stern charging of the doorman
to see that she reaches her apartment safely. She grows embarrassed, thinks perhaps that if not put off by her 'illness' I would
spend the night with her, which moves her to press upon me,
unasked, her telephone number. I bid her a solicitous good night
and take the cab back to my hotel, where I sleep."

No sex? No sex. How did he feel about the victim as a person?
"She was food."

This was his "hunting" of last night, he admits afterward, not
a made-up dream. No boasting in it, just telling. Telling me! Think:
I can go talk to Lucille, Mort, Doug, others about most of what
matters to me. Edward has only me to talk to and that for a
fee—what isolation! No wonder the stone, monumental face—only
those long, strong lips (his point of contact, verbal and physical-in-
fantasy, with world and with "food") are truly expressive. An
exciting narration; uncomfortable to find I felt not only empathy
but enjoyment. Suppose he picked up and victimized—even in
fantasy—Deb or Hilda, how would I feel then?

Later: truth—I also found this recital sexually stirring. Keep
visualizing how he looked finishing this "dream"—sat very still,
head up, look of thoughtful pleasure on his face. Like handsome
intellectual listening to music.

Kenny showed up unexpectedly at Floria's office on Monday, bursting with malevolent energy. She happened to be free, so she took
him—something was definitely up. He sat on the edge of his chair.

"I know why you're trying to unload me," he accused. "It's that new
one, the tall guy with the snooty look—what is he, an old actor or
something? Anybody could see he's got you itching for him."

"Kenny, when was it that I first spoke to you about terminating our
work together?" she said patiently.

"Don't change the subject. Let me tell you, in case you don't know
it: that guy isn't really interested, doctor, because he's a fruit. A faggot.
You want to know how I know?"

Oh Lord, she thought wearily, he's regressed to age ten. She could
see that she was going to hear the rest whether she wanted to or not.

What in God's name was the world like for Kenny, if he clung so frantically to her despite her failure to help him?

"Listen, I knew right away there was something flaky about him, so I followed him home from here to that hotel where he lives. I followed him the other afternoon, too. He walked around like he does a lot, and then he went into one of those ritzy movie houses on Third that open early and show risqué foreign movies—you know, Japs cutting each other's things off and glop like that. This one was French, though.

"Well, there was a guy came in, a Madison Avenue type carrying his attaché case, taking a work break or something. Your man moved over and sat down behind him and reached out and sort of stroked the guy's neck, and the guy leaned back, and your man leaned forward and started nuzzling at him, you know—kissing him.

"I saw it. They had their heads together and they stayed like that awhile. It was disgusting: complete strangers, without even 'Hello.' The Madison Avenue guy just sat there with his head back looking zonked, you know, just swept away, and what he was doing with his hands under the raincoat in his lap I couldn't see, but I bet you can guess.

"And then your fruity friend got up and walked out. I did, too, and I hung around a little outside. After a while the Madison Avenue guy came out looking all sleepy and loose, like after you-know-what, and he wandered off on his own someplace.

"What do you think now?" he ended, on a high, triumphant note.

Her impulse was to slap his face the way she would have slapped Deb-as-a-child for tattling. But this was a client, not a kid. God give me strength, she thought.

"Kenny, you're fired."

"You can't!" he squealed. "You can't! What will I—who can I—"

She stood up, feeling weak but hardening her voice. "I'm sorry. I absolutely cannot have a client who makes it his business to spy on other clients. You already have a list of replacement therapists from me."

He gaped at her in slack-jawed dismay, his eyes swimmy with tears.

"I'm sorry, Kenny. Call this a dose of reality therapy and try to learn from it. There are some things you simply will not be allowed to do." She felt stronger, better: it was done at last.

"I hate you!" He surged out of his chair, knocking it back against the wall. Threateningly, he glared at the fish tank, but, contenting himself with a couple of kicks at the nearest table-leg, he stamped out.

Floria buzzed Hilda: "No more appointments for Kenny, Hilda. You can close his file."

"Whoopee," Hilda said.

Poor, horrid Kenny. Impossible to tell what would happen to him, better not to speculate or she might relent, call him back . . . She had encouraged him, really, by listening instead of shutting him up and throwing him out before any damage was done.

Was it damaging to know the truth? In her mind's eye she saw a cream-faced young man out of a Black Thumb Vodka ad wander from a movie theater into daylight, yawning and rubbing absently at a sore spot on his neck . . .

She didn't even look at the telephone on the table or think about whom to call, now that she believed. No, she was going to keep quiet about Dr. Edward Lewis Weyland, her vampire.

Hardly alive at staff meeting, clinic, yesterday—people asking what's the matter, fobbed them off. Settled down today. Had to, to face him.

Asked him what he felt were his strengths. He said speed, cunning, ruthlessness. Animal strengths, I said. What about imagination, or is that strictly human? He defended at once: not human only. Lion, waiting at water-hole where no zebra yet drinks, thinks "Zebra—eat," therefore performs feat of imagining event yet-to-come. Self experienced as animal? Yes—reminded me that humans are also animals. Pushed for his early memories, he objected: "Gestalt is here-and-now, not history-taking." I insisted, citing anomalous nature of his situation; my own refusal to be bound by any one theoretical framework. He defends tensely: "Suppose I became lost there in memory, distracted from dangers of the present, left unguarded from those dangers?"

Speak for memory. He resists, but at length attempts it: " 'I am heavy with the multitudes of the past.' " Fingertips to forehead, propping up all that weight of lives. " 'So heavy, filling worlds of time laid down eon by eon, I accumulate, I persist, I demand recognition. I am as real as the life around you—more real, weightier, richer.' " His voice sinking, shoulders bowed, head in hands—I begin to feel pressure at the back of my own skull. " 'Let me in.' " Only a rough whisper now. " 'I offer beauty as well as terror. Let me in.' " Whispering also I suggest he reply to his memory. "Memory, you want to crush me," he groans. "You would overwhelm me with the cries of animals, the odor and jostle of bodies, old betrayals, dead joys, filth and anger from other times—I must concentrate on the danger now. Let me be." All I can take of this crazy conflict, I gabble us off onto something else. He looks up—relief? —follows my lead—where? Rest of session a blank.

No wonder sometimes no empathy at all—a species boundary! He

has to be utterly self-centered just to keep balance—self-centeredness of an animal. Thought just now of our beginning, me trying to push him to produce material, trying to control him, manipulate—no way, no way; so here we are, someplace else—I feel dazed, in shock, but stick with it—it's real.

Therapy with a dinosaur, a Martian.

"You call me 'Weyland' now, not 'Edward.' " I said first name couldn't mean much to one with no memory of being called by that name as a child, silly to pretend it signifies intimacy where it can't. I think he knows now that I believe him. Without prompting, told me truth of disappearance from Cayslin. No romance; he tried to drink from a woman who worked there, she shot him, stomach and chest. Luckily for him, small-calibre pistol, and he was wearing a lined coat over three-piece suit. Even so, badly hurt. (Midsection stiffness I noted when he first came—he was still in some pain at that time.) He didn't "vanish"—fled, hid, was found by questionable types who caught on to what he was, sold him "like a chattel" to someone here in the city. He was imprisoned, fed, put on exhibition—very privately—for gain. Got away. "Do you believe any of this?" Never asked anything like that before, seems of concern to him now. I said my belief or lack of same was immaterial; remarked on hearing a lot of bitterness.

Steepled his fingers, looked brooding at me over tips: "I nearly died there. No doubt my purchaser and his friends are still searching for me. Mind you, I had some reason at first to be glad of the attentions of the people who kept me prisoner. I was in no condition to fend for myself. They brought me food and kept me hidden and sheltered, whatever their motives. There are always advantages . . ."

Silence today started a short session. Hunting poor last night, Weyland still hungry. Much restless movement, watching goldfish darting in tank, scanning bookshelves. Asked him to be books. "I am old and full of knowledge, well-made to last long. You see only the title, the substance is hidden. I am a book that stays closed." Malicious twist of the mouth, not quite a smile: "This is a good game." Is he feeling threatened too—already "opened" too much to me? Too strung out with him to dig when he's skimming surfaces that should be probed. Don't know how to *do* therapy with Weyland—just have to let things happen, hope it's good. But what's "good"? Aristotle? Rousseau? Ask Weyland what's good, he'll say, "Blood."

Everything in a spin—these notes too confused, fragmentary—worthless for a book, just a mess, like me, my life. Tried to call Deb

last night, cancel visit. Nobody home, thank God. Can't tell her to stay away—but damn it—do not need complications now.

Floria went down to Broadway with Lucille to get more juice, cheese, and crackers for the clinic fridge. This week it was their turn to do the provisions, a chore that rotated among the staff. Their talk about grant proposals for the support of the clinic trailed off.

"Let's sit a minute," Floria said. They crossed to a traffic island in the middle of the avenue. It was a sunny afternoon, close enough to lunchtime so that the brigade of old people who normally occupied the benches had thinned out. Floria sat down and kicked a crumpled beer can and some greasy fast-food wrappings back under the bench.

"You look like hell but wide awake, at least," Lucille commented.

"Things are still rough," Floria said. "I keep hoping to get my life under control so I'll have some energy left for Deb and Nick and the kids when they arrive, but I can't seem to do it. Group was awful last night—a member accused me afterward of having abandoned them all. I think I have, too. The professional messes and the personal are all related somehow, they run into each other. I should be keeping them apart so I can deal with them separately, but I can't. I can't concentrate, my mind is all over the place. Except with Dracula, who keeps me riveted with astonishment when he's in the office and bemused the rest of the time."

A bus roared by, shaking the pavement and the benches. Lucille waited until the noise faded. "Relax about the group. They'd have defended you if you'd been attacked during the session. They'd all understand, even if you don't seem to: it's the summer doldrums, people don't want to work, they expect you to do it all for them. But don't push so hard. You're not a shaman who can magic your clients back into health."

Floria tore two cans of juice out of a six-pack and handed one to her. On a street corner opposite a violent argument broke out in typewriter-fast Spanish between two women. Floria sipped tinny juice and watched. She'd seen a guy last winter straddle another on that same corner and try to smash his brains out on the icy sidewalk. What's crazy, what's health?

"It's a good thing you dumped Chubs, anyhow," Lucille added. "I don't know what finally brought that on, but it's definitely a move in the right direction. What about Count Dracula? You don't talk about him much anymore. I thought I diagnosed a yen for his venerable body."

Floria shifted uncomfortably on the bench and didn't answer. If only she could deflect Lucille's sharp-eyed curiosity—

"Oh," Lucille said. "I see. You really are hot—or at least warm. Has he noticed?"

"I don't think so. He's not on the lookout for that kind of response from me. He says sex with other people doesn't interest him, and I think he's telling the truth."

"Weird," Lucille said. "What about *Vampire on My Couch?* Shaping up all right?"

"It's shaky, like everything else. I'm worried that I don't know how things are going to come out. I mean, Freud's wolf-man case was a success, as therapy goes. Will my vampire case turn out successfully?"

She glanced at Lucille's puzzled face, made up her mind, and plunged ahead. "Luce, think of it this way: suppose, just suppose, that my Dracula is for real, an honest-to-God vampire—"

"Oh, *shit!*" Lucille erupted in anguished exasperation. "Damn it, Floria, enough is enough—will you stop futzing around and get some help? Coming to pieces yourself and trying to treat this poor nut with a vampire fixation—how can you do him any good? No wonder you're worried about his therapy!"

"Please, just listen, help me think this out. My purpose can't be to cure him of what he is. Suppose vampirism isn't a defense he has to learn to drop? Suppose it's the core of his identity? Then what do I do?"

Lucille rose abruptly and marched away from her across the traffic, plunging through a gap between the rolling waves of cabs and trucks. Floria caught up with her on the next block.

"Listen, will you? Luce, you see the problem? I don't need to help him see who and what he is, he knows that perfectly well, and he's not crazy, far from it—"

"Maybe not," Lucille said grimly, "but you are. Don't dump this junk on me outside of office hours, Floria. I don't spend my time listening to nut-talk unless I'm getting paid."

"Just tell me if this makes psychological sense to you: he's healthier than most of us because he's always true to his identity, even when he's engaged in deceiving others. A fairly narrow, rigorous set of requirements necessary to his survival—that *is* his identity, and it commands him completely. Anything extraneous could destroy him. To go on living he has to act solely out of his own undistorted necessity, and if that isn't authenticity, what is? So he's healthy, isn't he?" She paused, feeling a sudden lightness in herself. "And that's the best sense I've been able to make of this whole business so far."

They were in the middle of the block. Lucille, who could not on her short legs outwalk Floria, turned on her suddenly. "What the hell do you think you're doing, calling yourself a therapist? For God's sake, Floria, don't try to rope me into this kind of professional irresponsibility. You're just dipping into your client's fantasies instead of helping him to handle them. That's not therapy, it's collusion. Have some sense! Admit you're over your head in troubles of your own, retreat to firmer ground—go get treatment for yourself!"

Floria angrily shook her head. When Lucille turned away and hurried on up the block toward the clinic, Floria let her go without trying to detain her.

Thought about Lucille's advice. After my divorce going back into therapy for a while did help, but now? Retreat again to being a client, like old days in training—so young, inadequate, defenseless then. Awful prospect. And I'd have to hand W. over to somebody else—who? I'm not up to handling him, can't cope, too anxious, yet with all the limitations we do good therapy together somehow. I offer: he's free to take, refuse, use as suits, as far as he's willing to go. I serve as resource while he does own therapy—isn't that therapeutic ideal, free of "shoulds," "shouldn'ts"?

Saw ballet with Mort, lovely evening—time out from W.—talking, singing, pirouetting all the way home, feeling safe as anything in the shadow of Mort-mountain, rolled later with that humming (off-key), sun-warm body.

Then today W. talked mechanics of blood-sucking while I thought cowardly thoughts about giving him notice, calling a halt. Doesn't bite, he says; has puncturing organ under tongue, hence no fangs. Half my mind saying, ah-hah, always wondered why movie vampire's victims have those two little holes in the throat, maybe 1 inch apart, while vampire has these huge canines 3 inches from each other at least. Other half screaming, Lucille's right, one (or both) here is crazy—*Get out!*

Then he says he saw me at Lincoln Center last night, avoided me because of Mort. W. is ballet fan! Started attending to pick up victims, now also because dance puzzles and pleases. "When a group dances well, the meaning is easy—the dancers make a visual complement to the music, all their moves necessary, coherent, and flowing. When a gifted soloist performs, the pleasure of making the moves is echoed in my own body. The soloist's absorption is total, much like my own in the actions of the hunt.

"But when a man and a woman dance together, something else happens. What is it? Sometimes one is hunter, one is prey, or they

shift these roles between them. Yet some other level of significance exists—I suppose to do with sex, and I feel it—a tugging sensation, here"—touched his solar plexus—"but I do not understand it."

Worked with his reactions to ballet. The response he feels to pas de deux is a kind of pull, "like hunger but not hunger." Of course he's baffled—Balanchine writes that the pas de deux is always a love story between man and woman. W. isn't man, isn't woman, yet the drama reaches him. His hands hovering as he spoke, fingers spread toward each other. Pointed this out. Body-work comes easier to him now: joined his hands, interlaced fingers, spoke for hands without prompting: "We are similar, we want the comfort of like closing to like." What would it be for him, to find—likeness, another of his kind? "Female?" Starts to tell me how unlikely this is—no, forget sex and pas de deux for now—just to find your like, another vampire. He springs up, agitated now. There are none, he insists.

But what would it be like? What would happen?

"I fear it!" Sits again, hands clenched. "I long for it." Silence. He watches goldfish, I watch him. I withhold fatuous attempt to pin down this insight, if that's what it is—what can I know about his insight? Suddenly he turns, studies me intently till I lose nerve, react, cravenly suggest that if I make him uncomfortable he may choose to switch to a male therapist. "Certainly not." More follows, all gold: "There is value to me in what we do here, Dr. Landauer, much against my earlier expectations. Although people talk appreciatively of honest speech they generally avoid it, and I myself have found scarcely any use for it at all. Your straightforwardness with me—and the straightforwardness you require in return—this is healthy in a life so dependent on deception as mine."

Sat there, wordless, much moved, thinking of what I don't show him—my upset life, seat-of-pants course with him and attendant strain, attraction to him—I'm holding out on him while he appreciates my honesty.

Hesitation, then lower-voiced: "Also, there are limits on my methods of self-discovery, short of turning myself over to a laboratory for vivisection. I have no others like myself to look at and learn from. Any tools that may help are worth much to me, and these games of yours are—potent."

Other stuff besides, not important. Important: he moves me and he draws me and he keeps on coming back. Hang in if he does.

Bad night—Kenny's aunt called: no bill from me this month, so if he's not seeing me, who's keeping an eye on him, where's he

hanging out? Much implied blame for what *might* happen. Absurd, but shook me up: I did fail Kenny. Called off group this week also; too much.

No, it was a *good* night—first dream in months I can recall, contact again with own depths—but disturbing. Dreamed myself in cab with W. in place of the woman from the Y. He put his hand not on my neck but breast—I felt intense sensual response in the dream, also anger and fear so strong they woke me.

Thinking about this: anyone leans toward him sexually, to him a sign his hunting technique has maneuvered prospective victim into range, maybe arouses his appetite for blood. I *don't want that.* "She was food." I am not food, I am a person. No thrill at languishing away in his arms in a taxi while he drinks my blood—that's disfigured sex, masochism. My sex response in dream signaled to me I would be his victim—I rejected that, woke up.

Mention of *Dracula* (novel). W. dislikes: meandering, inaccurate, those absurd fangs. Says he himself has when needed a sort of needle under his tongue, used to pierce skin. No offer to demonstrate, and no request from me. I brightly brought up historical Vlad Dracul—celebrated instance of Turkish envoys who, upon refusing to uncover to Vlad to show respect, were killed by spiking their hats to their skulls. "Nonsense," snorts W. "A clever ruler would use very small thumbtacks and dismiss the envoys to moan about the streets of Verna holding their tacked heads." First spontaneous play he's shown—took head in hands and uttered plaintive groans: "Ow, oh, ooh." I cracked up. W. reverted at once to usual dignified manner: "You can see that this would serve the ruler much more effectively as an object lesson against rash pride."

Later, same light vein: "I know why I'm a vampire; why are you a therapist?" Off balance as usual, said things about helping, mental health, etc. He shook his head: "And people think of a vampire as arrogant! You want to perform cures in a world which exhibits very little health of any kind—and it's the same arrogance with all of you. This one wants to be President or Class Monitor or Department Chairman or Union Boss, another must be first to fly to the stars or to transplant the human brain, and on and on. As for me, I wish only to satisfy my appetite in peace." And those of us whose appetite is for competence, for effectiveness? Thought of Green, treated eight years ago, went on to be indicted for running a hellish "home" for aged. I had helped him stay functional so he could destroy the helpless for profit.

W. not my first predator, only most honest and direct. Scared; not of attack by W., but of process we're going through. I'm

beginning to be up to it (?), but still—utterly unpredictable, impossible to handle or manage—Occasional stirrings of inward choreographer that used to shape my work so surely. Have I been afraid of that, holding it down in myself, choosing mechanical manipulation instead? Not a choice with W.—thinking no good, strategy no good, nothing left but instinct, clear and uncluttered responses if I can find them. Have to be my own authority with him, as he is always his own authority with a world in which he's unique. So work with W. not exhausting—exhilarating too, along with strain, fear.

Am I growing braver? Not much choice.

Park again today (air-conditioning out at office). Avoiding Lucille's phone calls from clinic (very reassuring that she calls despite quarrel, but don't want to take all this up with her again). Also meeting W. in open feels saner somehow—wild creatures belong outdoors? Sailboat pond N. of 72nd, lots of kids, garbage, one beautiful tall boat drifting.

W. maintains he remembers no childhood, no parents. I told him my astonishment, confronted by someone who never had a life of the previous generation (even adopted parent) shielding him from death—how naked we stand when the last shield falls. Got caught in remembering a death dream of mine, dream it now and then—couldn't concentrate, got scared, spoke of it—a dog tumbled under a passing truck, ejected to side of the road where it lay unable to move except to lift head and shriek—couldn't help. Shaking nearly to tears—remembered mother got into dream somehow—had blocked that at first. Didn't say it now. Tried to rescue situation, show W. how to work with a dream (sitting in vine arbor near band shell, some privacy).

He focused on my obvious shakiness: "The air vibrates constantly with the death-cries of countless animals large and small. What is the death of one dog?" Leaned close, speaking quietly, instructing. "Many creatures are dying in ways too dreadful to imagine. I am part of the world; I listen to the pain. You people claim to be above all that. You deafen yourselves with your own noise and pretend there's nothing else to hear. Then these screams enter your dreams, and you have to seek therapy because you have lost the nerve to listen."

Remembered myself, said, Be a dying animal. He refused: "You are the one who dreams this." I had a horrible flash, felt I was the dog—helpless, doomed, hurting—burst into tears. The great therapist, bringing her own hang-ups into session with client! Enraged with self, which did not help stop bawling.

W. disconcerted, I think; didn't speak. People walked past, glanced over, ignored us. W. said finally, "What is this?" Nothing, just the fear of death. "Oh, the fear of death. That's with me all the time. One must simply get used to it." Tears into laughter. Goddamn wisdom of the ages. He got up to go, paused: "And tell that stupid little man who used to precede me at your office to stop following me around. He puts himself in danger that way."

Kenny, damn it! Aunt doesn't know where he is, no answer on his phone. Idiot!

Sketching all night—useless. W. beautiful beyond the scope of line—the beauty of singularity, cohesion, rooted in absolute devotion to demands of his specialized body. In feeding (woman in taxi), utter absorption one wants from a man in sex—no score-keeping, no fantasies, just hot urgency of appetite, of senses, the moment by itself.

His sleeves worn rolled back today to the elbows—strong, sculptural forearms, the long bones curved in slightly, suggest torque, leverage. How old—?

Endurance: huge, rich cloak of time flows back from his shoulders like wings of a dark angel. All springs from, elaborates, the single, stark, primary condition: he is a predator who subsists on human blood. Harmony, strength, clarity, magnificence—all from that basic animal integrity. Of course I long for all that, here in the higgledy-piggledy hodge-podge of my life! Of course he draws me!

Wore no perfume today, deference to his keen, easily insulted sense of smell. He noticed at once, said curt thanks. Saw something bothering him, opened my mouth seeking desperately for right thing to say—up rose my inward choreographer, wide awake, and spoke plain from my heart: thinking on my floundering in some of our sessions—I am aware that you see this confusion of mine. I know you see by your occasional impatient look, sudden disengagement—yet you continue to reveal yourself to me (even shift our course yourself if it needs shifting and I don't do it). I think I know why. Because there's no place for you in world as you truly are. Because beneath your various facades your true self suffers; like all true selves, it wants, needs to be honored as real and valuable through acceptance by another. I try to be that other, but often you are beyond me. He rose, paced to window, looked back, burning at me. "If I seem sometimes restless or impatient, Dr. Landauer, it's not because of any professional shortcomings of yours. On the contrary—you are all too effective. The seductiveness, the distraction of our—human contact worries me. I fear for the ruthlessness that keeps me alive."

Speak for ruthlessness. He shook his head. Saw tightness in shoulders, feet braced hard against floor. Felt reflected tension in my own muscles.

Prompted him: " 'I resent—' "

"I resent your pretension to teach me about myself! What will this work that you do here make of me? A predator paralyzed by an unwanted empathy with his prey? A creature fit only for a cage and keeper?" He was breathing hard, jaw set. I saw suddenly the truth of his fear: his integrity is not human, but my work is specifically human, designed to make humans more human—what if it does that to him? Should have seen it before, should have seen it. No place left to go: had to ask him, in small voice, Speak for my pretension.

"No!" Eyes shut, head turned away.

Had to do it: Speak for me.

W. whispered, "As to the unicorn, out of your own legends— 'Unicorn, come lay your head in my lap while the hunters close in. You are a wonder, and for love of wonder I will tame you. You are pursued, but forget your pursuers, rest under my hand till they come and destroy you.' " Looked at me like steel. "Do you see? The more you involve yourself in what I am, the more you become the peasant with the torch!"

Two days later Doug came into town and had lunch with Floria.

He was a man of no outstanding beauty who was nevertheless attractive: he didn't have much chin and his ears were too big, but you didn't notice because of his air of confidence. His stability had been earned the hard way—as a gay man facing the straight world. Some of his strength had been attained with effort and pain in a group that Floria had run years earlier. A lasting affection had grown between herself and Doug. She was intensely glad to see him.

They ate near the clinic. "You look a little frayed around the edges," Doug said. "I heard about Jane Fennerman's relapse—too bad."

"I've only been able to bring myself to visit her once since."

"Feeling guilty?"

She hesitated, gnawing on a stale breadstick. The truth was, she hadn't thought of Jane Fennerman in weeks. Finally she said, "I must be."

Sitting back with his hands in his pockets, Doug chided her gently. "It's got to be Jane's fourth or fifth time into the nuthatch, and the others happened when she was in the care of other therapists. Who are you to imagine—to demand—that her cure lay in your hands? God may

be a woman, Floria, but she is not you. I thought the whole point was some recognition of individual responsibility—you for yourself, the client for himself or herself."

"That's what we're always saying," Floria agreed. She felt curiously divorced from this conversation. It had an old-fashioned flavor: Before Weyland. She smiled a little.

The waiter ambled over. She ordered bluefish. The serving would be too big for her depressed appetite, but Doug wouldn't be satisfied with his customary order of salad (he never was) and could be persuaded to help out.

He worked his way around to Topic A. "When I called to set up this lunch, Hilda told me she's got a crush on Weyland. How are you and he getting along?"

"My God, Doug, now you're going to tell me this whole thing was to fix me up with an eligible suitor!" She winced at her own rather strained laughter. "How soon are you planning to ask Weyland to work at Cayslin again?"

"I don't know, but probably sooner than I thought a couple of months ago. We hear that he's been exploring an attachment to an archaeology department at a Western school, some niche where I guess he feels he can have less responsibility, less visibility, and a chance to collect himself. Naturally, this news is making people at Cayslin suddenly eager to nail him down for us. Have you a recommendation?"

"Yes," she said. "Wait."

He gave her an inquiring look. "What for?"

"Until he works more fully through certain stresses in the situation at Cayslin. Then I'll be ready to commit myself about him." The bluefish came. She pretended distraction: "Good God, that's much too much fish for me. Douglas, come on and help me out here."

Hilda was crouched over Floria's file drawer. She straightened up, grim-looking. "Somebody's been in the office!"

What was this, had someone attacked her? The world took on a cockeyed, dangerous tilt. "Are you okay?"

"Yes, sure, I mean there are records that have been gone through. I can tell. I've started checking and so far it looks as if none of the files themselves are missing. But if any papers were taken out of them, that would be pretty hard to spot without reading through every folder in the place. Your files, Floria. I don't think anybody else's were touched."

Mere burglary; weak with relief, Floria sat down on one of the waiting-room chairs. But only her files? "Just my stuff, you're sure?"

Hilda nodded. "The clinic got hit too. I called. They see some new-looking scratches on the lock of your file drawer over there. Listen, you want me to call the cops?"

"First check as much as you can, see if anything obvious is missing."

There was no sign of upset in her office. She found a note on her table: Weyland had canceled his next appointment.

She buzzed Hilda's desk. "Hilda, let's leave the police out of it for the moment. Keep checking." She stood in the middle of the office, looking at the chair replacing the one he had broken, looking at the window where he had so often watched.

Relax, she told herself. There was nothing for him to find here or at the clinic.

She signaled that she was ready for the first client of the afternoon.

That evening she came back to the office after having dinner with friends. She was supposed to be helping set up a workshop for next month, and she'd been putting off even thinking about it, let alone doing any real work. She set herself to compiling a suggested bibliography for her section.

The phone light blinked.

It was Kenny, muffled and teary-voiced. "I'm sorry," he moaned. "The medicine just started to wear off. I've been trying to call you everyplace. God, I'm so scared—he was waiting in the alley."

"Who was?" she said, dry-mouthed. She knew.

"Him. The tall one, the faggot—only he goes with women too, I've seen him. He grabbed me. He hurt me. I was lying there a long time. I couldn't do anything. I felt so funny—like floating away. Some kids found me. Their mother called the cops. I was so cold, so scared—"

"Kenny, where are you?"

He told her which hospital. "Listen, I think he's really crazy, you know? And I'm scared he might—you live alone—I don't know—I didn't mean to make trouble for you. I'm so scared."

God damn you, you meant exactly to make trouble for me, and now you've bloody well made it. She got him to ring for a nurse. By calling Kenny her patient and using "Dr." in front of her own name without qualifying the title she got some information: two broken ribs, multiple contusions, a badly wrenched shoulder, and a deep cut on the scalp which Dr. Wells thought accounted for the blood-loss the patient seemed to have sustained. Picked up early today, the patient wouldn't say who had attacked him. You can check with Dr. Wells tomorrow, Dr.—?

Can Weyland think I've somehow sicked Kenny on him? No, he surely knows me better than that. Kenny must have brought this on himself.

She tried Weyland's number and then the desk at his hotel. He had closed his account and gone, providing no forwarding information.

Then she remembered: this was the night Deb and Nick and the kids were arriving. Oh, God. Next phone call.

The Americana was the hotel Deb had mentioned. Yes, Mr. and Mrs. Nicholas Redpath were registered in room whatnot. Ring please.

Deb's voice came shakily on the line. "I've been trying to call you." Like Kenny.

"You sound upset," Floria said, steadying herself for whatever calamity had descended: illness, accident, assault in the streets of the dark, degenerate city.

Silence, then a raggedy sob. "Nick's not here. I didn't phone you earlier because I thought he still might come, but I don't think he's coming, Mom." Bitter weeping.

"Oh, Debbie. Debbie, listen, you just sit tight, I'll be right down there."

The cab ride only took a few minutes. Debbie was still crying when Floria stepped into the room.

"I don't know, I don't know," Deb wailed, shaking her head. "What did I do wrong? He went away a week ago, to do some research he said, and I didn't hear from him, and half the bank money is gone—just half, he left me half. I kept hoping—they say most runaways come back in a few days or call up, they get lonely—I haven't told anybody—I thought since we were supposed to be here at this convention thing together, I'd better come, maybe he'd show up. But nobody's seen him, and there are no messages, not a word, nothing—"

"All right, all right, poor Deb," Floria said, hugging her.

"Oh God, I'm going to wake the kids with all this howling—" Deb pulled away, making a frantic gesture toward the door of the adjoining room. "It was so hard to get them to sleep—they were expecting Daddy to be here, I kept telling them he'd be here—" She rushed out into the hotel hallway. Floria followed, propping the door open with one of her shoes since she didn't know whether Deb had the key with her or not. They stood out there together, ignoring passers-by, huddling over Deb's weeping.

"What's been going on between you and Nick?" Floria said. "Have you two been sleeping together lately?"

Deb let out a squawk of agonized embarrassment, "Mo-*ther!*" and pulled away from her. Oh, hell, wrong approach.

"Come on, I'll help you pack and let's go—let Nick come looking for you. We'll leave word you're at my place." Floria firmly squashed down the miserable inner cry, How am I going to stand this?

"Oh, no, I can't move till morning now that I've got the kids settled down. Besides, there's one night's deposit on the rooms. Oh, Mom, what did I do?"

"You didn't do anything, hon," Floria said, patting her shoulder and thinking in some part of her mind, Oh boy, that's great, is that the best you can come up with in a crisis with all your training and experience? Your touted professional skills are not so hot lately, but this bad? Another part answered, Shut up, stupid, only a dope does therapy on her own family. Deb's come to her mother, not a shrink, so go ahead and be Mommy. If only Mommy had less pressure on her right now— but that was always the way: everything at once or nothing at all.

"Look, suppose I stay the night here with you?"

Deb shook the pale, damp-streaked hair out of her eyes with a determined, grown-up gesture. "No, thanks, Mom. Look, I'm so tired I'm just going to fall out now. You'll be getting a bellyful of all this when we move in on you tomorrow anyway. I can manage tonight, and besides—"

And besides, just in case Nick showed up, Deb didn't want Floria around complicating things; of course. Or in case the tooth-fairy dropped by.

Floria restrained an impulse to insist on staying: the impulse, she recognized, came from her own need not to be alone tonight. That was an inappropriate burden to load on Deb's shoulders.

"Okay," she said. "But look, Deb, I'll expect you to call me up first thing in the morning, whatever happens." And if I'm still alive, I'll answer the phone.

All the way home in the cab she knew with growing certainty that Weyland would be waiting for her there. He can't just walk away, she thought; he has to finish things with me. So let's get it over.

In the tiled hallway she hesitated, keys in hand. What about calling the cops to go inside with her? Absurd. You don't set the cops on a unicorn.

She unlocked and opened the door to the apartment and called inside, "All right, Weyland, where are you?"

Nothing. Of course not—the door was still open, and he would want

to be sure she was by herself. She stepped inside, shut the door, and snapped on a lamp as she walked into the living room.

He was sitting quietly on a radiator cover by the street window, his hands on his thighs. His appearance here in a new setting, her setting, this faintly-lit room in her home place, was startlingly intimate. She was sharply aware of the whisper of movement—his clothing, his shoe-soles against the carpet underfoot—as he shifted his posture.

"What would you have done if I'd brought somebody with me?" she said unsteadily. "Changed yourself into a bat and flown away?"

"Two things I must have from you," he said. "One is the bill of health that we spoke of when we began, though not, after all, for Cayslin College. I've made other plans. The story of my disappearance has of course filtered out along the academic grapevine so that even two thousand miles from here people will be wanting evidence of my mental soundness. Your evidence. I would type it myself and forge your signature, but I want your authentic tone and language. Please prepare a letter to the desired effect, addressed to these people."

He took something white from an inside pocket and held it out. She advanced and took the envelope from his extended hand. It was from the Western archaeology department that Doug had mentioned at lunch.

"Why not Cayslin?" she said. "They want you there."

"Have you forgotten your own suggestion that I find another job? That was a good idea after all. Your reference will serve me best out there—with a copy for my personnel file at Cayslin, naturally."

She put her purse down on the seat of a chair and crossed her arms. She felt reckless—the effect of stress and weariness, she thought, but it was an exciting feeling.

"The receptionist at the office does this sort of thing for me," she said.

He pointed. "I've been in your study. You have a typewriter there, you have stationery with your letterhead, you have carbon paper."

"What was the second thing you wanted?"

"Your notes on my case."

"Also at the—"

"You know that I've already been to both your workplaces, and the very circumspect jottings in your file on me are not what I mean. Others must exist: more detailed."

"What makes you think that?"

"How could you resist?" He mocked her. "You have encountered nothing like me in your entire professional life, and never shall again. Perhaps someday you hope to produce an article, even a book—a

memoir of something impossible that happened to you one summer—
you are an ambitious woman, Dr. Landauer."

Floria squeezed her crossed arms tighter against herself to quell her
shivering. "This is all just supposition," she said.

He took folded papers from his pocket: some of her thrown-aside
drawings of him, salvaged from the waste basket. "I found these. I think
there must be more. Fetch whatever there is for me, please."

"And if I refuse, what will you do? Beat me up the way you beat up
Kenny?"

Weyland said calmly, "I told you he should stop following me. This
is serious now. There are pursuers who intend me ill—my former
captors, of whom I told you. Whom do you think I keep watch for? No
records concerning me must fall into their hands. Don't bother protest-
ing to me your devotion to confidentiality. My pursuers would take
what they want, and be damned to your professional ethics. So I must
destroy all evidence you have about me before I leave the city."

Floria turned away and sat down by the coffee table, trying to think
beyond her fear. She breathed deeply against the fright trembling in her
chest.

"I see," he said dryly, "that you won't give me the notes; you don't
trust me to take them and go. You see some danger."

"All right, a bargain," she said. "I'll give you whatever I have on
your case if in return you promise to go straight out to your new job
and keep away from Kenny and my offices and anybody connected with
me—"

He was smiling slightly as he rose from the seat and stepped soft-
footed toward her over the rug. "Bargains, promises, negotiations—all
foolish, Dr. Landauer. I want what I came for."

She looked up at him. "But then how can I trust you at all? As soon
as I give you what you want—"

"What is it that makes you afraid—that you can't render me harmless to you? What a curious concern you show suddenly for your own
life and the lives of those around you! You are the one who led me to
take chances in our work together—to explore the frightful risks of
self-revelation. Didn't you see in the air between us the brilliant shimmer of those hazards? I thought your business was not smoothing the
world over but adventuring into it, discovering its true nature, and
closing valiantly with everything jagged, cruel, and deadly."

In the midst of her terror the inner choreographer awoke and
stretched. Floria rose to face the vampire.

"All right, Weyland, no bargains. I'll give you freely what you want."

Of course she couldn't make herself safe from him—or make Kenny or Lucille or Deb or Doug safe—any more than she could protect Jane Fennerman from the common dangers of life. Like Weyland, some dangers were too strong to bind or banish. "My notes are in the work room—come on, I'll show you. As for the letter you need, I'll type it right now and you can take it away with you."

She sat at the typewriter arranging paper, carbon sheets, and white-out, and feeling the force of his presence. Only a few feet away, just at the margin of the light from the gooseneck lamp by which she worked, he leaned against the edge of the long table that was twin to the table in her office. Open in his large hands was the notebook she had taken from the table drawer. When he moved his head over the notebook's pages, his glasses threw off pale glints.

She typed the heading and the date. How surprising, she thought, to find that she had regained her nerve here and now. When you dance as the inner coreographer directs, you act without thinking, not in command of events but in harmony with them. You yield control, accepting the chance that a mistake might be part of the design. The inner choreographer is always right but often dangerous: giving up control means accepting the possiblity of death. What I feared I have pursued right here to this moment in this room.

A sheet of paper fell out of the notebook. Weyland stooped and caught it up, glanced at it. "You had training in art?" Must be a sketch.

"I thought once I might be an artist," she said.

"What you chose to do instead is better," he said. "This making of pictures, plays, all art, is pathetic. The world teems with creation, most of it unnoticed by your kind just as most of the deaths are unnoticed. What can be the point of adding yet another tiny gesture? Even you, these notes—for what, a moment's celebrity?"

"You tried it yourself," Floria said. "The book you edited, *Notes on a Vanished People*." She typed: ". . . temporary dislocation resulting from a severe personal shock . . ."

"That was professional necessity, not creation," he said in the tone of a lecturer irritated by a question from the audience. With disdain he tossed the drawing on the table. "Remember, I don't share your impulse toward artistic gesture—your absurd frills—"

She looked up sharply. "The ballet, Weyland. Don't lie." She typed: ". . . exhibits a powerful drive toward inner balance and wholeness in a difficult life-situation. The steadying influence of an extraordinary basic integrity . . ."

He set the notebook aside. "My feeling for ballet is clearly some sort of aberration. Do you sigh to hear a cow calling in a pasture?"

"There are those who have wept to hear whales singing in the ocean."

He was silent, his eyes averted.

"This is finished," she said. "Do you want to read it?"

He took the letter. "Good," he said at length. "Sign it, please. And type an envelope for it." He stood closer, but out of arm's reach, while she complied. "You seem less frightened."

"I'm terrified but not paralyzed," she said and laughed, but the laugh came out like a gasp.

"Fear is useful. It has kept you at your best throughout our association. Have you a stamp?"

He took the letter and walked back into the living room. She took a deep breath. She got up, turned off the gooseneck lamp, and followed him.

"What now, Weyland?" she said softly. "A carefully arranged suicide so that I have no chance to retract what's in that letter or to reconstruct my notes?"

"It is a possibility," he observed—at the window again, always at the window, on watch. "Your doorman was sleeping in the lobby. He never saw me enter the building. Once inside I used the stairs, of course. The suicide rate among therapists is notoriously high. I looked it up."

"You have everything all planned?"

The window was open. He reached out and touched the metal grille that guarded it. One end of the grille swung creaking outward into the night air, like a gate opening. She visualized him sitting there waiting for her to come home, his powerful fingers patiently working the bolts at that side of the grille loose from the brick-and-mortar window frame. The hair lifted on the back of her neck.

He turned toward her again. She could see the end of the letter she had given him sticking palely out of his jacket pocket.

"Floria," he said meditatively. "You were named for a woman in the opera *Tosca,* isn't that so? At the end, doesn't she throw herself to her death from a high castle wall? People are careless about the names they give their children. I will not drink from you—I hunted today, and I fed. Still, to leave you living—is too dangerous."

A fire engine tore past below, siren screaming. When it had gone Floria said, "Listen, Weyland, you said it yourself: I can't make myself safe from you—I'm not strong enough to shove you out the window instead of being shoved out myself. Must you make yourself safe from me? Let me say this to you, without promises, demands, or pleadings:

I will not go back on what I wrote in that letter. I will not try to reconstruct my notes. I mean it. Be content with that."

"You tempt me to it," he murmured after a moment, "to go from here with you still alive behind me for the remainder of your little life—to leave woven into Dr. Landauer's quick mind those threads of my own life that I pulled for her . . . I want to be able sometimes to think of you thinking of me. But the risk is very great."

"Sometimes it's right to let the dangers live, to give them their place," she urged. "Didn't you tell me yourself a little while ago how risk makes us more heroic?"

He looked amused. "Are you instructing me in the virtues of danger? You are brave enough to know something, perhaps, about that, but I have studied danger all my life."

"A long, long life with more to come," she said, desperate to make him understand and believe her. "Not mine to jeopardize. There's no torch-brandishing peasant here; we left that behind long ago. Remember when you spoke for me? You said, 'For love of wonder.' That was true."

He leaned to turn off the lamp near the window. She thought that he had made up his mind and that when he straightened it would be to spring.

But instead of terror locking her limbs, from the inward choreographer came a rush of warmth and energy into her muscles and an impulse to turn toward him. Out of a harmony of desires she said swiftly, "Weyland, come to bed with me."

She saw his shoulders stiffen against the dim square of the window, his head lift in scorn. "You know I can't be bribed that way," he said contemptuously. "What are you up to? Are you one of those who come into heat at the sight of an upraised fist?"

"My life hasn't twisted me that badly, thank God," she retorted. "And if you've known all along how scared I've been, you must have sensed my attraction to you too, so you know it goes back to—very early in our work." Her mouth was dry as paper. She pressed quickly on, anxious to get it all said to him. "This is simply how I would like to mark the ending of our time together. This is the completion I want. Surely you feel something too, Weyland—curiosity at least?"

"Granted, your emphasis on the expressiveness of the body has instructed me," he admitted, and then he added lightly, "Isn't it extremely unprofessional to proposition a client?"

"Extremely, and I never do, but somehow now it feels right. For you to indulge in courtship that doesn't end in a meal would be unprofes-

sional too, but how would it feel to indulge anyway—just this once?"
Go softly now, he's intrigued but wary. "Since we started, you've
pushed me light-years beyond my profession. Now I want you to travel
all the way with me, Weyland. Let's be unprofessional together."

She turned and went into the bedroom, leaving the lights off. There
was a reflected light, cool and diffuse, from the glowing night air of the
great city. She sat down on the bed and kicked off her shoes. When she
looked up, he was in the doorway.

Hesitantly, he halted a few feet from her in the dimness, then came
and sat beside her. He would have lain down in his clothes, but she said
quietly, "You can undress. The front door's locked and there isn't
anyone here but us. You won't have to leap up and flee for your life."

He stood again and began to take off his clothes, which he draped
neatly over a chair. He said, "Suppose I am fertile with you; could you
conceive?"

By her own choice any such possibility had been closed off after Deb.
She said, "No," and that seemed to satisfy him.

She tossed her own clothes onto the dresser.

He sat down next to her again, his body silvery in the reflected light
and smooth, lean as a whippet and as roped with muscle. His cool thigh
pressed against her own fuller, darker one as he leaned across her and
carefully deposited his glasses on the bedtable. Then he turned toward
her, and she could just make out two puckerings of tissue in his skin.
Bullet scars, she thought, shivering.

He said, "But why do I wish to do this?"

"Do you?" She had to hold herself back from touching him.

"Yes." He stared at her. "How did you grow so real? The more I
spoke to you of myself, the more real you became."

"No more speaking, Weyland," she said gently. "This is body-work."

He lay back on the bed.

She wasn't afraid to take the lead. At the very least she could certainly do for him as well as he did for himself, and at the most, much better.
Her own skin was darker than his, a shadowy contrast where she
browsed over his body with her hands. Along the contours of his ribs
she felt knotted places, hollows—old healings, the tracks of time. The
tension of his muscles under her touch and the sharp sound of his
breathing stirred her. She lived the fantasy of sex with an utter stranger;
there was no one in the world so much a stranger as he. Yet there was
no one who knew him as well as she did, either. If he was unique, so
was she, and so was their confluence here.

The vividness of the moment inflamed her. His body responded. His

penis stirred, warmed, and thickened in her hand. He turned on his hip so that they lay facing each other, he on his right side, she on her left. When she moved to kiss him he swiftly averted his face: of course—to him the mouth was for feeding. She touched her fingers to his lips, signifying her comprehension.

He offered no caresses but closed his arms around her, his hands cradling the back of her head and neck. His shadowed face, deep-hollowed under brow and cheekbone, was very close to hers. From the parted lips that she must not kiss his quick breath came, roughened by groans of pleasure. At length he pressed his head against hers, inhaling deeply; taking her scent, she thought, from her hair and skin.

He entered her, hesitant at first, probing slowly and tentatively. She found this searching motion intensely sensuous, and clinging to him all along his sinewy length, she rocked with him through two hot, swelling waves of sweetness. She felt him strain tight against her, she heard him whine through clenched teeth.

Panting, they subsided and lay loosely interlocked. His head was tilted back; his eyes were closed. She had no desire to stroke him or to speak with him, only to rest spent against his body and absorb the sounds of his breathing, her breathing.

He did not lie long to hold or be held. Without a word he disengaged his body from hers and got up. He moved quietly about the bedroom, gathering his clothing, his shoes, the drawings, the notes from the work room. He dressed without lights. She listened in silence from the center of a deep repose.

There was no leave-taking. His tall figure passed and repassed the dark rectangle of the doorway, and then he was gone. The latch on the front door clicked shut.

Floria thought of getting up to secure the deadbolt. Instead she turned on her stomach and slept.

She woke as she remembered coming out of sleep as a youngster—peppy and clearheaded.

"Hilda, let's give the police a call about that break-in, so just in case something comes of it later we're on record as having reported it. You can tell them we don't have any idea who did it or why. And please make a photocopy of this letter carbon to send to Doug Sharpe up at Cayslin. Then you can put the carbon in Weyland's file and close it."

Hilda sighed. "Well, he was too old anyway."

He wasn't, my dear, but never mind.

In her office Floria picked up the morning's mail from her table. Her

glance strayed to the window where Weyland had so often stood. God, she was going to miss him; and God, how good it was to be restored to plain working days.

Only not yet. Don't let the phone ring, don't let the world push in here now. She needed to sit alone for a little and let her mind sort through the images left from—from the pas de deux with Weyland. It's the notorious morning-after, old dear, she told herself; just where have I been dancing, anyway?

In a clearing in the enchanted forest with the unicorn, of course, but not the way the old legends have it. According to them, hunters set a virgin to attract the unicorn by her chastity so that they can catch and kill him. My unicorn was the chaste one, come to think of it, and this lady meant no treachery. No, Weyland and I met hidden from the hunt, to celebrate a private mystery of our own . . .

Your mind grappled with my mind, my dark leg over your silver one, unlike closing with unlike across whatever likeness may be found: your memory pressing on my thoughts, my words drawing out your words in which you may recognize your life, my smooth palm gliding down your smooth flank . . .

Why, this will make me cry, she thought, blinking. And for what? Does an afternoon with the unicorn have any meaning for the ordinary days that come later? What has this passage with Weyland left me? Have I anything in my hands now besides the morning's mail?

What I have in my hands is my own strength, because I had to reach deep to find the strength to match him.

She put down the letters, noticing how on the backs of her hands the veins stood, pale shadows, under the thin skin. How can these hands be strong? Time was beginning to wear them thin and bring up the fragile inner structure in clear relief. That was the meaning of the last parent's death: that the child's remaining time has a limit of its own.

But not for Weyland. No graveyards of family dead lay behind him, no obvious and implacable ending of his own span threatened him. Time has to be different for a creature of an enchanted forest, as morality has to be different. He was a predator and a killer formed for a life of centuries, not decades; of secret singularity, not the busy hum of the herd. Yet his strength, suited to that non-human life, had revived her own strength. Her hands were slim, no longer youthful, but she saw now that they were strong enough.

For what? She flexed her fingers, watching the tendons slide under the skin. Strong hands don't have to clutch. They can simply open

She dialed Lucille's extension at the clinic.

"Luce? Sorry to have missed your calls lately. Listen, I want to start making arrangements to transfer my practice for a while. You were right, I do need a break, just as all my friends have been telling me. Will you pass the word for me to the staff over there today? Good, thanks. Also, there's the workshop coming up next month . . . yes. Are you kidding? They'd love to have you in my place. You're not the only one who's noticed that I've been falling apart, you know. It's awfully soon —can you manage, do you think? Luce, you are a brick and a lifesaver and all that stuff that means I'm very, very grateful."

Not so terrible, she thought, but only a start. Everything else remained to be dealt with. The glow of euphoria couldn't carry her for long. Already, looking down, she noticed jelly on her blouse, just like old times, and she didn't even remember having breakfast. If you want to keep the strength you've found in all this, you're going to have to get plenty of practice being strong. Try a tough one now.

She phoned Deb. "Of course you've slept late, so what? I did too, so I'm glad you didn't call and wake me up. Whenever you're ready—if you need some help moving uptown I can cancel here and come down —well, call if you change your mind. I left a house key for you with my doorman.

"And listen, hon, I've been thinking—how about all of us going up together to Nonnie's over the weekend? Then when you feel like it maybe you'd like to talk about what you'll do next. Yes, I've already started setting up some free time for myself. Think about it, love. Talk to you later."

Kenny's turn. "Kenny, I'll come by during visiting hours this afternoon."

"Are you okay?" he squeaked.

"I'm okay. But I'm not your mommy, Ken, and I'm not going to start trying to hold the big bad world off you again. I'll expect you to be ready to settle down seriously and choose a new therapist for yourself. We're going to get that done today once and for all. Have you got that?"

After a short silence he answered in a desolate voice, "All right."

"Kenny, nobody grown up has a mommy around to take care of things for them and keep them safe—not even me. You just have to be tough enough and brave enough yourself. See you this afternoon."

How about Jane Fennerman? No, leave it for now, we are not Wonder Woman, we can't handle that stress today as well.

Too restless to settle down to paperwork before the day's round of appointments began, she got up and fed the goldfish, then drifted to the

window and looked out over the city. Same jammed-up traffic down there, same dusty summer park stretching away uptown—yet not the same city, because Weyland no longer hunted there. Nothing like him moved now in those deep, grumbling streets. She would never come upon anyone there as alien as he—and just as well. Let last night stand as the end, unique and inimitable, of their affair. She was glutted with strangeness and looked forward frankly to sharing again in Mort's ordinary human appetite.

And Weyland—how would he do in that new and distant hunting ground he had found for himself? Her own balance had been changed. Suppose his once-perfect, solitary equilibrium had been altered too? Perhaps he had spoiled it by involving himself too intimately with another being—herself. And then he had left her alive—a terrible risk. Was this a sign of his corruption at her hands?

"Oh, no," she whispered fiercely, focusing her vision on her reflection in the smudged window-glass. Oh, no, I am not the temptress. I am not the deadly female out of legends whose touch defiles the hitherto unblemished being, her victim. If Weyland found some human likeness in himself, that had to be in him to begin with. Who said he was defiled anyway? Newly discovered capacities can be either strengths or weaknesses, depending on how you use them.

Very pretty and reassuring, she thought grimly; but it's pure cant. Am I going to retreat into mechanical analysis to make myself feel better?

She heaved open the window and admitted the sticky summer breath of the city into the office. There's your enchanted forest, my dear, all nitty-gritty and not one flake of fairy dust. You've survived here, which means you can see straight when you have to. Well, you have to now.

Has he been damaged? No telling yet, and you can't stop living while you wait for the answers to come in. I don't know all that was done between us, but I do know who did it: I did it, and he did it, and neither of us withdrew until it was done. We were joined in a rich complicity— he in the wakening of some flicker of humanity in himself, I in keeping and—yes—enjoying the secret of his implacable blood-hunger.

What that complicity means for each of us can only be discovered by getting on with living and watching for clues from moment to moment. His business is to continue from here and mine is to do the same, without guilt and without resentment. Doug was right: the aim is individual responsibility. From that effort not even the lady and the unicorn are exempt.

Shaken by a fresh upwelling of tears she thought bitterly, moving on

is easy enough for Weyland; he's used to it, he's had more practice. What about me? Yes, be selfish, woman—if you haven't learned that you've learned damn little.

The Japanese say that in middle age you should leave the claims of family, friends, and work, and go ponder the meaning of the universe while you still have the chance. Maybe I'll try just existing for a while, and letting grow in its own time my understanding of a universe that includes Weyland—and myself—among its possibilities.

Is that looking out for myself? Or am I simply no longer fit for living with family, friends, and work? Have *I* been damaged by *him*—by my marvelous, murderous monster?

Damn, she thought, I wish he were here, I wish we could talk about it. The light on her phone caught her eye; it was blinking the quick flashes that meant Hilda was signaling the imminent arrival of—not Weyland—the day's first client.

We're each on our own now, she thought, shutting the window and turning on the air-conditioner.

But think of me sometimes, Weyland, thinking of you.

AVRAM DAVIDSON
Sleep Well of Nights

"ARE THOSE lahvly young ladies with you, then?" the Red Cross teacher asked.

Limekiller evaded the question by asking another, a technique at least as old as the Book of Genesis. "Which way did they go?" he asked.

But it did not work this time. "Bless me if I saw them gow anywhere! They were both just standing on the corner as I went by."

Limekiller gave up not so easily. "Ah, but which corner?"

A blank look. "Why . . . *this* corner."

This corner was the corner of Grand Arawack and Queen Alexandra Streets in the Town of St. Michael of the Mountains, capital of Mountains District in the Colony of British Hidalgo. Fretwork galleries dripping with potted plants and water provided shade as well as free shower baths. These were the first and second streets laid out and had originally been deer trails; Government desiring District Commissioner Bartholomew "Bajan" Bainbridge to supply the lanes with names, he had, with that fund of imagination which helped build the Empire, called them First and Second Streets: it was rather a while before anyone in Government next looked at a map and then decided that numbered streets should run parallel to each other and not, as in this instance, across each other. And as the Grand Arawack Hotel was by that time built and as Alexandra (long-suffering consort of Fat Edward) was by that time Queen, thus they were renamed and thus had remained.

"St. Michael's" or "Mountains" Town, one might take one's pick, had once been a caravan city in miniature. The average person does not think of caravan cities being located in the Americas, and, for that matter, neither does anyone else. Nevertheless, trains of a hundred and

95

fifty mules laden with flour and rum and textiles and tinned foods
coming in, and with chicle and chicle and chicle going out, had been
common enough to keep anyone from bothering to count them each
time the caravans went by. The labor of a thousand men and a thousand
mules had been year by year spat out of the mouths of millions of North
Americans in the form of chewing gum.

So far as Limekiller knew, Kipling had never been in either Hidalgo,
but he might have thought to have been if one ignored biographical fact
and judged only by his lines,

> Daylong, the diamond weather,
> The high, unaltered blue—
> The smell of goats and incense
> And the mule-bell tinkling through.

Across from the hotel stood the abattoir and the market building.
The very early morning noises were a series of bellows, bleats, squeals,
and screams which drowned out cock-crow and were succeeded by the
rattle and clatter of vulture claws on the red-painted corrugated iron
roofs. Then the high voices of women cheapening meat. But all of these
had now died away. Beef and pork and mutton (sheep or goat) could
be smelled stewing and roasting now and then as the mild currents of
the air alternated the odors of food with those of woodsmoke. He even
thought he detected incense; there was the church spire nearby.

But there were certainly no young ladies around, lovely or otherwise.

There had been no very lengthy mule trains for a very long time.

There had been no flotillas of tunnel boats at the Town Wharf for
a long time, either, their inboard motors drawn as high-up in "tunnels"
within the vessels as possible to avoid the sand and gravel and boulders
which made river navigation so difficult on the upper reaches of the
Ningoon. No mule trains, no tunnel boats; no very great quantities of
chicle, and everything which proceeded to and from the colonial capital
of King Town and St. Michael's going now by truck along the rutted
and eroded Frontier Road. No Bay boat could ever, in any event, have
gotten higher up the river than the narrows called Bomwell's Boom;
and the *Sacarissa* (Jno. Limekiller, owner and Master and, usually—
save for Skippy the Cat—sole crew) was at the moment Hired Out.

She had been chartered to a pair of twosomes from a Lake Winnipeg
boat club, down to enjoy the long hours of sunshine. Jack had been glad
enough of the money but the charter had left him at somewhat of a loss:
leisure to him had for so long meant to haul his boat up and clean and

caulk and paint her: all things in which boatmen delight. Leisure without the boat was something new. Something else.

To pay his currently few debts had not taken long. He had considered getting Porter Portugal to sew a new suit of sails, but old P.P. was not a slot machine; you could not put the price into P.P.'s gifted hands and expect, after a reasonable (or even an unreasonable) period of time, for the sails to pop out. If Port-Port were stone sober he would not work and if dead drunk he *could* not work. The matter of keeping him supplied with just the right flow of old Hidalgo dark rum to, so to speak, oil the mechanism, was a nice task indeed: many boat owners, National, North American, or otherwise, had started the process with intentions wise and good: but Old Port was a crazy-foxy old Port and all too often had drunk them under the table, downed palm and needle, and vanished with the advance-to-buy-supplies into any one of the several stews which flourished on his trade. ("A debt of honor, me b'y," he would murmur, red-eyed sober, long days later. "Doesn't you gots to worry. I just hahs a touch ahv de ague, but soon as I bet-tah. . . .")

So that was *one* reason why John L. Limekiller had eventually decided to forget the new suit of sails for the time being.

Filial piety had prompted him to send a nice long letter home, but a tendency towards muscle spasms caused by holding a pen had prompted him to reduce the n.l.l. to a picture post card. He saw the women at the post office, one long and one short.

"What's a letter *cost,* to St. Michael's?" the Long was asking. "We *could, tele*phone for a reservation," the Short suggested. Jack was about to tell them, unsolicited, how fat the chance was of anybody in St. Michael's having a telephone *or* anything which could be reserved, let alone of understanding what a reservation was—then he took more than a peripheral look at them.

The Long had red hair and was wearing dungarees and a man's shirt. Not common, ordinary, just-plain-red: *cop*per-red. Worn in loops. Her shirt was blue with a faint white stripe. Her eyes were "the color of the sherry which the guests leave in the glass." Or don't, as the case may be. The Short could have had green hair in braids and been covered to her toes in a yashmak for all Jack noticed.

At that moment the clerk had asked him, "What fah you?"—a local, entirely acceptable usage, even commonplace, being higher than "What you want?" and lower than "You does want something?"—and by the time he had sorted out even to his own satisfaction that he wanted postage for a card to Canada and not, say, to send an armadillo by registered mail to Mauritius, and had completed the transaction in

haste and looked around, trying to appear casual, they were gone. Clean gone. Where they had been was a bright-eyed little figure in the cleanest rags imaginable, with a sprinkling of white hairs on its brown, nutcracker jaws.

Who even at once declared, " 'And now abideth faith, hope, and charity, these three, and the greatest of these is charity," you would not deny the Apostle Paul, would you, then, sir?"

"Eh? Uh . . . no," said Limekiller. Pretense cast aside, craning and gaping all around: *nothing*.

"Anything to offer me?" demanded the wee and ancient, with logic inexorable.

So there had gone a dime. And then and there had come the decision to visit St. Michael of the Mountains, said to be so different, so picturesque, hard upon the frontier of "Spanish" Hidalgo, and where (he reminded himself) he had after all *never been*.

Sometimes being lonely it bothers the way a tiny pebble in the shoe bothers: enough to stop and *do* something. But if one is very lonely indeed, then it becomes an accustomed thing. Only now did Limekiller bethink himself how lonely he had been. The boat and the Bay and the beastie-cat had been company enough. The average National boatman had a home ashore. The two men and two women even now aboard the *Sacarissa* in jammed-together proximity—they had each other. (And even now, considering another definition of the verb *to have* and the possible permutations of two males and two females made him wiggle like a small boy who has to *go*—). There was always, to be sure, the Dating Game, played to its logical conclusion, for a fee, at any one of the several hotels in King Town, hard upon the sea. But as for any of the ladies accompanying him anywhere on his boat . . .

"*Whattt?* You tink I ahm crazy? *Nut*ting like *dot*!"

Boats were gritty with sand to fill the boggy yards and lanes, smelly with fish. Boats had *no* connotations of romance.

Such brief affairs did something for his prostate gland ("Changing the acid," the English called it), but nothing whatsoever, he now realized, for his loneliness. Nor did conversation in the boatmen's bars, lately largely on the theme of, "New tax law, rum go up to 15¢ a glass, man!"

And so here he was, fifty miles from home, if King Town was "home"—and if the *Sacarissa* was home . . . well, who knew? St. Michael of the Mountains still had some faint air of its days as a port-and-caravan city, but that air was now faint indeed. Here the

Bayfolk (Black, White, Colored, and Clear) were outnumbered by Turks and 'Paniar's, and there were hardly any Arawack at all. (There seldom were, anywhere out of the sound and smell of the sea.) There were a lot of old wooden houses, two stories tall, with carved grillwork, lots of flowering plants, lots of hills: perhaps looking up and down the hilly lanes gave the prospects more quaintness and interest, perhaps even beauty, than they might have had, were they as level as the lanes of King Town, Port Cockatoo, Port Caroline, or Lime Walk. And, too, there were the mountains all about, all beautiful. And there was the Ningoon River, flowing round about the town in easy coils, all lovely, too: its name, though Indian in origin, allowing for any number of easy, Spanish-based puns:

"Suppose you drink de wat-tah here, sah, you *cahn-not* stay away!"

"*En otros paises, señor, otros lugares, dicen* mañana. *Pero, por acá, señor, se dice* ningun!"

And so forth.

Limekiller had perambulated every street and lane, had circumambulated town. Like every town and the one sole city in British Hidalgo, St. Michael's had no suburbs. It was clustered thickly, with scarcely even a vacant lot, and where it stopped being the Town of St. Michael of the Mountains, it stopped. Abruptly. *Here* was the Incorporation; *there* were the farms and fields; about a mile outside the circumambient bush began again.

He could scarcely beat every tree, knock on every door. He was too shy to buttonhole people, ask if they had seen a knockout redhead. So he walked. And he looked. And he listened. But he heard no women's voices, speaking with accent from north of the northern border of Mexico. Finally he grew a little less circumspect.

To Mr. John Paul Peterson, Prop., the Emerging Nation Bar and Club:

"Say . . . are there any other North Americans here in town?"

As though Limekiller had pressed a button, Mr. Peterson, who until that moment had been only amiable, scowled an infuriated scowl and burst out, "What the Hell they want come *here* for? You think them people *crazy*? They got richest countries in the world, which they take good care *keep* it that way; so why the Hell they want come *here*? Leave me ask you one question. Turn your head all round. You see them table? You see them booth? How many people you see sitting and drinking at them table and them booth?"

Limekiller's eyes scanned the room. The question was rhetorical. He sighed. "No one," he said, turning back to his glass.

Mr. Peterson smote the bar with his hand. "Exactly!" he cried. *"No one!* You not bloody damn fool, boy. You have good eye in you head. *Why* you see no one? Because no one can afford come here and drink, is why you see no one. People can scarce afford *eat*! Flour cost nine cent! Rice cost fif*teen* cent! Lard cost thirty-*four* cent! Brown sugar at nine cent and white sugar at eleven! D.D. milk twen-ty-one cent! And yet the tax going *up,* boy! The tax going *up!*"

A line stirred in Limekiller's mind. "Yes—and, 'Pretty soon *rum* going to cost fifteen cents,' " he repeated. Then had the feeling that (in that case) something was wrong with the change from his two-shillings piece. And with his having made this quotation.

"What you mean, *'fifteen cent'*?" demanded Mr. Peterson, in a towering rage. Literally, in a towering rage; he had been slumped on his backless chair behind the bar, now stood up to his full height . . . and it was a height, too.*"Whattt?* 'Fif-*teen*-cent?' You think this some damn dirty liquor booth off in the bush, boy? You think you got *swampy,* " referring to backwoods distilled goods, "in you glass? What *'fifteen cent'?'* No such *thing.* You got pure Governor Morgan in you glass, boy, never cost less than one shilling, and pretty soon going to be thirty cent, boy: thir-ty-*cent*! And for what? For the Queen can powder her nose with the extra five penny, boy?" Et cetera. Et cetera.

Edwin Rodney Augustine Bickerstaff, Royal British Hidalgo Police (sitting bolt-upright in his crisp uniform beneath a half-length photograph of the Queen's Own Majesty):

"Good afternoon, sir. May I help you, sir?"

"Uh . . . yes! I was wondering . . . uh . . . do you know if there are any North Americans in town?"

Police-sergeant Bickerstaff pondered the question, rubbed his long chin. "Any *North* Americans, you say sir?"

Limekiller felt obliged to define his terms. "Any Canadians or people from the States."

Police-sergeant Bickerstaff nodded vigorously. "Ah, now I understand you, sir. Well. That would be a matter for the Immigration Officer, wouldn't you agree, sir?"

"Why . . . I suppose. Is *he* in right now?" This was turning out to be more complex than he had imagined.

"Yes, sir. He *is* in. *Un*officially speaking, he is in. *I* am the police officer charged with the duties of Immigration Officer in the Mountains District, sir,"

"Well—"

"Three to four, sir."

Limekiller blinked. Begged his pardon. The police-sergeant smiled slightly. "Every evening from three to four, sir, pleased to execute the duties of Immigration Officer, sir. At the present time," he glanced at the enormous clock on the wall, with just a touch of implied proof, "I am carrying out my official duties as Customs Officer. *Have you anything to declare?*"

And, *So much for that suggestion,* Limekiller thought, a feeling of having only slightly been saved from having made a fool of himself tangible in the form of something warmer than sunshine round about his face and neck.

The middle-aged woman at the Yohan Yahanoglu General Mdse. Establishment store sold him a small bar of Fry's chocolate, miraculously unmelted. Jack asked, "Is there another hotel in town, besides the Grand?"

A touch of something like hauteur came over the still-handsome face of *Sra.* Yohanoglu. "Best you ahsk wan of the men," she said. And, which one of the men? *"Any men,"* said she.

So. Out into the sun-baked street went lonely Limekiller. Not that lonely at the moment, though, to want to find where the local hookers hung out. Gone too far to turn back. And, besides, turn back to *what?*

The next place along the street which was open was the El Dorado Club and Dancing (its sign, slightly uneven, said).

Someone large and burly thumped in just before he did, leaned heavily on the bar, "How much, *rum?*" he demanded.

The barkeep, a 'Paniard, maybe only one-quarter Indian (most of the Spanish-speaking Hidalgans were more than that), gave a slight yawn at this sudden access of trade. "Still only wan dime," he said. "Lahng as dees borrel lahst. When necessitate we broach nudder borrel, under new tox lah, *iay! Pobrecito! Going be fifteen cent!*"

"¡En el nombre del Queen!" proclaimed the other new customer, making the sign of the cross, then gesturing for a glass to be splashed.

Limekiller made the same gesture.

"What you vex weed de Queen, *varón?*" the barkeeper asked, pouring two fingers of "clear" into each glass. "You got new road, meb-be ah beet bum-py, but *new;* you got new wing on hospital, you got new generator for give ahl night, electricity: *whattt?* You teenk you hahv ahl dees, ahn not pay ah new tox? No sotch teeng!"

"No me hace falta, 'ahl dees," said the other customer. *"Resido en el* bush, where no hahv not-ting like dot."

The barkeep yawned again. *"Reside en el* bush? Why you not live like

old-time people? Dey not dreenk rum. Dey not smoke cigarette. Dey not use lahmp-*ile*. Ahn dey not pay toxes, not dem, no."

"Me no want leev like dot. *Whattt?* You cahl dot 'leev'?" He emptied his glass with a swallow, dismissed any suggestion that Walden Pond and its tax-free amenities might be his for the taking, turned to Limekiller his vast Afro-Indian face. "Filiberto Marín, señor, is de mahn to answer stranger question. Becahs God *love* de stranger, señor, ahn Filiberto Marín love *God*. Everybody know Filiberto Marín, ahn if anyone want know where he is, I am de mahn." Limekiller, having indeed questions, or at any rate, A Question, Limekiller opened his mouth.

But he was not to get off so easily. There followed a long, *long* conversation, or monologue, on various subjects, of which Filiberto Marín was the principal one. Filiberto Marín had once worked one entire year in the bush and was only home for a total of thirty-two days, a matter (he assured Jack) of public record. Filiberto Marín was born just over the line in Spanish Hidalgo, his mother being a Spanish Woman and his father a British Subject By Birth. Had helped build a canal, or perhaps it was *The* Canal. Had been in Spanish Hidalgo at the time of the next-to-last major revolution, during which he and his sweetheart had absquatulated for a more peaceful realm. Married *in church*! Filiberto Marín and his wife had produced one half a battalion for the British Queen! "Fifteen children—and *puros varónes*! Ahl son, señor! So fahst we have children! Sixty-two year old, and work more tasks one day dan any young man! An I now desires to explain we hunting and fishing to you, becahs you stranger here, so you ignorance not you fahlt, señor."

Limekiller kept his eyes in the mirror, which reflected the passing scene through the open door, and ordered two more low-tax rums; while Filiberto Marín told him how to cast nets with weights to catch mullet in the lagoons, they not having the right mouths to take hooks; how to catch turtle, the *tortuga blanca* and the striped turtle (the latter not being popular locally because it was striped)—

"What difference does the stripe mean, Don Filiberto?"

"*¡Seguro!* Exoctly!!" beamed Don Filiberto, and, never pausing, swept on: how to use raw beef skin to bait lobsters ("Dey cahl him *lobster,* but is really de *langusta,* child of de crayfish."), how to tell the difference in color between saltwater and freshwater ones; how to fix a dory, how to catch tortuga "by dive for him—"

"—You want to know how to cotch croc-o-*dile* by dive for him? Who

can tell you? Filiberto Marín will answer dose question," he said, and he shook Limekiller's hand with an awesome shake.

There seemed nothing boastful about the man. Evidently Filiberto Marín *did* know all these things and, out of a pure and disinterested desire to help a stranger, wanted merely to put his extensive knowledge at Jack's disposal. . . .

Of this much, Limekiller was quite clear the next day. He was far from clear, though, as to how he came to get there in the bush where many cheerful dark people were grilling strips of *barbacoa* over glowing coals—mutton it was, with a taste reminiscent of the best old-fashioned bacon, plus . . . well, *mutton.* He did not remember having later gone to bed, let alone to sleep. Nor know the man who came and stood at the foot of his bed, an elderly man with a sharp face which might have been cut out of ivory . . . this man had a long stick . . . a spear? . . . no . . .

Then Limekiller was on his feet. In the moon-speckled darkness he could see very little, certainly not another man. There was no lamp lit. He could hear someone breathing regularly, peacefully, nearby. He could hear water purling, not far off. After a moment, now able to see well enough, he made his way out of the cabin and along a wooden walkway. There was the Ningoon River below. A fine spray of rain began to fall; the river in the moonlight moved like watered silk. *What* had the man said to him? Something about showing him . . . showing him *what*? He could not recall at all. There had really been nothing menacing about the old man.

But neither had there been anything reassuring.

Jack made his way back into the cabin. The walls let the moonlight in, and the fine rain, too. But not so much of either as to prevent his falling asleep again.

Next day, passion—well, that was not exactly the right word—but what was? Infatuation? Scarcely even that. An uncommon interest in, plus a great desire for, an uncommonly comely young woman who also spoke his own language with familiar, or familiar enough, accents—oh, well—Hell!—whatever the *word* was, whatever his own state of mind had been, next morning had given way to something more like common sense. Common sense, then, told him that if the young woman (vaguely he amended this to the young women) had intended to come to St. Michael of the Mountains to stay at a hotel . . . or wherever it was, which they thought might take a reservation . . . had even considered *writing* for the reservation, well, they had not intended to come here at

once. In other words: enthusiasm (*that* was the word! . . . damn it
. . .) enthusiasm had made him arrive early.

So, since he was already *there,* he might as well relax and enjoy it.
—He was already *where?*

Filiberto Marín plunged his hands into the river and was noisily
splashing water onto his soapy face. Jack paused in the act of doing the
same thing for himself, waited till his host had become a trifle less
audible—*how* the man could snort!—"Don Fili, what is the name of this
place?"

Don Fili beamed at him, reached for the towel. "These place?" He
waved his broad hand to include the broad river and the broad clearing,
with its scattered fields and cabins. "These place, Jock, *se llame* Pahrot
Bend. You like reside here? Tell me, just. I build you house." He buried
his face in his towel. Jack had no doubt that the man meant exactly
what he said, gave another look around to see what was being so
openhandedly—and openheartedly—offered him; this time he looked
across to the other bank. Great boles of trees: Immense! Immense! The
eye grew lost and dizzy gazing upward toward the lofty, distant crowns.
Suddenly a flock of parrots, yellowheads, flew shrieking round and
round; then vanished.

Was it some kind of an omen? *Any* kind of an omen? To live here
would not be to live just anywhere. He thought of the piss-soaked bogs
which made up too large a part of the slums of King Town, wondered
how anybody could live *there* when anybody could live *here.* But *here*
was simply too far from the sea, and it was to live upon the sunwarm
sea that he had come to this small country, so far from his vast own
one. Still . . . might not be such a bad idea . . . well, not to *live* here
all the time. But . . . a smaller version of the not-very-large cabins of
the hamlet . . . a sort of country home . . . as it were . . . ha-ha
. . . well, why not? Something to think about . . . anyway.

"Crahs de river, be one nice spot for build you *cabanita,*" said Don
Filiberto, reading his mind.

"Mmm . . . what might it cost?" he could not help asking, even
though knowing whatever answer he might receive would almost certainly not in the long run prove accurate.

"Cahst?" Filiberto Marín, pulling his shirt over his huge dark torso,
considered. Cost, clearly, was not a matter of daily concern. Calculations, muttering from his mouth, living and audible thoughts, struggling to take form: "Cahst . . . May-be, ooohhh, say-*be* torty dollar?"

"Forty dollars?"

Don Filiberto started to shake his head, reconsidered. "I suppose

may-*be*. Not take lahng. May-be one hahf day, collect wild cane for make wall, bay *leaf* for make *techo,* roof. An may-be 'nother hahf day for put everything togedder. Cahst? So: Twenty dollar. Torty dollar. An ten dollar *rum*! Most eeem-por-tont!" He laughed. Rum! The oil which lubricates the neighbors' labors. A houseraising bee, Hidalgo style.

"And the land itself? The cost of the land?"

But Don Fili was done with figures. "What 'cahst of de lond'? Lond not cahst nah-ting. Lond belahng to Pike Es-tate."

A bell went ding-a-ling in Limekiller's ear. The Pike Estate. The great Pike Estate Case was the Jarndyce vs. Jarndyce of British Hidalgo. Half the lawyers in the colony lived off it. Was there a valid will? Were there valid heirs? Had old Pike died intestate? *¿Quien sabe?* There were barroom barristers would talk your ears off about the First Codicil and the Second Codicil and the Alleged Statement of Intention and the Holograph Document and all the rest of it. Limekiller had heard enough about the Pike Estate Case. He followed after Don Fili up the bank. Ah, but—

"Well, maybe nobody would bother me *now* if I had a cabin built there. But what about when the estate is finally settled?"

Marín waved an arm, as impatiently as his vast good nature would allow. "By dot time, *hijo mio,* what you care? You no hahv Squatter Rights by den? Meb-*be* you *dead* by den!"

Mrs. Don Filiberto, part American Indian, part East Indian, and altogether Amiable and Fat, was already fanning the coals on the raised fire-hearth for breakfast.

Nobody was boating back to town then, although earnest guarantees were offered that "by and by somebody" would *be* boating back, for sure. Limekiller knew such sureties. He knew, too, that he might certainly stay on with the Marín family at Parrot Bend until then—and longer—and be fully welcome. But he had after all come to "Mountains" for something else besides rural hospitality along the Ningoon River (a former Commissioner of Historical Sites and Antiquities had argued that the name came from an Indian word, or words, meaning Region of Bounteous Plenty; local Indians asserted that a more literal and less literary translation would be Big Wet). The fine rain of the night before began to fall again as he walked along, and soon he was soaked.

It did not bother him. By the time he got back into town the sun would have come out and dried him. Nobody bothered with oilskins or mackintoshes on the Bay of Hidalgo, nor did he intend to worry about

his lack of them here in the Mountains of Saint Michael Archangel and Prince of Israel.

Along the road (to give it its courtesy title) he saw a beautiful flurry of white birds—were they indeed cattle egrets? living in symbiosis, or commensality, with the cattle? was one, indeed, heavy with egg, "blown over from Africa"? Whatever their name or origin, they did follow the kine around, heads bobbing as they, presumably, ate the insects the heavy cloven hooves stirred up. But what did the *cattle* get out of it? Company?

The rain stopped, sure enough.

It was a beautiful river, with clear water, green and bending banks. He wondered how high the highest flood waters came. A "top gallon flood," they called that. Was there a hint of an old tradition that the highest floods would come as high as the topgallant sails of a ship? Maybe.

The rain began again. Oh, well.

An oilcloth serving as door of a tiny cabin was hauled aside and an old woman appeared and gazed anxiously at Jack. "Oh, sah, why you wahk around in dis eager rain?" she cried at him. "Best you come in, *bide,* till eet *stop!*"

He laughed. "It doesn't seem all that eager to me, Grandy," he said, "but thank you anyway."

In a little while it had stopped. *See?*

Further on, a small girl under a tree called, "Oh, see what beauty harse, meester!"

Limekiller looked. Several horses were coming from a stable and down the path to the river; they were indeed beautiful, and several men were discussing a sad story of how the malfeasance of a jockey (evidently not present) had lost first place in a recent race for one of them to the famous Tigre Rojo, the Red Tiger, of which even Limekiller, not a racing buff, had heard.

"Bloody b'y just raggedy-ahss about wid him, an so Rojo win by just a nose. Son of a beach!" said one of the men, evidently the trainer of *the* beauty horse, a big bay.

"—otherwise he beat any harse in British Hidalgo!"

"Oh, yes! Oh, yes, Mr. Ruy!—dot he would!"

Ruy, his dark face enflamed by the memory of the loss, grew darker as he watched, cried, "Goddammit, oh Laard Jesus Christ, b'y! Lead him by de *head* till he *in* de wahter, *den* lead him by rope! When you goin to learn?—an watch out for boulder!—you know what one bloody fool mon want me to do? Want me to *run* harse dis marnin—not even

just canter, he want *run* him!—No, *no,* b'y, just let him swim about be de best ting for him—

"Dis one harse no common harse—dis one harse foal by *Garobo,* from Mr. Pike *stud!* Just let him swim about, I say!"

The boy in the water continued, perhaps wisely, to say nothing, but another man now said, "Oh, yes. An blow aht de cold aht of he's head, too."

Mr. Ruy grunted, then, surveying the larger scene and the graceful sweep of it, he said, gesturing, "I cotch plenty fish in dis river—catfish, twenty-pound tarpon, too. I got nylon *line,* but three week now, becahs of race, I have no time for cotch fish." And his face, which had gradually smoothed, now grew rough and fierce again. "Bloody dom fool jockey b'y purely raggeddy-*ahss* around wid harse!" he cried. The other men sighed, shook their heads. Jack left them to their sorrow.

Here the river rolled through rolling pasture lands, green, with trees, some living and draped with vines, some dead and gaunt but still beautiful. The river passed a paddock of Brahma cattle like statues of weathered grey stone, beautiful as the trees they took the shade beneath, cattle with ears like leaf-shaped spearheads, with wattles and humps. Then came an even lovelier sight: black cattle in a green field with snow-white birds close by among them. Fat hogs, Barbados sheep, water meadows, sweet soft air.

He could see the higher roofs on the hills of the town, but the road seemed to go nowhere near there. Then along came a man who, despite his clearly having no nylon line, had—equally clearly—ample time to fish, carried his catch on a stick. "De toewn, sir? Straight acrahs de savannah, sir," he gestured, "is de road to toewn." And, giving his own interpretation to the text, *I will not let thee go unless thou bless me,* detained Limekiller with blessings of unsolicited information, mostly dealing with the former grandeur of St. Michael's Town, and concluding, "Yes, sir, in dose days hahv t'ree dahnce *hahll.* Twen-ty bar and club! Torkish Cat'edral w'open every day, sah—*every day!*—ahn . . ." he groped for further evidences of the glorious days of the past, "ahn ah fot fowl, sah, cahst two, t'ree shilling!"

Sic transit gloria mundi.

The room at the hotel was large and bare, and contained a dresser with a clouded mirror, a chair, and a bed with a broad mattress covered in red "brocade"; the sheet, however, would not encompass it. This was standard: the sheet never *would,* except in the highest of high class hotels. And as one went down the scale of classes and the size of the beds diminished so, proportionately, did the sheets: they were *always*

too narrow and too short. Curious, the way this was always so. (In the famous, or infamous, Hotel Pelican in King Town, sheets were issued on application only, at an extra charge, for the beds were largely pro forma. The British soldiers of the Right Royal Regiment, who constituted the chief patrons, preferred to ignore the bed and used the *wall*, would you believe it, for their erotic revels. If that was quite the right word.)

There was a large mahogany wardrobe, called a "press" in the best Dickensian tradition, but there were no hangers in it. There was a large bathroom off the hall but no towels and no soap, and the urinal was definitely out of order, for it was tied up with brown paper and string and looked like a twelve-pound turkey ready for the oven.

But all these shortcomings were made up for, by one thing which the Grand Hotel Arawack *did* have: out on the second-story verandah was a wide wooden-slatted swing of antique and heroic mold, the kind one used to see only at Auntie Mary's, deep in the interior of Prince Edward Island or other islands in time.—Did the Hiltons have wide wooden swings on their verandahs? Did the Hiltons have verandahs, for that matter?

Limekiller took his seat with rare pleasure: it was not every damned day that he could enjoy a nostalgia trip whilst at the same time rejoicing in an actual physical trip which was, really, giving him just as much pleasure. For a moment he stayed immobile. (Surely, Great-uncle Leicester was just barely out of sight, reading the Charlottetown newspaper, and damning the Dirty Grits?) Then he gave his long legs a push and was off.

Up! and the mountains displayed their slopes and foothills. *Down!* and the flowery lanes of town came into sight again. And, at the end of the lanes was the open square where stood the flagpole with the Union Jack and the National Ensign flapping in the scented breeze . . . and, also, in sight, and well in sight (Limekiller had chosen well) was the concrete bench in front of which the bus from King Town had to disembogue its passengers. If they came by bus, and come by bus they must (he reasoned), being certainly tourists and not likely to try hitching. Also, the cost of a taxi for fifty miles was out of the reach of anyone but a land speculator. No, by *bus,* and there was where the bus would stop.

"*Let me help you with your bags,*" he heard himself saying, ready to slip shillings into the hands of any boys brash enough to make the same offer.

There was only one fly in the ointment of his pleasure.

Swing as he would and as long as he would, no bus came.

"Bus? *Bus,* sir? *No,* sir. Bus ahlready come orlier today. Goin bock in evening. Come ahgain tomorrow."

With just a taste of bitterness, Limekiller said, *"Mañana."*

"¡Ah, Vd, si puede hablar en espanol, señor. Si-señor. Mañana viene el bus, otra vez.—Con el favor de Dios." An the creek don't rise, thought Limekiller.

Suddenly he was hungry. There was a restaurant in plain sight, with a bill of fare five feet tall painted on its outer wall: such menus were only there for, so to speak, authenticity. To prove that the place was indeed a restaurant. And not a cinema. Certainly no one would ever be able to order and obtain anything which was *not* painted on them.— Besides, the place was closed.

"Be open tonight, sir," said a passerby, observing him observing.

Jack grunted. "Think they'll *have* that tonight?" he asked, pointing at random to *Rost Muttons* and to *Beef Stakes.*

An emphatic shake of the head. *"No*-sir. Rice and beans."

Somewhere nearby someone was cooking something besides rice and beans. The passerby, noticing the stranger's blunt and sunburned nose twitch, with truly Christian kindness said, "But Tia Sani be open now."

"Tia Sani?"

"Yes-sir. Miss Sanita. Aunt Sue. Directly down de lane."

Tia Sani had no sign, no giant menu. However, Tia Sani was *open.*

Outside, the famous Swift Sunset of the Tropics dallied and dallied. There was no sense of urgency in Hidalgo, be it British or Spanish. There was the throb of the light-plant generator, getting ready for the night. Watchman, what of the night?—what put *that* into his mind? He swung the screen door, went in.

Miss Sani, evidently the trim grey little woman just now looking up towards him from her stove, did not have a single item of formica or plastic in her spotless place. Auntie Mary, back in P.E.I., would have approved. She addressed him in slow, sweet Spanish. "How may I serve you, sir?"

"What may I encounter for supper, señora?"

"We have, how do they call it in inglés, meat, milled, and formed together? ah! los mitbols! And also a *caldo* of meat with macaroni and verdants. Of what quality the meat? Of beef, señor."

Of course it was cheap, filling, tasty, and good.

One rum afterwards in a club. There might have been more than one, but just as the thought began to form (like a mitbol), someone ap-

proached the jukebox and slipped a coin into its slot—the only part of it not protected by a chickenwire cage against violent displays of dislike for whatever choice someone else might make. The management had been wise. At once, NOISE, slightly tinctured with music, filled the room. Glasses rattled on the bar. Limekiller winced, went out into the soft night.

Suddenly he felt sleepy. Whatever was there tonight would be there tomorrow night. He went back to his room, switched the sheet so that at least his head and torso would have its modest benefits, thumped the lumpy floc pillow until convinced of its being a hopeless task, and stretched out for slumber.

The ivory was tanned with age. The sharp face seemed a touch annoyed. The elder man did not exactly *threaten* Limekiller with his pole or spear, but . . . and why *should* Limekiller get up and go? Go *where*? For *what*? He had paid for his room, hadn't he? He wanted to sleep, didn't he? And he was damned well going to sleep, too. If old what's-his-name would only let him . . . off on soft green clouds he drifted. *Up* the river. *Down* the river. Old man smiled, slightly. And up the soft green mountains. Old man was frowning, now. Old man was—

"Will you get the Hell *out* of here?" Limekiller shouted, bolt upright in bed—poking him with that damned—

The old man was gone. The hotel maid was there. She was poking him with the stick of her broom. The light was on in the hall. He stared, feeling stupid and slow and confused. "Eh—?"

"You have bad *dream*," the woman said.

No doubt, he thought. Only—

"Uh, thanks. I—uh. Why did you poke me with the broomstick? And not just shake me?"

She snorted. "*Whattt?* You theenk I want *cotch* eet?"

He still stared. She smiled, slightly. *He* smiled, slightly, too. "Are bad dreams contagious, then?" he asked.

She nodded, solemnly, surprised that he should ask.

"Oh. Well, uh, then . . . then how about helping me have some *good* ones?" He took her, gently, by the hand. And, gently, pulled. She pulled her hand away. Gently. Walked towards the open door. Closed it.

Returned.

"Ahl right," she said. "We help each other." And she laughed.

He heard her getting up, in the cool of the early day. And he moved towards her, in body and speech. And fell at once asleep again.

Later, still early, he heard her singing as she swept the hall, with,

almost certainly, that same broom. He burst out and cheerfully grabbed at her. Only, it wasn't her. "What you want?" the woman asked. Older, stouter. Looking at him in mild surprise, but with no dislike or disapproval.

"Oh, I, uh, are, ah. Ha-ha. Hmm. Where is the other lady? Here last night? Works here?" He hadn't worded that as tactfully as he might have. But it didn't seem to matter.

"She? She not work here. She come help out for just one night. Becahs my sister, lahst night, she hahv wan lee pickney—gorl *beh*bee. So I go ahn she stay." The pronouns were a bit prolix, but the meaning was clear. "Now she go bock. Becahs truck fah go Macaw Falls di *leave,* señor." And, as she looked at the play of expression on his face, the woman burst into hearty, good-willed laughter. And bounced down the hall, still chuckling, vigorously plying her besom.

Oh, *well.*

And they *had* been *good* dreams, too.

Tia Sani was open. Breakfast: two fried eggs, buttered toast of thick-sliced home-baked bread, beans (mashed), tea with tinned milk, orange juice. Cost: $1.00, National Currency—say, 60¢, 65¢, US or Canadian. On the wall, benignly approving, the Queen, in her gown, her tiara, and her Smile of State; also, the National Premier, in open shirt, eyeglasses, and a much broader smile.

Jack found himself still waiting for the bus. *Despite* the Night Before. See (he told himself), so it *isn't* Just Sex. . . . Also waiting, besides the retired chicle-tappers and superannuated mahogany-cutters, all of them authorized bench-sitters, was a younger and brisker man.

"You are waiting for the bus, I take it," he now said.

"Oh, yes. Yes, I am."

And so was *he.* "I am expecting a repair part for my tractor. Because, beside my shop, I have a farm. You see my shop?" He companionably took Limekiller by the arm, pointed to a pink-washed building with the indispensable red-painted corrugated iron roof (indispensable because the rains rolled off them and into immense wooden cisterns) and overhanging gallery. "Well, I find that I cannot wait any longer, Captain Sneed is watching the shop for me, so I would like to ahsk you one favor. *If* you are here. *If* the bus comes. *Would* you be so kind as to give me a hail?"

Limekiller said, "Of course. Be glad to," suddenly realized that he had, after all, other hopes for *If* The Bus Come; hastily added, "And if not, I will send someone to hail you."

The dark (but not *local*-dark) keen face was split by a warm smile.

"Yes, do—Tony Mikeloglu," he added, giving Jack's hand a hearty, hasty shake; strode away. (Tony Mikeloglu could trust Captain Sneed not to pop anything under his shirt, not to raid the till, not to get too suddenly and soddenly drunk and smash the glass goods. But, suppose some junior customer were to appear during the owner's absence and, the order being added up and its price announced, pronounce the well-known words, *Ma say, "write eet doewn"*—could he trust Captain Sneed to demand cash and not "write it down?"—no, he could *not.*)

Long Limekiller waited, soft talk floating on around him, of oldtime "rounds" of sapodilla trees and tapping them for chicle, talk of "hunting"—that is, of climbing the tallest hills and scouting out for the telltale reddish sheen which mean mahogany—talk of the bush camps and the high-jinks when the seasons were over. But for them, now, all seasons were over, and it was only that: talk. Great-uncle Leicester had talked a lot, too; only *his* had been other trees, elsewhere.

Still, no bus.

Presently he became aware of feeling somewhat ill at ease, he could not say why. He pulled his long fair beard, and scowled.

One of the aged veterans said, softly, "Sir, de mon *hail*ing you."

With an effort, Limekiller focused his eyes. There. There in front of the pink store building. Someone in the street, calling, beckoning.

"De *Tork* hailing you, sir. Best go see what he want."

Tony Mikeloglu wanted to tell him something? Limekiller, with long strides strolled down to see. "I did not wish to allow you to remain standing in the sun, sir. I am afraid I did not ask your name. Mr. Limekiller?—Interesting name. Ah. Yes. My brother-in-law's brother has just telephoned me from King *Town,* Mr. Limekiller. I am afraid that the bus is not coming today. Break*down*?"

Under his breath, Limekiller muttered something coarse and disappointed.

"Pit-ty about the railroad," a deep voice said, from inside the store. "Klondike to Cape Horn. Excellent idea. Vi-sion. But they never built it. Pit-ty."

Limekiller shifted from one foot to another. Half, he would go back to the hotel. Half, he would go somewhere else. (They, she, no one was coming. What did it matter?) *Any*where. *Where?* But the problem was swiftly solved. Once again, and again without offense, the merchant took him by the arm. "Do not stand outside in the sun, sir. Do come *in*side the shop. In the shade. And have something cold to drink." And by this time Jack was already there. "Do you know Captain Sneed?"

Small, khaki-clad, scarlet-faced. Sitting at the counter, which was

serving as an unofficial bar. "I suppose you must have often wondered," said Captain Sneed, in a quarterdeck voice, "why the Spaniard didn't settle British Hidalgo when he'd settled everywhere *else* round about?"

"—Well—"

"Didn't know it was *here,* Old Boy! Couldn't have gotten here if he *did,* you see. First of all," he said, drawing on the counter with his finger dipped in the water which had distilled from his glass (Tony now sliding another glass, tinkling with, could it be?—yes, it was! Ice!—over to Jack, who nodded true thanks, sipped)—"First of all, you see, coming from east to west, there's Pharaoh's Reef—quite enough to make them sheer off south in a bit of a damned hurry, don't you see. Then there's the Anne of Denmark Island's Reef, even bigger! And suppose they'd *sail*ed south to avoid Anne of Denmark Island's Reef? Eh? What would they find, will you tell me that?"

"Carpenter's Reef . . . unless it's been moved," said Jack.

Sneed gave a great snort, went on, "*Exactly!* Well, then—now, even if they'd missed Pharaoh's Reef and got pahst it . . . even if they'd missed Anne of Denmark Island's Reef and got pahst it . . . even if they'd missed Carpenter's Reef and got pahst *it* . . . why, then there's that great long *Barrier* Reef, don't you see, one of the biggest in the world. (Of course, Australia's the biggest one. . . .) No. No, Old Boy. Only the British lads knew the way through the Reef, and you may be sure that *they* were not pahssing out the information to the Spaniard, no, ho-ho!"

Well (thought Jack, in the grateful shade of the shop), maybe so. It was an impressive thought, that, of infinite millions of coral polyps laboring and dying and depositing their stony "bones" in order to protect British Hidalgo (and, incidentally, though elsewhere, Australia) from "the Spaniard."

"Well!" Captain Sneed obliterated his watery map with a sweep of his hand. "Mustn't mind *me,* Old Boy. This is my own King Charles's head, if you want to know. It's just the damnable *cheek* of those Spaniards there, *there,* in Spanish Hidalgo, still claiming this blessed little land of ours as their own, when they had never even set their *foot* upon it!" And he blew out his scarlet face and actually said "Herrumph!"—a word which Jack had often seen but never, till now, actually heard.

And then Tony Mikeloglu, who had evidently gone through all, all of this many, many times before, said, softly, "My brother-in-law's brother had just told me on the telephone from King *Town*—"

"Phantom relay, it has—the telephone, you know—sorry, Tony,

forgive me—what does your damned crook of a kinsman tell you from King Town?"

". . . tells me that there is a rumor that the Pike Estate has finally been settled, you know."

Not *again*? *Always* . . . thought Limekiller.

But Captain Sneed said, Don't you believe it! "Oh. What? 'A rumor,' yes, well, you may believe *that*. Always a rumor. Why didn't the damned fellow make a proper will? Eh? For that matter, why don't *you*, Old Christopher?"

There was a sound more like a crackle of cellophane than anything else. Jack turned to look; there in an especially shadowy corner was a man even older, even smaller, than Captain Sneed; and exposed toothless gums as he chuckled.

"Yes, why you do not, Uncle Christopher?" asked Tony.

In the voice of a cricket who has learned to speak English with a strong Turkish accent, Uncle Christopher said that he didn't believe in wills.

"What's going to become of all your damned doubloons, then, when you go pop?" asked Captain Sneed. Uncle Christopher only smirked and shrugged. "Where have you concealed all that damned money which you accumulated all those years you used to peddle bad rum and rusty roast-beef tins round about the bush camps? Who's going to get it all, eh?"

Uncle Christopher went *hickle-hickle*. "I know who going get it," he said. *Sh'sh, sh'sh, sh'sh.* His shoulders, thin as a butterfly's bones, heaved his amusement.

"Yes, but *how* are they going to get it? What? How are you going to take care of that? Once you're dead."

Uncle Christopher, with a concluding crackle, said, "I going do like the Indians do. . . ."

Limekiller hadn't a clue what the old man meant, but evidently Captain Sneed had. "What?" demanded Captain Sneed. "Come now, come now, you don't really *believe* all that, do you? You *do*? You do! Tush. Piffle. The smoke of all those bush camps has addled your brains. Shame on you. Dirty old pagan. Disgusting. Do you call yourself a Christian and a member of a church holding the Apostolic Succession? *Stuff!*"

The amiable wrangle went on. And, losing interest in it, Limekiller once again became aware of feeling ill at ease. Or . . . was it . . . could it be? . . . *ill?*

In came a child, a little girl; Limekiller had seen her before. She was perhaps eight years old. *Where* had he seen her?

"Ah," said Mikeloglu, briskly the merchant again. "Here is me best customer. She going make me rich, not true, me Bet-ty gyel? What fah you, *chaparita*?"

White rice and red beans were for her, and some coconut oil in her own bottle was for her, and some tea and some chile peppers (not very much of any of these items, though) and the inevitable tin of milk. (The chief difference between small shops and large shops in St. Michael's was that the large ones had a much larger selection of tinned milk.) Tony weighed and poured, wrapped and tied. And looked at her expectantly.

She untied her handkerchief, knot by knot, and counted out the money. Dime by dime. Penny by penny. Gave them all a shy smile, left. "No fahget me when you rich, me Bet-ty gyel," Tony called after her. "Would you believe, Mr. Limekiller, she is one of the grand*children* of old Mr. Pike?"

"Then why isn't she rich already? Did the others get it all?—Oh. I forgot. Estate not settled."

Captain Sneed grunted. "Wouldn't help her even if the damned estate *were* settled. An outside child of an outside child. Couldn't inherit if the courts ever decide that he died intestate, and of course: no mention of her in any will . . . if there *is* any will . . ." *An outside child.* How well Jack knew that phrase by now. Marriage and giving in marriage was one thing in British Hidalgo; begetting and bearing of children, quite another thing. No necessary connection. "Do you have any children?" "Well, I has four children." Afterthought: "Ahnd t'ree oetside." Commonest thing in the world. Down here.

"What's wrong with you, Old Boy?" asked Captain Sneed. "You look quite dicky."

"Feel rotten," Limekiller muttered, suddenly aware of feeling so. "Bones all hurt."

Immediate murmurs of sympathy. And: "*Oh,* my. You weren't caught in that rain yesterday morning, were you?"

Jack considered. "Yesterday morning in the daytime. And . . . before . . . in the night time, too—Why?"

Sneed was upset. " '*Why?*' Why, when the rain comes down like that, from the north, at this time of year, they call it 'a fever rain. . . .'"

Ah. *That* was what the old woman had called out to him, urging him in out of the drizzle. *Bide,* she'd said. *Not* an "eager" rain—a *fever* rain!

"Some say that the rain makes the sanitary drains overflow. And

some say that it raises the mosquitoes. *I* don't know. And some laugh at the old people, for saying that. But *I* don't laugh. . . . You're not laughing, either, are you? Well. What are we going to do for this man, Mik? Doctor *in,* right now?"

But the District Medical Officer was not in right now. It was his day to make the rounds in the bush hamlets in one half of the circuit. On one other day he would visit the other half. And in between, he was in town holding clinics, walking his wards in the hospital there on one of the hills, and attending to his private patients. Uncle Christopher produced from somewhere a weathered bottle of immense pills which he assured them were quinine, shook it and rattled it like some juju gourd as he prepared to pour them out.

But Captain Sneed demurred. "Best save that till we can be sure that it is malaria. Not they use quinine nowadays. Mmm. No chills, no fever? Mmm. Let me see you to your room at the hotel." And he walked Limekiller back, saw him not only into his room but into his bed, called for "some decent sheets and some blankets, what sort of a kip are you running here, Antonoglu?" Antonoglu's mother, a very large woman in a dress as black and voluminous as the tents of Kedar, came waddling in with sighs and groans and applied her own remedy: a string of limes, to be worn around the neck. The maid aspersed the room with holy water.

"I shall go and speak to the pharmacist," Captain Sneed said, briskly. "What—?" For Limekiller, already feeling not merely rotten but *odd,* had beckoned to him. "Yes?"

Rotten, aching, odd or not, there was something that Limekiller wanted taken care of. "Would you ask anyone to check," he said, carefully. "To check the bus? The bus when it comes in. Two young ladies. One red-haired. When it comes in. Would you check. Ask anyone. Bus. Red-haired. Check. If no breakdown. Beautiful. Would you. Any. Please? Oh."

Captain Sneed and the others exchanged looks.

"Of course, Old Boy. Don't worry about it. All taken care of. Now." He had asked for something. It had not come. "What, not even a thermometer? *What?* Why, what do you *mean,* 'You had one but the children broke it'? *Get another one at once.* Do you wish to lose your license? Never mind. *I* shall get another one at once. *And* speak to the pharmacist. Antonoglu-*khan-um,* the moment he begins to sweat, or his teeth chatter, *send me word.*

"Be back directly," he said, over his shoulder.

But he was not back directly.

Juan Antonoglu was presently called away to take care of some incoming guests from the lumber camps. He repeated Captain Sneed's words to his mother, who, in effect, told him not to tell her how to make yogurt. She was as dutiful as anyone could be, and, after a while, her widower son's children coming home, duty called her to start dinner. She repeated the instructions to the maid, whose name was Purificación. Purificación watched the sick man carefully. Then, his eyes remaining closed, she tiptoed out to look for something certain to be of help for him, namely a small booklet of devotions to the Señor de Esquipulas, whose cultus was very popular in her native republic. But it began to drizzle again: out she rushed to, first, get the clothes off the line and, second, to hang them up in the lower rear hall.

Limekiller was alone.

The mahogany press had been waiting for this. It now assumed its rightful shape, which was that of an elderly gentleman rather expensively dressed in clothes rather old-fashioned in cut, and, carrying a long ... *something* ... in one hand, came over to Jack's bed and looked at him most earnestly. Almost reproachfully. Giving him a hand to help him out of bed, in a very few moments he had Limekiller down the stairs and then, somehow, they were out on the river; and then ... somehow ... they were *in* the river. No.

Not exactly.

Not at all.

They were *under* the river.

Odd.

Very odd.

A hundred veiled eyes looked at them.

Such a dim light. Not like anything familiar. Wavering. What was that. A crocodile. *I* am getting *out* of *here,* said Limekiller, beginning to sweat profusely. This was the signal for everyone to let Captain Sneed know. But nobody was there. Except Limekiller. And, of course, the old man.

And, of course, the crocodile.

And, it now became clear, *quite* a number of other creatures. All reptilian. Why was he not terrified, instead of being merely alarmed? He was in fact, now that he came to consider it, not even all that alarmed. The creatures were looking at him. But there was somehow nothing terrifying in this. It seemed quite all right for him to be there.

The old man made that quite clear.

Quite clear.

"Is he delirious?" the redhead asked. Not just plain ordinary red. *Copper*-red.

"I don't have enough Spanish to know if saying *'barba amarilla'* means that you're delirious, or not. Are you delirious?" asked the other one. The Short. Brown hair. Plain ordinary Brown.

" '*Barba amarilla*' means 'yellow beard,' " Limekiller explained. Carefully.

"Then you aren't delirious. I guess.—What does 'yellow beard' mean, in this context?"

But he could only shake his head.

"I mean, we can see that you do have a blond beard. Well, blond in *parts*. Is that your nickname? No."

Coppertop said, anxiously, "His pulse seems so *funny*, May!" She was the Long. So here they were. The Long and the Short of it. Them. He gave a sudden snort of laughter.

"An insane cackle if ever I heard one," said the Short. "Hm, *Hmm*. You're *right*, Felix. It *does* seem so funny. Mumping all *around* the place—Oh, hello!"

Old Mrs. Antonoglu was steaming slowly down the lake, all the other vessels bobbing as her wake reached them. *Very* odd. Because it still *was* old Mrs. Antonoglu in her black dress and not really the old Lake Mickinuckee ferry boat. And this wasn't a lake. Or a river. They were all back in his room. And the steam was coming from something in her hand.

Where was the old man with the sharp face? Tan old man. Clear. Things were far from *clear*, but—

"What I bring," the old woman said, slowly and carefully and heavily, just the way in which she walked, "I bring 'im to drink for 'ealth, poor sick! Call the . . . call the . . . country *yerba*," she said, dismissing the missing words.

The red-haired Long said, "Oh, good!"

Spoon by bitter spoonful she fed it to him. Sticks of something. Boiled in water. A lot of it dribbled down his beard. "Felix," what an odd name. She wiped it carefully with kleenex.

"But 'Limekiller' is just as odd," he felt it only fair to point out.

"Yes," said the Short. "You certainly are. How did you know we were coming? We weren't sure, ourselves. *Nor* do we know you. Not that it matters. We are emancipated women. Ride bicycles. But we don't smoke cheroots, and we are *not* going to open an actuarial office with distempered walls, and the nature of Mrs. Warren's profession does not bother us in the least: in fact, we have thought, now and then,

of entering it in a subordinate capacity. Probably *won't*, though. Still . . ."

Long giggled. Short said that the fact of her calling her Felix instead of *Felicia* shouldn't be allowed to give any wrong ideas. It was just that *Felicia* always sounded so goddamn silly. They were both talking at once. The sound was very comforting.

The current of the river carried them all off, and then it got so very still.

Quite early next morning.

Limekiller felt fine.

So he got up and got dressed. Someone, probably Purificación, had carefully washed his clothes and dried and ironed them. He hadn't imagined everything: there was the very large cup with the twigs of country *yerba* in it. He went downstairs in the early morning quiet, cocking an ear. Not even a buzzard scrabbled on the iron roof. There on the hall table was the old record book used as a register. On the impulse, he opened it. Disappointment washed over him. *John L. Limekiller, sloop* Sacarissa, *out of King Town.* There were several names after that, all male, all ending in *-oglu,* and all from the various lumber camps round about in the back bush: Wild Hog Eddy, Funny Gal Hat, Garobo Stream. . . .

Garobo.

Struck a faint echo. Too faint to bother with.

But no one named Felix. Or even *Felicia.* Or May.

Shite and onions.

There on the corner was someone.

"Lahvly morning," said someone. "Just come from hospital, seeing about the accident victims. Name is Pauls, George Pauls. Teach the Red Cross clahsses. British. You?"

"Jack Limekiller. Canadian. Have you seen two women, one a redhead?"

The Red Cross teacher *had* seen them, right there on that corner, but knew nothing more helpful than that. So, anyway, *that* hadn't been any delirium or dreams, either, *thank God.* (For how often had he not dreamed of fine friends and comely companions, only to wake and know that they had not been and would never be.)

At Tia Sani's. In came Captain Sneed. "*I say!* Terribly sorry! Shameful of me—I don't know how—Well. There'd been a motor accident, lorry overturned, eight people injured, so we all had to pitch in, there in hospital—Ah, by the *way.* I *did* meet your young ladies, thought

you'd imagined them, you know—District Engineer gave them a ride from King Town—I told them about you, went on up to hospital, then there was this damned accident—By the time we had taken care of them, poor chaps, fact is, I am *ashamed* to say, I'd forgotten all about you.—But you look all right, now." He scanned Limekiller closely. "Hm, still, you should see the doctor. I wonder. . . ."

He walked back to the restaurant door, looked up the street, looked down the street. *"Doc-tor!*—Here he comes now."

In came a slender Eurasian man; the District Medical Officer himself. (Things were *always* happening like that in Hidalgo. Sometimes it was, "You should see the Premier. Ah, here he comes now. *Prem-ier!"*) The D.M.O. felt Limekiller's pulse, pulled down his lower eyelid, poked at spleen and liver, listened to an account of yesterday. Said, "Evidently you have had a brief though severe fever. Something like the one-day flu. Feeling all right now? Good. Well, eat your usual breakfast, and if you can't hold it down, come see me at my office."

And was gone.

"Where are they now? The young women, I mean."

Captain Sneed said that he was blessed if he knew, adding immediately, "Ah. Here they come now."

Both talking at once, they asked Jack if he felt all right, assured him that he looked well, said they they'd spent the night at Government Guest House (there was one of these in every out-district capital and was best not confused with *Government House,* which existed only in the colonial capital itself: the Royal Governor lived there, and he was not prepared to put up guests below the rank of, well, *Gov*ernor).

"Mr. Boyd arranged it. We met him in King Town. He was coming here anyway," said Felix, looking long and lovely. "He's an engineer. He's . . . how would you describe him, May?"

"He's an engin*eer*," May said.

Felix's sherry-colored eyes met Limekiller's. "Come and live on my boat with me and we will sail the Spanish Main together and I will tell you all about myself and frequently make love to you," he said at once. Out loud, however, all he could say was, "Uh . . . thanks for wiping my beard last night . . . uh. . . ."

"Don't mention it," she said.

May said, "I want lots and lots of exotic foods for breakfast." She got two fried eggs, buttered toast of thick-sliced, home-baked bread, beans (mashed), tea, orange juice. "There is nothing *like* these exotic foods," she said.

Felix got egg on her chin. Jack took his napkin and wiped. She said

that turnabout was fair play. He said that one good turn deserved another. She asked him if he had ever been to Kettle Point Lagoon, said by They to be beautiful. A spirit touched his lips with a glowing coal.

"I am going there today!" he exclaimed. He had never heard of it.

"Oh, good! Then we can all go together!"

Whom did he see as they walked towards the river, but Filiberto Marín. Who greeted him with glad cries, and a wink, evidently intended as compliments on Jack's company. "Don Fili, can you take us to Kettle Point Lagoon?"

Don Fili, who had at once begun to nod, stopped nodding. "Oh, Juanito, only wan mon hahv boat which go to Kettle Point Lagoon, ahn dot is Very Big Bakeman. He get so *vex,* do anybody else try for go dot side, none ahv we odder boatmen adventure do it. But I bring you to him. May-be he go today. *Veremos.*"

Very Big Bakeman, so-called to distinguish him from his cousin, Big Bakeman, was very big indeed. What he might be like when "vex," Limekiller (no squab himself) thought he would pass up knowing.

Bakeman's was the only tunnel boat in sight, probably the only one still in service. His answer was short. "Not before Torsday, becahs maybe not enough wah-teh get me boat ahcross de bar. *Torsday,*" he concluded and, yawning, leaned back against the cabin. Monopolists the world over see no reason to prolong conversation with the public.

Felix said something which sounded like, "Oh, spit," but wasn't. Limekiller blinked. *Could* those lovely lips have uttered That Word? If so, he concluded without much difficulty, he would learn to like it. *Love* it. "Don Fili will take us to," he racked his brains, "somewhere just as interesting," he wound up with almost no pause. And looked at Don Fili, appealingly.

Filiberto Marín was equal to the occasion. "*Verdad.* In wan leetle while I going up de Right Branch. *Muy linda.* You will have pleasure. I telling Juanito about it, day before yesterday."

Limekiller recalled no such conversation, but he would have corroborated a deal with the devil, rather than let her out of his sight for a long while yet. He nodded knowingly. "Fascinating," he said.

"We'll get that nice lady to pack us a lunch."

Jack had a quick vision of Tia Sani packing them fried eggs, toast, beans, tea, and orange juice. But that nice lady fooled him. Her sandwiches were immense. Her eggs were deviled. She gave them *empenadas* and she gave them "crusts"—pastries with coconut and other sweet fillings—and then, behaving like aunts the whole world over, she ladled soup into a huge jar and capped it and handed it to Limekiller with the

caution to hold it like *this* so that it didn't leak. . . . Not having any intention to have his hands thus occupied the whole trip, he lashed it and shimmed it securely in the stern of Marín's boat.

He had barely known that the Ningoon River *had* two branches. Parrot Bend was on the left one, then. The dory, or dugout, in use today was the largest he had seen so far. Captain Sneed at once decided it had room enough for him to come along, too. Jack was not overjoyed at first. The elderly Englishman was *a decent sort.* But he talked, damn it! *How* he talked. Before long, however, Limekiller found he talked to May, which left Felix alone to talk to Jack.

"*John Lutwidge Limekiller,*" she said, having asked to see his inscribed watch. "there's a *name.* Beats Felicia Fox." *He* thought "fox" of all words in the world the most appropriate for her. He didn't say so. "—Why Lutwidge?"

"Lewis Carroll? Charles Lutwidge Dodgson, his real name? Distant cousin. Or so my Aunty Mary used to say."

This impressed her, anyway a little. "And what does Limekiller mean? How do you kill a lime? And *why*?"

"You take a limestone," he said, "and you burn it in a kil*n*. Often pronounced kill. Or, well, you *make* lime, for cement or whitewash or whatever, by burning stuff. Not just limestone. Marble. Oyster shells. Old orange rinds, maybe, I don't know, I've never done it. Family *name,*" he said.

She murmured, "I see. . . ." She wound up her sleeves. He found himself staring, fascinated, at a blue vein in the inside of her arm near the bend. Caught her gaze. Cleared his throat, sought for something subject-changing and ever so interesting and novel to say. "Tell me about yourself," was what he found.

She gave a soft sigh, looked up at the high-borne trees. There was another blue vein, in her *neck,* this time. Woman was one mass of sexy *veins,* damn it! He would simply lean over and he would kiss—"Well, I was an Art Major at Harrison State U. and I said the Hell with it and May is my cousin and she wanted to go someplace, too, and so we're here. . . . Look at the *bridge!*"

They looked at its great shadow, at its reflection, broken by the passing boat into wavering fragments and ripples. The bridge loomed overhead, so high and so impressive in this remote place, one might forget that its rotting road-planks, instead of being replaced, were merely covered with new ones . . . or, at the least, newer ones. "In ten years," they heard Captain Sneed say, "the roadbed will be ten feet tall . . . if it lasts that long."

May: "Be sure and let us know when it's going to fall and we'll come down and watch it. Ffff-*loppp*!—Like San Luis Rey."

"Like *whom*, my dear May?"

The river today was at middle strength: shallow-draft vessels could and still did navigate, but much dry shingle was visible near town. Impressions rushed in swiftly. The day was neither too warm nor too wet, the water so clear that Limekiller was convinced that he could walk across it. Felix lifted her hand, pointed in wordless wonder. There, on a far-outlying branch of a tree over the river was an absolutely monstrous lizard of a beautiful buff color; it could not have been less then five full feet from snout to end of tail, and the buff shaded into orange and into red along the spiky crenelations on the spiny back ridge. He had seen it before. *Had* he seen it before? He *had* seen it before.

"Iguana!" he cried.

Correction was polite but firm. "No, sir, Juanito. Iguana is *embra*, female. Dat wan be *macho*. Male. *Se llama 'garobo'*. . . ."

Something flickered in Limekiller's mind. "*¡Mira! ¡Mira!* Dat wan dere, *she* be iguana!" And that one there, smaller than the buff dragon, was of a beautiful blue-green-slate-grey color. "Usual," said Filiberto, "*residen en* de bomboo t'icket, which is why de reason is call in English, 'Bomboo chicken'. . . ."

"You *eat* it?"—Felix.

"Exotic *food*, exotic *food*!"—May.

"*Generalmente*, only de hine leg ahn de tail. But is very good to eat de she of dem when she have egg, because de egg so very nice eating, in May, June; but even noew, de she of dem have red egg, nice and hard. *Muy sabroso.*"

Jack turned and watched till the next bend hid the place from sight. After that he watched for them—he did not know why he watched for them, were they watching for *him*?—and he saw them at regular intervals, always in the topmost branches: immense. Why so high? Did they eat insects? And were there more insect to be taken, way up there? They surely did not eat *birds*? Some said, he now recalled in a vague way, that they ate only leaves; but were the top leaves so much more succulent? Besides, they seemed not to be eating anything at all, not a jaw moved. Questions perhaps not unanswerable, but, certainly, at the moment unanswered. Perhaps they had climbed so high only for the view: absurd.

"Didn't use to *be* so many of them, time was.—Eh, Fil?" asked

Captain Sneed. ("Correct, Copitan. Not.") "Only in the pahst five, six years . . . it seems. Don't *know* why. . . ."

But whatever, it made the river even more like a scene in a baroque faëry tale, with dragons, or, at least, dragonets, looking and lurking in the gigant trees.

The bed of the river seemed predominantly rocky, with some stretches of sand. The river ran very sinuously, with banks tending towards the precipitate, and the east bank was generally the higher. "When river get high," explained Don Fili, "she get white, ahn come up to de crutch of dem tree—" he pointed to a fork high up. "It can rise in wan hour. Ahn if she rise in de night, we people cahn loose we boat. Very . . . *peligroso* . . . dangerous—*¡Jesus María!* Many stick tear loose wid roots ahn ahl, even big stick like dot wan," he pointed to another massy trunk.

Here and there was open land, *limpiado*, "cleaned," they said here-abouts, for "cleared." "*Clear.* . . ." Something flickered in Limekiller's mind as he recollected this. Then it flickered away. There seemed, he realized, feeling odd about it, that quite a lot of flickering was and had been going on his mind. Nothing that would come into focus, though. The scenes of this Right Branch, now: why did they persist in seeming . . . almost . . . familiar? . . . when he had never been here before?

"What did you say just then, Don Fili?" he demanded, abruptly, not even knowing why he asked.

The monumental face half turned. "*¡Que?* What I just say, Juanito? Why . . . I say, too bod I forget bring ahlong my fisga, my pike . . . take some of dem iguana, garobo, cook dem fah you.—Fah *we*," he amended, as one of the women said, *Gik*.

"*We* would say, 'harpoon' ": Captain Sneed, judiciously. "Local term: 'pike.' "

The penny dropped. "Pike! Pike! It was a pike!" cried Limekiller. His body shook, suddenly, briefly. *Not* a lance or a spear. A pike!

They turned to look at him. Abashed, low-voiced, he muttered, "Sorry. Nothing. Something in a dream . . ." Shock was succeeded by embarrassment.

Felix, also low-voiced, asked, "Are you feverish again?" He shook his head. Then he felt her hand take his. His heart bounced. Then—Oh. She was only feeling his pulse. Evidently it felt all right. She started to release the hand. He took hers. She let it stay.

Captain Sneed said, "Speaking of Pike. All this land, all of it, far as the eye can reach, is part of the Estate of the Late Leopold Albert Edward Pike, you know, of fame and story and, for the last five or six

years, since he died, of interminable litigation. He made a great deal of money, out of all these precious hardwoods, and he put it all back into land—Did I know him? Of *course* I knew him! That is," he cleared his throat, "as well as *any*one knew him. Odd chap in a multitude of ways. *Damn*ably odd. . . ."

Of course that was not the end of the subject.

"Mr. Pike, he *reetch.* But he no di *trust* bonks. He say, bonks di go *bust,* mon. People say he'm, now-ah-days, bonks ahl *in*sure. Mr. Pike, he di say, Suh-pose *in*sure company di go bust, too? *¿Ai, como no?* Ahn he di say ah good word. He di say, 'Who shall guard de guards dem-selves?' "

Some one of the boatmen, who had theretofore said nothing, but silently plied his paddle, now spoke. "Dey say . . . Meester Pike . . . dey say, he *deal.* . . ." And his voice dropped low on this last word. Something went through all the boatmen at that. It was not exactly a shudder. But it was *there.*

Sneed cleared his throat again as though he were going to cry *Stuff!* or *Piffle!* Though what he said was, "Hm, I wouldn't go *that* far. He was pagan enough not to believe in our Devil, let alone try to deal with him. He did, well, he did, you know, study things better left unstudied . . . *my* opinion. Indian legends of a certain sort, things like that. Called it 'the *Old* Wisdom.' . . ."

Limekiller found his tongue. "Was he an Englishman?"

The matter was considered; heads were shaken. "He mosely *Blanco.* He *lee* bit *Indio.* And he hahv some lee bit *Block* generation in he'm too."

Sneed said, "His coloring was what they call in The Islands, *bright.* Light, in other words, you would say. Though color makes no difference here. Never *did.*"

Marín added, "What dey cahl Light, here we cahl Clear." He gestured towards shore, said, "Lime*stone.*" Much of the bankside was composed of that one same sort of rock, grey-white and in great masses, with many holes and caves: limestone was susceptible to such water-caused decay. In Yucatan the water had corroded deep pits in it, immense deep wells and pools.

"Now, up ahead," said Captain Sneed, "towards the right bank of the river is a sort of cove called Crocodile Pool—No No, ladies, no need for alarm. Just stay in the boat. And almost directly opposite the cove, is what's called the Garobo Church; you'll see why."

Often in the savannahs they saw the white egrets with the orange bills, usually ashore amidst the cattle. Another kind of egret seemed to

prefer the sand and gravel bars and the stumps or sawyers in midstream, and these were a distinctive shade of blue mixed with green, though lighter than the blue-green of the iguanas. Something like a blackbird took its perch and uttered a variety of long, sweet notes and calls.

Swallows skimmed and brighter colored birds darted and drank. And like great sentinels in livery, the great buff garobo-dragons peered down from the tall trees and the tall stones. Clouds of lemon-yellow and butter-yellow butterflies floated round the wild star-apples. *Here,* the stones lay in layers, like brickwork; *there,* the layers were warped and buckled, signs—perhaps—of some ancient strain or quake. But mostly, mostly, the stone rose and loomed and hung in bulbous worm-eaten masses. And over them, among them, behind them and between them, the tall cotton trees, the green-leaved cedars, the white-trunked Santa Maria, and the giant wild fig.

"Now, as to how you *catch* the crocodile," Captain Sneed answered an unasked question; "simple: one man stays in the dory and paddles her in a small circle, one or two men hold the *rope*—"

"—rope tie around odder mahn belly," Marín said.

"*Quite* so. And that chap *dives.* Machete in his *teeth.* And he ties up the croc and then he *tugs.* And then they haul them *up,* . . . you see. Simple."

Felix said, "Not *that* simple!"

May said, "Seems simple enough to me. Long as you've got a sound set of teeth."

Limekiller knew what was coming next. He had been here before. That was a mistake about his never having been here before, of course he had been here; never mind, Right Branch, Left Branch; or how else could he know? Down the steepy bluff a branch came falling with a crash of its *Crack!* falling with it; and the monstrous garobo hit the water with a tremendous sound and spray. It went *down* and it did not come up and it did not come *up.*

And then, distant but clear: the echo. And another echo. And—but that was too many echoes. Jack, who had been looking back, now turned. Spray was still flying up, falling down. *Ahead:* One after another the garobo were falling into the river. And then several at once, together. And then—

"Call *that,* 'The Garobo Church,' " said Captain Sneed.

That was an immense wild fig tree, hung out at an impossible angle; later, Limekiller was to learn that it had died of extreme age and of the storm which finally brought half of its roots out of the ground and

forward into the water and canted it, thus, between heaven, earth, and river. It was a skeletal and spectral white against the green *green* of the bush. Three separate and distinct ecologies were along that great tangled length of great gaunt tree: at *least* three!—things crept and crawled, leaped and lurched or lay quiescent, grew and decayed, lived and multiplied and died—and the topmost branches belonged to the iguana and the garobo—

—that were now abandoning it, as men might abandon a threatened ship. Crash! Crash! Down they came, simply letting go and falling. *Crash!*

Sound and spray.

"Won't the crocodiles *eat* them?" cried Felix, tightening her hold on Jack's hand.

The boatmen, to whom this was clearly no new thing, all shook their heads, said No.

"Dey goin *wahrn* he'm, *el legarto,* dot we comin. So dot he no come oet. So cahn tehk *care. Horita el tiene cuidado.*"

"Tush," said Sneed. "Pif-fle. Damned reptiles are simply getting out of our way, *they* don't know that we haven't any pike. Damned old creepy-crawlies. . . ."

Only the sound of their crashings, no other sound now, and Limekiller, saying in a calm flat voice, "Yes, of course," went out of his shirt and trousers and into the river.

He heard the men cry out, the women scream. But for one second only. Then the sounds muffled and died away. He was in the river. He saw a hundred eyes gazing at him. He swam, he felt bottom, he broke surface, he came up on his hands and knees. He did not try to stand. He was under the river. He was someplace else. Some place with a dim, suffused, wavering light. An odd place. A very odd place. With a very bad smell. He was alone. No, he was not. The garobo were all around and about him. The crocodile was very near up ahead of him. Something else was there, and he knew it had crawled there from the surface through a very narrow fissure. And some *thing* else was there. *That!* He had to take it and so he took it, wrenching it loose. It squilched, but it came. The crocodile gazed at him. The garobo moved aside for him. He backed away. He was in the water again. He—

"Into the *boat,* for Christ's sake!" old Sneed was shouting, his red face almost pale. The boatmen were reaching out to him, holding hands to be grasped by him, smacking the waters with their paddles and banging the paddles against the sides of the boat. The women looked like death. He gasped, spat, trod water, held up something—

—then it was in the boat. Then, all grace gone, he was half in and half out of the boat, his skin scraping the hard sides of it, struggling, being pulled and tugged, wet skin slipping. . . .

He was in the boat.

He leaned over the side, and, as they pulled and pressed, fearful of his going back again, he vomited into the waters.

Captain Sneed had never been so angry. "Well, what did you *expect* crocodile's den to smell like?" he demanded. "Attar of roses? Damndest foolishest crack-brainedest thing I ever saw—!"

Felix said, smoothing Jack's wet, wet hair, "*I* think it was *brave!*"

"You know nothing whatsoever about it, my dear child!—No, damn it, don't keep waving that damned old pipkin pot you managed to drag up, you damned Canuck! Seven hours under fire at Jutland, and I never had such an infernal shock, it was reckless, it was heedless, it was thoughtless, it was devil-may-care and a louse for the hangman; what was the *reason* for it, may I ask? To impress *whom*? Eh? *Me*? These good men? These young women? Why did you *do* it?"

All Limekiller could say was, "I dreamed that I had to."

Captain Sneed looked at him, mouth open. Then he said, almost in a mutter, "Oh, I say, poor old boy, he's still rambling, ill, *look*ed well enough, must have the *fever*. . . ." He was a moment silent. Then he blinked, gaped; almost in a whisper, he asked, "You *dreamed*. . . .Whom did you *see* in your dream?"

Limekiller shrugged. "Don't know who. . . . Oldish man. Sharp face. Tan. Old-fashioned clothes. Looked like a sort of a dandy, you might say."

And Captain Sneed's face, which had gone from scarlet to pink and then to scarlet again, now went muddy. They distinctly heard him swallow. Then he looked at the earthenware jar with its faded umber pattern. Then, his lips parting with a sort of dry smack: ". . . perhaps it *isn't* stuff and piffle, then. . . ."

Ashore.

Sneed had insisted that the police be present. It was customary in Hidalgo to use the police in many ways not customary in the northern nations: to record business agreements, for instance, in places where there were no lawyers. And to witness. Sergeant Bickerstaff said that he agreed with Sneed. He said, also, that he had seen more than one old Indian jar opened and that when they were not empty they usually contained mud and that when they did not contain *mud* they usually

contained "grahss-*seed,* cahrn-*ker*-nel, things like that. Never find any gold in one, not before *my* eye, no, sirs and ladies—But best you go ahead and open it."

The cover pried off, right-tight to the brim was a mass of dark and odorous substance, pronounced to be wild beeswax.

The last crumble of it evaded the knife, sank down into the small jar, which was evidently not filled but only plugged with it. They turned it upside down and the crumble of unbleached beeswax fell upon the table. And so did something else.

"Plastic," said May. "To think that the ancient Indians had invented plastic. Create a furor in academic circles. Invalidate God knows how many patents."

Sergeant Bickerstaff, unmoved by irony, said, "Best unwrop it, Coptain."

The plastic contained one dead wasp or similar insect, and two slips of paper. On one was written, in a firm old-fashioned hand, the words, *Page 36, Liber 100, Registers of Deeds of Gift, Mountains District.* The other was more complex. It seemed to be a diagram of sorts, and along the top and sides of it the same hand had written several sentences, beginning, *From the great rock behind Crocodile Cove and proceeding five hundred feet due North into the area called Richardson's Mahogany Lines. . . .*

It was signed, *L.A.E. Pike.*

There was a silence. Then Felix said, not exactly jumping up and down, but almost, her loops of coppery hair giving a bounce, "A treasure map! Jack! Oh, *good!*"

So far as he could recall, she had never called him by name before. His heart echoed: *Oh, good!*

Captain Sneed, pondering, seemingly by no means entirely recovered from his several shocks, but recovered enough, said:

"Too late to go poking about in the bush, today. First thing tomorrow, get some men, some machetes, axes, shovels—Eh?"

He turned to Police-sergeant Bickerstaff, who had spoken softly. And now repeated his words, still softly. But firmly. "First thing, sir. First thing supposed to be to notify the District Commissioner. Mister Jefferson Pike."

He was of course correct. As Captain Sneed agreed at once. Limekiller asked, "Any relation to the late Mr. Leopold Pike?" Bickerstaff nodded. "He is a bahstard son of the late Mr. Leopold Pike." The qualifying adjective implied neither insult nor disrespect. He said it as calmly, as mildly, as if he had said step-son. Cousin. Uncle. It was

merely a civil answer to a civil question. A point of identification had been raised, been settled.

D.C. Jefferson Pike was taller than his father had been, but the resemblance, once suggested, was evident. If any thoughts of an estate which he could never inherit were in his mind, they were not obvious. "Well, this is something new," was all his initial comment. Then, "I will ask my chief clark. . . . Roberts. Fetch us Liber 100, Register of Deeds of Gift. Oh, and see if they cannot bring some cups of tea for our visitors, please."

The tea was made and half drunk before Roberts, who did not look dilatory, returned, wiping dust and spiderwebs off the large old book. Which was now opened. Pages turned. "Well, well," said the District Commissioner. "This *is* something new!

"Don't know how they came to overlook *this,*" he wondered. "The lawyers," he added. "*Who* registered it? Oh. Ahah. I see. Old Mr. Athelny; been dead *several* years. And always kept his own counsel, too. Quite proper. Well." He cleared his throat, began to read:

> I, Leopold Albert Edward Pike, Woodcutter and Timber Merchant, Retired, a resident of the Town of Saint Michael of the Mountains, Mountains District, in the Colony of British Hidalgo, and a British subject by birth . . . do execute this Deed of Gift. . . . videlicet one collection of gold and silver coins, not being Coin of the Realm or Legal Tender, as follows, Item, one hundred pieces of eight reales, Item, fifty-five gold Lewises or louis d'or, Item . . .

He read them all, the rich and rolling old names, the gold moidores and gold mohurs, the golden guineas, the silver byzants and all the rest, as calmly as though he were reading off an inventory of office supplies; came finally to:

> and all these and any others which by inadvertancy may not be herein listed which are found in the same place and location I do hereby give and devise to one Elizabeth Mendoza also known as Betty Mendoza a.k.a. Elizabeth Pike a.k.a. Betty Pike, an infant now resident in the aforesaid Mountains District, which Gift I make for good and sufficient reason and of my own mere whim and fancy. . . .

Here the D.C. paused, raised his eyes, looked at Captain Sneed. Who nodded. Said, "His own sound and voice. Yes. How *like* him!"

* * *

... and fancy; the aforesaid collection of gold and silver coins being secured in this same District in a place which I do not herein designate or describe other than to say that it be situate on my own freehold lands in this same District. And if anyone attempt to resist or set aside this my Intention, I do herewith and hereafter declare that he, she or they shall not sleep well of nights.

After he had finished, there was a long pause. Then everybody began to talk at once. Then—

Sneed: Well, suppose we shall have to inform the lawyers, but don't see what *they* can do about it. Deed was executed whilst the old fellow was alive and has nothing to *do* with any question of the estate.

D.C. Pike: I quite agree with you. *Un*officially, of course. Officially, all I am to do is to make my report. The child? Why, yes, of course I know her. She is an outside child of my brother Harrison, who died even before the late Mr. Pike died. The late Mr. Pike seemed rather fond of her. The late Mr. Pike did, I believe, always give something to the child's old woman to keep her in clothes and find her food. As we ourselves have sometimes done, as best we could. But of course this will make a difference.

Sneed: As it *should.* As it *should.* He had put you big chaps to school and helped you make your own way in the world, but this was a mere babe. Do you suppose that he *knew* that such an estate was bound to be involved in litigation and that was why he tried to help the child with all this . . . this *treasure* business?

Marín: Mis-tah Pike, he ahlways give ah lahf ahn he say, nobody gweyn molest *he* treasure, *seguro,* no, becahs he di set such watchies roun ah-bote eet as no mahn adventure fi trifle wid day.

May: I can't help feeling that it's someone's cue to say, *"This all seems highly irregular."*

Roberts, Chief Clerk (softly but firmly): Oh, no, Miss. The Stamp Tax was paid according to regulations, Miss. *Everything seems in regular order, Miss.*

Watchies. A "watchie" was a watchman, sometimes registered as a private constable, thus giving him . . . Jack was not sure exactly what it gave him: except a certain status. But it was obvious that this was not what "the late Mr. Pike" had had in mind.

Finally, the District Commissioner said, "Well, well. Tomorrow is another day.—Richardson's Mahogany Lines! *Who* would have thought to look there? Nobody! It took eighty years after Richardson

cut down all the mahogany before it was worthwhile for anybody to go that side again. And . . . how long since the late Mr. Pike cut down the last of the 'new' mahogany? Ten to fifteen years ago. So it would be sixty-five to seventy-five years before anybody would have gone that side again. Even to *look*. Whatever we may find there would not have been stumbled upon before then, we may be sure. Well, Well.

"Sergeant Bickerstaff, please take these gentlemen's and ladies' statements. Meanwhile, perhaps we can have some further cups of tea. . . ."

Taking the statement, that action so dearly beloved of police officials wherever the Union Jack flies or has flown, went full smoothly. That is, until the moment (Limekiller later realized it was inevitable, but he had not been waiting for it, then), the moment when Sgt. Bickerstaff looked up, raised his pen, asked, "And what made you go and seek for this Indian jar, sir, which gave the clue to this alleged treasure, Mr. Limekiller? That is, in other words, how did you come to know that it was there?"

Limekiller started to speak. Fell silent beyond possibility of speech. But not Captain Sneed.

"He knew that it was there because Old Pike had dreamed it to him that it was there," said Captain Sneed.

Bickerstaff gave a *deep* nod, raised his pen. Set it down. Lifted it up. Looked at Jack. "This is the case, Mr. Limekiller, sir?"

Jack said, "Yes, it is." He had, so suddenly, realized it to be so.

"Doubt" was not the word for the emotion on the police-sergeant's face. "Perplexity," it was. He looked at his superior, the District Commissioner, but the District Commissioner had nothing to advise. It has been said by scholars that the Byzantine Empire was kept alive by its bureaucracy. Chief Clerk Roberts cleared his throat. In the tones of one dictating a routine turn of phrase, he produced the magic words.

" '*Acting upon information received,*' " he said, " '*I went to the region called Crocodile Cove, accompanied by,*' and so carry on from there, Sergeant Bickerstaff," he said.

In life, if not in literature, there is always anticlimax. By rights—by dramatic right, that is—they should all have gone somewhere and talked it all over. Talked it all out. And so tied up all the loose ends. But in fact there was nowhere for them all to go and do this. The police were finished when the statement was finished. District Officer Pike, who had had a long, hard day, did not suggest further cups of tea. Tia Sani's was closed. The Emerging Nation Bar and Club was closed, and

in the other clubs and bars local usage and common custom held that the presence of "ladies" was contra-indicated: so did common sense.

Wherever Captain Sneed lived, Captain Sneed was clearly not about to offer open house. "Exhausted," he said. And looked it. "Come along, ladies, I will walk along with you as far as the Guest House. Limekiller. Tomorrow."

What should Limekiller do? Carry them off to his landing at the Grand Arawack? Hospitality at Government Guest House, that relic of days when visitors, gaunt and sore from mule transport, would arrive at an even smaller St. Michael's, hospitality there was reported to be of a limited nature; but surely it was better than a place where the urinals were tied up in brown paper and string? (—Not that *they'd* use them anyway, the thought occurred.)

May said, "Well, if you get sick again, yell like Hell for us."

Felix said, reaching out her slender hand, whose every freckle he had come to know and love, she said, *"Will you be all right, Jack?" Will you be all right, Jack?* Not, mind you, *You'll be all right, Jack.* It was enough. (And if it wasn't, this was not the time and place to say what would be.)

"I'll be all right," he assured her.

But, back on his absurdly sheeted bed, more than slightly fearful of falling asleep at all, the river, the moment he closed his eyes, the river began to unfold before him, mile after beautiful and haunted mile. But this was a fairly familiar effect of fatigue. He had known it to happen with the roads and the wheatfields, in the Prairie Provinces.

It was on awakening to the familiar cockeling chorus of, *I make the sun to rise!* that he realized that he had not dreamed at all.

St. Michael's did not have a single bank; and, what was more—or less—it did not have a single lawyer. Attorneys for the Estate (alerted perhaps by the telephone's phantom relay) arrived early. But they did not arrive early enough . . . early enough to delay the digging. By the time the first lawyeriferous automobile came spinning to a stop before the local courthouse, the expedition was already on its way. The attorney for the Estate requested a delay, the attorneys for the several groups of claimants requested a delay. But the Estate's local agent had already given a consent, and the magistrate declined to set it aside. He did not, however, forbid them to attend.

Also in attendance was one old woman and one small girl. Limekiller thought that both of them looked familiar. And he was right. One was the same old woman who had urged him in out of the "fever rain." The

other was the child who had urged him to see "the beauty harse" and had next day made the meager purchases in Mikeloglu's shop ... whom the merchant had addressed as "Bet-ty me gyel," and urged her (with questionable humor) not to forget him when she was rich.

The crocodile stayed unvexed in his lair beneath the roots of the old Garobo Tree, though, seemingly, half the dragons along the river had dived to alert him.

To walk five hundred feet, *as a start,* is no great feat if one is in reasonable health. To cut and hack and ax and slash one's way through bush whose clearings require to be cleared twice a year if they are not to vanish: this is something else. However, the first five hundred feet proved to be the hardest (and hard enough to eliminate all but the hardiest of the lawyers). At the end of that first line they found their second marker: a lichen-studded rock growing right out of the primal bones of the earth. From there on, the task was easier. Clearly, though "the late Mr. Pike" had not intended it to be impossible, he had intended it to be difficult.

Sneed had discouraged, Marín had discouraged, others had discouraged May and Felix from coming: uselessly. Mere weight of male authority having proven to be obsolescent, Captain Sneed appealed to common sense. "My dear ladies," he pleaded, "can either of you handle a machete? Can either of you use an ax? Can—"

"Can either of us carry food?" was May's counter-question.

"*And* water?" asked Felix. "Both of us can," she said.

"Well, good for both of you," declared Captain Sneed, making an honorable capitulation of the fortress.

May had a question of her own. "Why do we all have to wear *boots*?" she asked, when there are hardly any wet places along here."

"Plenty tommy*goff,* Mees."

"Tommy Goff? Who is *he*?"

"Don't know who *he* was, common enough name, though, among English-speaking people in this part of the Caribbean. Don't know why they named a snake after the chap, either. . . ."

A slight pause. "A . . . snake . . . ?"

"And *such* a snake, too! The dreaded fer-de-lance, as they call it in the French islands."

"Uhh . . . *Poisonous*?"

Sneed wiped his sweating head, nodded his Digger-style bush hat. "*Deadly* poisonous. If it's in full venom, bite can kill a horse. Sometimes *does*. So do be exceedingly cautious. Please."

There was a further word on the subject, from Filiberto Marín. *"En castellano, se llame 'barba amarilla.' "*

This took a moment to sink in. Then one of the North Americans asked, "Doesn't that mean 'yellow beard'?"

"Quite right. In fact, the tommygoff's other name in English is 'yellow jaw.' But the Spanish is, literally, yes, it's yellow *beard.*"

All three North Americans said, as one, *"Oh."* And looked at each other with a wild surmise.

The noises went on all around them. *Slash—! Hack—!* And, *Chop! Chop! Chop!* After another moment, May went on, "Well, I must say that seems like quite a collection of watchies that your late Mr. Leopold Pike appointed. Crocodiles. Poison serpents. What else. Oh. Do garobo *bite?"*

"Bite your nose or finger off if you vex him from the front; yes."

May said, thoughtfully, "I'm not sure that I really *like* your late Mr. Leopold Pike—"

Another flash of daytime lightning. Limekiller said, and remembered saying it the day before in the same startled tone, videlicet: "Pike! Pike!" Adding, this time, *"Fer-de-lance . . . !"*

Felix gave him her swift look. Her face said, No, he was not feverish. . . . Next she said, "'*Fer,*' that's French for 'iron,' and . . . Oh. I see. Yes. Jesus. *Fer-de-lance,* lance-iron, or spear-head. Or spear-*point.* Or—"

"Or in other words," May wound up, *"Pike. . . ,* You dreamed that, too, small John?"

He swung his ax again, nodded. *Thunk.* "Sort of . . . one way or another." *Thunk.* "He had a, sort of a, pike with him." *Thunk.* "Trying to get his point—ha-ha—across. Did I dream the snake, too? Must have . . . I guess. . . ." *Thunk.*

"No. I do *not like* your late Mr. Leopold Pike."

Sneed declared a break. Took sips of water, slowly, carefully. Wiped his face. Said, "You might have liked Old Pike, though. A hard man in his way. Not without a sense of humor, though. And . . . after all . . . he hasn't hurt our friend John Limekiller . . . has he? Old chap Pike was simply trying to do his best for his dead son's child. May seem an odd way, to us. May *be.* Fact o'the matter: *Is.* Why didn't he do it another way? Who's to say. Didn't have too much trust in the law and the law's delays. I'll sum it up. *Pike liked to do things in his own way.* A lot of them were Indian ways. *Old* Indian ways. Used to burn copal gum when he went deer hunting. *A*lways got his deer. And as for *this* little business, well . . . the old Indians had no probate courts. What's the consequence? How does one guarantee that one's bequest reaches one's intended heir?

"Why . . . one *dreams* it to him! Or, for that matter, *her*. In this case, however, the *her* is a small child. So—"

One of the woodsmen put down his tin cup, and, thinking Sneed had done, said to Limekiller, "Mon, you doesn't holds de ox de same way we does. But you holds eet well. Where you learns dis?"

"Oh . . ." said Limekiller, vaguely, "I've helped cut down a very small part of Canada without benefit of chain saw. In my even younger days." Would he, too, he wondered, in his even older days, would he too ramble on about the trees he had felled?—the deeds he had done?

Probably.

Why not?

A wooden chest would have moldered away. An iron one would have rusted. Perhaps for these reasons the "collection of gold and silver coins, not being Coin of the Realm or Legal Tender," had been lodged in more Indian jars. Larger ones, this time. An examination of one of them showed that the contents were as described. Once again the machetes were put to use; branches, vines, ropes, were cut and trimmed. Litters, or slings, rough but serviceable, were made. Was some collective ethnic unconscious at work here? Had not the Incas, Aztecs, Mayas, ridden in palanquins?

Now for the first time the old woman raised her voice. "Ah! dis fah *you*, Bet-ty," she said, touching the ancient urns. "Bet-tah food. Fah *you*. Bet-tah house. Fah *you*. Bet-tah school. Fah *you*." Her gaze was triumphant. "*Ahl dis fah you!*"

One of the few lawyers who had not dropped out along the long, hard way, had a caveat. "Would the Law of Treasure Trove apply?" he wondered. "In which case, the Crown would own it. Although, to be sure, where there is no attempt at concealment The Crown would allow a finder's fee . . . Mr. Limekiller . . . ?"

And if anyone attempt to resist or set aside this my Intention, I do herewith and hereafter declare that he, she, or they shall not sleep well of nights. . . .

Limekiller said, "I'll pass."

And Captain Sneed cried, "Piffle! Tush! Was the Deed of Gift registered, or was it not? Was the Stamp Tax paid, or was it not?"

One of the policemen said, "If you have the Queen's head on your paper, you cahn't go wrong."

Nol. con.," the lawyer said. And said no more.

* * *

That had been that. The rest were details. (One of the details was found in one of the large jars: another piece of plastic-wrapped paper, on which was written in a now-familiar hand, *He who led you hither, he may now sleep well of nights.*) And in the resolution of these other details the three North Americans had no part. Nor had Marín and friends: back to Parrot Bend they went. Nor had Captain Sneed. "Holiday is over," he said. "If I don't get back to my farm, the wee-wee ants will carry away my fruit. Come and visit, all of you. Whenever you like. Anyone will tell you where it is," he said. And was gone, the brave old Digger bush-hat bobbing away down the lane: wearing an invisible plume.

And the major (and the minor) currents of life in St. Michael of the Mountains went on—as they had gone on for a century without them.

There was the inevitable letdown.

May said, with a yawn, "I need a nice, long rest. And I know just where I'm going to find it. *After* we get back to King Town. I'm going to take a room at that hotel near the National Library."

Felix asked, "Why?"

"*Why?* I'll be like a kid in a candy warehouse. Do you realize that on the second floor of the National Library is the largest collection of 19th century English novels which I have ever seen in any one place? EVerything EVer written by EVerybody. Mrs. Edgeworth, Mrs. Trollope, Mrs. Gaskell, Mrs. Oliphant, Mrs. This and Mrs. That."

"Mrs. That. *I* remember *her.* Say, she wasn't bad at all—"

"No, she *wasn't.* Although, personally, I prefer Mrs. This."

Felix and Limekiller found that they were looking at each other. *Speak now,* he told himself. *Aren't you tired of holding your own piece?* "And what are you going to be doing, then?" he asked.

She considered. Said she wasn't sure.

There was a silence.

"Did I tell you about my boat?"

"*No.* You didn't." Her look at him was a steady one. She didn't seem impatient. She seemed to have all the time in the world. "Tell me all about your boat," she said.

SIR H. RIDER HAGGARD
Black Heart and White Heart

1

A ZULU IDYLL

AT THE date of our introduction to him, Philip Hadden was a transport-rider and a trader in "the Zulu." Still on the right side of forty, in appearance he was singularly handsome: tall, dark, upright, with keen eyes, short-pointed beard, curling hair and clear-cut features. His life had been varied, and there were passages in it which he did not narrate even to his most intimate friends. He was of gentle birth, however, and it was said that he had received a public school and university education in England. At any rate he could quote the classics with aptitude on occasion, an accomplishment which, coupled with his refined voice and a bearing not altogether common in the wild places of the world, had earned for him among his rough companions the soubriquet of "The Prince."

However these things may have been, it is certain that he had emigrated to Natal under a cloud, and equally certain that his relatives at home were content to take no further interest in his fortunes. During the fifteen or sixteen years which he had spent in or about the colony, Hadden followed many trades, and did no good at any of them. A clever man, of agreeable and prepossessing manner, he always found it easy to form friendships and to secure a fresh start in life. But, by degrees, the friends were seized with a vague distrust of him; and, after a period of more or less application, he himself would close the opening that he had made by a sudden disappearance from the locality, leaving behind him a doubtful reputation and some bad debts.

Before the beginning of this story of one of the most remarkable episodes in his life, Philip Hadden was engaged for several years in transport-riding—that is, in carrying goods on ox wagons from Durban or Maritzburg to various points in the interior. A difficulty such as had

141

more than once confronted him in the course of his career, led to his temporary abandonment of this means of earning a livelihood. On arriving at the little frontier town of Utrecht in the Transvaal, in charge of two wagonloads of mixed goods consigned to a storekeeper there, it was discovered that out of six cases of brandy five were missing from his wagon. Hadden explained the matter by throwing the blame upon his Kaffir "boys," but the storekeeper, a rough-tongued man, openly called him a thief and refused to pay the freight on any of the load. From words the men came to blows, knives were drawn, and before anybody could interfere the storekeeper received a nasty wound in his side. That night, without waiting till the matter could be inquired into by the landdrost or magistrate, Hadden slipped away, and trekked back into Natal as quickly as his oxen would travel. Feeling that even here he was not safe, he left one of his wagons at Newcastle, loaded up the other with Kaffir goods—such as blankets, calico, and hardware—and crossed into Zululand, where in those days no sherrif's officer would be likely to follow him.

Being well acquainted with the language and customs of the natives, he did good trade with them, and soon found himself possessed of some cash and a small herd of cattle, which he received in exchange for his wares. Meanwhile news reached him that the man whom he had injured still vowed vengeance against him, and was in communication with the authorities in Natal. These reasons making his return to civilization undesirable for the moment, and further business being impossible until he could receive a fresh supply of trade stuff, Hadden like a wise man turned his thoughts to pleasure. Sending his cattle and wagon over the border to be left in charge of a native headman with whom he was friendly, he went on foot to Ulundi to obtain permission from the king, Cetywayo, to hunt game in his country. Somewhat to his surprise the Indunas, or headmen received him courteously—for Hadden's visit took place within a few months of the outbreak of the Zulu war in 1878, when Cetywayo was already showing unfriendliness to the English traders and others, though why the king did so they knew not.

On the occasion of his first and last interview with Cetywayo, Hadden got a hint of the reason. It happened thus. On the second morning after his arrival at the royal kraal, a messenger came to inform him that "the Elephant whose tread shook the earth" had signified that it was his pleasure to see him. Accordingly he was led through the thousands of huts and across the Great Place to the little enclosure where Cety-wayo, a royal-looking Zulu seated on a stool, and wearing a *kaross* of leopard skins, was holding an *indaba,* or conference, surrounded by his counsellors. The Induna who had conducted him to the august presence went down upon his hands and knees, and, uttering the royal salute of *Bayéte,* crawled forward to announce that the white man was waiting.

"Let him wait," said the king angrily; and, turning, he continued the discussion with his counsellors.

Now, as has been said, Hadden thoroughly understood Zulu; and when from time to time the king raised his voice, some of the words he spoke reached his ear.

"What!" Cetywayo said, to a wizened and aged man who seemed to be pleading with him earnestly; "am I a dog that these white hyenas should hunt me thus? Is not the land mine, and was it not my father's before me? Are not the people mine to save or to slay? I tell you that I will stamp out these little white men; my *impis* shall eat them up. I have said!"

Again the withered aged man interposed, evidently in the character of a peacemaker. Hadden could not hear his talk, but he rose and pointed toward the sea, while from his expressive gestures and sorrowful mien, he seemed to be prophesying disaster should a certain course of action be followed.

For a while the king listened to him, then he sprang from his seat, his eyes literally ablaze with rage.

"Hearken," he cried to the counsellor; "I have guessed it for long, and now I am sure of it. You are a traitor. You are Sompseu's* dog, and the dog of the Natal Government, and I will not keep another man's dog to bite me in my own house. Take him away!"

A slight involuntary murmur rose from the ring of *indunas,* but the old man never flinched, not even when the soldiers, who presently would murder him, came and seized him roughly. For a few seconds, perhaps five, he covered his face with the corner of the *kaross* he wore, then he looked up and spoke to the king in a clear voice.

"O King," he said, "I am a very old man; as a youth I served under Chaka the Lion, and I heard his dying prophecy of the coming of the white man. Then the white men came, and I fought for Dingaan at the battle of the Blood River. They slew Dingaan, and for many years I was the counsellor of Panda, your father. I stood by you, O King, at the battle of the Tugela, when its gray waters were turned to red with the blood of Umbulazi your brother, and of the tens of thousands of his people. Afterwards I became your counsellor, O King, and I was with you when Sompseu set the crown upon your head and you made

* Sir Theophilus Shepstone's.

promises to Sompseu—promises that you have not kept. Now you are weary of me, and it is well; for I am very old, and doubtless my talk is foolish, as it chances to the old. Yet I think that the prophecy of Chaka, your great-uncle, will come true, and that the white men will prevail against you and that through them you shall find your death. I would that I might have stood in one more battle and fought for you, O King, since fight you will, but the end which you choose is for me the best end. Sleep in peace, O King, and farewell. *Bayéte!*"*

For a space there was silence, a silence of expectation while men waited to hear the tyrant reverse his judgment. But it did not please him to be merciful, or the needs of policy outweighed his pity.

"Take him away," he repeated. Then, with a slow smile on his face and one word, "Good-night," upon his lips, supported by the arm of a soldier, the old warrior and statesman shuffled forth to the place of death.

Hadden watched and listened in amazement not unmixed with fear. "If he treats his own servants like this, what will happen to me?" he reflected. "We English must have fallen out of favor since I left Natal. I wonder whether he means to make war on us or what? If so, this isn't my place."

Just then the king, who had been gazing moodily at the ground, chanced to look up. "Bring the stranger here," he said.

Hadden heard him, and coming forward offered Cetywayo his hand in as cool and nonchalant a manner as he could command.

Somewhat to his surprise it was accepted. "At least, White Man," said the king, glancing at his visitor's tall spare form and cleanly cut face, "you are no *umfagozan* (low fellow); you are of the blood of chiefs."

"Yes, King," answered Hadden, with a little sigh, "I am of the blood of chiefs."

"What do you want in my country, White Man?"

"Very little, King. I have been trading here, as I daresay you have heard, and have sold all my goods. Now I ask your leave to hunt buffalo, and other big game, for a while before I return to Natal."

"I cannot grant it," answered Cetywayo, "you are a spy sent by Sompseu, or by the Queen's Induna in Natal. Get you gone."

"Indeed," said Hadden, with a shrug of his shoulders; "then I hope that Sompseu, or the Queen's Induna, or both of them, will pay me

---

* The royal salute of the Zulus.

when I return to my own country. Meanwhile I will obey you because I must, but I should first like to make you a present."

"What present?" asked the king. "I want no presents. We are rich here, White Man."

"So be it, King. It was nothing worthy of your taking, only a rifle."

"A rifle, White Man? Where is it?"

"Without. I would have brought it, but your servants told me that it is death to come armed before the 'Elephant who shakes the Earth.'"

Cetywayo frowned, for the note of sarcasm did not escape his quick ear.

"Let this white man's offering be brought; I will consider the thing."

Instantly the Induna who had accompanied Hadden darted to the gateway, running with his body bent so low that it seemed as though at every step he must fall upon his face. Presently he returned with the weapon in his hand and presented it to the king, holding it so that the muzzle was pointed straight at the royal breast.

"I crave leave to say, O Elephant," remarked Hadden in a drawling voice, "that it might be well to command your servant to lift the mouth of that gun from your heart."

"Why?" asked the king.

"Only because it is loaded, and at full cock, O Elephant, who probably desires to continue to shake the earth."

At these words the "Elephant" uttered a sharp exclamation, and rolled from his stool in a most unkingly manner, whilst the terrified Induna, springing backwards, contrived to touch the trigger of the rifle and discharge a bullet through the exact spot that a second before had been occupied by his monarch's head.

"Let him be taken away," shouted the incensed king from the ground, but long before the words had passed his lips the Induna, with a cry that the gun was bewitched, had cast it down and fled at full speed through the gate.

"He has already taken himself away," suggested Hadden, while the audience tittered. "No, King, do not touch it rashly; it is a repeating rifle. Look—" and lifting the Winchester, he fired the four remaining shots in quick succession into the air, striking the top of a tree at which he aimed with every one of them.

"*Wow*, it is wonderful!" said the company in astonishment.

"Has the thing finished?" asked the king.

"For the present it has," answered Hadden. "Look at it."

Cetywayo took the repeater in his hand, and examined it with caution, swinging the muzzle horizontally in an exact line with the stomachs of some of his most eminent Indunas, who shrank to this side and that as the barrel was brought to bear upon them.

"See what cowards they are, White Man," said the king with indignation, "they fear lest there should be another bullet in this gun."

"Yes," answered Hadden, "they are cowards indeed. I believe that if they were seated on stools they would tumble off them as it chanced to your Majesty to do just now."

"Do you understand the making of guns, White Man?" asked the king hastily, while the Indunas one and all turned their heads, and contemplated the fence behind them.

"No, King, I cannot make guns, but I can mend them."

"If I paid you well, White Man, would you stop here at my kraal, and mend guns for me?" asked Cetywayo anxiously.

"It might depend on the pay," answered Hadden; "but for a while I am tired of work, and wish to rest. If the king gives me the permission to hunt for which I asked, and men to go with me, then when I return perhaps we can bargain on the matter. If not, I will bid the king farewell, and journey to Natal."

"In order to make report of what he has seen and learned here," muttered Cetywayo.

At this moment the talk was interrupted, for the soldiers who had led away the old Induna returned at speed, and prostrated themselves before the king.

"Is he dead?" he asked.

"He has travelled the king's bridge," they answered grimly; "he died singing a song of praise of the king."

"Good," said Cetywayo, "that stone shall hurt my feet no more. Go, tell the tale of its casting away to Sompseu and to the Queen's Induna in Natal," he added with bitter emphasis.

"*Baba!* Hear our Father speak. Listen to the rumbling of the Elephant," said the Indunas taking the point, while one bolder than the rest added: "Soon we will tell them another tale, the white Talking Ones, a red tale, a tale of spears, and the regiments shall sing it in their ears."

At the words an enthusiasm caught hold of the listeners, as the sudden flame catches hold of dry grass. They sprang up, for the most of them were seated on their haunches, and stamping their feet upon the ground in unison, repeated:

Indaba ibomwu—indaba ye mikonto
Lizo dunyiswa nge impi ndhlebeni yaho.

(A red tale! A red tale! A tale of spears,
And the *impis* shall sing it in their ears.)

One of them, indeed, a great fierce-faced yellow, drew near to Hadden and shaking his fist before his eyes—fortunately being in the royal presence he had no assegai—shouted the sentences at him.

The king saw that the fire he had lit was burning too fiercely.

"Silence," he thundered in the deep voice for which he was remarkable, and instantly each man became as if he were turned to stone, only the echoes still answered back. "And the *impis* shall sing it in their ears—in their ears."

"I am growing certain that this is no place for me," thought Hadden; "if that scoundrel had been armed he might have temporarily forgotten himself. Hullo! who's this?"

Just then there appeared through the gate of the fence a splendid specimen of the Zulu race. The man, who was about thirty-five years of age, was arrayed in a full war dress of a captain of the Umcityu regiment. From the circlet of otter skin on his brow rose his crest of plumes, round his middle, arms and knees hung the long fringes of black oxtails, and in one hand he bore a little dancing shield, also black in color. The other was empty, since he might not appear before the king bearing arms. In countenance the man was handsome, and though just now they betrayed some anxiety, his eyes were genial and honest, and his mouth sensitive. In height he must have measured six foot two inches, yet he did not strike the observer as being tall, perhaps because of his width of chest and the solidity of his limbs, that were in curious contrast to the delicate and almost womanish hands and feet which so often mark the Zulu of noble blood. In short the man was what he seemed to be, a savage gentleman of birth, dignity and courage.

In company with him was another man plainly dressed in a moocha and a blanket, whose grizzled hair showed him to be over fifty years of age. His face also was pleasant and even refined, but the eyes were timorous, and the mouth lacked character.

"Who are these?" asked the king.

The two men fell on their knees before him, and bowed till their foreheads touched the ground—the while giving him his *sibonga* or titles of praise.

"Speak," he said impatiently.

"O King," said the young warrior, seating himself Zulu fashion. "I am Nahoon, the son of Zomba, a captain of the Umcityu, and this is my uncle, Umgona, the brother of one of my mothers, my father's youngest wife."

Cetywayo frowned. "What do you here away from your regiment, Nahoon?"

"May it please the king. I have leave of absence from the head captains, and I come to ask a boon of the king's bounty."

"Be swift, then, Nahoon."

"It is this, O King," said the captain with some embarrassment: "A while ago the king was pleased to make a *keshla* of me because of certain service that I did out yonder . . ." and he touched the black ring which he wore in the hair of his head. "Being now a ringed man and a captain, I crave the right of a man at the hands of the king—the right to marry."

"Right? Speak more humbly, son of Zomba; my soldiers and my cattle have no rights."

Nahoon bit his lip, for he had made a serious mistake.

"Pardon, O King. The matter stands thus: My uncle Umgona here has a fair daughter named Nanea, whom I desire to wife, and who desires me to husband. Awaiting the king's leave I am betrothed to her and in earnest of it I have paid to Umgona a *lobola* of fifteen head of cattle, cows and calves together. But Umgona has a powerful neighbor, an old chief named Maputa, the warden of the Crocodile Drift, who doubtless is known to the king, and this chief also seeks Nanea in marriage and harries Umgona, threatening him with many evils if he will not give the girl to him. But Umgona's heart is white toward me, and toward Maputa it is black, therefore together we come to crave this boon of the king."

"It is so; he speaks the truth," said Umgona.

"Cease," answered Cetywayo angrily. "Is this a time that my soldiers should seek wives in marriage, wives to turn their hearts to water? Know that but yesterday for this crime I commanded that twenty girls who had dared without my leave to marry men of the Undi regiment, should be strangled and their bodies laid upon the crossroads and with them the bodies of their fathers, that all might know their sin and be warned thereby. Ay, Umgona, it is well for you and for your daughter that you sought my word before she was given in marriage to this man. Now this is my award: I refuse your prayer, Nahoon, and since you, Umgona, are troubled with one whom you would not take as son-in-law, the old chief Maputa, I will free you from his importunity. The girl, says Nahoon, is fair—good, I myself will be gracious to her, and she shall be numbered among the wives of the royal house. Within thirty days from now, in the week of the next new moon, let her be delivered into the *Sigodhla,* the royal house of the women, and with her those cattle, the cows and the calves together, that Nahoon has given you, of which I fine him because he has dared to think of marriage without the leave of the king."

2

THE BEE PROPHESIES

" 'A DANIEL come to judgment' indeed," reflected Hadden, who had been watching this savage comedy with interest; "our lovesick friend has got more than he bargained for. Well, that comes of appealing to Caesar," and he turned to look at the two suppliants.

The old man, Umgona, merely started, then began to pour out sentences of conventional thanks and praise to the king for his goodness and condescension. Cetywayo listened to his talk in silence, and when he had done answered by reminding him tersely that if Nanea did not appear at the date named, both she and he, her father, would in due course certainly decorate a crossroad in their own neighborhood.

The captain, Nahoon, afforded a more curious study. As the fatal words crossed the king's lips, his face took on an expression of absolute astonishment, which was presently replaced by one of fury—the just fury of a man who suddenly has suffered an unutterable wrong. His whole frame quivered, the veins stood out in knots on his neck and forehead, and his fingers closed convulsively as though they were grasping the handle of a spear. Presently the rage passed away—for as well might a man be wroth with fate as with a Zulu despot—to be succeeded by a look of the most hopeless misery. The proud dark eyes grew dull, the copper-colored face sank in and turned ashen, the mouth drooped, and down one corner of it there trickled a little line of blood springing from the lip bitten through in the effort to keep silence. Lifting his hand in salute to the king, the great man rose and staggered rather than walked toward the gate.

As he reached it, the voice of Cetywayo commanded him to stop. "Stay," he said, "I have a service for you, Nahoon, that shall drive out of your head these thoughts of wives and marriage. You see this white man here; he is my guest, and would hunt buffalo and big game in the bush country. I put him in your charge; take men with you, and see that he comes to no hurt. See also that you bring him before me within a month, or your life shall answer for it. Let him be here at my royal kraal in the first week of the new moon—when Nanea comes—and then I will tell you whether or no I agree with you that she is fair. Go now, my child, and you, White Man, go also; those who are to accompany you shall be with you at the dawn. Farewell, but remember we meet again at the new moon, when we will settle what pay you shall receive as keeper of my guns. Do not fail me, White Man, or I shall send after you, and my messengers are sometimes rough."

"This means that I am a prisoner," thought Hadden, "but it will go hard if I cannot manage to give them the slip somehow. I don't intend to stay in this country if war is declared, to be pounded into *mouti* (medicine), or have my eyes put out, or any little joke of that sort."

Ten days had passed, and one evening Hadden and his escort were encamped in a wild stretch of mountainous country lying between the Blood and Unvunyana rivers, not more than eight miles from that "Place of the Little Hand" which within a few weeks was to become famous throughout the world by its native name of Isandhlwana. For three days they had been tracking the spoor of a small herd of buffalo that still inhabited the district, but as yet they had not come up with them. The Zulu hunters had suggested that they should follow the Unvunyana down toward the sea where game was more plentiful, but this neither Hadden, nor the captain, Nahoon, had been anxious to do, for reasons which each of them kept secret to himself. Hadden's object was to work gradually down to the Buffalo River across which he hoped to effect a retreat into Natal. That of Nahoon was to linger in the neighborhood of the kraal of Umgona, which was situated not very far from their present camping place, in the vague hope that he might find an opportunity of speaking with or at least of seeing Nanea, the girl to whom he was affianced, who within a few weeks must be taken from him, and given over to the king.

A more eerie-looking spot than that where they were encamped Hadden had never seen. Behind them lay a tract of land—half-swamp and half-bush—in which the buffalo were supposed to be hiding. Beyond, in lonely grandeur, rose the mountain of Isandhlwana, while in front was an amphitheater of the most gloomy forest, ringed round in the distance by sheer-sided hills. Into this forest there ran a river which drained the swamp, placidly enough upon the level. But it was not always level, for within three hundred yards of them it dashed suddenly over a precipice, of no great height but very steep, falling into a boiling rock-bound pool that the light of the sun never seemed to reach.

"What is the name of that forest, Nahoon?" asked Hadden.

"It is named *Emagudu*, 'The Home of the Dead,' " the Zulu replied absently, for he was looking toward the kraal of Nanea, which was situated an hour's walk away over the ridge to the right.

"The Home of the Dead! Why?"

"Because the dead live there, those whom we name the *Esemkofu*, the Speechless Ones, and with them other Spirits, the *Amahlosi*, from whom the breath of life has passed away, and who yet live on."

"Indeed," said Hadden, "and have you ever seen these ghosts?"

"Am I mad that I should go to look for them, White Man? Only the dead enter that forest, and it is on the borders of it that our people make offerings to the dead."

Followed by Nahoon, Hadden walked to the edge of the cliff and looked over it. To the left lay the deep and dreadful-looking pool, while close to the bank of it, placed upon a narrow strip of turf between the cliff and the commencement of the forest, was a hut.

"Who lives there?" asked Hadden.

"The great *Isanusi*—she who is named *Inyanga* or Doctoress; she who is named *Inyosi* (the Bee), because she gathers wisdom from the dead who grow in the forest."

"Do you think that she could gather enough wisdom to tell me whether I am going to kill any buffalo, Nahoon?"

"Mayhap, White Man, but," he added with a little smile, "those who visit the Bee's hive may hear nothing, or they may hear more than they wish for. The words of that Bee have a sting."

"Good; I will see if she can sting me."

"So be it," said Nahoon; and turning, he led the way along the cliff till he reached a native path which zig-zagged down its face.

By this path they climbed till they came to the sward at the foot of the descent, and walked up it to the hut which was surrounded by a low fence of reeds, enclosing a small courtyard paved with ant-heap earth beaten hard and polished. In this courtyard sat the Bee, her stool being placed almost at the mouth of the round opening that served as a doorway to the hut. At first all that Hadden could see of her, crouched as she was in the shadow, was a huddled shape wrapped round with a greasy and tattered catskin *kaross*, above the edge of which appeared two eyes, fierce and quick as those of a leopard. At her feet smouldered a little fire, and ranged around it in a semicircle were a number of human skulls, placed in pairs as though they were talking together, whilst other bones, to all appearance also human, were festooned about the hut and the fence of the courtyard.

"I see that the old lady is set up with the usual properties," thought Hadden, but he said nothing.

Nor did the witch doctoress say anything; she only fixed her beady eyes upon his face. Hadden returned the compliment, staring at her with all his might, till suddenly he became aware that he was vanquished in this curious duel. His brain grew confused, and to his fancy it seemed that the woman before him had shifted shape into the likeness of a colossal and horrid spider sitting at the mouth of her trap, and that these bones were the relics of her victims.

"Why do you not speak, White Man?" she said at last in a slow clear voice. "Well, there is no need, since I can read your thoughts. You are thinking that I who am called the Bee should be better named the Spider. Have no fear; I did not kill these men. What would it profit me when the dead are so many? I suck the souls of men, not their bodies, White Man. It is their living hearts I love to look on, for therein I read much and thereby I grow wise. Now what would you of the Bee, White Man, the Bee that labors in this Garden of Death, and—what brings *you* here, son of Zomba? Why are you not with the Umcityu now that they doctor themselves for the great war—the last war—the war of the white and the black—or if you have no stomach for fighting why are you not at the side of Nanea the tall, Nanea the fair?"

Nahoon made no answer, but Hadden said:

"A small thing, mother. I would know if I shall prosper in my hunting."

"In your hunting, White Man; what hunting? The hunting of game, of money, or of women? Well, one of them, for a-hunting you must ever be; that is your nature, to hunt and be hunted. Tell me now, how goes the wound of that trader who tasted of your steel yonder in the town of the Maboon (Boers)? No need to answer, White Man, but what fee, Chief, for the poor witch doctoress whose skill you seek," she added in a whining voice. "Surely you would not that an old woman should work without a fee?"

"I have none to offer you, mother, so I will be going," said Hadden, who began to feel himself satisfied with this display of the Bee's powers of observation and thought-reading.

"Nay," she answered with an unpleasant laugh, "would you ask a question, and not wait for the answer? I will take no fee from you at present, White Man; you shall pay me later on when we meet again," and once more she laughed. "Let me look in your face, let me look in your face," she continued, rising and standing before him.

Then of a sudden Hadden felt something cold at the back of his neck, and the next instant the Bee had sprung from him, holding between her thumb and finger a curl of dark hair which she had cut from his head. The action was so instantaneous that he had neither time to avoid nor to resent it, but stood still staring at her stupidly.

"That is all I need," she cried, "for like my heart my magic is white. Stay—son of Zomba, give me also of your hair, for those who visit the Bee must listen to her humming."

Nahoon obeyed, cutting a little lock from his head with the sharp edge of his assegai, though it was very evident that he did this not because he wished to do so, but because he feared to refuse.

Then the Bee slipped back her *kaross,* and stood bending over the fire before them, into which she threw herbs taken from a pouch that was bound about her middle. She was still a finely shaped woman, and she wore none of the abominations which Hadden had been accustomed to see upon the persons of witch doctoresses. About her neck, however, was a curious ornament, a small live snake, red and grey in hue, which her visitors recognized as one of the most deadly to be found in that part of the country. It is not unusual for Bantu witch doctors thus to decorate themselves with snakes, though whether or not their fangs have first been extracted no one seems to know.

Presently the herbs began to smoulder, and the smoke of them rose up in a thin straight stream, that, striking upon the face of the Bee, clung about her head enveloping it as though with a strange blue veil. Then of a sudden she stretched out her hands, and let fall the two locks of hair upon the burning herbs, where they writhed themselves to ashes like things alive. Next she opened her mouth, and began to draw the fumes of the hair and herbs into her lungs in great gulps; while the snake, feeling the influence of the medicine, hissed, and uncoiling itself from about her neck, crept upwards and took refuge among the black *saccaboola* feathers of her headdress.

Soon the vapors began to do their work; she swayed to and fro muttering, then sank back against the hut, upon the straw of which her head rested. Now the Bee's face was turned upwards toward the light, and it was ghastly to behold, for it had become blue in color, and the open eyes were sunken like the eyes of one dead, whilst above her forehead the red snake wavered and hissed, reminding Hadden of the Uraeus crest on the brow of statues of Egyptian kings. For ten seconds or more she remained thus, then she spoke in a hollow and unnatural voice:

"O Black Heart and body that is white and beautiful, I look into your heart, and it is black as blood, and it shall be black with blood. Beautiful white body with a black heart, you shall find your game and hunt it, and it shall lead you into the House of the Homeless, into the Home of the Dead, and it shall be shaped as a bull, it shall be shaped as a tiger, it shall be shaped as a woman whom kings and waters cannot harm. Beautiful white body and black heart, you shall be paid your wages, money for money, and blow for blow. Think of my word when the spotted cat purrs above your breast; think of it when the battle roars about you; think of it when you grasp your great reward, and for the last time stand face to face with the ghost of the dead in the Home of the Dead.

"O White Heart and black body, I look into your heart and it is white as milk, and the milk of innocence shall save it. Fool, why do you strike that blow? Let him be who is loved of the tiger, and whose love is as the love of a tiger, Ah! what face is that in the battle? Follow it, follow it, O swift of foot; but follow warily, for the tongue that has lies will never plead for mercy, and the hand that can betray is strong in war. White Heart, what is death? In death life lives, and among the dead you shall find the life you lost, for there awaits you she whom kings and waters cannot harm."

As the Bee spoke, by degrees her voice sank lower and lower till it was almost inaudible. Then it ceased altogether, and she seemed to pass from trance to sleep. Hadden, who had been listening to her with an amused and cynical smile, now laughed aloud.

"Why do you laugh, White Man?" asked Nahoon angrily.

"I laugh at my own folly in wasting time listening to the nonsense of that lying fraud."

"It is no nonsense, White Man."

"Indeed? Then will you tell me what it means?"

"I cannot tell you what it means yet, but her words have to do with a woman and a leopard, and with your fate and my fate."

Hadden shrugged his shoulders, not thinking the matter worth further argument, and at that moment the Bee woke up shivering, drew the red snake from her headdress and coiling it about her throat wrapped herself again in the greasy *kaross*.

"Are you satisfied with my wisdom, *Inkoos*?" she asked of Hadden.

"I am satisfied that you are one of the cleverest cheats in Zululand, mother," he answered coolly. "Now, what is there to pay?"

The Bee took no offense at this rude speech, though for a second or two the look in her eyes grew strangely like that which they had seen in those of the snake when the fumes of the fire made it angry.

"If the white lord says I am a cheat, it must be so," she answered, "for he of all men should be able to discern a cheat. I have said that I ask no fee—yet, give me a little tobacco from your pouch."

Hadden opened the bag of antelope hide and drawing some tobacco from it, gave it to her. In taking it she clasped his hand and examined the gold ring that was upon the third finger, a ring fashioned like a snake with two little rubies set in the head to represent the eyes.

"I wear a snake about my neck, and you wear one upon your hand, *Inkoos.* I should like to have this ring to wear upon my hand, so that the snake about my neck may be less lonely there."

"Then I am afraid you will have to wait till I am dead," said Hadden.

"Yes, yes," she answered in a pleased voice, "it is a good word. I will wait till you are dead and then I will take the ring, and none can say that I have stolen it, for Nahoon there will bear me witness that you gave me permission to do so."

For the first time Hadden started, since there was something about the Bee's tone that jarred upon him. Had she addressed him in her professional manner, he would have thought nothing of it; but in her cupidity she had become natural, and it was evident that she spoke from conviction, believing her own words.

She saw him start, and instantly changed her note.

"Let the white lord forgive the jest of a poor old witch doctoress," she said in a whining voice. "I have so much to do with Death that his name leaps to my lips," and she glanced first at the circle of skulls about her, then toward the waterfall that fed the gloomy pool upon whose banks her hut was placed.

"Look," she said simply.

Following the line of her outstretched hand Hadden's eyes fell upon two withered mimosa trees which grew over the falls almost at right angles to its rocky edge. These trees were joined together by a rude platform made of logs of wood lashed down with *riems* of hide. Upon this platform stood three figures: notwithstanding the distance and the spray of the fall, he could see that they were those of two men and a girl, for their shapes stood out distinctly against the fiery red of the sunset sky. One instant there were three, the next there were two—for the girl had gone, and something dark rushing down the face of the fall, struck the surface of the pool with a heavy thud, while a faint and piteous cry broke upon his ear.

"What is the meaning of that?" he asked, horrified and amazed.

"Nothing," answered the Bee with a laugh. "Do you not know, then, that this is the place where faithless women, or girls who have loved without the leave of the king, are brought to meet their death, and with them their accomplices. Oh! they die here thus each day, and I watch them die and keep the count of the number of them," and drawing a tally-stick from the thatch of the hut, she took a knife and added a notch to the many that appeared upon it, looking at Nahoon the while with a half-questioning, half-warning gaze.

"Yes, yes, it is a place of death," she muttered. "Up yonder the quick die day by day and down there"—and she pointed along the course of the river beyond the pool to where the forest began some two hundred yards from her hut—"the ghosts of them have their home. Listen!"

As she spoke, a sound reached their ears that seemed to swell from the dim skirts of the forests, a peculiar and unholy sound which it is impossible to define more accurately than by saying that it seemed beastlike, and almost inarticulate.

"Listen," repeated the Bee, "they are merry yonder."

"Who?" asked Hadden; "the baboons?"

"No, *Inkoos,* the *Amatongo*—the ghosts that welcome her who has just become of their number."

"Ghosts," said Hadden roughly, for he was angry at his own tremors, "I should like to see those ghosts. Do you think that I have never heard a troop of monkeys in the bush before, mother? Come, Nahoon, let us be going while there is light to climb the cliff. Farewell."

"Farewell *Inkoos,* and doubt not that your wish will be fulfilled. Go in peace *Inkoos*—to sleep in peace."

3

THE END OF THE HUNT

THE PRAYER of the Bee notwithstanding, Philip Hadden slept ill that night. He felt in the best of health, and his conscience was not troubling him more than usual, but rest he could not. Whenever he closed his eyes, his mind conjured up a picture of the grim witch doctoress, so strangely named the Bee and the sound of her evil-omened words as he had heard them that afternoon. He was neither a superstitious nor a timid man, and any supernatural beliefs that might linger in his mind were, to say the least of it, dormant. But do what he might, he could not shake off a certain eerie sensation of fear, lest there should be some grains of truth in the prophesyings of this hag. What if it were a fact that he was near his death, and that the heart which beat so strongly in his breast must soon be still for ever—no, he would not think of it. This gloomy place, and the dreadful sight which he saw that day, had upset his nerves. The domestic customs of these Zulus were not pleasant, and for his part he was determined to be clear of them so soon as he was able to escape the country.

In fact, if he could in any way manage it, it was his intention to make a dash for the border on the following night. To do this with a good prospect of success, however, it was necessary that he should kill a buffalo, or some other head of game. Then, as he knew well, the hunters with him would feast upon meat until they could scarcely stir, and that would be his opportunity. Nahoon, however, might not succumb to this temptation; therefore he must trust to luck to be rid of him. If it came to the worst, he could put a bullet through him, which he considered he would be justified in doing, seeing that in reality the man was his jailor. Should this necessity arise, he felt indeed that he could face it without undue compunction, for in truth he disliked Nahoon; at times he even hated him. Their natures were antagonistic, and he knew that the great Zulu distrusted and looked down upon him, and to be looked down upon by a savage "nigger" was more than his pride could stomach.

At the first break of dawn Hadden rose and roused his escort, who were still stretched in sleep around the dying fire, each man wrapped in his kaross or blanket. Nahoon stood up and shook himself, looking gigantic in the shadows of the morning.

"What is your will, *Umlungu* (white man), that you are up before the sun?"

"My will, *Muntumpofu* (yellow man), is to hunt buffalo," answered Hadden coolly. It irritated him that this savage should give him no title of any sort.

"Your pardon," said the Zulu reading his thoughts, "but I cannot call you *Inkoos* because you are not my chief, or any man's; still if the title 'white man' offends you, we will give you a name."

"As you wish," answered Hadden briefly.

Accordingly they gave him a name, *Inhlizin-mgama,* by which he was known among them thereafter, but Hadden was not best pleased when he found that the meaning of those soft-sounding syllables was

"Black Heart." That was how the *inyanga* had addressed him—only she used different words.

An hour later, and they were in the swampy bush country that lay behind the encampment searching for their game. Within a very little while Nahoon held up his hand, then pointed to the ground. Hadden looked; there, pressed deep in the marshy soil, and to all appearance not ten minutes old, was the spoor of a small herd of buffalo.

"I knew that we should find game today," whispered Nahoon, "because the Bee said so."

"Curse the Bee," answered Hadden below his breath. "Come on."

For a quarter of an hour or more they followed the spoor through thick reeds, till suddenly Nahoon whistled very softly and touched Hadden's arm. He looked up, and there, about two hundred yards away, feeding on some higher ground among a patch of mimosa trees, were the buffaloes—six of them—an old bull with a splendid head, three cows, a heifer and a calf about four months old. Neither the wind nor the nature of the veldt were favorable for them to stalk the game from their present position, so they made a detour of half a mile and very carefully crept toward them up the wind, slipping from trunk to trunk of the mimosas and when these failed them, crawling on their stomachs under cover of the tall *tambuti* grass. At last they were within forty yards, and a further advance seemed impracticable; for although he could not smell them, it was evident from his movements that the old bull heard some unusual sound and was growing suspicious. Nearest to Hadden, who alone of the party had a rifle, stood the heifer broadside on—a beautiful shot. Remembering that she would make the best beef, he lifted his Martini, and aiming at her immediately behind the shoulder, gently squeezed the trigger. The rifle exploded and the heifer fell dead, shot through the heart. Strangely enough the other buffaloes did not at once run away. On the contrary, they seemed puzzled to account for the sudden noise; and, not being to wind anything, lifted their heads and stared round them.

The pause gave Hadden space to get in a fresh cartridge and to aim again, this time at the old bull. The bullet struck him somewhere in the neck or shoulder, for he came to his knees, but in another second was up and having caught sight of the cloud of smoke he charged straight at it. Because of this smoke, or for some other reason, Hadden did not see him coming, and in consequence would most certainly have been trampled or gored, had not Nahoon sprung forward, at the imminent risk of his own life, and dragged him down behind an ant-heap. A moment more and the great beast had thundered by, taking no further notice of them.

"Forward," said Hadden, and leaving most of the men to cut up the heifer and carry the best of her meat to camp, they started on the blood spoor.

For some hours they followed the bull, till at last they lost the trail on a patch of stony ground thickly covered with bush, and exhausted by the heat, sat down to rest and to eat some *biltong* or sun-dried flesh which they had with them. They finished their meal, and were preparing to return to the camp, when one of the four Zulus who were with them went to drink at a little stream that ran at a distance of not more than ten paces away. Half a minute later they heard a hideous grunting noise and a splashing of water, and saw the Zulu fly into the air. All the while they were eating, the wounded buffalo had been lying in wait for them under a thick bush on the banks of the streamlet, knowing— cunning brute that he was—that sooner or later his turn would come. With a shout of consternation they rushed forward to see the bull vanish over the rise before Hadden could get a chance of firing at him, and to find their companion dying, for the great horn had pierced his lung.

"It is not a buffalo, it is a devil," the poor fellow gasped, and expired.

"Devil or not, I mean to kill it," exclaimed Hadden. So leaving the others to carry the body of their comrade to camp, he started on accompanied by Nahoon only. Now the ground was more open and the chase easier, for they sighted their quarry frequently, though they could not come near enough to fire. Presently they travelled down a steep cliff.

"Do you know where we are?" asked Nahoon, pointing to a belt of forest opposite. "That is *Emagudu,* the Home of the Dead—and look, the bull heads thither."

Hadden glanced round him. It was true; yonder to the left were the falls, the Pool of Doom, and the hut of the Bee.

"Very well," he answered; "then we must head for it too."

Nahoon halted. "Surely you would not enter there," he exclaimed.

"Surely I will," replied Hadden, "but there is no need for you to do so if you are afraid."

"I am afraid—of ghosts," said the Zulu, "but I will come."

So they crossed the strip of turf, and entered the haunted wood. It was a gloomy place indeed; great wide-topped trees grew thick there shutting out the sight of the sky; moreover, the air in it which no breeze stirred, was heavy with the exhalation of rotting foliage. There seemed to be no life here and no sound—only now and again a loathsome spotted snake would uncoil itself and glide away, and now and again a heavy rotten bough fell with a crash.

Hadden was too intent upon the buffalo, however, to be much impressed by his surroundings. He only remarked that the light would be bad for shooting, and went on.

They must have penetrated a mile or more into the forest when the sudden increase of blood upon the spoor told them that the bull's wound was proving fatal to him.

"Run now," said Hadden cheerfully.

"Nay, *hamba gachle*—go softly—" answered Nahoon, "the devil is dying, but he will try to play us another trick before he dies." And he went on peering ahead of him, cautiously.

"It is all right here, anyway," said Hadden, pointing to the spoor that ran straight forward printed deep in the marshy ground.

Nahoon did not answer, but stared steadily at the trunks of two trees a few paces in front of them and to their right. "Look," he whispered.

Hadden did so, and at length made out the outline of something brown that was crouched behind the trees.

"He is dead," he exclaimed.

"No," answered Nahoon, "he has come back on his own path and is waiting for us. He knows that we are following his spoor. Now if you stand here, I think that you can shoot him through the back between the tree trunks."

Hadden knelt down, and aiming very carefully at a point just below the bull's spine, he fired. There was an awful bellow, and the next instant the brute was up and at them. Nahoon flung his broad spear, which sank deep into its chest, then they fled this way and that. The buffalo stood still for a moment, its fore legs straddled wide and its head down, looking first after the one and then the other, till of a sudden it uttered a low moaning sound and rolled over dead, smashing Nahoon's assegai to fragments as it fell.

"There! he's finished," said Hadden, "and I believe it was your assegai that killed him. Hullo! what's that noise?"

Nahoon listened. In several quarters of the forest, but from how far away it was impossible to tell, there rose a curious sound, as of people calling to each other in fear but in no articulate language. Nahoon shivered.

"It is the *Esemkofu*," he said, "the ghosts who have no tongue, and who can only wail like infants. Let us be going; this place is bad for mortals."

"And worse for buffaloes," said Hadden, giving the dead bull a kick, "but I suppose that we must leave him here for your friends, the *Esemkofu,* as we have got meat enough, and can't carry his head."

So they started back towards the open country. As they threaded their way slowly through the tree trunks, a new idea came into Hadden's mind. Once out of this forest, he was within an hour's run of the Zulu border, and once over the Zulu border, he would feel a happier man than he did at that moment. As has been said, he had intended to attempt to escape in the darkness, but the plan was risky. All the Zulus might not overeat themselves and go to sleep, especially after the death of their comrade; Nahoon, who watched him day and night, certainly would not. This was his opportunity—there remained the question of Nahoon.

Well, if it came to the worst, Nahoon must die; it would be easy—he had a loaded rifle, and now that his assegai was gone, Nahoon had only a kerry. He did not wish to kill the man, though it was clear to him, seeing that his own safety was at stake, that he would be amply justified in so doing. Why should he not put it to him—and then be guided by circumstances?

Nahoon was walking across a little open space about ten paces ahead of him where Hadden could see him very well, whilst he himself was under the shadow of a large tree with low horizontal branches running out from the trunk.

"Nahoon," he said.

The Zulu turned round, and took a step toward him.

"No, do not move, I pray. Stand where you are, or I shall be obliged to shoot you. Listen now: do not be afraid for I shall not fire without warning. I am your prisoner, and you are charged to take me back to the king to be his servant. But I believe that a war is going to break out between your people and mine; and this being so, you will understand that I do not wish to go to the Cetywayo's kraal, because I should either come to a violent death there, or my own brothers will believe that I am a traitor and treat me accordingly. The Zulu border is not much more than an hour's journey away—let us say an hour and a half's: I mean to be across it before the moon is up. Now, Nahoon, will you lose me in the forest and give me this hour and a half's start—or will you stop here with that ghost people of whom you talk? Do you understand? No, please do not move."

"I understand you," answered the Zulu, in a perfectly composed voice, "and I think that was a good name which we gave you this morning, though, Black Heart, there is some justice in your words and more wisdom. Your opportunity is good, and one which a man named as you are should not let fall."

"I am glad to find that you take this view of the matter, Nahoon. And now will you be so kind as to lose me, and to promise not to look for me till the moon is up?"

"What do you mean, Black Heart?"

"What I say. Come, I have no time to spare."

"You are a strange man," said the Zulu reflectively. "You heard the king's order to me: would you have me disobey the order of the king?"

"Certainly, I would. You have no reason to love Cetywayo, and it does not matter to you whether or not I return to his kraal to mend guns there. If you think that he will be angry because I am missing, you had better cross the border also; we can go together."

"And leave my father and all my brethren to his vengeance? Black Heart, you do not understand. How can you, being so named? I am a soldier, and the king's word is the king's word. I hoped to have died fighting, but I am the bird in your noose. Come, shoot, or you will not reach the border before moonrise," and he opened his arms and smiled.

"If it must be, so let it be. Farewell, Nahoon, at least you are a brave man, but every one of us must cherish his own life," answered Hadden calmly.

Then with much deliberation he raised his rifle and covered the Zulu's breast.

Already—whilst his victim stood there still smiling, although a twitching of his lips betrayed the natural terrors that no bravery can banish—already his finger was contracting on the trigger, when of a sudden, as instantly indeed as though he had been struck by lightning, Hadden went down backwards, and behold! there stood upon him a great spotted beast that waved its long tail to and fro and glared down into his eyes.

It was a leopard—a tiger as they call it in Africa—which, crouched upon a bough of the tree above, had been unable to resist the temptation of satisfying its savage appetite on the man below. For a second or two there was silence, broken only by the purring, or rather the snoring sound made by the leopard. In those seconds, strangely enough, there sprang up before Hadden's mental vision a picture of the *inyanga* called *Inyosi* or the Bee, her deathlike head resting against the thatch of the hut, and her deathlike lips muttering "think of my word when the great cat purrs above your face."

Then the brute put out its strength. The claws of one paw it drove deep into the muscles of his left thigh, while with another it scratched at his breast, tearing the clothes from it and furrowing the flesh beneath. The sight of the white skin seemed to madden it, and in its fierce desire for blood it dropped its square muzzle and buried its fangs in its victim's shoulder. Next moment there was a sound of rushing feet and of a club falling heavily. Up reared the leopard with an angry snarl, up till it stood as high as the attacking Zulu. At him it came, striking out savagely and tearing the black man as it had torn the white. Again the kerry fell full on its jaws, and down it went backwards. Before it could rise again, or rather as it was in the act of rising, the heavy knob-stick struck it once more, and with fearful force, this time as it chanced, full on the nape of the neck, paralysing the brute. It writhed and bit and twisted, throwing up the earth and leaves, while blow after blow was rained upon it, till at length with a convulsive struggle and a stifled roar it lay still—the brains oozing from its shattered skull.

Hadden sat up, the blood running from his wounds.

"You have saved my life, Nahoon," he said faintly, "and I thank you."

"Do not thank me, Black Heart," answered the Zulu, "it was the king's word that I should keep you safely. Still this tiger has been hardly dealth with, for certainly *he* has saved *my* life," and lifting the Martini he unloaded the rifle.

At this juncture Hadden swooned away.

Twenty-four hours had gone by when, after what seemed to him to be but a little time of troubled and dreamful sleep, through which he could hear voices without understanding what they said, and feel himself borne he knew not whither, Hadden awoke to find himself lying upon a *kaross* in a large and beautifully clean Kaffir hut with a bundle of furs for a pillow. There was a bowl of milk at his side and tortured as he was by thirst, he tried to stretch out his arm to lift it to his lips, only to find to his astonishment that his hand fell back to his side like that of a dead man. Looking round the hut impatiently, he found that there was nobody in it to assist him, so he did the only thing which remained for him to do—he lay still. He did not fall asleep, but his eyes closed, and a kind of gentle torpor crept over him, half obscuring his recovered senses. Presently he heard a soft voice speaking; it seemed far away, but he could clearly distinguish the words.

"Black Heart still sleeps," the voice said, "but there is color in his face; I think that he will wake soon, and find his thoughts again."

"Have no fear, Nanea, he will surely wake, his hurts are not dangerous," answered another voice, that of Nahoon. "He fell heavily with the weight of the tiger on top of him, and that is why his senses have been shaken for so long. He went near to death, but certainly he will not die."

"It would have been a pity if he had died," answered the soft voice, "he is so beautiful; never have I seen a white man who was so beautiful."

"I did not think him beautiful when he stood with his rifle pointed at my heart," answered Nahoon sulkily.

"Well, there is this to be said," she replied, "he wished to escape from Cetywayo, and that is not to be wondered at," and she sighed. "Moreover he asked you to come with him, and it might have been well if you had done so, that is, if you would have taken me with you!"

"How could I have done it, girl?" he asked angrily. "Would you have me set at nothing the order of the king?"

"The king!" she replied raising her voice. "What do you owe to the king? You have served him faithfully, and your reward is that within a few days he will take me from you—me, who should have been your wife, and I must—I must . . ." And she began to weep softly, adding between her sobs, "If you loved me truly, you would think more of me and of yourself, and less of the Black One and his orders. Oh! let us fly, Nahoon, let us fly to Natal before this spear pierces me."

"Weep not, Nanea," he said; "why do you tear my heart in two between my duty and my love? You know that I am a soldier, and that I must walk the path whereon the king has set my feet. Soon I think I shall be dead, for I seek death, and then it will matter nothing."

"Nothing to you, Nahoon, who are at peace, but to me? Yet, you are right, and I know it, therefore forgive me, who am no warrior, but a woman who must also obey the will of the king." And she cast her arms about his neck, sobbing her fill upon his breast.

4

NANEA

PRESENTLY, MUTTERING something that the listener could not catch, Nahoon left Nanea, and crept out of the hut by its beehole entrance. Then Hadden opened his eyes and looked around him. The sun was sinking and a ray of its red light streaming through the little opening filled the place with a soft and crimson glow. In the center of the hut—supporting it—stood a thorn-wood roof-tree colored black by the smoke of the fire; and against this, the rich light falling full upon her, leaned the girl Nanea—a very picture of despair.

As is occasionally the case among Zulu women, she was beautiful—so beautiful that the sight of her went straight to the white man's heart, for a moment causing the breath to catch in his throat. Her dress was very simple. On her shoulders, hanging open in front, lay a mantle of soft white stuff edged with blue beads, about her middle was a buckskin moocha, also embroidered with blue beads, while around her forehead and left knee were strips of gray fur, and on her right wrist a shining bangle of copper. Her naked bronzed-hued figure was tall and perfect in its proportions; while her face had little in common with that of the ordinary native girl, showing as it did strong traces of the ancestral Arabian or Semitic blood. It was oval in shape, with delicate aquiline features, arched eyebrows, a full mouth, that drooped a little at the corners, tiny ears, behind which the wavy coal-black hair hung down to the shoulder, and the very loveliest pair of dark and liquid eyes that it is possible to imagine.

For a minute or more Nanea stood thus, her sweet face bathed in the sunbeam, while Hadden feasted his eyes upon its beauty. Then sighing heavily, she turned, and seeing that he was awake, started, drew her mantel over her breast and came, or rather glided, toward him.

"The chief is awake," she said in her soft Zulu accents. "Does he need aught?"

"Yes, Lady," he answered; "I need to drink, but alas! I am too weak."

She knelt down beside him, and supporting him with her left arm, with her right held the gourd to his lips.

How it came about Hadden never knew, but before that draught was finished a change passed over him. Whether it was a savage girl's touch, or her strange and fawnlike loveliness, or the tender pity in her eyes, matters not—the issue was the same. She struck some cord in his turbulent uncurbed nature, and of a sudden it was filled full with passion for her—a passion which if, not elevated, at least was real. He did not for a moment mistake the significance of the flood of feeling that surged through his veins. Hadden never shirked facts.

"By Heaven!" he said to himself. "I have fallen in love with a black beauty at first sight—more in love than I have ever been before. It's awkward, but there will be compensations. So much the worse for Nahoon, or for Cetywayo, or for both of them. After all, I can always get rid of her if she becomes a nuisance."

Then, in a fit of renewed weakness, brought about by the turmoil of his blood, he lay back upon the pillow of furs, watching Nanea's face while with a native salve of pounded leaves she busied herself dressing the wounds that the leopard had made.

It almost seemed as though something of what was passing in his mind communicated itself to that of the girl. At least, her hand shook a little at her task, and getting done with it as quickly as she could, she rose from her knees with a courteous "It is finished, *Inkoos*," and once more took up her position by the roof-tree.

"I thank you, Lady," he said; "your hand is kind."

"You must not call me lady, *Inkoos*," she answered, "I am no chieftainess, but only the daughter of a headman, Umgona."

"And named Nanea," he said. "Nay, do not be surprised. I have heard of you. Well, Nanea, perhaps you will soon become a chieftainess —up at the king's kraal yonder."

"Alas! and alas!" she said, covering her face with her hands.

"Do not grieve, Nanea, a hedge is never so tall and thick but that it can be climbed or crept through."

She let fall her hands and looked at him eagerly, but he did not pursue the subject.

"Tell me, how did I come here, Nanea?"

"Nahoon and his companions carried you, *Inkoos*."

"Indeed, I begin to be thankful to the leopard that struck me down. Well, Nahoon is a brave man, and he has done me a great service. I trust that I may be able to repay it—to you, Nanea."

This was the first meeting of Nanea and Hadden; but, although she did not seek them, the necessities of his sickness and of the situation brought about many another. Never for a moment did the white man waver in his determination to get into his keeping the native girl who had captivated him, and to attain his end he brought to bear all his powers and charm to detach her from Nahoon, and win her affections for himself. He was no rough wooer, however, but proceeded warily, weaving her about with a web of flattery and attention that must, he thought, produce the desired effect upon her mind. Without a doubt, indeed, it would have done so—for she was but a woman, and an untutored one—had it not been for a simple fact which dominated her whole nature. She loved Nahoon, and there was no room in her heart for any other man, white or black. To Hadden she was courteous and kindly but no more, nor did she appear to notice any of the subtle advances by which he attempted to win a foothold in her heart. For a while this puzzled him, but he remembered that the Zulu women do not usually permit themselves to show feeling toward an undeclared suitor. Therefore it became necessary that he should speak out.

His mind once made up, he had not to wait long for an opportunity. He was now quite recovered from his hurts, and accustomed to walk in the neighborhood of the kraal. About two hundred yards from Umgona's huts rose a spring, and thither it was Nanea's habit to resort in the evening to bring back drinking water for the use of her father's household. The path between this spring and the kraal ran through a patch of bush, where on a certain afternoon toward sundown Hadden took his seat under a tree, having first seen Nanea go down to the little stream as was her custom. A quarter of an hour later she reappeared carrying a large gourd upon her head. She wore no garment now except her moocha, for she had but one mantle and was afraid lest the water should splash it. He watched her advancing along the path, her hands resting on her hips, her splendid naked figure outlined against the westering sun, and wondered what excuse he could make to talk with her. As it chanced fortune favored him, for when she was near him a snake glided across the path in front of the girl's feet, causing her to spring backwards in alarm and overset the gourd of water. He came forward, and picked it up.

"Wait here," he said laughing; "I will bring it to you full."

"Nay, *Inkoos*," she remonstrated, "that is a woman's work."

"Among my people," he said, "the men love to work for the women," and he started for the spring, leaving her wondering.

Before he reached her again, he regretted his gallantry, for it was necessary to carry the handleless gourd upon his shoulder, and the contents of it spilling over the edge soaked him. Of this, however, he said nothing to Nanea.

"There is your water, Nanea, shall I carry it for you to the kraal?"

"Nay, *Inkoos*, I thank you, but give it to me, you are weary with its weight."

"Stay awhile, and I will accompany you. Ah! Nanea, I am still weak, and had it not been for you I think that I should be dead."

"It was Nahoon who saved you—not I, *Inkoos*."

"Nahoon saved my body, but you, Nanea, you alone can save my heart."

"You talk darkly, *Inkoos*."

"Then I must make my meaning clear, Nanea, I love you."

She opened her brown eyes wide.

"You, a white lord, love me, a Zulu girl? How can that be?"

"I do not know, Nanea, but it is so, and were you not blind you would have seen it. I love you, and I wish to take you to wife."

"Nay, *Inkoos,* it is impossible. I am already betrothed."

"Ay," he answered, "betrothed to the king."

"No, betrothed to Nahoon."

"But it is the king who will take you within a week; is it not so? And would you not rather that I should take you than the king?"

"It seems to be so, *Inkoos,* and I would rather go with you than with the king, but most of all I desire to marry Nahoon. It may be that I shall not be able to marry him, but if that is so, at least I will never become one of the king's women."

"How will you prevent it, Nanea?"

"There are waters in which a maid may drown, and trees upon which she can hang," she answered with a quick setting of the mouth.

"That would be a pity, Nanea, you are too fair to die."

"Fair or foul, yet I die, *Inkoos.*"

"No, no, come with me—I will find a way—and be my wife," and he put his arm about her waist, and strove to draw her to him.

Without any violence of movement, and with the most perfect dignity, the girl disengaged herself from his embrace.

"You have honored me, and I thank you, *Inkoos,*" she said quietly, "but you do not understand. I am the wife of Nahoon—I belong to Nahoon; therefore, I cannot look on any other man while Nahoon lives. It is not our custom, *Inkoos,* for we are not as the white women, but ignorant and simple, and when we vow ourselves to a man, we abide by that vow till death."

"Indeed," said Hadden; "and so now you go to tell Nahoon that I have offered to make you my wife."

"No, *Inkoos,* why should I tell Nahoon your secrets? I have said 'nay' to you, not 'yea', therefore he has no right to know," and she stopped to lift the gourd of water.

Hadden considered the situation rapidly, for his repulse only made him the more determined to succeed. Of a sudden under the emergency he conceived a scheme, or rather its rough outline. It was not a nice scheme, and some men might have shrunk from it, but as he had no intention of suffering himself to be defeated by a Zulu girl, he decided—with regret, it is true—that having failed to attain his ends by means which he considered fair, he must resort to others of more doubtful character.

"Nanea," he said, "you are a good and honest woman, and I respect you. As I have told you, I love you also, but if you refuse to listen to me there is nothing more to be said, and after all, perhaps it would be better that you should marry one of your own people. But, Nanea, you will never marry him, for the king will take you; and, if he does not give you to some other man, either you will become one of his 'sisters,' or to be free of him, as you say, you will die. Now hear me, for it is because I love you and wish your welfare that I speak thus. Why do you not escape into Natal, taking Nahoon with you, for there as you know you may live in peace out of reach of the arm of Cetywayo?"

"That is my desire, *Inkoos,* but Nahoon will not consent. He says that there is to be war between us and you white men, and he will not break the command of the king and desert from his army."

"Then he cannot love you much, Nanea, and at least you have to think of yourself. Whisper into the ear of your father and fly together, for be sure that Nahoon will soon follow you. Ay! and I myself will fly with you, for I too believe that there must be war, and then a white man in this country will be as a lamb among the eagles."

"If Nahoon will come, I will go, *Inkoos,* but I cannot fly without Nahoon; it is better I should stay here and kill myself."

"Surely then being so fair and loving him so well, you can teach him to forget his folly and to escape with you. In four days' time we must start for the king's kraal, and if you win over Nahoon, it will be easy for us to turn our faces southwards and cross the river that lies between the land of the Amazulu and Natal. For the sake of all of us, but most of all for your own sake, try to do this, Nanea, whom I have loved and whom I now would save. See him and plead with him as you know how, but as yet do not tell him that I dream of flight, for then I should be watched."

"In truth, I will, *Inkoos,*" she answered earnestly, "and oh! I thank you for your goodness. Fear not that I will betray you—first would I die. Farewell."

"Farewell, Nanea," and taking her hand he raised it to his lips.

Late that night, just as Hadden was beginning to prepare himself for sleep, he heard a gentle tapping at the board which closed the entrance to his hut.

"Enter," he said, unfastening the door, and presently by the light of the little lantern that he had with him, he saw Nanea creep into the hut, followed by the great form of Nahoon.

"*Inkoos,*" she said in a whisper when the door was closed again, "I have pleaded with Nahoon, and he has consented to fly; moreover, my father will come also."

"Is it so, Nahoon?" asked Hadden.

"It is so," answered the Zulu, looking down shamefacedly; "to save this girl from the king, and because the love of her eats out my heart, I have bartered away my honor. But I tell you, Nanea, and you, White Man, as I told Umgona just now, that I think no good will come of this flight, and if we are caught or betrayed, we shall be killed every one of us."

"Caught we can scarcely be," broke in Nanea anxiously, "for who could betray us, except the *Inkoos* here—"

"Which he is not likely to do," said Hadden quietly, "seeing that he desires to escape with you, and that his life is also at stake."

"That is so, Black Heart," said Nahoon, "otherwise I tell you that I should not have trusted you."

Hadden took no notice of this outspoken saying, but until very late that night they sat there together making their plans.

On the following morning Hadden was awakened by sounds of violent altercation. Going out of his hut he found that the disputants were Umgona and a fat and evil-looking Kaffir chief who had arrived at the kraal on a pony. This chief, he soon discovered, was named Maputa, being none other than the man who had sought Nanea in marriage and brought about Nahoon's and Umgona's unfortunate appeal to the king. At present he was engaged in abusing Umgona furiously, charging him with having stolen certain of his oxen and bewitched his cows so that they would not give milk. The alleged theft it was comparatively easy to disprove, but the wizardry remained a matter of argument.

"You are a dog, and a son of a dog," shouted Maputa, shaking his fat fist in the face of the trembling but indignant Umgona. "You promised me your daughter in marriage, then having vowed her to that *umfagozan* —that low lout of a soldier, Nahoon, the son of Zomba— you went, the two of you, and poisoned the king's ear against me, bringing me into trouble with the king, and now you have bewitched my cattle. Well, wait, I will be even with you, Wizard; wait till you wake up in the cold morning to find your fence red with fire, and the slayers standing outside your gates to eat up you and yours with spears—"

At this juncture Nahoon, who till now had been listening in silence, intervened with effect.

"Good," he said, "we will wait, but not in your company Chief Maputa. *Hamba*! (go)" and seizing the fat old ruffian by the scruff of his neck, he flung him backwards with such violence that he rolled over and over down the little slope.

Hadden laughed, and passed on toward the stream where he proposed to bathe. Just as he reached it, he caught sight of Maputa riding along the footpath, his head ring covered with mud, his lips purple and his black face livid with rage.

"There goes an angry man," he said to himself. "Now, how would it be . . ." and he looked upwards like one seeking an inspiration. It seemed to come; perhaps the devil finding it open whispered in his ear, at any rate—in a few seconds his plan was formed, and he was walking through the bush to meet Maputa.

"Go in peace, Chief," he said; "they seem to have treated you roughly up yonder. Having no power to interfere, I came away for I could not bear the sight. It is indeed shameful that an old and venerable man of rank should be struck into the dirt, and beaten by a soldier drunk with beer."

"Shameful, White Man!" gasped Maputa; "your words are true indeed. But wait a while. I, Maputa, will roll that stone over, I will throw that bull upon its back. When next the harvest ripens, this I promise, that neither Nahoon nor Umgona, nor any of his kraal shall be left to gather it."

"And how will you manage that, Maputa?"

"I do not know, but I will find a way. Oh! I tell you, a way shall be found."

Hadden patted the pony's neck meditatively, then leaning forward, he looked the chief in the eyes and said:

"What will you give me, Maputa, if I show you that way, a sure and certain one, whereby you may be avenged to the death upon Nahoon, whose violence I also have seen, and upon Umgona, whose witchcraft brought sore sickness upon me?"

"What reward do you seek, White Man?" asked Maputa eagerly.

"A little thing, Chief, a thing of no account, only the girl Nanea, to whom as it chances I have taken a fancy."

"I wanted her for myself, White Man, but he who sits at Ulundi has laid his hand upon her."

"That is nothing, Chief; I can arrange with him who 'sits at Ulundi.' It is with you who are great here that I wish to come to terms. Listen: if you grant my desire, not only will I fulfill yours upon your foes, but when the girl is delivered into my hands I will give you this rifle and a hundred rounds of cartridges."

Maputa looked at the sporting Martini, and his eyes glistened.

"It is good," he said; "it is very good. Often have I wished for such a gun that will enable me to shoot game, and to talk with my enemies from far away. Promise it to me, White Man, and you shall take the girl if I can give her to you."

"You swear it, Maputa?"

"I swear it by the head of Chaka, and the spirits of my fathers."

"Good. At dawn on the fourth day from now it is the purpose of Umgona, his daughter Nanea, and Nahoon, to cross the river into Natal by the drift that is called Crocodile Drift, taking their cattle with them and flying from the king. I also shall be of their company, for they know that I have learned their secret, and would murder me if I tried to leave them. Now you who are chief of the border and guardian of that drift, must hide at night with some men among the rocks in the shallows of the drift and await our coming. First Nanea will cross driving the cows and calves, for so it is arranged, and I shall help her; then will follow Umgona and Nahoon with the oxen and heifers. On these two you must fall, killing them and capturing the cattle, and afterwards I will give you the rifle."

"What if the king ask for the girl, White Man?"

"Then you shall answer that in the uncertain light you did not recognize her and so she slipped away from you; moreover, that at first you feared to seize the girl lest her cries should alarm the men and they should escape you."

"Good, but how can I be sure that you will give me the gun once you are across the river?"

"Thus: before I enter the ford I will lay the rifle and cartridges upon a stone by the bank, telling Nanea that I shall return to fetch them when I have driven over the cattle."

"It is well, White Man; I will not fail you."

So the plot was made, and after some further conversation upon points of detail, the two conspirators shook hands and parted.

"That ought to come off all right," reflected Hadden to himself as he plunged and floated in the waters of the stream, "but somehow I don't quite trust our friend Maputa. It would have been better if I could have relied upon myself to get rid of Nahoon and his respected uncle—a couple of shots would do it in the water. But then that would be murder and murder is unpleasant; whereas the other thing is only the delivery to justice of two base deserters, a laudable action in a military country. Also personal interference upon my part might turn the girl against me; while after Umgona and Nahoon have been wiped out by Maputa, she *must* accept my escort. Of course there is a risk, but in every walk of life the most cautious have to take risks at times."

As it chanced, Philip Hadden was correct in his suspicions of his coadjutor, Maputa. Even before that worthy chief reached his own kraal, he had come to the conclusion that the white man's plan, though attractive in some ways, was too dangerous, since it was certain that if the girl Nanea escaped, the king would be indignant. Moreover, the men he took with him to do the killing in the drift would suspect something and talk. On the other hand he would earn much credit with his majesty by revealing the plot, saying that he had learned it from the lips of the white hunter, whom Umgona and Nahoon had forced to participate in it, and of whose coveted rifle he must trust to chance to possess himself. An hour later two discreet messengers were bounding across the plains, bearing words from the Chief Maputa, the Warden of the Border, to the "great Black Elephant" at Ulundi.

5

THE DOOM POOL

FORTUNE SHOWED itself strangely favorable to the plans of Nahoon and Nanea. One of the Zulu captain's perplexities was as to how he should lull the suspicions and evade the vigilance of his own companions, who together with himself had been detailed by the king to assist Hadden in his hunting and to guard against his escape. As it chanced, however, on the day after the incident of the visit of Maputa, a messenger arrived from no less a person than the great military Induna, Tvingwayo ka Marolo, who afterwards commanded the Zulu army at Isandhlwana, ordering these men to return to their regiment the Umcityu Corps, which was to be placed upon full war footing. Accordingly Nahoon sent them, saying that he himself would follow with Black Heart in the course of a few days, as at present the white man was not sufficiently recovered from his hurts to allow of his travelling fast and far. So the soldiers went, doubting nothing.

Then Umgona gave it out that in obedience to the command of the king he was about to start for Ulundi, taking with him his daughter Nanea to be delivered over into the *Sigodhla,* and also those fifteen head of cattle that had been *lobola'd* by Nahoon in consideration of his forthcoming marriage, whereof he had been fined by Cetywayo. Under pretense that they required a change of veldt, the rest of his cattle he sent away in charge of a Basuto herd who knew nothing of their plans, telling him to keep them by the Crocodile Drift, as there the grass was good and sweet.

All preparations being completed, on the third day the party started, heading straight for Ulundi. After they had travelled some miles, however, they left the road and turning sharp to the right, passed unobserved of any through a great stretch of uninhabited bush. Their path now lay not far from the Pool of Doom, which, indeed, was close to Umgona's kraal, and the forest that was called Home of the Dead, but out of sight of these. It was their plan to travel by night, reaching the broken country near the Crocodile Drift on the following morning. Here they proposed to lie hid that day and through the night; then, having first collected the cattle which had preceded them, to cross the river at the break of dawn and escape into Natal. At least this was the plan of his companions; but, as we know, Hadden had another program, wherein after one last appearance two of the party would play no part.

During that long afternoon's journey Umgona, who knew every inch of the country, walked ahead driving the fifteen cattle and carrying in his hand, a long travelling stick of black and white *umzimbeet* wood, for in truth the old man was in a hurry to reach his journey's end. Next came Nahoon, armed with a broad assegai, but naked except for his moocha and necklet of baboon's teeth, and with him Nanea in her white bead-bordered mantle. Hadden, who brought up the rear, noticed that the girl seemed to be under the spell of an imminent apprehension, for from time to time she clasped her lover's arm, and looking up into his face, addressed him with vehemence, almost with passion.

Curiously enough, the sight touched Hadden, and once or twice he was shaken by so sharp a pang of remorse at the thought of his share in this tragedy, that he cast about in his mind seeking a means to unravel the web of death which he himself had woven. But ever that evil voice was whispering at his ear. It reminded him that he, the white *Inkoos,* had been refused by this dusky beauty, and that if he found a way to save him, within some few hours she would be the wife of the savage gentleman at her side, the man who had named him Black Heart and who despised him, the man whom he had meant to murder and who immediately repaid his treachery by rescuing him from the jaws of the leopard at the risk of his own life. Moreover, it was a law of Hadden's existence never to deny himself anything that he desired if it lay within his power to take it—a law which had led him always deeper into sin. In other respects, indeed, it had not carried him far, for in the past he had desired much, and he had won little; but this particular flower was to his hand, and he would pluck it. If Nahoon stood between him and the flower, so much the worse for Nahoon, and if it should wither in his grasp, so much the worse for the flower; it could always be thrown away. Thus it came about that, not for the first time in his life, Philip Hadden discarded the somewhat spasmodic prickings of conscience and listened to that evil whispering at his ear.

About half-past five o'clock in the afternoon the four refugees passed the stream that a mile or so down fell over the little precipice into the Doom Pool; and, entering a patch of thorn trees on the further side, walked straight into the midst of two-and-twenty soldiers, who were beguiling the tedium of expectancy by the taking of snuff and the smoking of *dakka* or native hemp. With these soldiers, seated on his pony, for he was too fat to walk, waited the Chief Maputa.

Observing that their expected guests had arrived, the men knocked out the *dakka* pipe, replaced the snuff boxes in the slits made in the lobes of their ears, and secured the four of them.

"What is the meaning of this, O King's soldiers," asked Umgona in a quavering voice. "We journey to the kraal of U'Cetywayo; why do you molest us?"

"Indeed. Wherefore then are your faces set toward the south? Does the Black One live in the south? Well, you will journey to another kraal presently," answered the jovial-looking captain of the party with a callous laugh.

"I do not understand," stammered Umgona.

"Then I will explain while you rest," said the captain. "The Chief Maputa yonder sent word to the Black One at Ulundi that he had learned of your intended flight to Natal from the lips of this white man, who had warned him of it. The Black One was angry, and despatched us to catch you and make an end of you. That is all. Come on now, quietly, and let us finish the matter. As the Doom Pool is near, your deaths will be easy."

Nahoon heard the words, and sprang straight at the throat of Hadden; but he did not reach it, for the soldiers pulled him down. Nanea heard them also, and turning, looked the traitor in the eyes; she said nothing, she only looked, but he could never forget that look. The white man for his part was filled with a fiery indignation against Maputa.

"You wicked villain," he gasped, whereat the chief smiled in a sickly fashion, and turned away.

Then they were marched along the banks of the stream till they reached the waterfall that fell into the Pool of Doom.

Hadden was a brave man after his fashion, but his heart quailed as he gazed into that abyss.

"Are you going to throw me in there?" he asked of the Zulu captain in a thick voice.

"You, White Man?" replied the soldier unconcernedly. "No, our orders are to take you to the king, but what he will do with you I do not know. There is to be war between your people and ours, so perhaps he means to pound you into medicine for the use of the witch doctors, or to peg you over an ant-heap as a warning to other white men."

Hadden received this information in silence, but its effect upon his brain was bracing, for instantly he began to search out some means of escape.

By now the party had halted near the two thorn trees that hung over the waters of the pool.

"Who dives first?" asked the captain of the Chief Maputa.

"The old wizard," he replied, nodding at Umgona; "then his daughter after him, and last of all this fellow," and he struck Nahoon in the face with his open hand.

"Come on, Wizard," said the captain, grasping Umgona by the arm, "and let us see how you can swim."

At the words of doom Umgona seemed to recover his self-command, after the fashion of his race.

"No need to lead me, soldier," he said, shaking himself loose, "who am old and ready to die." Then he kissed his daughter at his side, wrung Nahoon by the hand, and turning from Hadden with a gesture of contempt walked out upon the platform that joined the two thorn trunks. Here he stood for a moment looking at the setting sun, then suddenly, and without a sound, he hurled himself into the abyss below and vanished.

"That was a brave one," said the captain with admiration. "Can you spring too, girl, or must we throw you?"

"I can walk my father's path," Nanea answered faintly, "but first I crave leave to say one word. It is true that we were escaping from the king, and therefore by the law we must die; but it was Black Heart here who made the plot, and he who has betrayed us. Would you know why he has betrayed us? Because he sought my favor, and I refused him, and this is the vengeance that he takes—a white man's vengeance."

"*Wow!*" broke in the Chief Maputa, "this pretty one speaks truth, for the white man would have made a bargain with me under which Umgona, the wizard, and Nahoon, the soldier, were to be killed at the Crocodile Drift, and he himself suffered to escape with the girl. I spoke

him softly and said 'yes,' and then like a loyal man I reported to the
king."

"You hear," sighed Nanea. "Nahoon, fare you well, though presently
perhaps we shall be together again. It was I who tempted you from your
duty. For my sake you forgot your honor, and I am repaid. Farewell,
my husband, it is better to die with you than to enter the house of the
king's women," and Nanea stepped onto the platform.

Here, holding to a bough of one of the thorn trees, she turned and
addressed Hadden saying:

"Black Heart, you seem to have won the day, but me at least you lose
and—the sun is not yet set. After sunset comes the night, Black Heart,
and in that night I pray that you may wander eternally, and be given
to drink of my blood and the blood of Umgona my father, and the blood
of Nahoon my husband, who saved your life, and whom you have
murdered. Perchance, Black Heart, we may yet meet yonder—in the
House of the Dead."

Then uttering a low cry Nanea clasped her hands and sprang upwards and outwards from the platform. The watchers bent their heads
forward to look. They saw her rush headlong down the face of the fall
to strike the water fifty feet below. A few seconds, and for the last time,
they caught sight of her white garment glimmering on the surface of
the gloomy pool. Then the shadows and mist-wreaths hid it, and she
was gone.

"Now, husband," cried the cheerful voice of the captain, "yonder is
your marriage bed, so be swift to follow a bride who is so ready to lead
the way. *Wow!* but you are good people to kill, never have I had to do
with any who gave less trouble. You—" and he stopped, for mental
agony had done its work, and suddenly Nahoon went mad before his
eyes.

With a roar like that of a lion the great man cast off those who held
him and seizing one of them round the waist and thigh, he put out all
his terrible strength. Lifting him as though he had been an infant, he
hurled him over the edge of the cliff to find his death on the rocks of
the Pool of Doom. Then crying:

"Black Heart! your turn, Black Heart the traitor!" he rushed at
Hadden, his eyes rolling and foam flying from his lips, as he passed
striking the Chief Maputa from his horse with a backward blow of his
hand. Ill would it have gone with the white man if Nahoon had caught
him. But he could not come at him, for the soldiers sprang upon him
and notwithstanding his fearful struggles they pulled him to the

ground, as at certain festivals the Zulu regiments with their naked hands pull down a bull in the presence of the king.

"Cast him over before he can work more mischief," said a voice. But the captain cried out, "Nay, nay, he is sacred; the fire from Heaven has fallen on his brain, and we may not harm him, else evil would overtake us all. Bind him hand and foot, and bear him hence tenderly to where he can be cared for. Surely, I thought that these evildoers were giving us too little trouble, and thus it has proved."

So they set themselves to make fast Nahoon's hands and wrists, using as much gentleness as they might, for among the Zulus a lunatic is accounted holy. It was no easy task, and it took time.

Hadden glanced around him, and saw his opportunity. On the ground close beside him lay his rifle, where one of the soldiers had placed it, and about a dozen yards away Maputa's pony was grazing. With a swift movement, he seized the Martini and five seconds later he was on the back of the pony, heading for the Crocodile Drift at a gallop. So quickly indeed did he execute this masterly retreat, that occupied as they all were in binding Nahoon, for half a minute or more none of the soldiers noticed what had happened. Then Maputa chanced to see, and waddled after him to the top of the rise, screaming:

"The white thief, he has stolen my horse, and the gun too, the gun that he promised to give me."

Hadden, who by this time was a hundred yards away, heard him clearly, and a rage filled his heart. This man had made an open murderer of him; more, he had been the means of robbing him of the girl for whose sake he had dipped his hands in these iniquities. He glanced over his shoulder; Maputa was still running, and alone. Yes, there was time; at any rate he would risk it.

Pulling up the pony with a jerk, he leapt from its back, slipping his arms through the rein with an almost simultaneous movement. As it chanced, and as he had hoped would be the case, the animal was a trained shooting horse, and stood still. Hadden planted his feet firmly on the ground and drawing a deep breath, he cocked the rifle and covered the advancing chief. Now Maputa saw his purpose and with a yell of terror turned to fly. Hadden waited a second to get the sight fair on to his broad back, then just as the soldier appeared above the rise he pressed the trigger. He was a noted shot, and in this instance his skill did not fail him; for, before he heard the bullet tell, Maputa flung his arms wide and plunged to the ground dead.

Three seconds more, and with a savage curse, Hadden had remounted the pony and was riding for his life toward the river, which a while later he crossed in safety.

6

The Ghost of the Dead

When Nanea leapt from the dizzy platform that overhung the Pool of Doom, a strange fortune befell her. Close in to the precipice were many jagged rocks, and on these the waters of the fall fell and thundered, bounding from them in spouts of spray into the troubled depths of the foss beyond. It was on these stones that the life was dashed out of the bodies of the wretched victims who were hurled from above. But Nanea, it will be remembered, had not waited to be treated thus, and as it chanced the strong spring with which she had leapt to death carried her clear of the rocks. By a very little she missed the edge of them and striking the deep water head first like some practiced diver, she sank down and down till she thought that she would never rise again. Yet she did rise, at the end of the pool in the mouth of the rapid, along which she sped swiftly, carried down by the rush of the water. Fortunately there were no rocks here; and, since she was a skilful swimmer, she escaped the danger of being thrown against the banks.

For a long distance she was borne thus till at length she saw that she was in a forest, for trees cut off the light from the water, and their drooping branches swept its surface. One of these Nanea caught with her hand, and by the help of it she dragged herself from the River of Death whence none had escaped before. Now she stood upon the bank gasping but quite unharmed; there was not a scratch on her body; even her white garment was still fast about her neck.

But though she had suffered no hurt in her terrible voyage, so exhausted was Nanea that she could scarcely stand. Here the gloom was that of night, and shivering with cold she looked around helplessly to find some refuge. Close to the water's edge grew an enormous yellowwood tree, and to this she staggered—thinking to climb it, and seek shelter in its boughs where, as she hoped, she would be safe from wild beasts. Again fortune befriended her, for at a distance of a few feet from the ground there was a great hole in the tree which, she discovered, was hollow. Into this hole she crept, taking her chance of its being the home of snakes or other evil creatures, to find that the interior was wide and warm. It was dry also, for at the bottom of the cavity lay a foot or more of rotten tinder and moss brought there by rats or birds. Upon this tinder she lay down, and covering herself with the moss and leaves soon sank into sleep or stupor.

How long Nanea slept she did not know, but at length she was awakened by a sound as of guttural human voices talking in a language that she could not understand. Rising to her knees she peered out of the hole in the tree. It was night, but the stars shone brilliantly, and their light fell upon an open circle of ground close by the edge of the river. In this circle there burned a great fire, and at a little distance from the fire were gathered eight or ten horrible-looking beings, who appeared to be rejoicing over something that lay upon the ground. They were small in stature, men and women together, but no children, and all of them were nearly naked. Their hair was long and thin, growing down almost to the eyes, their jaws and teeth protruded and the girth of their black bodies was out of all proportion to their height. In their hands they held sticks with sharp stones lashed on to them, or rude hatchetlike knives of the same material.

Now Nanea's heart shrank within her, and she nearly fainted with fear, for she knew that she was in the haunted forest, and without a doubt these were the *Esemkofu,* the evil ghosts that dwelt therein. Yes, that was what they were, and yet she could not take her eyes off them—the sight of them held her with a horrible fascination. But if they were ghosts, why did they sing and dance like men? Why did they wave those sharp stones aloft, and quarrel and strike each other? And why did they make a fire as men do when they wish to cook food? More, what was it that they rejoiced over, that long dark thing which lay so quiet upon the ground? It did not look like a head of game, and it could scarcely be a crocodile, yet clearly it was food of some sort, for they were sharpening the stone knives in order to cut it up.

While she wondered thus, one of the dreadful-looking little creatures advanced to the fire, and taking from it a burning bough, held it over the thing that lay upon the ground, to give light to a companion who was about to do something to it with the stone knife. Next instant Nanea drew back her head from the hole, a stifled shriek upon her lips. She saw what it was now—it was the body of a man. Yes, and these were not ghosts; they were cannibals of whom when she was little, her mother had told her tales to keep her from wandering away from home.

But who was the man they were about to eat? It could not be one of themselves, for his stature was much greater. Oh! now she knew; it must be Nahoon, who had been killed up yonder, and whose dead body the waters had brought down to the haunted forest as they had brought her alive. Yes, it must be Nahoon, and she would be forced to see her husband devoured before her eyes. The thought of it overwhelmed her. That he should die by order of the king was natural, but that he should be buried thus? Yet what could she do to prevent it? Well, if it cost her her life, it should be prevented. At the worst they could only kill and eat her also, and now that Nahoon and her father were gone, being untroubled by any religious or spiritual hopes and fears, she was not greatly concerned to keep her own breath in her.

Slipping through the hole in the tree, Nanea walked quietly toward the cannibals—not knowing in the least what she should do when she reached them. As she arrived in line with the fire this lack of program came home to her mind forcibly, and she paused to reflect. Just then one of the cannibals looked up to see a tall and stately figure wrapped in a white garment which, as the flame-light flickered on it, seemed now to advance from the dense background of shadow, and now to recede into it. The poor savage wretch was holding a stone knife in his teeth when he beheld her, but it did not remain there long, for opening his great jaws he uttered the most terrified and piercing yell that Nanea had ever heard. Then the others saw her also, and presently the forest was ringing with shrieks of fear. For a few seconds the outcasts stood and gazed, then they were gone this way and that, bursting their path through the undergrowth like startled jackals. The *Esemkofu* of Zulu tradition had been routed in their own haunted home by what they took to be a spirit.

Poor *Esemkofu*! they were but miserable and starving bushmen who, driven into that place of ill omen many years ago, had adopted this means, the only one open to them, to keep the life in their wretched bodies. Here at least they were unmolested, and as there was little other food to be found amid that wilderness of trees, they took what the river brought them. When executions were few in the Pool of Doom, times were hard for them indeed—for then they were driven to eat each other. That is why there were no children.

As their inarticulate outcry died away in the distance, Nanea ran forward to look at the body that lay on the ground, and staggered back with a sigh of relief. It was not Nahoon, but she recognized the face for that of one of the party of executioners. How did he come here? Had Nahoon killed him? Had Nahoon escaped? She could not tell, and at the best it was improbable, but still the sight of this dead soldier lit her heart with a faint ray of hope, for how did he come to be dead if Nahoon had no hand in his death? She could not bear to leave him lying so near her hiding-place, however; therefore, with no small toil, she rolled the corpse back into the water, which carried it swiftly away. Then she returned to the tree, having first replenished the fire, and awaited the light.

At last it came—so much of it as ever penetrated this darksome den—and Nanea, becoming aware that she was hungry, descended from the tree to search for food. All day long she searched, finding nothing, till toward sunset she remembered that on the outskirts of the forest there was a flat rock where it was the custom of those who had been in any way afflicted, or who considered themselves or their belongings to be bewitched, to place propitiatory offerings of food wherewith the *Esemkofu* and *Amalhosi* were supposed to satisfy their spiritual cravings. Urged by the pinch of starvation, to this spot Nanea journeyed rapidly, and found to her joy that some neighboring kraal had evidently been in recent trouble, for the Rock of Offering was laden with cobs of corn, gourds of milk, porridge and even meat. Helping herself to as much as she could carry, she returned to her lair, where she drank of the milk and cooked meat and mealies at the fire. Then she crept back into the tree, and slept.

For nearly two months Nanea lived thus in the forest, since she could not venture out of it—fearing lest she should be seized, and for a second time taste of the judgment of the king. In the forest at least she was safe, for none dared enter there, nor did the *Esemkofu* give her further trouble. Once or twice she saw them, but on each occasion they fled shrieking from her presence—seeking some distant retreat, where they hid themselves or perished. Nor did food fail her, for finding that it was taken, the pious givers brought it in plenty to the Rock of Offering.

But, oh! the life was dreadful, and the gloom and loneliness coupled with her sorrows at times drove her almost to insanity. Still she lived on, though often she desired to die, for if her father was dead, the corpse she had found was not the corpse of Nahoon, and in her heart there still shone that spark of hope. Yet what she hoped for she could not tell.

When Philip Hadden reached civilized regions, he found that war was about to be declared between the Queen and Cetywayo, King of the Amazulu; also that in the prevailing excitement his little adventure with the Utrecht storekeeper had been overlooked or forgotten. He was the owner of two good buck wagons with spans of salted oxen, and at that time vehicles were much in request to carry military stores for the columns which were to advance into Zululand; indeed the transport authorities were glad to pay £90 a month for the hire of each wagon and to guarantee the owners against all loss of cattle. Although he was not desirous of returning to Zululand, this bait proved too much for Hadden, who accordingly leased out his wagons to the Commissariat, together with his own services as conductor and interpreter.

He was attached to No. 3 column of the invading force, which it may be remembered was under the immediate command of Lord Chelmsford, and on the 20 January, 1879, he marched with it by the road that runs from Rorke's Drift to the Indeni forest, and encamped that night beneath the shadow of the steep and desolate mountain known as Isandhlwana.

That day also a great army of King Cetywayo's, numbering twenty thousand men and more, moved down from the Upindo Hill and camped upon the stony plain that lies a mile and a half to the east of Isandhlwana. No fires were lit, and it lay there in utter silence, for the warriors were "sleeping on their spears."

With that *impi* was the Umcityu regiment, three thousand five hundred strong. At the first break of dawn the Induna in command of the Umcityu looked up from beneath the shelter of the black shield with which he had covered his body, and through the thick mist he saw a great man standing before him, clothed only in a moocha, a gaunt wild-eyed man who held a rough club in his hand. When he was spoken to, the man made no answer; he only leaned upon his club looking from left to right along the dense array of innumerable shields.

"Who is this *Silwana* (wild creature)?" asked the Induna of his captains wondering.

The captains stared at the wanderer, and one of them replied, "This is Nahoon-ka-Zomba, it is the son of Zomba who not long ago held rank in this regiment of the Umcityu. His betrothed, Nanea, daughter of Umgona, was killed together with her father by order of the Black One, and Nahoon went mad with grief at the sight of it, for the fire of Heaven entered his brain, and mad he has wandered ever since."

"What would you here, Nahoon-ka-Zomba?" asked the Induna.

Then Nahoon spoke slowly. "My regiment goes down to war against the white men, give me a shield and a spear, O Captain of the king, that I may fight with my regiment, for I seek a face in the battle."

So they gave him a shield and a spear, for they dared not turn away one whose brain was alight with the fire of Heaven.

When the sun was high that day, bullets began to fall among the ranks of the Umcityu. Then the black-shielded, black-plumed Umcityu arose, company by company, and after them arose the whole vast Zulu army, breast and horns together, and swept down in silence upon the doomed British camp, a moving sheen of spears. The bullets pattered on the shields, the shells tore long lines through the array, but they never halted nor wavered. Forward on either side shot out the horns of armed men, clasping the camp in an embrace of steel. Then as these began to close, out burst the war cry of the Zulus, and with the roar of a torrent and the rush of a storm, with a sound like the humming of a billion bees, wave after wave the deep breast of the *impi* rolled down upon the white men. With it went the black-shielded Umcityu and with them went Nahoon, the son of Zomba. A bullet struck him in the side, glancing from his ribs, he did not heed; a white man fell from his horse before him, he did not stab, for he sought but one face in the battle.

He sought—and at last he found. There, among the wagons where the spears were busiest, there standing by his horse and firing rapidly was Black Heart, he who had given Nanea his betrothed to death. Three soldiers stood between them, one of them Nahoon stabbed, and two he brushed aside; then he rushed straight at Hadden.

But the white man saw him come, and even through the mask of his madness he knew Nahoon again, and terror took hold of him. Throwing away the empty rifle, for his ammunition was spent, he leaped upon his horse and drove his spurs into its flanks. Away it went among the carnage, springing over the dead and bursting through the lines of shields, and after it came Nahoon, running long and low with head stretched forward and trailing spear, running as a hound runs when the buck is at view.

Hadden's first plan was to head for Rorke's Drift, but a glance to the left showed him that the masses of the Undi barred that way, so he fled straight on, leaving his path to fortune. In five minutes he was over a ridge, and there was nothing of the battle to be seen, in ten all sounds of it had died away, for few guns were fired in the dread race to Fugitive's Drift, and the assegai makes no noise. In some strange fashion, even at this moment, the contrast between the dreadful scene of blood and turmoil that he had left, and the peaceful face of Nature over which he was passing, came home to his brain vividly. Here birds sang and cattle grazed; here the sun shone undimmed by the smoke of cannon, only high up in the blue and silent air long streams of vultures could be seen winging their way to the Plain of Isandhlwana.

The ground was very rough, and Hadden's horse began to tire. He looked over his shoulder—there some two hundred yards behind came the Zulu, grim as Death, unswerving as Fate. He examined the pistol in his belt; there was but one undischarged cartridge left, all the rest had been fired and the pouch was empty. Well, one bullet should be enough for one savage: the question was should he stop and use it now? No, he might miss or fail to kill the man; he was on horseback and his foe on foot, surely he could tire him out.

A while passed, and they dashed through a little stream. It seemed familiar to Hadden. Yes, that was the pool where he used to bathe when he was the guest of Umgona, the father of Nanea; and there on the knoll to his right were the huts, or rather the remains of them, for they had been burnt with fire. What chance had brought him to this place, he wondered; then again he looked behind him at Nahoon, who seemed to read his thoughts, for he shook his spear and pointed to the ruined kraal.

On he went at speed for here the land was level, and to his joy he lost sight of his pursuer. But presently there came a mile of rocky ground, and when it was past, glancing back he saw that Nahoon was once more in his old place. His horse's strength was almost spent, but Hadden spurred it forward blindly, whither he knew not. Now he was travelling along a strip of turf and ahead of him he heard the music of a river, while to his left rose a high bank. Presently the turf belt bent inwards and there, not twenty yards away from him, was a Kaffir hut standing on the brink of a river. He looked at it, yes, it was the hut of that accursed *inyanga,* the Bee, and standing by the fence of it was none other than the Bee herself. At the sight of her the exhausted horse swerved violently, stumbled and came to the ground, where it lay panting. Hadden was thrown from the saddle but sprang to his feet unhurt.

"Ah! Black Heart, is it you? What news of the battle, Black Heart?" cried the Bee in a mocking voice.

"Help me, mother, I am pursued," he gasped.

"What of it, Black Heart, it is but by one tired man. Stand then and face him, for now Black Heart and White Heart are together again. You will not? Then away to the forest and seek shelter among the dead who await you there. Tell me, tell me, was it the face of Nanea that I saw beneath the waters a while ago? Good! bear my greetings to her when you two meet in the House of the Dead."

Hadden looked at the stream; it was in flood. He could not swim it, so followed by the evil laugh of the prophetess, he sped toward the forest. After him came Nahoon, his tongue hanging from his jaws like the tongue of a wolf.

Now he was in the shadow of the forest, but still he sped on following

the course of the river, till at length his breath failed, and he halted on
the further side of a little glade, beyond which a great tree grew.
Nahoon was more than a spear's throw behind him: therefore he had
time to draw his pistol and make ready.

"Halt, Nahoon," he cried, as once before he had cried; "I would
speak with you."

The Zulu heard his voice, and obeyed.

"Listen," said Hadden. "We have run a long race and fought a long
fight, you and I, and we are still alive both of us. Very soon, if you come
on, one of us must be dead, and it will be you, Nahoon, for I am armed
and as you know I can shoot straight. What do you say?"

Nahoon made no answer, but stood still at the edge of the glade, his
wild and glowering eyes fixed on the white man's face and his breath
coming in short gasps.

"Will you let me go, if *I* let *you* go?" Hadden asked once more. "I
know why you hate me, but the past cannot be undone, nor can the dead
be brought to earth again."

Still Nahoon made no answer, and his silence seemed more fateful
and more crushing than any speech; no spoken accusation would have
been so terrible in Hadden's ear. He made no answer, but lifting his
assegai he stalked grimly toward his foe.

When he was within five paces Hadden covered him and fired. Nahoon sprang aside, but the bullet struck him somewhere, for his right
arm dropped, and the stabbing spear that he held was jerked from it
harmlessly over the white man's head. But still making no sound, the
Zulu came on and gripped him by the throat with his left hand. For
a space they struggled terribly, swaying to and fro, but Hadden was
unhurt and fought with the fury of despair, while Nahoon had been
twice wounded, and there remained to him but one sound arm wherewith to strike. Presently forced to earth by the white man's iron
strength, the soldier was down, nor could he rise again.

"Now we will make an end," muttered Hadden savagely, and he
turned to seek the assegai, then staggered slowly back with starting eyes
and reeling gait. For there before him, still clad in her white robe, a
spear in her hand, stood the spirit of Nanea!

"Think of it," he said to himself, dimly remembering the words of
the *inyanga*, "when you stand face to face with the ghost of the dead
in the Home of the Dead."

There was a cry and a flash of steel; the broad spear leapt toward him
to bury itself in his breast. He swayed, he fell, and presently Black Heart

clasped that great reward which the word of the Bee had promised him.

"Nahoon! Nahoon!" murmured a soft voice, "awake, it is no ghost, but I—Nanea—I, your living wife, to whom my *Ehlose** has given it me to save you."

Nahoon heard and opened his eyes to look and his madness left him.

"Welcome, wife," he said faintly, "now I will live since Death has brought you back to me in the House of the Dead."

Today Nahoon is one of the Indunas of the English Government in Zululand, and there are children about his kraal. It was from the lips of none other than Nanea his wife that the teller of this tale heard its substance.

The Bee also lives and practices as much magic as she dares under the white man's rule. On her black hand shines a golden ring shaped like a snake with ruby eyes, and of this trinket the Bee is very proud.

* Guardian Spirit.

ROBERT E. HOWARD
Red Nails

1

THE SKULL ON THE CRAG

THE WOMAN on the horse reined in her weary steed. It stood with its legs wide-braced, its head drooping, as if it found even the weight of the gold-tassled, red-leather bridle too heavy. The woman drew a booted foot out of the silver stirrup and swung down from the gilt-worked saddle. She made the reins fast to the fork of a sapling, and turned about, hands on her hips, to survey her surroundings.

They were not inviting. Giant trees hemmed in the small pool where her horse had just drunk. Clumps of undergrowth limited the vision that quested under the somber twilight of the lofty arches formed by intertwining branches. The woman shivered with a twitch of her magnificent shoulders, and then cursed.

She was tall, full-bosomed, and large-limbed, with compact shoulders. Her whole figure reflected an unusual strength, without detracting from the femininity of her appearance. She was all woman, in spite of her bearing and her garments. The latter were incongruous, in view of her present environs. Instead of a skirt she wore short, wide-legged silk breeches, which ceased a hand's breadth short of her knees, and were upheld by a wide silken sash worn as a girdle. Flaring-topped boots of soft leather came almost to her knees, and a low-necked, wide-collared, wide-sleeved silk shirt completed her costume. On one shapely hip she wore a straight double-edged sword, and on the other a long dirk. Her unruly golden hair, cut square at her shoulders, was confined by a band of crimson satin.

Against the background of somber, primitive forest she posed with an unconscious picturesqueness, bizarre and out of place. She should have been posed against a background of sea clouds, painted masts, and wheeling gulls. There was the color of the sea in her wide eyes. And that was as it should have been, because this was Valeria of the Red Brotherhood, whose deeds are celebrated in song and ballad wherever seafarers gather.

She strove to pierce the sullen green roof of the arched branches and see the sky which presumably lay above it, but presently gave it up with a muttered oath.

Leaving her horse tied, she strode off toward the east, glancing back toward the pool from time to time in order to fix her route in her mind. The silence of the forest depressed her. No birds sang in the lofty boughs, nor did any rustling in the bushes indicate the presence of small animals. For leagues she had traveled in a realm of brooding stillness, broken only by the sounds of her own flight.

She had slaked her thirst at the pool, but now felt the gnawings of hunger and began looking about for some of the fruit on which she had sustained herself since exhausting the food originally in her saddlebags.

Ahead of her, presently, she saw an outcropping of dark, flintlike rock that sloped upward into what looked like a rugged crag rising among the trees. Its summit was lost to view amidst a cloud of encircling leaves. Perhaps its peak rose above the treetops, and from it she could see what lay beyond—if, indeed, anything lay beyond but more of this apparently illimitable forest through which she had ridden for so many days.

A narrow ridge formed a natural ramp that led up the steep face of the crag. After she had ascended some fifty feet, she came to the belt of leaves that surrounded the rock. The trunks of the trees did not crowd close to the crag, but the ends of their lower branches extended about it, veiling it with their foliage. She groped on in leafy obscurity, not able to see either above or below her; but presently she glimpsed blue sky, and a moment later came out in the clear, hot sunlight and saw the forest roof stretching away under her feet.

She was standing on a broad shelf which was about even with the treetops, and from it rose a spirelike jut that was the ultimate peak of the crag she had climbed. But something else caught her attention at the moment. Her foot had struck something in the litter of blown dead leaves which carpeted the shelf. She kicked them aside and looked down on the skeleton of a man. She ran an experienced eye over the bleached frame, but saw no broken bones nor any sign of violence. The man must have died a natural death; though why he should have climbed a tall crag to die she could not imagine.

She scrambled up to the summit of the spire and looked toward the horizons. The forest roof—which looked like a floor from her vantage point—was just as impenetrable as from below. She could not even see the pool by which she had left her horse. She glanced northward, in the direction from which she had come. She saw only the rolling green ocean stretching away and away, with just a vague blue line in the distance to hint of the hill range she had crossed days before, to plunge into this leafy waste.

West and east the view was the same; though the blue hill-line was lacking in those directions. But when she turned her eyes southward she stiffened and caught her breath. A mile away in that direction the forest thinned out and ceased abruptly, giving way to a cactus-dotted plain. And in the midst of that plain rose the walls and towers of a city. Valeria swore in amazement. This passed belief. She would not have been surprised to sight human habitations of another sort—the beehive-shaped huts of the black people, or the cliff-dwellings of the mysterious brown race which legends declared inhabited some country of this unexplored region. But it was a startling experience to come upon a walled city here so many long weeks' march from the nearest outposts of any sort of civilization.

Her hands tiring from clinging to the spirelike pinnacle, she let herself down on the shelf, frowning in indecision. She had come far—from the camp of the mercenaries by the border town of Sukhmet amidst the level grasslands, where desperate adventurers of many races guard the Stygian frontier against the raids that come up like a red wave from Darfar. Her flight had been blind, into a country of which she was wholly ignorant. And now she wavered between an urge to ride directly to that city in the plain, and the instinct of caution which prompted her to skirt it widely and continue her solitary flight.

Her thoughts were scattered by the rustling of the leaves below her. She wheeled catlike, snatched at her sword; and then she froze motionless, staring wide-eyed at the man before her.

He was almost a giant in stature, muscles rippling smoothly under his skin, which the sun had burned brown. His garb was similar to hers, except that he wore a broad leather belt instead of a girdle. Broadsword and poniard hung from his belt.

"Conan, the Cimmerian!" ejaculated the woman. "What are *you* doing on my trail?"

He grinned hardly, and his fierce blue eyes burned with a light any woman could understand as they ran over her magnificent figure, lingering on the swell of her splendid breasts beneath the light shirt, and the clear white flesh displayed between breeches and boot-tops.

"Don't you know?" he laughed. "Haven't I made my admiration for you plain ever since I first saw you?"

"A stallion could have made it no plainer," she answered disdainfully. "But I never expected to encounter you so far from the ale barrels and meatpots of Sukhmet. Did you really follow me from Zarallo's camp, or were you whipped forth for a rogue?"

He laughed at her insolence and flexed his mighty biceps.

"You know Zarallo didn't have enough knaves to whip me out of camp," he grinned. "Of course I followed you. Lucky thing for you, too, wench! When you knifed that Stygian officer, you forfeited Zarallo's favor and protection, and you outlawed yourself with the Stygians."

"I know it," she replied sullenly. "But what else could I do? You know what my provocation was."

"Sure," he agreed. "If I'd been there, I'd have knifed him myself. But if a woman must live in the war camps of men, she can expect such things."

Valeria stamped her booted foot and swore.

"Why won't men let me live a man's life?"

"That's obvious!" Again his eager eyes devoured her. "But you were wise to run away. The Stygians would have had you skinned. That officer's brother followed you; faster than you thought, I don't doubt. He wasn't far behind you when I caught up with him. His horse was better than yours. He'd have caught you and cut your throat within a few more miles."

"Well?" she demanded.

"Well what?" He seemed puzzled.

"What of the Stygian?"

"Why, what do you suppose?" he returned impatiently. "I killed him, of course, and left his carcass for the vultures. That delayed me, though, and I almost lost your trail when you crossed the rocky spurs of the hills. Otherwise I'd have caught up with you long ago."

"And now you think you'll drag me back to Zarallo's camp?" she sneered.

"Don't talk like a fool," he grunted. "Come, girl, don't be such a spitfire. I'm not like that Stygian you knifed, and you know it."

"A penniless vagabond," she taunted.

He laughed at her.

"What do you call yourself? You haven't enough money to buy a new seat for your breeches. Your disdain doesn't deceive me. You know I've commanded bigger ships and more men than you ever did in your life. As for being penniless—what rover isn't, most of the time? I've squandered enough gold in the seaports of the world to fill a galleon. You know that, too."

"Where are the fine ships and the bold lads you commanded, now?" she sneered.

"At the bottom of the sea, mostly," he replied cheerfully. "The Zingarans sank my last ship off the Shemite shore—that's why I joined Zarallo's Free Companions. But I saw I'd been stung when we marched to the Darfar border. The pay was poor and the wine was sour, and I don't like black women. And that's the only kind that came to our camp at Sukhmet—rings in their noses and their teeth filed—bah! Why did you join Zarallo? Sukhmet's a long way from salt water."

"Red Ortho wanted to make me his mistress," she answered sullenly. "I jumped overboard one night and swam ashore when we were anchored off the Kushite coast. Off Zabhela, it was. There a Shemite trader told me that Zarallo had brought his Free Companies south to guard the Darfar border. No better employment offered. I joined an east-bound caravan and eventually came to Sukhmet."

"It was madness to plunge southward as you did," commented Conan, "but it was wise, too, for Zarallo's patrols never thought to look for you in this direction. Only the brother of the man you killed happened to strike your trail."

"And now what do you intend doing?" she demanded.

"Turn west," he answered. "I've been this far south, but not this far east. Many days' traveling to the west will bring us to the open savannas, where the black tribes graze their cattle. I have friends among them. We'll get to the coast and find a ship. I'm sick of the jungle."

"Then be on your way," she advised. "I have other plans."

"Don't be a fool!" He showed irritation for the first time. "You can't keep on wandering through this forest."

"I can if I choose."

"But what do you intend doing?"

"That's none of your affair," she snapped.

"Yes, it is," he answered calmly. "Do you think I've followed you this far, to turn around and ride off empty-handed? Be sensible, wench, I'm not going to harm you."

He stepped toward her, and she sprang back, whipping out her sword.

"Keep back, you barbarian dog! I'll spit you like a roast pig!"

He halted, reluctantly, and demanded: "Do you want me to take that toy away from you and spank you with it?"

"Words! Nothing but words!" she mocked, lights like the gleam of the sun on blue water dancing in her reckless eyes.

He knew it was the truth. No living man could disarm Valeria of the Brotherhood with his bare hands. He scowled, his sensations a tangle of conflicting emotions. He was angry, yet he was amused and filled with admiration for her spirit. He burned with eagerness to seize that splendid figure and crush it in his iron arms, yet he greatly desired not to hurt the girl. He was torn between a desire to shake her soundly, and a desire to caress her. He knew if he came any nearer her sword would be sheathed in his heart. He had seen Valeria kill too many men in border forays and tavern brawls to have any illusions about her. He knew she was as quick and ferocious as a tigress. He could draw his broadsword and disarm her, beat the blade out of her hand, but the thought of drawing a sword on a woman, even without intent of injury, was extremely repugnant to him.

"Blast your soul, you hussy!" he exclaimed in exasperation. "I'm going to take off your—"

He started toward her, his angry passion making him reckless, and she poised herself for a deadly thrust. Then came a startling interruption to a scene at once ludicrous and perilous.

"*What's that?*"

It was Valeria who exclaimed, but they both started violently, and Conan wheeled like a cat, his great sword flashing into his hand. Back in the forest had burst forth an appalling medley of screams—the screams of horses in terror and agony. Mingled with their screams there came the snap of splintering bones.

"Lions are slaying the horses!" cried Valeria.

"Lions, nothing!" snorted Conan, his eyes blazing. "Did you hear a lion roar? Neither did I! Listen to those bones snap—not even a lion could make that much noise killing a horse."

He hurried down the natural ramp and she followed, their personal feud forgotten in the adventurers' instinct to unite against common peril. The screams had ceased when they worked their way downward through the green veil of leaves that brushed the rock.

"I found your horse tied by the pool back there," he muttered, treading so noiselessly that she no longer wondered how he had surprised her on the crag. "I tied mine beside it and followed the tracks of your boots. Watch, now!"

They had emerged from the belt of leaves, and stared down into the lower reaches of the forest. Above them the green roof spread its dusky canopy. Below them the sunlight filtered in just enough to make a jade-tinted twilight. The giant trunks of trees less than a hundred yards away looked dim and ghostly.

"The horses should be beyond that thicket, over there," whispered Conan, and his voice might have been a breeze moving through the branches. "Listen!"

Valeria had already heard, and a chill crept through her veins; so she unconsciously laid her white hand on her companion's muscular brown arm. From beyond the thicket came the noisy crunching of bones and the loud rending of flesh, together with the grinding, slobbering sounds of a horrible feast.

"Lions wouldn't make that noise," whispered Conan. "Something's eating our horses, but it's not a lion—Crom!"

The noise stopped suddenly, and Conan swore softly. A suddenly risen breeze was blowing from them directly toward the spot where the unseen slayer was hidden.

"Here it comes!" muttered Conan, half lifting his sword.

The thicket was violently agitated, and Valeria clutched Conan's arm hard. Ignorant of jungle lore, she yet knew that no animal she had ever seen could have shaken the tall brush like that.

"It must be as big as an elephant," muttered Conan, echoing her thought. "What the devil—" His voice trailed away in stunned silence.

Through the thicket was thrust a head of nightmare and lunacy. Grinning jaws bared rows of dripping yellow tusks; above the yawning mouth wrinkled a saurianlike snout. Huge eyes, like those of a python a thousand times magnified, stared unwinkingly at the petrified humans clinging to the rock above it. Blood smeared the scaly, flabby lips and dripped from the huge mouth.

The head, bigger than that of a crocodile, was further extended on a long scaled neck on which stood up rows of serrated spikes, and after it, crushing down the briars and saplings, waddled the body of a titan, a gigantic, barrel-bellied torso on absurdly short legs. The whitish belly almost raked the ground, while the serrated backbone rose higher than Conan could have reached on tiptoe. A long spiked tail, like that of a gargantuan scorpion, trailed out behind.

"Back up the crag, quick!" snapped Conan, thrusting the girl behind him. "I don't think he can climb, but he can stand on his hind legs and reach us—"

With a snapping and rending of bushes and saplings, the monster came hurtling through the thickets, and they fled up the rock before him like leaves blown before a wind. As Valeria plunged into the leafy screen a backward glance showed her the titan rearing up fearsomely on his massive hindlegs, even as Conan had predicted. The sight sent panic racing through her. As he reared, the beast seemed more gigantic than ever; his snouted head towered among the trees. Then Conan's iron hand closed on her wrist and she was jerked headlong into the blinding welter of the leaves, and out again into the hot sunshine above, just as the monster fell forward with his front feet on the crag with an impact that made the rock vibrate.

Behind the fugitives the huge head crashed through the twigs, and they looked down for a horrifying instant at the nightmare visage framed among the green leaves, eyes flaming, jaws gaping. Then the giant tusks clashed together futilely, and after that the head was withdrawn, vanishing from their sight as if it had sunk in a pool.

Peering down through broken branches that scraped the rock, they saw it squatting on its haunches at the foot of the crag, staring unblinkingly up at them.

Valeria shuddered.

"How long do you suppose he'll crouch there?"

Conan kicked the skull on the leaf-strewn shelf.

"That fellow must have climbed up here to escape him, or one like him. He must have died of starvation. There are no bones broken. That thing must be a dragon, such as the black people speak of in their legends. If so, it won't leave here until we're both dead."

Valeria looked at him blankly, her resentment forgotten. She fought down a surging of panic. She had proved her reckless courage a thousand times in wild battles on sea and land, on the blood-slippery decks of burning war ships, in the storming of walled cities, and on the trampled sandy beaches where the desperate men of the Red Brotherhood bathed their knives in one another's blood in their fights for leadership. But the prospect now confronting her congealed her blood. A cutlass stroke in the heat of battle was nothing; but to sit idle and helpless on a bare rock until she perished of starvation, besieged by a monstrous survival of an elder age—the thought sent panic throbbing through her brain.

"He must leave to eat and drink," she said helplessly.

"He won't have to go far to do either," Conan pointed out. "He's just gorged on horse meat and, like a real snake, he can go for a long time without eating or drinking again. But he doesn't sleep after eating, like a real snake, it seems. Anyway, he can't climb this crag."

Conan spoke imperturbably. He was a barbarian, and the terrible patience of the wilderness and its children was as much a part of him as his lusts and rages. He could endure a situation like this with a coolness impossible to a civilized person.

"Can't we get into the trees and get away, traveling like apes through the branches?" she asked desperately.

He shook his head. "I thought of that. The branches that touch the crag down there are too light. They'd break with our weight. Besides, I have an idea that devil could tear up any tree around here by its roots."

"Well, are we going to sit here on our rumps until we starve, like that?" she cried furiously, kicking the skull clattering across the ledge. "I won't do it! I'll go down there and cut his damned head off—"

Conan had seated himself on a rocky projection at the foot of the spire. He looked up with a glint of admiration at her blazing eyes and tense, quivering figure, but, realizing that she was in just the mood for any madness, he let none of his admiration sound in his voice.

"Sit down," he grunted, catching her by her wrist and pulling her down on his knee. She was too surprised to resist as he took her sword from her hand and shoved it back in its sheath. "Sit still and calm down. You'd only break your steel on his scales. He'd gobble you up at one gulp, or smash you like an egg with that spiked tail of his. We'll get out of this jam some way, but we shan't do it by getting chewed up and swallowed."

She made no reply, nor did she seek to repulse his arm from about her waist. She was frightened, and the sensation was new to Valeria of the Red Brotherhood. So she sat on her companion's—or captor's—knee with a docility that would have amazed Zarallo, who had ana-thematized her as a she-devil out of Hell's seraglio.

Conan played idly with her curly yellow locks, seemingly intent only upon his conquest. Neither the skeleton at his feet nor the monster crouching below disturbed his mind or dulled the edge of his interest.

The girl's restless eyes, roving the leaves below them, discovered splashes of color among the green. It was fruit, large, darkly crimson globes suspended from the boughs of a tree whose broad leaves were a peculiarly rich and vivid green. She became aware of both thirst and hunger, though thirst had not assailed her until she knew she could not descend from the crag to find food and water.

"We need not starve," she said. "There is fruit we can reach."

Conan glanced where she pointed.

"If we ate that we wouldn't need the bite of a dragon," he grunted. "That's what the black people of Kush call the Apples of Derketa. Derketa is the Queen of the Dead. Drink a little of the juice, or spill

it on your flesh, and you'd be dead before you could tumble to the foot
of this crag."

"Oh!"

She lapsed into dismayed silence. There seemed no way out of their
predicament, she reflected gloomily. She saw no way of escape, and
Conan seemed to be concerned only with her supple waist and curly
tresses. If he was trying to formulate a plan of escape he did not show
it.

"If you'll take your hands off me long enough to climb up on that
peak," she said presently, "you'll see something that will surprise you."

He cast her a questioning glance, then obeyed with a shrug of his
massive shoulders. Clinging to the spirelike pinnacle, he stared out over
the forest roof.

He stood a long moment in silence, posed like a bronze statue on the
rock.

"It's a walled city, right enough," he muttered presently. "Was that
where you were going, when you tried to send me off alone to the
coast?"

"I saw it before you came. I knew nothing of it when I left Sukhmet."

"Who'd have thought to find a city here? I don't believe the Stygians
ever penetrated this far. Could black people build a city like that? I see
no herds on the plain, no signs of cultivation, or people moving about."

"How could you hope to see all that, at this distance?" she demanded.

He shrugged his shoulders and dropped down on the shelf.

"Well, the folk of the city can't help us just now. And they might
not, if they could. The people of the Black Countries are generally
hostile to strangers. Probably stick us full of spears—"

He stopped short and stood silent, as if he had forgotten what he was
saying, frowning down at the crimson spheres gleaming among the
leaves.

"Spears!" he muttered. "What a blasted fool I am not to have thought
of that before! That shows what a pretty woman does to a man's mind."

"What are you talking about?" she inquired.

Without answering her question, he descended to the belt of leaves
and looked down through them. The great brute squatted below, watching the crag with the frightful patience of the reptile folk. So might one
of his breed have glared up at their troglodyte ancestors, treed on a
high-flung rock, in the dim dawn ages. Conan cursed him without heat,
and began cutting branches, reaching out and severing them as far from
the end as he could reach. The agitation of the leaves made the monster

restless. He rose from his haunches and lashed his hideous tail, snapping off saplings as if they had been toothpicks. Conan watched him warily from the corner of his eye, and just as Valeria believed the dragon was about to hurl himself up the crag again, the Cimmerian drew back and climbed up to the ledge with the branches he had cut. There were three of these, slender shafts about seven feet long, but not larger than his thumb. He had also cut several strands of tough, thin vine.

"Branches too light for spear-hafts, and creepers no thicker than cords," he remarked, indicating the foliage about the crag. "It won't hold our weight—but there's strength in union. That's what the Aquilonian renegades used to tell us Cimmerians when they came into the hills to raise an army to invade their own country. But we always fight by clans and tribes."

"What the devil has that got to do with those sticks?" she demanded.

"You wait and see."

Gathering the sticks in a compact bundle, he wedged his poniard hilt between them at one end. Then with the vines he bound them together and, when he had completed his task, he had a spear of no small strength, with a sturdy shaft seven feet in length.

"What good will that do?" she demanded. "You told me that a blade couldn't pierce his scales—"

"He hasn't got scales all over him," answered Conan. "There's more than one way of skinning a panther."

Moving down to the edge of the leaves, he reached the spear up and carefully thrust the blade through one of the Apples of Derketa, drawing aside to avoid the darkly purple drops that dripped from the pierced fruit. Presently he withdrew the blade and showed her the blue steel stained a dull purplish crimson.

"I don't know whether it will do the job or not," quoth he. "There's enough poison there to kill an elephant, but—well, we'll see."

Valeria was close behind him as he let himself down among the leaves. Cautiously holding the poisoned pike away from him, he thrust his head through the branches and addressed the monster.

"What are you waiting down there for, you misbegotten offspring of questionable parents?" was one of his more printable queries. "Stick your ugly head up here again, you long-necked brute—or do you want me to come down there and kick you loose from your illegitimate spine?"

There was more of it—some of it couched in eloquence that made Valeria stare, in spite of her profane education among the seafarers.

And it had its effect on the monster. Just as the incessant yapping of a dog worries and enrages more constitutionally silent animals, so the clamorous voice of a man rouses fear in some bestial bosoms and insane rage in others. Suddenly and with appalling quickness, the mastodonic brute reared up on its mighty hind legs and elongated its neck and body in a furious effort to reach this vociferous pigmy whose clamor was disturbing the primeval silence of its ancient realm.

But Conan had judged his distance with precision. Some five feet below him the mighty head crashed terribly but futilely through the leaves. And as the monstrous mouth gaped like that of a great snake, Conan drove his spear into the red angle of the jawbone hinge. He struck downward with all the strength of both arms, driving the long poniard blade to the hilt in flesh, sinew and bone.

Instantly the jaws clashed convulsively together, severing the triple-pieced shaft and almost precipitating Conan from his perch. He would have fallen but for the girl behind him, who caught his sword-belt in a desperate grasp. He clutched at a rocky projection, and grinned his thanks back at her.

Down on the ground the monster was wallowing like a dog with pepper in its eyes. He shook his head from side to side, pawed at it, and opened his mouth repeatedly to its widest extent. Presently he got a huge front foot on the stump of the shaft and managed to tear the blade out. Then he threw up his head, jaws wide and spouting blood, and glared up at the crag with such concentrated and intelligent fury that Valeria trembled and drew her sword. The scales along his back and flanks turned from rusty brown to a dull lurid red. Most horribly the monster's silence was broken. The sounds that issued from his blood-streaming jaws did not sound like anything that could have been produced by an earthly creation.

With harsh, grating roars, the dragon hurled himself at the crag that was the citadel of his enemies. Again and again his mighty head crashed upward through the branches, snapping vainly on empty air. He hurled his full ponderous weight against the rock until it vibrated from base to crest. And rearing upright he gripped it with his front legs like a man and tried to tear it up by the roots, as if it had been a tree.

This exhibition of primordial fury chilled the blood in Valeria's veins, but Conan was too close to the primitive himself to feel anything but a comprehending interest. To the barbarian, no such gulf existed between himself and other men, and the animals, as existed in the conception of Valeria. The monster below them, to Conan, was merely a form of life differing from himself mainly in physical shape. He attributed to it characteristics similar to his own, and saw in its wrath a counterpart of his rages, in its roars and bellowings merely reptilian equivalents to the curses he had bestowed upon it. Feeling a kinship with all wild things, even dragons, it was impossible for him to experience the sick horror which assailed Valeria at the sight of the brute's ferocity.

He sat watching it tranquilly, and pointed out the various changes that were taking place in its voice and actions.

"The poison's taking hold," he said with conviction.

"I don't believe it." To Valeria it seemed preposterous to suppose that anything, however lethal, could have any effect on that mountain of muscle and fury.

"There's pain in his voice," declared Conan. "First he was merely angry because of the stinging in his jaw. Now he feels the bite of the poison. Look! He's staggering. He'll be blind in a few more minutes. What did I tell you?"

For suddenly the dragon had lurched about and went crashing off through the bushes.

"Is he running away?" inquired Valeria uneasily.

"He's making for the pool!" Conan sprang up, galvanized into swift activity. "The poison makes him thirsty. Come on! He'll be blind in a few moments, but he can smell his way back to the foot of the crag, and if our scent's here still, he'll sit there until he dies. And others of his kind may come at his cries. Let's go!"

"Down there?" Valeria was aghast.

"Sure! We'll make for the city! They may cut our heads off there, but it's our only chance. We may run into a thousand more dragons on the way, but it's sure death to stay here. If we wait until he dies, we may have a dozen more to deal with. After me, in a hurry!"

He went down the ramp as swiftly as an ape, pausing only to aid his less agile companion, who, until she saw the Cimmerian climb, had fancied herself the equal of any man in the rigging of a ship or on the sheer face of a cliff.

They descended into the gloom below the branches and slid to the ground silently, though Valeria felt as if the pounding of her heart must surely be heard from far away. A noisy gurgling and lapping beyond the dense thicket indicated that the dragon was drinking at the pool.

"As soon as his belly is full he'll be back," muttered Conan. "It may take hours for the poison to kill him—if it does at all."

Somewhere beyond the forest the sun was sinking to the horizon. The forest was a misty twilight place of black shadows and dim vistas. Conan gripped Valeria's wrist and glided away from the foot of the crag. He made less noise than a breeze blowing among the tree trunks, but Valeria felt as if her soft boots were betraying their flight to all the forest.

"I don't think he can follow a trail," muttered Conan. "But if a wind blew our body-scent to him, he could smell us out."

"Mitra, grant that the wind blow not!" Valeria breathed.

Her face was a pallid oval in the gloom. She gripped her sword in her free hand, but the feel of the shagreen-bound hilt inspired only a feeling of helplessness in her.

They were still some distance from the edge of the forest when they heard a snapping and crashing behind them. Valeria bit her lip to check a cry.

"He's on our trail!" she whispered fiercely.

Conan shook his head.

"He didn't smell us at the rock, and he's blundering about through the forest trying to pick up our scent. Come on! It's the city or nothing now! He could tear down any tree we'd climb. If only the wind stays down—"

They stole on until the trees began to thin out ahead of them. Behind them the forest was a black impenetrable ocean of shadows. The ominous crackling still sounded behind them, as the dragon blundered in his erratic course.

"There's the plain ahead," breathed Valeria. "A little more and we'll—"

"Crom!" swore Conan.

"Mitra!" whispered Valeria.

Out of the south a wind had sprung up.

It blew over them directly into the black forest behind them. Instantly a horrible roar shook the woods. The aimless snapping and crackling of the bushes changed to a sustained crashing as the dragon came like a hurricane straight toward the spot from which the scent of his enemies was wafted.

"Run!" snarled Conan, his eyes blazing like those of a trapped wolf. "It's all we can do!"

Sailor's boots are not made for sprinting, and the life of a pirate does not train one for a runner. Within a hundred yards Valeria was panting and reeling in her gait, and behind them the crashing gave way to a rolling thunder as the monster broke out of the thickets and into the more open ground.

Conan's iron arm about the woman's waist half lifted her; her feet scarcely touched the earth as she was borne along at a speed she could never have attained herself. If he could keep out of the beast's way for a bit, perhaps that betraying wind would shift—but the wind held, and a quick glance over his shoulder showed Conan that the monster was almost upon them, coming like a war-galley in front of a hurricane. He thrust Valeria from him with a force that sent her reeling a dozen feet to fall in a crumpled heap at the foot of the nearest tree, and the Cimmerian wheeled in the path of the thundering titan.

Convinced that his death was upon him, the Cimmerian acted according to his instinct, and hurled himself full at the awful face that was bearing down on him. He leaped, slashing like a wildcat, felt his sword cut deep into the scales that sheathed the mighty snout—and then a terrific impact knocked him rolling and tumbling for fifty feet with all the wind and half the life battered out of him.

How the stunned Cimmerian regained his feet, not even he could have ever told. But the only thought that filled his brain was of the woman lying dazed and helpless almost in the path of the hurtling fiend, and before the breath came whistling back into his gullet he was standing over her with his sword in his hand.

She lay where he had thrown her, but she was struggling to a sitting posture. Neither tearing tusks nor trampling feet had touched her. It had been a shoulder or front leg that struck Conan, and the blind monster rushed on, forgetting the victims whose scent it had been following, in the sudden agony of its death throes. Headlong on its course it thundered until its low-hung head crashed into a gigantic tree in its path. The impact tore the tree up by the roots and must have dashed the brains from the misshapen skull. Tree and monster fell together, and the dazed humans saw the branches and leaves shaken by the convulsions of the creature they covered—and then grow quiet.

Conan lifted Valeria to her feet and together they started away at a reeling run. A few moments later they emerged into the still twilight of the treeless plain.

Conan paused an instant and glanced back at the ebon fastness behind them. Not a leaf stirred, nor a bird chirped. It stood as silent as it must have stood before Man was created.

"Come on," muttered Conan, taking his companion's hand. "It's touch and go now. If more dragons come out of the woods after us—"

He did not have to finish the sentence.

The city looked very far away across the plain, farther than it had looked from the crag. Valeria's heart hammered until she felt as if it would strangle her. At every step she expected to hear the crashing of the bushes and see another colossal nightmare bearing down upon them. But nothing disturbed the silence of the thickets.

With the first mile between them and the woods, Valeria breathed more easily. Her buoyant self-confidence began to thaw out again. The sun had set and darkness was gathering over the plain, lightened a little by the stars that made stunted ghosts out of the cactus growths.

"No cattle, no plowed fields," muttered Conan. "How do these people live?"

"Perhaps the cattle are in pens for the night," suggested Valeria, "and the fields and grazing-pastures are on the other side of the city."

"Maybe," he grunted. "I didn't see any from the crag, though."

The moon came up behind the city, etching walls and towers blackly in the yellow glow. Valeria shivered. Black against the moon the strange city had a somber, sinister look.

Perhaps something of the same feeling occurred to Conan, for he stopped, glanced about him, and grunted: "We stop here. No use coming to their gates in the night. They probably wouldn't let us in. Besides, we need rest, and we don't know how they'll receive us. A few hours' sleep will put us in better shape to fight or run."

He led the way to a bed of cactus which grew in a circle—a phenomenon common to the southern desert. With his sword he chopped an opening, and motioned Valeria to enter.

"We'll be safe from snakes here, anyhow."

She glanced fearfully back toward the black line that indicated the forest some six miles away.

"Suppose a dragon comes out of the woods?"

"We'll keep watch," he answered, though he made no suggestion as to what they would do in such an event. He was staring at the city, a few miles away. Not a light shone from spire or tower. A great black mass of mystery, it reared cryptically against the moonlit sky.

"Lie down and sleep. I'll keep the first watch."

She hesitated, glancing at him uncertainly, but he sat down cross-legged in the opening, facing toward the plain, his sword across his knees, his back to her. Without further comment she lay down on the sand inside the spiky circle.

"Wake me when the moon is at its zenith," she directed.

He did not reply nor look toward her. Her last impression, as she sank into slumber, was of his muscular figure, immobile as a statue hewn out of bronze, outlined against the low-hanging stars.

2

VALERIA AWOKE with a start, to the realization that a gray dawn was stealing over the plain.

She sat up, rubbing her eyes. Conan squatted beside the cactus, cutting off the thick pears and dexterously twitching out the spikes.

"You didn't awake me," she accused. "You let me sleep all night!"

"You were tired," he answered. "Your posterior must have been sore, too, after that long ride. You pirates aren't used to horseback."

"What about yourself?" she retorted.

"I was a *kozak* before I was a pirate," he answered. "They live in the saddle. I snatch naps like a panther watching beside the trail for a deer to come by. My ears keep watch while my eyes sleep."

And indeed the giant barbarian seemed as much refreshed as if he had slept the whole night on a golden bed. Having removed the thorns, and peeled off the tough skin, he handed the girl a thick, juicy cactus leaf.

"Skin your teeth in that pear. It's food and drink to a desert man. I was a chief of the Zuagirs once—desert men who live by plundering the caravans."

"Is there anything you haven't been?" inquired the girl, half in derision and half in fascination.

"I've never been king of an Hyborian kingdom," he grinned, taking an enormous mouthful of cactus. "But I've dreamed of being even that. I may be too, some day. Why shouldn't I?"

She shook her head in wonder at his calm audacity, and fell to devouring her pear. She found it not unpleasing to the palate, and full of cool and thirst-satisfying juice. Finishing his meal, Conan wiped his hands in the sand, rose, ran his fingers through his thick black mane, hitched up his sword belt and said:

"Well, let's go. If the people in that city are going to cut our throats they may as well do it now, before the heat of the day begins."

His grim humor was unconscious, but Valeria reflected that it might be prophetic. She too hitched her sword belt as she rose. Her terrors of the night were past. The roaring dragons of the distant forest were like a dim dream. There was a swagger in her stride as she moved off beside the Cimmerian. Whatever perils lay ahead of them, their foes would be men. And Valeria of the Red Brotherhood had never seen the face of the man she feared.

Conan glanced down at her as she strode along beside him with her swinging stride that matched his own.

"You walk more like a hillman than a sailor," he said. "You must be an Aquilonian. The suns of Darfar never burnt your white skin brown. Many a princess would envy you."

"I am from Aquilonia," she replied. His compliments no longer irritated her. His evident admiration pleased her. For another man to have kept her watch while she slept would have angered her; she had always fiercely resented any man's attempting to shield or protect her because of her sex. But she found a secret pleasure in the fact that this man had done so. And he had not taken advantage of her fright and the weakness resulting from it. After all, she reflected, her companion was no common man.

The sun rose behind the city, turning the towers to a sinister crimson.

"Black last night against the moon," grunted Conan, his eyes clouding with the abysmal superstition of the barbarian. "Blood-red as a threat of blood against the sun this dawn. I do not like this city."

But they went on, and as they went Conan pointed out the fact that no road ran to the city from the north.

"No cattle have trampled the plain on this side of the city," said he. "No plowshare has touched the earth for years, maybe centuries. But look: once this plain was cultivated."

Valeria saw the ancient irrigation ditches he indicated, half filled in places, and overgrown with cactus. She frowned with perplexity as her eyes swept over the plain that stretched on all sides of the city to the forest edge, which marched in a vast, dim ring. Vision did not extend beyond that ring.

She looked uneasily at the city. No helmets or spearheads gleamed on battlements, no trumpets sounded, no challenge rang from the towers. A silence as absolute as that of the forest brooded over the walls and minarets.

The sun was high above the eastern horizon when they stood before the great gate in the northern wall, in the shadow of the lofty rampart. Rust flecked the iron bracings of the mighty bronze portal. Spiderwebs glistened thickly on hinge and sill and bolted panel.

"It hasn't been opened for years!" exclaimed Valeria.

"A dead city," grunted Conan. "That's why the ditches were broken and the plain untouched."

"But who built it? Who dwelt here? Where did they go? Why did they abandon it?"

"Who can say? Maybe an exiled clan of Stygians built it. Maybe not.

It doesn't look like Stygian architecture. Maybe the people were wiped out by enemies, or a plague exterminated them."

"In that case their treasures may still be gathering dust and cobwebs in there," suggested Valeria, the acquisitive instincts of her profession waking in her; prodded, too, by feminine curiosity. "Can we open the gate? Let's go in and explore a bit."

Conan eyed the heavy portal dubiously, but placed his massive shoulder against it and thrust with all the power of his muscular calves and thighs. With a rasping screech of rusty hinges the gate moved ponderously inward, and Conan straightened and drew his sword. Valeria stared over his shoulder, and made a sound indicative of surprise.

They were not looking into an open street or court as one would have expected. The opened gate, or door, gave directly into a long, broad hall which ran away and away until its vista grew indistinct in the distance. It was of heroic proportions, and the floor of a curious red stone, cut in square tiles, that seemed to smolder as if with the reflection of flames. The walls were of a shiny green material.

"Jade, or I'm a Shemite!" swore Conan.

"Not in such quantity!" protested Valeria.

"I've looted enough from the Khitan caravans to know what I'm talking about," he asserted. "That's jade!"

The vaulted ceiling was of lapis lazuli, adorned with clusters of great green stones that gleamed with a poisonous radiance.

"Green fire-stones," growled Conan. "That's what the people of Punt call them. They're supposed to be the petrified eyes of those prehistoric snakes the ancients called Golden Serpents. They glow like a cat's eyes in the dark. At night this hall would be lighted by them, but it would be a hellishly weird illumination. Let's look around. We might find a cache of jewels."

"Shut the door," advised Valeria. "I'd hate to have to outrun a dragon down this hall."

Conan grinned, and replied: "I don't believe the dragons ever leave the forest."

But he complied, and pointed out the broken bolt on the inner side.

"I thought I heard something snap when I shoved against it. That bolt's freshly broken. Rust has eaten nearly through it. If the people ran away, why should it have been bolted on the inside?"

"They undoubtedly left by another door," suggested Valeria.

She wondered how many centuries had passed since the light of outer day had filtered into that great hall through the open door. Sunlight was finding its way somehow into the hall, and they quickly saw the source.

High up in the vaulted ceiling skylights were set in slot-like openings—translucent sheets of some crystalline substance. In the splotches of shadow between them, the green jewels winked like the eyes of angry cats. Beneath their feet the dully lurid floor smoldered with changing hues and colors of flame. It was like treading the floors of Hell with evil stars blinking overhead.

Three balustraded galleries ran along on each side of the hall, one above the other.

"A four-storied house," grunted Conan, "and this hall extends to the roof. It's long as a street. I seem to see a door at the other end."

Valeria shrugged her white shoulders.

"Your eyes are better than mine, then, though I'm accounted sharp-eyed among the sea-rovers."

They turned into an open door at random, and traversed a series of empty chambers, floored like the hall, and with walls of the same green jade, or of marble or ivory or chalcedony, adorned with friezes of bronze, gold, or silver. In the ceilings the green fire-gems were set, and their light was as ghostly and illusive as Conan had predicted. Under the witch-fire glow the intruders moved like specters.

Some of the chambers lacked this illumination, and their doorways showed black as the mouth of the Pit. These Conan and Valeria avoided, keeping always to the lighted chambers.

Cobwebs hung in the corners, but there was no perceptible accumulation of dust on the floor, or on the tables and seats of marble, jade, or carnelian which occupied the chambers. Here and there were rugs of that silk known as Khitan which is practically indestructible. Nowhere did they find any windows, or doors opening into streets or courts. Each door merely opened into another chamber or hall.

"Why don't we come to a street?" grumbled Valeria. "This palace or whatever we're in must be as big as the king of Turan's seraglio."

"They must not have perished of plague," said Conan, meditating upon the mystery of the empty city. "Otherwise we'd find skeletons. Maybe it became haunted, and everybody got up and left. Maybe—"

"Maybe, hell!" broke in Valeria rudely. "We'll never know. Look at these friezes. They portray men. What race do they belong to?"

Conan scanned them and shook his head.

"I never saw people exactly like them. But there's the smack of the East about them—Vendhya, maybe, or Kosala."

"Were you a king in Kosala?" she asked, masking her keen curiosity with derision.

"No. But I was a war chief of the Afghulis who live in the Himelian

mountains above the borders of Vendhya. These people favor the Kosalans. But why should Kosalans be building a city this far to west?"

The figures portrayed were those of slender, olive-skinned men and
women, with finely chiseled, exotic features. They wore filmy robes and
many delicate jeweled ornaments, and were depicted mostly in attitudes
of feasting, dancing, or lovemaking.

"Easterners, all right," grunted Conan, "but from where I don't
know. They must have lived a disgustingly peaceful life, though, or
they'd have scenes of wars and fights. Let's go up those stairs."

It was an ivory spiral that wound up from the chamber in which they
were standing. They mounted three flights and came into a broad
chamber on the fourth floor, which seemed to be the highest tier in the
building. Skylights in the ceiling illuminated the room, in which light
the firegems winked pallidly. Glancing through the doors they saw,
except on one side, a series of similarly lighted chambers. This other
door opened upon a balustraded gallery that overhung a hall much
smaller than the one they had recently explored on the lower floor.

"Hell!" Valeria sat down disgustedly on a jade bench. "The people
who deserted this city must have taken all their treasures with them.
I'm tired of wandering through these bare rooms at random."

"All these upper chambers seem to be lighted," said Conan. "I wish
we could find a window that overlooked the city. Let's have a look
through that door over there."

"You have a look," advised Valeria. "I'm going to sit here and rest
my feet."

Conan disappeared through the door opposite that one opening upon
the gallery, and Valeria leaned back with her hands clasped behind her
head, and thrust her booted legs out in front of her. These silent rooms
and halls with their gleaming green clusters of ornaments and burning
crimson floors were beginning to depress her. She wished they could
find their way out of the maze into which they had wandered and
emerge into a street. She wondered idly what furtive, dark feet had
glided over those flaming floors in past centuries, how many deeds of
cruelty and mystery those winking ceiling-gems had blazed down upon.

It was a faint noise that brought her out of her reflections. She was
on her feet with her sword in her hand before she realized what had
disturbed her. Conan had not returned, and she knew it was not he that
she had heard.

The sound had come from somewhere beyond the door that opened
on to the gallery. Soundlessly in her soft leather boots she glided

through it, crept across the balcony and peered down between the heavy balustrades.

A man was stealing along the hall.

The sight of a human being in this supposedly deserted city was a startling shock. Crouching down behind the stone balusters, with every nerve tingling, Valeria glared down at the stealthy figure.

The man in no way resembled the figures depicted on the friezes. He was slightly above middle height, very dark, though not Negroid. He was naked but for a scanty silk clout that only partly covered his muscular hips, and a leather girdle, a hand's breadth broad, about his lean waist. His long black hair hung in lank strands about his shoulders, giving him a wild appearance. He was gaunt, but knots and cords of muscles stood out on his arms and legs, without that fleshy padding that presents a pleasing symmetry of contour. He was built with an economy that was almost repellent.

Yet it was not so much his physical appearance as his attitude that impressed the woman who watched him. He slunk along, stooped in a semi-crouch, his head turning from side to side. He grasped a wide-tipped blade in his right hand, and she saw it shake with the intensity of the emotion that gripped him. He was afraid, trembling in the grip of some dire terror. When he turned his head she caught the blaze of wild eyes among the lank strands of black hair.

He did not see her. On tiptoe he glided across the hall and vanished through an open door. A moment later she heard a choking cry, and then silence fell again.

Consumed with curiosity, Valeria glided along the gallery until she came to a door above the one through which the man had passed. It opened into another, smaller gallery that encircled a large chamber.

This chamber was on the third floor, and it's ceiling was not so high as that of the hall. It was lighted only by the fire-stones, and their weird green glow left the spaces under the balcony in shadows.

Valeria's eyes widened. The man she had seen was still in the chamber.

He lay face down on a dark crimson carpet in the middle of the room. His body was limp, his arms spread wide. His curved sword lay near him.

She wondered why he should lie there so motionless. Then her eyes narrowed as she stared down at the rug on which he lay. Beneath and about him the fabric showed a slightly different color, a deeper, brighter crimson.

Shivering slightly, she crouched down closer behind the balustrade, intently scanning the shadows under the overhanging gallery. They gave up no secret.

Suddenly another figure entered the grim drama. He was a man similar to the first, and he came in by a door opposite that which gave upon the hall.

His eyes glared at the sight of the man on the floor, and he spoke something in a staccato voice that sounded like "Chicmec!" The other did not move.

The man stepped quickly across the floor, bent, gripped the fallen man's shoulder and turned him over. A choking cry escaped him as the head fell back limply, disclosing a throat that had been severed from ear to ear.

The man let the corpse fall back upon the blood-stained carpet, and sprang to his feet, shaking like a windblown leaf. His face was an ashy mask of fear. But with one knee flexed for flight, he froze suddenly, became as immobile as an image, staring across the chamber with dilated eyes.

In the shadows beneath the balcony a ghostly light began to glow and grow, a light that was not part of the fire-stone gleam. Valeria felt her hair stir as she watched it; for, dimly visible in the throbbing radiance, there floated a human skull, and it was from this skull—human yet appallingly misshapen—that the spectral light seemed to emanate. It hung there like a disembodied head, conjured out of night and the shadows, growing more and more distinct; human, and yet not human as she knew humanity.

The man stood motionless, an embodiment of paralyzed horror, staring fixedly at the apparition. The thing moved out from the wall and a grotesque shadow moved with it. Slowly the shadow became visible as a man-like figure whose naked torso and limbs shone whitely, with the hue of bleached bones. The bare skull on its shoulders grinned eyelessly, in the midst of its unholy nimbus, and the man confronting it seemed unable to take his eyes from it. He stood still, his sword dangling from nerveless fingers, on his face the expression of a man bound by the spells of a mesmerist.

Valeria realized that it was not fear alone that paralyzed him. Some hellish quality of that throbbing glow had robbed him of his power to think and act. She herself, safely above the scene, felt the subtle impact of a nameless emanation that was a threat to sanity.

The horror swept toward its victim and he moved at last, but only to drop his sword and sink to his knees, covering his eyes with his hands. Dumbly he awaited the stroke of the blade that now gleamed in the apparition's hand as it reared above him like Death triumphant over mankind.

Valeria acted according to the first impulse of her wayward nature. With one tigerish movement she was over the balustrade and dropping to the floor behind the awful shape. It wheeled at the thud of her soft boots on the floor, but even as it turned, her keen blade lashed down, and a fierce exultation swept her as she felt the edge cleave solid flesh and mortal bone.

The apparition cried out gurglingly and went down, severed through shoulder, breastbone and spine, and as it fell the burning skull rolled clear, revealing a lank mop of black hair and a dark face twisted in the convulsions of death. Beneath the horrific masquerade there was a human being, a man similar to the one kneeling supinely on the floor.

The latter looked up at the sound of the blow and the cry, and now he glared in wild-eyed amazement at the white-skinned woman who stood over the corpse with a dripping sword in her hand.

He staggered up, yammering as if the sight had almost unseated his reason. She was amazed to realize that she understood him. He was gibbering in the Stygian tongue, though in a dialect unfamiliar to her.

"Who are you? Whence come you? What do you in Xuchotl?" Then rushing on, without waiting for her to reply: "But you are a friend— goddess or devil, it makes no difference! You have slain the Burning Skull! It was but a man beneath it, after all! We deemed it a demon *they* conjured up out of the catacombs! *Listen!*"

He stopped short in his ravings and stiffened, straining his ears with painful intensity. The girl heard nothing.

"We must hasten!" he whispered. "*They* are west of the Great Hall! They may be all around us here! They may be creeping upon us even now!"

He seized her wrist in a convulsive grasp she found hard to break.

"Whom do you mean by 'they'?" she demanded.

He stared at her uncomprehendingly for an instant, as if he found her ignorance hard to understand.

"They?" he stammered vaguely. "Why—why, the people of Xotalanc! The clan of the man you slew. They who dwell by the eastern gate."

"You mean to say this city is inhabited?" she exclaimed.

"Aye! Aye!" He was writhing in the impatience of apprehension. "Come away! Come quick! We must return to Tecuhltli!"

"Where is that?" she demanded.

"The quarter by the western gate!" He had her wrist again and was pulling her toward the door through which he had first come. Great beads of perspiration dripped from his dark forehead, and his eyes blazed with terror.

"Wait a minute!" she growled, flinging off his hand. "Keep your hands off me, or I'll split your skull. What's all this about? Who are you? Where would you take me?"

He took a firm grip on himself, casting glances to all sides, and began speaking so fast his words tripped over each other.

"My name is Techotl. I am of Tecuhltli. I and this man who lies with his throat cut came into the Halls of Silence to try and ambush some of the Xotalancas. But we became separated and I returned here to find him with his gullet slit. The Burning Skull did it, I know, just as he would have slain me had you not killed him. But perhaps he was not alone. Others may be stealing from Xotalanc! The gods themselves blench at the fate of those they take alive!"

At the thought he shook as with an ague and his dark skin grew ashy. Valeria frowned puzzledly at him. She sensed intelligence behind this rigmarole, but it was meaningless to her.

She turned toward the skull, which still glowed and pulsed on the floor, and was reaching a booted toe tentatively toward it, when the man who called himself Techotl sprang forward with a cry.

"Do not touch it! Do not even look at it! Madness and death lurk in it. The wizards of Xotalanc understand its secret—they found it in the catacombs, where lie the bones of terrible kings who ruled in Xuchotl in the black centuries of the past. To gaze upon it freezes the blood and withers the brain of a man who understands not its mystery. To touch it causes madness and destruction."

She scowled at him uncertainly. He was not a reassuring figure, with his lean, muscle-knotted frame, and snaky locks. In his eyes, behind the glow of terror, lurked a weird light she had never seen in the eyes of a man wholly sane. Yet he seemed sincere in his protestations.

"Come!" he begged, reaching for her hand, and then recoiling as he remembered her warning. "You are a stranger. How you came here I do not know, but if you were a goddess or a demon, come to aid Tecuhltli, you would know all the things you have asked me. You must be from beyond the great forest, whence our ancestors came. But you are our friend, or you would not have slain my enemy. Come quickly, before the Xotalancas find us and slay us!"

From his repellent, impassioned face she glanced to the sinister skull, smoldering and glowing on the floor near the dead man. It was like a skull seen in a dream, undeniably human, yet with disturbing distor-

tions and malformations of contour and outline. In life the wearer of
that skull must have presented an alien and monstrous aspect. Life? It
seemed to possess some sort of life of its own. Its jaws yawned at her
and snapped together. Its radiance grew brighter, more vivid, yet the
impression of nightmare grew too; it was a dream; all life was a dream—
it was Techotl's urgent voice which snapped Valeria back from the dim
gulfs whither she was drifting.

"Do not look at the skull! Do not look at the skull!" It was a far cry
from across unreckoned voids.

Valeria shook herself like a lion shaking his mane. Her vision cleared.
Techotl was chattering: "In life it housed the awful brain of a king of
magicians! It holds still the life and fire of magic drawn from outer
spaces!"

With a curse Valeria leaped, lithe as a panther, and the skull crashed
to flaming bits under her swinging sword. Somewhere in the room, or
in the void, or in the dim reaches of her consciousness, an inhuman
voice cried out in pain and rage.

Techotl's hand was plucking at her arm and he was gibbering: "You
have broken it! You have destroyed it! Not all the black arts of Xotalanc
can rebuild it! Come away! Come away quickly, now!"

"But I can't go," she protested. "I have a friend somewhere near
by—"

The flare of his eyes cut her short as he stared past her with an
expression grown ghastly. She wheeled just as four men rushed through
as many doors, coverging on the pair in the center of the chamber.

They were like the others she had seen, the same knotted muscles
bulging on otherwise gaunt limbs, the same lank blue-black hair, the
same mad glare in their wide eyes. They were armed and clad like
Techotl, but on the breast of each was painted a white skull.

There were no challenges or war cries. Like blood-mad tigers the men
of Xotalanc sprang at the throats of their enemies. Techotl met them
with the fury of desperation, ducked the swipe of a wide-headed blade,
and grappled with the wielder, and bore him to the floor where they
rolled and wrestled in murderous silence.

The other three swarmed on Valeria, their weird eyes red as the eyes
of mad dogs.

She killed the first who came within reach before he could strike a
blow, her long straight blade splitting his skull even as his own sword
lifted for a stroke. She side-stepped a thrust, even as she parried a slash.
Her eyes danced and her lips smiled without mercy. Again she was

Valeria of the Red Brotherhood, and the hum of her steel was like a bridal song in her ears.

Her sword darted past a blade that sought to parry, and sheathed six inches of its point in a leather-guarded midriff. The man gasped agonizedly and went to his knees, but his tall mate lunged in, in ferocious silence, raining blow on blow so furiously that Valeria had no opportunity to counter. She stepped back coolly, parrying the strokes and watching for her chance to thrust home. He could not long keep up that flailing whirlwind. His arm would tire, his wind would fail; he would weaken, falter, and then her blade would slide smoothly into his heart. A sidelong glance showed her Techotl kneeling on the breast of his antagonist and striving to break the other's hold on his wrist and to drive home a dagger.

Sweat beaded the forehead of the man facing her, and his eyes were like burning coals. Smite as he would, he could not break past nor beat down her guard. His breath came in gusty gulps, his blows began to fall erratically. She stepped back to draw him out—and felt her thighs locked in an iron grip. She had forgotten the wounded man on the floor.

Crouching on his knees, he held her with both arms locked about her legs, and his mate croaked in triumph and began working his way around to come at her from the left side. Valeria wrenched and tore savagely, but in vain. She could free herself of this clinging menace with a downward flick of her sword, but in that instant the curved blade of the tall warrior would crash through her skull. The wounded man began to worry at her bare thigh with his teeth like a wild beast.

She reached down with her left hand and gripped his long hair, forcing his head back so that his white teeth and rolling eyes gleamed up at her. The tall Xotalanc cried out fiercely and leaped in, smiting with all the fury of his arm. Awkwardly she parried the stroke, and it beat the flat of her blade down on her head so that she saw sparks flash before her eyes, and staggered. Up went the sword again, with a low, beast-like cry of triumph—and then a giant form loomed behind the Xotalanc and steel flashed like a jet of blue lightning. The cry of the warrior broke short and he went down like an ox beneath the pole-ax, his brains gushing from his skull that had been split to the throat.

"Conan!" gasped Valeria. In a gust of passion she turned on the Xotalanc whose long hair she still gripped in her left hand. "Dog of hell!" Her blade swished as it cut the air in an upswinging arc with a blur in the middle, and the headless body slumped down, spurting blood. She hurled the severed head across the room.

"What the devil's going on here?" Conan bestrode the corpse of the

man he had killed, broadsword in hand, glaring about him in amazement.

Techotl was rising from the twitching figure of the last Xotalanc,
shaking red drops from his dagger. He was bleeding from the stab deep
in the thigh. He stared at Conan with dilated eyes.

"What is all this?" Conan demanded again, not yet recovered from
the stunning surprise of finding Valeria engaged in a savage battle with
these fantastic figures in a city he had thought empty and uninhabited.
Returning from an aimless exploration of the upper chambers to find
Valeria missing from the room where he had left her, he had followed
the sounds of strife that burst on his dumfounded ears.

"Five dead dogs!" exclaimed Techotl, his flaming eyes reflecting a
ghastly exultation. "Five slain! Five crimson nails for the black pillar!
The gods of blood be thanked!"

He lifted quivering hands on high, and then, with the face of a fiend,
he spat on the corpses and stamped on their faces, dancing in his
ghoulish glee. His recent allies eyed him in amazement, and Conan
asked, in the Aquilonian tongue: "Who is this madman?"

Valeria shrugged her shoulders.

"He says his name's Techotl. From his babblings I gather that his
people live at one end of this crazy city, and these others at the other
end. Maybe we'd better go with him. He seems friendly, and it's easy
to see that the other clan isn't."

Techotl had ceased his dancing and was listening again, his head
tilted sidewise, dog-like, triumph struggling with fear in his repellent
countenance.

"Come away, now!" he whispered. "We have done enough! Five dead
dogs! My people will welcome you! They will honor you! But come! It
is far to Tecuhltli. At any moment the Xotalancs may come on us in
numbers too great even for your swords."

"Lead the way," grunted Conan.

Techotl instantly mounted a stair leading up to the gallery, beckoning them to follow him, which they did, moving rapidly to keep on his
heels. Having reached the gallery, he plunged into a door that opened
toward the west, and hurried through chamber after chamber, each
lighted by skylights or green fire-jewels.

"What sort of a place can this be?" muttered Valeria under her
breath.

"Crom knows!" answered Conan. "I've seen *his* kind before, though.
They live on the shores of Lake Zuad, near the border of Kush. They're
a sort of mongrel Stygians, mixed with another race that wandered into

Stygia from the east some centuries ago and were absorbed by them. They're called Tlazitlans. I'm willing to bet it wasn't they who built this city, though."

Techotl's fear did not seem to diminish as they drew away from the chamber where the dead men lay. He kept twisting his head on his shoulder to listen for sounds of pursuit, and stared with burning intensity into every doorway they passed.

Valeria shivered in spite of herself. She feared no man. But the weird floor beneath her feet, the uncanny jewels over her head, dividing the lurking shadows among them, the stealth and terror of their guide, impressed her with a nameless apprehension, a sensation of lurking, inhuman peril.

"They may be between us and Tecuhltli!" he whispered once. "We must beware lest they be lying in wait!"

"Why don't we get out of this infernal palace, and take to the streets?" demanded Valeria.

"There are no streets in Xuchotl," he answered. "No squares nor open courts. The whole city is built like one giant palace under one great roof. The nearest approach to a street is the Great Hall which traverses the city from the north gate to the south gate. The only doors opening into the outer world are the city gates, through which no living man has passed for fifty years."

"How long have you dwelt here?" asked Conan.

"I was born in the castle of Tecuhltli thirty-five years ago. I have never set foot outside the city. For the love of the gods, let us go silently! These halls may be full of lurking devils. Olmec shall tell you all when we reach Tecuhltli."

So in silence they glided on with the green fire-stones blinking overhead and the flaming floors smoldering under their feet, and it seemed to Valeria as if they fled through Hell, guided by a dark-faced, lank-haired goblin.

Yet it was Conan who halted them as they were crossing an unusually wide chamber. His wilderness-bred ears were keener even than the ears of Techotl, whetted though these were by a lifetime of warfare in those silent corridors.

"You think some of your enemies may be ahead of us, lying in ambush?"

"They prowl through these rooms at all hours," answered Techotl, "as do we. The halls and chambers between Tecuhltli and Xotalanc are a disputed region, owned by no man. We call it the Halls of Silence. Why do you ask?"

"Because men are in the chambers ahead of us," answered Conan. "I heard steel clink against stone."

Again a shaking seized Techotl, and he clenched his teeth to keep them from chattering.

"Perhaps they are your friends," suggested Valeria.

"We dare not chance it," he panted, and moved with frenzied activity. He turned aside and glided through a doorway on the left which led into a chamber from which an ivory staircase wound down into darkness.

"This leads to an unlighted corridor below us!" he hissed, great beads of perspiration standing out on his brow. "They may be lurking there, too. It may all be a trick to draw us into it. But we must take the chance that they have laid their ambush in the rooms above. Come swiftly, now!"

Softly as phantoms they descended the stair and came to the mouth of a corridor black as night. They crouched there for a moment, listening, and then melted into it. As they moved along, Valeria's flesh crawled between her shoulders in momentary expectation of a sword-thrust in the dark. But for Conan's iron fingers gripping her arm she had no physical cognizance of her companions. Neither made as much noise as a cat would have made. The darkness was absolute. One hand, outstretched, touched a wall, and occasionally she felt a door under her fingers. The hallway seemed interminable.

Suddenly they were galvanized by a sound behind them. Valeria's flesh crawled anew, for she recognized it as the soft opening of a door. Men had come into the corridor behind them. Even with the thought she stumbled over something that felt like a human skull. It rolled across the floor with an appalling clatter.

"Run!" yelped Techotl, a note of hysteria in his voice, and was away down the corridor like a flying ghost.

Again Valeria felt Conan's hand bearing her up and sweeping her along as they raced after their guide. Conan could see in the dark no better than she, but he possessed a sort of instinct that made his course unerring. Without his support and guidance she would have fallen or stumbled against the wall. Down the corridor they sped, while the swift patter of flying feet drew closer and closer, and then suddenly Techotl panted: "Here is the stair! After me, quick! Oh, quick!"

His hand came out of the dark and caught Valeria's wrist as she stumbled blindly on the steps. She felt herself half dragged, half lifted up the winding stair, while Conan released her and turned on the steps, his ears and instincts telling him their foes were hard at their backs. *And the sounds were not all those of human feet.*

Something came writhing up the steps, something that slithered and rustled and brought a chill in the air with it. Conan lashed down with his great sword and felt the blade shear through something that might have been flesh and bone, and cut deep into the stair beneath. Something touched his foot that chilled like the touch of frost, and then the darkness beneath him was disturbed by a frightful thrashing and lashing, and a man cried out in agony.

The next moment Conan was racing up the winding staircase, and through a door that stood open at the head.

Valeria and Techotl were already through, and Techotl slammed the door and shot a bolt across it—the first Conan had seen since they had left the outer gate.

Then he turned and ran across the well-lighted chamber into which they had come, and as they passed through the farther door, Conan glanced back and saw the door groaning and straining under heavy pressure violently applied from the other side.

Though Techotl did not abate either his speed or his caution, he seemed more confident now. He had the air of a man who had come into familiar territory, within call of friends.

But Conan renewed his terror by asking: "What was that thing that I fought on the stairs?"

"The men of Xotalanc," answered Techotl, without looking back. "I told you the halls were full of them."

"This wasn't a man," grunted Conan. "It was something that crawled, and it was as cold as ice to the touch. I think I cut it asunder. It fell back on the men who were following us, and must have killed one of them in its death throes."

Techotl's head jerked back, his face ashy again. Convulsively he quickened his pace.

"It was the Crawler! A monster *they* have brought out of the catacombs to aid them! What it is, we do not know, but we have found our people hideously slain by it. In Set's name, hasten! If they put it on our trail, it will follow us to the very doors of Tecuhltli!"

"I doubt it," grunted Conan. "That was a shrewd cut I dealt it on the stair."

"Hasten! Hasten!" groaned Techotl.

They ran through a series of green-lit chambers, traversed a broad hall, and halted before a giant bronze door.

Techotl said: "This is Tecuhltli!"

3

THE PEOPLE OF THE FEUD

TECHOTL SMOTE on the bronze door with his clenched hand, and then turned sidewise, so that he could watch back along the hall.

"Men have been smitten down before this door, when they thought they were safe," he said.

"Why don't they open the door?" asked Conan.

"They are looking at us through the Eye," answered Techotl. "They are puzzled at the sight of you." He lifted his voice and called: "Open the door, Excelan! It is I, Techotl, with friends from the great world beyond the forest!—They will open," he assured his allies.

"They'd better do it in a hurry, then," said Conan grimly. "I hear something crawling along the floor beyond the hall."

Techotl went ashy again and attacked the door with his fists, screaming: "Open, you fools, open! The Crawler is at our heels!"

Even as he beat and shouted, the great bronze door swung noiselessly back, revealing a heavy chain across the entrance, over which spearheads bristled and fierce countenances regarded them intently for an instant. Then the chain was dropped and Techotl grasped the arms of his friends in a nervous frenzy and fairly dragged them over the threshold. A glance over his shoulder just as the door was closing showed Conan the long dim vista of the hall, and dimly framed at the other end an ophidian shape that writhed slowly and painfully into view, flowing in a dull-hued length from a chamber door, its hideous blood-stained head wagging drunkenly. Then the closing door shut off the view.

Inside the square chamber into which they had come heavy bolts were drawn across the door, and the chain locked into place. The door was made to stand the battering of a siege. Four men stood on guard, of the same lank-haired, dark-skinned breed as Techotl, with spears in their hands and swords at their hips. In the wall near the door there was a complicated contrivance of mirrors which Conan guessed was the Eye Techotl had mentioned, so arranged that a narrow, crystal-paned slot in the wall could be looked through from within without being discernible from without. The four guardsmen stared at the strangers with wonder, but asked no question, nor did Techotl vouchsafe any information. He moved with easy confidence now, as if he had shed his cloak of indecision and fear the instant he crossed the threshold.

"Come!" he urged his new-found friends, but Conan glanced toward the door.

"What about those fellows who were following us? Won't they try to storm that door?"

Techotl shook his head.

"They know they cannot break down the Door of the Eagle. They will flee back to Xotalanc, with their crawling fiend. Come! I will take you to the rulers of Tecuhltli."

One of the four guards opened the door opposite the one by which they had entered, and they passed through into a hallway which, like most of the rooms on that level, was lighted by both the slot-like skylights and the clusters of winking fire-gems. But unlike the other rooms they had traversed, this hall showed evidences of occupation. Velvet tapestries adorned the glossy jade walls, rich rugs were on the crimson floors, and the ivory seats, benches and divans were littered with satin cushions.

The hall ended in an ornate door, before which stood no guard. Without ceremony Techotl thrust the door open and ushered his friends into a broad chamber, where some thirty dark-skinned men and women lounging on satin-covered couches sprang up with exclamations of amazement.

The men, all except one, were of the same type as Techotl, and the women were equally dark and strange-eyed, though not unbeautiful in a weird dark way. They wore sandals, golden breastplates, and scanty silk skirts supported by gem-crusted girdles, and their black manes, cut square at their naked shoulders, were bound with silver circlets.

On a wide ivory seat on a jade dais sat a man and a woman who differed subtly from the others. He was a giant, with an enormous sweep of breast and the shoulders of a bull. Unlike the others, he was bearded, with a thick, blue-black beard which fell almost to his broad girdle. He wore a robe of purple silk which reflected changing sheens of color with his every movement, and one wide sleeve, drawn back to his elbow, revealed a forearm massive with corded muscles. The band which confined his blue-black locks was set with glittering jewels.

The woman beside him sprang to her feet with a startled exclamation as the strangers entered, and her eyes, passing over Conan, fixed themselves with burning intensity on Valeria. She was tall and lithe, by far the most beautiful woman in the room. She was clad more scantily even than the others; for instead of a skirt she wore merely a broad strip of gilt-worked purple cloth fastened to the middle of her girdle which fell below her knees. Another strip at the back of her girdle completed that part of her costume, which she wore with a cynical indifference. Her breast-plates and the circlet about her temples were adorned with gems. In her eyes alone of all the dark-skinned people there lurked no brooding gleam of madness. She spoke no word after her first exclamation; she stood tensely, her hands clenched, staring at Valeria.

The man on the ivory seat had not risen.

"Prince Olmec," spoke Techotl, bowing low, with arms outspread and the palms of his hands turned upward, "I bring allies from the world beyond the forest. In the Chamber of Tezcoti the Burning Skull slew Chicmec, my companion—"

"The Burning Skull!" It was a shuddering whisper of fear from the people of Tecuhltli.

"Aye! Then came I, and found Chicmec lying with his throat cut. Before I could flee, the Burning Skull came upon me, and when I looked upon it my blood became as ice and the marrow of my bones melted. I could neither fight nor run. I could only await the stroke. Then came this white-skinned woman and struck him down with her sword; and lo, it was only a dog of Xotalanc with white paint upon his skin and the living skull of an ancient wizard upon his head! Now that skull lies in many pieces, and the dog who wore it is a dead man!"

An indescribably fierce exultation edged the last sentence, and was echoed in the low, savage exclamations from the crowding listeners.

"But wait!" exclaimed Techotl. "There is more! While I talked with the woman, four Xotalancs came upon us! One I slew—there is the stab in my thigh to prove how desperate was the fight. Two the woman killed. But we were hard pressed when this man came into the fray and split the skull of the fourth! Aye! Five crimson nails there are to be driven into the pillar of vengeance!"

He pointed at a black column of ebony which stood behind the dais. Hundreds of red dots scarred its polished surface—the bright scarlet heads of heavy copper nails driven into the black wood.

"Five red nails for five Xotalanca lives!" exulted Techotl, and the horrible exultation in the faces of the listeners made them inhuman.

"Who are these people?" asked Olmec, and his voice was like the low, deep rumble of a distant bull. None of the people of Xuchotl spoke loudly. It was as if they had absorbed into their souls the silence of the empty halls and deserted chambers.

"I am Conan, a Cimmerian," answered the barbarian briefly. "This woman is Valeria of the Red Brotherhood, an Aquilonian pirate. We are deserters from an army on the Darfar border, far to the north, and are trying to reach the coast."

The woman on the dais spoke loudly, her words tripping in her haste. "You can never reach the coast! There is no escape from Xuchotl! You will spend the rest of your lives in this city!"

"What do you mean?" growled Conan, clapping his hand to his hilt and stepping about so as to face both the dais and the rest of the room. "Are you telling us we're prisoners?"

"She did not mean that," interposed Olmec. "We are your friends. We would not restrain you against your will. But I fear other circumstances will make it impossible for you to leave Xuchotl."

His eyes flickered to Valeria, and he lowered them quickly.

"This woman is Tascela," he said. "She is a princess of Tecuhltli. But let food and drink be brought our guests. Doubtless they are hungry, and weary from their long travels."

He indicated an ivory table, and after an exchange of glances, the adventurers seated themselves. The Cimmerian was suspicious. His fierce blue eyes roved about the chamber, and he kept his sword close to his hand. But an invitation to eat and drink never found him backward. His eyes kept wandering to Tascela, but the princess had eyes only for his white-skinned companion.

Techotl, who had bound a strip of silk about his wounded thigh, placed himself at the table to attend to the wants of his friends, seeming to consider it a privilege and honor to see after their needs. He inspected the food and drink the others brought in gold vessels and dishes, and tasted each before he placed it before his guests. While they ate, Olmec sat in silence on his ivory seat, watching them from under his broad black brows. Tascela sat beside him, chin cupped in her hands and her elbows resting on her knees. Her dark, enigmatic eyes, burning with a mysterious light, never left Valeria's supple figure. Behind her seat a sullen handsome girl waved an ostrich-plume fan with a slow rhythm.

The food was fruit of an exotic kind unfamiliar to the wanderers, but very palatable, and the drink was a light crimson wine that carried a heady tang.

"You have come from afar," said Olmec at last. "I have read the books of our fathers. Aquilonia lies beyond the lands of the Stygians and the Shemites, beyond Argos and Zingara; and Cimmeria lies beyond Aquilonia."

"We have each a roving foot," answered Conan carelessly.

"How you won through the forest is a wonder to me," quoth Olmec. "In bygone days a thousand fighting men scarcely were able to carve a road through its perils."

"We encountered a bench-legged monstrosity about the size of a mastodon," said Conan casually, holding out his wine goblet which Techotl filled with evident pleasure. "But when we'd killed it we had no further trouble."

The wine vessel slipped from Techotl's hand to crash on the floor. His dusky skin went ashy. Olmec started to his feet, an image of stunned amazement, and a low gasp of awe or terror breathed up from the others. Some slipped to their knees as if their legs would not support them. Only Tascela seemed not to have heard. Conan glared about him bewilderedly.

"What's the matter? What are you gaping about?"

"You—you slew the dragon-god?"

"God? I killed a dragon. Why not? It was trying to gobble us up."

"But dragons are immortal!" exclaimed Olmec. "They slay each other, but no man ever killed a dragon! The thousand fighting men of our ancestors who fought their way to Xuchotl could not prevail against them! Their swords broke like twigs against their scales!"

"If your ancestors had thought to dip their spears in the poisonous juice of Derketa's Apples," quoth Conan, with his mouth full, "and jab them in the eyes or mouth or somewhere like that, they'd have seen that dragons are no more immortal than any other chunk of beef. The carcass lies at the edge of the trees, just within the forest. If you don't believe me, go and look for yourself."

Olmec shook his head, not in disbelief but in wonder.

"It was because of the dragons that our ancestors took refuge in Xuchotl," said he. "They dared not pass through the plain and plunge into the forest beyond. Scores of them were seized and devoured by the monsters before they could reach the city."

"Then your ancestors didn't build Xuchotl?" asked Valeria.

"It was ancient when they first came into the land. How long it had stood here, not even its degenerate inhabitants knew."

"Your people came from Lake Zuad?" questioned Conan.

"Aye. More than half a century ago a tribe of the Tlazitlans rebelled against the Stygian king, and, being defeated in battle, fled southward. For many weeks they wandered over grasslands, desert and hills, and at last they came into the great forest, a thousand fighting men with their women and children.

"It was in the forest that the dragons fell upon them, and tore many to pieces; so the people fled in a frenzy of fear before them, and at last came into the plain and saw the city of Xuchotl in the midst of it.

"They camped before the city, not daring to leave the plain, for the night was made hideous with the noise of the battling monsters throughout the forest. They made war incessantly upon one another. Yet they came not into the plain.

"The people of the city shut their gates and shot arrows at our people from the walls. The Tlazitlans were imprisoned on the plain, as if the ring of the forest had been a great wall; for to venture into the woods would have been madness.

"That night there came secretly to their camp a slave from the city, one of their own blood, who with a band of exploring soldiers had wandered into the forest long before, when he was a young man. The dragons had devoured all his companions, but he had been taken into the city to dwell in servitude. His name was Tolkemec." A flame lighted the dark eyes at mention of the name, and some of the people muttered obscenely and spat. "He promised to open the gates to the warriors. He asked only that all captives taken be delivered into his hands.

"At dawn he opened the gates. The warriors swarmed in and the halls of Xuchotl ran red. Only a few hundred folk dwelt there, decaying remnants of a once great race. Tolkemec said they came from the east, long ago, from Old Kosala, when the ancestors of those who now dwell in Kosala came up from the south and drove forth the original inhabitants of the land. They wandered far westward and finally found this forest-girdled plain, inhabited then by a tribe of black people.

"These they enslaved and set to building a city. From the hills to the east they brought jade and marble and lapis lazuli, and gold, silver, and copper. Herds of elephants provided them with ivory. When their city was completed, they slew all the black slaves. And their magicians made a terrible magic to guard the city; for by their necromantic arts they re-created the dragons which had once dwelt in this lost land, and whose monstrous bones they found in the forest. Those bones they clothed in flesh and life, and the living beasts walked the earth as they walked it when time was young. But the wizards wove a spell that kept them in the forest and they came not into the plain.

"So for many centuries the people of Xuchotl dwelt in their city, cultivating the fertile plain, until their wise men learned how to grow fruit within the city—fruit which is not planted in soil, but obtains its nourishment out of the air—and then they let the irrigation ditches run dry, and dwelt more and more in luxurious sloth, until decay seized them. They were a dying race when our ancestors broke through the forest and came into the plain. Their wizards had died, and the people had forgot their ancient necromancy. They could fight neither by sorcery nor the sword.

"Well, our fathers slew the people of Xuchotl, all except a hundred which were given living into the hands of Tolkemec, who had been their slave; and for many days and nights the halls re-echoed to their screams under the agony of his tortures.

"So the Tlazitlans dwelt here, for a while in peace, ruled by the brothers Tecuhltli and Xotalanc, and by Tolkemec. Tolkemec took a girl of the tribe to wife, and because he had opened the gates, and because he knew many of the arts of the Xuchotlans, he shared the rule of the tribe with the brothers who had led the rebellion and the flight.

"For a few years, then, they dwelt at peace within the city, doing little but eating, drinking, and making love, and raising children. There was no necessity to till the plain, for Tolkemec taught them how to cultivate the air-devouring fruits. Besides, the slaying of the Xuchotlans broke the spell that held the dragons in the forest, and they came nightly and bellowed about the gates of the city. The plain ran red with the blood of their eternal warfare, and it was then that—" He bit his tongue in the midst of the sentence, then presently continued, but Valeria and Conan felt that he had checked an admission he had considered unwise.

"Five years they dwelt in peace. Then"—Olmec's eyes rested briefly on the silent woman at his side—"Xotalanc took a woman to wife, a woman whom both Tecuhltli and old Tolkemec desired. In his madness, Tecuhltli stole her from her husband. Aye, she went willingly enough. Tolkemec, to spite Xotalanc, aided Tecuhltli. Xotalanc demanded that she be given back to him, and the council of the tribe decided that the matter should be left to the woman. She chose to remain with Tecuhltli. In wrath Xotalanc sought to take her back by force, and the retainers of the brothers came to blows in the Great Hall.

"There was much bitterness. Blood was shed on both sides. The quarrel became a feud, the feud an open war. From the welter three factions emerged—Tecuhltli, Xotalanc, and Tolkemec. Already, in the days of peace, they had divided the city between them. Tecuhltli dwelt in the western quarter of the city, Xotalanc in the eastern, and Tolkemec with his family by the southern gate.

"Anger and resentment and jealousy blossomed into bloodshed and rape and murder. Once the sword was drawn there was no turning back; for blood called for blood, and vengeance followed swift on the heels of atrocity. Tecuhltli fought with Xotalanc, and Tolkemec aided first one and then the other, betraying each faction as it fitted his purposes. Tecuhltli and his people withdrew into the quarter of the western gate, where we now sit. Xuchotl is built in the shape of an oval. Tecuhltli, which took its name from its prince, occupies the western end of the oval. The people blocked up all doors connecting the quarter with the rest of the city, except one on each floor, which could be defended easily. They went into the pits below the city and built a wall cutting off the western end of the catacombs, where lie the bodies of the ancient Xuchotlans, and of those Tlazitlans slain in the feud. They dwelt as in a besieged castle, making sorties and forays on their enemies.

"The people of Xotalanc likewise fortified the eastern quarter of the city, and Tolkemec did likewise with the quarter by the southern gate. The central part of the city was left bare and uninhabited. Those empty halls and chambers became a battleground, and a region of brooding terror.

"Tolkemec warred on both clans. He was a fiend in the form of a human, worse than Xotalanc. He knew many secrets of the city he never told the others. From the crypts of the catacombs he plundered the dead of their grisly secrets—secrets of ancient kings and wizards, long forgotten by the degenerate Xuchotlans our ancestors slew. But all his magic did not aid him the night we of Tecuhltli stormed his castle and butchered all his people. Tolkemec we tortured for many days."

His voice sank to a caressing slur, and a faraway look grew in his eyes, as if he looked back over the years to a scene which caused him intense pleasure.

"Aye, we kept the life in him until he screamed for death as for a bride. At last we took him living from the torture chamber and cast him into a dungeon for the rats to gnaw as he died. From that dungeon, somehow, he managed to escape, and dragged himself into the catacombs. There without doubt he died, for the only way out of the catacombs beneath Tecuhltli is through Tecuhltli, and he never emerged by that way. His bones were never found, and the superstitious among our people swear that his ghost haunts the crypts to this day, wailing among the bones of the dead. Twelve years ago we butchered the people of Tolkemec, but the feud raged on between Tecuhltli and Xotalanc, as it will rage until the last man, the last woman is dead.

"It was fifty years ago that Tecuhltli stole the wife of Xotalanc. Half a century the feud has endured. I was born in it. All in this chamber, except Tascela, were born in it. We expect to die in it.

"We are a dying race, even as were those Xuchotlans our ancestors slew. When the feud began there were hundreds in each faction. Now we of Tecuhltli number only these you see before you, and the men who guard the four doors: forty in all. How many Xotalancas there are we do not know, but I doubt if they are much more numerous than we. For fifteen years no children have been born to us, and we have seen none among the Xotalancas.

"We are dying, but before we die we will slay as many of the men of Xotalanc as the gods permit."

And with his weird eyes blazing, Olmec spoke long of that grisly feud, fought out in silent chambers and dim halls under the blaze of the green fire-jewels, on floors smoldering with the flames of hell and splashed with deeper crimson from severed veins. In that long butchery a whole generation had perished. Xotalanc was dead, long ago, slain in a grim battle on an ivory stair. Tecuhltli was dead, flayed alive by the maddened Xotalancas who had captured him.

Without emotion Olmec told of hideous battles fought in black corridors, of ambushes on twisting stairs, and red butcheries. With a redder, more abysmal gleam in his deep dark eyes he told of men and women flayed alive, mutilated and dismembered, of captives howling under tortures so ghastly that even the barbarous Cimmerian grunted. No wonder Techotl had trembled with the terror of capture! Yet he had gone forth to slay if he could, driven by hate that was stronger than his fear. Olmec spoke further, of dark and mysterious matters, of black magic and wizardry conjured out of the black night of the catacombs, of weird creatures invoked out of darkness for horrible allies. In these things the Xotalancas had the advantage, for it was in the eastern catacombs where lay the bones of the greatest wizards of the ancient Xuchotlans, with their immemorial secrets.

Valeria listened with morbid fascination. The feud had become a terrible elemental power driving the people of Xuchotl inexorably on to doom and extinction. It filled their whole lives. They were born in it, and they expected to die in it. They never left their barricaded castle except to steal forth into the Halls of Silence that lay between the opposing fortresses, to slay and be slain. Sometimes the raiders returned with frantic captives, or with grim tokens of victory in fight. Sometimes they did not return at all, or returned only as severed limbs cast down before the bolted bronze doors. It was a ghastly, unreal nightmare existence these people lived, shut off from the rest of the world, caught together like rabid rats in the same trap, butchering one another through the years, crouching and creeping through the sunless corridors to maim and torture and murder.

While Olmec talked, Valeria felt the blazing eyes of Tascela fixed upon her. The princess seemed not to hear what Olmec was saying. Her expression, as he narrated victories or defeats, did not mirror the wild rage or fiendish exultation that alternated on the faces of the other Tecuhltli. The feud that was an obsession to her clansmen seemed meaningless to her. Valeria found her indifferent callousness more repugnant than Olmec's naked ferocity.

"And we can never leave the city," said Olmec. "For fifty years no one has left it except those—" Again he checked himself.

"Even without the peril of the dragons," he continued, "we who were born and raised in the city would not dare leave it. We have never set foot outside the walls. We are not accustomed to the open sky and the naked sun. No; we were born in Xuchotl, and in Xuchotl we shall die."

"Well," said Conan, "with your leave we'll take our chances with the dragons. This feud is none of our business. If you'll show us to the west gate we'll be on our way."

Tascela's hands clenched, and she started to speak, but Olmec interrupted her: "It is nearly nightfall. If you wander forth into the plain by night, you will certainly fall prey to the dragons."

"We crossed it last night, and slept in the open without seeing any," returned Conan.

Tascela smiled mirthlessly. "You dare not leave Xuchotl!"

Conan glared at her with instinctive antagonism; she was not looking at him, but at the woman opposite him.

"I think they dare," stated Olmec. "But look you, Conan and Valeria, the gods must have sent you to us, to cast victory into the laps of the Tecuhltli! You are professional fighters—why not fight for us? We have wealth in abundance—precious jewels are as common in Xuchotl as cobblestones are in the cities of the world. Some the Xuchotlans brought with them from Kosala. Some, like the firestones, they found in the hills to the east. Aid us to wipe out the Xotalancas, and we will give you all the jewels you can carry."

"And will you help us destroy the dragons?" asked Valeria. "With bows and poisoned arrows thirty men could slay all the dragons in the forest."

"Aye!" replied Olmec promptly. "We have forgotten the use of the bow, in years of hand-to-hand fighting, but we can learn again."

"What do you say?" Valeria inquired of Conan.

"We're both penniless vagabonds," he grinned hardily. "I'd as soon kill Xotalancas as anybody."

"Then you agree?" exclaimed Olmec, while Techotl fairly hugged himself with delight.

"Aye. And now suppose you show us chambers where we can sleep, so we can be fresh tomorrow for the beginning of the slaying."

Olmec nodded, and waved a hand, and Techotl and a woman led the adventurers into a corridor which led through a door off to the left of the jade dais. A glance back showed Valeria Olmec sitting on his throne, chin on knotted fist, staring after them. His eyes burned with a weird flame. Tascela leaned back in her seat, whispering to the sullen-faced maid, Yasala, who leaned over her shoulder, her ear to the princess's moving lips.

The hallway was not so broad as most they had traversed, but it was long. Presently the woman halted, opened a door, and drew aside for Valeria to enter.

"Wait a minute," growled Conan. "Where do I sleep?"

Techotl pointed to a chamber across the hallway, but one door farther down. Conan hesitated, and seemed inclined to raise an objection, but Valeria smiled spitefully at him and shut the door in his face. He muttered something uncomplimentary about women in general, and strode off down the corridor after Techotl.

In the ornate chamber where he was to sleep, he glanced up at the slot-like skylights. Some were wide enough to admit the body of a slender man, supposing the glass were broken.

"Why don't the Xotalancas come over the roofs and shatter those skylights?" he asked.

"They cannot be broken," answered Techotl. "Besides, the roofs would be hard to clamber over. They are mostly spires and domes and steep ridges."

He volunteered more information about the "castle" of Tecuhltli. Like the rest of the city it contained four stories, or tiers of chambers, with towers jutting up from the roof. Each tier was named; indeed, the people of Xuchotl had a name for each chamber, hall, and stair in the city, as people of more normal cities designate streets and quarters. In Tecuhltli the floors were named The Eagle's Tier, The Ape's Tier, The Tiger's Tier and The Serpent's Tier, in the order as enumerated, The Eagle's Tier being the highest, or fourth, floor.

"Who is Tascela?" asked Conan. "Olmec's wife?"

Techotl shuddered and glanced furtively about him before answering.

"No. She is—Tascela! She was the wife of Xotalanc—the woman Tecuhltli stole, to start the feud."

"What are you talking about?" demanded Conan. "That woman is beautiful and young. Are you trying to tell me that she was a wife fifty years ago?"

"Aye! I swear it! She was a full-grown woman when the Tlazitlans journeyed from Lake Zuad. It was because the king of Stygia desired her for a concubine that Xotalanc and his brother rebelled and fled into the wilderness. She is a witch, who possesses the secret of perpetual youth."

"What's that?" asked Conan.

Techotl shuddered again.

"Ask me not! I dare not speak. It is too grisly, even for Xuchotl!" And touching his finger to his lips, he glided from the chamber.

4

SCENT OF BLACK LOTUS

VALERIA UNBUCKLED her sword belt and laid it with the sheathed weapon on the couch where she meant to sleep. She noted that the doors were supplied with bolts, and asked where they led.

"Those lead into adjoining chambers," answered the woman, indicating the doors on right and left. "That one"—pointing to a copper-bound door opposite that which opened into the corridor—"leads to a corridor which runs to a stair that descends into the catacombs. Do not fear; naught can harm you here."

"Who spoke of fear?" snapped Valeria. "I just like to know what sort of harbor I'm dropping anchor in. No, I don't want you to sleep at the foot of my couch. I'm not accustomed to being waited on—not by women, anyway. You have my leave to go."

Alone in the room, the pirate shot the bolts on all the doors, kicked off her boots and stretched luxuriously out on the couch. She imagined Conan similarly situated across the corridor, but her feminine vanity prompted her to visualize him as scowling and muttering with chagrin as he cast himself on his solitary couch, and she grinned with gleeful malice as she prepared herself for slumber.

Outside, night had fallen. In the halls of Xuchotl the green fire-jewels blazed like the eyes of prehistoric cats. Somewhere among the dark towers, a night wind moaned like a restless spirit. Through the dim passages, stealthy figures began stealing, like disembodied shadows.

Valeria awoke suddenly on her couch. In the dusky emerald glow of the fire-gems she saw a shadowy figure bending over her. For a bemused instant the apparition seemed part of the dream she had been dreaming. She had seemed to lie on the couch in the chamber as she was actually lying, while over her pulsed and throbbed a gigantic black blossom so enormous that it hid the ceiling. Its exotic perfume pervaded her being, inducing a delicious, sensuous languor that was something more and less than sleep. She was sinking into scented billows of insensible bliss, when something touched her face. So supersensitive were her drugged senses, that the light touch was like a dislocating impact, jolting her rudely into full wakefulness. Then it was that she saw, not a gargantuan blossom, but a dark-skinned woman standing above her.

With the realization came anger and instant action. The woman turned lithely, but before she could run Valeria was on her feet and had caught her arm. She fought like a wildcat for an instant, and then subsided as she felt herself crushed by the superior strength of her captor. The pirate wrenched the woman around to face her, caught her chin with her free hand and forced her captive to meet her gaze. It was the sullen Yasala, Tascela's maid.

"What the devil were you doing bending over me? What's that in your hand?"

The woman made no reply, but sought to cast away the object. Valeria twisted her arm around in front of her, and the thing fell to the floor—a great black exotic blossom on a jade-green stem, large as a woman's head, to be sure, but tiny beside the exaggerated vision she had seen.

"The black lotus!" said Valeria between her teeth. "The blossom whose scent brings deep sleep. You were trying to drug me! If you hadn't accidentally touched my face with the petals, you'd have—why did you do it? What's your game?"

Yasala maintained a sulky silence, and with an oath Valeria whirled her around, forced her to her knees and twisted her arm up behind her back.

"Tell me, or I'll tear your arm out of its socket!"

Yasala squirmed in anguish as her arm was forced excruciatingly up between her shoulder blades, but a violent shaking of her head was the only answer she made.

"Slut!" Valeria cast her from her to sprawl on the floor. The pirate glared at the prostrate figure with blazing eyes. Fear and the memory of Tascela's burning eyes stirred in her, rousing all her tigerish instincts of self-preservation. These people were decadent; any sort of perversity might be expected to be encountered among them. But Valeria sensed here something that moved behind the scenes, some secret terror fouler than common degeneracy. Fear and revulsion of this weird city swept her. These people were neither sane nor normal; she began to doubt if they were even human. Madness smoldered in the eyes of them all—all except the cruel, cryptic eyes of Tascela, which held secrets and mysteries more abysmal than madness.

She lifted her head and listened intently. The halls of Xuchotl were as silent as if it were in reality a dead city. The green jewels bathed the chamber in a nightmare glow, in which the eyes of the woman on the floor glittered eerily up at her. A thrill of panic throbbed through Valeria, driving the last vestige of mercy from her fierce soul.

"Why did you try to drug me?" she muttered, grasping the woman's black hair, and forcing her head back to glare into her sullen, long-lashed eyes. "Did Tascela send you?"

No answer. Valeria cursed venomously and slapped the woman first on one cheek and then the other. The blows resounded through the room, but Yasala made no outcry.

"Why don't you scream?" demanded Valeria savagely. "Do you fear someone will hear you? Whom do you fear? Tascela? Olmec? Conan?"

Yasala made no reply. She crouched, watching her captor with eyes baleful as those of a basilisk. Stubborn silence always fans anger. Valeria turned and tore a handful of cords from a near-by hanging.

"You sulky slut!" she said between her teeth. "I'm going to strip you stark naked and tie you across that couch and whip you until you tell me what you were doing here, and who sent you!"

Yasala made no verbal protest, nor did she offer any resistance, as Valeria carried out the first part of her threat with a fury that her captive's obstinacy only sharpened. Then for a space there was no sound in the chamber except the whistle and crackle of hard-woven silken cords on naked flesh. Yasala could not move her fast-bound hands or feet. Her body writhed and quivered under the chastisement, her head swayed from side to side in rhythm with the blows. Her teeth were sunk into her lower lip and a trickle of blood began as the punishment continued. But she did not cry out.

The pliant cords made no great sound as they encountered the quivering body of the captive; only a sharp crackling snap, but each cord left a red streak across Yasala's dark flesh. Valeria inflicted the punishment with all the strength of her war-hardened arm, with all the mercilessness acquired during a life where pain and torment were daily happenings, and with all the cynical ingenuity which only a woman displays toward a woman. Yasala suffered more, physically and mentally, than she would have suffered under a lash wielded by a man, however strong.

It was the application of this feminine cyncism which at last tamed Yasala.

A low whimper escaped from her lips, and Valeria paused, arm lifted, and raked back a damp yellow lock. "Well, are you going to talk?" she demanded. "I can keep this up all night, if necessary!"

"Mercy!" whispered the woman. "I will tell."

Valeria cut the cords from her wrists and ankles, and pulled her to her feet. Yasala sank down on the couch, half reclining on one bare hip, supporting herself on her arm, and writhing at the contact of her smarting flesh with the couch. She was trembling in every limb.

"Wine!" she begged, dry-lipped, indicating with a quivering hand a gold vessel on an ivory table. "Let me drink. I am weak with pain. Then I will tell you all."

Valeria picked up the vessel, and Yasala rose unsteadily to receive it. She took it, raised it toward her lips—then dashed the contents full into the Aquilonian's face. Valeria reeled backward, shaking and clawing the stinging liquid out of her eyes. Through a smarting mist she saw Yaasala dart across the room, fling back a bolt, throw open the copper-bound door and run downn the hall. The pirate was after her instantly, sword out and murder in her heart.

But Yasala had the start, and she ran with the nervous agility of a woman who has just been whipped to the point of hysterical frenzy. She rounded a corner in the corridor, yards ahead of Valeria, and when the pirate turned it, she saw only an empty hall, and at the other end a door that gaped blackly. A damp moldly scent reeked up from it, and Valeria shivered. That must be the door that led to the catacombs. Yasala had taken refuge among the dead.

Valeria advanced to the door and looked down a flight of stone steps that vanished quickly into utter blackness. Evidently it was a shaft that led straight to the pits below the city, without opening upon any of the lower floors. She shivered slightly at the thought of the thousands of corpses lying in their stone crypts down there, wrapped in their moldering cloths. She had no intention of groping her way down those stone steps. Yasala doubtless knew every turn and twist of the subterranean tunnels.

She was turning back, baffled and furious, when a sobbing cry welled up from the blackness. It seemed to come from a great depth, but human words were faintly distinguishable, and the voice was that of a woman. "Oh, help! Help, in Set's name! Ahhh!" It trailed away, and Valeria thought she caught the echo of a ghostly tittering.

Valeria felt her skin crawl. What had happened to Yasala down there in the thick blackness? There was no doubt that it had been she who had cried out. But what peril could have befallen her? Was a Xotalanca lurking down there? Olmec had assured them that the catacombs below Tecuhltli were walled off from the rest, too securely for their enemies to break through. Besides, that tittering had not sounded like a human being at all.

Valeria hurried back down the corridor, not stopping to close the door that opened on the stair. Regaining her chamber, she closed the door and shot the bolt behind her. She pulled on her boots and buckled her sword-belt about her. She was determined to make her way to Conan's room and urge him, if he still lived, to join her in an attempt to fight their way out of that city of devils.

But even as she reached the door that opened into the corridor, a long-drawn scream of agony rang through the halls, followed by the stamp of running feet and the loud clangor of swords.

5

TWENTY RED NAILS

TWO WARRIORS lounged in the guardroom on the floor known as the Tier of the Eagle. Their attitude was casual, though habitually alert. An attack on the great bronze door from without was always a possibility, but for many years no such assault had been attempted on either side.

"The strangers are strong allies," said one. "Olmec will move against the enemy tomorrow, I believe."

He spoke as a soldier in a war might have spoken. In the miniature world of Xuchotl each handful of feudists was an army, and the empty halls between the castles was the country over which they campaigned.

The other meditated for a space.

"Suppose with their aid we destroy Xotalanc," he said. "What then, Xatmec?"

"Why," returned Xatmec, "we will drive red nails for them all. The captives we will burn and flay and quarter."

"But afterward?" pursued the other. "After we have slain them all? Will it not seem strange, to have no foes to fight? All my life I have fought and hated the Xotalancas. With the feud ended, what is left?"

Xatmec shrugged his shoulders. His thoughts had never gone beyond the destruction of their foes. They could not go beyond that.

Suddenly both men stiffened at a noise outside the door.

"To the door, Xatmec!" hissed the last speaker. "I shall look through the Eye—"

Xatmec, sword in hand, leaned against the bronze door, straining his ear to hear through the metal. His mate looked into the mirror. He started convulsively. Men were clustered thickly outside the door; grim, dark-faced men with swords gripped in their teeth—*and their fingers thrust into their ears.* One who wore a feathered headdress had a set of pipes which he set to his lips, and even as the Tecuhltli started to shout a warning, the pipes began to skirl.

The cry died in the guard's throat as the thin, weird piping penetrated the metal door and smote on his ears. Xatmec leaned frozen against the door, as if paralyzed in that position. His face was that of a wooden image, his expression one of horrified listening. The other guard, farther removed from the source of the sound, yet sensed the horror of what was taking place, the grisly threat that lay in that demoniac fifing. He felt the weird strains plucking like unseen fingers at the tissues of his brain, filling him with alien emotions and impulses of madness. But with a soul-tearing effort he broke the spell, and shrieked a warning in a voice he did not recognize as his own.

But even as he cried out, the music changed to an unbearable shrilling that was like a knife in the eardrums. Xatmec screamed in sudden agony, and all the sanity went out of his face like a flame blown out in a wind. Like a madman he ripped loose the chain, tore open the door and rushed out into the hall, sword lifted before his mate could stop him. A dozen blades struck him down, and over his mangled body the Xotalancas surged into the guardroom, with a long-drawn, blood-mad yell that sent the unwonted echoes reverberating.

His brain reeling from the shock of it all, the remaining guard leaped to meet them with goring spear. The horror of the sorcery he had just witnessed was submerged in the stunning realization that the enemy were in Tecuhltli. And as his spearhead ripped through a dark-skinned belly he knew no more, for a swinging sword crushed his skull, even as wild-eyed warriors came pouring in from the chambers behind the guardroom.

It was the yelling of men and the clanging of steel that brought Conan bounding from his couch, wide awake and broadsword in hand. In an instant he had reached the door and flung it open, and was glaring out into the corridor just as Techotl rushed up it, eyes blazing madly.

"The Xotalancas!" he screamed, in a voice hardly human. "*They are within the door!*"

Conan ran down the corridor, even as Valeria emerged from her chamber.

"What the devil is it?" she called.

"Techotl says the Xotalancas are in," he answered hurriedly. "That racket sounds like it."

With the Tecuhltli on their heels they burst into the throne room and were confronted by a scene beyond the most frantic dream of blood and fury. Twenty men and women, their black hair streaming, and the white skulls gleaming on their breasts, were locked in combat with the people of Tecuhltli. The women on both sides fought as madly as the men, and already the room and the hall beyond were strewn with corpses.

Olmec, naked but for a breech-clout, was fighting before his throne, and as the adventurers entered, Tascela ran from an inner chamber with a sword in her hand.

Xatmec and his mate were dead, so there was none to tell the Tecuhltli how their foes had found their way into their citadel. Nor was there any to say what had prompted that mad attempt. But the losses of the Xotalancas had been greater, their position more desperate, than the Tecuhltli had known. The maiming of their scaly ally, the destruction of the Burning Skull, and the news, gasped by a dying man, that mysterious white-skin allies had joined their enemies, had driven them to the frenzy of desperation and the wild determination to die dealing death to their ancient foes.

The Tecuhltli, recovering from the first stunning shock of the surprise that had swept them back into the throne room and littered the floor with their corpses, fought back with an equally desperate fury, while the door-guards from the lower floors came racing to hurl themselves into the fray. It was the deathfight of rabid wolves, blind, panting, merciless. Back and forth it surged, from door to dais, blades whickering and striking into flesh, blood spurting, feet stamping the crimson floor where redder pools were forming. Ivory tables crashed over, seats were splintered, velvet hangings torn down were stained red. It was the bloody climax of a bloody half-century, and every man there sensed it.

But the conclusion was inevitable. The Tecuhltli outnumbered the invaders almost two to one, and they were heartened by that fact and by the entrance into the mêlée of their light-skinned allies.

These crashed into the fray with the devastating effect of a hurricane plowing through a grove of saplings. In sheer strength no three Tlazitlans were a match for Conan, and in spite of his weight he was quicker on his feet than any of them. He moved through the whirling, eddying mass with the surety and destructiveness of a gray wolf amidst a pack of alley curs, and he strode over a wake of crumpled figures.

Valeria fought beside him, her lips smiling and her eyes blazing. She was stronger than the average man, and far quicker and more ferocious. Her sword was like a living thing in her hand. Where Conan beat down opposition by the sheer weight and power of his blows, breaking spears, splitting skulls and cleaving bosoms to the breastbone, Valeria brought into action a finesse of swordplay that dazzled and bewildered her antagonists before it slew them. Again and again a warrior, heaving high his heavy blade, found her point in his jugular before he could strike. Conan, towering above the field, strode through the welter smiting right and left, but Valeria moved like an illusive phantom, constantly shifting, and thrusting and slashing as she shifted. Swords missed her again and again as the wielders flailed the empty air and died with her point in their hearts or throats, and her mocking laughter in their ears.

Neither sex nor condition was considered by the maddened combatants. The five women of the Xotalancas were down with their throats cut before Conan and Valeria entered the fray, and when a man or woman went down under the stamping feet, there was always a knife ready for the helpless throat, or a sandaled foot eager to crush the prostrate skull.

From wall to wall, from door to door rolled the waves of combat, spilling over into adjoining chambers. And presently only Tecuhltli and their white-skinned allies stood upright in the great throne room. The survivors stared bleakly and blankly at each other, like survivors after Judgment Day or the destruction of the world. On legs wide-braced, hands gripping notched and dripping swords, blood trickling down their arms, they stared at one another across the mangled corpses of friends and foes. They had no breath left to shout, but a bestial mad howling rose from their lips. It was not a human cry of triumph. It was the howling of a rabid wolf-pack stalking among the bodies of its victims.

Conan caught Valeria's arm and turned her about.

"You've got a stab in the calf of your leg," he growled.

She glanced down, for the first time aware of a stinging in the muscles of her leg. Some dying man on the floor had fleshed his dagger with his last effort.

"You look like a butcher yourself," she laughed.

He shook a red shower from his hands.

"Not mine. Oh, a scratch here and there. Nothing to bother about. But that calf ought to be bandaged."

Olmec came through the litter, looking like a ghoul with his naked massive shoulders splashed with blood, and his black beard dabbled in crimson. His eyes were red, like the reflection of flame on black water.

"We have won!" he croaked dazedly. "The feud is ended! The dogs of Xotalanc lie dead! Oh, for a captive to flay alive! Yet it is good to look upon their dead faces. Twenty dead dogs! Twenty red nails for the black column!"

"You'd best see to your wounded," grunted Conan, turning away from him. "Here, girl, let me see that leg."

"Wait a minute!" she shook him off impatiently. The fire of fighting still burned brightly in her soul. "How do we know these are all of them? These might have come on a raid of their own."

"They would not split the clan on a foray like this," said Olmec, shaking his head, and regaining some of his ordinary intelligence. Without his purple robe the man seemed less like a prince than some repellent beast of prey. "I will stake my head upon it that we have slain them all. There were less of them than I dreamed, and they must have been desperate. But how came they in Tecuhltli?"

Tascela came forward, wiping her sword on her naked thigh, and holding in her other hand an object she had taken from the body of the feathered leader of the Xotalancas.

"The pipes of madness," she said. "A warrior tells me that Xatmec opened the door to the Xotalancas and was cut down as they stormed into the guardroom. This warrior came to the guardroom from the inner hall just in time to see it happen and to hear the last of a weird strain of music which froze his very soul. Tolkemec used to talk of these pipes, which the Xuchotlans swore were hidden somewhere in the catacombs with the bones of the ancient wizard who used them in his lifetime. Somehow the dogs of Xotalanc found them and learned their secret."

"Somebody ought to go to Xotalanc and see if any remain alive," said Conan. "I'll go if somebody will guide me."

Olmec glanced at the remnants of his people. There were only twenty left alive, and of these several lay groaning on the floor. Tascela was the only one of the Tecuhltli who had escaped without a wound. The princess was untouched, though she had fought as savagely as any.

"Who will go with Conan to Xotalanc?" asked Olmec.

Techotl limped forward. The wound in his thigh had started bleeding afresh, and he had another gash across his ribs.

"I will go!"

"No, you won't," vetoed Conan. "And you're not going either, Valeria. In a little while that leg will be getting stiff."

"I will go," volunteered a warrior, who was knotting a bandage about a slashed forearm.

"Very well, Yanath. Go with the Cimmerian. And you, too, Topal." Olmec indicated another man whose injuries were slight. "But first aid to lift the badly wounded on these couches where we may bandage their hurts."

This was done quickly. As they stooped to pick up a woman who had been stunned by a warclub, Olmec's beard brushed Topal's ear. Conan thought the prince muttered something to the warrior, but he could not be sure. A few moments later he was leading his companions down the hall.

Conan glanced back as he went out the door, at that shambles where the dead lay on the smoldering floor, blood-stained dark limbs knotted in attitudes of fierce muscular effort, dark faces frozen in masks of hate, glassy eyes glaring up at the green fire-jewels which bathed the ghastly scene in a dusky emerald witchlight. Among the dead the living moved aimlessly, like people moving in a trance. Conan heard Olmec call a woman and direct her to bandage Valeria's leg. The pirate followed the woman into an adjoining chamber, already beginning to limp slightly.

Warily the two Tecuhltli led Conan along the hall beyond the bronze door, and through chamber after chamber shimmering in the green fire. They saw no one, heard no sound. After they crossed the Great Hall which bisected the city from north to south, their caution was increased by the realization of their nearness to enemy territory. But chambers and halls lay empty to their wary gaze, and they came at last along a broad dim hallway and halted before a bronze door similar to the Eagle Door of Tecuhltli. Gingerly they tried it, and it opened silently under their fingers. Awed, they stared into the green-lit chambers beyond. For fifty years no Tecuhltli had entered those halls save as a prisoner going to a hideous doom. To go to Xotalanc had been the ultimate horror that could befall a man of the western castle. The terror of it had stalked through their dreams since earliest childhood. To Yanath and Topal that bronze door was like the portal of hell.

They cringed back, unreasoning horror in their eyes, and Conan pushed past them and strode into Xotalanc.

Timidly they followed him. As each man set foot over the threshold he stared and glared wildly about him. But only their quick, hurried breathing disturbed the silence.

They had come into a square guardroom, like that behind the Eagle

Door of Tecuhltli, and, similarly, a hall ran away from it to a broad chamber that was a counterpart of Olmec's throne room.

Conan glanced down the hall with its rugs and divans and hangings, and stood listening intently. He heard no noise, and the rooms had an empty feel. He did not believe there were any Xotalancas left alive in Xuchotl.

"Come on," he muttered, and started down the hall.

He had not gone far when he was aware that only Yanath was following him. He wheeled back to see Topal standing in an attitude of horror, one arm out as if to fend off some threatening peril, his distended eyes fixed with hypnotic intensity on something protruding from behind a divan.

"What the devil?" Then Conan saw what Topal was staring at, and he felt a faint twiching of the skin between his giant shoulders. A monstrous head protruded from behind the divan, a reptilian head, broad as the head of a crocodile, with down-curving fangs that project- ed over the lower jaw. But there was an unnatural limpness about the thing, and the hideous eyes were glazed.

Conan peered behind the couch. It was a great serpent which lay there limp in death, but such a serpent as he had never seen in his wanderings. The reek and chill of the deep black earth were about it, and its color was an indeterminable hue which changed with each new angle from which he surveyed it. A great wound in the neck showed what had caused its death.

"It is the Crawler!" whispered Yanath.

"It's the thing I slashed on the stair," grunted Conan. "After it trailed us to the Eagle Door, it dragged itself here to die. How could the Xotalancas control such a brute?"

The Tecuhltli shivered and shook their heads.

"They brought it up from the black tunnels *below* the catacombs. They discovered secrets unknown to Tecuhltli."

"Well, it's dead, and if they'd had any more of them, they'd have brought them along when they came to Tecuhltli. Come on."

They crowded close at his heels as he strode down the hall and thrust on the silver-worked door at the other end.

"If we don't find anybody on this floor," he said, "we'll descend into the lower floors. We'll explore Xotalanc from the roof to the catacombs. If Xotalanc is like Tecuhltli, all the rooms and halls in this tier will be lighted—what the devil!"

They had come into the broad throne chamber, so similar to that one in Tecuhltli. There were the same jade dais and ivory seat, the same divans, rugs and hangings on the walls. No black, red-scarred column stood behind the throne-dais, but evidences of the grim feud were not lacking.

Ranged along the wall behind the dais were rows of glass-covered shelves. And on those shelves hundreds of human heads, perfectly preserved, stared at the startled watchers with emotionless eyes, as they had stared for only the gods knew how many months and years.

Topal muttered a curse, but Yanath stood silent, the mad light growing in his wide eyes. Conan frowned, knowing that Tlazitlan sanity was hung on a hair-trigger.

Suddenly Yanath pointed to the ghastly relics with a twitching finger. "There is my brother's head!" he murmured. "And there is my father's younger brother! And there beyond them is my sister's eldest son!"

Suddenly he began to weep, dry-eyed, with harsh, loud sobs that shook his frame. He did not take his eyes from the heads. His sobs grew shriller, changed to frightful, high-pitched laughter, and that in turn became an unbearable screaming. Yanath was stark mad.

Conan laid a hand on his shoulder, and as if the touch had released all the frenzy in his soul, Yanath screamed and whirled, striking at the Cimmerian with his sword. Conan parried the blow, and Topal tried to catch Yanath's arm. But the madman avoided him and with froth flying from his lips, he drove his sword deep into Topal's body. Topal sank down with a groan, and Yanath whirled for an instant like a crazy dervish; then he ran at the shelves and began hacking at the glass with his sword, screeching blasphemously.

Conan sprang at him from behind, trying to catch him unaware and disarm him, but the madman wheeled and lunged at him, screaming like a lost soul. Realizing that the warrior was hopelessly insane, the Cimmerian sidestepped, and as the maniac went past, he swung a cut that severed the shoulder-bone and breast, and dropped the man dead beside his dying victim.

Conan bent over Topal, seeing that the man was at his last gasp. It was useless to seek to stanch the blood gushing from the horrible wound.

"You're done for, Topal," grunted Conan. "Any word you want to send to your people?"

"Bend closer," gasped Topal, and Conan complied—and an instant later caught the man's wrist as Topal struck at his breast with a dagger.

"Crom!" swore Conan. "Are you mad, too?"

"Olmec ordered it!" gasped the dying man. "I know not why. As we lifted the wounded upon the couches he whispered to me, bidding me to slay you as we returned to Tecuhltli—" And with the name of his clan on his lips, Topal died.

Conan scowled down at him in puzzlement. This whole affair had an aspect of lunacy. Was Olmec mad, too? Were all the Tecuhltli madder than he had realized? With a shrug of his shoulders he strode down the hall and out of the bronze door, leaving the dead Tecuhltli lying before the staring dead eyes of their kinsmen's heads.

Conan needed no guide back through the labyrinth they had traversed. His primitive instinct of direction led him unerringly along the route they had come. He traversed it as warily as he had before, his sword in his hand, and his eyes fiercely searching each shadowed nook and corner; for it was his former allies he feared now, not the ghosts of the slain Xotalancas.

He had crossed the Great Hall and entered the chambers beyond when he heard something moving ahead of him—something which gasped and panted, and moved with a strange, floundering, scrambling noise. A moment later Conan saw a man crawling over the flaming floor toward him—a man whose progress left a broad bloody smear on the smoldering surface. It was Techotl and his eyes were already glazing; from a deep gash in his breast blood gushed steadily between the fingers of his clutching hand. With the other he clawed and hitched himself along.

"Conan," he cried chokingly, "Conan! Olmec has taken the yellow-haired woman!"

"So that's why he told Topal to kill me!" murmured Conan, dropping to his knee beside the man, who his experienced eye told him was dying. "Olmec isn't as mad as I thought."

Techotl's groping fingers plucked at Conan's arm. In the cold, loveless, and altogether hideous life of the Tecuhltli, his admiration and affection for the invaders from the outer world formed a warm, human oasis, constituted a tie that connected him with a more natural humanity that was totally lacking in his fellows, whose only emotions were hate, lust, and the urge of sadistic cruelty.

"I sought to oppose him," gurgled Techotl, blood bubbling frothily to his lips. "But he struck me down. He thought he had slain me, but I crawled away. Ah, Set, how far I have crawled in my own blood! Beware, Conan! Olmec may have set an ambush for your return! Slay Olmec! He is a beast. Take Valeria and flee! Fear not to traverse the forest. Olmec and Tascela lied about the dragons. They slew each other years ago, all save the strongest. For a dozen years there has been only one dragon. If you have slain him, there is naught in the forest to harm you. He was the god Olmec worshipped; and Olmec fed human sacrifices to him, the very old and the very young, bound and hurled from the wall. Hasten! Olmec has taken Valeria to the Chamber of the—"

His head slumped down and he was dead before it came to rest on the floor.

Conan sprang up, his eyes like live coals. So that was Olmec's game, having first used the strangers to destroy his foes! He should have known that something of the sort would be going on in that black-bearded degenerate's mind.

The Cimmerian started toward Tecuhltli with reckless speed. Rapidly he reckoned the numbers of his former allies. Only twenty-one, counting Olmec, had survived that fiendish battle in the throne room. Three had died since, which left seventeen enemies with which to reckon. In his rage Conan felt capable of accounting for the whole clan single-handed.

But the innate craft of the wilderness rose to guide his berserk rage. He remembered Techotl's warning of an ambush. It was quite probable that the prince would make such provisions, on the chance that Topal might have failed to carry out his order. Olmec would be expecting him to return by the same route he had followed in going to Xotalanc.

Conan glanced up at a skylight under which he was passing and caught the blurred glimmer of stars. They had not yet begun to pale for dawn. The events of the night had been crowded into a comparatively short space of time.

He turned aside from his direct course and descended a winding staircase to the floor below. He did not know where the door was to be found that led into the castle on that level, but he knew he could find it. How he was to force the locks he did not know; he believed that the doors of Tecuhltli would all be locked and bolted, if for no other reason than the habits of half a century. But there was nothing else but to attempt it.

Sword in hand, he hurried noiselessly on through a maze of green-lit or shadowy rooms and halls. He knew he must be near Tecuhltli, when a sound brought him up short. He recognized it for what it was—a human being trying to cry out through a stifling gag. It came from somewhere ahead of him, and to the left. In those deathly-still chambers a small sound carried a long way.

Conan turned aside and went seeking after the sound, which continued to be repeated. Presently he was glaring through a doorway upon a weird scene. In the room into which he was looking a low rack-like frame of iron lay on the floor, and a giant figure was bound prostrate upon it. His head rested on a bed of iron spikes, which were already crimson-pointed with blood where they had pierced his scalp. A peculiar harness-like contrivance was fastened about his head, though in such a manner that the leather band did not protect his scalp from the spikes. This harness was connected by a slender chain to the mechanism that upheld a huge iron ball which was suspended above the captive's hairy breast. As long as the man could force himself to remain motionless the iron ball hung in its place. But when the pain of the iron points caused him to lift his head, the ball lurched downward a few inches. Presently his aching neck muscles would no longer support his head in its unnatural position and it would fall back on the spikes again. It was obvious that eventually the ball would crush him to a pulp, slowly and inexorably. The victim was gagged, and above the gag his great black ox-eyes rolled wildly toward the man in the doorway, who stood in silent amazement. The man on the rack was Olmec, prince of Tecuhltli.

6

THE EYES OF TASCELA

"WHY DID you bring me into this chamber to bandage my legs?" demanded Valeria. "Couldn't you have done it just as well in the throne room?"

She sat on a couch with her wounded leg extended upon it, and the Tecuhltli woman had just bound it with silk bandages. Valeria's red-stained sword lay on the couch beside her.

She frowned as she spoke. The woman had done her task silently and efficiently, but Valeria liked neither the lingering, caressing touch of her slim fingers nor the expression in her eyes.

"They have taken the rest of the wounded into the other chambers," answered the woman in the soft speech of the Tecuhltli women, which somehow did not suggest either softness or gentleness in the speakers. A little while before, Valeria had seen this same woman stab a Xotalanca woman through the breast and stamp the eyeballs out a wounded Xotalanca man.

"They will be carrying the corpses of the dead down into the catacombs," she added, "lest the ghosts escape into the chambers and dwell there."

"Do you believe in ghosts?" asked Valeria.

"I know the ghost of Tolkemec dwells in the catacombs," she answered with a shiver. "Once I saw it, as I crouched in a crypt among the bones of a dead queen. It passed by in the form of an ancient man with flowing white beard and locks, and luminous eyes that blazed in the darkness. It was Tolkemec; I saw him living when I was a child and he was being tortured."

Her voice sank to a fearful whisper: "Olmec laughs, but I *know* Tolkemec's ghost dwells in the catacombs! They say it is rats which gnaw the flesh from the bones of the newly dead—but ghosts eat flesh. Who knows but that—"

She glanced up quickly as a shadow fell across the couch. Valeria looked up to see Olmec gazing down at her. The prince had cleansed his hands, torso, and beard of the blood that had splashed them; but he had not donned his robe, and his great dark-skinned hairless body and limbs renewed the impression of strength bestial in its nature. His deep black eyes burned with a more elemental light, and there was the suggestion of a twitching in the fingers that tugged at his thick blue-black beard.

He stared fixedly at the woman, and she rose and glided from the chamber. As she passed through the door she cast a look over her shoulder at Valeria, a glance full of cynical derision and obscene mockery.

"She has done a clumsy job," criticized the prince, coming to the divan and bending over the bandage. "Let me see—"

With a quickness amazing in one of his bulk he snatched her sword and threw it across the chamber. His next move was to catch her in his giant arms.

Quick and unexpected as the move was, she almost matched it; for even as he grabbed her, her dirk was in her hand and she stabbed murderously at his throat. More by luck than skill he caught her wrist, and then began a savage wrestling-match. She fought him with fists, feet, knees, teeth, and nails, with all the strength of her magnificent body and all the knowledge of hand-to-hand fighting she had acquired in her years of roving and fighting on sea and land. It availed her nothing against his brute strength. She lost her dirk in the first moment of contact, and thereafter found herself powerless to inflict any appreciable pain on her giant attacker.

The blaze in his weird black eyes did not alter, and their expression filled her with fury, fanned by the sardonic smile that seemed carved upon his bearded lips. Those eyes and that smile contained all the cruel cynicism that seethes below the surface of a sophisticated and degenerate race, and for the first time in her life Valeria experienced fear of a man. It was like struggling against some huge elemental force; his iron arms thwarted her efforts with an ease that sent panic racing through her limbs. He seemed impervious to any pain she could inflict. Only once, when she sank her white teeth savagely into his wrist so that the blood started, did he react. And that was to buffet her brutally upon the side of the head with his open hand, so that stars flashed before her eyes and her head rolled on her shoulders.

Her shirt had been torn open in the struggle, and with cynical cruelty he rasped his thick beard across her bare breasts, bringing the blood to suffuse the fair skin, and fetching a cry of pain and outraged fury from her. Her convulsive resistance was useless; she was crushed down on a couch, disarmed and panting, her eyes blazing up at him like the eyes of a trapped tigress.

A moment later he was hurrying from the chamber, carrying her in his arms. She made no resistance, but the smoldering of her eyes showed that she was unconquered in spirit, at least. She had not cried out. She knew that Conan was not within call, and it did not occur to her that any in Tecuhltli would oppose their prince. But she noticed that Olmec went stealthily, with his head on one side as if listening for sounds of pursuit, and he did not return to the throne chamber. He carried her through a door that stood opposite that through which he had entered, crossed another room and began stealing down a hall. As she became convinced that he feared some opposition to the abduction, she threw back her head and screamed at the top of her lusty voice.

She was rewarded by a slap that half stunned her, and Olmec quickened his pace to a shambling run.

But her cry had been echoed and, twisting her head about, Valeria, through the tears and stars that partly blinded her, saw Techotl limping after them.

Olmec turned with a snarl, shifting the woman to an uncomfortable and certainly undignified position under one huge arm, where he held her writhing and kicking vainly, like a child.

"Olmec!" protested Techotl. "You cannot be such a dog as to do this thing! She is Conan's woman! She helped us slay the Xotalancas, and—"

Without a word Olmec balled his free hand into a huge fist and stretched the wounded warrior senseless at his feet. Stooping, and hindered not at all by the struggles and imprecations of his captive, he drew Techotl's sword from its sheath and stabbed the warrior in the breast. Then casting aside the weapon, he fled on along the corridor. He did not see a woman's dark face peer cautiously after him from behind a hanging. It vanished, and presently Techotl groaned and stirred, rose dazedly and staggered drunkenly away, calling Conan's name.

Olmec hurried on down the corridor, and descended a winding ivory staircase. He crossed several corridors and halted at last in a broad chamber whose doors were veiled with heavy tapestries, with one exception—a heavy bronze door similar to the Door of the Eagle on the upper floor.

He was moved to rumble, pointing to it: "That is one of the outer doors of Tecuhltli. For the first time in fifty years it is unguarded. We need not guard it now, for Xotalanc is no more."

"Thanks to Conan and me, you bloody rogue!" sneered Valeria, trembling with fury and the shame of physical coercion. "You treacherous dog! Conan will cut your throat for this!"

Olmec did not bother to voice his belief that Conan's own gullet had already been severed according to his whispered command. He was too utterly cynical to be at all interested in her thoughts or opinions. His flame-lit eyes devoured her, dwelling burningly on the generous expanses of clear white flesh exposed where her shirt and breeches had been torn in the struggle.

"Forget Conan," he said thickly. "Olmec is lord of Xuchotl. Xotalanc is no more. There will be no more fighting. We shall spend our lives in drinking and lovemaking. First let us drink!"

He seated himself on an ivory table and pulled her down on his knees, like a dark-skinned satyr with a white nymph in his arms. Ignoring her un-nymphlike profanity, he held her helpless with one great arm about her waist while the other reached across the table and secured a vessel of wine.

"Drink!" he commanded, forcing it to her lips, as she writhed her head away.

The liquor slopped over, stinging her lips, splashing down on her naked breasts.

"Your guest does not like your wine, Olmec," spoke a cool, sardonic voice.

Olmec stiffened; fear grew in his flaming eyes. Slowly he swung his great head about and stared at Tascela who posed negligently in the curtained doorway, one hand on her smooth hip. Valeria twisted herself about in his iron grip, and when she met the burning eyes of Tascela, a chill tingled along her supple spine. New experiences were flooding

Valeria's proud soul that night. Recently she had learned to fear a man; now she knew what it was to fear a woman.

Olmec sat motionless, a gray pallor growing under his swarthy skin. Tascela brought her other hand from behind her and displayed a small gold vessel.

"I feared she would not like your wine, Olmec," purred the princess, "so I brought some of mine, some I brought with me long ago from the shores of Lake Zuad—do you understand, Olmec?"

Beads of sweat stood out suddenly on Olmec's brow. His muscles relaxed, and Valeria broke away and put the table between them. But though reason told her to dart from the room, some fascination she could not understand held her rigid, watching the scene.

Tascela came toward the seated prince with a swaying, undulating walk that was mockery in itself. Her voice was soft, slurringly caressing, but her eyes gleamed. Her slim fingers stroked his beard lightly.

"You are selfish, Olmec," she crooned, smiling. "You would keep our handsome guest to yourself, though you knew I wished to entertain her. You are much at fault, Olmec!"

The mask dropped for an instant; her eyes flashed, her face was contorted and with an appalling show of strength her hand locked convulsively in his beard and tore out a great handful. This evidence of unnatural strength was no more terrifying than the momentary baring of the hellish fury that raged under her bland exterior.

Olmec lurched up with a roar, and stood swaying like a bear, his mighty hands clenching and unclenching.

"Slut!" His booming voice filled the room. "Witch! She-devil! Tecuhltli should have slain you fifty years ago! Begone! I have endured too much from you! This white-skinned wench is mine! Get hence before I slay you!"

The princess laughed and dashed the blood-stained strands into his face. Her laughter was less merciful than the ring of flint on steel.

"Once you spoke otherwise, Olmec," she taunted. "Once, in your youth, you spoke words of love. Aye, you were my lover once, years ago, and because you loved me, you slept in my arms beneath the enchanted lotus—and thereby put into my hands the chains that enslaved you. You know you cannot withstand me. You know I have but to gaze into your eyes, with the mystic power a priest of Stygia taught me, long ago, and you are powerless. You remember the night beneath the black lotus that waved above us, stirred by no worldly breeze; you scent again the unearthly perfumes that stole and rose like a cloud about you to enslave you. You cannot fight against me. You are my slave as you were that night—as you shall be so long as you shall live, Olmec of Xuchotl!"

Her voice had sunk to a murmur like the rippling of a stream running through starlit darkness. She leaned close to the prince and spread her long tapering fingers upon his giant breast. His eyes glazed, his great hands fell limply to his sides.

With a smile of cruel malice, Tascela lifted the vessel and placed it to his lips.

"Drink!"

Mechanically the prince obeyed. And instantly the glaze passed from his eyes and they were flooded with fury, comprehension and an awful fear. His mouth gaped, but no sound issued. For an instant he reeled on buckling knees, and then fell in a sodden heap on the floor.

His fall jolted Valeria out of her paralysis. She turned and sprang toward the door, but with a movement that would have shamed a leaping panther, Tascela was before her. Valeria struck at her with her clenched fist, and all the power of her supple body behind the blow. It would have stretched a man senseless on the floor. But with a lithe twist of her torso, Tascela avoided the blow and caught the pirate's wrist. The next instant Valeria's left hand was imprisoned and, holding her wrists together with one hand, Tascela calmly bound them with a cord she drew from her girdle. Valeria thought she had tasted the ultimate in humiliation already that night, but her shame at being manhandled by Olmec was nothing to the sensations that now shook her supple frame. Valeria had always been inclined to despise the other members of her sex; and it was overwhelming to encounter another woman who could handle her like a child. She scarcely resisted at all when Tascela forced her into a chair and, drawing her bound wrists down between her knees, fastened them to the chair.

Casually stepping over Olmec, Tascela walked to the bronze door and shot the bolt and threw it open, revealing a hallway without.

"Opening upon this hall," she remarked, speaking to her feminine captive for the first time, "there is a chamber which in old times was used as a torture room. When we retired into Tecuhltli, we brought most of the apparatus with us, but there was one piece too heavy to move. It is still in working order. I think it will be quite convenient now."

An understanding flame of terror rose in Olmec's eyes. Tascela strode back to him, bent and gripped him by the hair.

"He is only paralyzed temporarily," she remarked conversationally. "He can hear, think, and feel—aye, he can feel very well indeed!"

With which sinister observation she started toward the door, dragging the giant bulk with an ease that made the pirate's eyes dilate. She passed into the hall and moved down it without hesitation, presently disappearing with her captive into a chamber that opened into it, and whence shortly thereafter issued the clank of iron.

Valeria swore softly and tugged vainly, with her legs braced against the chair. The cords that confined her were apparently unbreakable.

Tascela presently returned alone; behind her a muffled groaning issued from the chamber. She closed the door but did not bolt it. Tascela was beyond the grip of habit, as she was beyond the touch of other human instincts and emotions.

Valeria sat dumbly, watching the woman in whose slim hands, the pirate realized, her destiny now rested.

Tascela grasped her yellow locks and forced back her head, looking impersonally down into her face. But the glitter in her dark eyes was not impersonal.

"I have chosen you for a great honor," she said. "You shall restore the youth of Tascela. Oh, you stare at that! My appearance is that of youth, but through my veins creeps the sluggish chill of approaching age, as I have felt it a thousand times before. I am old, so old I do not remember my childhood. But I was a girl once, and a priest of Stygia loved me, and gave me the secret of immortality and youth everlasting. He died, then—some said by poison. But I dwelt in my palace by the shores of Lake Zuad and the passing years touched me not. So at last a king of Stygia desired me, and my people rebelled and brought me to this land. Olmec called me a princess. I am not of royal blood. I am greater than a princess. I am Tascela, whose youth your own glorious youth shall restore."

Valeria's tongue clove to the roof of her mouth. She sensed here a mystery darker than the degeneracy she had anticipated.

The taller woman unbound the Aquilonian's wrists and pulled her to her feet. It was not fear of the dominant strength that lurked in the princess' limbs that made Valeria a helpless, quivering captive in her hands. It was the burning, hypnotic, terrible eyes of Tascela.

7

"WELL, I'M a Kushite!"

Conan glared down at the man on the iron rack.

"What the devil are *you* doing on that thing?"

Incoherent sounds issued from behind the gag and Conan bent and tore it away, evoking a bellow of fear from the captive; for his action the iron ball to lurch down until it nearly touched the broad breast.

"Be careful, for Set's sake!" begged Olmec.

"What for?" demanded Conan. "Do you think I care what happens to you? I only wish I had time to stay here and watch that chunk of iron grind your guts out. But I'm in a hurry. Where's Valeria?"

"Loose me!" urged Olmec. "I will tell you all!"

"Tell me first."

"Never!" The prince's heavy jaws set stubbornly.

"All right." Conan seated himself on a near-by bench. "I'll find her myself, after you've been reduced to a jelly. I believe I can speed up that process by twisting my sword-point around in your ear," he added, extending the weapon experimentally.

"Wait!" Words came in a rush from the captive's ashy lips. "Tascela took her from me. I've never been anything but a puppet in Tascela's hands."

"Tascela?" snorted Conan, and spat. "Why, the filthy—"

"No, no!" panted Olmec. "It's worse than you think. Tascela is old—centuries old. She renews her life and her youth by the sacrifice of beautiful young women. That's one thing that has reduced the clan to its present state. She will draw the essence of Valeria's life into her own body, and bloom with fresh vigor and beauty."

"Are the doors locked?" asked Conan, thumbing his sword edge.

"Aye! But I know a way to get into Tecuhltli. Only Tascela and I know, and she thinks me helpless and you slain. Free me and I swear I will help you rescue Valeria. Without my help you cannot win into Tecuhltli; for even if you tortured me into revealing the secret, you couldn't work it. Let me go, and we will steal on Tascela and kill her before she can work magic—before she can fix her eyes on us. A knife thrown from behind will do the work. I should have killed her thus long ago, but I feared that without her to aid us the Xotalancas would overcome us. She needed my help, too; that's the only reason she let me live this long. Now neither needs the other, and one must die. I

swear that when we have slain the witch, you and Valeria shall go free
without harm. My people will obey me when Tascela is dead."

Conan stooped and cut the ropes that held the prince, and Olmec slid
cautiously from under the great ball and rose, shaking his head like a
bull and muttering imprecations as he fingered his lacerated scalp.
Standing shoulder to shoulder the two men presented a formidable
picture of primitive power. Olmec was as tall as Conan, and heavier;
but there was something repellent about the Tlazitlan, something abysmal and monstrous that contrasted unfavorably with the clean-cut,
compact hardness of the Cimmerian. Conan had discarded the remnants of his tattered, blood-soaked shirt, and stood with his remarkable
muscular development impressively revealed. His great shoulders were
as broad as those of Olmec, and more cleanly outlined, and his huge
breast arched with a more impressive sweep to a hard waist that lacked
the paunchy thickness of Olmec's midsection. He might have been an
image of primal strength cut out of bronze. Olmec was darker, but not
from the burning of the sun. If Conan was a figure out of the dawn of
time, Olmec was a shambling, somber shape from the darkness of time's
pre-dawn.

"Lead on," demanded Conan. "And keep ahead of me. I don't trust
you any farther than I can throw a bull by the tail."

Olmec turned and stalked on ahead of him, one hand twitching
slightly as it plucked at his matted beard.

Olmec did not lead Conan back to the bronze door, which the prince
naturally supposed Tascela had locked, but to a certain chamber on the
border of Tecuhltli.

"This secret has been guarded for half a century," he said. "Not even
our own clan knew of it, and the Xotalancas never learned. Tecuhltli
himself built this secret entrance, afterward slaying the slaves who did
the work; for he feared that he might find himself locked out of his own
kingdom some day because of the spite of Tascela, whose passion for
him soon changed to hate. But she discovered the secret, and barred
the hidden door against him one day as he fled back from an unsuccessful raid, and the Xotalancas took him and flayed him. But once, spying
upon her, I saw her enter Tecuhltli by this route, and so learned the
secret."

He pressed upon a gold ornament in the wall, and a panel swung
inward, disclosing an ivory stair leading upward.

"This stair is built within the wall," said Olmec. "It leads up to a
tower upon the roof, and thence other stairs wind down to the various
chambers. Hasten!"

"After you, comrade!" retorted Conan satirically, swaying his broad-sword as he spoke, and Olmec shrugged his shoulders and stepped onto the staircase. Conan instantly followed him, and the door shut behind them. Far above a cluster of fire-jewels made the staircase a well of dusky dragon-light.

They mounted until Conan estimated that they were above the level of the fourth floor, and then came out into a cylindrical tower, in the domed roof of which was set the bunch of fire-jewels that lighted the stair. Through gold-barred windows, set with unbreakable crystal panes, the first windows he had seen in Xuchotl, Conan got a glimpse of high ridges, domes and more towers, looming darkly against the stars. He was looking across the roofs of Xuchotl.

Olmec did not look through the windows. He hurried down one of the several stairs that wound down from the tower, and when they had descended a few feet, this stair changed into a narrow corridor that wound tortuously on for some distance. It ceased at a steep flight of steps leading downward. There Olmec paused.

Up from below, muffled, but unmistakable, welled a woman's scream, edged with fright, fury, and shame. And Conan recognized Valeria's voice.

In the swift rage roused by that cry, and the amazement of wondering what peril could wring such a shriek from Valeria's reckless lips, Conan forgot Olmec. He pushed past the prince and started down the stair. Awakening instinct brought him about again, just as Olmec struck with his great mallet-like fist. The blow, fierce and silent, was aimed at the base of Conan's brain. But the Cimmerian wheeled in time to receive the buffet on the side of his neck instead. The impact would have snapped the vertebrae of a lesser man. As it was, Conan swayed back-ward, but even as he reeled he dropped his sword, useless at such close quarters, and grasped Olmec's extended arm, dragging the prince with him as he fell. Headlong they went down the steps together, in a revolving whirl of limbs and heads and bodies. And as they went, Conan's iron fingers found and locked in Olmec's bull-throat.

The barbarian's neck and shoulder felt numb from the sledge-like impact of Olmec's huge fist, which had carried all the strength of the massive forearm, thick triceps and great shoulder. But this did not affect his ferocity to any appreciable extent. Like a bulldog he hung on grimly, shaken and battered and beaten against the steps as they rolled, until at last they struck an ivory panel-door at the bottom with such an impact that they splintered it its full length and crashed through its ruins. But Olmec was already dead, for those iron fingers had crushed out his life and broken his neck as they fell.

Conan rose, shaking the splinters from his great shoulder, blinking blood and dust out of his eyes.

He was in the great throne room. There were fifteen people in that room besides himself. The first person he saw was Valeria. A curious black altar stood before the throne-dais. Ranged about it, seven black candles in golden candlesticks sent up oozing spirals of thick green smoke, disturbingly scented. These spirals united in a cloud near the ceiling, forming a smoky arch above the altar. On that altar lay Valeria, stark naked, her white flesh gleaming in shocking contrast to the glistening ebon stone. She was not bound. She lay at full length, her arms stretched out above her head to their fullest extent. At the head of the altar knelt a young man, holding her wrists firmly. A young woman knelt at the other end of the altar, grasping her ankles. Between them she could neither rise nor move.

Eleven men and women of Tecuhltli knelt dumbly in a semicircle, watching the scene with hot, lustful eyes.

On the ivory throne-seat Tascela lolled. Bronze bowls of incense rolled their spirals about her; the wisps of smoke curled about her naked limbs like caressing fingers. She could not sit still; she squirmed and shifted about with sensuous abandon, as if finding pleasure in the contact of the smooth ivory with her sleek flesh.

The crash of the door as it broke beneath the impact of the hurtling bodies caused no change in the scene. The kneeling men and women merely glanced incuriously at the corpse of their prince and at the man who rose from the ruins of the door, then swung their eyes greedily back to the writhing white shape on the black altar. Tascela looked insolently at him, and sprawled back on her seat, laughing mockingly.

"Slut!" Conan saw red. His hands clenched into iron hammers as he started for her. With his first step something clanged loudly and steel bit savagely into his leg. He stumbled and almost fell, checked in his headlong stride. The jaws of an iron trap had closed on his leg, with teeth that sank deep and held. Only the ridged muscles of his calf saved the bone from being splintered. The accursed thing had sprung out of the smoldering floor without warning. He saw the slots now, in the floor where the jaws had lain, perfectly camouflaged.

"Fool!" laughed Tascela. "Did you think I would not guard against your possible return? Every door in this chamber is guarded by such traps. Stand there and watch now, while I fulfill the destiny of your handsome friend! Then I will decide your own."

Conan's hand instinctively sought his belt, only to encounter an empty scabbard. His sword was on the stair behind him. His poniard was lying back in the forest, where the dragon had torn it from his jaw. The steel teeth in his leg were like burning coals, but the pain was not as savage as the fury that seethed in his soul. He was trapped, like a wolf. If he had had his sword he would have hewn off his leg and crawled across the floor to slay Tascela. Valeria's eyes rolled toward him with mute appeal, and his own helplessness sent red waves of madness surging through his brain.

Dropping on the knee of his free leg, he strove to get his fingers between the jaws of the trap, to tear them apart by sheer strength. Blood started from beneath his fingernails, but the jaws fitted close about his leg in a circle whose segments jointed perfectly, contracted until there was no space between his mangled flesh and the fanged iron. The sight of Valeria's naked body added flame to the fire of his rage.

Tascela ignored him. Rising languidly from her seat she swept the ranks of her subjects with a searching glance, and asked: "Where are Xamec, Zlanath and Tachic?"

"They did not return from the catacombs, princess," answered a man. "Like the rest of us, they bore the bodies of the slain into the crypts, but they have not returned. Perhaps the ghost of Tolkemec took them."

"Be silent, fool!" she ordered harshly. "The ghost is a myth."

She came down from her dais, playing with a thin gold-hilted dagger. Her eyes burned like nothing on the hither side of hell. She paused beside the altar and spoke in the tense stillness.

"Your life shall make me young, white woman!" she said. "I shall lean upon your bosom and place my lips over yours, and slowly—ah, slowly!—sink this blade through your heart, so that your life, fleeing your stiffening body, shall enter mine, making me bloom again with youth and with life everlasting!"

Slowly, like a serpent arching toward its victim, she bent down through the writhing smoke, closer and closer over the now motionless woman who stared up into her glowing dark eyes—eyes that grew larger and deeper, blazing like black moons in the swirling smoke.

The kneeling people gripped their hands and held their breath, tense for the bloody climax, and the only sound was Conan's fierce panting as he strove to tear his leg from the trap.

All eyes were glued on the altar and the white figure there; the crash of a thunderbolt could hardly have broken the spell, yet it was only a low cry that shattered the fixity of the scene and brought all whirling about—a low cry, yet one to make the hair stand up stiffly on the scalp. They looked, and they saw.

Framed in the door to the left of the dais stood a nightmare figure. It was a man, with a tangle of white hair and a matted white beard that fell over his breast. Rags only partly covered his gaunt frame, revealing half-naked limbs strangely unnatural in appearance. The skin was not like that of a normal human. There was a suggestion of *scaliness* about it, as if the owner had dwelt long under conditions almost antithetical to those conditions under which human life ordinarily thrives. And there was nothing at all human about the eyes that blazed from the tangle of white hair. They were great gleaming disks that stared unwinkingly, luminous, whitish, and without a hint of normal emotion or sanity. The mouth gaped, but no coherent words issued—only a high-pitched tittering.

"Tolkemec!" whispered Tascela, livid, while the others crouched in speechless horror. "No myth, then, no ghost! Set! You have dwelt for twelve years in darkness! Twelve years among the bones of the dead! What grisly food did you find? What mad travesty of life did you live, in the stark blackness of that eternal night? I see now why Xamec and Zlanath and Tachic did not return from the catacombs—and never will return. But why have you waited so long to strike? Were you seeking something, in the pits? Some secret weapon you knew was hidden there? And have you found it at last?"

That hideous tittering was Tolkemec's only reply, as he bounded into the room with a long leap that carried him over the secret trap before the door—by chance, or by some faint recollection of the ways of Xuchotl. He was not mad, as a man is mad. He had dwelt apart from humanity so long that he was no longer human. Only an unbroken thread of memory embodied in hate and the urge for vengeance had connected him with the humanity from which he had been cut off, and held him lurking near the people he hated. Only that thin string had kept him from racing and prancing off for ever into the black corridors and realms of the subterranean world he had discovered, long ago.

"You sought something hidden!" whispered Tascela, cringing back. "And you have found it! You remember the feud! After all these years of blackness, you remember!"

For in the lean hand of Tolkemec now waved a curious jade-hued wand, on the end of which glowed a knob of crimson shaped like a pomegranate. She sprang aside as he thrust it out like a spear, and a beam of crimson fire lanced from the pomegranate. It missed Tascela, but the woman holding Valeria's ankles was in the way. It smote between her shoulders. There was a sharp crackling sound and the ray of fire flashed from her bosom and struck the black altar, with a snapping of blue sparks. The woman toppled sidewise, shriveling and withering like a mummy even as she fell.

Valeria rolled from the altar on the other side, and started for the opposite wall on all fours. For hell had burst loose in the throne room of dead Olmec.

The man who had held Valeria's hands was the next to die. He turned to run, but before he had taken half a dozen steps, Tolkemec, with an agility appalling in such a frame, bounded around to a position that placed the man between him and the altar. Again the red fire-beam flashed and the Tecuhltli rolled lifeless to the floor, as the beam completed its course with a burst of blue sparks against the altar.

Then began slaughter. Screaming insanely the people rushed about the chamber, caroming from one another, stumbling and falling. And among them Tolkemec capered and pranced, dealing death. They could not escape by the doors; for apparently the metal of the portals served like the metal-veined stone altar to complete the circuit for whatever hellish power flashed like thunderbolts from the witch-wand the ancient waved in his hand. When he caught a man or a woman between him and a door or the altar, that one died instantly. He chose no special victim. He took them as they came, with his rags flapping about his wildly gyrating limbs, and the gusty echoes of his tittering sweeping the room above the screams. And bodies fell like falling leaves about the altar and at the doors. One warrior in desperation rushed at him, lifting a dagger, only to fall before he could strike. But the rest were like crazed cattle, with no thought for resistance, and no chance of escape.

The last Tecuhltli except Tascela had fallen when the princess reached the Cimmerian and the girl who had taken refuge beside him. Tascela bent and touched the floor, pressing a design upon it. Instantly the iron jaws released the bleeding limb and sank back into the floor.

"Slay him if you can!" she panted, and pressed a heavy knife into his hand. "I have no magic to withstand him!"

With a grunt he sprang before the women, not heeding his lacerated leg in the heat of the fighting lust. Tolkemec was coming toward him, his weird eyes ablaze, but he hesitated at the gleam of the knife in Conan's hand. Then began a grim game, as Tolkemec sought to circle about Conan and get the barbarian between him and the altar or a metal door, while Conan sought to avoid this and drive home his knife. The women watched tensely, holding their breath.

There was no sound except the rustle and scrape of quick-shifting feet. Tolkemec pranced and capered no more. He realized that grimmer game confronted him than the people who had died screaming and fleeing. In the elemental blaze of the barbarian's eyes he read an intent deadly as his own. Back and forth they weaved, and when one moved the other moved as if invisible threads bound them together. But all the time Conan was getting closer and closer to his enemy. Already the coiled muscles of his thighs were beginning to flex for a spring, when Valeria cried out. For a fleeting instant a bronze door was in line with Conan's moving body. The red line leaped, searing Conan's flank as he twisted aside, and even as he shifted he hurled the knife. Old Tolkemec went down, truly slain at last, the hilt vibrating on his breast.

Tascela sprang—not toward Conan, but toward the wand where it shimmered like a live thing on the floor. But as she leaped, so did Valeria, with a dagger snatched from a dead man; and the blade, driven with all the power of the pirate's muscles, impaled the princess of Tecuhltli so that the point stood out between her breasts. Tascela screamed once and fell dead, and Valeria spurned the body with her heel as it fell.

"I had to do that much, for my own self-respect!" panted Valeria, facing Conan across the limp corpse.

"Well, this cleans up the feud," he grunted. "It's been a hell of a night! Where did these people keep their food? I'm hungry."

"You need a bandage on that leg." Valeria ripped a length of silk from a hanging and knotted it about her waist, then tore off some smaller strips which she bound efficiently about the barbarian's lacerated limb.

"I can walk on it," he assured her. "Let's begone. It's dawn, outside this infernal city. I've had enough of Xuchotl. It's well the breed exterminated itself. I don't want any of their accursed jewels. They might be haunted."

"There is enough clean loot in the world for you and me," she said, straightening to stand tall and splendid before him.

The old blaze came back in his eyes, and this time she did not resist as he caught her fiercely in his arms.

"It's a long way to the coast," she said presently, withdrawing her lips from his.

"What matter?" he laughed. "There's nothing we can't conquer. We'll have our feet on a ship's deck before the Stygians open their ports for the trading season. And then we'll show the world what plundering means!"

JOHN JAKES
Storm in a Bottle

1

THE TRAIN of seven two-wheeled carts creaked around another corner, and the big, yellow-haired barbarian still standing stubbornly upright in the fourth vehicle let out a growl of surprise.

His scarred hands reached automatically for the cart's side-rail, closed. Veins stood out; a long, clotted sword wound down his left forearm began to ooze scarlet again.

One of the small, pelt-clad men crowded into the same cart grumbled when the bigger man accidentally stepped on his foot. In response, the barbarian moved his wrists closer together. The hateful chain-links hanging between iron wrist-cuffs momentarily formed a sort of noose. The barbarian's eyes left no doubt about whose neck the iron noose would fit.

The little, foul-smelling complainer glanced away, looking for sympathy from his companions in the creaking vehicle. The barbarian paid no more attention. Standing tall, he was the only prisoner in all seven carts who did not wear scabrous-looking fur clothing, and whose body was not matted with dark, wiry hair.

For a moment the barbarian forgot his seething rage at being captured, subdued, chained out on the arid plateau two days ago. He was diverted by the sight revealed when the caravan rounded the corner, passing from stifling shadow to the full glare of the sun.

The big man saw a broad avenue, imposingly paved, heat-hazed. The avenue stretched into the distance past shops, public marts, fountained cul-de-sacs where no water ran. At the avenue's far end rose massive buildings of yellow stone, larger and higher than any other structures in the walled city.

The barbarian took note of artfully-sculpted idols lining both sides

of the avenue at one-square intervals. All the statues were identical; all
were of the same transparent crystal. The image was that of a seated
human figure with the head of a long-snouted animal. The creature's
open jaws held a thin disc. From the ferocity of the expression, it was
clear that the half-beast was about to crunch the disc between its fangs.
The image was repeated endlessly, pedestal after crystal-topped pedestal, up the sweltering avenue beneath the cloudless noon sky.

Soldiers of the lord to whose slaving party Brak the barbarian had
fallen prey jogged their mounts along the line of seven carts, occasionally cracking short whips. But listlessly. Their dust-covered faces and
dust-dulled armor were evidence of the long trek in across the waste-
land with the prisoners. On the left wrist of each soldier, from the
mounted leader and his subcommanders to the two dozen accompanying foot, a simple bronze bracelet shot off red-gold glints.

Men and women of the city watched the little caravan from positions
beneath awnings and on balconies. Some of the watchers wore elegant
robes, others more common cloth.

A boy with one leg missing hobbled forward on a crutch and lobbed
a stone at the cart in which Brak rode. The big barbarian stiffened, then
realized the stone was not for him, but for the pack of bent, sullen-eyed
little men crouched at his calves like stunted trees surrounding one that
had grown straight.

The rock struck a man near Brak. He yelped, jumped up, began to
clash his chain and screech at the watchers. His guttural speech was
incomprehensible, but not his fury.

Instantly, three mounted officers converged on the cart, began to arc
their whips onto the backs of the prisoners. The little men cringed and
shrieked. The tip of one lash flicked Brak's face. With a deep-chested
yell, he caught the whip's end and yanked, all his humiliation and
self-disgust surfacing as he hauled the surprised officer out of his saddle.

The officer swore, scrabbling in the street on hands and knees. He
struggled to free his short-sword. But his fellow officers repaid the
barbarian's outburst for him. They pressed their mounts in closer to the
cart, whose driver had brought it to an abrupt halt and leaped down
out of range of Brak's flailing chains. In a moment, the stifling air
resounded with the methodical cracking of whips.

Brak made abortive grabs at one or two. Futile. He closed his eyes
and gripped the cart rail, trying not to shudder at each new welt laid
atop the others criss-crossing his back. He would show them he was not
like these dog-men whimpering at his feet. Above all, he would not cry
out.

And somehow, he would escape the accursed chains dangling between his wrists like the weight of the world—

"Enough."

The voice Brak had heard before sliced through the cracking of the whips, and another sound—the murmurings of the city people as they surged forward to stare at the strange, savage figure of the hulk-shouldered man who wore a lion-hide around his middle and his hair in a long yellow braid down his back.

Brak took another lash as the commander shouted again, *"Enough!"*

The whips laid off. Brak opened his eyes to stare into the thin, leather-cheeked face of the young and dusty veteran to whom he had been presented—beaten to his knees—after his capture.

The commander sidled his mount nearer, shook his head wearily:

"You will cast your life away, then? I told you there was a chance for you, outlander—"

"A chance to wear your chains," Brak said, and spat.

The spittle struck the commander's breastplate, barely dampening the yellow dust. The commander straightened in his saddle, fingers closing tighter around the butt of his whip.

Then, as if from weariness, or fear, or both, he slumped, letting the insult pass.

"You have the strength to keep fighting back but I haven't the strength to keep fighting you," the commander sighed. "We'll let someone else drub you into line. Just be thankful you're not like the rest of the filth we caught. Then you wouldn't even have the opportunity of manful service. You'd be put three floors underground, turning the grind-wheels for the rest of your life."

"I have no part of this fight between you and your lice-ridden enemies!" Brak snarled, gesturing at the glare-eyed little men crouched around him. His chains clinked. "I was a traveler harming no one. I was set upon—!"

The commander shrugged. "We've gone over it before. I'll not debate. While the foes of Lord Magnus yap around his heels—" cruelly, he kicked one of the little men through the uprights of the cart side, "—our fighting companies need every recruit." He held up his left arm. The bronze bracelet flashed. "I've explained your choice. Wear one of these—or a grave-cloth."

He cracked his whip, shouting to the head of the caravan:

"Move on, damn you! We've had fourteen days of this sun!"

"And so have we, and more!" a woman cried from the crowd. "If the

Children of the Smoke can't bring the Worldbreaker down with spears,
they'll bring him down with magic."

The commander glanced down at the crone. "No rain, then?"

"Does it look like we've been cleansed with rain? Refreshed?" someone else yelled. "The Children of the Smoke have bewitched the sky!"

"*Ah!*" The commander gestured angrily. "They have no wizards—"

"Then why does the plain of Magnus burn?" another voice jeered.
"Why do the reservoirs go dry? Tell us that, captain!"

Others joined the clamor. Brak thought a riot might erupt on the
spot. Nearly a hundred people started shoving and jostling the cart. But
the soldiers drove them back with cuts of their whips and jabs of their
short-swords.

Wearily, Brak reflected that it all had the quality of a nightmare. The
heat haze blurred everything, including the snowy ramparts of the
Mountains of Smoke far eastward. Those mountains supposedly guarded the approaches to the world's rim, and hid the homes of whatever
gods ruled these so-called civilized lands.

During the sweltering ride across the plateau to the city, Brak had
seen once-fertile fields that were parched, their crops stunted. He had
listened to grumbling conversations of the soldiers in the heat of
evening and learned that his fellow prisoners, all sharp teeth and matted
hair and hateful eyes, belonged to a large nomadic tribe from the
foothills of those distant mountains. Every few years, the tribe tried to
gain more lands belonging to the lord who ruled the plateau. It had been
Brak's misfortune to be captured and cast among the enemy while he
was continuing his long journey southward to golden Khurdisan, where
he was bound to seek his fortune—

Some inquisitive soul in the crowd pointed at Brak. "Who is he?
Where's he from?"

"He says the wild steppes of the north," a soldier answered.

"Kill him—his presence is another bad omen!" the cry rang back.

"No worse than no rain for a three-month," snarled the soldier,
riding on.

The cart driver resumed his place and the caravan again moved down
the dusty avenue between the crystal images of the man-beast with the
disc in its mouth. Brak mastered his fury as best he could, though the
new and old whip-wounds, a webwork on his muscled back, made it
difficult. So did the scowls of the soldiers, the taunts of the crowd—

The soldiers had slain his pony in the capture. Broken his broadsword. And chained him. Again he looked yearningly east, toward the
cool blue spires rising above the rooftops and the city wall. The Moun-

tains of Smoke, white-crowned. Beyond that barrier, he'd been told, lay down-sloping passes that led into the south—

But he would never see them unless he escaped his chains. Kept his temper—and his life.

He clenched his upper teeth on his lower lip, tasting his own briny sweat, and squinted into the hellish glare of noonday, and saw certain curious things he had not seen before.

2

MOST OF the citizens abroad in this obviously prosperous city looked wan, frightened. Brak noted another curiosity as the cart rolled past one of the crystal statues. The disc in the mouth of the beast-headed figure had a horizontal crack across its center. He thought this a flaw until he perceived that the discs of several more statues were similarly designed.

He signaled a soldier. The man rode in, but not too close. Brak asked: "Why is the round thing in the statute's mouth shown broken?"

"Because that is the god-image of Lord Magnus, idiot. Once he held all of creation in his possession—to break or preserve as he saw fit. Now he's an old man. And his wizard, Ool, has no spells against whatever damned magic is being worked on this land."

Brak wiped his sweat-running neck. "You mean no rain."

The soldier nodded. "Without it, the reservoirs go empty. The crops perish. It's never happened before. Not in a hundred years, or a hundred again. This was a green and pleasant land before the parching of the skies."

Brak jerked a hand to indicate the bent, hairy heads around his knees. "And the sorcerers of your enemies worked the enchantment?"

"They have no sorcerers!" the soldier rasped back. "Nothing but old medicine women who birth babies."

Or they had no sorcerers until now, Brak thought. But he kept the retort to himself—because the more closely he looked, the more clearly he could discern the tiredness and terror lurking in the eyes of military man and civilian alike.

Once more he stared down at his chained wrists while the carts lurched nearer the jumble of yellow buildings at the avenue's end. He understood one more thing now. In addition to a tribe of enemies and a magical blight that was decimating city and countryside alike, the kingdom was also burdened with a lord who thought mightily of himself. Enough, anyway, to build endless replicas of a savage image of himself, and plant in its jaws a representation of the World—

That was what it looked like, eh? Brak had never seen it depicted before.

All the emerging circumstances only heightened his determination to escape. But he would take his time, be cunning and careful—

If he survived this particular ride. He didn't care for the expressions of the men and women lining the avenue. They continued to murmur and point at him. He was an omen, and not a favorable one—

Under those hostile glares, a total weariness descended on him suddenly. Maybe this *was* the end after all. Maybe he was fated to die chained and helpless in a country whose strutting lord appeared close to defeat. Worldbreaker indeed! In all the land he'd traversed thus far, Brak had never heard the name.

Another jarring memory reinforced his new pessimism. What about the toll he had exacted for his capture? How would they settle with him for that?

Head lowered, he was staring at the dusty paving-stones rolling by when the shadow of the horse of an attending soldier suddenly vanished.

Shrieks, oaths from both sides of the avenue—

Sudden chittering barks of pleasure from the little prisoners in the carts—

And Brak jerked his head up to gasp while horror shivered his sweaty spine.

In the center of the sky, the sun was disappearing.

A smear of gray widened, dulling the light. Tendrils of the strange cloud reached toward all points on the horizon at once—and what had been noon became stifling twilight almost instantly.

The cart horses reacted to the uproar, neighed, pawed the air. One driver jumped down and fled into an alley, not looking back—

There was no wind, no roar of storm. Only that awesome gray cloud spreading and spreading from the apex of heaven. The commotion along the boulevard turned to hysterical tumult.

Darkening, the cloud seemed to race past the city's walls toward the mountains and the wasted plain in the other direction. A young woman fell to her knees, rent the garments over her breasts, shrieked—

Brak whirled. On his left, he saw a chilling sight: the gigantic statue of the lord with creation in his mouth began to fill with some dark red substance, translucent, *like blood*—

And the redness was rising in every statue along the avenue.

Kicking his horse, the harried young commander raced up and down the line, lashing his whip to keep the crowd back:

"There's no danger. No danger! It's only another of the enemy's magical apparitions—"

But the crystal images kept darkening, like the sky. The red climbed from the waist toward the head. Noon turned to night. All around Brak, the Children of the Smoke still barked and chittered—though many of them now looked fully as frightened as the citizens of the city.

The whipping and the oaths of the soldiers proved futile. The maddened crowds began to surge forward again. Suddenly Brak realized their objective. Another accusing hand pointed his way:

"You brought a polluted pagan through the gates. *That's the reason for all this—!*"

"Stand back, he's a military prisoner!" the commander yelled, just before being buffetted from his horse. The mob surged around the cart, all hateful eyes, clawing hands. Brak felt the left wheel lift.

The Children of the Smoke began to gibber and slaver as the cart tilted. Brak knew what would happen. Tumbled into that mob, he'd be torn apart—

As the cart tilted even more sharply, he jumped wide, heedless of where he landed. Both feet came down on a fat man's shoulder. As Brak continued his fall, hands tore at him. But his weight crashed him through to the pavement.

For a moment he was ringed by dirty feet, the hems of dusty robes. Then he glanced up from hands and knees and saw a ring of almost insane faces. Old, young, male, female—and above them, a sky turned nearly to ebony—

Peripherally, he saw one of the crystal statues. By now it was red to the tips of the beast-head's ears.

"Sacrifice the pagan to drive out the darkness!" a man screamed, lunging.

Brak had no weapon save the length of chain hanging between his hands. He fought to his feet, pressed his wrists together, began to swing them in a circle, whipping them around, faster and faster. The chain opened a man's cheek. Blood gushed. A knife raked Brak's shoulder. He darted away, keeping the chain swinging.

Another man ventured too close. The end of the chain pulped one eyeball. The man dropped, howling—

And then, it seemed, the splendid boulevard of Lord Magnus the Worldbreaker became utter bedlam.

The mob poured at Brak from all directions, a blur of distorted faces, yapping mouths, glazed eyes that promised murder. So this was to be the end, was it? Dying a victim of some accursed magic in which he had no hand, but for which he was being blamed and punished—

The crystal statues had filled completely, scarlet from pedestal to snout-tip. Even the cracked discs of creation were suffused with the evil-looking red. The arch of heaven was dark gray from end to end. Brak abandoned all his former resolve to preserve his life so that he might escape. Now he only wanted to sell his life expensively. If these deranged fools would kill him, they would not do so easily—

Whir and *crack,* the chain whirled. A forearm snapped; a scalp dripped gore. Brak kicked, snarled, spat, worked the chain until he could barely see, so thick was the sweat clogging on his eyelids. Although the sky had blackened, the air had not cooled. He fought in some dim, steaming inferno—

A hand grabbed his ankle. He stamped down, hard. His attacker shrieked, held up ruined, boneless fingers. Whir and *crack,* the chain sliced the air—and suddenly his tormenters began to retreat from his savage figure: from the whip of his long yellow braid; from the flying fur-puff at the end of the lion's tail at his waist; from that brain-spattered chain swinging, *scything*—

A way opened. He lunged through full speed, crashing into one of the statue pedestals. Behind him, the crowd bayed its anger. The crowd was growing larger as more and more citizens poured in from intersecting avenues. In a moment, backed against the pedestal, Brak was surrounded.

He whirled, leaped high, started to clamber upward, his thighs bloody from the nail-marks of hands that clawed him. He gained the top of the pedestal, teetered there, feeling the cool of the crystal against his back. To gain momentum for flailing the chain down at the enraged faces and the hands straining to reach him, he whipped the iron links back over his left shoulder—

The chain smashed against the statue. A prolonged glassy crackling modulated into a sudden loud thunderclap. Light smote Brak's eyes, blinding.

Noon light—

The illusion-cloud in the heavens was gone. Below him, terrorized people dropped to their knees, shielded their eyes—

The chain clinked down across Brak's shoulder. Panting, he curled his toes around the pedestal's edge and squinted across the avenue. There, another statue of Lord Magnus the Worldbreaker was crystal-bright, empty of scarlet.

So was every similar image along the avenue.

"You cursed fools—!" Flaying about with his whip, the commander, on horseback again, rode through the mob. "We tried to tell you it was only a wizard's illusion!"

"From where?" someone screamed.

"From the enemy who will conquer!" another cried.

"And *he* dispelled it," the commander said, reining up just below an exhausted Brak leaning against the image. The commander had a puzzling, almost sad expression on his face. "The chain's blow did it—"

The officer gestured with his whip. Brak craned his buzzing head around, saw a crystalline webbing of cracks running through the bent left knee of the seated figure. Again he felt the clutch of inexplicable dread. The darkness and the rising red had indeed been potent mind-spells. No scarlet ran out from the statue. It was solid.

The commander's smile was feeble. "The end of a short and glorious career," he said. "Now you must be taken to Lord Magnus himself. For the one crime of killing three of my men when you were captured—and the greater crime of profaning an image of the lord."

"*Profaning—!*" Brak screamed, gripping the statute to keep from falling. "The chain broke the statue and the spell and that's an *offense?*"

"Regrettably so. I have no choice but to present you to Lord Magnus for sentence of execution."

In the hot noon silence, while the kneeling, cringing throng peered at Brak through fingers or across the uplifted sleeves of robes, the commander looked sick at heart. For a moment his eyes locked with Brak's, as if begging understanding. Brak was too full of rage. He twisted his head around and spat on the webwork of the smashed crystal. He was done; he knew it. The defilement of the idol brought pleasure.

With another, somehow-sad gesture, the commander raised his whip to signal his stunned men forming up on the rim of the terrorized mob. He pointed to Brak and said:

"Drag him down."

3

In the largest of the immense buildings he'd glimpsed from afar, Brak the barbarian was conducted into an echoing hall and thrust to his knees by the tense commander. The vast, high-windowed chamber was an inferno of early afternoon shadows. The air was oppressive. Brak had great difficulty breathing.

On the journey to the great complex of yellow stone, Brak had several times entertained the idea of trying to break free. But each time, he'd decided to wait. Partly out of self-interest; partly from a sort of morbid curiosity. Before his life was taken away, he wanted to set eyes on this lord who styled himself Worldbreaker.

And there was always a faint, formless hope that if he were clever enough—though in what way, he couldn't yet say—he might save himself. The prospect made it seem sensible for him to check his impulse to fight and run.

"You may raise your head to the lord," whispered the decidedly nervous commander who stood next to the kneeling barbarian. Brak obeyed.

All he saw at first was a step. Then another; and eight more, each revealed as his gaze traveled up to a throne that had once been splendid, but was now all green-tinged bronze.

The lower portion of the throne was a massive chair. Its high, solid back rose upward and jutted out over the throne-seat to form the gigantic head and snout of the lord's image, complete with cracked disc in its jaws. In the shelter of this canopy sat the Worldbreaker.

A small, thick-chested man. So short his plain, worn soldier's boots barely touched the floor. He wore a military kilt and the familiar bronze bracelet of the army on his left wrist. He looked more like a member of the foot troops than he did a king.

He had a squarish, strong-featured face, much lined. Pure white hair hung to his shoulders. Prepared to be contemptuous, Brak found it hard somehow. The ruler did not adorn himself ostentatiously, though perhaps only because of the heat, which was causing the three or four dozen court officials and military men surrounding the throne's base to shift from foot to foot, mop their sweated cheeks with kerchiefs and sigh frequently.

Two things about Lord Magnus the Worldbreaker impressed Brak deeply—and alarmed him as well. One was the man's grave, pitiless stare. The other was his body. Calves and thighs, forearms and shoulders and trunk were a war-map of the past. Mountain ranges and valleys of scar tissue created a whole geography of battle on the flesh of the ruler. He was, Brak sensed, no commander who had sent his armies ahead to fight. He had led them.

"You may address the lord," said a man who glided into sight from the gloom at one side of the great throne.

"Thanks be to you, oh sexless one," returned the commander, genuflecting. Brak peered at this new personage who had taken a place at the lord's right hand.

The newcomer was a tall, heavily robed man of middle years. He looked overweight. He had an oval, curiously hairless head, opaque eyes, flesh as white as the belly of a new-caught fish. Under the man's basilisk stare, Brak shivered.

The commander spoke to the ruler on the throne:

"With great Ool's leave given, Lord Magnus, I beg to report a most unfortunate occurrence on the avenue—"

Ool, Brak thought. *So this gelded creature is the ruler's wizard?* An odd specimen indeed. While the others in the chamber were obviously suffering from the heat, Ool's pasty white jowls and ivory forehead remained dry. His hands were completely hidden within the voluminous linen of his crossed sleeves.

Lord Magnus gave a tired nod:

"I saw, Captain Xeraph. From the watch-roof I saw the dark heavens and the red-running idols. A footman brought word of the desecration of one of them." The little man's gaze hardened, raking Brak up and down. "This is the pagan slave who worked the damage?"

Suddenly Brak was on his feet. "No, lord. I'm no man's slave. I was set on by your human carrion, caught and trussed up with these—" He rattled his iron chainlinks.

Ool whispered, "Be silent, barbarian, or you will be slain where you stand."

"I'll be damned before I'll be silent!" Brak yelled.

The hairless wizard inclined his pale head. Three spearmen started clattering down the throne steps, weapons pointed at Brak's chest. The barbarian braced for the attack.

"Hold."

The single, powerful syllable from Lord Magnus checked the spearmen's descent. They swung, looked upward for further instructions. Ool nodded acquiescence, but unhappily; he nibbled at his underlip and treated Brak to a baleful glare.

"You have a ready tongue for a captive," said Lord Magnus in a toneless voice that might have been threatening, or might not. Brak could not tell; nor read that old, scarred countenance. "And you have no knowledge, evidently, that my image is sacred?"

"But shattering it shattered the spell," Brak retorted, glancing pointedly at the pasty-jowled Ool. The man remained impassive. Brak finished, "No one else seemed able to do that."

"Aye, the darkness rolled back," Magnus agreed. "The darkness which cannot be—" his mouth wrenched, a quick, sour imitation of a smile, "—since our mortal enemies have no enchanters to work such spells. None at all! Therefore we cannot be plagued. What happened is impossible—*everything* is impossible!" he shouted, slamming a horn-hard palm on the throne's curved arm.

At that moment Brak sensed just how much rage must be seething under that gnarled old exterior. It was a rage like his own. Although Brak did not care for this lord and never would, he did not precisely hate him, either. It was a puzzling circumstance he did not fully understand.

Lord Magnus went on, "The Children cannot work wizardries against us, therefore all I see is a deception. The water-channels dry and silted—a deception. The people maddened and near to revolt—deception. The noon heavens like midnight—and a chain that breaks the illusion—no, none of it's real. Perhaps not even you, eh, outlander?"

Brak rattled his chains, "Take these off and I'll show you my hands are real. You'll see how real when they close on the throats of your jackals."

The commander, Captain Xeraph, gulped audibly. Gasps and oaths rippled through the crowd clustered near the throne. Swords snicked out of scabbards. Abruptly, Lord Magnus laughed.

The sound was quick, harsh—and stunned everyone, including the big barbarian. With effort, he stared the ruler down. Neither man blinked.

"You seem determined to die quickly," Lord Magnus said.

"It appears I have no choice in the matter, lord." Mocking: "I violated your holy image—"

"And," put in the hairless Ool, his calm tone belying the animosity Brak saw in his eyes, "if our intelligence may be trusted, slew three of Captain Xeraph's best when they took you prisoner."

"Aye," Brak nodded. "Because they had no reason to seize me."

"The fact that you crossed my boundary-marker is reason enough," Lord Magnus advised.

"To you, lord. To a traveler bound to Khurdisan—no."

Magnus lifted one scar-crusted hand, scratched his sweaty chin where a beard stubble already showed white after the day's razoring. "Cease your glowering and grimacing, kindly! Don't you wonder why you're not dead by now? You apparently fail to recognize a chance to survive when it's presented to you."

In the little man's dark eyes, Brak saw nothing he could comprehend. A plot was weaving. But what kind of plot, he could not tell. Still, something in him seized at the half-offered promise. He felt hope for the first time.

The ghoul-white face of Ool the sexless looked stark. *Careful,* Brak thought. *Do not appear over-eager—*

He licked his sweaty lips, said:

"I do not understand the lord's meaning, that's true. But I understand little or nothing of what has befallen me. I tell you again—there was no reason for me to be imprisoned. Or brought to your city in bondage."

"You deny that a man can be slain for killing three soldiers of a land through which he travels?" Magnus asked.

"I was attacked!"

"You deny a man can be punished for desecrating the sacred law of such a land?"

"I never broke your image on purpose. Only accidentally, while trying to save myself from the mob."

"And you broke the darkness too," Magnus mused. Suddenly a finger stabbed out, pointing down. Brak saw that the finger was a toughened stub at the end; lopped off at the first knuckle long ago.

"What is your name, outlander? Where did you journey from? Most important—how did you come by the power that broke the darkness?"

The big barbarian answered, "Lord, I'm called Brak. My home was once the northern steppes. My people cast me out for mocking their gods—"

"Ah, you make a habit of that!" said Magnus, the corners of his mouth twisting again.

"When the rules of such gods defy a man's own good sense, yes. I am bound south for Khurdisan—or I was," he added with a smoldering glance at the uncomfortable Captain Xeraph. "As to why and how I was able to rend the darkness in the sky—" *Careful!* He spaced the next words with deliberate slowness. "—I ask leave not to say."

Ool chuckled, a dry, reedy sound. "In other words, you confirm that you have no real powers."

Staring fiercely at the wizard, Brak replied, "I neither confirm it nor deny it, magician. After I am dead you may make up your own mind."

Again Magnus laughed. He studied Brak closely, said at last:

"But perhaps—as I hinted—there is another way. For the first time, I am besieged by forces against which my host and my chariots will not avail. You are a bold man, barbarian. Strong-looking to boot. You *seem* to have thaumaturgic skills—whether by training or by accident, you don't care to reveal. Very well—"

Magnus stood. Brak realized just how short the old man really was. But his ridged shoulders and scarmarked belly looked tough as iron.

"You cannot guess the extremes to which we have gone to overcome this plague of dryness. A plague that can destroy this kingdom as the pitiful clubs and daggers of the Children of the Smoke never could before. So despite your crimes, my rude friend—and because you staved off carnage in the streets—I will strike you a bargain."

Cold and shrewd, the eyes of the Worldbreaker pierced down from the sweaty gloom around the throne.

"You will not die. You will not wear chains—"

Brak's heart almost burst at the sudden, unexpected reprieve; then he heard the jarring conclusion:

"If you can bring down the rain."

"Bring down the—?"

He wanted to laugh. He couldn't. He was too appalled by the sudden snapping of the trap.

"Open the heavens!" Magnus exclaimed, his voice genuinely power-ful now. "Darken the skies—but this time, so they flood the land with downpour. Unbind the spell of the Children of the Smoke—whatever it is, and from wherever it comes—and you'll neither die nor wear chains again. That is my concession and my promise, Brak barbarian. Whether you have true or only chance powers, we shall now discover. I warn you, none has succeeded so far in undoing the plague spell. My own wizard is helpless—" A lifted hand made Ool bristle; more softly, Magnus went on, "Though not through any lack of daily effort and industry, I must hasten to add. Now—"

He directed his gaze at the astounded young commander.

"While we test the barbarian, Captain Xeraph, you shall be his guardian and constant companion. Let him not out of your sight for a moment, or your own life is forfeit."

The commander went white. Brak started to protest that he had been lured into a hopeless snare, but Magnus gestured:

"I have already given you a great concession. Keep silent and ask for nothing more."

He turned his back, starting to leave by circling the throne. After a quick glance down the stairs at Brak, the eunuch Ool plucked his lord's forearm. Annoyed, Magnus stopped.

Ool leaned in, whispered. Magnus pondered. Then he wheeled around, said to Brak:

"One further condition—and a wise one, I think. You have two days and two nights to make it rain, no more."

Again Brak sensed the old fighter's desperation; glimpsed it in his eyes just before the Worldbreaker vanished behind the throne, Ool gliding after him, a white specter—

Leaving Brak to reflect dismally that he would have been better off to have been killed outright.

4

"BALLS OF the gods, will you pick a piece and move it?" shouted Captain Xeraph, jumping up. He stalked through the arch to the little balcony overlooking the city and, a floor below, a courtyard shared by four barracks buildings.

Perched on a stool much too small for his bulk, Brak looked with bleary eyes at the out-of-humor officer pacing back and forth just beyond the arch. Xeraph was stripped down to his kilt. Both occupants of the tiny officer's apartment in the yellow stone complex were sticky with perspiration, even though the sun had simmered out of sight hours ago. But another light limned the officer's profile as he leaned on the balcony rail and gazed at the night city.

The rooftops were outlined by red glares from half a dozen locations. The roaring of mobs and the crashes of mass destruction carried through the still air. Xeraph's right hand strayed absently to the bracelet on his left wrist as he stared at the fires with something akin to longing.

The captain's apartment consisted of two narrow rooms. Both rooms were sparsely furnished. But the addition of a pallet for Xeraph's semiprisoner badly cramped the main room. The master of the quarters swung suddenly, glaring—another challenge for Brak to get on with his move.

The huge yellow-haired man picked up the tail of his lion-clout, used it to wipe sweat from his nose, then draped it over one muscled thigh so it hung between his legs. He reached down for the wine jar beside his bare feet.

He tilted the jug, drank deeply of the dry red wine, heedless of the way it dripped down his chin onto his massive chest. Putting the jar aside again, he peered fuzzily at the playing board set on a low block of stone.

The board featured a pattern of squares in two colors. On the squares sat oddly-carved wood pieces of different designs. Half the pieces were lacquered dark green. The others had been left unfinished.

For two hours, Captain Xeraph had been trying to teach him the confusing game. Eating little and drinking much after the disastrous interview with Magnus earlier in the day, Brak had no head for it. Even sober, he had decided, he probably couldn't comprehend it.

But Xeraph was so obviously upset by his enforced confinement with a prisoner that Brak made one more effort. He picked up one of his pieces, the one named—let's see, could he remember?—the fortress.

Xeraph watched him slide the piece to the adjoining square. With a curse, the captain stormed back into the room, snatched up the piece and shook it in Brak's face:

"This is the wizard, you idiot! The wizard cannot move in that pattern. I must have explained it ten times!"

Brak's temper let go. Growling, he lifted a corner of the playing board. Several pieces fell off. With a sweep of his thick arm, he scattered the rest, then flung the board on the floor.

"Take your playthings and throw 'em in the pit!" Brak shouted, his eyes ugly. The hateful chains clinked between his wrists.

For a moment he thought Captain Xeraph would grab his short-sword from the scabbard hanging on a wall peg. Xeraph's neck muscles bunched. But he managed control. He sighed a long, disgusted sigh:

"I shouldn't expect some unlettered foreigner to master a game played by civilized gentlemen. But gods! I'm already sick of tending you—!"

"I didn't ask to be penned up here!" Brak screamed back, and again it seemed as if the two would go for each other's throat. Then, sighing again, Xeraph slumped, as if the heat, the effort of argumentation, were too much.

He sprawled on Brak's pallet while the latter stood glowering and fingering the chain.

"Well, one night's almost done," Xeraph said in a gloomy tone. "One more, and two days, and Magnus will take your head." His eyes sought Brak's. He almost sounded sorrowful: "You have no spells to bring rain, do you?"

Brak's answer was a terse, "Of course not. Why the darkness lifted when I smashed the idol, I don't know. Your lord's a desperate man—he admitted it himself. I have seen men in similar predicaments grow rash and foolish. That's what happened when your lord offered me that ridiculous bargain for my life."

Xeraph clucked his tongue. "The lord's too old—that's what they're all saying. Believe me, Magnus has no lack of courage—"

"His scars prove that."

"—but for once, the odds are too overwhelming. He can't cope with the magic with which the Children have cursed us."

"Nor, apparently, can his own wizard, despite those efforts to which Magnus referred. How does the eunuch try to bring down rain and end the drought?"

The officer shrugged. "To watch Ool do whatever he does—mix potions, wail at the sky—is forbidden to all but a few young boys who attend him. They are specially selected and, I might add, perverted." Xeraph's mouth quirked in distaste. "Every day, Ool rides out in his chariot, that much I know. He goes toward the channel that once brought sweet rainwater from the lower slopes of the Mountains of Smoke." Xeraph gestured eastward. "Somewhere out there, Ool tries to undo the curse—in secret." The captain concluded sarcastically, "Like to discover some of his methods, would you?"

"They sound worthless. On the other hand, since I have no powers of my own, I've thought of the idea. I don't intend to spend the rest of the allotted time pacing this room and drinking myself into oblivion."

That amused Xeraph. "Oh, you think you can improve upon Ool's performance, do you? Acquire magical skills like that?" He snapped his fingers.

Brak scowled. "I doubt it. But there must be an answer somewhere. And if it lies in magic, what better place to begin the search than with Ool?"

"You don't give up easily," Xeraph said, not without admiration. Brak simply stared at the litter of game pieces scattered around his thoroughly dirty feet. Xeraph harrumphed. "Brak, there is no answer! Except this. The rain won't come. And you'll die. Then the rest of us. This time—" Restless, he rose and wandered back to the balcony.

"—this time I think the Worldbreaker himself will be broken. And all of his kingdom in the bargain."

Suddenly Xeraph's voice grew louder: "They're already going mad! Drinking, rioting, setting fires—"

"And you feel you should be out there helping to quell it."

Xeraph spun. "Yes! That duty, I understand. This—" His gesture swept the lamplit chamber resentfully. "It's fool's work."

Speaking out of genuine feeling, Brak said, "Captain, I am sorry the lot fell to you."

"No apologies," Xeraph cut him off. "I obey orders. It's a bad twist of fate's twine, that's all. We've had nothing else for months—why should I expect a change?"

Once more the young officer leaned on the railing, staring in dismay at the sullen scarlet silhouettes of the city's rooftops. His eyes picked up red reflections, simmered with frustration. Hopelessness.

Brak resumed his place on the stool. He picked up a wooden piece which, if his wine-buzzing head served him, represented a male ruler. He asked:

"Has Lord Magnus no trusted advisers to help point the way out of this difficult situation? No generals—?"

"He is the general," Xeraph returned. "He is the government, the chief judge—everything. Before, his shoulders have always been strong enough, his mind quick enough—"

The statement somehow fitted with Brak's appraisal of the tough little warrior. The barbarian studied the piece in his sweat-glistening palm a moment longer.

"The lord hasn't even a wife to counsel him?" he wanted to know.

"He did, many years ago—why go into all this?" Xeraph said irritably.

"I don't know," Brak admitted. "Except that I don't want to be killed."

Xeraph managed an exhausted smile. "That, at least, is something we have in common."

"We were talking of Magnus. He has no sons—?"

Xeraph shook his head. "No issue at all." Briefly, then, he narrated the story of Magnus's consort, a queen whose name he could not even recall because she had died forty years earlier, well before Xeraph himself had been born. But legend said the lord's wife had been exceedingly lovely and desirable.

Lord Magnus had been away on a campaign to harry the Children of the Smoke, who were making one of their abortive advances into his territory. A soldier in the small detachment left behind to garrison the city—"Name unknown, identity unknown," Xeraph commented—entered the apartment of the lord's wife by stealth one night. Presumably drunk, he raped her.

"The lady cried out and the terrified fool cut her throat. There was a great melee in the darkness. The soldier was pursued. Another captain who died only a six-month ago was on duty in the palace at the time, and swore he caught the offender for a moment. Claimed he ran him through with a spear. But the man ultimately escaped in the confusion —to perish of his wound in some back alley, presumably. His corpse was never found. And as I say, his name remains unknown to this day. Magnus was so exercised with grief, he could never take another woman to his side, except for serving girls for single nights of pleasure. Even that stopped five or six years ago," Xeraph finished unhappily.

Brak set the lord-piece aside in favor of the piece he had moved wrongly before: the wizard.

"And this court magician—do you think he serves the Worldbreaker well?"

Xeraph shrugged. "If not well, then faithfully and diligently, at least. You heard the lord say as much. Ool was a wandering shaman, I'm told. He came to court a long time ago, and stayed. Until now, he's always seemed proficient in minor spells and holy rituals. But this particular curse has proved too large for his powers—as it has for the lord's. And so we'll be destroyed—"

"Unless it rains."

Captain Xeraph glanced away.

Brak walked to the balcony, looking out into the flame-shot dark. Thinking aloud, he said, "Perhaps I would indeed do well to observe this Ool at work. It's possible I might find inspiration! Discover powers I never knew I had—"

At first Xeraph's expression showed surprise. This was quickly replaced by new annoyance:

"I told you, Brak—observance of the wizard's private mysteries is forbidden. Just as entering his quarters is forbidden."

Brak shook his head. The long yellow braid bobbed gently against his lash-marked back. "When my life is forfeit, nothing's forbidden."

Again Xeraph couldn't contain a half-admiring smile: "Gods, what a determined lout you are. In better times, Lord Magnus could use a hundred like you in his fighting companies."

"I mean to be free of these chains, captain, not serve your lord or any other."

"What about the lord who takes life?" Xeraph retorted. "It's him you'll be serving at sunset the day after tomorrow! Look—why risk more trouble with Ool? You've admitted you have no arcane talents—"

"But I repeat, I won't sit and wait to be executed. If you can think of a better idea than observing the wizard, tell me and I'll do it."

"We'll do it," Xeraph corrected. "Remember, if I lose sight of you—" Matter-of-factly, he stroked an index finger across his sweat-blackened throat. In the distance, another huge crash rent the night. A column of flame and sparks shot heavenward. Somewhere a mob bayed like a beast.

Finally, Brak gave a crisp nod. "Well, then—tomorrow, when I'm rested—and sober—I mean to find this water channel where master Ool tries his futile spells. You can either let me blunder there alone, or you can go with me and fulfill the lord's charge that you keep watch on me."

"You could never pass the city gates without me."

"Don't be too sure, captain."

Slowly Xeraph wiped his palms down his lean thighs. He gave Brak a steady look. Not defying him. Testing:

"But what if I say no to your excursion, my friend?"

"I will go anyway."

"I might stop you."

"You might try," Brak replied softly.

In truth, he felt that the plan was exactly like all other plans afloat in the capital of Magnus the Worldbreaker: worthless. But he had no other alternative in mind.

He felt like an animal hunted by mounted men and dogs. With certain doom at his heels, he was still unwilling to stop and await death. He preferred motion—even though it was empty of solid hope or solid purpose. At least doing something might temporarily dispel the morbid thoughts of his future—besides, perhaps the scheme wasn't so foolish after all.

The wizard Ool presented curious contradictions. If he had entrenched himself at the court with his magical proficiency in the past, why had his talents suddenly proved wanting? Having experienced firsthand the abilities of both lesser and greater wizards, Brak could understand how Ool might not be competent to overcome the drought spell. Yet it was still odd that none around Lord Magnus raised the question of why Ool failed. They merely accepted it.

Perhaps they were too occupied with the tangible, pressing dangers of an advancing enemy and a populace in near-revolt. Perhaps the outside viewpoint of a stranger was required to see past distractions to simple, essential questions—

Such was the puzzle of Ool. Brak's hard, sweating face confirmed his resolve concerning the matter.

All at once, Captain Xeraph bowed to that, and laughed:

"Damn you for an insolent rogue, Brak—all right, we'll go. At sunrise." He kicked at the fallen playpieces and added, with a smile that bore no malice, "It can't be any more useless than trying to teach a thick-skulled foreigner this noble game."

Brak smiled a bleak smile in return and reached for the wine jar. Out in the city, more burning buildings began to fall, crashing—

5

THE SUN ate cruelly at Brak's body, promising painful burns by night-fall. With Captain Xeraph, he was crouched at the foot of a ridge some distance east of the city. The wall, some rooftops and columns of smoke could still be seen through clouds of dust blowing across empty, desiccated fields.

Like Brak, Captain Xeraph had cast aside the coarse cowled cloak each had worn to slip through the city gates shortly after dawn. Xeraph's presence had permitted them to leave with only a brief questioning. The discarded cloaks lay under a stone now, snapping and fluttering at their feet.

Xeraph wore a plain artisan's kilt. Except for his short-sword and the bronze bracelet which could not be removed, there was nothing to mark him as a military man.

He looked fearful as Brak peered toward the jumbled boulders along the ridge-top. Both men could clearly hear the strange sounds coming from the far side.

Brak knew why Xeraph was upset. What they were about to do was forbidden. Yet as Brak listened, the sounds seemed more odd than alarming; a mystery more than a menace.

He heard the creak of wheels, the rattle of hoofs. Now louder, then fading—exactly like the furious thudding of beaten drumheads. A voice chanted an incomprehensible singsong.

"I am going up to look, captain," Brak said.

Xeraph swallowed. "Very well, we'll—" Abruptly: "No, I'll stay here."

He shoved the point of his sword against Brak's throat. The barbarian edged away quickly but carefully. Xeraph's trembling hand might cause an accident.

"Don't get out of sight, understand?"

Xeraph darted a nervous glance around the sere horizon. Further east stood a farmstead, abandoned in the blowing dust. Hoofs and wheels, drums and chanting grew louder again. Brak gave a tight nod, turned and began to clamber up the hillside.

He moved cautiously, with the craft of the steppe-born hunter. Twice he stopped still and cursed, as the damnable chains between his wrists clinked too loudly.

He turned once to see Captain Xeraph staring up at him with an absolutely terrified expression. Brak hardened his heart and continued his climb. Whatever lay on the other side of the ridge was not sacred to him. And in his travels toward Khurdisan's golden crescent in the far south, he had encountered many marvels and enchantments. He did not precisely fear the sight of an inept wizard.

At length he worked himself between two boulders, his lips already dry and cracked from the heat. He looked out and down—

And blinked in astonishment.

As Xeraph had said, an immense, stone-lined channel lay below. It stretched east toward the mountains, west toward the city. The channel was filled with blowing dust.

Along a track on the far side, an imposing gold-chased chariot drawn by four white horses raced at furious speed. Brak counted five people in the oversized car, in addition to the driver.

Gripping the car's front rail, his voluminous robes flying behind him, stood Ool the magician, head thrown back. It was Ool uttering that weird, ululating chant.

Behind him, swaying and knocking against one another, was a quartet of boys with pudgy pink legs, ringleted hair, soft hands and generally feminine appearance. One had a pair of drums suspended on a strap around his neck. Another pounded the skin drumhead with padded beaters. A third picked up lengths of wood from the floor of the car and set them afire with a torch. The fourth threw the fresh-lit firebrands out of the car while Ool continued to chant.

Brak swore a foul oath. The whole expedition had been wasted. He had seen a similar ceremony in his youth in the wild lands of the north—and if this was all Ool could muster to open the heavens and relieve the drought, he was a poor wizard indeed.

The chariot continued to race along beside the channel, traveling a short way eastward before wheeling back again. Ool kept up his sing-song chant. The drums pounded. The torches arched out of the car every which way—

Despairing, Brak watched only a few moments longer. Just as the chariot completed its course away on his left and turned back toward his vantage point, he prepared to rejoin Xeraph. The chariot swept along beside the channel—and a gust of wind caught the magician's gown, flattened his sleeves back against his forearms. Suddenly Brak's belly flip-flopped. He stared through the sweat running off his eyebrows. Stared and stared as the chariot raced nearer, boiling dust out behind—

Firebrands scattered sparks. The drums *thud-thudded.* Brak squinted against the sun-glare, watching Ool's hands gripping the rail of the car—

As the chariot swept past, a thin suspicion became an alarming possibility.

The chariot thundered on, the drum-throbs and hoof-rattles and wheel-creaks diminishing again. Brak scrambled up, avoiding Captain Xeraph's anxious gaze from the bottom of the ridge.

What should he do? Go instantly to Lord Magnus?

No, he'd never be believed. He was an outlander with no status except the useless one of prisoner. Automatically, he would be counted a liar.

And if Ool heard of an accusation, he would probably move against the barbarian in some secret way. Have him slain before the time limit expired—

Yet Brak knew he had to act. Gazing into the dusty sunlight, he let his mind cast up images of the magician in the chariot. White cheeks. Jowls jiggling, soft and flabby. And the hands; the momentarily bared hands and forearms—those Brak saw most vividly of all.

Not a little frightened, he clambered down. Xeraph clutched his arm: "What did you see?"

"Trumpery," Brak said with a curt wave, wanting no hint of his suspicion to show on his face. "Magic such as the pathetic shamans of my own land practiced in hopes of changing the weather—"

Briefly he described the sights he'd observed—except for Ool's revealed hands.

Captain Xeraph was baffled by the details Brak reported. He asked for further explanation.

"They beat drums and throw torches helter-skelter to simulate thunder and lightning. Along with that, Ool howls some spell or other. The idea is to summon storms by imitating them. I've never seen it work before and I venture it won't work now."

Because, whispered a cold little serpent voice in his mind, *it is not meant to work.*

"Captain Xeraph," he said, "we must immediately—"

He stopped. Would this plain soldier who dealt in simple, fundamental concepts such as marching formations and use of weapons understand what he did not fully understand himself? Certainly he could not prove so much as one jot of his suspicion—yet. An accusation now, even presented to one such as Xeraph who, Brak felt, half-trusted him, would only bring ridicule.

Brow furrowed, Xeraph stared at him. "Must what, outlander? Finish what you started to say."

At last Brak knew what he must do. *Tonight.* Tonight would provide the only hours of darkness left.

But as he realized what he had to do—and do alone—he felt dismayed. If he took the risk, followed out the sketchy plan already in mind, he might put Captain Xeraph's life in jeopardy. And while he would never be fond of any captor, Xeraph was at least more agreeable than most.

Still, his own life was in jeopardy too. That made the difference.

"We must immediately return to the city," Brak concluded, a hasty lie. He felt the shame of a betrayer, the dread of the night's work waiting. "I saw nothing but a eunuch doing child's magic."

Xeraph looked relieved. They crept away from the ridge. The drumming and chanting and chariot-clatter faded.

Cloaked again, they trudged west in the heat. Each was silent, but for different reasons.

6

A NIGHT and a day. Like some drunken balladeer's refrain, the words kept coming to Brak's thoughts as he lay tensely on his pallet, counting time. *A night and a day—*

Outside, steamy darkness; his final night was perhaps half gone already. On the morrow, he would have no more chance. The light of the simmering sky would make his desperate gamble impossible. *A night and a day to make it rain—*

No, he amended in the grim silence of his thoughts, *a night—this night—to discover why it does* not *rain.*

At last, the stertorous breathing of Captain Xeraph subsided in the adjoining room. Brak rolled over, raised himself on an elbow, then bunched his legs beneath him.

Slowly he rose to a standing position. His body was already slicked with perspiration. The fall of the sun had brought no relief, no coolness. Through the arch that led to the apartment's regular bedchamber, the sounds of Xeraph thrashing came again.

As he stole barefoot toward the peg where Xeraph's sword-scabbard hung, Brak tried to remember the position of the hilt—about half way up the wall, wasn't it? He kept moving, cautiously—

Another pace.

Another.

Three more to go.

Then two.

He froze.

Soldiers were crossing the courtyard below the balcony. Three or four of them, he couldn't be certain. They were singing an obscene barracks ditty.

At last a heavy door closed. Brak moved again, wondering that the men of Lord Magnus had the heart to sing while the red of last night's fires still flickered throughout one quarter of the sky. A vast tenement section had been set ablaze, Xeraph had reported after the evening meal. The flaming devastation had yet to be contained—

Well, perhaps the soldiers of Magnus drank heaviest and sang loudest when they were powerless against certain defeat.

He listened. The courtyard was silent.

He lifted his hand, groping for the hilt of the shortsword. But somehow, while his attention had been distracted by the noises below, he had lost his precise sense of distances in the dark. Reaching out, he felt the back of his right hand collide suddenly with the hilt while his fingers closed on empty air. The scabbard knocked the wall. Loudly—

For a moment he held absolutely still, breath sucked in. But the damage was done. Wakened by the noisy thump against the intervening wall, Xeraph muttered a questioning monosyllable.

Brak didn't debate with himself for long. There would be no arguing with Xeraph. The captain would forbid what he'd planned. He jerked the short-sword from the scabbard, heedless of the racket of his chain. He pivoted and plunged toward the balcony.

Behind him he heard Xeraph thrash, call out. Then Brak caught the *slap-slap* of running feet.

One thick, scarred leg hooked over the low balcony wall as Xeraph rushed from the darkened apartment. Both hands on the hilt, Brak whipped up the short-sword, turning the blade just so and hammering it down in what he hoped would be a felling but not wounding blow.

Again he cursed his bad luck. He could tell the blow was mis-aimed. Xeraph was moving too fast, cursing him as a damned trickster—

The sword-flat thwacked and slid away. Captain Xeraph let out a loud, hurt cry as he crumpled.

Brak listened again, hoping that the doorkeeper on the floor below was drowsing in his booth. But again luck eluded him. The distant rapping of boots signaled the doorkeeper climbing the inner stairs to investigate the cry.

Brak faced a terrible decision. Remain—and fail. Or go on, and leave Xeraph to be discovered. Minus his prisoner. The barbarian knew what Xeraph's punishment would be—

In the hot darkness, Brak's face hardened. He would try to complete his night errand swiftly. Come back to Xeraph in time.

But if he failed—

Well, better not to think of that.

Xeraph was a decent, kindly jailer. But something deeper and darker within the huge barbarian swept that consideration aside. Something deeper, darker—and as heavy as the chains between his wrists.

The doorkeeper hammered outside Xeraph's apartment. A querulous voice inquired whether something was amiss. Xeraph, a fallen lump, stirred. Groaned. Brak's face was pitiless, a mask for his regret as he swung his other leg over and dropped toward the courtyard.

He would save Xeraph if he could. But above all, he would not live in chains.

7

INFURIATED BY the series of unlucky circumstances that had so far wrecked all but the basic thrust of his plan, Brak landed in a jarring crouch. He did his best to muffle the clinking links against his naked belly, at the same time maneuvering to keep from being cut by the sword.

He heard the doorkeeper knocking more insistently now. He bolted for the far side of the quadrangle, and a passage that would lead to a second, larger yard in the palace complex.

The knocking and shouting continued. Brak dodged into the passage just as a lamp was lit in another officer's apartment. The whole area would be awake soon. Damn and damn again!

Racing down the passage, he checked where the wall ended. He flattened his naked back against stone that still radiated heat. Behind him, more lamps bobbed. Shouts of genuine alarm were being raised.

He forced his concentration ahead. Saw a tired, limping soldier crossing the dark square on guard duty. The man walked with infernal slowness. Would he hear the commotion—?

Brak's breath hissed in and out of his lungs, a low, bestial sound. His eyes picked up some of the scarlet glare in the cloudless sky. Like a preying animal, he watched and counted time's destructive passage. If the soldier reacted to the distant noise from the officer's quarters—or if he about-faced to recross the square instead of proceeding on rounds elsewhere, Brak intended to kill him.

But the man did vanish inside a lantern-hung doorway. Perhaps he'd heard the racket and didn't care. Perhaps he wanted a drink of cool wine to break the night's sticky monotony. Whatever the reason, he was gone.

Whipping his head left and right, Brak checked for anyone else who might be observing him. He saw no one. He broke from cover, dashed toward the outer staircase of the two-story yellow building directly opposite.

On the second floor of that structure, he had learned via a casual inquiry to Xeraph, Ool the eunuch had his quarters. The floor below was occupied by the two dozen pink-lipped boys who served him. No one else was permitted to enter the building, Xeraph said. No other servants. Not even Lord Magnus.

Panting, Brak reached the exterior steps, crouched at the bottom, peering upward. He expected to see a guard posted on the terrace entrance to Ool's apartment. He saw no one.

Taking a tight grip on the sword's hilt, he began to climb, muffling the clinking chain as best he could. Time was running too fast for complete caution—

He still had no clear notion of what he expected to find, should he be lucky enough to penetrate Ool's private quarters. Evidence of treachery—but in what form? He couldn't predict.

Still, he was convinced his suspicions had some foundation. So he took the stairs three at a time.

By the time he neared the top, he wondered whether Ool's position was so secure, and his powers so feared, that he needed no personal guards. Somehow, Brak couldn't believe that. Yet, conscious of Xeraph's peril, he didn't pause to ponder the question—

He reached the terrace, immediately turned right toward a doorless arch where thin hangings stirred slowly. Deep in the dark of the apartment beyond, he saw white light flicker. He heard a small, hollow rumbling, mysterious and inexplicable, that somehow made his spine crawl.

A slithering noise spun him around.

He sucked in a startled breath at the sight of one—no, two—gods, *three* of the plump-faced boys rising from the shadow of the terrace railing. Had they been squatted there all along? Because of his haste and the darkness, Brak had missed them.

Their peculiar bright eyes glistened with red reflections from the sky. One boy giggled, shuffled a sandaled foot forward. Pressed against him, his companions followed suit.

The three advanced another step with those gleeful, half-mad expressions on their faces. *Were they drugged assassins*—?

Wary, awaiting attack, Brak was in one way reassured. Ool's quarters were, in fact, guarded. Because he had something to conceal?

In a wet, lisping voice, one of the round-faced trio said, "No one may enter to disturb the slumber of the sexless one."

"I think this says otherwise," Brak growled, giving the short-sword a flourish.

From the apartment he heard that preternatural rumbling again. The white-fleshed boys interlocked their hands and laughed at him. High-pitched, feminine giggles—

They were not armed. *But they were laughing at him!*

He backed up a pace, dread grabbing at his bowels. The trio kept mincing toward him, hands clutching hands. The faces suddenly glowed paste-white, illuminated by that strange radiance flaring inside the apartment—

Somehow, Brak's eyes misted. He blinked. No, the trouble was not in his eyes. A fog seemed to be forming around the boys.

The middle boy opened his mouth to laugh again. And Brak's brain shrieked nameless terror as that mouth began to *grow*—

Began to stretch upward, downward, to both sides simultaneously, becoming a huge, spectral monstrosity with sharp, filed teeth that gleamed wet with spittle. *Teeth the size of Brak's own head—*

Suddenly there were three giant, slavering mouths, each swollen outward from the head of a boy. There was a mouth on his left, another on his right, one directly ahead—all three arching forward to bite his skull and crack it—

Enchantments! Brak's mind screamed. *Illusions! They need no weapons because Ool taught them to guard with spells—*

Yet his own terror was real. So was the horrendous *craack* as the gigantic, disembodied central mouth clashed its teeth together, almost taking off his left arm.

Brak could see nothing of the trio of boys now. Only the formless mist in which the distended mouths were the sole perverted reality. Huge pink-lipped maws, clicking and grimacing and coming closer, left and right and ahead, *closer—*

The left mouth clashed its teeth three times. Then an immense, serpentine tongue shot from the maw and licked the lower lip in anticipation. A spittle-gob the size of fist dripped from the tongue's end—

Mesmerized with dread, Brak barely heard the noise on his right. He jerked his head around just in time to see the mouth arching over him, the gigantic teeth straining apart in preparation for the death-bite. Brak's brain howled his mortal fear. Yet something else within him still cried out:

Spells! Mind-dreams! You have seen them before! FIGHT THEM—

Both hands on the blade-hilt, he somehow found strength to hurl himself beneath the closing jaws—*CRAACK*—and stab into the mist as far as his chained arms would permit. Somewhere in that ghostly whorl of mind-smoke, the tip of his sword struck solid flesh—

A human shriek, bubbling and wild, roiled the smoke suddenly. The grinding mouth that had almost closed on him vanished.

The images of the other two began to shimmer and grow dim. Through the smoke he perceived a dying boy sprawled on the terrace flags, black-looking blood pouring out of his stabbed throat.

The mouth facing Brak flew at him, sharp-filed teeth wide open. But this time Brak fought his own hysteria more successfully, braced his legs and stabbed into the mist beneath the apparition—

And it too vanished, simultaneously with a cry of mortal hurt.

One phantom left—and that image was feeble. Through the vile, immense tongue, Brak glimpsed the reddened heavens of the city. He tossed his sword to his left hand, extended both arms as far as he could, and killed the unseen boy behind the snapping mouth—

Which shrank and puffed away, leaving three sad, suetlike bodies in a bloodied heap.

Gasping, Brak wiped sweat from his eyes. His heart pounded so heavily that it almost brought physical pain. Surely the cries of the boy-guards with their devilish mind projections had wakened the sleeper in the apartment. And others near the square—

Brak peered over the stone railing, saw the lone soldier pacing listlessly again. The only sounds the big barbarian heard were the drag of the soldier's boots and—behind him—that strange, hollow crashing that reverberated into stillness.

He leaned down, prodded one of the forlorn corpses. His fingers came away sticky with warm blood. No, the obscene mouths had not been real. But the briefly-invisible bodies that had tasted his iron had been real. That in itself was a reassurance of sanity, giving him the courage to turn, take three steps, raise his short-sword to touch the edge of one of the hangings and lift it—

Again that eerie white light flickered and danced deep in the apartment's gloom.

Brak tried to discern the light's source. It seemed to radiate from behind another drapery. But he couldn't be sure.

He listened again.

Silence. Where was Ool?

If Brak had somehow slain the evil boys without a sound, perhaps the wizard had not been awakened. Perhaps all the noises he'd heard during the struggle had been illusions too. The thought emboldened him to the point of taking one step past the hanging. From the concealment of the distant drapery, the hollow booming sounded once more.

Brak's backbone crawled as a sibilant voice spoke:

"Even in sleep, my mind is linked with those of my protectors. Their power comes from my thoughts, you see. When they died, I awakened. To give you a fitting reception, my curious outlander."

On the last word spoken by the unseen Ool, the short-sword in Brak's right hand burned. He screamed and let go.

The blade flew toward the ceiling, lighting the whole splendidly-furnished apartment for one bizarre instant. The sword turned molten, dripping. Dollops of glowing fire struck the apartment's tiles and burned smoking pits into them.

Brak dodged back from the fire-shower, seeing beyond it the hairless body of Ool standing beside his canopied bed, naked save for a loin-wrapping of linen that matched the whiteness of his flesh.

The last droplets of the destroyed sword struck the tiles and hissed out. But not before Brak had glimpsed the damning evidence again:

Ool's left wrist did bear the mark Brak thought he had seen when the wind blew back the wizard's sleeves in the chariot—

The mark was a scarred ridge of tissue circling the left wrist. Once, the man's flesh had been bound by a tight bracelet.

"You have come to perish, then," smiled Ool. "I shan't disappoint you—"

Immense, invisible hands created with no more than a blink of Ool's basilisk eyes lifted Brak and hurled him to the floor. His ears rang as he hit. His body went numb with pain.

Slowly, the pale wizard advanced toward the place where the big barbarian lay writhing, trying to regather his strength. With a little purse of his lips, Ool lifted one bare foot and placed it on Brak's sweating chest. With his right hand he made a quick mesmeric pass.

Instantly, Brak felt as though the weight of a building pressed down on him. He clenched his teeth, lashed his head from side to side, growled savagely—

But he could not move. He was held by the magical weight of Ool's soft, clammy foot.

From where he sprawled, Brak saw the magician's obscenely white shine in the glare from behind the far curtain. Ool the sexless one lifted his left forearm, displayed the scarred wrist almost mockingly.

"Is this what you came to see, outlander? Well—" An exquisite shrug. "Look your last."

8

BRAK THE barbarian lay helpless under that pasty white foot, his arms and legs and trunk tingling faintly. The pain of his hard fall was diminishing. But he was still unable to move. He was prisoned not by visible weight, but by the weight of Ool's arcane talents.

From what Brak could see of Ool, whenever the white light-source flared behind the distant curtain, the wizard continued to act amused. At length he gave voice to that amusement:

"You played boldly before my Lord Magnus, that I'll put to your credit. But you were foredoomed. Consider it an act of mercy on my part when I suggested you be allowed only two days and nights to work your nonexistent magic. No one can draw down the rain because I have gathered and held it. There."

A supple, almost boneless gesture with the left hand—toward the rumbling light-source.

"For the Children of the Smoke," Brak gasped out.

"Ultimately," Ool agreed. "But in chief, for myself. You see—" the whitish lips hardened into a cruel line, "—years ago, the Worldbreaker took something from me that represented irredeemable loss. Not by his own hand did he take it from me. But the hand which did the deed was his instrument. So I fled west to the lands of Shend, and for several years I discipled myself to their great wizards. I had some natural talent, I discovered—most humans do. Perhaps even you. But such talents lie dormant for lack of training and development. Had I not been so blessed, however, I would have sought another means of revenging myself. In any case, when my preparations were complete, I returned to his court as a different man. Unrecognized. My plan was to gain the confidence of Lord Magnus. Thus I served him well and faithfully for years—"

"Until the time when you were ready to strike against him."

Ool nodded. "You have a sharper wit than the few northlanders I've encountered. You have brains you put to use—guessing, puzzling out answers—yes, you're right. I waited. Always maintaining secret communication with the Children. Always urging *them* to wait until their numbers were great enough—and Lord Magnus was old, his powers failing. The hour came finally, as I knew it would," Ool said with another purse of the moist lips. "In a few weeks—a month or two—but soon, the Children will sweep out of the east. By then, the maddened people within these walls will have no more heart or strength to resist. Even the army will rise, I imagine. Such is the miraculous power of nature's rain—and the lack thereof."

"Was—" Brak thrashed again. But the supernatural weight seemed to restrain every part of him. "—was it you, then, who blackened the sky and filled the crystal idols with what looked like blood?"

"Of course." Ool smiled. "There will be additional—ah—demonstrations of that sort before I send my last signal to the Children. Alas, you spoiled that particular illusion. The blow from your chain, I think. Breaking the idol, it broke the projective trance. I was lying yonder—" he indicated the rumpled bedclothes that exuded a sweet but somehow foul perfume, "—arranging it all with my mind. Of a sudden, I was jolted awake. Much the same thing happened when you killed my dear little guards. But enough of that. Although you are the loser and I am the winner in this small contest—"

He smiled again, seeing the glare in Brak's eyes. Again the big barbarian tried to move; futile. The naked foot held him. He could do nothing but clench and unclench his fists.

"—I respect certain of your qualities. I would like to know this much. What brought you here? These rooms are forbidden, even to the lord. I made sure of that long ago, so I could pursue my—private ventures undisturbed."

"The sight of the scar brought me," Brak said. "And certain things repeated by Captain Xeraph—"

Ool's hairless brows quirked, the back and sides of his oval head illuminated by another glare from behind the drape. "But when did you see the scar, pray? In public, I keep my hands forever hid in full sleeves."

"I spied on your so-called spell-working at the water-channel yesterday. While you were in the chariot, the wind blew your gown aside as the car went by the rocks where I was watching."

Ool was genuinely amused.

"I don't doubt your own people cast you out, my friend. No spellworker of small talent could abide a man of your perceptions observing his mummery."

"But the holding back of the rain is no mummery—"

"I told you, I have not held it back," Ool corrected, crooking one pudgy finger in an almost schoolmasterish way. "I have imprisoned it. That, too, I learned in Shend, and thought it an excellent major weapon at the proper time. That time, mercifully, has come."

"Will—" Again Brak forced out each word. "Will you rule the Children when they take over the Worldbreaker's kingdom?"

After a thoughtful pause, Ool replied, "I think not. I'll advise them, no doubt. Influence them. But the real savor of this victory will come long before I find myself in such a position." The white-oval face wrenched. "My only desire is to bring down that swilling, posturing little war-cock!"

"At least—" Brak struggled to breathe. "—at least he'll die a man. Which is more than you can ever claim."

Ool's pale face contorted. He shrilled an almost feminine scream, leaning over. One wrathful hand slapped Brak's face. The blow was sharp, vicious. But the big barbarian hardly felt it; he felt something more important. Something for which he'd hoped and gambled with the gasped insult—

He felt the shift in weight on his chest. The pressure lessened ever so little. Still bent over, Ool was prey now. If he could strike fast enough—

Brak's chained hands came up. An inch. Another. Faster, rising—

By leaning to strike Brak's face, Ool had somehow weakened the occult weight. Brak could shift his trunk a little, raise one shoulder up in the same instant he seized Ool's left ankle with both hands, and wrenched.

Heaving against the phantom power holding him down, Brak managed to hurl the wizard off balance. Ool toppled backwards, linen wrap flying.

The wizard reeled into a taboret, collapsed it as he fell, floundering and shrieking. Brak struggled to his feet, his huge, rope-muscled body washed by the white glare from behind the drapery. The hollow boom rolled through the chamber as Brak drove himself toward that curtain and the secret it concealed—

Behind him, Ool squealed and gibbered in rage. At any moment Brak expected some ensorcelled bolt of fire to strike him, char the flesh off his bones, burn him dead. His leaping strides were long, fear-driven—

Ool still flopped about on hands and knees, not yet fully recovered from his upsetting. Brak's hands closed on the white-shimmering drapery, coarse stuff. He tugged. Rings clattered. Fabric tore—

With a cry of terror, Brak flung up an arm to shield his eyes.

On a low stone pedestal in an alcove stood a flask of strangely opalescent glass. The flask, stoppered, was no more than four hands high. Inside—*inside*—

Brak's skin crawled. His mouth tasted the bile of nauseous terror as he watched miniature stormclouds whirl and tumble within the flask.

The clouds moved with incredible speed, smashing the side of the glass prison, turning under and smashing again. Tiny lightning bolts sizzled and spat within the flask, spending themselves against the sides in unearthly fire-showers—

As Ool had said: the storms of heaven, magically imprisoned.

Noise behind him. The wizard scrambling up—

Terrified almost witless, Brak grabbed at the awful flask, heard Ool shriek:

"Do not touch it—!"

The flask vibrated in Brak's hand, shooting off its white glare of prisoned lightnings, booming the sound of captured thunder. The flask cast a sickly white aura between the barbarian and the sorcerer, who was framed against the terrace where his dead guardians lay. Ool's supple white hands rose in the beginning of what Brak knew would be a last, death-bringing spell-cast—

He hurled the flask with all his strength.

Ool saw it flying at him, white and thundering. The motions of his spell dissolved into frantic, fending gestures. He managed to hit the flask, deflect it. But when he saw the direction, he screamed and screamed—

The flask fell toward the floor.

Struck the tiles.

Shattered—

A cataclysm of lightbursts and thunderclaps smote Brak's brain and body. Unleashed winds picked him up, tossed him toward the splitting ceiling, tumbled him and bounced him off a wall while noise drummed, glare burned, shrieking gale-winds funneled skyward—

The whirlwind dropped Brak through white-glaring darkness, smashing the sense out of him an instant after he heard Ool's final scream drowned in the roar of furious, downpouring rain.

9

BLOODIED, ONLY half in possession of his senses, wracked with pain yet forcing himself to drag the flaccid white corpse by its ankle, Brak the barbarian sought the hall of Lord Magnus the Worldbreaker.

It was not hard to find. Drums hammered. Pipes skirled. Joyous, almost hysterical voices whooped and sang as he came limping up a long, empty corridor where torches blew and sheeting rain gusted in through high slot windows.

Staggering, Brak dropped to one knee. He released Ool's ankle, held both palms against his eyelids, fighting back the pain.

He had wakened in the apartment, finding half the ceiling caved away. The snapped end of a beam had crushed Ool's skull. Behind him along the ghostly corridor, Brak could see a trail of red and gray paste where Ool's head had dragged.

For his part, Brak had been prisoned beneath a rubble-heap, badly knocked and gashed, but with no detectable damage besides general pain and a sharper one that might indicate a shattered bone somewhere in his left leg. He could barely support himself on that side.

Some of Ool's boy guardians had come creeping upstairs fearfully. At the sight of their dead master, they fled into the night. Brak had pulled himself up and out of the ruins of the ceiling from which the prisoned storm-forces had escaped to spread and deluge the land with the rain; rain that even now rivered loudly off the palace rooftop. He'd hauled Ool's shattered body through empty squares and courtyards while his pain-dulled mind perceived cries of jubilation from streets and palace buildings alike.

Now he gained his feet again. He saw a turning in the corridor just ahead. He clutched Ool's ankle, shambled on, drenched by a gust of rain through a window he passed. Cold, clean rain pouring down on the kingdom of Lord Magnus the Worldbreaker—

Weaving on his feet, struggling against the agony that seared his whole left side, Brak limped to the entrance of the huge hall, and waited.

A thousand people thronged there, it seemed, reveling. They axed open wine casks, lay beneath the pouring red streams, bathing in them. Others whooped and danced impromptu steps: soldiers and courtiers, ladies and serving-maids alike—

One wine-drenched bawd saw Brak slouched in the great doorway and screamed.

The merrymaking ended. Heads turned. Mouths gaped.

Like some great wounded animal, Brak the barbarian dragged his victim on, up through a long, quickly-opened aisle of faces to the foot of the beast-throne where Magnus the Worldbreaker sat, wine cup in hand.

The rain drummed and hammered in the dark night outside. Magnus's lined face bore a disbelieving look as he stared down at the grim, bloodied hulk of a man who, with his good right foot, rolled the wizard's corpse to the base of the throne stairs and then simply stared upward.

"Was it you who brought the rain—at the price of my wizard's life?" Magnus asked, as if he couldn't quite countenance it. Ripples of amazement noised through the crowd, stilled suddenly by the lord's upraised hand.

At first Brak could manage no more than a single, pain-wracked shake of his head. Then he said:

"I only freed what your treacherous magician prisoned inside a flask with a powerful spell—to bring this kingdom down. Many—"

Brak saw three lords seated on the throne. Then two. He rubbed his eyes; fought the hurt spearing up his left side; stiffened his injured leg so he wouldn't totter and fall.

"—many years ago, I was told, a soldier ravished your wife, and escaped. But not before a spear gave him a wound. Look at the wizard's arm, which he has kept concealed from you—from everyone—since the first day he came to your court. Once he wore your bracelet. Pull away his waist linen—" This Brak had already done, back in the apartment, to verify his suspicion. "A spear that struck in darkness robbed him of what a man can afford to lose least of all—"

He swayed, dizzy, as soldiers and courtiers ran forward to strip the corpse and expose the sexless, scarred ruin at the joining of Ool's pale legs.

A woman fainted. The linen was hastily replaced.

Lord Magnus gazed down in wonder and loathing. Brak forced out more hoarse words:

"He escaped to the land of Shend, and there learned sorceries. He returned and gained your favor under the name by which you knew him. For years he conspired with the Children of the Smoke, until the arrival of the hour he deemed opportune to—" A wracking cough that started deep in his belly nearly spilled Brak over. "—to bring you down. All this I will repeat in detail at—some better time." Glowering, he swung his head left and right. He missed the one face he sought: "Where is Captain Xeraph?"

"In the dungeons, being drawn on the wheel for permitting your escape."

"I struck him by surprise. He had no chance—let him go."

Silence.

"*I said let him go!*"

Lord Magnus signaled. Two senior officers dashed for a portal as Brak went on:

"Before I make my departure, I will explain fully how I destroyed the man who would have destroyed you, lord. But I want your leave—" Again a terrible, sick spell of dizziness swept him. The pain climbed through his left leg and his torso to eat at his brain. He braced his gashed left leg, dug horny nails into his palms: fresh pain, to sting his senses alive again.

"—to claim what you promised me if the rain came down in two days and two nights. That I will be free of your bondage."

Suddenly, horrifyingly, in the small, scarred face of Lord Magnus the Worldbreaker whose booted feet did not reach the floor in front of his throne, there was both cheerfulness and cunning. In the rain-hissing silence, the lord said:

"Barbarian, you heard me amiss. I spoke exactly this. *You will not die. You will not wear chains.* I never said you would go free. In fact I never intended that at all—and chose my words accordingly. I am ever in need of stout, quick-witted fighters—and will number you among such from this day forward. Instead of chains, you will only wear the bronze bracelet of my army."

10

FROM SOMEWHERE deep in his hurt body, Brak's cry of betrayal bellowed out:

"The gods damn you for deception—*I will escape!*"

Looking down on his new thrall with scarcely-concealed admiration, Lord Magnus gave a tired, pleased nod.

"Accepted. I will prevent it, if I can."

It made no difference to Brak the barbarian that he knew why Lord Magnus had deceived him, and would impress him into service. In his terrible pain, he felt only hatred. Faces, forms, firelight from socketed torches swam together and melted into darkness as he threw his head back and let out one long, baying howl of animal rage.

Lunging, he tried to climb the throne stairs to his captor. But he was too weak. He fell back, sprawling over the corpse of Ool. His mind darkened swiftly—

There was sudden stillness except for the hammer of the rain. The unconscious barbarian's right arm slipped off the dead magician's shoulder where it had rested, and struck the floor with a last faint clattering of chain.

FRITZ LEIBER
Ill Met in Lankhmar

SILENT AS specters, the tall and the fat thief edged past the dead, noose-strangled watch-leopard, out the thick, lock-picked door of Jengao the Gem Merchant, and strolled east on Cash Street through the thin black night-smog of Lankhmar.

East on Cash it had to be, for west at Cash and Silver was a police post with unbribed guardsmen restlessly grounding and rattling their pikes.

But tall, tight-lipped Slevyas, master thief candidate, and fat, darting-eyed Fissif, thief second class, with a rating of talented in double-dealing, were not in the least worried. Everything was proceeding according to plan. Each carried thonged in his pouch a smaller pouch of jewels of the first water only, for Jengao, now breathing stertoriously inside and senseless from the slugging he'd suffered, must be allowed, nay, nursed and encouraged to build his business again and so ripen it for another plucking. Almost the first law of the Thieves' Guild was never to kill the hen that laid eggs with a ruby in the yolk.

The two thieves also had the relief of knowing that they were going straight home now, not to a wife, Arath forbid!—or to parents and children, all gods forfend!—but to Thieves' House, headquarters and barracks of the almighty Guild, which was father to them both and mother too, though no woman was allowed inside its ever-open portal on Cheap Street.

In addition there was the comforting knowledge that although each was armed only with his regulation silver-hilted thief's knife, they were nevertheless most strongly convoyed by three reliable and lethal bravoes hired for the evening from the Slayers' Brotherhood, one moving well ahead of them as point, the other two well behind as rear guard and chief striking force.

And if all that were not enough to make Slevyas and Fissif feel safe and serene, there danced along soundlessly beside them in the shadow of the north curb a small, malformed or at any rate somewhat large-headed shape that might have been a very small dog, a somewhat undersized cat, or a very big rat.

True, this last guard was not an absolutely unalloyed reassurance. Fissif strained upward to whisper softly in Slevyas' long-lobed ear, "Damned if I like being dogged by that familiar of Hristomilo, no matter what security he's supposed to afford us. Bad enough that Krovas did employ or let himself be cowed into employing a sorcerer of most dubious, if dire, reputation and aspect, but that—"

"Shut your trap!" Slevyas hissed still more softly.

Fissif obeyed with a shrug and employed himself in darting his gaze this way and that, but chiefly ahead.

Some distance in that direction, in fact just short of Gold Street, Cash was bridged by an enclosed second-story passageway connecting the two buildings which made up the premises of the famous stone-masons and sculptors Rokkermas and Slaarg. The firm's buildings themselves were fronted by very shallow porticoes supported by unnecessarily large pillars of varied shape and decoration, advertisements more than structural members.

From just beyond the bridge came two low, brief whistles, a signal from the point bravo that he had inspected that area for ambushes and discovered nothing suspicious and that Gold Street was clear.

Fissif was by no means entirely satisfied by the safety signal. To tell the truth, the fat thief rather enjoyed being apprehensive and even fearful, at least up to a point. So he scanned most closely through the thin, sooty smog the frontages and overhangs of Rokkermas and Slaarg.

On this side the bridge was pierced by four small windows, between which were three large niches in which stood—another advertisement —three life-size plaster statues, somewhat eroded by years of weather and dyed varyingly tones of dark gray by as many years of smog. Approaching Jengao's before the burglary, Fissif had noted them. Now it seemed to him that the statue to the right had indefinably changed. It was that of a man of medium height wearing cloak and hood, who gazed down with crossed arms and brooding aspect. No, not indefinably quite—the statue was a more uniform dark gray now, he fancied, cloak, hood, and face; it seemed somewhat sharper featured, less eroded; and he would almost swear it had grown shorter!

Just below the niches, moreover, there was a scattering of gray and raw white rubble which he didn't recall having been there earlier. He strained to remember if during the excitement of the burglary, the unsleeping watch-corner of his mind had recorded a distant crash, and now he believed it had. His quick imagination pictured the possibility of a hole behind each statue, through which it might be given a strong push and so tumbled onto passersby, himself and Slevyas specifically, the right-hand statue having been crashed to test the device and then replaced with a near twin.

He would keep close watch on all the statues as he and Slevyas walked under. It would be easy to dodge if he saw one start to over-balance. Should he yank Slevyas out of harm's way when that happened? It was something to think about.

His restless attention fixed next on the porticoes and pillars. The latter, thick and almost three yards tall, were placed at irregular inter-vals as well as being irregularly shaped and fluted, for Rokkermas and Slaarg were most modern and emphasized the unfinished look, random-ness, and the unexpected.

Nevertheless it seemed to Fissif, that there was an intensification of unexpectedness, specifically that there was one more pillar under the porticoes than when he had last passed by. He couldn't be sure which pillar was the newcomer, but he was almost certain there was one.

The enclosed bridge was close now. Fissif glanced up at the right-hand statue and noted other differences from the one he'd recalled. Although shorter, it seemed to hold itself more strainingly erect, while the frown carved in its dark gray face was not so much one of philo-sophic brooding as sneering contempt, self-conscious cleverness, and conceit.

Still, none of the three statues toppled forward as he and Slevyas walked under the bridge. However, something else happened to Fissif at that moment.

One of the pillars winked at him.

The Gray Mouser turned round in the right-hand niche, leaped up and caught hold of the cornice, silently vaulted to the flat roof, and crossed it precisely in time to see the two thieves emerge below.

Without hesitation he leaped forward and down, his body straight as a crossbow bolt, the soles of his ratskin boots aimed at the shorter thief's fat-buried shoulder blades, though leading him a little to allow for the yard he'd walk while the Mouser hurtled toward him.

In the instant that he leaped, the tall thief glanced up over-shoulder and whipped out a knife, though making no move to push or pull Fissif out of the way of the human projectile speeding toward him.

More swiftly than one would have thought he could manage, Fissif whirled round then and thinly screamed, "Slivikin!"

The ratskin boots took him high in the belly. It was like landing on a big cushion. Writing aside from Slevyas' thrust, the Mouser somersaulted forward, and as the fat thief's skull hit a cobble with a dull *bong* he came to his feet with dirk in hand, ready to take on the tall one.

But there was no need. Slevyas, his eyes glazed, was toppling too.

One of the pillars had sprung forward, trailing a voluminous robe. A big hood had fallen back from a youthful face and long-haired head. Brawny arms had emerged from the long, loose sleeves that had been the pillar's topmost section. While the big fist ending one of the arms had dealt Slevyas a shrewd knockout punch on the chin.

Fafhrd and the Gray Mouser faced each other across the two thieves sprawled senseless. They were poised for attack, yet for the moment neither moved.

Fafhrd said, "Our motives for being here seem identical."

"Seem? Surely must be!" the Mouser answered curtly, fiercely eyeing this potential new foe, who was taller by a head than the tall thief.

"You said?"

"I said, 'Seem? Surely must be!' "

"How civilized of you!" Fafhrd commented in pleased tones.

"Civilized?" the Mouser demanded suspiciously, gripping his dirk tighter.

"To care, in the eye of action, exactly what's said," Fafhrd explained. Without letting the Mouser out of his vision, he glanced down. His gaze traveled from the pouch of one fallen thief to that of the other. Then he looked up at the Mouser with a broad, ingenuous smile.

"Fifty-fifty?" he suggested.

The Mouser hesitated, sheathed his dirk, and rapped out, "A deal!" He knelt abruptly, his fingers on the drawstrings of Fissif's pouch. "Loot you Slivikin," he directed.

It was natural to suppose that the fat thief had been crying his companion's name at the end.

Without looking up from where he knelt, Fafhrd remarked, "That . . . ferret they had with them. Where did it go?"

"Ferret?" the Mouser answered briefly. "It was a marmoset!"

"Marmoset," Fafhrd mused. "That's a small tropical monkey, isn't it? Well, might have been—I've never been south—but I got the impression that—"

The silent, two-pronged rush which almost overwhelmed them at that instant really surprised neither of them. Each had unconsciously been expecting it.

The three bravoes racing down upon them in concerted attack, all with swords poised to thrust, had assumed that the two highjackers would be armed at most with knives and as timid in weapons-combat as the general run of thieves and counter-thieves. So it was they who were thrown into confusion when with the lightning speed of youth the Mouser and Fafhrd sprang up, whipped out fearsomely long swords, and faced them back to back.

The Mouser made a very small parry in carte so that the thrust of the bravo from the east went past his left side by only a hair's breadth. He instantly riposted. His adversary, desperately springing back, parried in turn in carte. Hardly slowing, the tip of the Mouser's long, slim sword dropped under that parry with the delicacy of a princess curtsying and then leaped forward and a little upward and went between two scales of the bravo's armored jerkin and between his ribs and through his heart and out his back as if all were angel food cake.

Meanwhile Fafhrd, facing the two bravoes from the west, swept aside their low thrusts with somewhat larger, down-sweeping parries in seconde and low prime, then flipped up his sword, as long as the Mouser's but heavier, so that it slashed through the neck of his right-hand adversary, half decapitating him. Then dropping back a swift step, he readied a thrust for the other.

But there was no need. A narrow ribbon of bloodied steel, followed by a gray glove and arm, flashed past him from behind and transfixed the last bravo with the identical thrust the Mouser had used on the first.

The two young men wiped their swords. Fafhrd brushed the palm of his open right hand down his robe and held it out. The Mouser pulled off his right-hand gray glove and shook it. Without word exchanged, they knelt and finished looting the two unconscious thieves, securing the small bags of jewels. With an oily towel and then a dry one, the Mouser sketchily wiped from his face the greasy ash-soot mixture which had darkened it.

Then, after only a questioning eye-twitch east on the Mouser's part and a nod from Fafhrd, they swiftly walked on in the direction Slevyas and Fissif and their escort had been going.

After reconnoitering Gold Street, they crossed it and continued east on Cash at Fafhrd's gestured proposal.

"My woman's at the Golden Lamprey," he explained.

"Let's pick her up and take her home to meet my girl," the Mouser suggested.

"Home?" Fafhrd inquired politely.

"Dim Lane." the Mouser volunteered.

"Silver Eel?"

"Behind it. We'll have some drinks."

"I'll pick up a jug. Never have too much juice."

"True. I'll let you."

Fafhrd stopped, again wiped right hand on robe, and held it out. "Name's Fafhrd."

Again the Mouser shook it. "Gray Mouser," he said a touch defiantly, as if challenging anyone to laugh at the sobriquet.

"Gray Mouser, eh?" Fafhrd remarked. "Well, you killed yourself a couple of rats tonight."

"That I did." The Mouser's chest swelled and he threw back his head. Then with a comic twitch of his nose and a sidewise half-grin he admitted, "You'd have got your second man easily enough. I stole him from you to demonstrate my speed. Besides, I was excited."

Fafhrd chuckled. "You're telling me? How do you suppose I was feeling?"

Once more the Mouser found himself grinning. What the deuce did this big fellow have that kept him from putting on his usual sneers?

Fafhrd was asking himself a similar question. All his life he'd mistrusted small men, knowing his height awakened their instant jealousy. But this clever little chap was somehow an exception. He prayed to Kos that Vlana would like him.

On the northeast corner of Cash and Whore a slow-burning torch shaded by a broad, gilded spiral cast a cone of light up into the thickening black night-smog and another cone down on the cobbles before the tavern door. Out of the shadows into the second cone stepped Vlana, handsome in a narrow black velvet dress and red stockings, her only ornaments a silver-hilted dagger in a silver sheath and a silver-worked black pouch, both on a plain black belt.

Fafhrd introduced the Gray Mouser, who behaved with an almost fawning courtesy. Vlana studied him boldly, then gave him a tentative smile.

Fafhrd opened under the torch the small pouch he'd taken off the tall thief. Vlana looked down into it. She put her arms around Fafhrd, hugged him tight and kissed him soundly. Then she thrust the jewels into the pouch on her belt.

When that was done, he said, "Look, I'm going to buy a jug. You tell her what happened, Mouser."

When he came out of the Golden Lamprey he was carrying four jugs in the crook of his left arm and wiping his lips on the back of his right hand. Vlana frowned. He grinned at her. The Mouser smacked his lips at the jugs. They continued east on Cash. Fafhrd realized that the frown was for more than the jugs and the prospect of stupidly drunken male revelry. The Mouser tactfully walked ahead.

When his figure was little more than a blob in the thickening smog, Vlana whispered harshly, "You had two members of the Thieves' Guild knocked out cold and you didn't cut their throats?"

"We slew three bravoes," Fafhrd protested by way of excuse.

"My quarrel is not with the Slayers' Brotherhood, but that abominable guild. You swore to me that whenever you had the chance—"

"Vlana! I couldn't have the Gray Mouser thinking I was an amateur counter-thief consumed by hysteria and blood lust."

"Well, he told me that *he'd* have slit their throats in a wink, if he'd known I wanted it that way."

"He was only playing up to you from courtesy."

"Perhaps and perhaps not. But you knew and you didn't—"

"Vlana, shut up!"

Her frown became a rageful glare, then suddenly she laughed widely, smiled twitchingly as if she were about to cry, mastered herself and smiled more lovingly. "Pardon me, darling," she said. "Sometimes you must think I'm going mad and sometimes I believe I am."

"Well, don't," he told her shortly. "Think of the jewels we've won instead. And behave yourself with our new friends. Get some wine inside you and relax. I mean to enjoy myself tonight. I've earned it."

She nodded and clutched his arm in agreement and for comfort and sanity. They hurried to catch up with the dim figure ahead.

The Mouser, turning left, led them a half square north on Cheap Street to where a narrower way went east again. The black mist in it looked solid.

"Dim Lane," the Mouser explained.

Vlana said, "Dim's too weak—too *transparent* a word for it tonight," with an uneven laugh in which there were still traces of hysteria and which ended in a fit of strangled coughing.

She gasped out, "Damn Lankhmar's night-smog! What a hell of a city!"

"It's the nearness here of the Great Salt Marsh," Fafhrd explained. And he did indeed have part of the answer. Lying low betwixt the

Marsh, the Inner Sea, the River Hlal, and the southern grain fields
watered by canals fed by the Hlal, Lankhmar with its innumerable
smokes was the prey of fogs and sooty smogs.

About halfway to Carter Street, a tavern on the north side of the lane
emerged from the murk. A gape-jawed serpentine shape of pale metal
crested with soot hung high for a sign. Beneath it they passed a door
curtained with begrimed leather, the slit in which spilled out noise,
pulsing torchlight, and the reek of liquor.

Just beyond the Silver Eel the Mouser led them through an inky
passageway outside the tavern's east wall. They had to go single file,
feeling their way along rough, slimily bemisted brick.

"Mind the puddle," the Mouser warned. "It's deep as the Outer Sea."

The passageway widened. Reflected torchlight filtering down
through the dark mist allowed them to make out only the most general
shape of their surroundings. Crowding close to the back of the Silver
Eel rose a dismal, rickety building of darkened brick and blackened,
ancient wood. From the fourth story attic under the ragged-guttered
roof, faint lines of yellow light shone around and through three tightly
latticed windows. Beyond was a narrow alley.

"Bones Alley," the Mouser told them.

By now Vlana and Fafhrd could see a long, narrow wooden outside
stairway, steep yet sagging and without a rail, leading up to the lighted
attic. The Mouser relieved Fafhrd of the jugs and went up it quite
swiftly.

"Follow me when I've reached the top," he called back. "I think it'll
take your weight, Fafhrd, but best one of you at a time."

Fafhrd gently pushed Vlana ahead. She mounted to the Mouser
where he now stood in an open doorway, from which streamed yellow
light that died swiftly in the night-smog. He was lightly resting a hand
on a big, empty, wrought-iron lamp-hook firmly set in a stone section
of the outside wall. He bowed aside, and she went in.

Fafhrd followed, placing his feet as close as he could to the wall, his
hands ready to grab for support. The whole stairs creaked ominously
and each step gave a little as he shifted his weight onto it. Near the top,
one step gave way with the muted crack of half-rotted wood. Gently
as he could, he sprawled himself hand and knee on as many steps as
he could get, to distribute his weight, and cursed sulphurously.

"Don't fret, the jugs are safe," the Mouser called down gayly.

Fafhrd crawled the rest of the way and did not get to his feet until
he was inside the doorway. When he had done so, he almost gasped
with surprise.

It was like rubbing the verdigris from a cheap brass ring and revealing a rainbow-fired diamond of the first water. Rich drapes, some twinkling with embroidery of silver and gold, covered the walls except where the shuttered windows were—and the shutters of those were gilded. Similar but darker fabrics hid the low ceiling, making a gorgeous canopy in which the flecks of gold and silver were like stars. Scattered about were plump cushions and low tables, on which burned a multitude of candles. On shelves against the walls were neatly stacked like small logs a vast reserve of candles, numerous scrolls, jugs, bottles, and enameled boxes. In a large fireplace was set a small metal stove, neatly blacked, with an ornate firepot. Also set beside the stove was a tidy pyramid of thin, resinous torches with frayed ends—fire-kindlers and other pyramids of small, short logs and gleamingly black coal.

On a low dais by the fireplace was a couch covered with cloth of gold. On it sat a thin, pale-faced, delicately handsome girl clad in a dress of thick violet silk worked with silver and belted with a silver chain. Silver pins headed with amethysts held in place her high-piled black hair. Round her shoulders was drawn a wrap of snow-white serpent fur. She was leaning forward with uneasy-seeming graciousness and extending a narrow white hand which shook a little to Vlana, who knelt before her and now gently took the proffered hand and bowed her head over it, her own glossy, straight, dark-brown hair making a canopy, and pressed its back to her lips.

Fafhrd was happy to see his woman playing up properly to this definitely odd, though delightful situation. Then looking at Vlana's long, red-stockinged leg stretched far behind her as she knelt on the other, he noted that the floor was everywhere strewn—to the point of double, treble, and quadruple overlaps—with thick-piled, close-woven, many-hued rugs of the finest quality imported from the Eastern Lands. Before he knew it, his thumb had shot toward the Gray Mouser.

"You're the Rug Robber!" he proclaimed. "You're the Carpet Crimp!—and the Candle Corsair too!" he continued, referring to two series of unsolved thefts which had been on the lips of all Lankhmar when he and Vlana had arrived a moon ago.

The Mouser shrugged impassive-faced at Fafhrd, then suddenly grinned, his slitted eyes a-twinkle, and broke into an impromptu dance which carried him whirling and jigging around the room and left him behind Fafhrd, where he deftly reached down the hooded and long-sleeved huge robe from the latter's stooping shoulders, shook it out, carefully folded it, and set it on a pillow.

The girl in violet nervously patted with her free hand the cloth of gold beside her, and Vlana seated herself there, carefully not too close, and the two women spoke together in low voices, Vlana taking the lead.

The Mouser took off his own gray, hooded cloak and laid it beside Fafhrd's. Then they unbelted their swords, and the Mouser set them atop folded robes and cloak.

Without those weapons and bulking garments, the two men looked suddenly like youths, both with clear, close-shaven faces, both slender despite the swelling muscles of Fafhrd's arms and calves, he with long red-gold hair falling down his back and about his shoulders, the Mouser with dark hair cut in bangs, the one in brown leather tunic worked with copper wire, the other in jerkin of coarsely woven gray silk.

They smiled at each other. The feeling each had of having turned boy all at once made their smiles embarrassed. The Mouser cleared his throat and, bowing a little, but looking still at Fafhrd, extended a loosely spread-fingered arm toward the golden couch and said with a preliminary stammer, though otherwise smoothly enough, "Fafhrd, my good friend, permit me to introduce you to my princess. Ivrian, my dear, receive Fafhrd graciously if you please, for tonight he and I fought back to back against three and we conquered."

Fafhrd advanced, stooping a little, the crown of his red-gold hair brushing the be-starred canopy, and knelt before Ivrian exactly as Vlana had. The slender hand extended to him looked steady now, but was still quiveringly a-tremble, he discovered as soon as he touched it. He handled it as if it were silk woven of the white spider's gossamer, barely brushing it with his lips, and still felt nervous as he mumbled some compliments.

He did not sense that the Mouser was quite as nervous as he, if not more so, praying hard that Ivrian would not overdo her princess part and snub their guests, or collapse in trembling or tears, for Fafhrd and Vlana were literally the first beings that he had brought into the luxurious nest he had created for his aristocratic beloved—save the two love birds that twittered in a silver cage hanging to the other side of the fireplace from the dais.

Despite his shrewdness and cynicism, it never occurred to the Mouser that it was chiefly his charming but preposterous coddling of Ivrian that was making her doll-like.

But now as Ivrian smiled at last, the Mouser relaxed with relief, fetched two silver cups and two silver mugs, carefully selected a bottle of violet wine, then with a grin at Fafhrd uncorked instead one of the jugs the Northerner had brought, and near-brimmed the four gleaming vessels and served them all four.

With no trace of stammer this time, he toasted, "To my greatest theft to date in Lankhmar, which willy-nilly I must share fifty-fifty with"— He couldn't resist the sudden impulse—"with this great, long-haired, barbarian lout here!" And he downed a quarter of his mug of pleasantly burning wine fortified with brandy.

Fafhrd quaffed off half of his, then toasted back, "To the most boastful and finical little civilized chap I've ever deigned to share loot with," quaffed off the rest, and with a great smile that showed white teeth, held out his empty mug.

The Mouser gave him a refill, topped off his own, then set that down to go to Ivrian and pour into her lap from their small pouch the gems he'd filched from Fissif. They gleamed in their new, enviable location like a small puddle of rainbow-hued quicksilver.

Ivrian jerked back a-tremble, almost spilling them, but Vlana gently caught her arm, steadying it. At Ivrian's direction, Vlana fetched a blue-enameled box inlaid with silver, and the two of them transferred the jewels from Ivrian's lap into its blue velvet interior. Then they chatted on.

As he worked through his second mug in smaller gulps, Fafhrd relaxed and began to get a deeper feeling of his surroundings. The dazzling wonder of the first glimpse of this throne room in a slum faded, and he began to note the ricketiness and rot under the grand overlay.

Black, rotten wood showed here and there between the drapes and loosed its sick, ancient stinks. The whole floor sagged under the rugs, as much as a span at the center of the room. Threads of night-smog were coming through the shutters, making evanescent black arabesques against the gilt. The stones of the large fireplace had been scrubbed and varnished, yet most of the mortar was gone from between them; some sagged, others were missing altogether.

The Mouser had been building a fire there in the stove. Now he pushed in all the way the yellow-flaring kindler he'd lit from the fire-pot, hooked the little black door shut over the mounting flames, and turned back into the room. As if he'd read Fafhrd's mind, he took up several cones of incense, set their peaks a-smolder at the fire-pot, and placed them about the room in gleaming, shallow brass bowls. Then he stuffed silken rags in the widest shutter-cracks, took up his silver mug again, and for a moment gave Fafhrd a very hard look.

Next moment he was smiling and lifting his mug to Fafhrd, who was doing the same. Need of refills brought them close together. Hardly moving his lips, the Mouser explained, "Ivrian's father was a duke. I slew him. A most cruel man, cruel to his daughter too, yet a duke, so that Ivrian is wholly unused to fending for herself. I pride myself that I maintain her in grander state than her father did with all his servants."

Fafhrd nodded and said amiably, "Surely you've thieved together a charming little place."

From the couch Vlana called in her husky contralto, "Gray Mouser, your Princess would hear an account of tonight's adventure. And might we have more wine?"

Ivrian called, "Yes, please, Mouser."

The Mouser looked to Fafhrd for the go-ahead, got the nod, and launched into his story. But first he served the girls wine. There wasn't enough for their cups, so he opened another jug and after a moment of thought uncorked all three, setting one by the couch, one by Fafhrd where he sprawled now on the pillowy carpet, and reserving one for himself. Ivrian looked apprehensive at this signal of heavy drinking ahead, Vlana cynical.

The Mouser told the tale of counter-thievery well, acting it out in part, and with only the most artistic of embellishments—the ferret-marmoset before escaping ran up his body and tried to scratch out his eyes—and he was interrupted only twice.

When he said, "And so with a whish and a snick I bared Scalpel—" Fafhrd remarked, "Oh, so you've nicknamed your sword as well as yourself?"

The Mouser drew himself up. "Yes, and I call my dirk Cat's Claw. Any objections? Seem childish to you?"

"Not at all. I call my own sword Graywand. Pray continue."

And when he mentioned the beastie of uncertain nature that had gamboled along with the thieves (and attacked his eyes!), Ivrian paled and said with a shudder, "Mouser! That sounds like a witch's familiar!"

"Wizard's," Vlana corrected. "Those gutless Guild-villains have no truck with women, except as fee'd or forced vehicles for their lust. But Krovas, their current king, is noted for taking *all* precautions, and might well have a warlock in his service."

"That seems most likely; it harrows me with dread," the Mouser agreed with ominous gaze and sinister voice, eagerly accepting any and all atmospheric enhancements of his performance.

When he was done, the girls, eyes flashing and fond, toasted him and Fafhrd for their cunning and bravery. The Mouser bowed and eye-twinklingly smiled about, then sprawled him down with a weary sigh, wiping his forehead with a silken cloth and downing a large drink.

After asking Vlana's leave, Fafhrd told the adventurous tale of their escape from Cold Corner—he from his clan, she from an acting troupe —and of their progress to Lankhmar, where they lodged now in an actors' tenement near the Plaza of Dark Delights. Ivrian hugged herself to Vlana and shivered large-eyed at the witchy parts of his tale.

The only proper matter he omitted from his account was Vlana's fixed intent to get a monstrous revenge on the Thieves' Guild for torturing to death her accomplices and harrying her out of Lankhmar when she'd tried freelance thieving in the city before they met. Nor of course did he mention his own promise—foolish, he thought now—to help her in this bloody business.

After he'd done and got his applause, he found his throat dry despite his skald's training, but when he sought to wet it, he discovered that his mug was empty and his jug too, though he didn't feel in the least drunk—he had talked all the liquor out of him, he told himself, a little of the stuff escaping in each glowing word he'd spoken.

The Mouser was in like plight and not drunk either—though inclined to pause mysteriously and peer toward infinity before answering question or making remark. This time he suggested, after a particularly long infinity-gaze, that Fafhrd accompany him to the Eel while he purchased a fresh supply.

"But we've a lot of wine left in *our* jug," Ivrian protested. "Or at least a little," she amended. It did sound empty when Vlana shook it. "Besides, you've wine of all sorts here."

"Not this sort, dearest, and first rule is never mix 'em," the Mouser explained, wagging a finger. "That way lies unhealth, aye, and madness."

"My dear," Vlana said, sympathetically patting her wrist, "at some time in any good party all the men who are really men simply have to go out. It's extremely stupid, but it's their nature and can't be dodged, believe me."

"But, Mouser, I'm scared. Fafhrd's tale frightened me. So did yours —I'll hear that familiar a-scratch at the shutters when you're gone, I know I will!"

"Darlingest," the Mouser said with a small hiccup, "there is all the Inner Sea, all the Land of the Eight Cities, and to boot all the Trollstep Mountains in their sky-scraping grandeur between you and Fafhrd's Cold Corner and its silly sorcerers. As for familiars, pish!—they've never in the world been anything but the loathy, all-too-natural pets of stinking old women and womanish old men."

Vlana said merrily, "Let the sillies go, my dear. 'Twill give us chance for a private chat, during which we'll take 'em apart from wine-fumey head to restless foot."

So Ivrian let herself be persuaded, and the Mouser and Fafhrd slipped off, quickly shutting the door behind them to keep out the night-smog, and the girls heard their light steps down the stairs.

Waiting for the four jugs to be brought up from the Eel's cellar, the two newly met comrades ordered a mug each of the same fortified wine, or one near enough, and ensconced themselves at the least noisy end of the long serving counter in the tumultuous tavern. The Mouser deftly kicked a rat that thrust black head and shoulders from his hole.

After each had enthusiastically complimented the other on his girl, Fafhrd said diffidently, "Just between ourselves, do you think there might be anything to your sweet Ivrian's notion that the small dark creature with Slivikin and the other Guild-thief was a wizard's familiar, or at any rate the cunning pet of a sorcerer, trained to act as go-between and report disasters to his master or to Krovas?"

The Mouser laughed lightly. "You're building bug-bears—formless baby ones unlicked by logic—out of nothing, dear barbarian brother, if I may say so. How could that vermin make useful report? I don't believe in animals that talk—except for parrots and such birds, which only . . . parrot.

"Ho, there, you back of the counter! Where are my jugs? Rats eaten the boy who went for them days ago? Or he simply starved to death while on his cellar quest? Well, tell him to get a swifter move on and brim us again!

"No, Fafhrd, even granting the beastie to be directly or indirectly a creature of Krovas, and that it raced back to Thieves' House after our affray, what would that tell them there? Only that something had gone wrong with the burglary at Jengao's."

Fafhrd frowned and muttered stubbornly, "The furry slinker might, nevertheless, somehow convey our appearances to the Guild masters, and they might recognize us and come after us and attack us in our homes."

"My dear friend," the Mouser said condolingly, "once more begging your indulgence, I fear this potent wine is addling your wits. If the Guild knew our looks or where we lodged, they'd have been nastily on our necks days, weeks, nay, months ago. Or conceivably you don't know that their penalty for freelance thieving within the walls of Lankhmar is nothing less than death, after torture, if happily that can be achieved."

"I know all about that, and my plight is worse even than yours,"

Fafhrd retorted, and after pledging the Mouser to secrecy, told him the tale of Vlana's vendetta against the Guild and her deadly serious dreams of an all-encompassing revenge.

During his story the four jugs came up from the cellar, but the Mouser only ordered that their earthenware mugs be refilled.

Fafhrd finished, "And so, in consequence of a promise given by an infatuated and unschooled boy in a southern angle of the Cold Waste, I find myself now as a sober—well, at other times—man being constantly asked to make war on a power as great as that of Lankhmar's overlord, for as you may know the Guild has locals in all other cities and major towns of this land. I love Vlana dearly and she is an experienced thief herself, but on this one topic she has a kink in her brains, a hard knot neither logic nor persuasion can even begin to loosen."

"Certes t'would be insanity to assault the Guild direct, your wisdom's perfect there," the Mouser commented. "If you cannot break your most handsome girl of this mad notion, or coax her from it, then you must stoutly refuse e'en her least request in that direction."

"Certes I must," Fafhrd agreed with great emphasis and conviction. "I'd be an idiot taking on the Guild. Of course, if they should catch me, they'd kill me in any case for freelancing and highjacking. But wantonly to assault the Guild direct, kill one Guild-thief needlessly—lunacy entire!"

"You'd not only be a drunken, drooling idiot, you'd questionless be stinking in three nights at most from that emperor of diseases, Death. Malicious attacks on her person, blows directed at the organization, the Guild requires tenfold what she does other rule-breaking, freelancing included. So, no least giving-in to Vlana in this one matter."

"Agreed!" Fafhrd said loudly, shaking the Mouser's iron-thewed hand in a near crusher grip.

"And now we should be getting back to the girls," the Mouser said.

"After one more drink while we settle the score. Ho, boy!"

"Suits."

Vlana and Ivrian, deep in excited talk, both started at the pounding rush of footsteps up the stairs. Racing behemoths could hardly have made more noise. The creaking and groaning were prodigious, and there were the crashes of two treads breaking. The door flew open and their two men rushed in through a great mushroom top of night-smog which was neatly sliced off its black stem by the slam of the door.

"I told you we'd be back in a wink," the Mouser cried gayly to Ivrian, while Fafhrd strode forward, unmindful of the creaking floor, crying, "Dearest heart, I've missed you sorely," and caught up Vlana despite her voiced protests and pushing-off and kissed and hugged her soundly before setting her back on the couch again.

Oddly, it was Ivrian who appeared to be angry at Fafhrd then, rather than Vlana, who was smiling fondly if somewhat dazedly.

"Fafhrd, sir," she said boldly, her little fists set on her narrow hips, her tapered chin held high, her dark eyes blazing, "my beloved Vlana has been telling me about the unspeakably atrocious things the Thieves' Guild did to her and to her dearest friends. Pardon my frank speaking to one I've only met, but I think it quite unmanly of you to refuse her the just revenge she desires and fully deserves. And that goes for you too, Mouser, who boasted to Vlana of what you would have done had you but known, all the while intending only empty ingratiation. You who in like case did not scruple to slay my very own father!"

It was clear to Fafhrd that while he and the Gray Mouser had idly boozed in the Eel, Vlana had been giving Ivrian a doubtless empurpled account of her grievances against the Guild and playing mercilessly on the naive girl's bookish, romantic sympathies and high concept of knightly honor. It was also clear to him that Ivrian was more than a little drunk. A three-quarters empty flask of violet wine of far Kiraay sat on the low table next the couch.

Yet he could think of nothing to do but spread his big hands helplessly and bow his head, more than the low ceiling made necessary, under Ivrian's glare, now reinforced by that of Vlana. After all, they *were* in the right. He *had* promised.

So it was the Mouser who first tried to rebut.

"Come now, pet," he cried lightly as he danced about the room, silk-stuffing more cracks against the thickening night-smog and stirring up and feeding the fire in the stove, "and you too, beauteous Lady Vlana. For the past month Fafhrd has by his highjackings been hitting the Guild-thieves where it hurts them most—in their purses a-dangle between their legs. Come, drink we up all." Under his handling, one of the new jugs came uncorked with a pop, and he darted about brimming silver cups and mugs.

"A merchant's revenge!" Ivrian retorted with scorn, not one whit appeased, but rather enangered anew. "At the least you and Fafhrd must bring Vlana the head of Krovas!"

"What would she *do* with it? What *good* would it be except to spot the carpets?" the Mouser plaintively inquired, while Fafhrd, gathering his wits at last and going down on one knee, said slowly, "Most respected Lady Ivrian, it is true I solemnly promised my beloved Vlana I would help her in her revenge, but if Mouser and I should bring Vlana the head of Krovas, she and I would have to flee Lankhmar on the instant, every man's hand against us. While you infallibly would lose this fairyland Mouser has created for love of you and be forced to do likewise, be with him a beggar on the run for the rest of your natural lives."

While Fafhrd spoke, Ivrian snatched up her new-filled cup and drained it. Now she stood up straight as a soldier, her pale face flushed, and said scathingly, "*You count the cost!* You speak to me of *things*—" She waved at the many-hued splendor around her, "—of mere property, however costly—when *honor* is at stake. You gave Vlana *your word.* Oh, is knighthood wholly dead?"

Fafhrd could only shrug again and writhe inside and gulp a little easement from his silver mug.

In a master stroke, Vlana tried gently to draw Ivrian down to her golden seat again. "Softly, dearest," she pled. "You have spoken nobly for me and my cause, and believe me, I am most grateful. Your words revived in me great, fine feelings dead these many years. But of us here, only you are truly an aristocrat attuned to the highest proprieties. We other three are naught but thieves. Is it any wonder some of us put safety above honor and word-keeping, and most prudently avoid risking our lives? Yes, we are three thieves and I am outvoted. So please speak no more of honor and rash, dauntless bravery, but sit you down and—"

"You mean, they're both *afraid* to challenge the Thieves' Guild, don't you?" Ivrian said, eyes wide and face twisted by loathing. "I always thought my Mouser was a nobleman first and a thief second. Thieving's nothing. My father lived by cruel thievery done on rich wayfarers and neighbors less powerful than he, yet he was an aristocrat. Oh, you're *cowards,* both of you! *Poltroons!* " she finished, turning her eyes flashing with cold scorn first on the Mouser, then on Fafhrd.

The latter could stand it no longer. He sprang to his feet, face flushed, fists clenched at his sides, quite unmindful of his down-clattered mug and the ominous creak his sudden action drew from the sagging floor.

"*I am not a coward!*" he cried. "I'll dare Thieves' House and fetch you Krovas' head and toss it with blood a-drip at Vlana's feet. I swear that by my sword Graywand here at my side!"

He slapped his left hip, found nothing there but his tunic, and had to content himself with pointing tremble-armed at his belt and scabbarded sword where they lay atop his neatly folded robe—and then picking up, refilling splashily, and draining his mug.

The Gray Mouser began to laugh in high, delighted, tuneful peals.

All stared at him. He came dancing up beside Fafhrd, and still smiling widely, asked, "*Why not?* Who speaks of fearing the Guild-thieves? Who becomes upset at the prospect of this ridiculously easy exploit, when all of us know that all of them, even Krovas and his ruling clique, are but pygmies in mind and skill compared to me or Fafhrd here? A wondrously simple, foolproof scheme has just occurred to me for penetrating Thieves' House, every closet and cranny. Stout Fafhrd and I will put it into effect at once. Are you with me, Northerner?"

"Of course I am," Fafhrd responded gruffly, at the same time frantically wondering what madness had gripped the little fellow.

"Give me a few heartbeats to gather needed props, and we're off!" the Mouser cried. He snatched from shelf and unfolded a stout sack, then raced about, thrusting into it coiled ropes, bandage rolls, rags, jars of ointment and unction and unguent, and other oddments.

"But you can't go *tonight*," Ivrian protested, suddenly grown pale and uncertain-voiced. "You're both . . . in no condition to."

"You're both *drunk*," Vlana said harshly. "Silly drunk—and that way you'll get naught in Thieves' House but your deaths. Fafhrd! Control yourself!"

"Oh, no," Fafhrd told her as he buckled on his sword. "You wanted the head of Krovas heaved at your feet in a great splatter of blood, and that's what you're going to get, like it or not!"

"Softly, Fafhrd," the Mouser interjected, coming to a sudden stop and drawing tight the sack's mouth by its strings. "And softly you too, Lady Vlana, and my dear princess. Tonight I intend but a scouting expedition. No risks run, only the information gained needful for planning our murderous strike tomorrow or the day after. So no head-choppings whatsoever tonight. Fafhrd, you hear me? Whatever may hap, hist's the word. And don your hooded robe."

Fafhrd shrugged, nodded, and obeyed.

Ivrian seemed somewhat relieved. Vlana too, though she said, "Just the same you're both drunk."

"All to the good!" the Mouser assured her with a mad smile. "Drink may slow a man's sword-arm and soften his blows a bit, but it sets his wits ablaze and fires his imagination, and those are the qualities we'll need tonight."

Vlana eyed him dubiously.

Under cover of this confab Fafhrd made quietly yet swiftly to fill once more his and the Mouser's mugs, but Vlana noted it and gave him such a glare that he set down mugs and uncorked jug so swiftly his robe swirled.

The Mouser shouldered his sack and drew open the door. With a casual wave at the girls, but no word spoken, Fafhrd stepped out on the tiny porch. The night-smog had grown so thick he was almost lost to view. The Mouser waved four fingers at Ivrian, then followed Fafhrd.

"Good fortune go with you," Vlana called heartily.

"Oh, be careful, Mouser," Ivrian gasped.

The Mouser, his figure slight against the loom of Fafhrd's, silently drew shut the door.

Their arms automatically gone around each other, the girls waited for the inevitable creaking and groaning of the stairs. It delayed and delayed. The night-smog that had entered the room dissipated and still the silence was unbroken.

"What can they be doing out there?" Ivrian whispered. "Plotting their course?"

Vlana impatiently shook her head, then disentangled herself, tiptoed to the door, opened it, descended softly a few steps, which creaked most dolefully, then returned, shutting the door behind her.

"They're gone," she said in wonder.

"I'm frightened!" Ivrian breathed and sped across the room to embrace the taller girl.

Vlana hugged her tight, then disengaged an arm to shoot the door's three heavy bolts.

In Bones Alley the Mouser returned to his pouch the knotted line by which they'd descended from the lamp hook. He suggested, "How about stopping at the Silver Eel?"

"You mean and just *tell* the girls we've been to Thieves' House?" Fafhrd asked.

"Oh, no," the Mouser protested. "But you missed your stirrup cup upstairs—and so did I."

With a crafty smile Fafhrd drew from his robe two full jugs.

"Palmed 'em, as 'twere, when I set down the mugs. Vlana sees a lot, but not all."

"You're a prudent, far-sighted fellow," the Mouser said admiringly. "I'm proud to call you comrade."

Each uncorked and drank a hearty slug. Then the Mouser led them west, they veering and stumbling only a little, and then north into an even narrower and more noisome alley.

"Plague Court," the Mouser said.

After several preliminary peepings and peerings, they staggered swiftly across wide, empty Crafts Street and into Plague Court again. For a wonder it was growing a little lighter. Looking upward, they saw stars. Yet there was no wind blowing from the north. The air was deathly still.

In their drunken preoccupation with the project at hand and mere locomotion, they did not look behind them. There the night-smog was thicker than ever. A high-circling nighthawk would have seen the stuff converging from all sections of Lankhmar in swift-moving black rivers and rivulets, heaping, eddying, swirling, dark and reeking essence of Lankhmar from its branding irons, braziers, bonfires, kitchen fires and warmth fires, kilns, forges, breweries, distilleries, junk and garbage fires innumerable, sweating alchemist's and sorcerers' dens, crematoriums, charcoal burners' turfed mounds, all those and many more . . . converging purposefully on Dim Lane and particularly on the Silver Eel and the rickety house behind it. The closer to that center it got, the more substantial the smog became, eddy-strands and swirl-tatters tearing off and clinging like black cobwebs to rough stone corners and scraggly surfaced brick.

But the Mouser and Fafhrd merely exclaimed in mild, muted amazement at the stars and cautiously zigzagging across the Street of the Thinkers, called Atheist Avenue by moralists, continued up Plague Court until it forked.

The Mouser chose the left branch, which trended northwest.

"Death Alley."

After a curve and recurve, Cheap Street swung into sight about thirty paces ahead. The Mouser stopped at once and lightly threw his arm against Fafhrd's chest.

Clearly in view across Cheap Street was the wide, low, open doorway of Thieves' House, framed by grimy stone blocks. There led up to it two steps hollowed by the treading of centuries. Orange-yellow light spilled out from bracketed torches inside. There was no porter or guard in sight, not even a watchdog on a chain. The effect was ominous.

"Now how do we get into the damn place?" Fafhrd demanded in a hoarse whisper. "That doorway stinks of traps."

The Mouser answered, scornful at last, "Why, we'll walk straight through that doorway you fear." He frowned. "Tap and hobble, rather. Come on, while I prepare us."

As he drew the skeptically grimacing Fafhrd back down Death Alley until all Cheap Street was again cut off from view, he explained, "We'll pretend to be beggars, members of *their* guild, which is but a branch of the Thieves' Guild and reports in to the Beggarmasters at Thieves' House. We'll be new members, who've gone out by day, so it'll not be expected that the Night Beggarmaster will know our looks."

"But we don't look like beggars," Fafhrd protested. "Beggars have awful sores and limbs all a-twist or lacking altogether."

"That's just what I'm going to take care of now," the Mouser chuckled, drawing Scalpel. Ignoring Fafhrd's backward step and wary glance, the Mouser gazed puzzledly at the long tapering strip of steel he'd bared, then with a happy nod unclipped from his belt Scalpel's scabbard furbished with ratskin, sheathed the sword and swiftly wrapped it up, hilt and all, spirally, with the wide ribbon of a bandage roll dug from his sack.

"There!" he said, knotting the bandage ends. "Now I've a tapping cane."

"What's that?" Fafhrd demanded. "And why?"

The Mouser laid a flimsy black rag across his own eyes and tied it fast behind his head.

"Because I'll be blind, that's why." He took a few shuffling steps, tapping the cobbles ahead with wrapped sword—gripping it by the quillons, or cross guard, so that the grip and pommel were up his sleeve—and groping ahead with his other hand. "That look all right to you?" he asked Fafhrd as he turned back. "Feels perfect to me. Bat-blind!—eh? Oh, don't fret, Fafhrd—the rag's but gauze. I can see through it—fairly well. Besides, I don't have to convince anyone inside Thieves' House I'm actually blind. Most Guild-beggars fake it, as you must know. Now what to do with you? Can't have you blind also—too obvious, might wake suspicion." He uncorked his jug and sucked inspiration. Fafhrd copied this action, on principle.

The Mouser smacked his lips and said, "I've got it! Fafhrd, stand on your right leg and double up your left behind you at the knee. Hold!—don't fall on me! Avaunt! But steady yourself by my shoulder. That's right. Now get that left foot higher. We'll disguise your sword like mine, for a crutch cane—it's thicker and'll look just right. You can also steady yourself with your other hand on my shoulder as you hop—the halt leading the blind. But higher with that left foot! No, it just doesn't come off—I'll have to rope it. But first unclip your scabbard."

Soon the Mouser had Graywand and its scabbard in the same state as Scalpel and was tying Fafhrd's left ankle to his thigh, drawing the rope cruelly tight, though Fafhrd's wine-numbed nerves hardly registered it. Balancing himself with his steel-cored crutch cane as the Mouser worked, he swigged from his jug and pondered deeply.

Brilliant as the Mouser's plan undoubtedly was, there did seem to be drawbacks to it.

"Mouser," he said, "I don't know as I like having our swords tied up, so we can't draw 'em in emergency."

"We can still use 'em as clubs," the Mouser countered, his breath hissing between his teeth as he drew the last knot hard. "Besides, we'll have our knives. Say, pull your belt around until your knife is behind your back, so your robe will hide it sure. I'll do the same with Cat's Claw. Beggars don't carry weapons, at least in view. Stop drinking now, you've had enough. I myself need only a couple swallows more to reach my finest pitch."

"And I don't know as I like going hobbled into that den of cutthroats. I can hope amazingly fast, it's true, but not as fast as I can run. Is it really wise, think you?"

"You can slash yourself loose in an instant," the Mouser hissed with a touch of impatience and anger. "Aren't you willing to make the least sacrifice for art's sake?"

"Oh, very well," Fafhrd said, draining his jug and tossing it aside. "Yes, of course I am."

"Your complexion's too hale," the Mouser said, inspecting him critically. He touched up Fafhrd's features and hands with pale gray grease paint, then added wrinkles with dark. "And your garb's too tidy." He scooped dirt from between the cobbles and smeared it on Fafhrd's robe, then tried to put a rip in it, but the material resisted. He shrugged and tucked his lightened sack under his belt.

"So's yours," Fafhrd observed, and crouching on his right leg got a good handful of muck himself. Heaving himself up with a mighty effort, he wiped the stuff off on the Mouser's cloak and gray silken jerkin too.

The small man cursed, but, "Dramatic consistency," Fafhrd reminded him. "Now come on, while our fires and our stinks are still high." And grasping hold of the Mouser's shoulder, he propelled himself rapidly toward Cheap Street, setting his bandaged sword between cobbles well ahead and taking mighty hops.

"Slow down, idiot," the Mouser cried softly, shuffling along with the speed almost of a skater to keep up, while tapping his (sword) cane like mad. "A cripple's supposed to be *feeble*—that's what draws the sympathy."

Fafhrd nodded wisely and slowed somewhat. The ominous empty doorway slid again into view. The Mouser tilted his jug to get the last of his wine, swallowed awhile, then choked sputteringly. Fafhrd snatched and drained the jug, then tossed it over shoulder to shatter noisily.

They hop-shuffled across Cheap Street and without pause up the two worn steps and through the doorway, past the exceptionally thick wall. Ahead was a long, straight, high-ceilinged corridor ending in a stairs and with doors spilling light at intervals and wall-set torches adding their flare, but empty all its length.

They had just got through the doorway when cold steel chilled the neck and pricked a shoulder of each of them. From just above, two voices commanded in unison, "Halt!"

Although fired—and fuddled—by fortified wine, they each had wit enough to freeze and then very cautiously look upward.

Two gaunt, scarred, exceptionally ugly faces, each topped by a gaudy scarf binding backhair, looked down at them from a big, deep niche just above the doorway. Two bent, gnarly arms thrust down the swords that still pricked them.

"Gone out with the noon beggar-batch, eh?" one of them observed. "Well, you'd better have a high take to justify your tardy return. The Night Beggarmaster's on a Whore Street furlough. Report above to Krovas. Gods, you stink! Better clean up first, or Krovas will have you bathed in live steam. Begone!"

The Mouser and Fafhrd shuffled and hobbled forward at their most authentic. One niche-guard cried after them, "Relax, boys! You don't have to put it on here."

"Practice makes perfect," the Mouser called back in a quavering voice. Fafhrd's fingerends dug his shoulder warningly. They moved along somewhat more naturally, so far as Fafhrd's tied-up leg allowed. Truly, thought Fafhrd, Kos of the Dooms seemed to be leading him direct to Krovas and perhaps head-chopping *would* be the order of the night. And now he and the Mouser began to hear voices, mostly curt and clipped ones, and other noises.

They passed some doorways they'd liked to have paused at, yet the most they dared do was slow down a bit more.

Very interesting were some of those activities. In one room young boys were being trained to pick pouches and slit purses. They'd approach from behind an instructor, and if he heard scuff of bare foot or felt touch of dipping hand—or, worst, heard *clunk* of dropped leaden mockcoin—that boy would be thwacked.

In a second room, older student thieves were doing laboratory work in lock picking. One group was being lectured by a grimy-handed graybeard, who was taking apart a most complex lock piece by weighty piece.

In a third, thieves were eating at long tables. The odors were tempting, even to men full of booze. The Guild did well by its members.

In a fourth, the floor was padded in part and instruction was going on in slipping, dodging, ducking, tumbling, tripping, and otherwise foiling pursuit. A voice like a sergeant-major's rasped, "Nah, nah, nah! You couldn't give your crippled grandmother the slip. I said duck, not genuflect to holy Arth. Now this time—"

By that time the Mouser and Fafhrd were halfway up the end stairs, Fafhrd vaulting somewhat laboriously as he grasped curving banister and swaddled sword.

The second floor duplicated the first, but was as luxurious as the other had been bare. Down the long corridor lamps and filagreed incense pots pendent from the ceiling alternated, diffusing a mild light and spicy smell. The walls were richly draped, the floor thick-carpeted. Yet this corridor was empty too and, moreover, *completely* silent. After a glance at each other, they started off boldly.

The first door, wide open, showed an untenanted room full of racks of garments, rich and plain, spotless and filthy, also wig stands, shelves of beards and such. A disguising room, clearly.

The Mouser darted in and out to snatch up a large green flask from the nearest table. He unstoppered and sniffed it. A rotten-sweet gardenia-reek contended with the nose-sting of spirits of wine. The Mouser sloshed his and Fafhrd's fronts with this dubious perfume.

"Antidote to muck," he explained with the pomp of a physician, stoppering the flask. "Don't want to be parboiled by Krovas. No, no, no."

Two figures appeared at the far end of the corridor and came toward them. The Mouser hid the flask under his cloak, holding it between elbow and side, and he and Fafhrd continued boldly onward.

The next three doorways they passed were shut by heavy doors. As they neared the fifth, the two approaching figures, coming on arm-in-arm, became distinct. Their clothing was that of noblemen, but their faces those of thieves. They were frowning with indignation and suspicion, too, at the Mouser and Fafhrd.

Just then, from somewhere between the two man-pairs, a voice began to speak words in a strange tongue, using the rapid monotone priests employ in a routine service, or some sorcerers in their incantations.

The two richly clad thieves slowed at the seventh doorway and looked in. Their progress ceased altogether. Their necks strained, their eyes widened. They paled. Then of a sudden they hastened onward, almost running, and by-passed Fafhrd and the Mouser as if they were furniture. The incantatory voice drummed on without missing a beat.

The fifth doorway was shut, but the sixth was open. The Mouser peeked in with one eye, his nose brushing the jamb. Then he stepped forward and gazed inside with entranced expression, pushing the black rag onto his forehead for better vision. Fafhrd joined him.

It was a large room, empty so far as could be told of human and animal life, but filled with most interesting things. From knee-high up, the entire far wall was a map of the city of Lankhmar. Every building and street seemed depicted, down to the meanest hovel and narrowest court. There were signs of recent erasure and redrawing at many spots, and here and there little colored hieroglyphs of mysterious import.

The floor was marble, the ceiling blue as lapis lazuli. The side walls were thickly hung, the one with all manner of thieves' tools, from a huge, thick, pry-bar that looked as if it could unseat the universe, to a rod so slim it might be an elf-queen's wand and seemingly designed to telescope out and fish from a distance for precious gauds on milady's spindle-legged, ivory-topped vanity table. The other wall had pad-locked to it all sorts of quaint, gold-gleaming and jewel-flashing objects, evidently mementos chosen for their oddity from the spoils of memora-ble burglaries, from a female mask of thin gold, breathlessly beautiful in its features and contours but thickly set with rubies simulating the spots of the pox in its fever stage, to a knife whose blade was wedged-shaped diamonds set side by side and this diamond cutting-edge looking razor-sharp.

In the center of the room was a bare round table of ebony and ivory squares. About it were set seven straight-backed but well-padded chairs, the one facing the map and away from the Mouser and Fafhrd being higher backed and wider armed than the others—a chief's chair, likely that of Krovas.

The Mouser tiptoed forward, irresistibly drawn, but Fafhrd's left hand clamped down on his shoulder.

Scowling his disapproval, the Northerner brushed down the black rag over the Mouser's eyes again and with his crutch-hand thumbed ahead, then set off in that direction in most carefully calculated, silent hops. With a shrug of disappointment the Mouser followed.

As soon as they had turned away from the doorway, a neatly black-bearded, crop-haired head came like a serpent's around the side of the highest-backed chair and gazed after them from deep-sunken yet glint-ing eyes. Next a snake-supple, long hand followed the head out, crossed thin lips with ophidian forefinger for silence, and then finger-beckoned the two pairs of dark-tunicked men who were standing to either side of the doorway, their backs to the corridor wall, each of the four

gripping a curvy knife in one hand and a dark leather, lead-weighted
bludgeon in the other.

When Fafhrd was halfway to the seventh doorway, from which the
monotonous yet sinister recitation continued to well, there shot out
through it a slender, whey-faced youth, his narrow hands clapped over
his mouth, under terror-wide eyes, as if to shut in screams or vomit,
and with a broom clamped in an armpit, so that he seemed a bit like
a young warlock about to take to the air. He dashed past Fafhrd and
the Mouser and away, his racing footsteps sounding rapid-dull on the
carpeting and hollow-sharp on the stairs before dying away.

Fafhrd gazed back at the Mouser with a grimace and shrug, then
squatting one-legged until the knee of his bound-up leg touched the
floor, advanced half his face past the doorjamb. After a bit, without
otherwise changing position, he beckoned the Mouser to approach. The
latter slowly thrust half his face past the jamb, just above Fafhrd's.

What they saw was a room somewhat smaller than that of the great
map and lit by central lamps that burnt blue-white instead of customary
yellow. The floor was marble, darkly colorful and completely whorled.
The dark walls were hung with astrological and anthropomantic charts
and instruments of magic and shelved with cryptically labeled porcelain
jars and also with vitreous flasks and glass pipes of the oddest shapes,
some filled with colored fluids, but many gleamingly empty. At the foot
of the walls, where the shadows were thickest, broken and discarded
stuff was irregularly heaped, as if swept out of the way and forgot, and
here and there opened a large rathole.

In the center of the room and brightly illuminated by contrast was
a long table with thick top and many stout legs. The Mouser thought
fleetingly of a centipede and then of the bar at the Eel, for the table top
was densely stained and scarred by many a spilt elixir and many a deep
black burn by fire or acid or both.

In the midst of the table an alembic was working. The lamp's flame—
deep blue, this one—kept a-boil in the large crystal cucurbit a dark,
viscid fluid with here and there diamond glints. From out of the thick,
seething stuff, strands of a darker vapor streamed upward to crowd
through the cucurbit's narrow mouth and stain—oddly, with bright
scarlet—the transparent head and then, dead black now, flow down the
narrow pipe from the head into a spherical crystal receiver, larger even
than the cucurbit, and there curl and weave about like so many coils
of living black cord—an endless, skinny, ebon serpent.

Behind the left end of the table stood a tall, yet hunch-backed man
in black robe and hood, which shadowed more than hid a face of which

the most prominent features were a long, thick, pointed nose with out-jutting, almost chinless mouth. His complexion was sallow-gray like sandy clay. A short-haired, bristly, gray beard grew high on his wide cheeks. From under a receding forehead and bushy gray brows, wide-set eyes looked intently down at an age-browned scroll, which his disgustingly small clubhands, knuckles big, short backs gray-bristled, ceaselessly unrolled and rolled up again. The only move his eyes ever made, besides the short side-to-side one as he read the lines he was rapidly intoning, was an occasional glance at the alembic.

On the other end of the table, beady eyes darting from the sorcerer to the alembic and back again, crouched a small black beast, the first glimpse of which made Fafhrd dig fingers painfully into the Mouser's shoulder and the latter almost gasp, but not from the pain. It was most like a rat, yet it had a higher forehead and closer-set eyes, while its forepaws, which it constantly rubbed together in what seemed restless glee, looked like tiny copies of the sorcerer's clubhands.

Simultaneously yet independently, Fafhrd and the Mouser each became certain it was the beast which had gutter-escorted Slivikin and his mate, then fled, and each recalled what Ivrian had said about a witch's familiar and Vlana about the likelihood of Krovas employing a warlock.

The tempo of the incantation quickened; the blue-white flames brightened and hissed audibly; the fluid in the cucurbit grew thick as lava; great bubbles formed and loudly broke; the black rope in the receiver writhed like a nest of snakes; there was an increasing sense of invisible presences; the supernatural tension grew almost unendurable, and Fafhrd and the Mouser were hard put to keep silent the open-mouthed gapes by which they now breathed, and each feared his heart-beat could be heard yards away.

Abruptly the incantation peaked and broke off, like a drum struck very hard, then instantly silenced by palm and fingers outspread against the head. With a bright flash and dull explosion, cracks innumerable appeared in the cucurbit; its crystal became white and opaque, yet it did not shatter or drip. The head lifted a span, hung there, fell back. While two black nooses appeared among the coils in the receiver and suddenly narrowed until they were only two big black knots.

The sorcerer grinned, let the end of the parchment roll up with a snap, and shifted his gaze from the receiver to his familiar, while the latter chittered shrilly and bounded up and down in rapture.

"Silence, Slivikin! Comes now *your* time to race and strain and sweat," the sorcerer cried, speaking pidgin Lankhmarese now, but so rapidly and in so squeakingly high-pitched a voice that Fafhrd and the Mouser could barely follow him. They did, however, both realize they had been completely mistaken as to the identity of Slivikin. In moment of disaster, the fat thief had called to the witch-beast for help rather than to his human comrade.

"Yes, master," Slivikin squeaked back no less clearly, in an instant revising the Mouser's opinions about talking animals. He continued in the same fife-like, fawning tones, "Harkening in obedience, Hristomilo."

Hristomilo ordered in whiplash pipings, "To your appointed work! See to it you summon an ample sufficiency of feasters!—I want the bodies stripped to skeletons, so the bruises of the enchanted smog and all evidence of death by suffocation will be vanished utterly. But forget not the loot! On your mission, now—depart!"

Slivikin, who at every command had bobbed his head in manner reminiscent of his bouncing, now squealed, "I'll see it done!" and gray lightning-like, leaped a long leap to the floor and down an inky rathole.

Hristomilo, rubbing together his disgusting clubhands much as Slivikin had his, cried chucklingly, "What Slevyas lost, my magic has re-won!"

Fafhrd and the Mouser drew back out of the doorway, partly for fear of being seen, partly in revulsion from what they had seen and heard, and in poignant if useless pity for Slevyas, whoever he might be, and for the other unknown victims of the rat-like and conceivably rat-related sorcerer's deathspells, poor strangers already dead and due to have their flesh eaten from their bones.

Fafhrd wrested the green bottle from the Mouser and, though almost-gagging on the rotten-flowery reek, gulped a large, stinging mouthful. The Mouser couldn't quite bring himself to do the same, but was comforted by the spirits of wine he inhaled.

Then he saw, beyond Fafhrd, standing before the doorway to the map room, a richly clad man with gold-hilted knife jewel-scabbarded at his side. His sunken-eyed face was prematurely wrinkled by responsibility, overwork, and authority, and framed by neatly cropped black hair and beard. Smiling, he silently beckoned them with a serpentine gesture.

The Mouser and Fafhrd obeyed, the latter returning the green bottle to the former, who recapped it and thrust it under his left elbow with well-concealed irritation.

Each guessed their summoner was Krovas, the Guild's Grandmaster. Once again Fafhrd marveled, as he hobbledehoyed along, reeling and belching, how Kos or the Fates were guiding him to his target tonight.

The Mouser, more alert and more apprehensive too, was reminding himself that they had been directed by the niche-guards to report to Krovas, so that the situation, if not developing quite in accord with his own misty plans, was still not deviating disastrously.

Yet not even his alertness, nor Fafhrd's primeval instincts, gave them forewarning as they followed Krovas into the map room.

Two steps inside, each of them was shoulder-grabbed and bludgeon-menaced by a pair of ruffians further armed with knives tucked in their belts.

"All secure, Grandmaster," one of the ruffians rapped out.

Krovas swung the highest-backed chair around and sat down, eyeing them cooly.

"What brings two stinking, drunken beggar-guildsmen into the top-restricted precincts of the masters?" he asked quietly.

The Mouser felt the sweat of relief bead his forehead. The disguises he had brilliantly conceived were still working, taking in even the head man, though he had spotted Fafhrd's tipsiness. Resuming his blind-man manner, he quavered, "We were directed by the guard above the Cheap Street door to report to you in person, great Krovas, the Night Beggarmaster being on furlough for reasons of sexual hygiene. Tonight we've made good haul!" And fumbling in his purse, ignoring as far as possible the tightened grip on his shoulders, he brought out a golden coin and displayed it tremble-handed.

"Spare me your inexpert acting," Krovas said sharply. "I'm not one of your marks. And take that rag off your eyes."

The Mouser obeyed and stood to attention again insofar as his pin-ioning would permit, and smiling the more seeming carefree because of his reawakening uncertainties. Conceivably he wasn't doing quite as brilliantly as he'd thought.

Krovas leaned forward and said placidly yet piercingly, "Granted you were so ordered, why were you spying into a room beyond this one when I spotted you?"

"We saw brave thieves flee from that room," the Mouser answered pat. "Fearing that some danger threatened the Guild, my comrade and I investigated, ready to scotch it."

"But what we saw and heard only perplexed us, great sir," Fafhrd appended quite smoothly.

"I didn't ask you, sot. Speak when you're spoken to," Krovas snapped at him. Then, to the Mouser, "You're an overweening rogue, most presumptuous for your rank. Beggars claim to protect thieves indeed! I'm of a mind to have you both flogged for your spying, and again for your drunkenness, aye, and once more for your lies."

In a flash the Mouser decided that further insolence—and lying, too—rather than fawning, was what the situation required. "I am a most presumptuous rogue indeed, sir," he said smugly. Then he set his face solemn. "But now I see the time has come when I must speak darkest truth entire. The Day Beggarmaster suspects a plot against your own life, sir, by one of your highest and closest lieutenants—one you trust so well you'd not believe it, sir. He told us that! So he set me and my comrade secretly to guard you and sniff out the verminous villain."

"More and clumsier lies!" Krovas snarled, but the Mouser saw his face grow pale. The Grandmaster half rose from his seat. "Which lieutenant?"

The Mouser grinned and relaxed. His two captors gazed sideways at him curiously, losing their grip a little. Fafhrd's pair seemed likewise intrigued.

The Mouser then asked coolly, "Are you questioning me as a trusty spy or a pinioned liar? If the latter, I'll not insult you with one more word."

Krovas' face darkened. "Boy!" he called. Through the curtains of an inner doorway, a youth with the dark complexion of a Kleshite and clad only in a black loincloth sprang to kneel before Krovas, who ordered, "Summon first my sorcerer, next the thieves Slevyas and Fissif," whereupon the dark youth dashed into the corridor.

Krovas hesitated a moment in thought, then shot a hand toward Fafhrd. "What do you know of this drunkard? Do you support your mate's crazy tale?"

Fafhrd merely sneered his face and folded his arms, the still-slack grip of his captors permitting it, his sword-crutch hanging against his body from his lightly gripping hand. Then he scowled as there came a sudden shooting pain in his numbed, bound-up left leg, which he had forgotten.

Krovas raised a clenched fist and himself wholly from his chair, in prelude to some fearsome command—likely that Fafhrd and the Mouser be tortured, but at that moment Hristomilo came gliding into the room, his feet presumably taking swift, but very short steps—at any rate his black robe hung undisturbed to the marble floor despite his slithering speed.

There was a shock at his entrance. All eyes in the map room followed him, breaths were held, and the Mouser and Fafhrd felt the horny hands that gripped them shake just a little. Even Krovas' tense expression became also guardedly uneasy.

Outwardly oblivious to this reaction to his appearance, Hristomilo, smiling thin-lipped, halted close to one side of Krovas' chair and inclined his hood-shadowed rodent face in the ghost of a bow.

Krovas asked sharply yet nervously, gesturing toward the Mouser and Fafhrd, "Do you know these two?"

Hristomilo nodded decisively. "They just now peered a befuddled eye each at me," he said, "whilst I was about that business we spoke of. I'd have shooed them off, reported them, save such action would have broken my spell, put my words out of time with the alembic's workings. The one's a Northerner, the other's features have a southern cast—from Tovilyis or near, most like. Both younger than their now-looks. Freelance bravoes, I'd judge 'em, the sort the Brotherhood hires as extras when they get at once several big guard and escort jobs. Clumsily disguised now, of course, as beggars."

Fafhrd by yawning, the Mouser by pitying headshake tried to convey that all this was so much poor guesswork. The Mouser even added a warning glare, brief as lightning, to suggest to Krovas that the conspiring lieutenant might be the Grandmaster's own sorcerer.

"That's all I can tell you without reading their minds," Hristomilo concluded. "Shall I fetch my lights and mirrors?"

"Not yet." Krovas faced the Mouser and said, "Now speak truth, or have it magicked from you and then be whipped to death. Which of my lieutenants were you set to spy on by the Day Beggarmaster? But you're lying about that commission, I believe?"

"Oh, no," the Mouser denied it guilelessly. "We reported our every act to the Day Beggarmaster and he approved them, told us to spy our best and gather every scrap of fact and rumor we could about the conspiracy."

"And he told me not a word about it!" Krovas rapped out. "If true, I'll have Bannat's head for this! But you're lying, aren't you?"

As the Mouser gazed with wounded eyes at Krovas, a portly man limped past the doorway with help of a gilded staff. He moved with silence and aplomb.

But Krovas saw him. "Night Beggarmaster!" he called sharply. The limping man stopped, turned, came crippling majestically through the door. Krovas stabbed a finger at the Mouser, then Fafhrd. "Do you know these two, Flim?"

The Night Beggarmaster unhurriedly studied each for a space, then shook his head with its turban of cloth of gold. "Never seen either before. What are they? Fink beggars?"

"But Flim wouldn't know us," the Mouser explained desperately, feeling everything collapsing in on him and Fafhrd. "All our contacts were with Bannat alone."

Flim said quietly, "Bannat's been abed with the swamp ague this past ten-day. Meanwhile I have been Day Beggarmaster as well as Night."

At that moment Slevyas and Fissif came hurrying in behind Flim. The tall thief bore on his jaw a bluish lump. The fat thief's head was bandaged above his darting eyes. He pointed quickly at Fafhrd and the Mouser and cried, "There are the two that slugged us, took our Jengao loot, and slew our escort."

The Mouser lifted his elbow and the green bottle crashed to shards at his feet on the hard marble. Gardenia-reek sprang swiftly through the air.

But more swiftly still the Mouser, shaking off the careless hold of his startled guards, sprang toward Krovas, clubbing his wrapped-up sword.

With startling speed Flim thrust out his gilded staff, tripping the Mouser, who went heels over head, midway seeking to change his involuntary somersault into a voluntary one.

Meanwhile Fafhrd lurched heavily against his left-hand captor, at the same time swinging bandaged Graywand strongly upward to strike his right-hand captor under the jaw. Regaining his one-legged balance with a mighty contortion, he hopped for the loot-wall behind him.

Slevyas made for the wall of thieves' tools, and with a muscle-crack-ing effort wrenched the great pry-bar from its padlocked ring.

Scrambling to his feet after a poor landing in front of Krovas' chair, the Mouser found it empty and the Thief King in a half-crouch behind it, gold-hilted dagger drawn, deep-sunk eyes coldly battle-wild. Spin-ning around, he saw Fafhrd's guards on the floor, the one sprawled senseless, the other starting to scramble up, while the great Northerner, his back against the wall of weird jewelry, menaced the whole room with wrapped-up Graywand and with his long knife, jerked from its scabbard behind him.

Likewise drawing Cat's Claw, the Mouser cried in trumpet-voice of battle, "Stand aside, all! He's gone mad! I'll hamstring his good leg for you!" And racing through the press and between his own two guards, who still appeared to hold him in some awe, he launched himself with flashing dirk at Fafhrd, praying that the Northerner, drunk now with battle as well as wine and poisonous perfume, would recognize him and guess his stratagem.

Graywand slashed well above his ducking head. His new friend not only guessed, but was playing up—and not just missing by accident, the Mouser hoped. Stopping low by the wall, he cut the lashings on Fafhrd's left leg. Graywand and Fafhrd's long knife continued to spare him. Springing up, he headed for the corridor, crying overshouldered to Fafhrd, "Come on!"

Hristomilo stood well out of his way, quietly observing. Fissif scuttled toward safety. Krovas stayed behind his chair, shouting, "Stop them! Head them off!"

The three remaining ruffian guards, at last beginning to recover their fighting-wits, gathered to oppose the Mouser. But menacing them with swift feints of his dirk, he slowed them and darted between—and then just in the nick of time knocked aside with a downsweep of wrapped-up Scalpel Flim's gilded staff, thrust once again to trip him.

All this gave Slevyas time to return from the tools-wall and aim at the Mouser a great swinging blow with the massive pry-bar. But even as that blow started, a very long, bandaged and scabbarded sword on a very long arm thrust over the Mouser's shoulder and solidly and heavily poked Slevyas high on the chest, jolting him backwards, so that the pry-bar's swing was short and sang past harmlessly.

Then the Mouser found himself in the corridor and Fafhrd beside him, though for some weird reason still only hopping. The Mouser pointed toward the stairs. Fafhrd nodded, but delayed to reach high, still on one leg only, and rip off the nearest wall a dozen yards of heavy drapes, which he threw across the corridor to baffle pursuit.

They reached the stairs and started up the next flight, the Mouser in advance. There were cries behind, some muffled.

"Stop hopping, Fafhrd!" the Mouser ordered querulously. "You've got two legs again."

"Yes, and the other's still dead," Fafhrd complained. "Ahh! Now feeling begins to return to it."

A thrown knife whished between them and dully clinked as it hit the wall point-first and stone powder flew. Then they were around the bend.

Two more empty corridors, two more curving flights, and then they saw above them on the last landing a stout ladder mounting to a dark, square hole in the roof. A thief with hair bound back by a colorful handkerchief—it appeared to be the door guards' identification— menaced the Mouser with drawn sword, but when he saw there were two of them, both charging him determinedly with shining knives and strange staves or clubs, he turned and ran down the last empty corridor.

The Mouser, followed closely by Fafhrd, rapidly mounted the ladder and vaulted up through the hatch into the star-crusted night.

He found himself near the unrailed edge of a slate roof which slanted enough to have made it look most fearsome to a novice roof-walker, but safe as houses to a veteran.

Turning back at a bumping sound, he saw Fafhrd prudently hoisting the ladder. Just as he got it free, a knife flashed up close past him out of the hatch.

It clattered down near them and slid off the roof. The Mouser loped south across the slates and was halfway from the hatch to that end of the roof when the faint chink came of the knife striking the cobbles of Murder Alley.

Fafhrd followed more slowly, in part perhaps from a lesser experience of roofs, in part because he still limped a bit to favor his left leg, and in part because he was carrying the heavy ladder balanced on his right shoulder.

"We won't need that," the Mouser called back.

Without hesitation Fafhrd heaved it joyously over the edge. By the time it crashed in Murder Alley, the Mouser was leaping down two yards and across a gap of one to the next roof, of opposite and lesser pitch. Fafhrd landed beside him.

The Mouser led them at almost a run through a sooty forest of chimneys, chimney pots, ventilators with tails that made them always face the wind, black-legged cisterns, hatch covers, bird houses, and pigeon traps across five roofs, until they reached the Street of the Thinkers at a point where it was crossed by a roofed passageway much like the one at Rokkermas and Slaarg's.

While they crossed it at a crouching lope, something hissed close past them and clattered ahead. As they leaped down from the roof of the bridge, three more somethings hissed over their heads to clatter beyond. One rebounded from a square chimney almost to the Mouser's feet. He picked it up, expecting a stone, and was surprised by the greater weight of a leaden ball big as two doubled-up fingers.

"They," he said, jerking thumb overshoulder, "lost no time in getting slingers on the roof. When roused, they're good."

Southeast then through another black chimney-forest toward a point on Cheap Street where upper stories overhung the street so much on either side that it would be easy to leap the gap. During this roof-traverse, an advancing front of night-smog, dense enough to make them cough and wheeze, engulfed them and for perhaps sixty heartbeats the Mouser had to slow to a shuffle and feel his way, Fafhrd's hand on his shoulder. Just short of Cheap Street they came abruptly and completely out of the smog and saw the stars again, while the black front rolled off northward behind them.

"Now what the devil was that?" Fafhrd asked and the Mouser shrugged.

A nighthawk would have seen a vast thick hoop of black night-smog blowing out in all directions from a center near the Silver Eel.

East of Cheap Street the two comrades soon made their way to the ground, landing back in Plague Court.

Then at last they looked at each other and their trammeled swords and their filthy faces and clothing made dirtier still by roof-soot, and they laughed and laughed and laughed, Fafhrd roaring still as he bent over to massage his left leg above and below knee. This hooting self-mockery continued while they unwrapped their swords—the Mouser as if his were a surprise package—and clipped their scabbards once more to their belts. Their exertions had burnt out of them the last mote and atomy of strong wine and even stronger stenchful perfume, but they felt no desire whatever for more drink, only the urge to get home and eat hugely and guzzle hot, bitter gahveh, and tell their lovely girls at length the tale of their mad adventure.

They loped on side by side.

Free of night-smog and drizzled with starlight, their cramped surroundings seemed much less stinking and oppressive than when they had set out. Even Bones Alley had a freshness to it.

They hastened up the long, creaking, broken-treaded stairs with an easy carefulness, and when they were both on the porch, the Mouser shoved at the door to open it with surprise-swiftness.

It did not budge.

"Bolted," he said to Fafhrd shortly. He noted now there was hardly any light at all coming through the cracks around the door, nor had any been noticeable through the lattices—at most, a faint orange-red glow. Then with sentimental grin and in fond voice in which only the ghost of uneasiness lurked, he said, "They've gone to sleep, the unworrying wenches!" He knocked loudly thrice and then cupping his lips called softly at the door crack, "Hola, Ivrian! I'm home safe. Hail, Vlana! Your man's done you proud, felling Guild-thieves innumerable with one foot tied behind his back!"

There was no sound whatever from inside—that is, if one discounted a rustling so faint it was impossible to be sure of it.

Fafhrd was wrinkling his nostrils. "I smell vermin."

The Mouser banged on the door again. Still no response.

Fafhrd motioned him out of the way, hunching his big shoulder to crash the portal.

The Mouser shook his head and with a deft tap, slide, and a tug removed a brick that a moment before had looked to be a firm-set part of the wall beside the door. He reached in all his arm. There was the scrape of a bolt being withdrawn, then another, then a third. He swiftly recovered his arm and the door swung fully inward at touch.

But neither he nor Fafhrd rushed in at once, as both had intended to, for the indefinable scent of danger and the unknown came puffing out along with an increased reek of filthy beast and a slight, sickening sweet scent that though female was no decent female perfume.

They could see the room faintly by the orange glow coming from the small oblong of the open door of the little, well-blacked stove. Yet the oblong did not sit properly upright but was unnaturally a-tilt—clearly the stove had been half overset and now leaned against a side wall of the fireplace, its small door fallen open in that direction.

By itself alone, that unnatural angle conveyed the entire impact of a universe overturned.

The orange glow showed the carpets oddly rucked up with here and there ragged black circles a palm's breadth across, the neatly stacked candles scattered about below their shelves along with some of the jars and enameled boxes, and—above all—two black, low, irregular, longish heaps, the one by the fireplace, the other half on the golden couch, half at its foot.

From each heap there stared at the Mouser and Fafhrd innumerable pairs of tiny, rather widely set, furnace-red eyes.

On the thickly carpeted floor on the other side of the fireplace was a silver cobweb—a fallen silver cage, but no love birds sang from it.

There was the faint scrape of metal as Fafhrd made sure Graywand was loose in his scabbard.

As if that tiny sound had beforehand been chosen as the signal for attack, each instantly whipped out sword and they advanced side by side into the room, warily at first, testing the floor with each step.

At the screech of the swords being drawn, the tiny furnace-red eyes had winked and shifted restlessly, and now with the two men's approach they swiftly scattered pattering, pair by red pair, each pair at the forward end of a small, low, slender, hairless-tailed black body, and each making for one of the black circles in the rugs, where they vanished.

Indubitably the black circles were ratholes newly gnawed up through the floor and rugs, while the red-eyed creatures were black rats.

Fafhrd and the Mouser sprang forward, slashing and chopping at them in a frenzy, cursing and human-snarling besides.

They sundered few. The rats fled with preternatural swiftness, most of them disappearing down holes near the walls and the fireplace.

Also Fafhrd's first frantic chop went through the floor and on his third step, with an ominous crack and splintering, his leg plunged through the floor to his hip. The Mouser darted past him, unmindful of further crackings.

Fafhrd heaved out his trapped leg, not even noting the splinter-scratches it got and as unmindful as the Mouser of the continuing creakings. The rats were gone. He lunged after his comrade, who had thrust a bunch of kindlers into the stove, to make more light.

The horror was that, although the rats were all gone, the two longish heaps remained, although considerably diminished and, as now shown clearly by the yellow flames leaping from the tilted black door, changed in hue—no longer were the heaps red-beaded black, but a mixture of gleaming black and dark brown, a sickening purple-blue, violet and velvet black and snow-serpent white, and the reds of stockings and blood and bloody flesh and bone.

Although hands and feet had been gnawed bone-naked, and bodies tunneled heart-deep, the two faces had been spared. But that was not good, for they were purple-blue from death by strangulation, lips drawn back, eyes bulging, all features contorted in agony. Only the black and very dark brown hair gleamed unchanged—that and the white, white teeth.

As each man stared down at his love, unable to look away despite the waves of horror and grief and rage washing higher and higher in him, each saw a tiny black strand uncurl from the black depression ringing each throat and drift off, dissipating, toward the open door behind them—two strands of night-smog.

With a crescendo of crackings the floor sagged three spans more in the center before arriving at a new temporary stability.

Edges of centrally tortured minds noted details: That Vlana's silver-hilted dagger skewered to the floor a rat, which, likely enough, overeager had approached too closely before the night-smog had done its magic work. That her belt and pouch were gone. That the blue-enameled box inlaid with silver, in which Ivrian had put the Mouser's share of the highjacked jewels, was gone too.

The Mouser and Fafhrd lifted to each other white, drawn faces, which were quite mad, yet completely joined in understanding and purpose. No need for Fafhrd to explain why he stripped off his robe and hood, or why he jerked up Vlana's dagger, snapped the rat off it with a wrist-flick, and thrust it in his belt. No need for the Mouser to tell why he searched out a half dozen jars of oil and after smashing three of them in front of the flaming stove, paused, thought, and stuck the other three in the sack at his waist, adding to them the remaining kindlers and the fire-pot, brimmed with red coals, its top lashed down tight.

Then, still without word exchanged, the Mouser reached into the fireplace and without a wince at the burning metal's touch, deliberately tipped the flaming stove forward, so that it fell door-down on oil-soaked rugs. Yellow flames sprang up around him.

They turned and raced for the door. With louder crackings than any before, the floor collapsed. They desperately scrambled their way up a steep hill of sliding carpets and reached door and porch just before all behind them gave way and the flaming rugs and stove and all the firewood and candles and the golden couch and all the little tables and boxes and jars—and the unthinkably mutilated bodies of their first loves—cascaded into the dry, dusty, cobweb-choked room below, and the great flames of a cleansing or at least obliterating cremation began to flare upward.

They plunged down the stairs, which tore away from the wall and collapsed in the dark as they reached the ground. They had to fight their way over the wreckage to get to Bones Alley.

By then the flames were darting their bright lizard-tongues out of the shuttered attic windows and the boarded-up ones in the story just below. By the time they reached Plague Court, running side by side at top speed, the Silver Eel's fire alarm was clanging cacophonously behind them.

They were still sprinting when they took the Death Alley fork. Then the Mouser grappled Fafhrd and forced him to a halt. The big man struck out, cursing insanely, and only desisted—his white face still a lunatic's—when the Mouser cried panting, "Only ten heartbeats to arm us!"

He pulled the sack from his belt and keeping tight hold of its neck, crashed it on the cobbles—hard enough to smash not only the bottles of oil, but also the fire-pot, for the sack was soon flaming at its base.

Then he drew gleaming Scalpel and Fafhrd Graywand, and they raced on, the Mouser swinging his sack in a great circle beside him to fan its flames. It was a veritable ball of fire burning his left hand as they dashed across Cheap Street and into Thieves' House, and the Mouser, leaping high, swung it up into the great niche above the doorway and let go of it.

The niche-guards screeched in surprise and pain at the fiery invader of their hidey-hole.

Student thieves poured out of the door ahead at the screeching and foot-pounding, and then poured back as they saw the fierce point of flames and the two demon-faced on-comers brandishing their long, shining swords.

One skinny little apprentice—he could hardly have been ten years old—lingered too long. Graywand thrust him pitilessly through, as his big eyes bulged and his small mouth gaped in horror and plea to Fafhrd for mercy.

Now from ahead of them there came a weird, wailing call, hollow and hair-raising, and doors began to thud shut instead of spewing forth the armed guards Fafhrd and the Mouser prayed would appear to be skewered by their swords. Also, despite the long, bracketed torches looking newly renewed, the corridor was darkening.

The reason for this last became clear as they plunged up the stairs. Strands of night-smog appeared in the stairwell, materializing from nothing, or the air.

The strands grew longer and more tangible. They touched and clung nastily. In the corridor above they were forming from wall to wall and from ceiling to floor, like a gigantic cobweb, and were becoming so substantial that the Mouser and Fafhrd had to slash them to get through, or so their two maniac minds believed. The black web muffled a little a repetition of the eerie, wailing call, which came from the seventh door ahead and this time ended in a gleeful chittering and cackling as insane as the emotions of the two attackers.

Here, too, doors were thudding shut. In an ephemeral flash of rationality, it occurred to the Mouser that it was not he and Fafhrd the thieves feared, for they had not been seen yet, but rather Hristomilo and his magic, even though working in defense of Thieves' House.

Even the map room, whence counterattack would most likely erupt, was closed off by a huge oaken, iron-studded door.

They were now twice slashing the black, clinging, rope-thick spider-web for every single step they drove themselves forward. While midway between the map and magic rooms, there was forming on the inky web, ghostly at first but swiftly growing more substantial, a black spider as big as a wolf.

The Mouser slashed heavy cobweb before it, dropped back two steps, then hurled himself at it in a high leap. Scalpel thrust through it, striking amidst its eight new-formed jet eyes, and it collapsed like a daggered bladder, loosing a vile stink.

Then he and Fafhrd were looking into the magic room, the alchemist's chamber. It was much as they had seen it before, except some things were doubled, or multiplied even further.

On the long table two blue-boiled cucurbits bubbled and roiled, their heads shooting out a solid, writhing rope more swiftly than moves the black swamp-cobra, which can run down a man—and not into twin receivers, but into the open air of the room (if any of the air in Thieves' House could have been called open then) to weave a barrier between their swords and Hristomilo, who once more stood tall though hunchbacked over his sorcerous, brown parchment, though this time his exultant gaze was chiefly fixed on Fafhrd and the Mouser, with only an occasional downward glance at the text of the spell he drummingly intoned.

While at the other end of the table, in web-free space, there bounced not only Slivikin, but also a huge rat matching him in size in all members except the head.

From the ratholes at the foot of the walls, red eyes glittered and gleamed in pairs.

With a bellow of rage Fafhrd began slashing at the black barrier, but the ropes were replaced from the cucurbit heads as swiftly as he sliced them, while the cut ends, instead of drooping slackly, now began to strain hungrily toward him like constrictive snakes or strangle-vines.

He suddenly shifted Graywand to his left hand, drew his long knife and hurled it at the sorcerer. Flashing toward its mark, it cut through three strands, was deflected and slowed by a fourth and fifth, almost halted by a sixth, and ended hanging futilely in the curled grip of a seventh.

Hristomilo laughed cacklingly and grinned, showing his huge, upper incisors, while Slivikin chittered in ecstasy and bounded the higher.

The Mouser hurled Cat's Claw with no better result—worse, indeed, since his action gave two darting smog-strands time to curl hamperingly around his sword-hand and stranglingly around his neck. Black rats came racing out of the big holes at the cluttered base of the walls.

Meanwhile other strands snaked around Fafhrd's ankles, knees and left arm, almost toppling him. But even as he fought for balance, he jerked Vlana's dagger from his belt and raised it over his shoulder, its silver hilt glowing, its blade brown with dried rat's-blood.

The grin left Hristomilo's face as he saw it. The sorcerer screamed strangely and importuningly then, and drew back from his parchment and the table, and raised clawed clubhands to ward off doom.

Vlana's dagger sped unimpeded through the black web—its strands even seemed to part for it—and betwixt the sorcerer's warding hands, to bury itself to the hilt in his right eye.

He screamed thinly in dire agony and clawed at his face.

The black web writhed as if in death spasm.

The cucurbits shattered as one, spilling their lava on the scarred table, putting out the blue flames even as the thick wood of the table began to smoke a little at the lava's edge. Lava dropped with *plops* on the dark marble floor.

With a faint, final scream Hristomilo pitched forward, hands clutched to his eyes above his jutting nose, silver dagger-hilt protruding between his fingers.

The web grew faint, like wet ink washed with a gush of clear water.

The Mouser raced forward and transfixed Slivikin and the huge rat with one thrust of Scalpel before the beasts knew what was happening. They too died swiftly with thin screams, while all the other rats turned tail and fled back down their holes swift almost as black lightning.

Then the last trace of night-smog or sorcery-smoke vanished, and Fafhrd and the Mouser found themselves standing alone with three dead bodies amidst a profound silence that seemed to fill not only this room but all Thieves' House. Even the cucurbit-lava had ceased to move, was hardening, and the wood of the table no longer smoked.

Their madness was gone and all their rage, too—vented to the last red atomy and glutted to more than satiety. They had no more urge to kill Krovas or any other thieves than to swat flies. With horrified inner-eye Fafhrd saw the pitiful face of the child-thief he'd skewered in his lunatic anger.

Only their grief remained with them, diminished not one whit, but rather growing greater—that and an ever more swiftly growing revulsion from all that was around them: the dead, the disordered magic room, all Thieves' House, all of the city of Lankhmar to its last stinking alleyway.

With a hiss of disgust the Mouser jerked Scalpel from the rodent cadavers, wiped it on the nearest cloth, and returned it to its scabbard. Fafhrd likewise sketchily cleansed and sheathed Graywand. Then the two men picked up their knife and dirk from where they'd dropped to the floor when the web had dematerialized, though neither glanced at Vlana's dagger where it was buried. But on the sorcerer's table they did notice Vlana's black velvet, silver-worked pouch and belt, and Ivrian's blue-enameled box inlaid with silver. These they took.

With no more word than they had exchanged back at the Mouser's burnt nest behind the Eel, but with a continuing sense of their unity of purpose, their identity of intent, and of their comradeship, they made their way with shoulders bowed and with slow, weary steps which only very gradually quickened out of the magic room and down the thick-carpeted corridor, past the map room's wide door now barred with oak and iron, and past all the other shut, silent doors, down the echoing stairs, their footsteps speeding a little; down the bare-floored lower corridor past its closed, quiet doors, their footsteps resounding loudly no matter how softly they sought to tread; under the deserted, black-scorched guard-niche, and so out into Cheap Street, turning left and north because that was the nearest way to the Street of the Gods, and there turning right and east—not a waking soul in the wide street except for one skinny, bent-backed apprentice lad unhappily swabbing the flagstones in front of a wine shop in the dim pink light beginning to seep from the east, although there were many forms asleep, a-snore and a-dream in the gutters and under the dark porticoes—yes, turning right and east down the Street of the Gods, for that way was the Marsh Gate, leading to Causey Road across the Great Salt Marsh; and the Marsh Gate was the nearest way out of the great and glamorous city that was now loathsome to them, a city of beloved, unfaceable ghosts—indeed, not to be endured for one more stabbing, leaden heartbeat than was necessary.

MICHAEL MOORCOCK
The Lands Beyond the World

1

HIS BONE-WHITE, long-fingered hand upon a carved demon's head in black-brown hardwood (one of the few such decorations to be found anywhere about the vessel), the tall man stood alone in the ship's fo'csle and stared through large, slanting, crimson eyes at the mist into which they moved with a speed and sureness to make any mortal mariner marvel and become incredulous.

There were sounds in the distance, incongruent with the sounds of even this nameless, timeless sea: thin sounds, agonized and terrible, for all that they remained remote—yet the ship followed them, as if drawn by them; they grew louder—pain and despair were there, but terror was predominant.

Elric had heard such sounds echoing from his cousin Yyrkoon's sardonically named "Pleasure Chambers" in the days before he had fled the responsibilities of ruling all that remained of the old Melnibonéan Empire. These were the voices of men whose very souls were under siege; men to whom death meant not mere extinction, but a continuation of existence, forever in thrall to some cruel and supernatural master. He had heard men cry so when his salvation and his nemesis, his great black battle-blade Stormbringer, drank their souls.

He did not savor the sound: he hated it, turned his back away from the source and was about to descend the ladder to the main deck when he realized that Otto Blendker had come up behind him. Now that Corum had been borne off by friends with chariots which could ride upon the surface of the water, Blendker was the last of those comrades to have fought at Elric's side against the two alien sorcerers Gagak and Agak.

349

Blendker's black, scarred face was troubled. The ex-scholar, turned hireling sword, covered his ears with his huge palms.

"Ach! By the Twelve Symbols of Reason, Elric, who makes that din? It's as though we sail close to the shores of Hell itself!"

Prince Elric of Melniboné shrugged. "I'd be prepared to forego an answer and leave my curiosity unsatisfied, Master Blendker, if only our ship would change course. As it is, we sail closer and closer to the source."

Blendker grunted his agreement. "I've no wish to encounter whatever it is that causes those poor fellows to scream so! Perhaps we should inform the Captain."

"You think he does not know where his own ship sails?" Elric's smile had little humor.

The tall black man rubbed at the inverted V-shaped scar which ran from his forehead to his jawbones. "I wonder if he plans to put us into battle again?"

"I'll not fight another for him." Elric's hand moved from the carved rail to the pommel of his runesword. "I have business of my own to attend to, once I'm back on real land."

A wind came from nowhere. There was a sudden rent in the mist. Now Elric could see that the ship sailed through rust-colored water. Peculiar lights gleamed in that water, just below the surface. There was an impression of creatures moving ponderously in the depths of the ocean and, for a moment, Elric thought he glimpsed a white, bloated face not dissimilar to his own—a Melnibonéan face. Impulsively he whirled, back to the rail, looking past Blendker as he strove to control the nausea in his throat.

For the first time since he had come aboard the Dark Ship he was able clearly to see the length of the vessel. Here were the two great wheels, one beside him on the foredeck, one at the far end of the ship on the rear deck, tended now as always by the Steersman, the Captain's sighted twin. There was the great mast bearing the taut black sail, and fore and aft of this, the two deck cabins, one of which was entirely empty (its occupants having been killed during their last landfall) and one of which was occupied only by himself and Blendker. Elric's gaze was drawn back to the Steersman and not for the first time the albino wondered how much influence the Captain's twin had over the course of the Dark Ship. The man seemed tireless, rarely, to Elric's knowledge, going below to his quarters which occupied the stern deck as the Captain's occupied the foredeck. Once or twice Elric or Blendker had tried to involve the Steersman in conversation, but he appeared to be as dumb as his brother was blind.

The cryptographic, geometrical carvings covering all the ship's wood and most of its metal, from sternpost to figurehead, were picked out by the shreds of pale mist still clinging to them (and again Elric wondered if the ship actually generated the mist normally surrounding it) and, as he watched, the designs slowly turned to pale pink fire as the light from that red star, which forever followed them, permeated the overhead cloud.

A noise from below. The Captain, his long red-gold hair drifting in a breeze which Elric could not feel, emerged from his cabin. The Captain's circlet of blue jade, worn like a diadem, had turned to something of a violet shade in the pink light, and even his buff-colored hose and tunic reflected the hue—even the silver sandals with their silver lacing glittered with the rosy tint.

Again Elric looked upon that mysterious blind face, as unhuman, in the accepted sense, as his own, and puzzled upon the origin of the one who would allow himself to be called nothing but "Captain."

As if at the Captain's summons, the mist drew itself about the ship again, as a woman might draw a froth of furs about her body. The red star's light faded, but the distant screams continued.

Did the Captain notice the screams now for the first time, or was this a pantomime of surprise. His blind head tilted, a hand went to his ear. He murmured in a tone of satisfaction: "Aha!" The head lifted. "Elric?"

"Here," said the albino. "Above you."

"We are almost there, Elric."

The apparently fragile hand found the rail of the companionway. The Captain began to climb.

Elric faced him at the top of the ladder. "If it's a battle . . ."

The Captain's smile was enigmatic, bitter. "It was a fight—or shall be one."

". . . we'll have no part of it," concluded the albino firmly.

"It is not one of the battles in which my ship is directly involved," the blind man reassured him. "Those whom you can hear are the vanquished—lost in some future which, I think, you will experience close to the end of your present incarnation."

Elric waved a dismissive hand. "I'll be glad, Captain, if you would cease such vapid mystification. I'm weary of it."

"I'm sorry it offends you. I answer literally, according to my instincts."

The Captain, going past Elric and Otto Blendker so that he could stand at the rail, seemed to be apologizing. He said nothing for a while but listened to the disturbing and confused babble from the mist. Then he nodded, apparently satisfied.

"We'll sight land shortly. If you would disembark and seek your own world, I should advise you to do so now. This is the closest we shall ever come again to your plane."

Elric let his anger show. He cursed, invoking Arioch's name, and put a hand upon the blind man's shoulder. "What? You cannot return me directly to my own plane?"

"It is too late." The Captain's dismay was apparently genuine. "The ship sails on. We near the end of our long voyage."

"But how shall I find my world. I have no sorcery great enough to move me between the spheres! And demonic assistance is denied me here."

"There is one gateway to your world," the Captain told him. "That is why I suggest you disembark. Elsewhere there are none at all. Your sphere and this one intersect directly."

"But you say this lies in my future?"

"Be sure—you will return to your own time. Here you are timeless. It is why your memory is so poor. It is why you remember so little of what befalls you. Seek for the gateway—it is crimson and it emerges from the sea off the coast of the island."

"Which island?"

"The one we approach."

Elric hesitated. "And where shall you go, when I have landed?"

"To Tanelorn," said the Captain. "There is something I must do there. My brother and I must complete our destiny. We carry cargo as well as men. Many will try to stop us now, for they fear our cargo. We might perish, but yet we must do all we can to reach Tanelorn."

"Was that not, then, Tanelorn, where we fought Agak and Gagak?"

"That was nothing more than a broken dream of Tanelorn, Elric."

The Melnibonéan knew that he would receive no more information from the Captain.

"You offer me a poor choice—to sail with you into danger and never see my own world again, or to risk landing on yonder island inhabited, by the sound of it, by the damned and those which prey upon the damned!"

The Captain's blind eyes moved in Elric's direction. "I know," he said softly. "But it is the best I can offer you, nonetheless."

The screams, the imploring, terrified shouts, were closer now, but there were fewer of them. Glancing over the side Elric thought he saw a pair of armored hands rising from the water; there was foam, red-flecked and noxious, and there was yellowish scum in which pieces of frightful flotsam drifted; there were broken timbers, scraps of canvas, tatters of flags and clothing, fragments of weapons and, increasingly, there were floating corpses.

"But where was the battle?" Blendker whispered, fascinated and horrified by the sight.

"Not on this plane," the Captain told him. "You see only the wreckage which has drifted over from one world to another."

"Then it was a supernatural battle?"

The Captain smiled again. "I am not omniscient. But, yes, I believe there were supernatural agencies involved. The warriors of half a world fought in the sea-battle—to decide the fate of the multiverse. It is—or will be—one of the decisive battles to determine the fate of Mankind, to fix Man's destiny for the coming Cycle."

"Who were the participants?" asked Elric, asking the question in spite of his resolve. "What were the issues as they understood them?"

"You will know in time, I think." The Captain's head faced the sea again.

Blendker sniffed the air. "Ach! It's foul!"

Elric, too, found the odor increasingly unpleasant. Here and there now the water was lit by guttering fires which revealed the faces of the drowning, some of whom still managed to cling to pieces of blackened driftwood. Not all the faces were human (though they had the appearance of having, once, been human): Things with the snouts of pigs and of bulls raised twisted hands to the Dark Ship and grunted plaintively for succor, but the Captain ignored them and the Steersman held his course.

Fires spluttered and water hissed; smoke mingled with the mist. Elric had his sleeve over his mouth and nose and was glad that the smoke and mist between them helped obscure the sights, for as the wreckage grew thicker not a few of the corpses he saw reminded him more of reptiles than of men, their pale, lizard bellies spilling something other than blood.

"If that is my future," Elric told the Captain, "I've a mind to remain on board, after all."

"You have a duty, as have I," said the Captain quietly. "The future must be served, as much as the past and the present."

Elric shook his head. "I fled the duties of an Empire because I sought freedom," the albino told him. "And freedom I must have."

"No," murmured the Captain. "There is no such thing. Not yet. Not for us. We must go through much more before we can even begin to guess what freedom is. The price for the knowledge alone is probably higher than any you would care to pay at this stage of your life. Indeed, life itself is often the price."

"I also sought release from metaphysics when I left Melniboné," said Elric. "I'll fetch the rest of my gear and take the land that's offered. With luck this Crimson Gate will be quickly found and I'll be back amongst dangers and torments which will, as least, be familiar."

"It is the only decision you could have made." The Captain's blind head turned towards Blendker. "And you, Otto Blendker? What shall you do?"

"Elric's world is not mine and I like not the sound of those screams. What can you promise me, sir, if I sail on with you?"

"Nothing but a good death." There was regret in the Captain's voice.

"Death is the promise we're all born with, sir. A good death is better than a poor one. I'll sail on with you."

"As you like. I think you're wise." The Captain sighed. "I'll say farewell to you, then, Elric of Melniboné. You fought well in my service and I thank you."

"Fought for what?" Elric asked.

"Oh, call it Mankind. Call it Fate. Call it a dream or an ideal, if you wish."

"Shall I never have a clearer answer?"

"Not from me. I do not think there is one."

"You allow a man little faith." Elric began to descend the companionway.

"There are two kinds of faith, Elric. Like freedom, there is a kind which is easily kept but proves not worth the keeping and there is a kind which is hard-won. I agree, I offer little of the former."

Elric strode towards his cabin. He laughed, feeling genuine affection for the blind man at that moment. "I thought I had a penchant for such ambiguities, but I have met my match in you, Captain."

He noticed that the Steersman had left his place at the wheel and was swinging out a boat on its davits, preparatory to lowering it.

"Is that for me?"

The Steersman nodded.

Elric ducked into his cabin. He was leaving the ship with nothing but that which he had brought aboard, only his clothing and his armor were in a poorer state of repair than they had been, and his mind was in a considerably greater state of confusion.

Without hesitation he gathered up his things, drawing his heavy cloak about him, pulling on his gauntlets, fastening buckles and thongs, then he left the cabin and returned to the deck. The Captain was pointing through the mist at the dark outlines of a coast. "Can you see land, Elric?"

"I can."

"You must go quickly, then."

"Willingly."

Elric swung himself over the rail and into the boat. The boat struck the side of the ship several times, so that the hull boomed like the beating of some huge funeral drum. Otherwise there was silence now upon the misty waters and no sign of wreckage.

Blendker saluted him. "I wish you luck, comrade."

"You, too, Master Blendker."

The boat began to sink towards the flat surface of the sea, the pulleys of the davits creaking. Elric clung to the rope, letting go as the boat hit the water. He stumbled and sat down heavily upon the seat, releasing the ropes so that the boat drifted at once away from the Dark Ship. He got out the oars and fitted them into their rowlocks.

As he pulled toward the shore he heard the Captain's voice calling to him, but the words were muffled by the mist and he would never know, now, if the blind man's last communication had been a warning or merely some formal pleasantry. He did not care. The boat moved smoothly through the water; the mist began to thin, but so, too, did the light fade.

Suddenly he was under a twilight sky, the sun already gone and stars appearing. Before he had reached the shore it was already completely dark, with the moon not yet risen, and it was with difficulty that he beached the boat on what seemed flat rocks, and stumbled inland until he judged himself safe enough from any inrushing tide.

Then, with a sigh, he lay down, thinking just to order his thoughts before moving on; but, almost instantly, he was asleep.

2

ELRIC DREAMED.

He dreamed not merely of the end of his world but of the end of an entire cycle in the history of the cosmos. He dreamed that he was not only Elric of Melniboné but that he was other men, too—men who were pledged to some numinous cause which even they could not describe. And he dreamed that he had dreamed of the Dark Ship and Tanelorn and Agak and Gagak while he lay exhausted upon a beach somewhere beyond the borders of Pikarayd and when he woke up he was smiling sardonically, congratulating himself for the possession of a grandiose imagination. But he could not clear his head entirely of the impression left by that dream.

This shore was not the same, so plainly something had befallen him—perhaps he had been drugged by slavers, then later abandoned when they found him not what they expected? But, no, the explanation would not do. If he could discover his whereabouts, he might also recall the true facts.

It was dawn, for certain. He sat up and looked about him.

He was sprawled upon a dark, sea-washed limestone pavement, cracked in a hundred places, the cracks so deep that the small streams of foaming saltwater rushing through these many narrow channels made raucous what would otherwise have been a very still evening.

Elric climbed to his feet, using his scabbarded runesword to steady himself. His bone-white lids closed for a moment over his crimson eyes as he sought, again, to recollect the events which had brought him here.

He recalled his flight from Pikarayd, his panic, his falling into a coma of hopelessness, his dreams. And, because he was evidently neither dead nor a prisoner, he could at least conclude that his pursuers had, after all, given up the chase, for if they had found him they would have killed him.

Opening his eyes and casting about him, he remarked the peculiar blue quality of the light (doubtless a trick of the sun behind the gray clouds) which made the landscape ghastly and gave the sea a dull, metallic look.

The limestone terraces which rose from the sea and stretched above him shone intermittently like polished lead. On an impulse he held his hand to the light and inspected it. The normally lusterless white of his skin was now tinged with a faint, bluish luminosity. He found it pleasing and smiled as a child might smile, in innocent wonder.

He had expected to be tired, but he now realised that he felt unusually refreshed, as if he had slept long after a good meal, and, deciding not to question the fact of this fortunate (and unlikely) gift, he determined to climb the cliffs in the hope that he might get some idea of his bearings before he decided which direction he would take.

Limestone could be a little treacherous, but it made easy climbing, for there was almost always somewhere that one terrace met another.

He climbed carefully and steadily, finding many footholds, and seemed to gain considerable height quite quickly, yet it was noon before he had reached the top and found himself standing at the edge of a broad, rocky plateau which fell away sharply to form a close horizon. Beyond the plateau was only the sky. Save for sparse, brownish grass, little grew here and there were no signs at all of human habitation. It was now, for the first time, that Elric realized the absence of any form of wildlife. Not a single seabird flew in the air, not an insect crept through the grass. Instead, there was an enormous silence hanging over the brown plain.

Elric was still remarkably untired, so he decided to make the best use he could of his energy and reach the edge of the plateau in the hope that, from there, he would sight a town or a village. He pressed on, feeling no lack of food and water, and his stride was singularly energetic, still, but he had misjudged his distance and the sun had begun to set well before his journey to the edge was completed. The sky on all sides turned a deep, velvety blue and the few clouds that there were in it were also tinged blue, and now, for the first time, Elric realized that the sun itself was not its normal shade, that it burned blackish purple, and he wondered again if he still dreamed.

The ground began to rise sharply and it was with some effort that he walked, but before the light had completely faded he was on the steep flank of a hill, descending towards a wide valley which, though bereft of trees, contained a river which wound through rocks and russet turf and bracken. After a short rest, Elric decided to press on, although night had fallen, and see if he could reach the river where he might, at least, drink and, possibly, in the morning, find fish to eat.

Again, no moon appeared to aid his progress and he walked for two or three hours in a darkness which was almost total, stumbling occasionally into large rocks, until the ground leveled and he felt sure he had reached the floor of the valley.

He had developed a strong thirst by now and was feeling somewhat hungry, but decided that it might be best to wait until morning before seeking the river when, rounding a particularly tall rock, he saw, with some astonishment, the light of a camp fire.

Hopefully this would be the fire of a company of merchants, a trading caravan on its way to some civilized country which would allow him to travel with it, perhaps in return for his services as a mercenary swordsman (it would not be the first time, since he had left Melniboné, that he had earned his bread in such a way).

Yet Elric's old instincts did not desert him: he approached the fire cautiously and let no one see him. Beneath an overhang of rock, made shadowy by the flame's light, he stood and observed the group of fifteen or sixteen men who sat or lay close to the fire, playing some kind of game involving dice and slivers of numbered ivory.

Gold, bronze, and silver gleamed in the firelight as the men staked large sums on the fall of a die and the turn of a slip of ivory.

Elric guessed that, if they had not been so intent on their game, these men must certainly have detected his approach, for they were not, after all, merchants. By the evidence, they were warriors, wearing scarred leather and dented metal, their weapons ready to hand, yet they belonged to no army—unless it be an army of bandits—for they were of all races and (oddly) seemed to be from various periods in the history of the Young Kingdoms.

It was as if they had looted some scholar's collection of relics. An axman of the later Lormyrian Republic, which had come to an end some two hundred years ago, lay with his shoulder rubbing the elbow of a Chalalite bowman, from a period roughly contemporary with Elric's own. Close to the Chalalite sat a short Ilmioran infantryman of a century past. Next to him was a Filkharian in the barbaric dress of that nation's earliest times. Tarkeshites, Shazarians, Vilmirians, all mingled and the only thing they had in common, by the look of them, was a villainous, hungry cast to their features.

In other circumstances Elric might have skirted this encampment and moved on, but he was so glad to find human beings of any sort that he ignored the disturbing incongruities of the group, but yet he remained content to watch them.

One of the men, less unwholesome than the others, was a bulky, black-bearded, bald-headed sea warrior clad in the casual leathers and silks of the people of the Purple Towns. It was when this man produced a large, gold Melnibonéan wheel—a coin not minted, as most coins, but carved by craftsmen to a design both ancient and intricate—that Elric's caution was fully conquered by his curiosity.

Very few of those coins existed in Melniboné and none, that Elric had heard of, outside; for the coins were not used for trade with the Young Kingdoms. They were prized, even by the nobility of Melniboné.

It seemed to Elric that the bald-headed man could only have acquired the coin from another Melnibonéan traveler—and Elric knew of no other Melnibonéan who shared his penchant for exploration. His wariness dismissed, he stepped into the circle.

If he had not been completely obsessed by the thought of the Melnibonéan wheel he might have taken some satisfaction in the sudden scuffle to arms which resulted. Within seconds, the majority of the men were on their feet, their weapons drawn.

For a moment, the gold wheel was forgotten. His hand upon his runesword's pommel, he presented the other in a placatory gesture.

"Forgive the interruption, gentlemen. I am but one tired fellow soldier who seeks to join you. I would beg some information and purchase some food, if you have it to spare."

On foot, the warriors had an even more ruffianly appearance. They grinned among themselves, entertained by Elric's courtesy but not impressed by it.

One, in the feathered helmet of a Pan Tangian seachief, with features to match—swarthy, sinister—pushed his head forward on its long neck and said banteringly:

"We've company enough, white-face. And few here are overfond of the man-demons of Melniboné. You must be rich."

Elric recalled the animosity with which Melnibonéans were regarded in the Young Kingdoms, particularly by those from Pan Tang who envied the Dragon Isle her power and her wisdom and, of late, had begun crudely to imitate Melniboné.

Increasingly on his guard, he said evenly: "I have a little money."

"Then we'll take it, demon." The Pan Tangian presented a dirty palm just below Elric's nose as he growled: "Give it over and be on your way."

Elric's smile was polite and fastidious, as if he had been told a poor joke.

The Pan Tangian evidently thought the joke better than did Elric, for he laughed heartily and looked to his nearest fellows for approval.

Coarse laughter infected the night and only the bald-headed, black-bearded man did not join in the jest, but took a step or two backward, while all the others pressed forward.

The Pan Tangian's face was close to Elric's own; his breath was foul and Elric saw that his beard and hair were alive with lice, yet he kept his head, replying in the same equable tone:

"Give me some decent food—a flask of water—some wine, if you have it—and I'll gladly give you the money I have."

The laughter rose and fell again as Elric continued:

"But if you would take my money and leave me with naught—then I must defend myself. I have a good sword."

The Pan Tangian strove to imitate Elric's irony. "But you will note, Sir Demon, that we outnumber you. Considerably."

Softly the albino spoke: "I've noticed that fact, but I'm not disturbed by it," and he had drawn the black blade even as he finished speaking, for they had come at him with a rush.

And the Pan Tangian was the first to die, sliced through the side, his vertebrae sheered, and Stormbringer, having taken its first soul, began to sing.

A Chalalite died next, leaping with stabbing javeline poised, on the point of the runesword, and Stormbringer murmured with pleasure.

But it was not until it had sliced the head clean off a Filkharian pikemaster that the sword began to croon and come fully to life, black fire flickering up and down its length, its strange runes glowing.

Now the warriors knew they battled sorcery and became more cautious, yet they scarcely paused in their attack, and Elric, thrusting and parrying, hacking and slicing, needed all of the fresh, dark energy the sword passed on to him.

Lance, sword, ax, and dirk were blocked, wounds were given and received, but the dead had not yet outnumbered the living when Elric found himself with his back against the rock and nigh a dozen sharp weapons seeking his vitals.

It was at this point, when Elric had become somewhat less than confident that he could best so many, that the bald-headed warrior, ax in one gloved hand, sword in the other, came swiftly into the firelight and set upon those of his fellows closest to him.

"I thank you, sir!" Elric was able to shout, during the short respite this sudden turn produced. His morale improved, he resumed the attack.

The Lormyrian was cloven from hip to pelvis as he dodged a feint; a Filkharian, who should have been dead four hundred years before, fell with the blood bubbling from lips and nostrils, and the corpses began to pile one upon the other. Still Stormbringer sang its sinister battlesong and still the runesword passed its power to its master so that with every death Elric found strength to slay more of the soldiers.

Those who remained now began to express their regret for their hasty attack. Where oaths and threats had issued from their mouths, now came plaintive petitions for mercy and those who had laughed with such bold braggadocio now wept like young girls, but Elric, full of his old battle-joy, spared none.

Meanwhile the man from the Purple Towns, unaided by sorcery, put ax and sword to good work and dealt with three more of his one-time comrades, exulting in his work as if he had nursed a taste for it for some time.

"*Yoi!* But this is worthwhile slaughter!" cried the black-bearded one.

And then that busy butchery was suddenly done and Elric realized that none were left save himself and his new ally who stood leaning on his ax, panting and grinning like a hound at the kill, replacing a steel skullcap upon his pate from where it had fallen during the fight, and wiping a bloody sleeve over the sweat glistening on his brow, and saying, in a deep, good-humored tone:

"Well, now, it is we who are wealthy, of a sudden."

Elric sheathed Stormbringer still reluctant to return to its scabbard. "You desire their gold. Is that why you aided me?"

The black-bearded soldier laughed. "I owed them a debt and had been biding my time, waiting to pay. These rascals are all that were left of a pirate crew which slew everyone aboard my own ship when we wandered into strange waters—they would have slain me had I not told them I wished to join them. Now I am revenged. Not that I am above taking the gold, since much of it belongs to me and my dead brothers. It will go to their wives and their children when I return to the Purple Towns."

"How did you convince them not to kill you, too?" Elric sought amongst the ruins of the fire for something to eat. He found some cheese and began to chew upon it.

"They had no captain or navigator, it seemed. None are real sailors at all, but coast-huggers, based upon this island. They were stranded here, you see, and had taken to piracy as a last resort, but were too terrified to risk the open sea. Besides, after the fight, they had no ship. We had managed to sink that as we fought. We sailed mine to this shore, but provisions were already low and they had no stomach for setting sail without full holds, so I pretended that I knew this coast (may the Gods take my soul if I ever see it again after this business) and offered to lead them inland to a village they might loot. They had heard of no such village, but believed me when I said it lay in a hidden valley. That way I prolonged my life while I waited for the opportunity to be revenged upon them. It was a foolish hope, I know. Yet," grinning, "as it happened, it was well founded, after all! Eh?"

The black-bearded man glanced a little warily at Elric, uncertain of what the albino might say, hoping, however, for comradeship, though it was well known how haughty Melnibonéans were. Elric could tell that all these thoughts went through his new acquaintance's mind; he had seen many others make similar calculations. So he smiled openly and slapped the man on the shoulder.

"You saved my life, also, my friend. We are both fortunate."

The man sighed in relief and slung his ax upon his back "Aye—lucky's the word. But shall our luck hold, I wonder?"

"You do not know the island at all?"

"Nor the waters, either. How we came to them I'll never guess. Enchanted waters, though, without question. You've seen the color of the sun?"

"I have."

"Well," the seaman bent to remove a pendant from around the Pan Tangian's throat, "you'd know more about enchantments and sorceries than I. How came you here, Sir Melnibonéan?"

"I know not. I fled from some who hunted me. I came to a shore and could flee no further. Then I dreamed a great deal. When next I awoke I was on the shore again, but of this island."

"Spirits of some sort—maybe friendly to you—took you to safety, away from your enemies."

"That's just possible," Elric agreed, "for we have many allies amongst the elementals. I am called Elric and I am self-exiled from Melniboné. I travel because I believe I have something to learn from the folk of the Young Kingdoms. I have no power, save what you see . . ."

The black-bearded man's eyes narrowed in appraisal as he pointed at himself with his thumb. "I'm Smiorgan Baldhead, once a sealord of the Purple Towns. I commanded a fleet of merchantmen. Perhaps I still do. I shall not know until I return—if I ever do return."

"Then let us pool our knowledge and our resources, Smiorgan Baldhead, and make plans to leave this island as soon as we can."

Elric walked back to where he saw traces of the abandoned game, trampled into the mud and the blood. From amongst the dice and the ivory slips, the silver and the bronze coins, he found the gold Melnibonéan wheel. He picked it up and held it in his outstretched palm. The wheel almost covered the whole palm. In the old days, it had been the currency of kings.

"This was yours, friend?" he asked Smiorgan.

Smiorgan Baldhead looked up from where he was still searching the Pan Tangian for his stolen possessions. He nodded.

"Aye. Would you keep it as part of your share?"

Elric shrugged. "I'd rather know from whence it came. Who gave it you?"

"It was not stolen. It's Melnibonéan, then?"

"Yes."

"I guessed it."

"From whom did you obtain it?"

Smiorgan straightened up, having completed his search. He scratched at a slight wound on his forearm. "It was used to buy passage on our ship—before we were lost—before the raiders attacked us."

"Passage? By a Melnibonéan?"

"Maybe," said Smiorgan. He seemed reluctant to speculate.

"Was he a warrior?"

Smiorgan smiled in his beard. "No. It was a woman gave that to me."

"How came she to take passage?"

Smiorgan began to pick up the rest of the money. "It's a long tale and, in part, a familiar one to most merchant sailors. We were seeking new markets for our goods and had equipped a good sized fleet, which I commanded, as the largest shareholder." He seated himself casually upon the big corpse of the Chalalite and began to count the money. "Would you hear the the tale or do I bore you already?"

"I'd be glad to listen."

Reaching behind him, Smiorgan pulled a wine flask from the belt of the corpse and offered it to Elric who accepted it and drank sparingly of a wine which was unusually good.

Smiorgan took the flask when Elric had finished. "That's part of our cargo," he said. "We were proud of it. A good vintage, eh?"

"Excellent. So you set off from the Purple Towns?"

"Aye. Going east towards the Unknown Kingdoms. We sailed due east for a couple of weeks, sighting some of the bleakest coasts I have ever seen, and then we saw no land at all for another week. That was when we entered a stretch of water we came to call the Roaring Rocks —like the Serpent's Teeth off Shazar's coast, but much greater in expanse, and larger, too. Huge volcanic cliffs which rose from the sea on every side and around which the waters heaved and boiled and howled with a fierceness I've rarely experienced. Well, in short, the fleet was dispersed and at least four ships were lost on those rocks. At last we were able to escape those waters and found ourselves becalmed and alone. We searched for our sister ships for a while and then decided to give ourselves another week before turning for home, for we had no liking to go back into the Roaring Rocks again. Low on provisions, we sighted land at last—grassy cliffs and hospitable beaches and, inland, some signs of cultivation, so we knew we had found civilization again. We put into a small fishing port and satisfied the natives—who spoke no tongue used in the Young Kingdoms—that we were friendly. And that was when the woman approached us."

"The Melnibonéan woman?"

"If Melnibonéan she was. She was a fine-looking woman, I'll say that. We were short of provisions, as I told you, and short of any means of purchasing them, for the fishermen desired little of what we had to trade. Having given up our original quest, we were content to head westward again."

"The woman?"

"She wished to buy passage to the Young Kingdoms—and was content to go with us as far as Menii, our home port. For her passage she gave us two of those wheels. One was used to buy provisions in the town—Graghin, I think it was called—and after making repairs we set off again."

"You never reached the Purple Towns?"

"There were more storms—strange storms. Our instruments were useless, our lodestones were of no help to us at all. We became even more completely lost than before. Some of my men argued that we had gone beyond our own world altogether. Some blamed the woman, saying she was a sorceress who had no intention of going to Menii. But I believed her. Night fell and seemed to last forever until we sailed into a calm dawn beneath a blue sun. My men were close to panic—and it takes much to make my men panic—when we sighted the island. As we headed for it those pirates attacked us in a ship which belonged to history—it should have been on the bottom of the ocean, not on the surface. I've seen pictures of such craft in murals on a temple wall in Tarkesh. In ramming us, she stove in half her port side and was sinking even when they swarmed aboard. They were desperate, savage men, Elric—half-starved and blood-hungry. We were weary after our voyage but fought well. During the fighting the woman disappeared, killed herself, maybe, when she saw the stamp of our conquerors. After a long fight only myself and one other, who died soon after, were left. That was when I became cunning and decided to wait for revenge."

"The woman had a name?"

"None she would give. I have thought the matter over and suspect that, after all, we were used by her. Perhaps she did not seek Menii and the Young Kingdoms. Perhaps it was this world she sought, and, by sorcery, led us here."

"This world? You think it different to our own?"

"If only because of the sun's strange color. Do you not think so, too? You, with your Melnibonéan knowledge of such things, must believe it?"

"I have dreamed of such things," Elric admitted, but he would say no more.

"Most of the pirates thought as I—they were from all the ages of the Young Kingdoms. That much I discovered. Some were from the earliest years of the era, some from our own time—and some were from the future. Adventurers, most of them, who, at some stage in their lives, sought a legendary land of great riches which lay on the other side of an ancient gateway, rising from the middle of the ocean, but they found themselves trapped here, unable to sail back through this mysterious gate. Others had been involved in sea fights, thought themselves drowned and woken up on the shores of the island. Many, I suppose, had once had reasonable virtues, but there is little to support life on the island and they had become wolves, living off one another or any ship unfortunate enough to pass, inadvertently, through this gate of theirs."

Elric recalled part of his dream. "Did any call it the 'Crimson Gate'?"

"Several did, aye."

"And yet the theory is unlikely, if you'll forgive my skepticism," Elric said. "As one who has passed through the Shade Gate to Ameeron . . ."

"You know of other worlds, then?"

"I've never heard of this one. And I am versed in such matters. That is why I doubt the reasoning. And yet, there was the dream . . ."

"Dream?"

"Oh, it was nothing. I am used to such dreams and give them no significance."

"The theory cannot seem surprising to a Melnibonéan, Elric!" Smiorgan grinned again. "It's I who should be skeptical, not you."

And Elric replied, half to himself: "Perhaps I fear the implications more." He lifted his head and, with the shaft of a broken spear, began to poke at the fire. "Certain ancient sorcerers of Melniboné proposed that an infinite number of worlds coexist with our own. Indeed, my dreams, of late, have hinted as much!" He forced himself to smile. "But I cannot afford to believe such things. Thus, I reject them."

"Wait for the dawn," said Smiorgan Baldhead. "The color of the sun shall prove the theory."

"Perhaps it will prove only that we both dream," said Elric. The smell of death was strong in his nostrils. He pushed aside those corpses nearest to the fire and settled himself to sleep.

Smiorgan Baldhead had begun to sing a strong yet lilting song in his own dialect, which Elric could scarcely follow.

"Do you sing of your victory over your enemies?" the albino asked.

Smiorgan paused for a moment, half amused. "No, Sir Elric, I sing to keep the shades at bay. After all, these fellows' ghosts must still be lurking nearby, in the dark, so little time has passed since they died."

"Fear not," Elric told him. "Their souls are already eaten."

But Smiorgan sang on, and his voice was louder, his song more intense, than ever it had been before.

Just before he fell asleep, Elric thought he heard a horse whinny, and he meant to ask Smiorgan if any of the pirates had been mounted, but he fell asleep before he could do so.

3

RECALLING LITTLE of his voyage on the Dark Ship, Elric would never know how he came to reach the world in which he now found himself. In later years he would recall most of these experiences as dreams and, indeed, they seemed dreamlike even as they occurred.

He slept uneasily, and, in the morning, the clouds were heavier, shining with that strange, leaden light, though the sun itself was obscured. Smiorgan Baldhead of the Purple Towns was pointing upwards, already on his feet, speaking with quiet triumph:

"Will that evidence suffice to convince you, Elric of Melniboné?"

"I am convinced of a quality about the light—possibly about this terrain—which makes the sun appear blue," Elric replied. He glanced with distaste at the carnage around him. The corpses made a wretched sight and he was filled with a nebulous misery that was neither remorse nor pity.

Smiorgan's sigh was sardonic. "Well, Sir Skeptic, we had best retrace my steps and seek my ship. What say you?"

"I agree," the albino told him.

"How far had you marched from the coast when you found us?" Elric told him.

Smiorgan smiled. "You arrived in the nick of time, then. I should have been most embarrassed by today if the sea had been reached and I could show my pirate friends no village! I shall not forget this favor you have done me, Elric. I am a Count of the Purple Towns and have much influence. If there is any service I can perform for you when we return, you must let me know."

"I thank you," Elric said gravely. "But first we must discover a means of escape."

Smiorgan had gathered up a satchel of food, some water and some wine. Elric had no stomach to make his breakfast among the dead, so he slung the satchel over his shoulder. "I'm ready," he said.

Smiorgan was satisfied. "Come—we go this way."

Elric began to follow the sealord over the dry, crunching turf. The steep sides of the valley loomed over them, tinged with a peculiar and unpleasant greenish hue, the result of the brown foliage being stained by the blue light from above. When they reached the river, which was narrow and ran rapidly through boulders giving easy means of crossing, they rested and ate. Both men were stiff from the previous night's fighting; both were glad to wash the dried blood and mud from their bodies in the water.

Refreshed, the pair climbed over the boulders and left the river behind, ascending the slopes, speaking little so that their breath was saved for the exertion. It was noon by the time they reached the top of the valley and observed a plain not unlike the one which Elric had first crossed. Elric now had a fair idea of the island's geography: it resembled the top of a mountain, with an indentation near the center which was the valley. Again he became sharply aware of the absence of any wildlife and remarked on this to Count Smiorgan, who agreed that he had seen nothing—no bird, fish nor beast since he had arrived.

"It's a barren little world, friend Elric, and a misfortune for a mariner to be wrecked upon its shores."

They moved on, until the sea could be observed meeting the horizon in the far distance.

It was Elric who first heard the sound behind them, recognizing the steady thump of the hooves of a galloping horse, but when he looked back over his shoulder he could see no sign of a rider, nor anywhere that a rider could hide. He guessed that, in his tiredness, his ears were betraying him. It had been thunder that he had heard.

Smiorgan strode implacably onward, though he, too, must have heard the sound.

Again it came. Again, Elric turned. Again he saw nothing.

"Smiorgan? Did you hear a rider?"

Smiorgan continued to walk without looking back. "I heard," he grunted.

"You have heard it before?"

"Many times since I arrived. The pirates heard it, too, and some believed it their nemesis—an Angel of Death seeking them out for retribution."

"You don't know the source?"

Smiorgan paused, then stopped, and when he turned his face was grim. "Once or twice I have caught a glimpse of a horse, I think. A tall horse—white—richly dressed—but with no man upon his back. Ignore it, Elric, as I do. We have larger mysteries with which to occupy our minds!"

"You are afraid of it, Smiorgan?"

He accepted this. "Aye. I confess it. But neither fear nor speculation will rid us of it. Come!"

Elric was bound to see the sense of Smiorgan's statement and he accepted it, yet, when the sound came again, about an hour later, he could not resist turning. Then he thought he glimpsed the outline of a large stallion, caparisoned for riding, but that might have been nothing more than an idea Smiorgan had put in his mind.

The day grew colder and in the air was a peculiar, bitter odor. Elric remarked on the smell to Count Smiorgan and learned that this, too, was familiar.

"The smell comes and goes, but it is usually here in some strength."

"Like sulphur," said Elric.

Count Smiorgan's laugh had much irony in it, as if Elric made reference to some private joke of Smiorgan's own. "Oh, aye! Sulphur right enough!"

The drumming of hooves grew louder behind them as they neared the coast and at last Elric, and Smiorgan too, turned round again, to look.

And now a horse could be seen plainly—riderless, but saddled and bridled, its dark eyes intelligent, its beautiful white head held proudly.

"Are you still convinced of the absence of sorcery here, Sir Elric?" Count Smiorgan asked with some satisfaction. "The horse was invisible. Now it is visible." He shrugged the battle-ax on his shoulder into a better position. "Either that, or it moves from one world to another with ease, so that all we mainly hear are its hoofbeats."

"If so," said Elric sardonically, eyeing the stallion, "it might bear us back to our own world."

"You admit, then, that we are marooned in some Limbo?"

"Very well, yes. I admit the possibility."

"Have you no sorcery to trap the horse?"

"Sorcery does not come so easily to me, for I have no great liking for it," the albino told him.

As they spoke, they approached the horse, but it would let them get no closer. It snorted and moved backward, keeping the same distance between them and itself.

At last, Elric said: "We waste time, Count Smiorgan. Let's get to your ship with speed and forget blue suns and enchanted horses as quickly as we may. Once aboard the ship I can doubtless help you with a little incantation or two, for we'll need aid of some sort if we're to sail a large ship by ourselves."

They marched on, but the horse continued to follow them. They came to the edge of the cliffs, standing high above a narrow, rocky bay in which a battered ship lay at anchor. The ship had the high, fine lines of a Purple Towns merchantman, but its decks were piled with shreds of torn canvas, pieces of broken rope, shards of timber, torn-open bales of cloth, smashed wine-jars, and all manner of other refuse, while in several places her rails were smashed and two or three of her yards had splintered. It was evident that she had been through both storms and sea-fights and it was a wonder that she still floated.

"We'll have to tidy her up as best we can, using only the mains'l for motion," mused Smiorgan. "Hopefully we can salvage enough food to last us . . ."

"Look!" Elric pointed, sure that he had seen someone in the shadows near the afterdeck. "Did the pirates leave any of their company behind?"

"None."

"Did you see anyone on the ship, just then?"

"My eyes play filthy tricks on my mind," Smiorgan told him. "It is this damned blue light. There is a rat or two aboard, that's all. And that's what you saw."

"Possibly." Elric looked back. The horse appeared to be unaware of them as it cropped the brown grass. "Well, let's finish the journey."

They scrambled down the steeply sloping cliff-face and were soon on the shore, wading through the shallows for the ship, clambering up the slippery ropes which still hung over the sides and, at last, setting their feet with some relief upon the deck.

"I feel more secure already," said Smiorgan. "This ship was my home for so long!" He searched through the scattered cargo until he found an unbroken winejar, carved off the seal and handed it to Elric. Elric lifted the heavy jar and let a little of the good wine flow into his mouth. As Count Smiorgan began to drink, Elric was sure he saw another movement near the afterdeck, and he moved closer.

Now he was certain that he heard strained, rapid breathing—like the breathing of one who sought to stifle their need for air rather than be detected. They were slight sounds, but the albino's ears, unlike his eyes, were sharp. His hand ready to draw his sword, he stalked towards the source of the sound, Smiorgan now behind him.

She emerged from her hiding place before he reached her. Her hair hung in heavy, dirty coils about her pale face; her shoulders were slumped and her soft arms hung limply at her sides, while her dress was stained and ripped.

As Elric approached, she fell on her knees before him. "Take my life," she said humbly, "but I beg you—do not take me back to Saxif D'Aan, though I know you must be his servant or his kinsman."

"It's she!" cried Smiorgan in astonishment. "It's our passenger. She must have been in hiding all this time."

Elric stepped forward, lifting up the girl's chin so that he could study her face. There was a Melnibonéan cast about her features, but she was, to his mind, of the Young Kingdoms; she lacked the pride of a Melnibonéan woman, too. "What name was that you used, girl?" he asked kindly. "Did you speak of Saxif D'Aan? Earl Saxif D'Aan of Melniboné?"

"I did, my lord."

"Do not fear me as his servant," Elric told her. "And as for being a kinsman, I suppose you could call me that—on my mother's side—or rather my great-grandmother's side. He was an ancestor. He must have been dead for two centuries, at least!"

"No," she said. "He lives, my lord."

"On this island?"

"This island is not his home, but it is in this plane that he exists. I sought to escape him through the Crimson Gate. I fled through the gate in a skiff, reached the town where you found me, Count Smiorgan, but he drew me back once I was aboard your ship. He drew me back and the ship with me. For that, I have remorse—and for what befell your crew. Now I know he seeks me. I can feel his presence growing nearer."

"Is he invisible," Smiorgan asked suddenly. "Does he ride a white horse?"

She gasped. "You see! He *is* near! Why else should the horse appear on this island?"

"He rides it?" Elric asked.

"No, no! He fears the horse almost as much as I fear him. The horse pursues him!"

Elric produced the Melnibonéan gold wheel from his purse. "Did you take these from Earl Saxif D'Aan?"

"I did."

The albino frowned.

"Who is this man, Elric?" Count Smiorgan asked. "You describe him as an ancestor—yet he lives in this world. What do you know of him?"

Elric weighed the large gold wheel in his hand before replacing it in his pouch. "He was something of a legend in Melniboné. His story is part of our literature. He was a great sorcerer—one of the greatest— and he fell in love. It's rare enough for Melnibonéans to fall in love, as others understand the emotion, but rarer for one to have such feelings for a girl who was not even of our own race. She was half-Melnibonéan, so I heard, but from a land which was, in those days, a Melnibonéan possession, a western province close to Dharijor. She was bought by him in a batch of slaves he planned to use for some sorcerous experi- ment, but he singled her out, saving her from whatever fate it was the others suffered. He lavished his attention upon her, giving her every- thing. For her, he abandoned his practices, retired to live quietly away from Imrryr, and I think she showed him a certain affection, though she did not seem to love him. There was another, you see, called Carolak, as I recall, and also half-Melnibonéan, who had become a mercenary in Shazar and risen in the favor of the Shazarian court. She had been pledged to this Carolak before her abduction . . ."

"She loved him?" Count Smiorgan asked.

"She was pledged to marry him, but let me finish my story . . ." Elric continued: "Well, at length Carolak, now a man of some substance, second only to the king in Shazar, heard of her fate and swore to rescue her. He came with raiders to Melniboné's shores and, aided by sorcery, sought out Saxif D'Aan's palace. That done, he sought the girl, finding her at last in the apartments Saxif D'Aan had set aside for her use. He told her that he had come to claim her as his bride, to rescue her from persecution. Oddly, the girl resisted, suggesting that she had been too long a slave in the Melnibonéan harem to readapt to the life of a princess in the Shazarian court. Carolak scoffed at this and seized her. He managed to escape the castle and had the girl over the saddle of his horse and was about to rejoin his men on the coast when Saxif D'Aan detected them. Carolak, I think, was slain, or else a spell was put on him, but Saxif D'Aan, in his terrible jealousy and certain that the girl had planned the escape with a lover, ordered her to die upon the Wheel of Chaos—a machine rather like that coin in design. Her limbs were broken slowly and Saxif D'Aan sat and watched, through long days, while she died. Her skin was peeled from her flesh, and Earl Saxif D'Aan observed every detail of her punishment. Soon it was evident that the drugs and sorcery used to sustain her life were failing and Saxif D'Aan ordered her taken from the Wheel of Chaos and laid upon a couch. 'Well,' he said, 'you have been punished for betraying me and I am glad. Now you may die.' And he saw that her lips, blood-caked and frightful, were moving, and he bent to hear her words."

"Those words? Revenge? An oath?" asked Smiorgan.

"Her last gesture was an attempt to embrace him. And the words were those she had never uttered to him before, much as he had hoped that she would. She said simply, over and over again, until the last breath left her: 'I love you. I love you. I love you.' And then she died."

Smiorgan rubbed at his beard. "Gods! What then? What did your ancestor do?"

"He knew remorse."

"Of course!"

"Not so, for a Melnibonéan. Remorse is a rare emotion with us. Few have ever experienced it. Torn by guilt, Earl Saxif D'Aan left Melniboné, never to return. It was assumed that he had died in some remote land, trying to make amends for what he had done to the only creature he had ever loved. But now, it seems, he sought the Crimson Gate, perhaps thinking it an opening into Hell."

"But why should he plague me!" the girl cried. "I am not she! My name is Vassliss. I am a merchant's daughter, from Jharkor. I was voyaging to visit my uncle in Vilmir when our ship was wrecked. A few of us escaped in an open boat. More storms seized us. I was flung from the boat and was drowning when . . ." she shuddered—"when *his* galley found me. I was grateful, then . . ."

"What happened?" Elric pushed the matted hair away from her face and offered her some of their wine. She drank gratefully.

"He took me to his palace and told me that he would marry me, that I should be his Empress forever and rule beside him. But I was frightened. There was such pain in him—and such cruelty, too. I thought he must devour me, destroy me. Soon after my capture, I took the money and the boat and fled for the gateway, which he had told me about . . ."

"You could find this gateway for us?" Elric asked.

"I think so. I have some knowledge of seamanship, learned from my father. But what would be the use, sir? He would find us again and drag us back. And he must be very near, even now."

"I have a little sorcery myself," Elric assured her, "and will pit it against Saxif D'Aan's, if I must." He turned to Count Smiorgan. "Can we get a sail aloft quickly?"

"Fairly quickly."

"Then let's hurry, Count Smiorgan Baldhead. I might have the means of getting us through this Crimson Gate and free from any further involvement in the dealings of the dead!"

4

WHILE COUNT Smiorgan and Vassliss of Jharkor watched, Elric lowered himself to the deck, panting and pale. His first attempt to work sorcery in this world had failed and had exhausted him.

"I am further convinced," he told Smiorgan, "that we are in another plane of existence, for I should have worked my incantations with less effort."

"You have failed."

Elric rose with some difficulty. "I shall try again."

He turned his white face skyward; he closed his eyes; he stretched out his arms and his body tensed as he began the incantation again, his voice growing louder and louder, higher and higher, so that it resembled the shrieking of a gale.

He forgot where he was; he forgot his own identity; he forgot those who were with him as his whole mind concentrated upon the summoning. He sent his call out beyond the confines of the world, into that strange plane where the elementals dwelled—where the powerful creatures of the air could still be found—the *sylphs* of the breeze, and the *sharnahs,* who lived in the storms, and the most powerful of all, the *h'Haarshanns,* creatures of the whirlwind.

And now at last some of them began to come at his summons, ready to serve him as, by virtue of an ancient pact, the elementals had served his forefathers. And slowly the sail of the ship began to fill, and the timbers creaked, and Smiorgan raised the anchor, and the ship was sailing away from the island, through the rocky gap of the harbor, and out into the open sea, still beneath a strange, blue sun.

Soon a huge wave was forming around them, lifting up the ship and carrying it across the ocean, so that Count Smiorgan and the girl marveled at the speed of their progress, while Elric, his crimson eyes open now, but blank and unseeing, continued to croon to his unseen allies.

Thus the ship progressed across the waters of the sea, and at last the island was out of sight and the girl, checking their position against the position of the sun, was able to give Count Smiorgan sufficient information for him to steer a course.

As soon as he could, Count Smiorgan went up to Elric, who still straddled the deck, still as stiff-limbed as before, and shook him.

"Elric! You will kill yourself with this effort. We need your friends no longer!"

At once the wind dropped and the wave dispersed and Elric, gasping, fell to the deck.

"It is harder here," he said. "It is so much harder here. It is as if I have to call across far greater gulfs than any I have known before."

And then Elric slept.

He lay in a warm bunk in a cool cabin. Through the porthole filtered diffused blue light. He sniffed. He caught the odor of hot food and, turning his head, saw that Vassliss stood there, a bowl of broth in her hands. "I was able to cook this," she said. "It will improve your health. As far as I can tell, we are nearing the Crimson Gate. The seas are always rough around the gate, so you will need your strength."

Elric thanked her pleasantly and began to eat the broth as she watched him.

"You are very like Saxif D'Aan," she said. "Yet harder in a way— and gentler, too. He is so remote. I know why that girl could never tell him that she loved him."

Elric smiled. "Oh, it's nothing more than a folktale, probably, the story I told you. This Saxif D'Aan could be another person altogether— or an imposter, even, who has taken his name—or a sorcerer. Some sorcerers take the names of other sorcerers, for they think it gives them more power."

There came a cry from above, but Elric could not make out the words.

The girl's expression became alarmed. Without a word to Elric, she hurried from the cabin.

Elric, rising unsteadily, followed her up the companionway.

Count Smiorgan Baldhead was at the wheel of his ship and he was pointing towards the horizon behind them. "What do you make of that, Elric?"

Elric peered at the horizon, but could see nothing. Often his eyes were weak, as now. But the girl said in a voice of quiet despair:

"It is a golden sail."

"You recognize it?" Elric asked her.

"Oh, indeed I do. It is the galleon of Earl Saxif D'Aan. He has found us. Perhaps he was lying in wait along our route, knowing we must come this way."

"How far are we from the Gate?"

"I am not sure."

At that moment, there came a terrible noise from below, as if something sought to stave in the timbers of the ship.

"It's in the forward hatches!" cried Smiorgan. "See what it is, friend Elric! But take care, man!"

Cautiously Elric prized back one of the hatch covers and peered into the murky fastness of the hold. The noise of stamping and thumping continued and, as his eyes adjusted to the light, he saw the source.

The white horse was there. It whinnied as it saw him, almost in greeting.

"How did it come aboard?" Elric asked. "I saw nothing. I heard nothing."

The girl was almost as white as Elric. She sank to her knees beside the hatch, burying her face in her arms.

"He has us! He has us!"

"There is still a chance we can reach the Crimson Gate in time," Elric reassured her. "And once in my own world, why I can work much stronger sorcery to protect us."

"No," she sobbed, "it is too late. Why else would the white horse be here. He knows that Saxif D'Aan must soon board us."

"He'll have to fight us before he shall have you," Elric promised her.

"You have not seen his men. Cutthroats all. Desperate and wolfish! They'll show you no mercy. You would be best advised to hand me over to Saxif D'Aan at once and save yourselves. You'll gain nothing from trying to protect me. But I'd ask you a favor."

"What's that?"

"Find me a small knife to carry, that I may kill myself as soon as I know you two are safe."

Elric laughed, dragging her to her feet. "I'll have no such melodramatics from you, lass! We stand together. Perhaps we can bargain with Saxif D'Aan."

"What have you to barter?"

"Very little. But he is not aware of that."

"He can read your thoughts, seemingly. He has great powers!"

"I am Elric of Melniboné. I am said to possess a certain facility in the sorcerous arts, myself."

"But you are not as single-minded as Saxif D'Aan," she said simply. "Only one thing obsesses him—the need to make me his consort."

"Many girls would be flattered by the attention—glad to be an Empress with a Melnibonéan Emperor for a husband." Elric was sardonic.

She ignored his tone. "That is why I fear him so," she said in a murmur. "If I lost my determination for a moment, I could love him. I should be destroyed! It is what *she* must have known!"

5

THE GLEAMING galleon, sails and sides all gilded so that it seemed the sun itself pursued them, moved rapidly upon them while the girl and Count Smiorgan watched aghast and Elric desperately attempted to recall his elemental allies, without success.

Through the pale blue light the golden ship sailed relentlessly in their wake. Its proportions were monstrous, its sense of power vast, its gigantic prow sending up huge, foamy waves on both sides as it sped silently towards them.

With the look of a man preparing himself to meet death, Count Smiorgan Baldhead of the Purple Towns unslung his battle-ax and loosened his sword in its scabbard, setting his little metal cap upon his bald pate. The girl made no sound, no movement at all, but she wept.

Elric shook his head and his long, milk-white hair formed a halo around his face for a moment. His moody, crimson eyes began to focus on the world around him. He recognized the ship; it was of a pattern with the golden battle-barges of Melniboné—doubtless the ship in which Earl Saxif D'Aan had fled his homeland, searching for the Crimson Gate. Now Elric was convinced that this must be that same Saxif D'Aan and he knew less fear than did his companions, but considerably greater curiosity. Indeed, it was almost with nostalgia that he noted the ball of fire, like a natural comet, glowing with green light, come hissing and spluttering towards them, flung by the ship's forward catapult. He half expected to see a great dragon wheeling in the sky overhead, for it was with dragons and gilded battlecraft like these that Melniboné had once conquered the world.

The fireball fell into the sea a few inches from their bow and was evidently placed there deliberately, as a warning.

"Don't stop!" cried Vassliss. "Let the flames slay us! It will be better!"

Smiorgan was looking upwards. "We have no choice. Look! He has banished the wind, it seems."

They were becalmed. Elric smiled a grim smile. He knew now what the folk of the Young Kingdoms must have felt when his ancestors had used these identical tactics against them.

"Elric?" Smiorgan turned to the albino. "Are these your people? That ship's Melnibonéan without question!"

"So are the methods," Elric told him. "I am of the blood royal of Melniboné. I could be Emperor, even now, if I chose to claim my throne. There is some small chance that Earl Saxif D'Aan, though an ancestor, will recognize me and, therefore, recognize my authority. We are a conservative people, the folk of the Dragon Isle."

The girl spoke through dry lips, hopelessly: "He recognizes only the authority of the Lords of Chaos, who give him aid."

"All Melnibonéans recognize that authority," Elric told her with a certain humor.

From the forward hatch, the sound of the stallion's stamping and snorting increased.

"We're besieged by enchantments!" Count Smiorgan's normally ruddy features had paled. "Have you none of your own, Prince Elric, you can use to counter them?"

"None, it seems."

The golden ship loomed over them. Elric saw that the rails, high overhead, were crowded not with Imrryrian warriors but with cut-throats equally as desperate as those he had fought upon the island, and, apparently, drawn from the same variety of historical periods and nations. The galleon's long sweeps scraped the sides of the smaller vessel as they folded, like the legs of some water insect, to enable the grappling irons to be flung out. Iron claws bit into the timbers of the little ship and the brigandly crowd overhead cheered, grinning at them, menacing them with their weapons.

The girl began to run to the seaward side of the ship, but Elric caught her by the arm.

"Do not stop me, I beg you!" she cried. "Rather, jump with me and drown!"

"You think that death will save you from Saxif D'Aan?" Elric said. "If he has the power you say, death will only bring you more firmly into his grasp!"

"Oh!" The girl shuddered and then, as a voice called down to them from one of the tall decks of the gilded ship, she gave a moan and fainted into Elric's arms, so that, weakened as he was by his spell-working, it was all that he could do to stop himself falling with her to the deck.

The voice rose over the coarse shouts and guffaws of the crew. It was pure, lilting and sardonic. It was the voice of a Melnibonéan, though it spoke the common tongue of the Young Kingdoms, a corruption, in itself, of the speech of the Bright Empire.

"May I have the captain's permission to come aboard?"

Count Smiorgan growled back: "You have us firm, sir! Don't try to disguise an act of piracy with a polite speech!"

"I take it I have your permission then." The unseen speaker's tone remained exactly the same.

Elric watched as part of the rail was drawn back to allow a gangplank, studded with golden nails to give firmer footing, to be lowered from the galleon's deck to theirs.

A tall figure appeared at the top of the gangplank. He had the fine features of a Melnibonéan nobleman, was thin, proud in his bearing, clad in voluminous robes of cloth-of-gold, an elaborate helmet in gold and ebony upon his long, auburn locks. He had gray-blue eyes, pale, slightly flushed skin, and he carried, so far as Elric could see, no weapons of any kind.

With considerable dignity, Earl Saxif D'Aan began to descend, his rascals at his back. The contrast between this beautiful intellectual and those he commanded was remarkable. Where he walked with straight back, elegant and noble, they slouched, filthy, degenerate, unintelligent, grinning with pleasure at their easy victory. Not a man amongst them showed any sign of human dignity; each was overdressed in tattered and unclean finery, each had at least three weapons upon his person, and there was much evidence of looted jewelry, of noserings, earrings, bangles, necklaces, toe- and finger-rings, pendants, cloak-pins and the like.

"Gods!" murmured Smiorgan. "I've rarely seen such a collection of scum, and I thought I'd encountered most kinds in my voyages. How can such a man bear to be in their company?"

"Perhaps it suits his sense of irony," Elric suggested.

Earl Saxif D'Aan reached their deck and stood looking up at them to where they still positioned themselves, in the poop. He gave a slight bow. His features were controlled and only his eyes suggested something of the intensity of emotion dwelling within him, particularly as they fell upon the girl in Elric's arms.

"I am Earl Saxif D'Aan of Melniboné, now of the Islands Beyond the Crimson Gate. You have something with you which is mine. I would claim it from you."

"You mean the Lady Vassliss of Jharkor?" Elric said, his voice as steady as Saxif D'Aan's.

Saxif D'Aan seemed to note Elric for the first time. A slight frown crossed his brow and was quickly dismissed. "She is mine," he said. "You may be assured that she will come to no harm at my hands."

Elric, seeking some advantage, knew that he risked much when he next spoke, in the High Tongue of Melniboné, used between those of the blood royal. "Knowledge of your history does not reassure me, Saxif D'Aan."

Almost imperceptibly, the golden man stiffened and fire flared in his gray-blue eyes. "Who are you, to speak the Tongue of Kings? Who are you, who claims knowledge of my past?"

"I am Elric, son of Sadric, and I am the four-hundred-and-twenty-eighth Emperor of the folk of R'lin K'ren A'a, who landed upon the Dragon Isle ten thousand years ago. I am Elric, your Emperor, Earl Saxif D'Aan, and I demand your fealty." And Elric held up his right hand, upon which still gleamed a ring set with a single Actorios stone, the Ring of Kings.

Earl Saxif D'Aan now had firm control of himself again. He gave no sign that he was impressed. "Your sovereignty does not extend beyond your own world, noble emperor, though I greet you as a fellow monarch." He spread his arms so that his long sleeves rustled. "This world is mine. All that exists beneath the blue sun do I rule. You trespass, therefore, in my domain. I have every right to do as I please."

"Pirate pomp," muttered Count Smiorgan, who had understood nothing of the conversation but had gathered something of what passed by the tone. "Pirate braggadocio. What does he say, Elric?"

"He convinces me that he is not, in your sense, a pirate, Count Smiorgan. He claims that he is ruler of this plane. Since there is apparently no other, we must accept his claim."

"Gods! Then let him behave like a monarch and let us sail safely out of his waters!"

"We may—if we give him the girl."

Count Smiorgan shook his head. "I'll not do that. She's my passenger, in my charge. I must die rather than do that. It is the Code of the Sealords of the Purple Towns."

"You are famous for your adherence to that Code," Elric said. "As for myself, I have taken this girl into my protection and, as hereditary emperor of Melniboné, I cannot allow myself to be browbeaten."

They had conversed in a murmur, but, somehow, Earl Saxif D'Aan had heard them.

"I must let you know," he said evenly, in the common tongue, "that the girl is mine. You steal her from me. Is that the action of an Emperor?"

"She is not a slave," Elric said, "but the daughter of a free merchant in Jharkor. You have no rights upon her."

Earl Saxif D'Aan said: "Then I cannot open the Crimson Gate for you. You must remain in my world forever."

"You have closed the gate? Is it possible?"

"To me."

"Do you know that the girl would rather die than be captured by you, Earl Saxif D'Aan? Does it give you pleasure to instill such fear?"

The golden man looked directly into Elric's eyes as if he made some cryptic challenge. "The gift of pain has ever been a favorite gift amongst our folk, has it not? Yet it is another gift I offer her. She calls herself Vassliss of Jharkor, but she does not know herself. I know her. She is Gratyesha, Princess of Fwem-Omeyo, and I would make her my bride."

"How can it be that she does not know her own name?"

"She is reincarnated—soul and flesh are identical—that is how I know. And I have waited, Emperor of Melniboné, for many scores of years for her. Now I shall not be cheated of her."

"As you cheated yourself, two centuries past, in Melniboné?"

"You risk much with your directness of language, brother monarch!" There was a hint of a warning in Saxif D'Aan's tone, a warning much fiercer than any implied by the words.

"Well," Elric shrugged, "you have more power than we. My sorcery works poorly in your world. Your ruffians outnumber us. It should not be difficult for you to take her from us."

"You must give her to me. Then you may go free, back to your own world and your own time."

Elric smiled. "There is sorcery here. She is no reincarnation. You'd bring your lost love's spirit from the netherworld to inhabit this girl's body. Am I not right? That is why she must be given freely, or your sorcery will rebound upon you—or might—and you would not take the risk."

Earl Saxif D'Aan turned his head away so that Elric might not see his eyes. "She is the girl," he said, in the High Tongue. "I know that she is. I mean her soul no harm. I would merely give it back its memory."

"Then it is stalemate," said Elric.

"Have you no loyalty to a brother of the royal blood?" Saxif D'Aan murmured, still refusing to look at Elric.

"You claimed no such loyalty, as I recall, Earl Saxif D'Aan. If you accept me as your emperor, then you must accept my decisions. I keep the girl in my custody. Or you must take her by force."

"I am too proud."

"Such pride shall ever destroy love," said Elric, almost in sympathy. "What now, King of Limbo? What shall you do with us?"

Earl Saxif D'Aan lifted his noble head, about to reply, when from the hold the stamping and the snorting began again. His eyes widened. He looked questioningly at Elric, and there was something close to terror in his face.

"What's that? What have you in the hold?"

"A mount, my lord, that is all," said Elric equably.

"A horse? An ordinary horse?"

"A white one. A stallion, with bridle and saddle. It has no rider."

At once Saxif D'Aan's voice rose as he shouted orders for his men. "Take those three aboard our ship. This one shall be sunk directly. Hurry! Hurry!"

Elric and Smiorgan shook off the hands which sought to seize them and they moved towards the gangplank, carrying the girl between them, while Smiorgan muttered: "At least we are not slain, Elric. But what becomes of us now?"

Elric shook his head. "We must hope that we can continue to use Earl Saxif D'Aan's pride against him, to our advantage, though the gods alone know how we shall resolve the dilemma."

Earl Saxif D'Aan was already hurrying up the gangplank ahead of them.

"Quickly," he shouted. "Raise the plank!"

They stood upon the decks of the golden battle-barge and watched as the gangplank was drawn up, the length of rail replaced.

"Bring up the catapults," Saxif D'Aan commanded. "Use lead. Sink that vessel at once!"

The noise from the forward hold increased. The horse's voice echoed over ships and water. Hooves smashed at timber and then, suddenly, it came crashing through the hatch-covers, scrambling for purchase on the deck with its front hooves, and then standing there, pawing at the planks, its neck arching, its nostrils dilating and its eyes glaring, as if ready to do battle.

Now Saxif D'Aan made no attempt to hide the terror on his face. His voice rose to a scream as he threatened his rascals with every sort of horror if they did not obey him with utmost speed. The catapults were dragged up and huge globes of lead were lobbed onto the decks of Smiorgan's ship, smashing through the planks like arrows through parchment so that almost immediately the ship began to sink.

"Cut the grappling hooks!" cried Saxif D'Aan, wrenching a blade from the hand of one of his men and sawing at the nearest rope. "Cast loose—quickly!"

Even as Smiorgan's ship groaned and roared like a drowning beast, the ropes were cut. The ship keeled over at once, and the horse disappeared.

"Turn about!" shouted Saxif D'Aan. "Back to Fhaligarn and swiftly, or your souls shall feed my fiercest demons!"

There came a peculiar, high-pitched neighing from the foaming water, as Smiorgan's ship, stern uppermost, gasped and was swallowed. Elric caught a glimpse of the white stallion, swimming strongly.

"Go below!" Saxif D'Aan ordered, indicating a hatchway. "The horse can smell the girl and thus is doubly difficult to lose."

"Why do you fear it?" Elric asked. "It is only a horse. It cannot harm you."

Saxif D'Aan uttered a laugh of profound bitterness. "Can it not, brother monarch? Can it not?"

As they carried the girl below, Elric was frowning, remembering a little more of the legend of Saxif D'Aan, of the girl he had punished so cruelly, and of her lover, Prince Carolak. The last he heard of Saxif D'Aan was the sorcerer crying:

"More sail! More sail!"

And then the hatch had closed behind them and they found themselves in an opulent Melnibonéan day-cabin, full of rich hangings, precious metal, decorations of exquisite beauty and, to Count Smiorgan, disturbing decadence. But it was Elric, as he lowered the girl to a couch, who noticed the smell.

"Augh! It's the smell of a tomb—of damp and mold. Yet nothing rots. It is passing peculiar, friend Smiorgan, is it not?"

"I scarcely noticed, Elric." Smiorgan's voice was hollow. "But I would agree with you on one thing. We are entombed. I doubt we'll live to escape this world now."

6

AN HOUR had passed since they had been forced aboard. The door had been locked behind them and, it seemed, Saxif D'Aan was too preoccupied with escaping the white stallion to bother with them. Peering through the lattice of a porthole, Elric could look back to where their ship had been sunk. They were many leagues distant, already, yet he still thought, from time to time, that he saw the head and shoulders of the stallion above the waves.

Vassliss had recovered and sat pale and shivering upon the couch.

"What more do you know of that horse?" Elric asked her. "It would be helpful to me if you could recall anything you have heard."

She shook her head. "Saxif D'Aan spoke little of it, but I gather he fears the rider more than he does the horse."

"Ah!" Elric frowned. "I suspected it! Have you ever seen the rider?"

"Never. I think that Saxif D'Aan has never seen him, either. I think he believes himself doomed if that rider should ever sit upon the white stallion."

Elric smiled to himself.

"Why do you ask so much about the horse?" Smiorgan wished to know.

Elric shook his head. "I have an instinct, that is all. Half a memory. But I'll say nothing and think as little as I may, for there is no doubt Saxif D'Aan, as Vassliss suggests, has some power of reading the mind."

They heard a footfall above, descending to their door. A bolt was drawn and Saxif D'Aan, his composure fully restored, stood in the opening, his hands in his golden sleeves.

"You will forgive, I hope, the peremptory way in which I sent you here. There was danger which had to be averted at all costs. As a result, my manners were not all that they should have been."

"Danger to us?" Elric asked. "Or to you, Earl Saxif D'Aan."

"In the circumstances, to all of us, I assure you."

"Who rides the horse?" Smiorgan asked bluntly. "And why do you fear him?"

Earl Saxif D'Aan was master of himself again, so there was no sign of a reaction. "That is very much my private concern," he said softly. "Will you dine with me now?"

The girl made a noise in her throat and Earl Saxif D'Aan turned piercing eyes upon her. "Gratyesha, you will want to cleanse yourself and make yourself beautiful again. I will see that facilities are placed at your disposal."

"I am not Gratyesha," she said. "I am Vassliss, the merchant's daughter."

"You will remember," he said. "In time, you will remember." There was such certainty, such obsessive power in his voice that even Elric experienced a frisson of awe. "The things will be brought to you, and you may use this cabin as your own until we return to my palace on Fhaligarn. My lords . . ." he indicated that they should leave.

Elric said: "I'll not leave her, Saxif D'Aan. She is too afraid."

"She fears only the truth, brother."

"She fears you and your madness."

Saxif D'Aan shrugged insouciantly. "I shall leave first then. If you would accompany me, my lords . . ." He strode from the cabin and they followed.

Elric said, over his shoulder: "Vassliss, you may depend upon my protection." And he closed the cabin doors behind him.

Earl Saxif D'Aan was standing upon the deck, exposing his noble face to the spray which was flung up by the ship as it moved with supernatural speed through the sea.

"You called me mad, Prince Elric? Yet you must be versed in sorcery, yourself?"

"Of course. I am of the blood royal. I am reckoned knowledgeable in my own world."

"But here? How well does your sorcery work?"

"Poorly, I'll admit. The spaces between the planes seems greater."

"Exactly. But I have bridged them. I have had time to learn how to bridge them."

"You are saying that you are more powerful than am I?"

"It is a fact, is it not?"

"It is. But I did not think we were about to indulge in sorcerous battles, Earl Saxif D'Aan."

"Of course. Yet, if you were to think of besting me by sorcery, you would think twice, eh?"

"I should be foolish to contemplate such a thing at all. It could cost me my soul. My life, at least."

"True. You are a realist, I see."

"I suppose so."

"Then we can progress on simpler lines, to settle the dispute between us."

"You propose a duel?" Elric was surprised.

Earl Saxif D'Aan's laughter was light. "Of course not—against your sword? That has power in all worlds, though the magnitude varies."

"I am glad that you are aware of that," Elric said significantly.

"Besides," added Earl Saxif D'Aan, his golden robes rustling as he moved a little nearer to the rail, "you would not kill me—for only I have the means of your escaping this world."

"Perhaps we'd elect to remain," said Elric.

"Then you would be my subjects. But, no—you would not like it here. I am self-exiled. I could not return to my own world now, even if I wished to do so. It has cost me much, my knowledge. But I would found a dynasty here, beneath the blue sun. I must have my wife, Prince Elric. I must have Gratyesha."

"Her name is Vassliss," said Elric obstinately.

"She thinks it is."

"Then it is. I have sworn to protect her, as has Count Smiorgan. Protect her we shall. You will have to kill us all."

"Exactly," said Earl Saxif D'Aan with the air of a man who has been coaching a poor student towards the correct answer to a problem. "Exactly. I shall have to kill you all. You leave me with little alternative, Prince Elric."

"Would that benefit you?"

"It would. It would put a certain powerful demon at my service for a few hours."

"We should resist."

"I have many men. I do not value them. Eventually, they would overwhelm you. Would they not?"

Elric remained silent.

"My men would be aided by sorcery," added Saxif D'Aan. "Some would die, but not too many, I think."

Elric was looking beyond Saxif D'Aan, staring out to sea. He was sure that the horse still followed. He was sure that Saxif D'Aan knew, also.

"And if we gave up the girl?"

"I should open the Crimson Gate for you. You would be honored guests. I should see that you were borne safely through, even taken safely to some hospitable land in your own world, for even if you passed through the gate there would be danger. The storms."

Elric appeared to deliberate.

"You have only a little time to make your decision, Prince Elric. I had hoped to reach my palace, Fhaligarn, by now. I shall not allow you very much longer. Come, make your decision. You know I speak the truth."

"You know that I can work some sorcery in your world, do you not?"

"You summoned a few friendly elementals to your aid, I know. But at what cost? Would you challenge me directly?"

"It would be unwise of me," said Elric.

Smiorgan was tugging at his sleeve. "Stop this useless talk. He knows that we have given our word to the girl and that we *must* fight him!"

Earl Saxif D'Aan sighed. There seemed to be genuine sorrow in his voice. "If you are determined to lose your lives . . ." he began.

"I should like to know why you set such importance upon the speed with which we make up our minds," Elric said. "Why cannot we wait until we reach Fhaligarn?"

Earl Saxif D'Aan's expression was calculating, and again he looked full into Elric's crimson eyes. "I think you know," he said, almost inaudibly.

But Elric shook his head. "I think you give me too much credit for intelligence."

"Perhaps."

Elric knew that Saxif D'Aan was attempting to read his thoughts; he deliberately blanked his mind, and suspected that he sensed frustration in the sorcerer's demeanor.

And then the albino had sprung at his kinsman, his hand chopping at Saxif D'Aan's throat. The earl was taken completely off guard. He tried to call out, but his vocal chords were numbed. Another blow, and he fell to the deck, senseless.

"Quickly, Smiorgan," Elric shouted, and he had leapt into the rigging, climbing swiftly upwards to the top yards. Smiorgan, bewildered, followed, and Elric had drawn his sword, even as he reached the crow's nest, driving upwards through the rail so that the lookout was taken in the groin scarcely before he realized it.

Next, Elric was hacking at the ropes holding the mainsail to the yard. Already a number of Saxif D'Aan's ruffians were climbing after them.

The heavy golden sail came loose, falling to envelop the pirates and take several of them down with it.

Elric climbed into the crow's nest and pitched the dead man over the rail in the wake of his comrades. Then he had raised his sword over his head, holding it in his two hands, his eyes blank again, his head raised to the blue sun, and Smiorgan, clinging to the mast below, shuddered as he heard a peculiar crooning come from the albino's throat.

More of the cutthroats were ascending, and Smiorgan hacked at the rigging, having the satisfaction of seeing half a score go flying down to break their bones on the deck below, or be swallowed by the waves.

Earl Saxif D'Aan was beginning to recover, but he was still stunned.

"Fool!" he was crying. "Fool!" But it was not possible to tell if he referred to Elric or to himself.

Elric's voice became a wail, rhythmical and chilling, as he chanted his incantation, and the strength from the man he had killed flowed into him and sustained. His crimson eyes seemed to flicker with fires of another, nameless color, and his whole body shook as the strange runes shaped themselves in a throat which had never been made to speak such sounds.

His voice became a vibrant groan as the incantation continued, and Smiorgan, watching as more of the crew made efforts to climb the mainmast, felt an unearthly cold creep through him.

Earl Saxif D'Aan screamed from below:

"You would not dare!"

The sorcerer began to make passes in the air, his own incantation tumbling from his lips, and Smiorgan gasped as a creature made of smoke took shape only a few feet below him. The creature smacked its lips and grinned and stretched a paw, which became flesh even as it moved, towards Smiorgan. He hacked at the paw with his sword, whimpering.

"Elric!" cried Count Smiorgan, clambering higher so that he grasped the rail of the crow's nest. "Elric! He sends demons against us now!"

But Elric ignored him. His whole mind was in another world, a darker, bleaker world even than this one. Through gray mists, he saw a figure, and he cried a name. "Come!" he called in the ancient tongue of his ancestors. "Come!"

Count Smiorgan cursed as the demon became increasingly substantial. Red fangs clashed and green eyes glared at him. A claw stroked his boot and no matter how much he struck with his sword, the demon did not appear to notice the blows.

There was no room for Smiorgan in the crow's nest, but he stood on the outer rim, shouting with terror, desperate for aid. Still Elric continued to chant.

"Elric! I am doomed!"

The demon's paw grasped Smiorgan by his ankle.

"Elric!"

Thunder rolled out at sea; a ball of lightning appeared for a second and then was gone. From nowhere there came the sound of a horse's hooves pounding, and a human voice shouting in triumph.

Elric sank back against the rail, opening his eyes in time to see Smiorgan being dragged slowly downward. With the last of his strength he flung himself forward, leaning far out to stab downwards with Stormbringer. The runesword sank cleanly into the demon's right eye and it roared, letting go of Smiorgan, striking at the blade which drew its energy from it and, as that energy passed into the blade and thence to Elric, the albino grinned a frightful grin so that, for a second, Smiorgan became more frightened of his friend than he had been of the demon. The demon began to dematerialize, its only means of escape from the sword which drank its life force, but more of Saxif D'Aan's rogues were behind it, and their blades rattled as they sought the pair.

Elric swung himself back over the rail, balanced precariously on the yard as he slashed at their attackers, yelling the old battle-cries of his people. Smiorgan could do little but watch. He noted that Saxif D'Aan was no longer on deck and he shouted urgently to Elric:

"Elric! Saxif D'Aan. He seeks out the girl."

Elric now took the attack to the pirates, and they were more than anxious to avoid the moaning runesword, some even leaping into the sea rather than encounter it. Swiftly the two leapt from yard to yard until they were again upon the deck.

"What does he fear? Why does he not use more sorcery?" panted Count Smiorgan, as they ran towards the cabin.

"I have summoned the one who rides the horse," Elric told him. "I had so little time—and I could tell you nothing of it, knowing that Saxif D'Aan would read my intention in your mind, if he could not in mine!"

The cabin doors were firmly secured from the inside. Elric began to hack at them with the black sword.

But the door resisted as it should not have resisted. "Sealed by sorcery and I've no means of unsealing it," said the albino.

"Will he kill her?"

"I don't know. He might try to take her into some other plane. We must—"

Hooves clattered on the deck and the white stallion reared behind them, only now it had a rider, clad in bright purple and yellow armor. He was bareheaded and youthful, though there were several old scars upon his face. His hair was thick and curly and blond and his eyes were a deep blue.

He drew tightly upon his reins, steadying the horse. He looked piercingly at Elric. "Was it you, Melnibonéan, who opened the pathway for me?"

"It was."

"Then I thank you, though I cannot repay you."

"You have repaid me," Elric told him, then drew Smiorgan aside as the rider leaned forward and spurred his horse directly at the closed doors, smashing through as though they were rotted cotton.

There came a terrible cry from within and then Earl Saxif D'Aan, hampered by his complicated robes of gold, rushed from the cabin, seizing a sword from the hand of the nearest corpse, darting Elric a look not so much of hatred but of bewildered agony, as he turned to face the blond rider.

The rider had dismounted now and came from the cabin, one arm around the shivering girl, Vassliss, one hand upon the reins of his horse, and he said, sorrowfully:

"You did me a great wrong, Earl Saxif D'Aan, but you did Gratyesha an infinitely more terrible one. Now you must pay."

Saxif D'Aan paused, drawing a deep breath, and when he looked up again, his eyes were steady, his dignity had returned.

"Must I pay in full?" he said.

"In full."

"It is all I deserve," said Saxif D'Aan. "I escaped my doom for many years, but I could not escape the knowledge of my crime. She loved me, you know. Not you."

"She loved us both, I think. But the love she gave you was her entire soul and I should not want that from any woman."

"You would be the loser, then."

"You never knew how much she loved you."

"Only—only afterwards . . ."

"I pity you, Earl Saxif D'Aan." The young man gave the reins of his horse to the girl, and he drew his sword. "We are strange rivals, are we not?"

"You have been all these years in Limbo, where I banished you—in that garden on Melniboné?"

"All these years. Only my horse could follow you. The horse of Tendric, my father, also of Melniboné, and also a sorcerer."

"If I had known that, then, I'd have slain you cleanly and sent the horse to Limbo."

"Jealousy weakened you, Earl Saxif D'Aan. But now we fight as we should have fought then—man to man, with steel, for the hand of the one who loves us both. It is more than you deserve."

"Much more," agreed the sorcerer. And he brought up his sword to lunge at the young man who, Smiorgan guessed, could only be Prince Carolak himself.

The fight was predetermined. Saxif D'Aan knew that, if Carolak did not. Saxif D'Aan's skill in arms was up to the standard of any Melnibonéan nobleman, but it could not match the skill of a professional soldier, who had fought for his life time after time.

Back and forth across the deck, while Saxif D'Aan's rascals looked on in open-mouthed astonishment, the rivals fought a duel which should have been fought and resolved two centuries before, while the girl they both plainly thought was the reincarnation of Gratyesha watched them with as much concern as might her original have watched when Saxif D'Aan first encountered Prince Carolak in the gardens of his palace, so long ago.

Saxif D'Aan fought well, and Carolak fought nobly, for on many occasions he avoided an obvious advantage, but at length Saxif D'Aan threw away his sword, crying: "Enough. I'll give you your vengeance, Prince Carolak. I'll let you take the girl. But you'll not give me your damned mercy—you'll not take my pride."

And Carolak nodded, stepped forward, and struck straight for Saxif D'Aan's heart.

The blade entered clean and Earl Saxif D'Aan should have died, but he did not. He crawled along the deck until he reached the base of the mast, and he rested his back against it, while the blood pumped from the wounded heart. And he smiled.

"It appears," he said faintly, "that I cannot die, so long have I sustained my life by sorcery. I am no longer a man."

He did not seem pleased by this thought, but Prince Carolak, stepping forward and leaning over him, reassured him. "You will die," he promised, "soon."

"What will you do with her—with Gratyesha."

"Her name is Vassliss," said Count Smiorgan insistently. "She is a merchant's daughter, from Jharkor."

"She must make up her own mind," Carolak said, ignoring Smiorgan.

Earl Saxif D'Aan turned glazed eyes on Elric. "I must thank you," he said. "You brought me the one who could bring me peace, though I feared him."

"Is that why, I wonder, your sorcery was so weak against me," Elric said. "Because you wished Carolak to come and release you from your guilt."

"Possibly, Elric. You are wiser in some matters, it seems, than am I."

"What of the Crimson Gate?" Smiorgan growled. "Can that be opened? Have you still the power, Earl Saxif D'Aan?"

"I think so." From the folds of his bloodstained garments of gold, the sorcerer produced a large crystal which shone with the deep colors of a ruby. "This will not only lead you to the gate, it will enable you to pass through, only I must warn you . . ." Saxif D'Aan began to cough. "The ship—" he gasped, "the ship—like my body—has been sustained by means of sorcery—therefore . . ." His head slumped forward. He raised it with a huge effort and stared beyond them at the girl who still held the reins of the white stallion. "Farewell, Gratyesha, Princess of Fwem-Omeyo. I loved you." The eyes remained fixed upon her, but they were dead eyes now.

Carolak turned back to look at the girl. "How do you call yourself, Gratyesha?"

"They call me Vassliss," she told him. She smiled up into his youthful, battle-scarred face. "That is what they call me, Prince Carolak."

"You know who I am?"

"I know you now."

"Will you come with me, Gratyesha? Will you be my bride, at last, in the strange new lands I have found, beyond the world?"

"I will come," she said.

He helped her up into the saddle of his white stallion and climbed so that he sat behind her. He bowed to Elric of Melniboné. "I thank you again, Sir Sorcerer, though I never thought to be helped by one of the royal blood of Melniboné."

Elric's expression was not without humor. "In Melniboné," he said, "I'm told it's tainted blood."

"Tainted with mercy, perhaps."

"Perhaps."

Prince Carolak saluted them. "I hope you find peace, Prince Elric, as I have found it."

"I fear my peace will more resemble that which Saxif D'Aan found," Elric said grimly. "Nonetheless, I thank you for your good words, Prince Carolak."

Then Carolak, laughing, had ridden his horse for the rail, leapt it, and vanished.

There was a silence upon the ship. The remaining ruffians looked uncertainly, one to the other. Elric addressed them:

"Know you this—I have the key to the Crimson Gate—and only I have the knowledge to use it. Help me sail the ship, and you'll have freedom from this world! What say you?"

"Give us our orders, captain," said a toothless individual, and he cackled with mirth. "It's the best offer we've had in a hundred years or more!"

7

IT WAS Smiorgan who first saw the Crimson Gate. He held the great red gem in his hand and pointed ahead.

"There! There, Elric! Saxif D'Aan has not betrayed us!"

The sea had begun to heave with huge, turbulent waves and, with the mainsail still tangled upon the deck, it was all that the crew could do to control the ship, but the chance of escape from the world of the blue sun made them work with every ounce of energy and, slowly, the golden battle-barge neared the towering crimson pillars.

The pillars rose from the gray, roaring water, casting a peculiar light upon the crests of the waves. They appeared to have little substance, and yet stood firm against the battering of the tons of water lashing around them.

"Let us hope they are wider apart than they look," said Elric. "It would be a hard enough task steering through them in calm waters, let alone this kind of sea."

"I'd best take the wheel, I think," said Count Smiorgan, handing Elric the gem, and he strode back up the tilting deck, climbing to the covered wheelhouse and relieving the frightened man who stood there.

There was nothing Elric could do but watch as Smiorgan turned the huge vessel into the waves, riding the tops as best he could, but sometimes descending with a rush which made Elric's heart rise to his mouth. All around them, then, the cliffs of water threatened, but the ship was taking another wave before the main force of water could crash onto her decks. For all this, Elric was quickly soaked through and, though sense told him he would be best below, he clung to the rail, watching as Smiorgan steered the ship with uncanny sureness towards the Crimson Gate.

And then the deck was flooded with red light and Elric was half blinded. Gray water flew everywhere; there came a dreadful scraping sound, then a snapping as oars broke against the pillars. The ship shuddered and began to turn, sideways to the wind, but Smiorgan forced her round and suddenly the quality of the light changed subtly,

though the sea remained as turbulent as ever and Elric knew, deep
within him, that overhead, beyond the heavy clouds, a yellow sun was
burning again.

But now there came a creaking and a crashing from within the bowels
of the battle-barge. The smell of mold, which Elric had noted earlier,
became stronger, almost overpowering.

Smiorgan came hurrying back, having handed over the wheel. His
face was pale again. "She's breaking up, Elric," he called out, over the
noise of the wind and the waves. He staggered as a huge wall of water
struck the ship and snatched away several planks from the deck. "She's
falling apart, man!"

"Saxif D'Aan tried to warn us of this!" Elric shouted back. "As he
was kept alive by sorcery, so was his ship. She was old before he sailed
her to that world. While there, the sorcery which sustained her remained strong—but on this plane it has no power at all. Look!" And
he pulled at a piece of the rail, crumbling the rotten wood with his
fingers. "We must find a length of timber which is still good."

At that moment a yard came crashing from the mast and struck the
deck, bouncing, then rolling towards them.

Elric crawled up the sloping deck until he could grasp the spar and
test it. "This one's still good. Use your belt or whatever else you can
and tie yourself to it!"

The wind wailed through the disintegrating rigging of the ship; the
sea smashed at the sides, driving great holes below the waterline.

The ruffians who had crewed her were in a state of complete panic,
some trying to unship small boats which crumbled even as they swung
them out, others lying flat against the rotted decks and praying to
whatever gods they still worshipped.

Elric strapped himself to the broken yard as firmly as he could and
Smiorgan followed his example. The next wave to hit the ship full-on
lifted them with it, cleanly over what remained of the rail and into the
chilling, shouting waters of that terrible sea.

Elric kept his mouth tight shut against swallowing too much water
and reflected on the irony of his situation. It seemed that, having
escaped so much, he was to die a very ordinary death, by drowning.

It was not long before his senses left him and he gave himself up to
the swirling and somehow friendly waters of the ocean.

He awoke, struggling.

There were hands upon him. He strove to fight them off, but he was
too weak. Someone laughed, a rough, good-humored sound.

The water no longer roared and crashed around him. The wind no longer howled. Instead there was a gentler movement. He heard waves lapping against timber. He was aboard another ship.

He opened his eyes, blinking in warm, yellow sunlight. Red-cheeked Vilmirian sailors grinned down at him. "You're a lucky man—if man you be!" said one.

"My friend?" Elric sought for Smiorgan.

"He was in better shape than were you. He's down in Duke Avan's cabin now."

"Duke Avan?" Elric knew the name but, in his dazed condition, could remember nothing to help him place the man. "You saved us?"

"Aye. We found you both drifting, tied to a broken yard carved with the strangest designs I've ever seen. A Melnibonéan craft, was she?"

"Yes, but rather old."

And with a smile, more tranquil than most, he fell back into his slumbers.

JANET MORRIS
A Man and His God

1

SOLSTICE STORMS and heat lightning beat upon Sanctuary, washing the dust from the gutters and from the faces of the mercenaries drifting through town on their way north where (seers proclaimed and rumor corroborated) the Rankan Empire would soon be hiring multitudes, readying for war.

The storms doused cookfires, west of town, where the camp followers and artificers that Sanctuary's ramshackle facilities could not hold had overflowed. There squatted, under stinking ill-tanned hide pavilions, custom weaponers catering to mercenaries whose eyes were keener than the most carefully wax-forged iron and whose panoplies must bespeak their whereabouts in battle to their comrades; their deadly efficacy to strangers and combatants; the dear cost of their hire to prospective employers. Fine corselets, cuirasses ancient and modern, custom's best axes and swords, and helmetry with crests dyed to order could be had in Sanctuary that summer; but the downwind breeze had never smelled fouler than after wending through their press.

Here and there among the steaming firepots siegecrafters and commanders of fortifications drilled their engineers, lest from idleness picked men be suborned by rival leaders seeking to upgrade their corps. To keep order here, the Emperor's halfbrother Kadakithis had only a handful of Rankan Hell-Hounds in his personal guard, and a local garrison staffed by indigenous Ilsigs, conquered but not assimilated. The Rankans called the Ilsigs "Wrigglies," and the Wrigglies called the Rankans naked barbarians and their women worse, and not even the rain could cool the fires of that age-old rivalry.

On the landspit north of the lighthouse, rain had stopped work on Prince Kadakithis's new palace. Only a man and horse, both bronze, both of heroic proportions, rode the beach. Doom criers of Sanctuary, who once had proclaimed their town "just left of heaven," had changed their tune: they had dubbed Sanctuary Death's Gate and the one man, called Tempus, Death Himself.

He was not. He was a mercenary, envoy of a Rankan faction desirous of making a change in emperors; he was a Hell-Hound, by Kadakithis's good offices; and marshal of palace security, because the prince, not meant to triumph in his governorship/exile, was understaffed. Of late Tempus had become a royal architect, for which he was as qualified as any man about, having fortified more towns than Kadakithis had years. The prince had proposed the site; the soldier examined it and found it good. Not satisfied, he had made it better, dredging deep with oxen along the shore while his imported fortifications crews raised double walls of baked brick filled with rubble and faced with stone. When complete, these would be deeply crenelated for archers, studded with gatehouses, double-gated and sheer. Even incomplete, the walls which barred the folk from spit and lighthouse grinned with a death's head smirk toward the town, enclosing granaries and stables and newly whited barracks and a spring for fresh water: if War came hither, Tempus proposed to make Him welcome for a long and arduous siege.

The fey, god's breath weather might have stopped work on the construction, but Tempus worked without respite, always: it eased the soul of the man who could not sleep and who had turned his back upon his god. This day, he awaited the arrival of Kadakithis and that of his own anonymous Rankan contact, to introduce emissary to possible figurehead, to put the two together and see what might be seen.

When he had arranged the meeting, he had yet walked in the shelter of the god Vashanka's arm. Now, things had changed for him and he no longer cared to serve Vashanka, the Storm God, who regulated kingship. If he could, he was going to contrive to be relieved of his various commissions and of his honor bond to Kadakithis, freed to go among the mercenaries to whom his soul belonged (since he had it back) and put together a cohort to take north and lease to the highest bidder. He wanted to wade thigh-deep in gore and guts and see if, just by chance, he might manage to find his way back through the shimmering dimensional gate beyond which the god had long ago thrust him, back into the world and into the age to which he was born.

Since he knew the chances of that were less than Kadakithis becoming Emperor of Upper and Lower Ranke, and since the god's gloss of rationality was gone from him, leaving him in the embrace of the curse, yet lingering, which he had originally become the god's suppliant to thwart, he would settle for a small mercenary corps of his own choosing, from which to begin building an army that would not be a puerile jest, as Kadakithis's forces were at present. For this he had been contacted, to this he had agreed. It remained only to see to it that Kadakithis agreed.

The mercenary who was a Hell-Hound scolded the horse, who did not like its new weighted shoes or the water surging around its knees, white as its stockings. Like the horse, Kadakithis was only potential in quest of actualization; like the horse, Kadakithis feared the wrong things, and placed his trust in himself only, an untenable arrogance in horse or man, when the horse must go to battle and the man also. Tempus collected the horse up under him, shifting his weight, pulling the red-bronze beast's head in against its chest, until the combination of his guidance and the toe-weights on its hooves and the waves' kiss showed the horse what he wanted. Tempus could feel it in the stallion's gaits; he did not need to see the result: like a dancer, the sorrel lifted each leg high. Then it gave a quizzical snort as it sensed the power to be gained from such a stride: school was in session. Perhaps, despite the four white socks, the horse would suit. He lifted it with a touch and a squeeze of his knees into a canter no faster than another horse might walk. "Good, good," he told it, and from the beach came the *pat-pat* of applause.

Clouds split; sunrays danced over the wrack-strewn shore and over the bronze stallion and its rider, stripped down to plated loinguard, making a rainbow about them. Tempus looked up, landward to where a lone eunuch clapped pink palms together from one of Prince Kadakithis's chariots. The rainbow disappeared, the clouds suppressed the sun, and in a wrap of shadow the enigmatic Hell-Hound (whom the eunuch knew from his own experience to be capable of regenerating a severed limb and thus veritably eternal; and who was indubitably deadlier than all the mercenaries descended on Sanctuary like flies upon a day-old carcass) trotted the horse up the beach to where the eunuch in the chariot was waiting on solid ground.

"What are you doing here, Sissy? Where is your lord, Kadakithis?" Tempus stopped his horse well back from the irascible pair of blacks in their traces. This eunuch was near their color: a Wriggly. Cut young and deftly, his answer came in a sweet alto:

"Lord Marshall, most daunting of Hell-Hounds, I bring you His Majesty's apologies, and true word, if you will heed it."

The eunuch, no more than seventeen, gazed at him longingly. Kadakithis had accepted this fancy toy from Jubal, the slaver, despite the slavemaster's own brand on its high rump, and the deeper dangers implied by the identity of its fashioner. Tempus had marked it, when first he heard its lilting voice in the palace, for he had heard that voice before. Foolish, haughty, or merely pressed beyond a bedwarmer's ability to cope: no matter; this creature of Jubal's, he had long wanted. Jubal and Tempus had been making private war, the more fierce for being undeclared, since Tempus had first come to Sanctuary and seen the swaggering, masked killers Jubal kept on staff terrorizing whom they chose on the town's west side. Tempus had made those masked murderers his private game stock, the west end of Sanctuary his personal preserve, and the campaign was on. Time and again, he had dispatched them. But tactics change, and Jubal's had become too treacherous for Tempus to endure, especially now with the northern insurrection half out of its egg of rumor. He said to the parted lips awaiting his permission to speak and to the deer-soft eyes doting on his every move that the eunuch might dismount the car, prostrate itself before him, and from there deliver its message.

It did all of those, quivering with delight like a dog enraptured by the smallest attention, and said with its forehead to the sand: "My lord, the Prince bids me say he has been detained by Certain Persons, and will be late, but means to attend you. If you were to ask me why that was, then I would have no choice but to admit to you that the three most mighty magicians, those whose names cannot be spoken, came down upon the summer palace in billows of blackest smoke and foul odors, and that the fountains ran red and the sculptures wept and cried, and frogs jumped upon my lord in his bath, all because the Hazards are afraid that you might move to free the slayer-of-sorcerers called Cime before she comes to trial. Although my master assured them that you would not, that you had said nothing to him about this woman, when I left they still were not satisfied, but were shaking walls and raising shades and doing all manner of wizardly things to demonstrate their concern."

The eunuch fell quiet, awaiting leave to rise. For an instant there was total silence, then the sound of Tempus's slithering dismount. Then he said: "Let us see your brand, pretty one," and with a wiggling of its upthrust rump the eunuch hastened to obey.

It took Tempus longer than he had estimated to wrest a confession from the Wriggly, from the Ilsig who was the last of his line and at the end of his line. It did not make cries of pleasure or betrayal or agony, but accepted its destiny as good Wrigglies always did, writhing soundlessly.

When he let it go, though the blood was running down its legs and it saw the intestine like wet parchment caught in his fingernails, it wept with relief, promising to deliver his exhortation posthaste to Kadaki-this. It kissed his hand, pressing his palm against its beardless cheek, never realizing that it was, itself, his message, or that it would be dead before the sun set.

2

KNEELING TO wash his arm in the surf, he found himself singing a best-forgotten funerary dirge in the ancient argot all mercenaries learn. But his voice was gravelly and his memories were treacherous thickets full of barbs, and he stopped as soon as he realized that he sang. The eunuch would die because he remembered its voice from the workshop of despicable Kurd, the frail and filthy vivisectionist, while he had been an experimental animal therein. He remembered other things, too: he remembered the sear of the branding iron and the smell of flesh burning and the voices of two fellow guardsmen, the Hell Hounds Zalbar and Razkuli, piercing the drugmist through holes the pain poked in his stupor. And he recalled a protracted and hurtful healing, shut away from any who might be overawed to see a man regrow a limb. Mending, he had brooded, seeking certainty, some redress fit to his grievance. But he had not been sure enough to act. Now, after hearing the eunuch's tale, he was certain. When Tempus was certain, Destiny got out its ledger.

But what to write therein? His instinct told him it was Black Jubal he wanted, not the two Hell-Hounds; that Razkuli was a nonentity and Zalbar, like a raw horse, was merely in need of schooling. Those two had single-handedly arranged for Tempus's snuff to be drugged, for him to be branded, his tongue cut out, then sold off to wicked little Kurd, there to languish interminably under the knife? He could not credit it. Yet the eunuch had said—and in such straits no one lies—that though Jubal had gone to Zalbar for help in dealing with Tempus, the slave trader had known nothing of what fate the Hell Hounds had in mind for their colleague. Never mind it; Jubal's crimes were voluminous. Tempus would take him for espionage—that punishment could only be administered once. Then personal grudges must be put aside: it is unseemly to hold feuds with the dead.

But if not Jubal, then who had written Tempus's itinerary for Hell? It sounded, suspiciously, like the god's work. Since he had turned his back upon the god, things had gone from bad to worse. And if Vashanka had not turned His face away from Tempus even while he lay helpless, the god had not stirred to rescue him (though any limb lopped off him still grew back, any wound he took healed relatively quickly, as men judge such things). No, Vashanka, his tutelary, had not hastened to aid him. The speed of Tempus's healing was always in direct proportion to the pleasure the god was taking in His servant. Vashanka's terrible rebuke had made the man wax terrible, also. Curses and unholy insults rang down from the mind of the god and up from the mind of the man who then had no tongue left with which to scream. It had taken Hanse the thief, young Shadowspawn, chancemet and hardly known, to extricate him from interminable torture. Now he owed more debt than he liked to Shadowspawn, and Shadowspawn knew more about Tempus than even that backstreeter could want to know, so that the thief's eyes slid away, sick and mistrustful, when Tempus would chance upon him in the Maze.

But even then, Tempus's break with divinity was not complete. Hopefully, he stood as Vashanka in the recreation of the Ten-Slaying and Seduction of Azyuna, thinking to propitiate the god while saving face—to no avail. Soon after, hearing that his sister, Cime, had been apprehended slaying sorcerers wantonly in their beds, he had thrown the amulet of Vashanka, which he had worn since former times, out to sea from this very shore—he had had no choice. Only so much can be borne from men, so much from gods. Zalbar, had he the wit, would have revelled in Tempus's barely hidden reaction to his news that the fearsome mage-killer was now in custody, her diamond rods locked away in the Hall of Judgement awaiting her disposition.

He growled to him, thinking about her, her black hair winged with gray, in Sanctuary's unsegregated dungeons where any syphilitic rapist could have her at will, while he must not touch her at all, or raise hand to help her lest he start forces in motion he could not control. His break with the god stemmed from her presence in Sanctuary, at his endless wandering as Vashanka's minion had stemmed from an altercation he had over her with a mage. If he went down into the pits and took her, the god would be placated; he had no desire to reopen relations with Vashanka, who had turned His face away from His servant. If Tempus brought her out under his own aegis, he would have the entire Mage-guild at his throat; he wanted no quarrel with the Adepts. He had told her not to slay them here, where he must maintain order and the letter of the law.

By the time Kadakithis arrived in that very same chariot, its braces sticky with Wriggly blood, Tempus was in a humor darker than the drying clots, fully as dark as the odd, round cloud coming fast from the northeast.

Kadakithis's noble Rankan visage was suffused with rage, so that his skin was darker than his pale hair: "But why? In the name of all the gods, what did the poor little creature ever do to you? You owe me a eunuch, and an explanation." He tapped his lacquered nails on the chariot's bronze rim.

"I have a perfect replacement in mind," smiled Tempus smoothly, "my lord. As for why . . . all eunuchs are duplicitous. This one was an information conduit to Jubal. Unless you would like to invite the slaver to policy sessions and let him stand behind those ivory screens where your favorites eavesdrop as they choose, I have acted well within my prerogatives as marshal. If my name is attached to your palace security, then your palace *will* be secure."

"Bastard! How dare you even imply that *I* should apologize to *you*? When will you treat me with the proper amount of respect? You tell me all eunuchs are treacherous, the very breath after offering me another one!"

"I am giving you respect. Reverence I reserve for better men than I. When you have attained that dignity, we shall both know it: you will not have to ask. Until then, either trust or discharge me." He waited, to see if the prince would speak. Then he continued: "As to the eunuch I offer as replacement, I want you to arrange for his training. You like Jubal's work; send to him saying yours has met with an accident and you wish to tender another into his care to be similarly instructed. Tell him you paid a lot of money for it, and you have high hopes."

"You have such a eunuch?"

"I will have it."

"And you expect me to conscion your sending of an agent in there— aye, to aid you—without knowing your plan, or even the specifics of the Wriggly's confession?"

"Should you know, my lord, you would have to approve, or disapprove. As it lies, you are free of onus."

The two men regarded each other, checked hostility jumping between them like Vashanka's own lightning in the long, dangerous pause.

Kadakithis flicked his purple mantle over his shoulder. He squinted past Tempus, into the waning day. "What kind of cloud is that?"

Tempus swung around in his saddle, then back. "That should be our friend from Ranke."

The prince nodded. "Before he arrives, then, let us discuss the matter of the female prisoner Cime."

Tempus's horse snorted and threw its head, dancing in place. "There is nothing to discuss."

"But . . .? Why did you not come to me about it? I could have done something, previously. Now, I cannot . . ."

"I did not ask you. I am not asking you." His voice was a blade on whetstone, so that Kadakithis pulled himself up straight. "It is not for me to take a hand."

"Your own sister? You will not intervene?"

"Believe what you will, *prince.* I will not sift through gossip with any man, be he prince or king."

The prince lost hold, then, having been "princed" too often back in Ranke, and berated the Hell-Hound.

The man sat quite still upon the horse the prince had given him, garbed only in his loinguard though the day was fading, letting his gaze full of festering shadows rest in the prince's until Kadakithis trailed off, saying, ". . . the trouble with you is that anything they say about you could be true, so a man knows not what to believe."

"Believe in accordance with your heart," the voice like grinding stone suggested, while the dark cloud came to hover over the beach.

It settled, seemingly, into the sand, and the horses shied back, necks outstretched, nostrils huge. Tempus had his sorrel up alongside the chariot team and was leaning down to take the lead-horse's bridle when an earsplitting clarion came from the cloud's transluscent center.

The Hell-Hound raised his head then, and Kadakithis saw him shiver, saw his brow arch, saw a flicker of deepset eyes within their caves of bone and lid. Then again Tempus spoke to the chariot horses, who swiveled their ears toward him and took his counsel, and he let loose the lead-horse's bridle and spurred his own between Kadakithis's chariot and what came out of the cinereous cloud which had been so long descending upon them in opposition to the prevailing wind:

The man on the horse who could be seen within the cloud waved: a flash of scarlet glove, a swirl of burgundy cloak. Behind his tasseled steed he led another, and it was this second gray horse who again challenged the other stallions on the beach, its eyes full of fire. Farther back within the cloud, stonework could be seen, masonry like none in

Sanctuary, a sky more blue and hills more virile than any Kadakithis knew.

The first horse, reins flapping, was emerging, nose and neck casting shadows upon solid Sanctuary sand; then its hooves scattered grains, and the whole of the beast, and its rider, and the second horse he led on a long tether, stood corporeal and motionless before the Hell-Hound, while behind, the cloud whirled in upon itself and was gone with an audible "pop."

"Greetings, Riddler," said the rider in burgundy and scarlet, as he doffed his helmet with its blood-dark crest to Tempus.

"I did not expect you, Abarsis. What could be so urgent?"

"I heard about the Trôs horse's death, so I thought to bring you another, better auspiced, I hope. Since I was coming anyway, our friends suggested I bring what you require. I have long wanted to meet you." Spurring his mount forward, he held out his hand.

Red stallion and iron gray snaked arched necks, thrusting forth clacking teeth, wide-gaped jaws emitting squeals to go with flattened ears and rolling eyes. Above horse hostilities could be heard snatches of low wordplay, parry and riposte: ". . . disappointed that you could not build the temple." ". . . welcome to take my place here and try. The foundations of the temple grounds are defiled, the priest in charge more corrupt than even politics warrants. I wash my hands . . ." ". . . with the warring imminent, how can you . . .?" "Theomachy is no longer my burden." "That cannot be so." ". . . hear about the insurrection, or take my leave!" ". . . His name is unpronounceable, and that of his empire, but I think we all shall learn it so well we will mumble it in our sleep . . ." "I don't sleep. It is a matter of the right field officers, and men young enough not to have fought upcountry the last time." "I am meeting some Sacred Band members here, my old team. Can you provision us?" "Here? Well enough to get to the capital and do it better. Let me be the first to . . ."

Kadakithis, forgotten, cleared his throat.

Both men stared at the prince severely, as if a child had interrupted adults. Tempus bowed low in his saddle, arm outswept. The rider in reds with the burnished cuirass tucked his helmet under his arm and approached the chariot, handing the second horse's tether to Tempus as he passed by.

"Abarsis, presently of Ranke," said the dark, cultured voice of the armored man, whose hair swung black and glossy on a young bull's neck. His line was old, one of court graces and bas-relief faces and upswept, regal eyes that were disconcertingly wise and as gray-blue as the huge horse Tempus held with some difficulty. Ignoring the squeals of just-met stallions, the man continued: "Lord Prince, may all be well with you, with your endeavors and your holdings, eternally. I bear reaffirmation of our bond to you." He held out a purse, fat with coin.

Tempus winced, imperceptibly, and took wraps of the gray horse's tether, drawing its head close with great care, until he could bring his fist down hard between its ears to quiet it.

"What is this? There is enough money here to raise an army!" scowled Kadakithis, tossing the pouch lightly in his palm.

A polite and perfect smile lit the northern face, so warmly handsome, of the Rankan emissary. "Have you not told him, then, O Riddler?"

"No, I thought to, but got no opportunity. Also, I am not sure whether we will raise it, or whether that is my severance pay." He threw a leg over the sorrel's neck and slid down it, butt to horse, dropped its reins and walked away down the beach with his new Trôs horse in hand.

The Rankan hooked his helmet carefully on one of the saddle's silver rosettes. "You two are not getting on, I take it. Prince Kadakithis, you must be easy with him. Treat him as he does his horses; he needs a gentle hand."

"He needs his comeuppance. He has become insufferable! What is this money? Has he told you I am for sale? I am not!"

"He has turned his back on his god and the god is letting him run. When he is exhausted, the god will take him back. You found him pleasant enough, previously, I would wager. He has been set upon by your own staff, men to whom he was sworn and who gave oaths to him. What do you expect? He will not rest easy until he has made that matter right."

"What is this? My men? You mean that long unexplained absence of his? I admit he is changed. But how do you know what he would not tell me?"

A smile like sunrise lit the elegant face of the armored man. "The god tells me what I need to know. How would it be, for him to come running to you with tales of feuding among your ranks like a child to his father? His honor precludes it. As for the . . . funds . . . you hold, when we sent him here, it was with the understanding that should he feel you would make a king, he would so inform us. This, I was told you knew."

"In principle. But I cannot take a gift so large."

"Take a loan, as others before you have had to do. There is no time now for courtship. To be capable of *becoming* a king insures no seat of kingship, these days. A king must be more than a man, he must be a hero. It takes many men to make a hero, and special times. Opportunities approach, with the upcountry insurrection and a new empire rising beyond the northern range. Were you to distinguish yourself in combat, or field an army that did; we who seek a change could rally around you publicly. You cannot do it with what you have, the emperor has seen to that."

"At what rate am I expected to pay back this loan?"

"Equal value, nothing more. If the prince, my lord, will have patience, I will explain all to Your Majesty's satisfaction. That, truly, is why I am come."

"Explain away, then."

"First, one small digression, which touches a deeper truth. You must have some idea who and what the man you call Tempus is, I am sure you have heard it from your wizards and from his enemies among the officials of the Mageguild. Let me add to that this: Where he goes, the god scatters His blessings. By the cosmological rules of state cult and kingship, He has invested this endeavor with divine sanction by his presence. Though he and the god have their differences, without him, no chance remains that you might triumph. My father found that out. Even sick with his curse, he is too valuable to waste, unappreciated. If you would rather remain a princeling forever, and let the empire slide into ruin apace, just tell me and I will take word home. We will forget this matter of the kingship and this corollary matter of a small standing army, and I will release Tempus. He would as soon it, I assure you."

"Your *father?* Who in the God's Eye *are* you?"

"Ah, my arrogance is unforgivable; I thought you would know me. We are all so full of ourselves, these days, it is no wonder events have come to such a pass. I am Man of the God in Upper Ranke, Sole Friend to the Mercenaries, the hero, Son of the Defender, and so forth."

"High Priest of Vashanka."

"In the Upper Land."

"My family and yours thinned each other's line," stated Kadakithis baldly, no apology, no regret in his words. Yet he looked differently upon the other, thinking they were of an age, both wielding wooden swords in shady courts while the slaughter raged, far off at the fronts.

"Unto eradication," remarked the dark young man. "But we did not contest, and now there is a different enemy, a common threat. It is enough."

"And you and Tempus have never met?"

"He knew my father. And when I was ten, and my father died and our armies were disbanded, he found a home for me. Later, when I came to the god and the mercenaries' guild, I tried to see him. He would not meet with me." He shrugged, looking over his shoulder at the man walking the blue-gray horse into blue-gray shadows falling over the blue-black sea. "Everyone has his hero, you know. A god is not enough for a whole man; he craves a fleshly model. When he sent to me for a horse, and the god approved it, I was elated. Now, perhaps, I can do more. The horse may not have died in vain, after all."

"I do not understand you, Priest."

"My Lord, do not make me too holy. I am Vashanka's priest: I know many requiems and oaths, and thirty-three ways to fire a warrior's bier. They call me Stepson, in the mercenaries' guild. I would be pleased if you would call me that, and let me talk to you at greater length about a future in which your destiny and the wishes of the Storm God, our Lord, could come to be the same."

"I am not sure I can find room in my heart for such a god; it is difficult enough to pretend to piety," grated Kadakithis, squinting after Tempus in the dusk.

"You will, you will," promised the priest, and dismounted his horse to approach Tempus's ground-tied sorrel. Abarsis reached down, running his hand along the beast's white-stocking'd leg. "Look, Prince," he said, craning his neck up to see Kadakithis's face as his fingers tugged at the gold chain wedged in the weight-cleat on the horse's shoe. At the end of the chain, sandy but shining gold, was an amulet. "The god wants him back."

3

THE MERCENARIES drifted into Sanctuary dusty from their westward trek or blue-lipped from their rough sea passage and wherever they went they made hellish what before had been merely dissolute. The Maze was no longer safe for pickpocket or pander; usurer and sorcerer scuttled in haste from street to doorway, where before they had swaggered virtually unchallenged, crime lords in fear of nothing.

Now the whores walked bowlegged, dreamy-eyed, parading their new finery in the early hours of the morning while most mercenaries slept; the taverns changed shifts but feared to close their doors, lest a mercenary find that an excuse to take offense. Even so early in the day, the inns were full of brawls and the gutters full of casualties. The garrison soldiers and the Hell-Hounds could not be omnipresent: wherever they were not, mercenaries took sport, and they were not in the Maze this morning.

Though Sanctuary had never been so prosperous, every guild and union and citizen's group had sent representatives to the palace at sunrise to complain.

Lastel, a/k/a One-Thumb, could not understand why the Sanctuarites were so unhappy. Lastel was very happy: he was alive and back at the Vulgar Unicorn tending bar, and the Unicorn was making money, and money made Lastel happy, always. Being alive was something Lastel had not fully appreciated until recently, when he had spent aeons dying a subjective death in thrall to a spell he had paid to have laid upon his own person, a spell turned against him by the sons of its deceased creator, Mizraith of the Hazard class, and dispelled by he-knew-not-whom. Though every night he expected his mysterious benefactor to sidle up to the bar and demand payment, no one ever came and said: "Lastel, I saved you. I am the one. Now show your gratitude." But he knew very well that someday soon, someone would. He did not let this irritation besmirch his happiness. He had gotten a new shipment of Caronne krrf (black, pure drug, foil stamped, a full weight of it, enough to set every mercenary in Sanctuary at the kill) and it was so good that he considered refraining from offering it on the market. Having considered, he decided to keep it all for himself, and so was very happy indeed, no matter how many fistfights broke out in the bar, or how high the sun was, these days, before he got to bed . . .

Tempus, too, was happy that morning, with the magnificent Trôs horse under him and signs of war all around him. Despite the hour, he saw enough rough hoplites and dour artillery fighters with their crankbows (whose springs were plaited from women's hair) and their quarrels (barbed and poisoned) to let him know he was not dreaming: these did not bestir themselves from daydreams! The war was real to them. And any one of them could be his. He felt his troop levy money cuddled tight against his groin, and he whistled tunelessly as the Trôs horse threaded his way toward the Vulgar Unicorn.

One-Thumb was not going to be happy much longer.

Tempus left the Trôs horse on its own recognizance, dropping the reins and telling it, "Stay." Anyone who thought it merely ripe for stealing would learn a lesson about the strain which is bred only in Syr from the original line of Trôs's.

There were a few locals in the Unicorn, most snoring over tables along with other, bagged trash ready to be dragged out into the street.

One-Thumb was behind his bar, big shoulders slumped, washing mugs while watching everything through the bronze mirror he had had installed over his stock.

Tempus let his heels crack against the board and his armor clatter: he had dressed for this, from a box he had thought he might never again open. The wrestler's body which Lastel had built came alert, pirouetted smoothly to face him, staring unabashedly at the nearly god-sized apparition in leopard-skin mantle and helmet set with boar's tusks, wearing an antique enameled breastplate and bearing a bow of ibex-horn morticed with a golden grip.

"*What* in Azyuna's twat are *you*?" bellowed One-Thumb, as every waking customer he had hastened to depart.

"I," said Tempus, reaching the bar and removing his helmet so that his yarrow-honey hair spilled forth, "am Tempus. We have not chanced to meet." He held out a hand whose wrist bore a golden bracer.

"Marshal," acknowledged One-Thumb, carefully, his pate creasing with his frown. "It is good to know you are on our side. But you cannot come in here . . . My—"

"I am here, *Lastel.* While you were so inexplicably absent, I was often here, and received the courtesy of service without charge. But now I am not here to eat or drink with those who recognize me for one who is fully as corrupt as are they themselves. There are those who know where you were, *Lastel,* and why—and *one* who broke the curse that bound you. Truly, if you had cared, you could have found out." Twice, Tempus called One-Thumb by his true name, which no palace personage or Mazedweller should have known enough to do.

"Marshal, let us go to my office." Lastel fairly ramped behind his bar.

"No time, krrf-dealer. Mizraith's sons, Stefab and Marype; Mark-mor: those three and more were slain by the woman Cime who is in the pits awaiting sentence. I thought that you should know."

"What are you saying? You want me to break her out? Do it your-self."

"No one," said the Hell-Hound, "can break anyone out of the palace. I am in charge of security there. If she were to escape, I would be very busy explaining to Kadakithis what went wrong. And tonight I am having a reunion here with fifty of my old friends from the mercenaries' guild. I would not want anything to spoil it. And, too, I ask no man to take me on faith, or go where I have not been." He grinned like the Destroyer, gesturing around. "You had better order in extra. And half a piece of krrf, your courtesy to me, of course. Once you have seen my men when well in hand, you will be better able to conjecture what might happen should they get out of hand, and weigh your alternatives. Most men I solicit find it to their benefit to work in accord with me. Should you deem it so for you, we will fix a time, and discuss it."

Not the cipher's meaning, nor the plan it shrouded, nor the threat that gave it teeth were lost on the man who did not like to be called "Lastel" in the Maze. He bellowed: "You are addled. You cannot do this. I cannot do that! As for krrf, I know nothing about . . . any . . . krrf."

But the man was gone, and Lastel was trembling with rage, thinking he had been in purgatory too long; it had eroded his nerves!

4

WHEN THE dusk cooled the Maze, Shadowspawn ducked into the Unicorn. One-Thumb was not in evidence; Two-Thumbs was behind the bar.

He sat with the wall supporting him, where the story-teller liked to sit, and watched the door, waiting for the crowd to thicken, tongues to loosen, some caravan driver to boast of his wares. The mercenaries were no boon to a thief, but dangerous playmates, like Kadakithis's palace women. He did not want to be intrigued; he was being distracted moment by moment. As a consequence, he was very careful to keep his mind on business, so that he would not come up hungry next Ilsday, when his funds, if not increased, would run out.

Shadowspawn was dark as iron and sharp like a hawk; a cranked crossbow, loaded with cold bronze and quarrels to spare. He wore knives where a professional wears them, and sapphire and gold and crimson to draw the eye from his treasured blades.

Sanctuary had spawned him: he was hers, and he had thought nothing she did could surprise him. But when the mercenaries arrived as do clients to a strumpet's house, he had been hurt like a whore's bastard when first he learns how his mother feeds him.

It was better, now; he understood the new rules.

One rule was: get up and give them your seat. Hanse *gave* no one his seat. He might recall pressing business elsewhere, or see someone he just had to hasten over to greet. Tonight, he remembered nothing earlier forgotten; he saw no one he cared to bestir himself to meet. He prepared to defend his place as seven mercenaries filled the doorway with plumes and pelts and hilts and mail, and looked his way. But they went in a group to the bar, though one, in a black mantle, with iron at chest and head and wrists, pointed directly to him like a man sighting his arrow along an outstretched arm.

The man talked to Two-Thumbs awhile, took off his helmet with its horsehair crests that seemed blood-red, and approached Hanse's table alone. A shiver coursed the thief's flesh, from the top of his black thatch to his toetips.

The mercenary reached him in a dozen swinging strides, drawing a stabbing sword as he came on. If not for the fact that the other hand held a mug, Shadowspawn would have aired iron by the time the man (or youth from his smooth, heartshaped face) spoke: "Shadowspawn, called Hanse? I am Stepson, called Abarsis. I have been hoping to find you." With a grin full of dazzling teeth, the mercenary put the ivory-hilted sword flat in the wet-rings on the table, and sat, both hands well in evidence, clasped under his chin.

Hanse gripped his beltknife tightly. Then the panic-flash receded, and time passed, instead of piling all its instants terrifyingly on top of one another. Hanse knew that he was no coward, that he was plagued by flashbacks from the two times he had been tapped with the fearstick of Vashanka, but his chest was heaving, and the mercenary might see. He slumped back, for camouflage. The mercenary with the expensive taste in accouterments could be no older than he. And yet, only a king's son could afford such a blade as that before him. He reached out hesitantly to touch its silvered guard, its garnet pommel, his gaze locked in the sellsword's soulless pale one, his hand slipping closer and closer to the elegant sword of its own accord.

"Ah, you do like it then," said Stepson. "I was not sure. You will take it, I hope. It is customary in my country, when meeting a man who has performed heroically to the benefit of one's house, to give a small token." He withdrew a silver scabbard from his belt, laid it with the sword, which Hanse put down as if burned.

"What did I ever do for you?"

"Did you not rescue the Riddler from great peril?"

"Who?"

The tanned face grinned ingenuously. "A truly brave man does not boast. I understand. Or is it a deeper thing? That—"He leaned forward; he smelled sweet like new-mown hay"—is truly what I need to know. Do you comprehend me?"

Hanse gave him an eagle's look, and shook his head slowly, his fingers flat on the table, near the magnificent sword that the mercenary

Stepson had offered to give him. *The Riddler?* He knew no one of that name.

"Are you protecting him? There is no need, not from me. Tell me, Shadowspawn, are you and Tempus lovers?"

"Mother—!" His favorite knife leapt into his palm, unbidden. He looked at it in his own grasp in consternation, and dropped his other hand over it, and began paring his nails. *Tempus! The Riddler?* Hanse's eyes caressed the covetable blade. "I helped him out, once or twice, that's all."

"That is good," the youth across from him approved. "Then we will not have to fight over him. And, too, we could work a certain bargain, service for service, that would make me happy and you, I modestly estimate, a gentleman of ease for at least six months."

"I'm listening," said Shadowspawn, taking a chance, commending his knife to its sheath. The short sword too, he handled, fitting it in the scabbard and drawing it out, fascinated by the alert scrutiny of Abarsis the Stepson's six companions.

When he began hearing the words "diamond rods" and "Hall of Judgment" he waxed uneasy. But by then, he could not see any way that he could allow himself to appear less than heroic in the pale, blue-gray eyes of the Stepson. Not when the amount of money Stepson had offered hung in the balance, not when the nobly fashioned sword he had been given as if it were merely serviceable proclaimed the flashy mercenary's ability to *pay* that amount. But too, if he would pay that, he would pay more. Hanse was not so enthralled by the mercenaries' mystique to hasten into one's pay without some good Sanctuary barter. Watching Stepson's six formidable companions, waiting like purebred hunting dogs curried for show, he spied a certain litheness about them, an uncanny cleanliness of limb and nearness of girded hips. Close friends, these. Very close.

Abarsis's sonorous voice had ceased, waiting for Hanse's response. The disconcertingly pale eyes followed Hanse's stare, frank now, to his companions.

"Will you say yea, then, friend of the Riddler? And become my friend, also? These other friends of mine await only your willingness to embrace you as a brother."

"I own," Hanse muttered.

Abarsis raised one winged brow. "So? They are members of a Sacred Band, my old one; most prized officers; heroes, every pair." He judged Hanse's face. "Can it be you do not have the custom, in the south? From your mien I must believe it." His voice was liquid, like deep running water. "These men, to me and to their chosen partners, have sworn to forsake life before honor, to stand and never retreat, to fall where they fight if need be, shoulder to shoulder. There is no more hallowed tryst than theirs. Had I a thousand such, I would rule the earth."

"Which one is yours?" Hanse tried not to sneer, to be conversational, unshaken, but his eyes could find no comfortable place to rest, so that at last he took up the gift-sword and examined the hieratic writing on its blade.

"None. I left them, long ago, when my partner went up to heaven. Now I have hired them back, to serve a need. It is strictly a love of spirit, Hanse, that is required. And only in Sacred Bands is a mercenary asked so much."

"Still, it's not my style."

"You sound disappointed."

"I am. In your offer. Pay me twice that, and I will get the items you desire. As for your friends, I don't care if you bugger them each twice daily. Just as long as it's not part of my job and no one thinks I am joining any organizations."

A swift, appreciative smile touched Abarsis. "Twice, then. I am at your mercy."

"I stole those diamond rods once before, for Tem—, for the Riddler. He'll just give them back to her, after she does whatever it is she does for him. I had her once, and she did nothing for me that any other whore would not do."

"You *what?* Ah, you do not know about them, then? Their legend, their curse?"

"Legend? Curse? I knew she was a sorceress. Tell me about it! Am I in any danger? You can forget the whole idea, about the rods. I keep shut of sorcery."

"Hardly sorcery, no need to worry. They cannot transmit any of it. When he was young and she was a virgin, he was a prince and a fool of ideals. I heard it that the god is his true father, and thus she is *not* his sibling, but you know how legends are. As a princess, her sire looked for an advantageous marriage. An archmage of a power not seen any- more made an offer, at about the time the Riddler renounced his claim to the throne and retired to a philosopher's cave. She went to him begging aid, some way out of an unacceptable situation, and convinced him that should she be deflowered, the mage would not want her, and of all men the Riddler was the only one she trusted with the task; anyone else would despoil her. She seduced him easily, for he had loved her all his young life and that unacceptable attraction to flesh of his flesh was part of what drove him from his primogeniture. She loved nothing but herself; some things never change. He was wise enough to know he brought destruction upon himself, but men are prone to ruin from women. In passion, he could not think clearly; when it left him he went to Vashanka's altar and threw himself upon it, consigning his fate to the god. The god took him up, and when the archmage appeared with four eyes spitting fire and four mouths breathing fearful curses, the god's aegis partly shielded him. Yet, the curse holds. He wanders eternally bringing death to whomever loves him and being spurned by whomsoever he shall love. She must offer herself for pay to any comer, take no gift of kindness on pain of showing all her awful years, incapable of giving love as she has always been. So thus, the gods, too, are barred to her, and she is truly damned."

Hanse just stared at Stepson, whose voice had grown husky in the telling, when the mercenary left off.

"Now, will you help me? Please. He would want it to be you."

Hanse made a sign.

"*Would* want it to be me?" the thief frowned. "He does not *know* about this?" There came the sound of Shadowspawn's bench scraping back.

Abarsis reached out to touch the thief's shoulder, a move quick as lightning and soft as a butterfly's landing. "One must do for a friend what the friend cannot do for himself. With such a man, opportunities of this sort come seldom. If not for him, or for your price, or for whatever you hold sacred, do this thing for me, and I will be eternally in your debt."

A sibilant sound, part impatience, part exasperation, part irritation, came sliding down Shadowspawn's hawkish nose.

"Hanse?"

"You are going to surprise him with this deed, done? What if he has no taste for surprises? What if you are wrong, and he refrains from aiding her because he prefers her right where she is? And besides, I am staying away from him and his affairs."

"No surprise: I will tell him once I have arranged it. I will make you one more offer: Half again the doubled fee you suggested, to ease your doubts. But that is my final bid."

Shadowspawn squinted at the heartshaped face of Stepson. Then, without a word, he scooped up the short stabbing sword in its silver sheath, and found it a home in his belt. "Done," said Hanse.

"Good. Then, will you meet my companions?" The long-fingered,

graceful hand of Stepson, called Abarsis, made a gesture that brought
them, all smiles and manly welcomes, from their exile by the bar.

5

KURD, THE vivisectionist who had tried his skills on Tempus, was
found a fair way from his adobe workshop, his gut stretched out for
thirty feet before him: he had been dragged by the entrails; the hole cut
in his belly to pull the intestines out was made by an expert: a mercenary had to be at fault. But there were so many mercenaries in Sanctuary, and so few friends of the vivisectionist, that the matter was not
pursued.

The matter of the Hell-Hound Razkuli's head, however, was much
more serious. Zalbar (who knew why both had died and at whose
hands, and who feared for his own life) went to Kadakithis with his
friend's staring eyes under one arm, sick and still tasting vomit, and told
the prince how Tempus had come riding through the gates at dawn and
called up to him where he was checking pass-bys in the gatehouse:
"Zalbar, I've a message for you."

"Yo!" Zalbar had waved.

"Catch," Tempus laughed, and threw something up to him while the
gray horse reared, uttered a shrill, demonic scream, and clattered off
by the time Zalbar's hand had said *head: human;* and his eyes had said,
head: Razkuli's and then begun to fill with tears.

Kadakithis listened to his story, looking beyond him out the window
the entire time. When Zalbar had finished, the prince said, "Well, I
don't know what you expected, trying to take him down so clumsily."

"But he said it was a message for me," Zalbar entreated, caught his
own pleading tone, scowled and straightened up.

"Then take it to heart, man. I can't allow you two to continue
feuding. If it is anything other than simple feuding, I do not want to
know about it. Stepson, called Abarsis, told me to expect something like
this! I demand a stop to it!"

"*Stepson!*" Tall, lank Zalbar snarled like a man invoking a vengeful
god in close fighting. "An ex-Sacred Bander looking for glory and death
with honor, in no particular order! *Stepson* told you? The Slaughter
Priest? My lord prince, you are keeping deadly company these days!
Are all the gods of the armies in Sanctuary, then, along with their

familiars, the mercenary hordes? I had wanted to discuss with you what could be done to curb them—"

"Zalbar," interrupted Kadakithis firmly. "In the matter of gods, I hold firm: I do not believe in them. In the matter of mercenaries, let them be. You broach subjects too sensitive for your station. In the matter of Tempus, I will talk to him. You change your attitude. Now, if that is *all* . . .?"

It *was* all. It was nearly the end of Zalbar the Hell-Hound's entire career; he almost struck his commander-in-chief. But he refrained, though he could not utter even a civil goodbye. He went to his billet and he went into the town, and he worked wrath out of himself, as best he could. The dregs he washed away with drink, and after that he went to visit Myrtis, the whoremistress of Aphrodisia House who knew how to soothe him. And she, seeing his heart breaking and his fists shaking, asked him nothing about why he had come, after staying away so long, but took him to her breast and healed what she might of his hurts, remembering that all the protection he provided her and good he did for her, he did because of a love spell she had bought and cast on him long since, and thus she owed him at least one night to match his dreams.

6

TEMPUS HAD gone among his own kind, after he left the barracks. He had checked in at the guild hostel north of the palace, once again in leopard and bronze and iron, and he was welcome there.

Why he had kept himself from it for so long, he could not have reasoned, unless it was that without these friends of former times the camaraderie would not have been as sweet.

He went to the sideboard and got hot mulled wine from a krater, sprinkling in goat's cheese and grain, and took the posset to a corner, so the men could come to him as they would.

The problem of the eunuch was still unsolved; finding a suitable replacement was not going to be easy: there were not many eunuchs in the mercenaries' guild. The clubroom was red as dying day and dark as backlit mountains, and he felt better for having come. So, when Abarsis, high priest of Upper Ranke, left his companions and approached, but did not sit among, the mercenaries Tempus had collected, he said to the nine that he would see them at the appointed time, and to the iron-clad one:

"Life to you, Stepson. Please join me."

"Life to you, Riddler, and everlasting glory." Cup in hand, he sipped pure water, eyes hardly darker never leaving Tempus's face. "Is it Sanctuary that has driven you to drink?" He indicated the posset.

"The dry soul is wisest? Not at the empire's anus, where the water is chancy. Anyway, those things I said long ago and far away: do not hold me to any of that."

The smooth cheek of Stepson ticced. "I must," he murmured. "You are the man I have emulated. All my life I have listened after word of you and collected intelligence of you and studied what you left us in legend and stone in the north. Listen: 'War is sire of all and king of all, and some He has made gods and some men, some bond and some free'. Or: 'War is ours in common; strife is justice; all things come into being and pass away through strife'. You see, I know your work, even those other names you have used. Do not make me speak them. I would work with you, O Sleepless One. It will be the pinnacle of my career." He flashed Tempus a bolt of naked entreaty, then his gaze flickered away and he rushed on: "You need me. Who else will suit? Who else here has a brand and gelding's scars? *And* time in the arena as a gladiator, like Jubal himself? Who could intrigue him, much less seduce him among these? And though I—"

"No."

Abarsis dug in his belt and tossed a golden amulet onto the table. "The god will not give you up; this was caught in the sorrel's new shoe. That teacher of mine whom you remember . . .?"

"I know the man," Tempus said grimly.

"He thinks that Sanctuary is the endpoint of existence; that those who come here are damned beyond redemption; that Sanctuary is Hell."

"Then how is it, Stepson," said Tempus almost kindly, "that folk experience fleshly death here? So far as I know, I am the only soul in Sanctuary who suffers eternally, with the possible exception of my sister, who may not have a soul. Learn not to listen to what people say, priest. A man's own mistakes are load enough, without adding others'."

"Then *let me* be your choice! There is no time to find some other eunuch." He said it flatly, without bitterness, a man fielding logic. "I can also bring you a few fighters whom you might not know and who would not dare, on their own, to approach you. My Sacred Band yearns to serve you. You dispense your favor to provincials and foreigners who

barely recognize their honor! Give it to me, who craves little else
. . . ! The prince who would be king, will not expose me, but pass me
on to Jubal as an untrained boy. I am a little old for it, but in Sanctuary,
those niceties seem not to matter. I have increased your lot here. You
owe me this opportunity."

Tempus stirred his cooling posset with a finger. "That prince
. . ." Changing the subject, he sighed glumly, a sound like rattling bones.
"He will never be a Great King, such as your father. Can you tell me
why the god is taking such an interest?

"The god will tell you, when you make of the Trôs horse a sacrifice.
Or some person. Then He will be mollified. You know the ritual. If it
be a man you choose, I will gladly volunteer . . . Ah, you understand
me, now? I do not want to frighten you . . ."

"Take no thought of it."

"Then . . . though I risk your displeasure, yet I say it: I love you. One
night with you would be a surfeit, to work under you is my long-held
dream. Let me do this, which none can do better, which no *whole* man
can do for you at all!"

"I cede you the privilege, since you value it so; but there is no telling
what Jubal's hired hawk-masks might do to the eunuch we send in
there."

"With your blessing and the god's, I am fearless. And you will be
close by, busy attacking Black Jubal's fortress. While you are arresting
the slavemaster for his treasonous spying, whosoever will make good
the woman's escape. I understand your thought; I have arranged for the
retrieval of her weapons."

Tempus chuckled. "I hardly know what to say."

"Say you look kindly upon me, that I am more than a bad memory
to you."

Shaking his head, Tempus took the amulet Abarsis held out to him.
"Come then, Stepson, we will see what part of your glorious expectations we can fulfill."

7

IT WAS said, ever after, that the Storm God took part in the sack of
the slaver's estate. Lightning crawled along the gatehouses of its defen-
sive wall and rolled in balls through the inner court and turned the

oaken gates to ash. The ground rumbled and buckled and bucked and great crumbling cracks appeared in its inner sanctum, where the slaver dallied with the glossy-haired eunuch Kadakithis had just sent up for training. It was profligate waste to make a fancy boy out of such a slave: the arena had muscled him up and time had grown him up, and to squeeze the two or three remaining years of that sort of pleasure out of him seemed to the slaver a pity. If truth be known, blood like his came so rarely to the slavepens that gelding him was a sin against future generations: had Jubal gotten him early on—when the cuts had been made, at nine, or ten—he would have raised him with great pains and put him to stud. But his brand and tawny skin smacked of northern mountains and high wizards' keeps where the wars had raged so savagely that no man was proud to remember what had been done there, on either side.

Eventually, he left the eunuch chained by the neck to the foot of his bed and went to see what the yelling and the shouting and the blue flashes and the quivering floorboards could possibly mean.

What he saw from his threshhold he did not understand, but he came striding back, stripping off his robe as he passed by the bed, rushing to arm himself and do battle against the infernal forces of this enemy, and, it seemed, the whole of the night.

Naphtha fireballs came shooting over his walls into the courtyard; flaming arrows torqued from spring-wound bows; javelins and swordplay glittered nastily, singing as they slew in soft susurrusings Jubal had hoped never to hear there.

It was eerily quiet: no shouting, not from his hawk-masks, or the adversaries; the fire crackled and the horses snorted and groaned like the men where they fell.

Jubal recollected the sinking feeling he had had in his stomach when Zalbar had confided to him that the bellows of anguish emanating from the vivisectionist's workshop were the Hell-Hound Tempus's agonies, the forebodings he had endured when a group of his beleaguered sellswords went after the man who killed those who wore the mask of Jubal's service for sport, and failed to down him.

That night, it was too late for thinking. There was time enough only for wading into the thick of battle (if he could just find it: the attack was from every side, out of darkness); hollering orders; mustering point leaders (two); and appointing replacements for the dead (three). Then he heard whoops and abysmal screams and realized that someone had let the slaves out of their pens; those who had nothing to lose bore haphazard arms, but sought only death with vengeance. Jubal, seeing wide, white rimmed eyes and murderous mouths and the new eunuch from Kadakithis's palace dancing ahead of the pack of them, started to run. The key to its collar had been in his robe; he remembered discarding it, within the eunuch's reach.

He ran in a private wash of terror, in a bubble through which other sounds hardly penetrated, but where his breathing reverberated stentorian, rasping, and his heart gonged loud in his ears. He ran looking back over his shoulder, and he saw some leopard-pelted apparition with a horn bow in hand come sliding down the gatehouse wall. He ran until he reached the stable, until he stumbled over a dead hawk-mask, and then he heard everything, cacophonously, that had been so muted before: swords rasping; panoplies rattling; bodies thudding and greaved men running; quarrels whispering bright death as they passed through the dark press; javelins ringing as they struck helm or shield suddenly limned in lurid fiery light.

Fire? Behind Jubal flame licked out the stable windows and horses whistled their death screams.

The heat was singeing. He drew his sword and turned in a fluid motion, judging himself as he was wont to do when the crowds had been about him in applauding tiers and he must kill to live to kill another day, and do so pleasingly.

He felt the thrill of it, the immediacy of it, the joy of the arena, and as the pack of freed slaves came shouting, he picked out the prince's eunuch and reached to wrest a spear from the dead hawk-mask's grip. He hefted it, left-handed, to cast, just as the man in leopard pelt and cuirass and a dozen mercenaries came between him and the slaves, cutting him off from his final refuge, the stairs to the westward wall.

Behind him, the flames seemed hotter, so that he was glad he had not stopped for armor. He threw the spear, and it rammed home in the eunuch's gut.

The leopard leader came forward, alone, sword tip gesturing three times, leftward.

Was it Tempus, beneath that frightful armor? Jubal raised his own blade to his brow in acceptance, and moved to where his antagonist indicated, but the leopard leader was talking over his shoulder to his front-line mercenaries, three of whom were clustered around the downed eunuch. Then one archer came abreast of the leader, touched his leopard pelt. And that bowman kept a nocked arrow on Jubal, while the leader sheathed his sword and walked away, to join the little knot around the eunuch.

Someone had broken off the haft; Jubal heard the grunt and the snap of wood and saw the shaft discarded. Then arrows whizzed in quick succession into both his knees and beyond the shattering pain, he knew nothing more.

8

TEMPUS KNELT over Abarsis, bleeding out his life naked in the dirt. "Get me light," he rasped. Tossing his helmet aside, he bent down until his cheek touched Stepson's knotted, hairless belly. The whole bronze head of the spear, barbs and all, was deep in him. Under his lowest rib, the shattered haft stuck out, quivering as he breathed. The torch was brought; the better light told Tempus there was no use in cutting the spearhead loose; one flange was up under the low rib; vital fluids oozed out with the youth's blood. Out of age-old custom, Tempus lay his mouth upon the wound and sucked the blood and swallowed it, then raised his head and shook it to those who waited with a hot blade and hopeful, silent faces. "Get him some water, no wine. And give him some air."

They moved back and as the Sacred Bander who had been holding Abarsis's head put it down, the wounded one murmured; he coughed, and his frame shuddered, one hand clutching spasmodically at the spear. "Rest now, Stepson. You have got your wish. You will be my sacrifice to the god." He covered the youth's nakedness with his mantle, taking the gory hand from the broken haft, letting it fasten on his own.

Then the blue-gray eyes of Abarsis opened in a face pale with pain, and something else: "I am not frightened, with you and the god beside me."

Tempus put an arm under his head and gathered him up, pulling him across his lap. "Hush, now."

"Soon, soon," said the paling lips. "I did well for you. Tell me so . . . that you are content. O Riddler, so well do I love you, I go to my god singing your praises. When I meet my father, I will tell him . . . I . . . fought beside you."

"Go with more than that, Stepson," whispered Tempus, and leaned forward, and kissed him gently on the mouth, and Abarsis breathed out his soul while their lips yet touched.

9

Now, HANSE had gotten the rods with no difficulty, as Stepson had promised he would be able to do, citing Tempus's control of palace personnel as surety. And afterward, the young mercenary's invitation to come and watch them fight up at Jubal's rang in his head until, to banish it, he went out to take a look.

He knew it was foolish to go, for it was foolish even to *know,* but he knew that he wanted to be able to say, "Yes, I saw. It was wonderful," the next time he saw the young mercenary, so he went very carefully and cautiously. If he were stopped, he would have all of Stepson's Sacred Band as witnesses that he had been at Jubal's, and nowhere near the palace and its Hall of Judgment.

He knew those excuses were flimsy, but he wanted to go, and he did not want to delve into why: the lure of mercenary life was heady in his nostrils; if he admitted how sweet it seemed, he might be lost. If he went, perchance he would see something not so sweet, or so intoxicating, something which would wash away all this talk of friendship and honor. So he went, and hid on the roof of a gatehouse abandoned in the confusion. Thus he saw all that transpired.

When he could in safety leave his roost, he followed the pair of gray horses bearing Tempus and the corpse ridgeward, stealing the first mount he came to that looked likely.

The sun was risen when Tempus reached the ridgetop and called out behind: "Whoever you are, ride up," and set about gathering branches to make a bier.

Hanse rode to the edge of the outcropping of rock on which Tempus piled wood and said: "Well, accursed one, are you and your god replete? Stepson told me all about it."

The man straightened up, eyes like flames, and put his hand to the small of his back: "What do you want, Shadowspawn? A man who is respectful does not sling insults over the ears of the dead. If you are here for him, then welcome. If you are here for me, I assure you, your timing is ill."

"I *am* here for him, *friend.* What think you, that I would come here to console you in your grief when it was his love for you that he died of? He asked me," Hanse continued, not dismounting, "to get these. He was going to give them to you." He reached for the diamond rods, wrapped in hide, he had stolen.

"Stay your hand, and your feelings. Both are misplaced. Do not judge

what you do not understand. As for the rods, Abarsis was mistaken as
to what I wanted done with them. If you are finishing your first mercenary's commission, then give them to One-Thumb. Tell him they are
for his benefactor. Then it is done. Someone of the Sacred Band will
seek you out and pay you. Do not worry about that. Now, if you would
honor Abarsis, dismount." The struggle obvious in Tempus's face for
control was chilling, where nothing unintentioned was ever seen. "Otherwise, please leave now, friend, *while* we are yet friends. I am in no
mood for living boys today."

So Hanse slid from the horse and stalked over to the corpse stage-
whispering, "Mouth me no swill, Doomface. If this is how your friends
fare, I'd as soon be relieved of the honor," and flipped back the shroud.
"His eyes are open." Shadowspawn reached out to close them.

"Don't. Let him see where he goes."

They glared a time at each other above the staring corpse while a
red-tailed hawk circled overhead, its shadow caressing the pale, dead
face.

Then Hanse knelt stiffly, took a coin from his belt, slid it between
Stepson's slightly parted lips, and murmured something low. Rising, he
turned and strode to his stolen horse and scrambled clumsily astride,
reining it round and away without a single backward glance.

When Tempus had the bier all made, and Abarsis arranged on it to
the last glossy hair, and a spark nursed to consuming flame, he stood
with clenched fists and watering eyes in the billows of smoke. And
through his tears, he saw the boy's father, fighting oblivious from his
car, his charioteer fallen between his legs, that time Tempus had hacked
off an enemy's arm to save him from the ax it swung; he saw the
witchbitch of a sorceress the king had wed in the black hills to make
alliance with what could not be had by force; he saw the aftermath of
that, when the wild woman's spawn was out of her and every loyal
general took a hand in her murder before she laid their commander out
in state. He saw the boy, wizard-haired and wise, running to Tempus's
chariot for a ride, grasping his neck, laughing, kissing like the northern
boys had no shame to do; all this before the Great King discharged his
armies and retired home to peace, and Tempus rode south to Ranke,
an empire hardly whelped and shaky on its prodigious feet. And Tempus saw the field he had taken against a monarch, once his liege:
Masters change. He had not been there when they had got the Great
King, dragged him down from his car and begun the Unending Deaths
that proved the Rankans barbarians second to none. It was said by
those who *were* there that he stood it well enough until his son was

castrated before his eyes, given off to a slaver with ready collar
... When he had heard, Tempus had gone searching among the sacked
towns of the north, where Ranke wrought infamy into example, legends
better than sharp javelins at discouraging resistance. And he saw Abarsis in the slaver's kennel, the boy's look of horror that a man of the
armies would see what had been done to him. No glimmer of joy
invaded the gaunt child's face turned up to him. No eager hands out-
flung to their redeemer; a small, spent hero shuffled across soiled straw
to meet him, slave's eyes gauging without fear just what he might expect
from this man, who had once been among his father's most valued, but
was now only one more Rankan enemy. Tempus remembered picking
the child up in his arms, hating how little he weighed, how sharp his
bones were; and that moment when Abarsis at last believed he was safe.
About a boy's tears, Abarsis had sworn Tempus to secrecy. About the
rest, the less said, the better. He had found him foster parents, in the
rocky west by the sea temples where Tempus himself was born, and
where the gods still made miracles upon occasion. He had hoped somehow the gods would heal what love could not. Now, they had done it.

He nodded, having passed recollection like poison, watching the fire
burn down. Then, for the sake of the soul of Stepson, called Abarsis,
and under the aegis of his flesh, Tempus humbled himself before Vashanka and came again into the service of his god.

10

HANSE, HIDDEN below on a shelf, listening and partaking of the funeral
of his own fashion, upon realizing what he was overhearing, spurred the
horse out of there as if the very god whose thunderous voice he had
heard were after him.

He did not stop until he reached the Vulgar Unicorn. There, he shot
off the horse in a dismount which was a fall disguised as a vault, slapped
the beast smartly away, telling it hissingly to go home, and slipped
inside with such relief as his favorite knife must feel when he sheathed
it.

"One-Thumb," Hanse called out, making for the bar, "What is going
on out there?" There had been soldierly commotion at the Common
Gate.

"You haven't heard?" scoffed the night-turned-day barman. "Some prisoners escaped from the palace dungeon, certain articles were thieved from the Hall of Judgment, and none of the regular security officers were around to get their scoldings."

Looking at the mirror behind the bar, Hanse saw the ugly man grin without humor. Gaze locked to mirror-gaze, Hanse drew the hide-wrapped bundle from his tunic. "These are for you. You are supposed to give them to your benefactor." He shrugged to the mirror.

One-Thumb turned and wiped the dishrag along the shining bar and when the rag was gone, the small bundle was gone, also. "Now, what do you want to get involved in something like this for? You think you're moving up? You're not. Next time, when it's this sort of thing, come around the back. Or, better, don't come at all. I thought you had more sense."

Hanse's hand smacked flat and loud upon the bar. "I have taken enough offal for one day, cupbearer. Now I tell you what you do, Wide-Belly: You take what I brought you and your sage counsel, and you wrap it all together, and then you squat on it!" And stiff-kneed as a roused cat, Shadowspawn stalked away, toward the door, saying over his shoulder: "As for sense, I thought *you* had more."

"I have my business to think of," called out One-Thumb, too boldly for a whine.

"Ah, yes! So have I, so have I."

11

LAVENDER AND lemon dawn light bedizened the white-washed barracks' walls and colored the palace parade grounds.

Tempus had been working all night, out at Jubal's estate where he was quartering his mercenaries away from town and Hell-Hounds and Ilsig garrison personnel. He had fifty there, but twenty of them were paired members of three different Sacred Bands: Stepson's legacy to him. The twenty had convinced the thirty nonallied operatives that "Stepsons" would be a good name for their squadron, and for the cohort it would eventually command should things go as everyone hoped.

He would keep the Sacred Band teams and spread the rest throughout the regular army, and throughout the prince's domain. They would find what clay they chose, and mold a division from it of which the spirit of Abarsis, if it were not too busy fighting theomachy's battles in heaven, could look upon with pride.

The men had done Tempus proud, already, that night at Jubal's, and thereafter; and this evening when he had turned the corner round the slave barracks the men were refitting for livestock, there it had been, a love-note written in lamb's blood two cubits high on the encircling protective wall: "*War is all and king of all, and all things come into being out of strife.*"

Albeit they had not gotten it exactly right, he had smiled, for though the world and the boyhood from out of which he had said such audacious things was gone to time, Stepson, called Abarsis, and his legacy of example and followers made Tempus think that perhaps (oh just perhaps) he, Tempus, had not been so young, or so foolish, as he had lately come to think that he had been. And if thus the man, then his epoch, too, was freed of memory's hindsightful taint.

And the god and he were reconciled: This pushed away his curse and the shadow of distress it cast ever before him. His troubles with the prince had subsided. Zalbar had come through his test of fire and returned to stand his duty, thinking deeply, walking quietly. His courage would mend. Tempus knew his sort.

Jubal's disposition he had left to Kadakithis. He had wanted to take the famous ex-gladiator's measure in single combat, but there was no fitness in it now, since the man would never be quick on his feet, should he live to regain the use of them.

Not that the world was as ridiculously beautiful as was the arrogant summer morning which did not understand that it was a Sanctuary morning and therefore should at least be gory, garish, or full of flies buzzing about his head. No, one could find a few thorns in one's path, still. There was Shadowspawn, called Hanse, exhibiting unseemly and proprietary grief over Abarsis whenever it served him, yet not taking a billet among the Stepsons that Tempus had offered. Privately, Tempus thought he might yet come to it, that he was trying to step twice into the same river. When his feet chilled enough, he would step out onto the banks of manhood. If he could sit a horse better, perhaps his pride would let him join in where now, because of that, he could only sneer.

Hanse, too, must find his own path. He was not Tempus's problem, though Tempus would gladly take on that burden should Shadowspawn ever indicate a desire to have help toting it.

His sister, Cime, however, *was* his problem, his alone, and the enormity of that conundrum had him casting about for any possible solution, taking pat answers up and putting them down like gods move seeds from field to field. He could kill her, rape her, deport her; he could not ignore her, forget her, or suffer along without confronting her.

That she and One-Thumb had become enamored of one another was something he had not counted on. Such a thing had never occurred to him.

Tempus felt the god rustling around in him, the deep cavernous sensing in his most private skull that told him the deity was going to speak. *Silently!* he warned the god. They were uneasy with each other, yet, like two lovers after a trial separation.

We can take her, mildly, and then she will leave. You cannot tolerate her presence. Drive her off. I will help thee, spake Vashanka.

"Must you be so predictable, Pillager?" Tempus mumbled under his breath, so that Abarsis's Trôs horse swiveled its ears back to eavesdrop. He slapped its neck, and told it to continue on straight and smartly. They were headed toward Lastel's modest eastside estate.

Constancy is one of My attributes, jibed the god in Tempus's head meaningfully.

"You are not getting her, O Ravening One. You who are never satisfied, in this one thing, will not triumph. What would we have between us to keep it clear who is whom? I cannot allow it."

You will, said Vashanka so loud in his head that he winced in his saddle and the Trôs horse broke stride, looking reproachfully about at him to see what that shift of weight could possibly be construed to mean.

Tempus stopped the horse in the middle of the cool shadowed way on that beautiful morning and sat stiffly a long while, conducting an internal battle which had no resolution.

After a time, he swung the horse back in its tracks, kicked it into a lope toward the barracks from which he had just come. Let her stay with One-Thumb, if she would. She had come between him and his god before. He was not ready to give her to the god, and he was not ready to give himself back into the hands of his curse, rip asunder what had been so laboriously patched together and at such great cost. He thought of Abarsis, and Kadakithis, and the refractory upcountry peoples, and he promised Vashanka any other woman the god should care to choose before sundown. Cime would keep, no doubt, right where she was. He would see to it that Lastel saw to her.

Abarsis's Trôs horse snorted softly, as if in agreement, single-footing through Sanctuary's better streets toward the barracks. But the Trôs horse could not have known that by this simple decision its rider had attained to a greater victory than in all the wars of all the empires he had ever labored to increase. No, the Trôs horse whose belly quivered between Tempus's knees as it issued a blaring trumpet to the dusty air did so not because of its rider's triumph over self and god, but out of pure high spirits, as horses always will praise a fine day dawned.

ANDRE NORTON
Spider Silk

1

THE BIG Storm in the Year of the Kobold came late, long past the month when such fury was to be expected. This was all part of that evil which the Guardians had drawn upon Estcarp when they summoned up their greatest power to blast and twist the mountain lands, seal off passes through which had come the invasion from Karsten.

Rannock lay open to that storm. Only the warning dream-sending to the Wise Woman, Ingvarna, drew a portion of the women and children to the higher lands, there to watch with fear and trembling the sea's fierce assault upon the coast. So high dashed those waves that water covered and boiled about the Serpent Teeth of the upper ledges. Only here, in pockets among the Tor rocks, could a fugitive crouch in almost mindless terror, awaiting the end.

Of the fishing fleet which had set out yesterday morn, who had any hopes now of its return save perhaps a scattering of wreckage, playthings of the storm waves?

There was left only a handful of old men and boys, and one or two such as Herdrek, the Twist-Leg, the village smith. For Rannock was as poor in men as it was in all else since the war years had ravaged Estcarp. To the north perched Alizon, a hawk ready to be unleashed upon its neighbor; from the south Karsten boiled and bubbled, if aught was still left alive beyond the wrecked mountain passages.

Men who had marched with the Borderers under Lord Simon Tregarth or served beneath the Banners of the Witch Women of Es—where were they? Long since, their kin had given up any hope of their return. There had been no true peace in this land since old Nabor (who could count his years at more than a hundred) had been in his green youth.

It was Nabor now who battled the strength of the wind to the Tor,

433

dragged himself up to stand, hunched shoulder to shoulder, with Ing-varna. As she, he looked to the sea uneasily. That she expected still their own fleet, he could not believe, foresighted as all knew her to be.

Waves mounted, to pound giant fists against the rock. Nabor caught sight of a ship rising and falling near the Serpent's dread fangs. Then a huge swell whirled it over those sharp threats into the comparative calm beyond. Nabor sighed with the relief of a seaman who had wit-nessed a miracle, life won from the very teeth of rock death. Also, Rannock had the right of storm wrack. If that ship survived so far, its cargo was forfeit now to any who could bring it to shore. He half-turned to seek the shelter of the Tor hollows, rouse Herdrek, the others, with this promise of fortune.

However, Ingvarna turned her head. Through the drifts of rain her eyes held his. There was a warning in her steady gaze. "One comes—" He saw her lips shape the words rather than voice them above the roar of wind and wave.

At the same moment, there was such a crash as equaled the drum of thunder, the lash of lightning. The strange ship might have beaten the menace of the reef's fangs, but now had been driven halfway up the beach, where it was fast breaking up under the hammer blows of the surf.

Herdrek stumped out to join them. "It is a raider," he commented during a lull of the wind. "Perhaps one of the Sea Wolves of Alizon." He spat at the wreck below.

Ingvarna was already scrambling over the rocks towards the shore, as if what lay there were of vast importance. Herdrek shouted after her a warning, but she did not even turn her head. With a curse at the folly of females, which a second later he devoutly hoped the Wise Woman had not been able to pick out of the air, the smith followed her, two of the lads venturing in his wake.

At least when they reached the shore level, the worst of the storm was spent. Waves drew a torn seaweed veil around the broken vessel. Herdrek made fast a rope about his waist, gave dire warnings to his followers to keep a tight hold upon it. Then he ventured into the surf, using that cordage from wind-rent sails, hanging in loops down the shattered sides, to climb aboard.

There was a hatch well tamped down, roped shut. He drew belt knife to slash the fastening.

"Ho!" His voice rolled hollowly into the dark beneath him. "Anyone below?"

A thin cry answered, one which might issue from the throat of a seabird such as already coasted over the subsiding surface of the sea on hunt for the bounty of the storm. Yet he thought not. Gingerly, favoring his stiff leg, the smith lowered himself into the stinking hold. What he found there made him retch, and then heated in him dull anger against those who had mastered this vessel. She had been a slaver, such as Rannock's men had heard tell of—dealing in live cargo.

But of that cargo, only one survived. Her, Herdrek carried gently from the horror of that prison. A little maid, her small arms no more than skin slipped glovelike on bones, her eyes great, gray, and blankly open. Ingvarna took the strange child from the smith as one who had the authority of clan and home hearth, wrapping the little one's thin, shivering body in her own warm cloak.

From whence Dairine came, those of Rannock never learned. That slavers raided far was no secret. Also, the villagers soon discovered the child was blind. Ingvarna, though she was a Wise One, greatly learned in herbs and spells, the setting of bones, the curing of wounds, shook her head sadly over that discovery, saying that the child's blindness came from no hurt of body. Rather, she must have looked upon some things so horrible that thereafter her mind closed and refused all sight.

Though she must have been six or seven winters old, yet also speech seemed riven from her, and only fear was left to be her portion. Although the women of Rannock would have tried to comfort her, yet secretly in their hearts they were willing that she bide with Ingvarna, who treated her oddly, they thought. For the Wise Woman did not strive to make life easier in any way for the child. Rather, from the first, Ingvarna treated the sea waif not as one maimed in body, and perhaps in mind, but rather as she might some daughter of the village whom she had chosen to be her apprentice in the harsh school of her own learning.

These years were bleak for Rannock. Full half the fleet did not return from out of the maw of that storm. Nor did any of the coastwise traders come. The following winter was a lean one. But in those dark days, Dairine showed first her skill. Though her eyes might not see what her fingers wrought, yet she could mend fishing nets with such cleverness that even the experienced women marveled.

And in the following spring, when the villagers husked the loquth balls to free their seeds for new plantings, Dairine busied herself with the silken inner fibers, twisting and turning those. Ingvarna had Herdrek make a small spindle, and showed the child how this tool might be best put to work.

Good use did Dairine make of it, too. Her small, birdclaw fingers drew out finer thread than any had achieved before, freer from knotting than any the villagers had seen. Yet never seemed she satisfied, but strove ever to make her spinning yet finer, more smooth.

The Wise Woman continued her fosterling's education in other ways, teaching her to use her fingers, her nose, in the herb garden. Dairine learnt easily the spelling which was part of a Wise Woman's knowledge. She absorbed such very quickly, yet always there was about her an impatience. When she made mistakes, then her anger against herself was great. The greatest when she tried to explain some tool or need which she seemed unable to describe but for which she evinced a need.

Ingvarna spoke to Herdrek (who was now village elder), saying that perhaps the craft of the Wise Woman might aid in regaining a portion of Dairine's lost memory. When he demanded why she had not voiced such a matter before, Ingvarna answered gravely:

"This child is not blood of our blood, and she was captive to the sea wolves. Have we the right to recall to her past horrors? Perhaps Gunnore, who watches over all womankind, has taken away her memory of the past in pity. If so—"

He bit his thumb, watching Dairine as she paced back and forth before the loom which he had caused to be set up for her, now and then halting to slap her hand upon the frame in frustration. It seemed as if she longed to force the heavy wood into another pattern which would serve her better.

"I think that she grows more and more unhappy," he agreed slowly. "At first she seemed content. Now there are times when she acts as a snow cat encaged against her will. I do not like to see her so."

The Wise Woman nodded. "Well enough. In my mind, this is a right choice."

Ingvarna went to the girl, taking both her hands, drawing her around so that she might look directly into those blind eyes. At Ingvarna's touch, Dairine stood still. "Leave us!" the Wise Woman commanded the smith.

Early that evening as Herdrek stood at his forge, Dairine walked into the light of his fire. She came to him unhesitatingly. So acute was her hearing that she often startled the villagers by her recognition of another presence. Now she held out her hands to him as she might to a father she loved. And he knew all was well.

By midsummer, when the loquths had flowered and their blossoms dropped, Dairine went often into the fields, fingering the swelling bolls. Sometimes she sang, queer, foreign-tongued words, as if the plants were children (now knee height, and then shoulder height) who must be amused and cherished.

Herdrek had changed her loom as the girl suggested might be done. From Ingvarna, she learned the mysteries of dyes, experimenting on her own. She had no real friend among the few children of the dying village. Firstly, because she did not range much afield, save with Ingvarna, of whom most were in awe. Secondly, because her actions were strange and she seemed serious and more adult than the years they believed to be hers.

In the sixth year after her coming, a Sulcar ship put in at Rannock, the first strange vessel they had sighted since the wreck of the slaver. Its captain brought news that the long war was at last over.

The defeat of the Karsten invaders, who so drained the powers of the rulers of Estcarp, had been complete. Koris of Gorm was now Commander of Estcarp, since so many of the Guardians had perished when they turned the full extent of their power upon the enemy. Yet the land was hardly at peace. The sea wolves of the coast had been augmented by ships of the broken and defeated navy of Karsten. And as in times of chaos, other wolfheads, without any true lands or allegiance, now ravaged the land wherever they might. Though the forces under Captain General Koris sought to protect the boundaries, yet to clearly defeat such hit-and-run raids was yet well beyond the ability of any defending force.

The Sulcar Captain was impressed by the latest length of Dairine's weaving, offering for it, when he bargained with Ingvarna, a much better price than he had thought to pay out in this forgotten village. He was much interested also in the girl, speaking to her slowly in several tongues. However, she answered him only in the language of Estcarp, saying she knew no other.

Still, he remarked privately to Ingvarna that somewhere in the past he had seen those like unto her, though where and when during his travels he could not bring to mind. Still, he thought that she was not of common stock.

It was a year later that the Wise Woman wrought the best she could for her sea-gift foundling.

No one knew how old Ingvarna was, for the Wise Woman showed no advance of age, as did those less learned in the many uses of herbs and medicants. But it was true that she walked more slowly, and that she no longer went alone when she sought out certain places of Power, taking Dairine ever with her. What the two did there no one knew, for who would spy on any woman with the Witch Talent?

On this day, the few fishing boats had taken to sea before dawn. At moonrise the night before, the Wise Woman and her fosterling had gone inland to visit a certain very ancient place. There Ingvarna kindled a fire which burned not naturally red, but rather blue. Into those flames, she tossed small, tightly bound bundles of dried herbs so that the smoke which arose was heavily scented. But she watched not that fire. Rather, a slab of stone set behind its flowering. That stone had a surface like unto glass, the color of a fine sword blade.

Dairine stood a little behind the Wise Woman. Though Ingvarna had taught her so much over the years, to make her other senses serve her in place of her missing sight, so that her fingers were ten eyes, her nostrils, her ears could catch scent and sound to an extent far outreaching the skill of ordinary mankind; yet at moments such as this, the longing to be as others awoke in her a sense of loss so dire that to her eyes came tears, flowing silently down her cheeks. Much Ingvarna had given her. Still, she was not as the others of Rannock. And ofttimes loneliness settled upon her as a burdensome cloak. Now the girl sensed that Ingvarna planned for her some change. But that it would make her see as others saw—that she could not hope for.

She heard clearly the chanting of the Wise Woman. The odor of the burning herbs filled her nose, now and then made her gasp for a less heavy lungful of air. Then came a command, not given in words, nor by some light touch against her arm and shoulder. But into her mind burst an order and Dairine walked ahead, her hands outstretched, until her ten fingers flattened against a throbbing surface. Warm it was, near to a point which would sear her flesh, while its throb was in twin beat to her own heart. Still, Dairine stood firm, while the chant of the Wise Woman came more faintly, as if the girl had been shifted from farther away in space from her foster mother.

Then she felt an inward flow from the surface she touched, a warmth which spread along her hands, her wrists, up her arms. Fainter still came the voice of Ingvarna petitioning on her behalf, strange and half-forgotten powers.

Slowly the warmth receded. But how long Dairine had stood so wedded to that surface she could not see, the girl never knew. Except that there came a moment when her hands fell, as if too heavily burdened for her to raise.

"What is done, is done." Ingvarna's voice at the girl's left sounded as weighted as Dairine's hands felt. "All I have to give, this I have freely shared with you. Though being blind as men see blindness, yet you have sight such as few can own to. Use it well, my fosterling."

From that day it became known that Dairine did indeed have strange powers of "seeing"—through her hands. She could take up a thing which had been made and tell you of the maker, of how long since it had been wrought. A shred of fleece from one of the thin-flanked hill sheep put into her fingers would enable her to guide an anxious owner to where the lost flock member had strayed.

There was one foretelling which she would not do, after she came upon its secret by chance only. For she had taken the hand of little Hulde during the Harvest Homing dance. Straightway thereafter, Dairine dropped her grasp upon the child's small fingers, crying out and shrinking away from the villagers, to seek out Ingvarna's house and therein hide herself. Within the month, Hulde had died of a fever. Thereafter, the girl used her new sight sparingly, and always with a fear plain to be seen haunting her.

In the Year of the Weldworm, when Dairine passed into young womanhood, Ingvarna died, swiftly. As if foreseeing another possible end, she summoned death as one summons a servant to do one's bidding.

Though Dairine was no true Wise Woman, yet thereafter she took on many of the duties of her foster mother. Within a month after the Wise Woman's burial, the Sulcar ship returned.

As the Captain told the forgotten village the news of the greater world, his eyes turned ever to Dairine, her hands busy with thread she spun as she listened. Among those of the village, she was indeed one apart, with her strange silver-fair hair, silver-light eyes.

Sibbald Ortis, Sibbald the Wrong-Handed—thus they had named him after a sea battle had lopped off his hand, and a smith in another land had made him one of metal—was that captain. He was new come to command and young—though he had lived near all his life at sea after the manner of his people.

Peace, after a fashion, he told them, had encompassed the land at last. For Koris of Gorm now ruled Estcarp with a steady hand. Alizon had been defeated in some invasion that nation had attempted overseas. And Karsten was in chaos, one prince or lord always rising against another. While the sea wolves were being hunted down, one after another, to a merciless end.

Having made clear that he was in Rannock on lawful business, the Captain now turned briskly to the subject of trade. What had they, if anything, which would be worth stowage in his own ship?

Herdrek was loathe to spread their poverty before these strangers. Also, he wanted, with a desire he could hardly conceal, some of the tools and weapons he had seen in casual use among them. Yet what had Rannock? Fish dried to take them through a lean winter, some woven lengths of wool.

The villagers would be hard put even to give these visitors guest-right, with the feast they were entitled to. And to fail in that was to deny their own heritage.

Dairine, listening to the Captain, had wished she dared touch his hand, and thus learn what manner of a man he was who had journeyed so far and seen so much. A longing was born in her to be free of the narrow, well-known ways of Rannock, to see what lay beyond in the world. Her fingers steadily twirled her thread, but her thoughts were elsewhere.

Then she lifted her head a little, for she knew someone was now standing at her side. There was the tang of sea-salted leather, and other odors. This was a stranger, one of the Sulcar men.

"You work that thread with skill, maid."

She recognized the Captain's voice. "It is my skill, Lord Captain."

"They tell me that fate has served you harshly," he spoke bluntly then. But she liked him the better for that bluntness.

"Not so, Lord Captain. These of Rannock have been ever kind. And I was fosterling to their Wise Woman. Also, my hands serve well, if my eyes are closed upon this world. Come, you, and see!" She spoke with pride as she arose from her stool, thrusting her spindle into her girdle.

Thus Dairine brought him to the cottage which was hers, sweet within for all its scents of herbs. She gestured to where stood the loom Herdrek had made her.

"As you see, Lord Captain, I am not idle, even though I may be blind."

For she knew that there, in the half-done web, there was no mistake.

Ortis was silent for a moment. Then she heard the hiss of his breath expelled in wonder.

"But this is weaving of the finest! There is no fault in color or pattern. . . . How can this be done?"

"With one's two hands, Lord Captain!" She laughed. "Here, give me a possession of yours that I may show you better how fingers can be eyes."

Within her there was a new excitement, for something told her that this was a moment of importance in her life. She heard then a faint swish as if some bit of woven stuff were being shaken free. A clinging length was pressed into the hand she held out.

"Tell me," he commanded, "from whence came this, and how was it wrought?"

Back and forth between her fingers, the girl slipped the ribband of silken stuff.

Woven—yes. But her "seeing" hands built no mind picture of human fingers at the business. No, strangely ill-formed were those members engaged in the weaving. And so swift were they also that they seemed to blur. No woman, as Dairine knew women, had fashioned this. But female—strongly, almost fiercely female.

"Spider silk—" She was not aware that she had spoken aloud until she heard the sound of her own words. "Yet not quite spider. A woman weaving—still, not a woman. . . ."

She raised the ribband to her cheek. There was a wonder in such weaving which brought to life in her a fierce longing to know more and more.

"You are right." The Captain's voice broke her preoccupation with that need to learn. "This comes from Usturt. And had a man but two full bolts of it within his cargo, he could count triple profits from such a voyage alone."

"Where lies Usturt?" Dairine demanded. If she could go there—learn what could be learned. "And who are the weavers? I do not see them as beings like unto our own people."

She heard his breath hiss again. "To see the weavers," he said in a low voice, "is death. They hate all mankind—"

"Not so, Lord Captain!" Dairine answered him then. "It is not mankind that they hate—it is all males." For from the strip between her fingers came that knowledge.

For a moment she was silent. Did he doubt her?

"At least no man sails willingly to Usturt," he replied. "I had that length from one who escaped with his bare life. He died upon our deck shortly after we fished him from a waterlogged raft."

"Captain," she stroked the silk, "you have said that this weaving is a true treasure. My people are very poor and grow poorer. If one were to learn the secret of such weaving, might not good come of it?"

With a sharp jerk he took the ribband from her.

"There is no such way."

"But there is!" Her words came in an eager tumble, one upon the other. "Women—or female things—wove this. They might treat with a woman—one who was already a weaver."

Great, calloused hands closed upon her shoulders.

"Girl, not for all the gold in Karsten would I send any woman into

Usturt! You know not of what you speak. It is true that you have gifts
of the Talent. But you are no confirmed Guardian, and you are blind.
What you suggest is such a folly—Aye, Vidruth, what is it now?"

Dairine had already sensed that someone had approached.

"The tide rises. For better mooring, Captain, we need move beyond
the rocks."

"Aye. Well, girl, may the Right Hand of Lraken be your shield.
When a ship calls, no captain lingers."

Before she could even wish him well, he was gone. Retreating, she
sat down on her hard bench by the loom. Her hands trembled, and from
her eyes the tears seeped. She felt bereft, as if she had had for a space
a treasure and it had been torn from her. For she was certain that her
instinct had been right, that if any could have learned the secret of
Usturt, she was that one.

Now, when she put a hand out to finger her own weaving, the web
on the loom seemed coarse, utterly ugly. In her mind, she held queer
vision of a deeply forested place in which great, sparkling webs ran in
even strands from tree to tree.

Through the open door puffed a wind from the sea. Dairine lifted her
face to it as it tugged at her hair.

"Maid!"

She was startled. Even with her keen ears, she had not heard anyone
approach so loud was the wind-song.

"Who are you?" she asked quickly.

"I am Vidruth, maid, mate to Captain Ortis."

She arose swiftly. "He has thought more upon my plan?" For she
could see no other reason for the seaman to seek her out in this fashion.

"That is so, maid. He awaits us now. Give me your hand—so.
. . ."

Fingers grasped hers tightly. She strove to free her hand. This man—
there was that in him which was—wrong—Then out of nowhere, came
a great, smothering cloak, folded about her so tightly she could not
struggle. There were unclean smells to affront her nostrils, but the worst
was that this Vidruth had swung her up across his shoulder so that she
could have been no more than a bundle of trade goods.

2

So was she brought aboard what was certainly a ship, for in spite of the muffling of the cloak, Dairine used her ears, her nose. However, in her mind, she could not sort out her thoughts. Why had Captain Ortis so vehemently, and truthfully (for she had read that truth in his touch), refused to bring her? Then this man of his had come to capture her as he might steal a woman during some shore raid?

The Sulcarmen were not slave traders, that was well known. Then why?

Hands pulled away the folds of the cloak at last. The air she drew thankfully into her lungs was not fresh, rather tainted with stinks which made her feel unclean even to sniff. She thought that her prison must lie deep within the belly of the ship.

"Why have you done this?" Dairine asked of the man she could hear breathing heavily near her.

"Captain's orders," he answered, leaning so close she not only smelt his uncleanly body, but gathered with that a sensation of heat. "He has eyes in his head, has the Captain. You be a smooth-skinned, likely wench—"

"Let her be, Wak!" That was Vidruth.

"Aye, Captain," the other answered with a slur of sly contempt. "Here she be, safe and sound—"

"And here she stays, Wak, safe from your kind. Get out!"

There was a growl from Wak, as if he were close to questioning the other's right to so order him. Then Dairine's ears caught a sound which might have been that of a panel door sliding into place.

"You are not the Captain," she spoke into the silence between them.

"There has been a change of command," he returned. "The Captain, he has not brought us much luck in months agone. When we learned that he would not try to better his fortune—he was—"

"Killed!"

"Not so. Think you we want a blood feud with all his clan? The Sulcarmen take not lightly to those who let the red life out of some one of their stock."

"I do not understand. You are all Sulcar—"

"That we are not, girl. The world has changed since those ruled the waves about the oceans. They were fighters and fighting men get killed. The Kolder they fought, and they blew up Sulcarkeep in that fighting, taking the enemy—but also too many of their own—on into the Great

Secret. Karsten they fought, and they were at the taking of Gorm, aye. Then they have patrolled against the sea wolves of Alizon. Men they have lost, many men. Now if they take a ship out of harbor, they do it with others than just their kin to raise sails and set the course. No, we do not kill Sibbald Ortis, we may need him later. But he is safe laid.

"Now let us to the business between us, girl. I heard the words you spoke with Ortis. Also did I learn much about you from those starvelings who live in Rannock. You have some of the Talents of the Wise Women, if you cannot call upon the full Power, blind as you are. You yourself said it—if any can treat with those devil females of Usturt, it must be one such as you.

"Think on that spider silk, girl. You held that rag that Ortis has. And you can do mighty things, unless all those at Rannock are crazed in their wits. Which I do not believe. This is a chance which a man may have offered to him but once in a lifetime."

She heard the greed in his voice. And perhaps that greed would be her protection. Vidruth would take good care to keep her safe. Just as he held somewhere Sibbald Ortis for a like reason.

"Why did you take me so, if your intentions are good? If you heard my words to the Captain, you know I would have gone willingly."

He laughed. "Do you think those shore-side halflingmen would have let you go? With three-quarters of the Guardians dead, their own Wise Woman laid also in her grave shaft, would they willingly have surrendered to us even your small Talent? The whole land is hard pressed now for any who hold even a scrap of the Power.

"No matter. They will welcome you back soon enough after you have learned the secret of Usturt. If it then still be in your mind to go to them."

"But how do you know that in Usturt I shall work for you?"

"Because you will not want the Captain to be given over to them. They do not have a pleasant way with captives."

There was fear behind his words, a fear born of horror, which he fought to control.

"Also, if you do not do as we wish, we can merely sail and leave you on Usturt for the rest of your life. No ship goes there willingly. A long life for you perhaps, girl, alone with none of your own kind—think of that."

He was silent for a moment before he added, "It is a bargain, girl, one we swear to keep. You deal with the weavers, we take you back to Rannock, or anywhere else you name. The Captain, he can be set ashore with you even. No more harm done. And a portion of the silk for your own. Why, you can buy all of Rannock and make yourself a Keep lady!"

"There is one thing—" She was remembering Wak. "I am not such a one as any of your men can take at his will. Know you not what happens then to any Talent I may possess?"

When Vidruth answered her, there was a deep note of menace in his voice, though it was not aimed at her.

"All men know well that the Talent departs from a woman who lies with a man. None shall trouble you."

"So be it," she returned, with an outward calm it was hard for her to assume. "Have you the bit of silk? Let me learn from it what I can."

She heard him move away the grate of whatever door kept snug her prison. As that sound ceased, she put out her hands to explore. The cubby was small, there was a shelflike bunk against the wall, a stool which seemed bolted to the deck, nought else. Did they have Captain Ortis pent in such a hole also? And how had this Vidruth managed so well the take-over of the Captain's command? What she had read of Sibbald Ortis during their brief meeting had not been such as to lead her to think he was one easily overcome by an enemy.

But she was sitting quietly on the stool when Vidruth returned to drop the length of ribband across her quiet hands.

"Learn all you can," he urged her. "We have two days of sail if this wind continues to favor us, then we shall raise Usturt. Food, water, what you wish, shall be brought to you, and there is a guard without so that you need not be troubled."

With the silk between her hands, Dairine concentrated upon what it could tell her. She had no illusions concerning Vidruth. To him and the others, she was only a tool to their hands. Because she was sightless, he might undervalue her, for all his talk of Talent and Power. She had discovered many times in the past that such was so.

Deliberately, Dairine closed out the world about her, shut her ears to creak of timber, wash of wave, her nose to the many smells which offended it. Once more her "sight" turned inward. She could "see" the blur of those hands (which were not quite hands) engaged in weaving. Colors she had no words to describe were clear and bright. For the material she saw so was not one straight length of color, but shimmered from one shade to another.

Dairine tried now to probe beyond that shift of color to the loom from which it had come. She had an impression of tall, dark shafts. Those were not of well-planed and smooth wood; no, they had the crooked surface of—trees—standing trees!

The hands—concentrate now upon the moving hands of the weaver.

But the girl had only reached that point of recognition when there was a knock to distract her concentration. Exasperated, she turned her head to the door of the cubby.

"Come!"

Again the squeak of hinge, the sound of boots, the smell of sea-wet leather and man-skin. The newcomer cleared his throat as if ill at ease.

"Lady, here is food."

She swirled the ribband about her wrist, put out her hands, for suddenly she was hungry and athirst.

"By your leave, lady," he fitted the handle of a mug into her right hand, placed a bowl on the palm of the other. "There is a spoon. It is only ship's ale, lady, and stew."

"My thanks," she said in return. "And what name do you go by, ship's man?"

"Rothar, lady. I am a blank shield and no real seaman. But since I know no trade but war, one venture is nigh as good as another."

"Yet of this venture you have some doubts." She had set the mug on the deck, kept upright between her worn sandals. Now she seized his hand, held it to read. For it seemed to Dairine that she must not let this opportunity of learning more of Vidruth's followers go, and she sensed that this Rothar was not of the same ilk as Wak.

"Lady"—his voice was very low and swift—"they say that you have knowledge of herb craft. Why then has Vidruth not taken you to the Captain that you may learn what strange, swift illness struck him down?"

There was youth in the hand Dairine held and not, she believed, any desire to deceive.

"Where lies the Captain?" she asked in as low a voice.

"In his cabin. He is fevered and raves. It is as if he has come under some ensorcelment and—"

"Rothar!" From the door, another voice sharp as an order. The hand she held jerked free from hers. But not before she had felt the spring of fear.

"I promised no man shall trouble you. Has this cub been at such tricks?" Vidruth demanded.

"Not so." Dairine was surprised her voice remained so steady. "He has been most kind in bringing me food and drink, both of which I needed."

"And having done so—out!" Vidruth commanded. "Now"—she

heard the door close behind the other—"what have you learned, girl, from this piece of silk?"

"I have had but a little time, lord. Give me more. I must study it."

"See that you do" was his order as he also departed.

He did not come again, nor did Rothar ever once more bring her food. She thought, though, of what the young man had said concerning the Captain. Vidruth's tale made her believe that the whole ship's company had been behind the mate's scheme to take command and sail to Usturt. There were herbs which, put in a man's food or drink, could plunge him into the depths of fever. If she could only reach the Captain, she would know. But there was no faring forth from this cubby.

Now and again Vidruth would suddenly appear to demand what more she had learned from the ribband. There was such an avid greediness in his questions that sometimes rising uneasiness nearly broke through her control. At last she answered with what she believed to be the truth.

"Have you never heard, Captain, that the Talent cannot be forced? I have tried to read from this all which I might. But this scrap was not fashioned by a race such as ours. An alien nature cannot be so easily discovered. For all my attempts, I cannot build a mind picture of these people. What I see clearly is only the weaving."

When he made no answer, Dairine continued:

"This is a thing not of the body, but the mind. Along such a road one creeps as a babe, one does not race as one full grown."

"You have less than a day now. Before sundown, Usturt shall rise before us. I know only what I have heard tell of witch powers, and that may well be changed by the telling and retelling. Remember, girl, your life can well ride on your 'seeing'!"

She heard him go. The ribband no longer felt so light and soft. Rather, it had taken on the heaviness of a slave chain binding her to his will. She ate ship's biscuits from the plate he had brought her. It was true time was passing, and she had done nothing of importance.

Oh, she could now firmly visualize the loom and see the silk come into being beneath the flying fingers. But the body behind those hands, that she could not see. Nor did any of the personality of the weavers who had made that which she held come clear to her, for all her striving.

Captain Ortis—he came in the reading, for he had held this. And Vidruth also. There was a third who was more distant, lying hid under a black cloud of fear. Was this day or night? She had lost track of time. That the ship still ran before the wind, she sensed.

Then—she was not alone in the cubby! Yet she had not heard the warning creak of the door. Fear kept her tense, hunched upon the stool, listening with all her might.

"Lady?"

Rothar! But how had he come?

"Why are you here?" Dairine had to wet her lips with her tongue before she could shape those words.

"They move now to put you ashore on Usturt, lady! Captain Ortis, he came up leaning on Vidruth's arm, his body all atremble. He gives no orders, only Vidruth. Lady, there is some great wrong here—for we are at Usturt. And Vidruth commands. Such is not right."

"I knew that I must go to Usturt," she returned. "Rothar, if you have any allegiance to your captain, know he is a prisoner to Vidruth in some manner, even as I have been. And if I do not do as Vidruth says, there will be greater trouble—death—"

"You do not understand." His voice was very husky. "There are monsters on this land. To see them even, they say, makes a man go mad!"

"But I shall not see them," Dairine reminded him. "How long do I have?"

"Some moments yet."

"Where am I and how did you get here?"

"You are in the treasure hold, below the Captain's own cabin. I have used the secret opening to reach you as this is the first time Vidruth and the Captain have been out of it. Now they must watch carefully for the entrance to the inner reef."

"Can you get me into the Captain's cabin?" If, in those moments, she might discover what hold Vidruth had over Captain Ortis, she perhaps would be able to help a man she trusted.

"Give me your hands, then, lady. I fear we have very little time."

She reached out, and her wrists were instantly caught in a hold tight enough to be painful, but she made no sound of complaint. Then she found herself pulled upward with a vast heave as if Rothar must do this all in a single effort. When he set her on her feet once more, she sensed she was in a much larger space. And there was the fresh air from the sea blowing in as if through some open port.

But the air was not enough to hide from her that telltale scent—a scent of evil.

"Let me go, touch me not now," she told Rothar. "I seek that which must be found, and your slightest touch will confuse my course."

Slowly she turned away from the wind, facing to her right.

"What lies before me?"

"The Captain's bed, lady."

Step by step she approached in that direction. The sniff of evil was stronger. What it might be she had no idea, for though Ingvarna had taught her to distinguish that which was of the shadow, she knew little more. The fetid odor of some black sorcery was rank.

"The bed," she ordered now, "do you strip off its coverings. If you find aught which is strange, be sure you do not touch it with your hand. Rather, use something of iron, if you can, to pluck it forth. And then throw it quickly into the sea."

He asked no questions, but she could hear his hurried movements. And then—

"There is a—a root, most misshapen. It lies under the pillow, lady."

"Wait!" Perhaps the whole of that bed place was now impregnated by what evil had been introduced. To destroy its source might not be enough. "Bundle all—pillow, coverings—give them to the sea!" she ordered. "Let me back then into the treasure cubby, and if there be time, make the bed anew. I do not know what manner of ensorcelment has been wrought here. But it is of the Shadow, not of the Power. Take care that you keep yourself also from contact with it."

"That will I do of a certainty, lady!" His answer was fervent. "Stand well back, I will get rid of this."

She retreated, hearing the click of his sea boots on the planking as he passed her toward the source of the sea wind.

"Now"—he was back at her side—"I shall see you safe, lady. Or as safe as you can be until the Captain comes to his mind once more and Vidruth be removed from command."

His hands closed upon her, lowered her back down into the cubby. She listened intently. But if he closed that trap door, and she was sure that he had, it had fallen into place without a sound.

3

SHE HAD not long to wait, for the opening on the floor level of the cubby was opened and she recognized Vidruth's step.

"Listen well, girl," he commanded. "Usturt is an island, one of a string of islands, reaching from the shore. At one time, they may all have been a part of the coast. But now some are only bare rock with such a wash of sea around them as no man can pass. So think not that you have any way of leaving save by our favor. We shall set you ashore and keep down-sea thereafter. But when you have learned what we wish, then return to the shore and there leave three stones piled one upon another. . . ."

To Dairine, his arrangements seemed to be not well thought out. But she questioned nothing. What small hopes she had she could only pin on Rothar and the Captain. Vidruth's hand tightened about her arm. He drew her to a ladder, set her hands upon its rungs.

"Climb, girl. And you had better play well your part. There are those among us who fear witchcraft and say there is only one certain way to disarm a witch. That, you have heard. . . ."

She shivered. Yes, there was a way to destroy a witch—by enjoying the woman. All men were well versed in that outrage.

"Rothar shall set you ashore," Vidruth continued. "And we shall watch your going. Think not to talk him out of his orders, for there is no place elsewhere. . . ."

Dairine was on the deck now, heard the murmur of voices. Where stood Captain Ortis? Vidruth gave her no time to try to sort out the sounds. Under his compelling, the girl came up against the rail. Then Vidruth caught her up as if she were a small child and lowered her until other hands steadied her, easing her down upon a plank seat.

Around her was the close murmur of the sea, and she could hear the grate of oars within their locks.

"Do you believe me witch, Rothar?" she asked.

"Lady, I do not know what you are. But that you are in danger with Vidruth, that I can swear to. If the Captain comes into his own mind again—"

He broke off and then continued. "Through the war, I have come to hate any act which makes man or woman unwillingly serve another. There is no future before me, for I am wastage of war, having no trade save that of killing. Therefore, I will do what I may to help you and the Captain."

"You are young to speak so, of being without a future."

"I am old in killing," he told her bleakly. "And of such men as Vidruth leads, I have seen amany. Lady, we are near the shore. And those on the ship watch us well. When I set you on the beach, take forth carefully what you find in my belt, hide it from all. It is a knife made of the best star-steel, fashioned by the hand of Hamraker himself. Not mine in truth, but the Captain's."

Dairine did as he ordered when he carried her from the sand-smoothing waves to the drier reach beyond. Memory stirred in her. Once there had been such a knife and—firelight had glinted on it—

"No!" she cried aloud to deny memory. Yet her fingers remained curled about that hilt.

"Yes!" He might not understand her inner turmoil, but his hold on her tightened. "You must keep it."

"Walk straight ahead," he told her. "Those on the ship have the great dart caster trained on you. There are trees ahead—within those, there the spiders are said to be. But, lady, though I dare not move openly in your aid now, for that would bring me quick death to no purpose, yet what I can do, that I shall."

Uncertainty held Dairine. She felt naked in this open which she did not know. Yet she must not appear concerned to those now watching her. She had the ribband of silk looped about her wrist. And within the folds of her skirt, she held also the knife. Turning her head slightly from one side to another, she listened with full concentration, walking slowly forward against the drag of the sand.

Coolness ahead—she must be entering the shade of the trees. She put out her hand, felt rough bark, slid around it, setting the trunk as a barrier between that dart thrower of which Rothar had warned, and her back.

Then she knew, as well as if her eyes could tell her, that it was not alone the ship's company who watched. She was moving under observation of someone—or something—else. Dairine used her sense of perception, groping as she did physically with her hands, seeking what that might be.

A moment later she gasped with shock. A strong mental force burst through the mind door she had opened. She felt as if she had been caught in a giant hand, raised to the level of huge eyes which surveyed her outwardly and inwardly.

Dairine swayed, shaken by that nonphysical touch, search. It was nonhuman. Yet she realized, as she fought to recover her calm, it was not inimical—yet.

"Why come you here, female?"

In Dairine's mind, the word shaped clearly. Still, she could build up no mental picture of her questioner. She faced a little to the right, held out the hand about which she had bound the ribband.

"I seek those able to weave such beauty," she replied aloud, wondering if they could hear, or understand, her words.

Again that sensation of being examined, weighed. But this time she stood quiet, unshaken under it.

"You think this thing beautiful?" Again the mind question.

"Yes."

"But you have not eyes to see it." Harshly that came, as if to deny her claim.

"I have not eyes, that is the truth. But my fingers have been taught to serve me in their place. I, too, weave, but only after the manner of my own people."

Silence, then a touch on the back of her hand, so light and fleeting Dairine was not even sure she had really felt it. The girl waited, for she understood this was a place with its own manner of barriers, and she might continue only if those here allowed it.

Again a touch on her hand, but this time it lingered. Dairine made no attempt to grasp, though she tried to read through that contact. And saw only bright whirls.

"Female, you may play with threads after the crude fashion of your kind. But call yourself not a weaver!" There was arrogance in that.

"Can one such as I learn the craft as your people know it?"

"With hands as clumsy as this?" There came a hard rap across her knuckles. "Not possible. Still, you may come, see with your fingers what you cannot hope to equal."

The touch slid across her hand, became a sinewy band about her wrist as tight as the cuff of a slave chain. Dairine knew now there was no escape. She was being drawn forward. Oddly, though she could not read the nature of the creature who guided her, there flowed from its contact a sharp mental picture of the way ahead.

This was a twisted path. Sometimes she brushed against the trunks of trees; again she sensed they crossed clear areas—until she was no longer sure in what direction the beach now lay.

At last they came into an open space where there was some protection other than branches and leaves overhead to ward off the sun. Her ears picked up small, scuttling sounds.

"Put out your hand!" commanded her guide. "Describe what you find before you."

Dairine obeyed, moving slowly and with caution. Her fingers found a solid substance, not unlike the barked tree trunk. Only, looped about it, warp lines of thread were stretched taut. She transferred her touch to those lines, tracing them to another bar. Then she knelt, fingering the length of cloth. This was smooth as the ribband. A single thread led away—that must be fastened to the shuttle of the weaver.

"So beautiful!"

For the first time since Ingvarna had trained her, Dairine longed for actual sight. The need to *see* burned in her. Color—somehow as she touched the woven strip, the fact of color came to her. Yet all she could "read" of the weaver was a blur of narrow, nonhuman hands.

"Can you do such, you who claim to be a weaver?"

"Not this fine." Dairine answered with the truth. "This is beyond anything I have ever touched."

"Hold out your hands!" This time Dairine sensed that the order had not come from her guide, but another.

The girl spread out her fingers, palms up. There followed a featherlight tracing on her skin along each finger, gliding across her palm.

"It is true. You are a weaver—after a fashion. Why do you come to us, female?"

"Because I would learn." Dairine drew a deep breath. What did Vidruth's idea of trade matter now? This was of greater importance. "I would learn from those who can do this."

She continued to kneel, waiting. There was communication going on about her, but none she could catch and hold with either eye or mind. If these weavers would shelter her, what need had she to return to Vidruth? Rothar's plans? Those were too uncertain. If she won the good will of these, she had shelter against the evil of her own kind.

"Your hands are clumsy, you have no eyes." That was like a whiplash. "Let us see what you *can* do, female."

A shuttle was thrust into her hand. She examined it carefully by touch. Its shape was slightly different from those she had always known, but she could use it. Then she surveyed, the same way, the web on the loom. The threads of both warp and woof were very fine, but she concentrated until she could indeed "see" what hung there. Slowly she began to weave, but it took a long time and what she produced in her half inch of fabric was noticeably unlike that of the beginning.

Her hands shaking, the girl sat back on her heels, frustrated. All her pride in her past work was wiped out. Before these, she was a child beginning a first ragged attempt to create cloth.

Yet when she had relaxed from concentrating on her task and was aware once more of those about her, she did not meet the contempt she had expected. Rather, a sensation of surprise.

"You are one perhaps who can be taught, female," came that mind voice of authority. "If you wish."

Dairine turned her face eagerly in the direction from which she believed that message had come. "I do wish, Great One!"

"So be it. But you will begin even as our hatchlings, for you are not yet a weaver."

"That I agree." The girl ran her fingers ruefully across the fabric before her.

If Vidruth expected her return into his power now—she shrugged. And let Rothar concentrate upon the Captain and his own plight. What seemed of greatest importance to her was that she must be able to satisfy these weavers.

They seemed to have no real dwelling except this area about their looms. Nor were there any furnishings save the looms themselves. And those stood in no regular pattern. Dairine moved cautiously about, memorizing her surroundings by touch.

Though she sensed a number of beings around her, none touched her, mind or body. And she made no advances in turn, somehow knowing such would be useless.

Food they did bring her, fresh fruit. And there were some finger-lengths of what she deemed dried meat. Perhaps it was better she did not know the origin of that.

She slept when she tired on a pile of woven stuff, not quite as silky as that on the looms, yet so tightly fashioned she thought it might pass the legendary test of carrying water within its folds. Her sleep was dreamless. And when she awoke, she found it harder to remember the men or the ship, even Rothar or the Captain. Rather, they were like some persons she had known once in distant childhood, for the place of the weavers was more and more hers. And she *must* learn. To do that was a fever burning in her.

There was a scuttling sound and then a single order:

"Eat!"

Dairine groped before her, found more of the fruit. Even before she was quite finished, there came a twitch on her skirt.

"This ugly thing covering your body, you cannot wear it for thread gathering."

Thread gathering? She did not know the meaning of that. But it was true that her skirt, if she moved out of the open space about the looms, caught on branches. She arose and unfastened her girdle, the lacings of her bodice, allowed the dress to slip away into a puddle about her feet. Wearing only her brief chemise, Dairine felt oddly free. But she sought out her girdle again, wrapped it around her slim waist, putting there within the knife.

There came one of those light touches, and she faced about.

"Thread hangs between the trees"—her guide gave a small tug—"touch it with care. Shaken, it will become a trap. Prove that you have the lightness of fingers to be able to learn from us."

No more instructions came. Dairine realized they must be again testing her. She must prove she was able to gather this thread. Gather it how? Just as she questioned that, something was pushed into her hand. She discovered she held a smooth rod, the length of her lower arm. This must be a winder for the thread.

Now there was a grasp again on her wrist, drawing her away from the looms, on under the trees. Even as her left hand brushed a tree trunk came the order:

"Thread!"

There would be no profit in blind rushing. She must concentrate all her well-trained perceptive sense to aid her to find thread here.

Into her mind slid a very dim picture. Perhaps that came from the very far past which she never tried to remember. A green field lay open under the morning sun and on it were webs pearled with dew. Was what she sought allied to the material of such webs?

Who could possibly harvest the fine threads of such webs? A dark depression weighed upon Dairine. She wanted to hurl the collecting rod from her, to cry aloud that no one could do such a thing.

Then she had a vision of Ingvarna standing there. That lack of self-pity, that belief in herself which the Wise Woman had fostered, revived. To say that one could not do a thing before one ever tried was folly.

In the past her sense of perception had only located for her things more solid than a tree-hung thread. But now it must serve her better.

Under her bare feet, for she had left her sandals with her dress, lay a soft mass of long-fallen leaves. Around here there appeared to be no ground growth—only the trees.

Dairine paused, advancing her hand until her fingertips rested on bark. With caution, she slid that touch up and around the trunk. A faint impression was growing in her. Here was what she sought.

Then—she found the end of a thread. The rest of it was stretched out and away from the tree. With infinite care, Dairine broke the thread, putting the freed end to the rod. To her vast relief, it adhered there as truly as it had to the tree trunk. Now. . . . She did not try to touch the thread, but she wound slowly, with great care, moving to keep the strand taut before her, evenly spread on the rod.

Round and round—then her hand scraped another tree trunk. Dairine gave a sigh of relief, hardly daring to believe she had been successful in harvesting her first thread. But one was little enough, and she must not grow overconfident. Think only of the thread! She found another end and, with the same slow care, began once more to wind.

To those without sight, day is as night, night is as day. Dairine no longer lived within the time measure of her own kind. She went forth between intervals of sleep and food to search for the tree-looped thread, wondering if she so collected something manufactured by the weavers themselves or a product of some other species.

Twice she made the error she had been warned against, had moved too hastily, with overconfidence, shaken the thread. Thus she found herself entrapped in a sticky liquid which flowed along the line, remaining fast caught until freed by a weaver.

Though she was never scolded, each time her rescuer projected an aura of such disdain for this clumsiness that Dairine cringed inwardly.

The girl had early learned that the weavers were all female. What they did with the cloth they loomed, she had not yet discovered. They certainly did not use it all, neither had she any hint that they traded it elsewhere. Perhaps the very fact of creation satisfied some need rampant in them.

Those who, like her, hunted threads were the youngest of this nonhuman community. Yet she was able to establish no closer communication with them than she did with the senior weavers.

Once or twice there was an uneasy hint of entrapment about her life in the loom place. Why did everything which had happened before she arrived now seem so distant and of such negligible account?

If the weavers did not speak to her save through mind speech—and that rarely—they were not devoid of voices, for those at the looms hummed. Though the weird melody they so evoked bore little resemblance to human song, it became a part of one. Even Dairine's hand moved to its measure and by it her thoughts were lulled. In all the world, there were only the looms, the thread to be sought for them—only this was of any importance.

There came a day when they gave her an empty loom and left her to thread it. Even in the days of her life in the village, this had been a matter which required her greatest dexterity and concentration. Now, as she worked with unfamiliar bars, it was even worse. She threaded until her fingertips were sore, her head aching from such single-minded using of perception, while all about her the humming of the weavers urged her on and on.

When fatigue closed in upon her, she slept. And she paused to eat only because she knew that her body must have fuel. At last she knew that she had finished, for good or ill.

Now her fingers, as she rubbed her aching head, were stiff. It was difficult to flex them. Still, the hum set her body swaying in answer to its odd rhythm.

To Dairine's surprise, no weaver came to inspect her work, to say whether it was adequately or poorly done. When she had rested so that she could once more control her fingers, she began to weave. As she did so, she discovered that she too hummed, echoing the soft sound about her.

As she worked, there was a renewal of energy within her. Maybe her hands did not move as swiftly as the blur of elongated fingers she had seen in her mind, but they followed the rhythm of the hum and they seemed sure and knowing, not as if her own will but some other force controlled them. She was weaving—well or ill she did not know or care. It was enough that she kept to the beat of the quiet song.

Only when she reached the end of her thread supply, and sat with an empty shuttle in her hand, did Dairine rouse, as one from a dream. Her whole body ached, her hand fell limply on her knee. In her was the sharpness of hunger. There was no longer to be heard the hum of the others.

The girl arose stiffly, stumbled to her sleeping place. There was food which she mouthed before she lay down on the cloth, her face turned up to whatever roof was between her and the sky, feeling drained, exhausted—all energy gone from her body, as was logical thought from her mind.

4

DAIRINE AWOKE into fear, her hands were clenched, long shivers shook her body. The dream which had driven her into consciousness abruptly faded, leaving only a sense of terror behind. However, it had broken the spell of the weavers, her memory was once more sharp and clear.

How long had she been here? What had happened when she had not returned to the shore? Had the ship under Vidruth's control left, thinking her lost? And Rothar? the Captain?

Slowly she turned her head from side to side, aware of something else. Though she could not see them, she knew that the looms ringing her in were vacant, the weavers were gone!

Now Dairine believed she must have been caught in some invisible web, and had only this moment broken free. Why had she chosen to come here? Why had she remained? The ribband of stuff was gone from her wrist—had that set some ensorcelment upon her?

Fool! She could not see as the rest of the world saw. Now it appeared that even her carefully fostered sense of perception had, in some manner, deceived her. As Dairine arose, her hand brushed the loom where she had labored for so long. Curiosity made her stoop to finger the width her efforts had created. Not quite as smooth as the ribband, but far, far better than her first attempt.

Only—where were the weavers? The shadow of terror lingering from her dream sent her moving purposefully about the clearing. Each loom was empty, the woven cloth gone. She kicked against something— groped to find it. A collecting rod for thread.

"Where—where are you?" she dared to call aloud. The quiet seemed so menacing she longed to set her back to some tree, to raise a defense. Against whom—or what?

Dairine did not believe that Vidruth and his men would dare to penetrate the wood. But did the weavers have other enemies, and had fled those, not taking the trouble to warn her?

Breathing faster, she set hand on the hilt of the knife at her girdle. Where *were* they? Her call had echoed so oddly that she dared not try again. Only her fear grew as she tried to listen.

There was the rustle of tree leaves. Nothing else. Nor could she pick up by mind touch any suggestion of another life form nearby. Should she believe that the cloth missing from each loom meant her co-workers had left for an ordered purpose, not in flight? Would she be able to track them?

Never before had she put to such a use that sense Ingvarna had trained in her. Also, that the weavers had their own guards, Dairine was well aware. She was not sure that she herself mattered enough in their eyes for them to set any defense against her seeking their company. Suppose, with a collecting rod in her hand, she was to leave the loom place as if on the regular mission of hunting thread?

First she must have food. That she located, by scent, in two bins. The fruit was too soft, overripe, and there was none of the dried sticks left. But she ate all she could.

Then, rod conspicuously in hand, the girl ventured into the woods. All the nearby threads must have been harvested, her questing fingers could find none as she played out her game for any who might watch.

And there *were* watchers! Not the weavers, for the impression these gave her was totally different—more feeble sparks as compared to a well-set fire. As she moved, so did they, hovering near, yet making no attempt to come in contact with her.

She discovered a thread on a tree. Skillfully, she wound it on her rod, took so a second and third. However, at the next, she flinched away. Any thread anchored here must have been disturbed, for she smelled the acrid odor of the sticky coating.

The next two trees supported similarly gummed threads. Did that mean these had been prepared to keep her prisoner? Dairine turned a little. Already, she was out of familiar territory. Thus she expected to meet at any moment opposition, either from the threads or those watchers.

Next was a tree free of thread. Trusting to her sense of smell, she sought another opening, hoping that the unthreaded trees would mark a trail. Though she moved a little faster, she kept to her pretense of seeking threads from each tree she encountered. The watchers had not left her, though she picked up no betraying sound, only knew they were there.

Another free tree—this path was a zigzag puzzle. And she had to go so slowly. One more free tree, and then, from her left, a sound at last—a faint moaning.

It was human, that sound, enough to feed her fear. This—somehow this all seemed a shadow out of her now-forgotten dream. In her dream she had known the sufferer—

Dairine halted. The watchers were drawing in. She could tell they had amassed between her and the direction from which the moan came. Thus she had a choice—to ignore the sound or to try to circle around.

No sign, make no sign that she heard. Keep on hunting for threads—strive to deceive the watchers. All her nature rebelled against abandoning one who might be in trouble, even if he were one of Vidruth's men.

She put out her hand as if searching for thread, more than half expecting to touch a sticky web. From those watchers she believed she picked up an answering sensation of uncertainty. This might be her only chance.

Her fingers closed about a thick band of woven stuff. That led in turn downward to a bag, the flap of the top turned over and stuck to the fabric so tightly she could not open it. The bag was very large, pulling down the branch from which it was suspended. And within in—something had been imprisoned!

Dairine jerked back. She did not know if she had cried out. What was sealed within that bag, her perception told her, had been alive, was now only newly dead. She forced herself to run fingers once more along the surface of the dangling thing. Too small—surely too small to be a man!

Now that the girl knew no human was so encased, she wanted no greater knowledge of the contents. As she stepped away, her shoulder grazed a second bag. She realized that she moved among a collection of them, and all they held was death.

Only, she could still hear that moaning. And it was human. Also, at last the watchers had dropped behind. As if this place were one they dared not enter.

Those bags—Dairine hated to brush against them. Some seemed far lighter than others and twirled about dizzily as she inadvertently touched them. Others dipped heavily with their burdens.

The moans—

The girl made herself seek what hung before her now. Her collecting rod was in her girdle. In its place, she held the knife. When she touched this last bag, feeble movement answered. There was a muffled cry which Dairine was sure was one for help.

She ripped at the silk with knife point. The tightly woven fabric gave reluctantly, this was no easily torn material. She hacked and pulled until she heard a half-stifled cry!

"For Sul's sake—"

Dairine dragged away the slashed silk. There was indeed a man ensnared. However, about him now was sticky web, for its acrid scent was heavy on the air. Against that, her knife was of no avail. To touch such would only make her prisoner, too.

She gathered up the folds of the torn bag and, using pieces to shield her fingers, tore and worried at the web. To her relief, she was succeeding. She could feel that his own struggles to throw off his bonds were more successful.

Also, she knew whom she fought to free—Rothar! It was as if he had been a part of that dream she could not remember.

Dairine spoke his name, asking him if he were near free.

"Yes. Though I still hang. But that now is a small matter—"

Dairine heard a threshing movement, then the sound of his weight touching the ground. His breath hissed heavily in and out.

"Lady, in nowise could you have come at a better time." His hand closed about her arm. She felt him sway and then recover balance.

"You are hurt?"

"Not so. Hungry and needful of a drink. I do not know how long I have hung in that larder. The Captain—he will think us both dead."

"Larder!" That one grim word struck her like a blow.

"Did you not know? Yes, this is the spider females' larder, where they preserve their males—"

Dairine fought rising nausea. Those bags of silk, the beautifully woven silk! And to be used so.

"There is someone—something—out there," he said.

The watchers, her protective sense, alerted her. They were now moving in again.

"Can you see them?" Dairine asked.

"Not clearly." Then he changed that to "Yes!"

"They have throwing cords of web, such as they used on me before. No blade can cut those—"

"The bag!"

"What do you mean?"

Covered with the bag's rent material, she had been able to pull loose his bindings. Those sticky cords could not find purchase against the woven silk. As she explained that, her knife was wrenched from her hold and she heard sounds of ripping.

The watchers—as Rothar worked to empty other bags, Dairine strove to perceive them by mind. They had neared, but once more had halted, as if this were a place which they feared to enter even if ordered to do so to hold the humans captive.

"They spin their lines now," Rothar told her. "They plan to wall us in."

"Let them believe us helpless," she commanded.

"But you think we are not?"

"With the bags, perhaps not."

If she could only *see!* Dairine could have cried aloud in her frustration. Who were the watchers? She was sure they were not the weavers themselves. Perhaps these were the ones who supplied the thread she had harvested so carefully in the past.

Rothar once more was back at her side, a bundle of silk from plundered bags. The girl dared not let herself remember *what* had been in those bags.

"Tell me," she said, "what is the nature of those spinning out there?"

She could sense his deep aversion, revulsion. "Spiders. Giant spiders. They are furred and the size of hounds."

"What are they doing?"

"They are enwebbing an opening. Beyond that on either side are already nets. Now they are disappearing. Only one is left, hanging in the center of the fresh web."

Through her grasp on his wrist, Dairine could read his thoughts, his mind picture, even more clearly, to add to the scene his words had built for her.

"Those others may have gone to summon the weavers"—she made an alarming guess. "So for the present, we have only that one guard to deal with."

"And the web—"

She loosed her hold upon him, clutched a length of the raggedly cut silk. "This we must bind about our bodies. Do not touch the web save with this between your flesh and it."

"I understand."

Dairine moved forward. "I must loose the web," she told him. "The guard will be your matter. Lead me to a tree where the web is anchored."

His hand was on her shoulders. Under his gentle urging, she was guided to the left, was moved forward step by cautious step.

"The tree is directly before you now, lady. Have no fear of the guard." His promise was grim.

"Remember, let nothing of the web touch your flesh."

"Be sure I am well shielded," he assured her.

She fingered rough bark, around her hand and arm the silk was well and tightly anchored. There—she had discovered the end of an anchoring thread. But this was far stronger and thicker than any she had harvested before.

"Ha!" Rothar gave a cry—was no longer beside her.

Dairine found a second thread, felt vibrations along it. The guard must be making ready to defend its web. However, she must concentrate on the finding of each thread, of breaking such loose from the tree.

There was no way for her to know how many threads she must snap so. From her right came the sound of scuffling, heavy breathing.

"Ah!" Rothar's voice fiercely triumphant. "The thing is safely dead, lady. You are right, the cords it threw at me were well warded by the cloth."

"Keep watch. Those which were with it may still return," she warned.

"That I know!" he agreed.

The girl moved as swiftly as she could, discovering thread ends, snapping them. Not only might the spiders return, but the weavers. And them she feared even more.

"The web is down," he told her.

However, she felt little relief at what might be a small victory.

"Lady, now it would be well to wrap our feet and legs with this silk, they could well lay ground webs for our undoing."

"Yes!" She had not thought of that, only of the threading cords from tree to tree.

"Let me get more silk."

Dairine stood waiting, her whole body tense as she strained to use ears and inner senses to assess what might lie in wait beyond. Then he was back and, with no by-your-leave, busied himself wrapping her feet and legs with lengths of silk, tying the strips tightly in places.

While she, who had once so loved the ribband Captain Ortis had shown her, wanted to shrink from any touch of that stuff. Save now it might be their salvation.

"That is the best I can do." He released her foot after tying a last knot about her ankle. "Do you hear aught, lady?"

"Not yet. But they will come."

"Who—what are the weavers?" he asked.

"I know not. But they do not hold our kind high in esteem."

He laughed shortly. "How well do I know that! Yet they did you no harm."

"Because, I think, I am without sight, and also a female who knows a little of their own trade. They are proud of their skill and wished to impress me."

"Shall we go then?"

"We must watch for trees bare of threads."

"Those I can see, lady. Perhaps trusting in my kind of sight, we can go the quicker. There has been much happened. The Captain, though he is still weak, again commands his ship. Vidruth is—dead. But the Captain could not get that scum which his mate has signed to come ashore. And only he can hold them in control."

"Thus you alone are here?"

He did not answer her directly. "Set your hand to my belt. And I shall take heed in my going, I promise," was all he said.

Such a journey was humiliating for Dairine. So long had it been since she must turn to one of her kind as a guide. But she knew that he was right.

So Captain Ortis, released from the evil spell, had taken command. She wondered briefly how Vidruth had died, there had been a queer little hesitancy in Rothar's telling of that. For now she must put her mind on what lay immediately before them. That the weavers would allow them to escape easily she did not believe.

A moment later she knew she was right. They were once more under observation, she sensed. This new, stronger contact was not that of the watchers.

"They come!" she warned.

"We must reach the shore! It is among the trees that they set their traps. And I have a signal fire built there, ready to be lighted, which will bring in the *Sea Raven*."

"Can you see any such traps?"

She could feel his impatience and doubt in the slight contact of her fingers against his body where they were hooked about his belt.

"No. But there are no straight trails among the trees. Webs hang here and there; one can only dodge back and forth between those."

Dairine was given no warning, had no time to loose her hold. Rothar suddenly fell forward and down, bearing her with him. Her side scraped painfully against a broken end of branch. It was as if the very earth under them had opened.

5

THE SMELL of freshly turned soil was thick in her nostrils. She lay against Rothar and he was moving. In spite of her bruises, the jarring shock of that fall, Dairine sat up. Where they had landed she did not know, but she guessed they were now under the surface of the ground.

"Are you hurt?" asked her companion.

"No. And you?"

"My arm caught under me when I landed. I hope it is only a bad bruising and no break. We are in one of their traps. They had it coated over." There was a note of self-disgust bleak in his voice.

Dairine was glad he had told her the bald truth. Rising to her feet, the girl put out her hands to explore the pit. Freshly dug, the earth of its sides was moist and sticky. Here and there a bit of root projected. Could they use such to pull themselves out? Before she could ask that of Rothar, words shot harshly into her mind.

"Female, why have you stolen this meat from us?"

Dairine turned her head toward the opening which must be above. So close that voice, she could believe that a head bobbed there, eyes watched them gloatingly.

"I know not your meaning," she returned with all the spirit she could summon. "*This* is a man of my people, one who came seeking me because he felt concern."

"That with you is our meat!"

Cold menace in that message brought not fear, but a growing anger to Dairine. She would not accept that any man was—*meat*. These weavers—she had considered them creatures greater than herself because of the beauty they created, because of their skill. She had accepted their arrogance because she also accepted that she was inferior in that skill.

Yet to what purpose did they put their fine creations? Degrading and loathsome usage by her own belief. With a flash of true understanding, she was now certain that she had not been free here, never so until she had awakened in the deserted loom place. They had woven about her thoughts a web of ensorcelment which had bound her to them and their ways, just as at this moment they had entrapped her body.

"No man is your meat," she returned.

What answered her then was no mind words, rather a blast of uncontrolled fury. She swayed under that mental blow, but she did not fall. Rothar called out her name, his arm was about her, holding her steady.

"Do not fear for me," she said and tried to loosen her grip. This was her battle. Her foot slipped in the soft earth of the pit and she stumbled. She flung out her arms to keep herself off the wall. There was a sharp pain just above her eyes, and then only blackness in which she was totally lost.

Heat—heat of blazing fire. And through it screaming—terrible screaming—which tortured her ears. There was no safety left in the world. She had curled herself into a small space of blessed dark, hiding. But she could still see—see with her *eyes!* No, she would not look, she dared not look—at the swords in the firelight—at the thing streaming with blood which hung whimpering from two knives driven like hooks into the wall to hold it upright. She willed herself fiercely *not* to see.

"Dairine! Lady!"

"No—" She screamed her denial. "I will not look!"

"Lady!"

"I will not—"

There were flashes of color about her. No mind pictures these—the fire, the blood, the swords—

"Dairine!"

A face, wavery, as if she saw it mirrored in troubled water, a man's face. His sword—he would lift the sword and then—

"No!" she screamed again.

A sharp blow rocked her head from side to side. Oddly enough, that steadied her sight. A man's face near hers, yes, but no fire, no sword dripping blood, no wall against which a thing hung whimpering.

He held her gently, his eyes searching hers.

They—they were not—not in the Keep of Trin. Dairine shuddered; memory clung about her as a foul cloak. Trin was long, long ago. There had been the sea, and then Ingvarna and Rannock. And now—now they were on Usturt. She was not sure what had happened.

But she *saw*.

Had Ingvarna believed that some day this sight would return to her? Not sight totally destroyed, but sight denied by a child who had been forced to look upon such horrors that she would not let herself face the true world openly again.

Her sight had returned. But that was not what the weavers had intended. No, their burst of mind fury had been sent to cut her down. Not death had they given her, but new life.

Then *she*, who had sent that thrust of mind power, looked over and down upon the prey.

Dairine battled her fear. No retreat this time. She must make herself face this new horror. Ingvarna's teachings went deep, had strengthened her for this very moment of her life, as if the Wise Woman had been enabled to trace the years ahead and know what would aid her fosterling.

The girl did not raise her hand but she struck back, her new-found sight centering upon that horror of a countenance. Human it was in dreadful part, arachnoid in another, such as to send one witless with terror. And the thought strength of the weaver was gathering to blast Dairine.

Those large, many-faceted eyes blinked. Dairine's did not.

"Be ready," the girl said to Rothar, "they are preparing to take us."

Down into the pit whirled sticky web lines hurled by the weaver's spider servants. Those caught and clung to root ends and then fell upon the two.

"Let them think for this moment," Dairine said, "that we are helpless."

He did not question her as more and more of the lines dropped upon them, lying over their arms, legs. Dull gray was the cloth which they had wound about them. That had none of the shimmering quality her mind had given to it. Perhaps the evil use to which this had been put had killed that opalescence.

While the cords fell, the girl did not shift her gaze, but met straightly the huge, alien eyes, those cold and deadly eyes, of the weaver. In and in, Dairine aimed her power, that power Ingvarna had fostered in her, boring deep to reach the brain behind the eyes. Untrained in most of the Wise Woman's skills, she intuitively knew that this was her only form of attack, an attack which must also serve as defense.

Were those giant eyes dulling a little? The girl could not be sure, she could not depend upon her newly restored sight.

About them, the web lengths had ceased to fall. But there was new movement around the lip of the pit above.

Now! Gathering all her strength, pulling on every reserve she believed she might have, Dairine launched a direct thought blow at the weaver. That weird figure writhed, uttered a cry which held no note of human in it. For a moment, it hunched so. Then that misshapen, nightmare body fell back, out of Dairine's range of sight. She was aware of no more mental pressure. No, instead came a weak panic, a fear which wiped away all the weaver's strength.

"They—they are going!" Rothar cried out.

"For a while perhaps." Dairine still held the creatures of the loom in wary respect. They had not thought her a worthy foe, so perhaps they had not unleashed against her all that they might. But while the weavers were still bewildered, shaken, at least she and Rothar had gained time.

The young man beside her was already shaking off the cords. Those curled limply away from his fabric-covered body, just as they fell from hers as he jerked at them. She blinked. Now that the necessity for focusing her eyes on the weaver was past, Dairine found it hard to see. It was a distinct effort for her to fasten on any one object, bring that into clear shape. This was something she must learn, even as she had learned to make her fingers see for her.

Though he winced as he tried to use his left arm, Rothar won out of the pit by drawing on the root ends embedded in the soil. Then he unbuckled his belt and lowered it for her aid.

Out of the earth prison, Dairine stood still for a long moment, turning her head right and left. She could not see them in the dusky shadows among the trees, yet they were there, weavers, spinners, both. But she sensed also that they were still shaken, as if all their strength of purpose had lain only in the will of the one she had temporarily bested.

All were that weaver's own brood—the arachnoid-human, the arachnoid complete. They were subject to the Great One's will, her thoughts controlled them, and they were her tools, the projections of herself.

Until the Great Weaver regained her own balance, these would be no menace. But how long could such a respite last for those she would make her prey?

Dairine saw mistily a brighter patch ahead, sunlight fighting the dusk of this now-sinister wood.

"Come!" Rothar reached for her hand, clasped it tight. "The shore must lie there!"

The girl allowed him to draw her forward, away from the leaderless ones.

"The signal fire," he was saying. "But let me give light to that and the Captain will bring in the ship."

"Why did you come—alone from that ship?" Dairine asked suddenly, as they broke out of the shade of the forest into a hard brilliance of the sun upon the sand. So hurting was that light that she needs must shelter her eyes with her hand.

Peering between her fingers, Dairine saw him shrug. "What does it matter how a man who is already dead dies? There was a chance to reach you. The Captain could not take it, for that rogue's spell left him too weak, though he raged against it. None other could he trust—"

"Except you. You speak of yourself as a man already dead, yet you are not. I was blind—now I see. I think Usturt has given us both that which we dare not throw lightly away."

His somber face, in which his eyes were far too old and shadowed, became a little lighter as he smiled.

"Lady, well do they speak of your powers. You are of the breed who may make a man believe in anything, even perhaps himself. And there lies our signal waiting."

He gestured to a tall heap of driftwood. In spite of the slippage of the sand under his enwrapped feet, he left her side and ran toward it.

Dairine followed at a slower pace. There was the Captain and there was this Rothar who risked his life, even though he professed to find that of little matter. Perhaps now there would be others to touch upon her life, mayhap even her heart in years to come. She had these years to weave, and she must do so with care, matching each strand to another in brightness, as all had heretofore been wrought in darkness. The past was behind her. There was no need to glance back over her shoulder unto the dusk of the woods. Rather must she search out seaward whence would come the next strand to add to her pattern of weaving.

THOMAS BURNETT SWANN
Where is the Bird of Fire?

1

I AM very old by the counting of my people, the Fauns—ten full years. Hardly a boyhood, men would say, but we are the race with cloven hooves and pointed, furry ears, descendants of the great god Faunus who roamed with Saturn in the Golden Age. Like the goats, our cousins, we count ten years a lifetime.

And in my years, I have seen the beginning of Rome, a city on the Palatine which Romulus says will straddle the orange Tiber and spread west to the Tyrrhenian Sea, south through the new Greek settlement at Cumae to the tip of Italy, and north through Etruria to the land of the Gauls. Romulus, the Wolf, says these things, and I believe him, because with one exception he has never failed. Now, however, I do not wish to speak of Romulus, but of his twin brother, Remus, who was also part of the beginning. Remus, the bird of fire. With a reed pen, I will write his story on papyrus and trust it to the coffers of time which, cool in the earth, endure and preserve.

My people have wandered the hills and forests of Central Italy since the reign of Saturn: the blue-rocked Apennines where the Tiber springs, and the forests of beech and oak where Dryads comb green hair in the sun-dappled branches. When invaders arrived from Africa and from the tall Alps to the north, Saturn withdrew to a land where the Fauns could not follow him. Forsaken, they remained in Italy, together with the Dryads in their leafy houses.

A Faun's life has always been brief and simple. We wear no clothes to encumber our movements except, in the winter months which have no name, a covering of wolf skin. Our only weapon is a simple sling with a hempen cord. We have no females of our own and must propagate by enticing maidens from the walled towns. I was born to an Alba

Longan who had come to draw water from the Numicus River, outside her city.

Because the city was bowed under King Amulius, a tyrant who some years before had stolen the throne from his kindly brother Numitor and imprisoned him in the palace, she was willing to stay, for a little, with my father in the woods. But when she gave birth to me and saw my cloven hooves and pointed ears, she cried, "I would rather nurse a goat!" and hurried back to her town and its tyrannical king. I was left to be reared by a band of Fauns, who had built a small encampment in the woods, with branches raised on stakes to shelter them from the rains of Jupiter, and a low palisade to guard against marauding wolves or unfriendly shepherds.

It was night and we had built a fire, not only to cook our supper but to comfort ourselves in the loneliness of the black woods. Evil forces had come with the flight of Saturn, Lemures or ghosts and blood-sucking Striges. My father, holding nine black beans in his mouth, made the circuit of our camp and spat them out one by one, mumbling each time, "With this I ransom me and mine." The Lemures, it was said by the shepherds who had taught him the custom, followed and ate the beans and were appeased.

This done, he bathed his hands in a clay vessel of water, clanged together two copper cooking pots left by my mother, and said, "Good Folks, get you gone." At six months old—five years or so in human terms—I was much impressed with my father's ritual. He had never shown me the least affection, but neither had anyone else, and a Faun's place, I judged, was to be brave and clever, not affectionate.

My father looked very gallant confronting the ghosts and very wise since, even while facing them bravely, he spoke with discretion. The other Fauns, eight of them, gnarled, brown, hairy creatures as old, one would think, as the oaks of the forest, squatted on their hooves and watched with admiration and also impatience, since they had not yet enjoyed their supper of roasted hares and myrtle berries.

But scarcely had my father uttered "Good Folks" than a tree trunk crashed through the thin palisade and figures ran through the opening and thrashed among us with wooden staves. Lemures, I thought at first, but their staves and goatskin loin cloths marked them as shepherds. I heard the names "Romulus" and "Wolf" applied to the same man and guessed him to be their leader, the brawniest and the youngest.

The first thing they did was to stamp out our fire. I scrambled to shelter in a thicket of witch grass and watched with round-eyed terror and with ears quivering above my head. By the light of smoldering embers, I saw my father struck to the ground by Romulus himself. I roused myself and scurried to his side, but Romulus's brawny arms scooped me into the air. He raised me above his head, opened his mouth, and gave the high thin wail of a hunting she-wolf. Then with the camp in shambles and the Fauns either fallen or staggering, he leaped through the broken fence with me in his arms, and his shepherds followed him, hugging roasted hares.

I gave my captor a sharp kick with my hoof, but he squeezed me so hard that I gasped for breath, and I thought it best to lie still.

Through the woods we raced; through oak trees older than Saturn, and feathery cypresses like Etruscan maidens dancing to soundless flutes. At last the earth became marshy and Romulus's sandals squished in the sodden grass. I had heard my father speak of this malarial country near the Tiber, and I held my breath to avoid the poisonous vapors. Finally I grew faint and gulped in breaths, expecting the air to burn as it entered my lungs. Throughout the journey, Romulus never seemed short of breath, never stumbled, never rested.

We began to climb and soon reached the summit of what I guessed to be that hill of shepherds, the Palatine. On a broad plateau, hearth fires flickered through the doorways of circular huts. The jogging motion of my captor made the fires seem to dance and sway, and I blinked my eyes to make sure that they were real and not some feverish dream implanted by the swamp. From their pens of stone, pigs grunted and cattle lowed in resentment at being awakened.

One of the huts, the largest, seemed to belong to Romulus. We entered through a low door—though Romulus stooped, he brushed my ears against the lintel—and I found myself in a windowless, goat-smelling room with an earthen floor baked hard by the central fire. Romulus thrust me against a wall where a goat was nibbling a pile of straw. A hole in the roof allowed some smoke to escape, but some remained, and I waited for my eyes to stop watering before I could get a clear look at my captor.

I saw that the powerful arms which had held me belonged to one little more than a boy (at the time, of course, he looked overpoweringly adult, but still the youngest in the hut). Yet he was tall, broad, with muscular legs and with muscles tight across the bare abdomen above his loin cloth. A thin adolescent down darkened his chin, but the furrow between his eyebrows suggested ambitions beyond his years. His crow-black hair, unevenly cropped about an inch from his scalp, rioted in curls.

He stood in the firelight and laughed, and I dimly understood even then why men twice his age could follow and call him Wolf. His handsome face held a wolf's cruelty, together with its preternatural strength. Had I been older, I might have seen also a wolf's fierce tenderness toward those it loves; for this boy, though he loved rarely, could love with great tenacity. As it was, I thought him cruel and powerful, nothing more, and I cowered in terror.

An aged shepherd, his long white hair bound in a fillet behind his head, rose from the fire when Romulus entered with his five men. The five immediately began to laugh and boast about their victory over my people. But when Romulus spoke, the others were silent.

"The Fauns were driving out spirits, Faustulus," he explained to the old man. "Their leader said, 'Good Folks, get you gone,' and in we come! See, I have captured a baby."

"In a year he will be full grown," said Faustulus, whose face, though wrinkled like a brick shattered in a kiln, held an ageless dignity. He was no mere shepherd, I later found, but a man of learning from Carthage. Shipwrecked near the mouth of the Tiber, he had wandered inland to take shelter with herdsmen and married a girl named Larentia. When his rustic bride hesitated to return with him to Carthage, he remained with her people and learned their trade.

"What will you do with him then? Your nocturnal games are childish, Romulus. They bring you no closer to the throne of Alba Longa."

Romulus frowned. "Everything I do, Faustulus, brings me closer to the throne. Tonight we wrestle with Fauns. Tomorrow, soldiers. My men need practice."

His ominous tone and the thought of what he had done to my father made me tremble. I burrowed into the hay where the goat seemed unlikely to eat (a foul-smelling beast, cousin though he was!) and peered out between wisps of straw.

Romulus saw my terror. To Faustulus he said, "You ask me what I will do with our captive. Eat him, before he grows up! Goat flesh cooked on a spit." When Faustulus seemed ill-disposed to the joke (or serious intention, I was not sure which), Romulus addressed a young shepherd with the stupid, flattened eyes of a ram. "Faustulus, it seems, is not hungry. What about you, Celer?"

Winking at Romulus, Celer felt my arms and muttered, "Too thin, too thin. Fatten him first, eh?" His speech was thick and slow, as if he were speaking with a mouthful of wine.

Romulus seemed to debate. "No," he said finally. "He may be thin, but I am hungry. And I want to make a belt of his ears." With that he hoisted me from the ground and lowered me toward the fire by the stump of my tail! I lay very still until I felt the flames singe my ears. Then I began to bleat, and Romulus and the ram-eyed Celer threw back their heads in merriment.

A voice spoke from the doorway, low but forceful. "Put him down, Romulus."

Romulus turned and, recognizing the speaker, tossed me back into the straw. With one tremendous bound he reached the door and embraced his brother.

"Remus," he cried, "I thought they had kept you in Veii!"

Remus returned his brother's embrace with enthusiasm, though his slight frame was almost engulfed by Romulus's massive hug. Like the others, he wore a loin cloth, but of wool, not goatskin, and dyed to the green of the woodpecker which haunts the forests of Latium. Over his shoulder hung a bow, and at his side, a quiver of arrows, their bronze nocks enwreathed with feathers to match his loin cloth. When I saw his hair, bound with a fillet but spilling in silken fire behind his head, I caught my breath. Picus, the woodpecker god, I thought. Who except gods and Gauls, in this part of Italy, had yellow hair (and Etruscan ladies, with the help of their famous cosmetics)?

He released himself from Romulus's hug and walked over to my nest of straw. I squirmed away from him. A god he might be, but after all I had been kidnapped and almost cooked by his brother. I need not have feared him, however. He lifted me in his arms as my mother might if she had not disliked my ears. He cradled me against his smooth bronze chest—fragrant with clover as if he had slept in a meadow—and stroked the fur of my ears, smoothing it toward the tips.

"Little Faun," he said. "Don't be afraid. Tomorrow I will take you back to your people."

"Take him back!" protested Romulus. "I caught him myself."

"Fauns are not animals," said Remus. "At least, not entirely. They have lived in this forest for centuries, and we have no right to capture their children." He pointed to Romulus's bloody stave. "Or fight their fathers."

"They enjoy a fight as much as we do," shrugged Romulus. "We knocked them about a bit, nothing more. If I don't train my shepherds, how can they capture a city?" He grinned broadly, his sharp white teeth glittering in the firelight. "If we don't take the city, what will we do for women?" Celer and the others—except Faustulus—whooped their approval. I was later to learn that these young shepherds, driven from Alba Longa and other towns of Latium for minor crimes, were womanless, and that Romulus had promised a house in the city and a wife for every man. Romulus winked at Celer. "My brother knows much of animals, but nothing of women. We will find him a girl when we take Alba Longa—a saucy wench with breasts like ripe pomegranates."

"Brother," said Remus, a slow smile curving his lips. "What do *you* know of pomegranates? You must have been gardening beyond the Palatine!"

"I know!" cried Celer. "I know about them! The girls I remember—"

"And the girls I imagine," sighed Remus.

"Remember, imagine," said Romulus. "One is as bad as the other. But once we take the city—! Now, brother, tell us about your journey to Veii."

Romulus and the others seated themselves around the fire, while Remus remained standing. Clearly there had been an urgent purpose behind his visit to Veii, the Etruscan city twelve miles to the north. Even at my age, I sensed that purpose and, crouching at his feet, awaited his words more eagerly than those of my father when he told me stories of Dryads and river goddesses. What I failed to understand at the time was later clarified for me by Remus.

The brothers, it seemed, claimed to be sons of the war god Mars and a Vestal princess, Rhea, daughter of that same King Numitor whom Amulius had deposed and imprisoned in the palace. As Remus spoke, I learned how these royal twins in exile longed, above everything, to seize the throne of Alba Longa and restore their grandfather or rule in his place. Remus had gone to Veii to ask the *lucomo* or king to back their cause. It was a brazen thing for a young Latin shepherd, even a deposed prince, to seek audience with an Etruscan king and ask him to make war against a Latin city. But Romulus and Remus, after all, were very young.

I passed into the city (said Remus) with farmers taking shelter for the night. The palace astonished me. Its walls were of purple stucco, and terra cotta sphinxes flanked the entrance. I told the guards that I wished to see their king; that I could speak only with him. Would they tell him that Remus, exiled prince of Alba Longa, sought an audience.

"Yellow Hair," one of them said. "Our king is a jolly man. I will take him word. Your boldness will make him laugh."

After a long time, the guard returned and said that the king would see me now—in his banquet hall. In the great hall, the ceiling was painted with winged monsters and strange enormous cats. The king was lying on a couch with a young woman at his side. She was almost unrobed. He motioned me to a couch next to him and laid his arm, heavy with amber and gold, on my shoulder.

"Remus," he said, "I have heard your story from shepherds who once served Amulius but now serve me. They told me how your mother, the Vestal Rhea, bore you to the God Mars and was buried alive for breaking her vow of chastity. How her uncle, King Amulius, ordered the shepherd Faustulus to drown you in the Tiber, but the shepherd set you adrift in a hollow log. How the log came ashore and a she-wolf suckled you in her cave and a woodpecker brought you berries, until Faustulus found and reared you as his own children.

"The story, it seems, is widely known in the country, though Amulius himself believes you long dead—for tyrants are rarely told the truth. I greet you as the prince you are. But we of Veii want peace with Rome, our closest neighbor. Lead your shepherds against Amulius, if you must, and pray to Mars that the townspeople rise to help you. When you have captured the city, come to me again and we shall sign treaties of amity. Until then, let us be friends but not allies."

I looked closely into his face, the short pointed beard, black as a vulture, the arched eyebrows, the almond eyes, and saw that he would not change his mind. I took my leave and followed the basalt road through the great arched gate and returned to you.

Romulus sprang to his feet, narrowly avoiding my ears. "No help from Veii then. And we are not yet strong enough alone. Thirty shepherds at most, even if we scour the countryside." He fingered the stubble on his chin, as if craving the ample beard—and the years—of a man. "We shall have to wait at least a year before we attack," he continued, with the heavy weariness of one who was not used to waiting —who, at seventeen, was something of a leader already and covetous of wider leadership. "Gather more shepherds around us. Send scouts to the city and feel out the mood of the crowd." Neither Romulus nor Remus had visited Alba Longa: their royal blood made it difficult to pass as herdsmen. "Father Mars, let it not be long!"

He strode to the corner of the hut where a wreathed bronze spear, green with age, lay apart like a holy relic. Mars, as everyone knows, manifests himself in spears and shields. "One day soon, Great Father, let me say to you: 'Mars, awaken!' "

"But even if we take the city," asked Remus, "will our grandfather let us rule? The throne is rightfully his."

"He is very old," said Romulus. "When he steps aside—and he will, very soon—we will build a temple to Mars and train an army even the Etruscans will fear."

"And offer asylum to slaves, and even to birds and animals."

"Oh, Remus," chided his brother. "This is a *city* we will rule, not a menagerie! For once, forget your animals."

"But the city can learn from the forest! Remember when I cured your fever with berries last year? A bear showed them to me, growing beside the Tiber."

Romulus shook his head. "Remus," he smiled, "we shall have our problems ruling together. I sometimes wish that I had no brother or that I did not love him above all men. But let us capture the city—then we shall plan our government. Now it is late. Almost Cockcrow time."

With a warm goodnight to Romulus and Faustulus, Remus gathered me in his arms and left the hut. Of course I could walk quite by myself, but rather than lose my ride I said nothing. Stumbling a bit with his burden, he descended the bank of the Palatine toward the Tiber, which looped like an adder in the starlight and swelled in places as if digesting a meal. Near the foot of the hill we entered the mouth of a cave where a small fire burned on a raised clay hearth. Remus stirred the fire.

"I hate the dark," he said. "It is sad with spirits. People who died like my mother, without proper rites."

Sleepily I looked around me and saw that the earthen floor had been covered with rushes and clover, that a pallet of clean white wool lay in the corner, and that earthen pots lined the opposite wall. There was no one in the cave, but a large dog lay asleep beyond the fire. As we entered, the animal awoke and opened its eyes. A dog indeed! An immense wolf, its yellow-gray fur matted with age, rose on its haunches and faced us. Whether it snarled or grinned, I could not be sure. When Remus bent to deposit me on the pallet, I refused at first to let go of his neck.

"Lie still, little Faun," he laughed. "This is Luperca, my foster mother. It was she who found Romulus and me on the bank of the Tiber and brought us to this very cave. She is very old now. Sometimes she walks in the woods, but at night she shares my cave and my supper." He knelt beside her and stroked her black-rimmed ears. In looking back, I can see the nobility of the scene, this boy with slender hands and hair as yellow as sunflowers, the aged wolf that had suckled him in this very cave. But at six months old, I saw only a flea-bitten animal which monopolized my friend's attention.

"My name is Sylvan," I said haughtily. They were the first words I had spoken since my capture.

"I did not know you could talk," he laughed, rising from my rival and coming to lie beside me.

"Nobody asked me," I said, less haughty now that he had answered my summons. As the firelight dwindled, he talked of Alba Longa and how, when he ruled the city with Romulus, Fauns would be as welcome as men.

"You have surely seen the city," he said, and before I could tell him yes, that my father had carried me once to see the walls and pointed, "That is where your mother ran off to," he continued. "It is a very small city, really just a town. But its houses are white and clean, and its temple to Vesta is as pure as the goddess's flame. It is now an unhappy city. Amulius is a harsh ruler. He killed my mother, Sylvan. He laughed when she told him that Mars was my father: 'You have broken your vow,' he said, and buried her alive in the earth. Faustulus saw her before she died. Just a girl, really. Bewildered but proud. She looked at Amulius with her large black eyes and said: 'Mars is my husband and he will look after my sons.'

"Everyone believed her except Amulius. You see why I hate him. And I have other reasons. He taxes the vintners a third of their wine and the shepherds a fourth of their sheep. What do they get in return? The protection of his soldiers—when they are not stealing wine and sheep! But Sylvan, forgive me. I am keeping you awake with problems beyond your months. Sleep little Faun. Tomorrow I will take you home."

But I already knew that I did not wish to return to my people.

<h1 style="text-align:center">2</h1>

TWELVE MONTHS had passed. Growing two inches a month, I had reached a Faun's full height of five feet. Sometimes I looked in the stream that flowed near our cave and admired my reflection, for Fauns are vain as long as they resemble young saplings, and until they begin to grow gnarled—alas, too quickly—like the oaks of Saturn. My skin was the bronze of Etruscan shields. I wore my ears proudly, waving their silken fur above my head. I combed my tail with a hazel branch and kept it free from thistles and burrs. Remus was eighteen now but soon I would overtake him. Together with Luperca, I still shared his cave and we often hunted together, I with a sling, he with a bow and arrow. But at his insistence we hunted only the lower animals, and then from necessity—the hare and the wild pig. Bears and deer and even wolves had nothing to fear from us. Sometimes on these hunts I saw my father and called to him in passing. The first time he stopped to speak with me. I saw the scar which Romulus's staff had left between his ears. He looked much older than I remembered and a little stooped.

"Is it well with you?" he asked, ignoring Remus.

"Yes, Father," I answered, half expecting him to embrace me. For I had grown used to Remus's affection.

But family ties among Fauns are usually shallow; we live such a little time. "Good," he said. "I thought they might have killed you." He galloped into the forest.

On the Palatine Hill, new huts had risen near that of Romulus and Faustulus. Sabine shepherds had moved there from a neighboring hill, the Quirinal (named for their spear god, Quirinus), and also thieves and murderers from the forest, whom Romulus welcomed too readily into his group. When Remus objected, Romulus argued that thieves, much more than shepherds, could help to capture a town. They could move with stealth and strike with sudden fury.

As shepherds, of course, the brothers must care for a large herd of cattle and sheep, leading them from pasture to pasture both on and below the Palatine, guarding them from wolves and bears, and making sacrifice to the deities called the Pales. The herds they tended belonged to an Alba Longan named Tullius, who often sent an overseer from the city to count or examine his animals; hence, our source of news about Amulius and his increasing tyrannies.

One day the overseer complained that the king had doubled taxes, the next, that his soldiers had insulted a Vestal or executed a boy for petty theft. The soldiers numbered a thousand—all the able bodied men in town were subject to duty at one time or another—and by no means the whole number approved of Amulius or victimized civilians. But a hard core, rewarded with land, cattle, or armor (there was no coinage yet in Latium), served Amulius willingly.

Inflamed by word from the city, Romulus left his herds in the care of sheep dogs and drilled his men; he taught them how to climb rocky cliffs like city walls or move with the swiftness of wolves. On the hill called Aventine, Remus taught them to whittle bows from hickory limbs and feather their arrows for deadly accuracy.

One day, when Remus was resting from both the herds and the training of archers, we had an adventure which seemed at the time unrelated to war and conquest, though it later proved vastly important. I found Remus standing under the fig tree near the mouth of his cave.

He called it the Fig-Tree of Rumina, the goddess who protected suck-ling infants, because he felt that she had watched over him and Romu-lus while they fed from the she-wolf.

Finding him preoccupied, I crept up silently, seized his waist, and rolled him to the grass. My disadvantage in such matches was my tail, which he liked to take hold of and jerk until I begged for mercy. This morning, however, I had caught him by surprise, and soon I was sitting on his chest, triumphant. Already I had grown to outweigh him, with my hooves and my slim but sinewy body.

"Enough," he gasped. "Let me up!" I rose and we fell against each other, laughing and catching our breath.

"The next time you turn your back," he swore, "I will pull out your tail by the roots!" Suddenly he became serious. "Sylvan, my bees are dying."

He had found the bees in a poorly concealed log, stunned them with smoke, and removed them to a hollow in the fig tree, safe from hungry bears and shepherds. For awhile they had seemed to thrive and Remus had been delighted, taking their honey only when they had enough to spare. But now—

"Look," he said, drawing me to the tree which lifted its broad rough leaves to a remarkable forty feet. "The bees are very ill."

I stood beside him, my hand on his shoulder, and peered up into the tree. The bees were carrying off their dead in great numbers. Two of them, overwhelmed by the weight of a third, fell to the ground at my feet.

"They look beyond our help," I said. "But there are other hives, Remus. There will be no lack of honey."

"But I am fond of *these*," he protested, turning to face me. "They are my friends, Sylvan. Not once have they stung me, even when I took their honey." He looked so troubled, so young and vulnerable, that I was speechless. In the year I had known him he had hardly changed. His face was still beardless, his hair like woven sunlight. Who could explain how this blond, green-eyed boy, so different from Romulus, had been born to a dark Latin Mother? Only Mars knew the answer. Yet Rhea, the gentle Vestal, and not the warlike Mars, seemed more truly his parent.

"Wait," I said. "Fauns love honey and sometimes keep bees. My father will know what to do."

We went to find him in the forest south of the Aventine. Though a Faun without clothes and with only a slingshot to encumber me, I could barely keep pace with Remus, who raced through the woods as if he

wore wings. As a matter of fact, he had sewn his loin cloth with those
same woodpecker feathers he used to wreathe his arrows.

"Remus, take pity," I gasped. "I expect you to rise through the
treetops!"

Remus laughed. "They say a woodpecker fed me when I was small."

"And gave you his wings."

In the deepest part of the forest, the trees were tall as hills and older
than Saturn. What they had seen had left them weary—bent, twisted,
and sagging—but still powerful. Oaks were the oldest, but ilex trees,
too, and gray-barked beeches mixed sunlight and shadows in a venerable mist of limbs. Blue-eyed owls hooted among the leaves and magpies,
birds of good omen, chattered in hidden recesses. A woodpecker burned
his small green flame against the greater fire of the forest, and Remus
pointed to him excitedly. "It was one like that who fed me berries."

Remus might have wandered for days without finding my father, but
Fauns have an instinct in the woods and I led him straight to our camp.

Outside the palisade, I bleated like a goat to signify kinship with
those behind the barrier. A section was lifted aside and a Faun, knotty
and mottled like the underside of a rock, filled the entrance. His ears
quivered with suspicion.

"It is Sylvan," I said. "Will you tell Nemus, my father, I wish to see
him?"

The Faun vanished without a word. Another took his place. To
human eyes—to Remus, as he later confessed—there was nothing to
distinguish this Faun from the first. But I knew my father by the scar
on his head and by the length of his ears—they were very long, even
for a Faun.

"Sylvan," he said without emotion. "You want me?"

"Yes, Father. This is Remus, my friend."

"I have seen you together."

"We need your help. Remus's bees are dying. We hoped you could
help us save them. The hive is well placed. But a sickness has taken
them. They are carrying off their dead."

Nemus thought a moment. "Ah," he said. "You must find a Dryad."

"A Dryad, Father?"

"Yes. They speak to the bees. They know all cures."

"But Dryads are rare. I have never seen one."

"I have," said Nemus proudly. "Her hair was the color of oak leaves,
and her skin, like milk—" He broke off, as if embarrassed by his own
enthusiasm. "But I will tell you where to look. Two miles to the south

of this camp, there is a circle of oaks. Some say Saturn planted them. At any rate, one is inhabited by a Dryad. Which one I cannot say. I saw her dipping water from a spring and followed her to a ruined altar among the oaks. There she escaped me. You must hide in the bushes and watch the bees for an hour or more. In the tree where the most of them light will be your Dryad. Taking her nectar, you know. But tell me, Sylvan, why are these bees so important? Let them die. There are others."

Remus answered for me. "They are friends. We like to hear them work outside our cave. Now they are almost quiet."

"Friends, you call them? You are one of the Old Ones, aren't you, boy? Your hair is ripe barley, but your heart might have lived with Saturn. In the old time, there was love in the forest. So the records of my people say. A scrawl on a stone, a picture, an image of clay—always they tell of love. Fauns, men and animals living in harmony." He turned to his son.

"Look after him, Sylvan. Help him to find his Dryad. Help him always. He is one who is marked to be hurt."

I reached out and touched my father on the shoulder, as I often touched Remus. He seemed surprised, whether pleased or offended I could not say. When he turned his back, we went to find our Dryad.

There was the ring of oaks, just as he had said. Not the most ancient trees, if planted by Saturn, but old nonetheless. In their midst rose a pile of crumbling stones which had once formed an altar. Fingertips of sun touched the stones and live plants overrunning them, white narcissi with red-rimmed coronas, spiny-leafed acanthuses, and jonquils yellow as if the sunlight had flowered into the petals. We did not explore the altar however, and risk discovery by the Dryad, but crouched in some bushes beyond the oaks and watched for bees.

Soon a faint buzzing tingled my ears. I cocked them toward the sound and nudged Remus. A swarm of bees was approaching the ring of oaks. We watched them circle and vanish in the oak tree nearest the altar, a large tree with a trunk perhaps twenty feet wide at the base, and a welter of greenery high in the air. Yes, it could easily house a Dryad. I started to rise, but Remus grasped my tail.

"No," he whispered. "Your father said to watch where the *most* bees go."

We waited, I fretfully, since a minute to a man seems like ten to a Faun. Soon I grew sleepy and, using Remus's back for a pillow, slept until he shook me.

"Three swarms have entered that tree and left again," he said. "No other tree has attracted so many. That must be the one."

We rose and walked to the tree in question. "We forgot to ask your father how to get inside," Remus said, staring at the great trunk. Apparently the bees had entered through a hole invisible to us and far above our heads. The trunk was much too rough and broad to climb, and there were no branches within reach of our hands. We circled the base, prodding among the roots for an entrance, but succeeded only in dislodging a turquoise lizard that ran over Remus's sandal and flickered toward the altar.

Thoughtful, Remus stared after him. "Your father lost sight of the Dryad near the altar." We followed the lizard to the crumbling stones and began to kick among the rubble, careful, however, not to crush the jonquils or narcissi. A field mouse, poised for escape, stared at us from the tallest stone. A honey bee surged from a shaken jonquil.

"Sylvan," Remus cried at last. "I think we have found it!" Eagerly he brushed aside bushes and, head first, squirmed into an opening just large enough for one body at a time. I followed him without enthusiasm. Such holes concealed poisonous adders as well as harmless lizards and mice.

The walls were smooth; neither roots nor rocks tore at our bodies. But the journey seemed long and the blackness grew oppressive. I imagined an adder with every bend of the tunnel.

Suddenly Remus stood up and pulled me beside him. We had entered the trunk of a tree, the Dryad's tree, I hoped. Far above our heads, a light shone roundly through an opening. Climbing toward the light, wooden rungs had been carved in the side of the trunk.

"We have found it," he cried, joyfully pulling my tail. "We have found her house!"

"I hope she is more accessible than her house," I muttered.

We started to climb and at once I felt dizzy, since the tree was very tall. I consoled myself that our Dryad would perhaps be beautiful. I had heard that they remained young until they died with their trees. Remus and I saw no women on the Palatine, and imagination was a poor substitute. I had seen him scratching pictures on the walls of our cave, Rumina and other goddesses. He invariably drew them young, beautiful, radiant, the image of Woman in his own young heart. Did such a woman await us now?

Through the circular opening, we drew ourselves into a room which roughly followed the shape of the trunk. Small round windows cut in the walls admitted sunshine. A couch stood across the room, with feet

like a lion's and a silken coverlet prancing with warriors. The air
smelled of living wood, and white narcissus petals carpeted the floor.
Somewhat hesitantly we advanced into the room. At once I collided
with a table and almost upset a lamp like a twisted dragon. Remus,
meanwhile, had settled in a backless chair.

"It is citrus wood from Carthage," he said. "I saw one like it in Veii.
But where is the Dryad?"

"The ladder continues," I noted, hastily ridding myself of the dragon
lamp. "There must be a second room over our head."

Remus walked to the ladder. "I will call her. She must not think we
are robbers."

But he did not have to call, for we heard footsteps descending the
ladder. I lifted the sling from my neck in case the Dryad should be
armed. Aeneas, after all, had found a race of fierce Amazons in Italy.
Dryads who lived alone, Amazons or not, must know how to fight for
their trees.

The Dryad paused at the foot of the ladder and faced us. She was
diminutive even to a five-foot Faun—no taller than four herself. Her
hair fell long and loosely over her shoulders, green hair, a dark leaf-
green that in the shadows looked black, but where the sunlight struck
it smoldered like jade that travelers bring from the East. Her mouth was
pink and small; her skin, the pure fresh white of goat's milk. A brown
linen robe, bordered with tiny acorns, rippied to sandaled feet.

She waited for us to speak and explain ourselves. When we said
nothing—what could we say? our invasion was evident—she spoke
herself, slowly as if out of practice, but with great precision.

"You have violated my house. I was sleeping above when your
clumsy sandals woke me. May Janus, the door-god, curse you with evil
spirits!"

"I am sorry we woke you," said Remus. "As for violating your house,
we were not sure it *was* a house until we found this room. Then we
forgot ourselves in its beauty." He paused. "We have come to ask a
favor."

"A favor?" she cried. "I can guess the favor you mean." She fixed
her glare on me. "You are the worst, you Fauns. Did it never occur to
you to cover your loins, as your friend does?"

"If you notice my nakedness," I said proudly, "perhaps it is because
you admire it. Dryads need men, and Fauns need women. Why should
they not be friends?"

"I have banqueted kings," she spat. "Shall I frolic with strangers who
blunder in from the woods—a Faun and a shepherd?"

"We only want to ask you about our bees." Remus blinked, a small hurt child scolded for a deed he has not committed. He stepped toward her and she did not move. "Our bees are dying and we want you to heal them." They stared at each other. Then, incredibly, unpredictably even to me, he took her in his arms. Like the scolded child who does the very thing of which he has been accused, he kissed her small pink lips. Quick as an adder her hand rose—for the first time I saw the dagger—and raked down his side.

With a cry he withdrew, staring not at his blood-streaked side but at her, and not with anger but shame at his own affront. I seized the knife before she could use it again and caught her, struggling in my arms. Furious because she had hurt my friend, I pressed her wrists cruelly until she lay still. I felt her breasts against my flesh, and then, before I could want her too much myself, said, "Remus, she is yours. Kiss her again!"

"Let her go," he said.

"But Remus, she attacked you. She deserves what she feared."

"Sylvan, let her go," he said, a small boy, baffled, defeated, but not to be disobeyed. I released her. She stared at the streak down his side.

"Please," he said to her. "My bees are dying. Tell me what to do for them."

She drew him into the clear light of a window and dabbed the blood with a corner of her robe. "Burn galbanum under the hive and carry them clusters of raisins in leaves of thyme. They will heal and grow strong again." Then she took a long, unhurried look at him, and I might have been in another oak, for all they noticed me. "You are very young. At first you were hidden in the shadows. When you kissed me, I was sure you were like the rest."

"I am," he said. "I came to ask you about my bees, but I forgot them. I wanted your body. You made me think of grass and flowers in the hot sun. I am like the rest."

"But you told your friend to release me. Why weren't you angry when I hurt you?"

"I was. With myself."

She held his face between her hands. "You are fragrant from the forest. You have lain in clover, I think. Like Aeneas, the Trojan. I loved him, you know. He came to me just as you have. All Latium rang with his triumphs—Turnus defeated, Camilla's Amazons put to rout! He sat on my couch and said, 'Mellonia, I am tired. Since the sack of Troy I have wandered and fought. I have lost my wife and my father and forsaken a queen of Carthage. And I am tired.'

"I took his head between my hands and kissed him, my prince, my warrior. In the years that followed, I watched him grow old. He married the princess Lavinia to found a royal line here in Latium. But he died in my arms, an old man with hair like a white waterfall. And I cursed this tree which kept me young. I wanted to die with Aeneas. The years passed and I did not give myself, even in loneliness. I have waited for another Aeneas."

She turned away from him and stared through a window at a swarm of bees approaching the tree. "They are bringing me honey. My little friends. Your friends too." She faced him again.

"Why are you young? Aeneas was gray when he came to me, older than I in wars and loves, though younger in years. Now I am ancient. But you are young. You cannot have waited for anything very long. Your eyes are naked, a child's. You have not learned to hide your thoughts. You want me and fear me. I could stab you with words more sharply than with this dagger. Why do you come here young and virginal? I will make you old. My face is a girl's, but my eyes are tired with waiting."

Like round-built merchant ships laden with precious oils, the bees invaded the room and unloaded their nectar in a cup of agate. She held out her hand and some of them lit in her palm. "To me, Remus, you are like the bees. Their life is six weeks."

"Then help me to be like Aeneas!"

She reached up to him and loosened the fillet which bound his hair. "It spills like sunflowers. I am cold, so cold. Give me your sunflowers, Remus. Prince of Alba Longa!"

"You know me?"

"Not at first. Only when I had hurt you. I knew you by your yellow hair and your gentleness. The forest speaks of you, Remus. With love."

Their voices blended with the whirr of bees, and the scent of nectar throbbed in my nostrils like a sweet intoxicant. I had lingered too long. I backed down the ladder and returned to the pile of stones.

Much later, when Remus stepped from the tunnel, he said, "Sylvan, you are crying!"

"I am *not* crying," I protested. "Fauns don't cry. We take things as they come and make light of everything. A bramble bush scratched my eyes and made them water."

He looked doubtful but did not press me. In fact, he said little even after we left the circle of oaks and plunged into the forest.

"The Dryad," I asked. "Was she hospitable?" I pressed him with the hope that he would speak of her lightly, as a woman possessed and forgotten. I wanted him to reassure me that I was not replaced in his heart by a bad-tempered Dryad older than Aeneas!

"Yes."

"Remus," I chided. "Your spirits seem mildewed. Have you nothing to tell me about Mellonia?"

It was almost as if the aged Faustulus were speaking. "What is there to say about love? It isn't happiness, altogether; it is sadness too. It is simply possession."

"I should think you would feel like wrestling," I said. "Or drawing one of your goddesses. Or swimming the Tiber. You don't look possessed to me, you look vacant."

"I am thinking of many things," he said. "Yesterday, I wanted to punish the man who had killed my mother, and I wanted to be king for the sake of Fauns and wolves and runaway slaves. Now I want to be king for her sake also."

We were nearing the Palatine. At the mouth of our cave, he stopped and faced me and placed his hands on my shoulders.

"Sylvan, why were you crying back there?"

"I told you," I snapped.

"Did you think she had driven you out of my heart, little Faun?"

He had not called me "little Faun" since that night a year—ten years—ago, when Romulus stole me from my camp. "Yes," I said, losing control of my tears. "And not to a girl but a witch! Or squirrel, I should say, the way she lives in a tree. Remus, she will bite you yet." Being half goat, I always saw people as animals.

He did not laugh at me and try to make light of my tears, but touched his fingers, lightly as butterflies, to my ear. "In the circle of oaks," he said, "there were jonquils and narcissi growing together. There was room for both. Do you understand what I am saying, Sylvan?"

Just then the ram-eyed Celer hurried toward us down the hill. If anything, his eyes had grown flatter and more stupid with the passing year.

"Remus," he called in his thick slurred way. "News from the city! Romulus wants you in his hut."

IN THE early dusk, the hill lay shadowed and strange, and the hut of Romulus seemed misted to stone. Solemn and dignified, sheep roamed the paths and, pausing, were hardly separable from the low rocks which Vulcan, it was said, had thrust from his caverns in a fiery temper. Shepherds and those who had recently joined them, Romulus's latest recruits, loitered in small groups talking about the day's work or tomorrow's drill. The newcomers held apart from the original shepherds. Their garb was the same simple loin cloth, but their faces, though mostly young, were scared and sullen. One, I knew, was a murderer who had fled from Lavinium after killing his wife; another, a parricide from the new Greek colony at Cumae. It was men like these whom Remus wished to bar from the Palatine, and Romulus welcomed because they knew how to fight.

When the wife-killer saw me, he bleated like a goat. Remus wheeled in anger but I shoved him toward Romulus's hut. He must not fight on my account.

"You sound like a frog," I called good-naturedly. "Do it like this." And I bleated so convincingly that she-goats answered from every direction.

A figure loomed toward us, a tall ship scudding in a sea of mist. It was Romulus. To me he nodded, to Remus he smiled.

"Brother," he said. "Gaius is here from the city. He has brought us news." We walked into his hut, where a small, bearded man who reminded me of a water bug, so freely did he skip about the room, was telling a story he seemed to have told several times and would no doubt tell again. His eyes sparkled when he saw Remus and me, a new audience.

"Remus," he said. "And Sylvan, is it not? Listen to what I have seen! I met Numitor in the market yesterday with two attendants. Lately Amulius has allowed him considerable freedom. To appease the people, I expect, and keep them from growling about taxes. Anyway, a half-grown sheep dog was barking at one of Amulius's soldiers. A friendly dog, wanting to play. But the soldier did not. He raised his spear and drove it through the animal's heart. Numitor cried out in anger and raised his staff to strike the man. The soldier, far from cowed, drew his sword, but a barber and a vintner intervened while Numitor's attendants hurried him back to the palace.

"As the old man disappeared, I heard him shout, 'If my grandsons had lived, there would be no soldiers!' Everyone who had watched the scene—myself included—was stirred by Numitor's courage. And everyone wished that there were truly grandsons to drive the soldiers from the street."

With a vigorous skip, he ended his story and smote Remus's shoulder for emphasis. Remus's emotion was evident. His eyes, wide and troubled, mirrored the flames from the hearth: mournful lights in a green, sad forest. As far as I knew, no one had told the overseer the boy's real identity. But Gaius watched him with unusual interest. Perhaps he had overheard the shepherds.

Sparing Gaius the temptation to repeat his story, Romulus led him to the door. "It is bad news you bring us, Gaius. Thank Jove we are kingless here! Do you wonder we stay in the country?"

Gaius smiled ironically. Doubtless he guessed that most of Romulus's men and Romulus himself avoided the city for reasons that had nothing to do with a fondness for the countryside.

"When I think of Amulius," he sighed, "I am tempted to stay here with you. They call him The Toad, you know, though he calls himself The Bear. But Tullius, my master, depends on me. His herds have multiplied, Romulus. I shall take him good news." With a backward wave, he bobbed down the Palatine.

In Romulus's hut, Faustulus, Celer, the twins, and I gathered by the fire to evaluate Gaius's news. On such occasions, Remus always included me, though the first time both Romulus and Celer had objected to the presence of a Faun.

"We have waited with patience," Romulus said with unsuppressed excitement. "Now the mood of the city seems right. They will flock to our side the minute they know us! But they have to be told who we are, and our grandfather is the one to tell them. First we must identify ourselves to him. I will go to Alba Longa tomorrow and get an audience."

"But he lives in Amulius's palace," cried the aged Faustulus bent like a hickory bow but taut, like the rest of us, with the spirit of revolt. "How can you get an audience?"

"He is right," said Remus. "You can't simply walk to the palace as I did in Veii and ask to see Numitor. Amulius's guards are much too suspicious. Your height and bearing set you apart at once. I should be the one to go."

"You, Remus? What about your hair? Blond men in Latium are as rare as virgins in Etruria. They will take you for a spy from the Gauls! Even if they don't, how will you gain an audience with Numitor?"

"I have thought what I would do for some time. First I will dye my hair dark brown. You know the umber that's dug from the banks of the Tiber? I will rub some in my hair and disguise the color. Then I will steal one of Numitor's cows. His shepherds will catch me and take me to Numitor. In the theft of cows, the owner and not the king has the right to pass judgment. Amulius will have no hand in this unless Numitor turns me over to him. I don't believe he will."

"No," said Romulus, "it is much too dangerous. I won't let you take the risk."

Usually I wanted to kick him with both my hooves. Now I wanted to embrace him.

"Remus is right," said that idiot, Celer, mouthing his usual monosyllables. "Old men love him. He's soft and polite. Let him go, Romulus. I have a stake in this too."

Yes, I thought, cattle, women, and a house in town. That's all you want. What do you know about government? Remus, my friend, even if you win the city, you will not have won your justice.

"It is settled then," said Remus with a finality that ended argument.

"And I will help you," I said.

"No, I will do it alone. Fauns are not popular in Latium. The shepherds might kill you right off."

Romulus looked troubled. He stroked his beginning beard and furrowed his brow. This fierce, ambitious young man, who feared neither wolves nor warriors, was unashamedly afraid for his brother. At last, like a father sending his son to fight the Gauls, he placed his hands on Remus's shoulders and said, "Go then, Brother. But while you are gone, I will gather the shepherds. We will be ready to attack the city when you return with word from Numitor. If you don't return within three days, we will attack anyway. The gate is strong, but the walls aren't high to shepherds who live on hills."

"Or to shepherds led by princes," said Faustulus proudly, drawing the twins to his side. "For eighteen years I have called you my sons. In fact, since I found you in the cave at the breast of Luperca. After you had fed, she let me take you—she, your second mother, knew that the time had come for a third. And I carried you back to this very hut and to Larentia, my wife. When Larentia died a year later, I brought you up myself. Now, like the wolf, I must step aside and return you to your grandfather. You will not shame him."

In our cave the next morning, Remus veiled his head in a cloak and addressed a prayer to the god Bonus Eventus, whose image he had scratched on the wall. No one knew the god's true appearance, but Remus had made him young and round-cheeked, with a spray of barley in his hand. Holding out his arms and quite oblivious to Luperca and me, Remus prayed:

"Bonus Eventus, god who brings luck to the farmer with his barley and his olive trees, bring me luck too; send me safely to my grandfather!"

After the prayer, he set a cup of milk before the image, for everyone knows that the gods, whether human as Remus and the Etruscans supposed, or bodiless powers in the wind, the rock, the tree, demand offerings of food. (Luperca eyed the milk, and I hoped that the god drank quickly!) Then he attended to his bees, burning galbanum under the hive and carrying them raisins in thyme.

"Look after them, will you?" he asked. "And Luperca too. You may have to feed her from your hands. She is very feeble." (Not too feeble to drink that milk, I thought.) "And Sylvan. Will you tell Mellonia where I have gone? I had meant to visit her today."

I stamped my hoof in protest. "The squirrel lady?"

"Goddess," he corrected.

"Goddess? She will live no longer than her tree!"

"But her tree has lived hundreds of years, and will live hundreds more. Till Saturn returns. Then he will find her another."

"Is that what she told you? What about lightning? And floods? And woodcutters?"

"Your ears are quivering," he grinned. "They always do when you are angry." And he began to stroke them with his irresistible fingers. "You will see Mellonia? Promise me, Sylvan."

"Don't do that," I cried. "You know how it tickles."

"But you like to be tickled."

"That's my point. You can make me promise anything."

"Would you rather I yanked your tail?"

"All right, all right. I will see Mellonia. Now go and steal your cow."

Of course I had meant all along to help him. My problem was how to remain hidden until he had begun his theft, then run out and implicate myself and share his capture. I followed his tracks at a safe distance. In the marshes, I was careful not to let my hooves squish noisily, and among the Sabine burial mounds, some fresh, some covered with grass, I steeled myself not to take fright at the presence of spirits and break into a gallop. I was careful to keep a tree or a hill between us.

He moved rapidly, as always, but his tracks and my keen sense of hearing kept me on his trail.

Numitor's shepherds lay asleep in the shade, three gnarled men as ancient as their master, who, it was said, hired only the old to work for him because the young reminded him of his lost daughter and grandsons. At the feet of the shepherds lay an aged sheep dog who also seemed to be sleeping. I hid behind an ilex tree and waited for developments.

Remus advanced into the herd and singled out a thin, black cow with a shrunken udder. The dog stared at him sleepily as the three shepherds continued to drowse.

"Ho there, cow, off with you!" Remus cried, scuffing through the bushes with a great racket. Like a child chasing geese, he seemed to enjoy himself.

The dog made no move until he saw the shepherds open their eyes. Then he hobbled forward and warily circled the intruder. The men rubbed their eyes and began to shout, "Thief, thief!" Remus pretended to be bewildered by their cries and ran in circles around the cow. I sprang from my ilex tree and joined him.

"I told you not to come," he whispered, as angry as I had ever seen him.

"Two of them," croaked a shepherd. "And one a Faun. They might have made off with the herd!"

They cautiously approached the spot where we circled the cow, who, unperturbed by our sallies, continued her breakfast of grass, while the dog, preening himself on his vigilance, barked from a bed of lupine.

"Brave dog, brave Balbus," the shepherds muttered, stroking the animal on its flea-bitten head. One of them fetched some leathern thongs from a lean-to beside the pasture.

"Now," said the least infirm of the three, who seemed their leader. "Tie their hands."

Without resistance, we offered our hands. While a shepherd bound them, the leader waved his staff threateningly and the dog rushed in and out barking, then withdrew to catch his breath.

"They are just boys," said our binder, craning his neck and squinting for a clear look. "Need we take them to Numitor in town? It's such a long walk, Julius. A good thrashing may be all they need."

Remus hurried to speak. "My father thrashed me once. That is why I ran away. It made me rebellious. No, I am afraid you must take us to Numitor, unless you want every cow stolen and sold to the Etruscans across the river." He looked very fierce and tilted his head as if to look down in scorn on these men who dared call him just a boy. "And my friend here, the Faun. Would you believe it! Young as he is, he has already carried off six maidens." He added wickedly, "I have carried off seven. But then, I am older."

"Boys they may be," sighed the leader, "but dangerous ones. Numitor will have to judge. Can the two of you get them to town while Balbus and I watch the herds?"

The old men looked at each other and then toward town, as if weighing the effect of twenty-four miles on their weathered ankles. One of them prodded Remus with his staff, the other me. We lurched forward obligingly. "We will try," they sighed.

"Give them a whack if they talk," advised the leader, and off we went to find Numitor.

Alba Longa, the city of Romulus's and Remus's dream, which I myself had seen only from the woods at the foot of its plateau, was in truth a modest walled town of five thousand people. Its rock walls, though tall, were starting to crumble, and its streets grew grass between their cobblestones. Nevertheless the houses glittered whitely with plaster and looked to us both like little palaces.

"And their roots," Remus whispered. "They are covered with *baked clay shingles.*" We were used, of course, to the thatched roofs of shepherd huts. "No danger of fire, no rain soaking through."

"Ho there, thieves, get on with you," our captors shouted, and prodded us with their staves. Everywhere the people stared at our advance, to the obvious pleasure of the shepherds, who cried the more loudly, "Ho there!" A vestal with a black Etruscan vase almost spilled her water. A vintner dropped his pig-skin of wine and a thin red stream trickled among the cobblestones. There were barbers in stalls by the road, and sellers of vegetables holding great melons in their hands; children, sheep dogs, and asses; and, brash and numerous, the soldiers of Amulius. In most Latin cities, I knew, there was no standing army, no soldiers except in wartime. But Amulius's men, brandishing spears tipped with bronze, marched through the city as if to say, "We march on the king's business, and it is not for civilians to inquire its nature."

"Ho there," shouted our captors once too often, and a soldier swatted them both on the head with the shaft of his spear. "Be quiet, old men. You are near the palace." Chastened, the shepherds fell silent and ceased to prod us.

To the left lay the temple of Vesta, raised by Etruscan architects on a stone platform, with four square pillars across the front. Its pediment twinkled with orange terra cotta but not with the images beloved by the Etruscans, for the Latin goddess Vesta lived in the flame of her hearth and had no physical semblance. Opposite the temple crouched the palace of Amulius, a low white rectangle distinguished only by size from the houses we had passed. It was whispered that one day Amulius hoped to build a true Etruscan palace, multi-colored instead of white, with frescoes and colonnades, from the cattle he took in taxes; he would trade them to the Etruscans for architects and stone.

As a start, at least, he had flanked his gate with bronze Etruscan lions, slender and lithe-legged, their tails looped over to touch their backs, their eyes almond-shaped like those of the men who had made them. In front of the lions stood a pair of human guards, only less lordly than the animals.

"Have you business in the king's palace?" one of them demanded. His jerkin was leather, his crested helmet, bronze.

Our captors had not recovered their composure since the scene with the soldier. They stammered awkwardly and Remus had to speak for them.

"They caught us stealing Numitor's cattle. They want to receive his judgment."

At mention of Numitor, the guards softened. One of them leaned into the gate and called, and a withered attendant appeared from the interior. Guard and attendant whispered together; attendant disappeared and shortly returned. He led us down a hallway supported by wooden timbers and into a garden behind the palace, enclosed on three sides by a brick wall. Roses rioted in vermilion chaos and crocuses spilled like golden goblets. It was the first flower garden I had ever seen. I wanted to roll in the blossoms, thorns and all, and kick my hooves in the air. Then I saw the king of the garden and forgot to dream. He sat in a backless chair and stared into a milky pool. His white curving hair was hardly distinguishable from his robes, which billowed around his feet and hid his sandals.

He seemed unaware of us. The attendant drew his attention. "Prince, your shepherds have brought two thieves to receive justice."

He raised his head and looked at us without expression. His face was as yellow and cracked as papyrus, laid in a tomb by pharaohs older than Saturn; god-men ruling the Nile before the Etruscans had passed through Egypt and brought her lore to Italy. A face like papyrus whose writing had been erased by time; inscrutable.

"Bring them forward," he said. We knelt and Remus took his hand.

"My king," he said, nothing more, but with infinite sincerity.

Numitor withdrew his hand and motioned the boy to rise. "I am not your king," he said stiffly. "I never was. You are much too young—the age of my grandsons, had they lived. And they were born after I had lost my throne. Tell me, boy, why did you steal my cattle?"

"Because I wanted to see you."

"To see me? I don't understand."

"As a thief, I knew they would bring me to receive your judgment."

"You were right. Before I deliver judgment, what favor do you ask? I warn you, I have few to give."

"Your blessing. Your love."

"An old man loves his children. I have none. His grandchildren. I have none. My heart has rid itself of love. A nest without swallows. But what is your name? Something about you stirs me to remember—"

"A shepherd named me Remus, and my brother, Romulus. We are twins."

The names, of course, were meaningless to him, but he caught at Remus's last word. "Twins, you say?"

"Soon after we were born, our mother was buried in a pit and we were taken to be drowned in the Tiber. But Faustulus saved us and made us his sons."

Numitor groaned and surged to his feet, like the geysers of Vulcan, white with borax, which roar from the earth and shudder in the air.

"What are you saying?" he thundered. "You lie as well as steal. I saw my grandsons when Amulius took them from my daughter. One had dark hair, darker than yours. One had gold, gold like this flower." He crushed a crocus under his sandal. "A gift from the god, his father. Which are you?"

"The gold-haired." Remus fell to his knees and ducked his head in the pool, which began to run rivulets of brown. He rose and shook out his hair. Though streaked with umber, it glittered yellowly like gold among veins of iron.

I watched the papyrus mask. The worn and time-veined surface trembled and softened, the forgotten language of love spoke in misting eyes. He ran his hand through Remus's hair and felt the molten umber between his fingers.

"Time," he said. "Give me time. I am not used to tears. They burn like wine." An old man sightless with tears, he took the boy in his arms. "Rhea," he whispered, "your son has come back to me."

"You are a senile old fool," a voice croaked from the door. "This boy has played a trick on you. He should be taught a lesson."

I recognized Amulius though I had never seen him. I knew him from the veined toad eyes which never blinked, the hunched and dwarfish shape. Amulius the Toad.

"Guards!" he called.

"Go to Romulus," Remus whispered. "I will hold them off."

Behind me a prince and a tyrant grappled in roses and thorns. With a single thrust of my hooves, I clutched the top of the wall and drew myself up the bricks. "Bonus Eventus," I prayed, "help me to bring him help!"

4

I LANDED in a narrow street behind the palace and my hooves clattered on the cobblestones. An old woman, carrying melons from market, paused in surprise, then trudged down the street with a shrug that seemed to say: "Let Amulius protect his own palace. If Fauns can rob it, good for them." There was no one else in sight, but an ass, tethered to a stake, watched me vacantly. His master, it seemed, had business in the shop of a dyer, which reeked with decaying trumpet shells, much prized for their purple dye.

Remus had given me seconds. As soon as the guards overpowered him, they would follow me or send their friends. I must reach the gate quickly; I must run. But a running Faun, in a city of soldiers, would look suspicious. They would take me for a thief. Nibbling grass between the stones, the tethered ass browsed in the sun. I loosed his rope and kicked him with the full force of my hoof. He galloped down the street.

"Whoa, whoa," I shouted, galloping after him as if to recover my own escaping property. Round a bend he sped and into the central street and straight toward the towers of the gate. When he slowed, I slowed. When he quickened, I quickened and yelled "Whoa!" A hand reached out to stop him; I caught my breath; but he burst free and charged for the gate. The guards laughed and spurred him on with a slap to his flank and a cry of "Giddyap!" Upsetting a potter's cart, laden with orange clay lamps, I hurried after him.

"May thieves crack your skull," cried the potter. I waved without looking back and raced down the hill toward the forest. To the left of me, Lake Albanus glittered in the afternoon sun, and skiffs of hollowed alder poised like dragonflies on its molten turquoise. Ahead of me dusky cypresses signaled the path to the Palatine.

I found Romulus with Celer and the herd at the foot of the Palatine. When I told him what had happened, he turned very pale and drove his staff into the ground.

"I *knew* I should have gone."

"Never mind," I consoled. "Who can say no to Remus?"

"If they harm him, I will burn the city! Celer, watch the cattle." He hurried me up the hill, making plans as he went. "We will attack tonight. In the dark, we may be able to climb the walls before we are seen."

"But the people won't know us. Remus had no chance to tell Numitor about our plan."

"No matter. We can't delay. Once in the city, we will shout his name—'Long live Numitor!'—and hope to rally support."

Romulus was right, we could not delay. But what could we do against walls and soldiers? If we battered down the gate with a tree, soldiers would surely be waiting. If we climbed the walls, they might see us and still be waiting. Since Alba Longa stands on a ridge, it is difficult to reach the walls without detection, even at night. I said nothing; Romulus knew the dangers. But I could not risk Remus's life with such a puny effort.

I descended the Palatine and headed for the cave. I wanted to think. On the way I passed Celer with the herd. He leaned against a rock, staff in hand and a straw between his teeth. Complacent oaf, I thought. Calm as a sheep when Remus's life is in danger.

"So they shut the Woodpecker in a cage," he grinned. "Big games tonight, eh?" Before I could hoof him, he changed the subject. "Sylvan, I hear you found a Dryad. Where's her tree?"

"She is Remus's Dryad," I said indignantly.

"And yours," he smirked. "And mine, if you show me her tree."

"North of the Quirinal," I lied. "An ilex tree with a lightning mark on the trunk." I lowered my ears to muffle his answer and hurried to the cave. Inside, I threw myself on a pallet of clover, but the fragrance reminded me of Remus and clouded my thoughts. I paced the floor. Luperca crept from the rear of the cave and pressed against my leg. I knelt and took her head in my hands.

"Luperca," I said. "Remus has gone to the city. They have taken him captive. What shall I do?" She looked at me with such intelligence that I felt she understood my words; she began to whine and I wished that I understood hers.

Then I heard a swarming of bees outside the cave. I walked out and looked at the hive in the fig tree. Mellonia's remedy had worked. The bees were recovering their health. Mellonia! She was the one to help Remus. She had cured his bees. Might she not have secrets to release him from prison? After all, she had loved Aeneas, the incomparable warrior. I galloped for the circle of oaks. Behind me a conch shell boomed from the Palatine, and I knew that Romulus was summoning his men.

I stood at the foot of her oak and called: "Mellonia, I have come from Remus." No answer.

Again I called. A voice, muffled by branches, answered. "I am coming down. Wait for me by the altar."

In a surprisingly short time, she emerged from the tunnel. She was not the Mellonia I remembered, hard and queenly, but a pale tree child blinking in the alien sun. She raised a hand to shelter her eyes.

"He is hurt?"

"No. But Amulius has taken him prisoner." I told her about his capture.

"What does Romulus mean to do?"

I explained his plan—as much as I knew.

"Romulus's shepherds," she sighed. "I have seen them drilling in the woods. They are brave but they have no armor. They have no spears. Only their staves and bows. What good are bows against walls, or in fighting hand to hand through the streets? They will cost Remus his life."

"Mellonia," I cried desperately. "You can save him. I know you can."

She touched my cheek with the tips of her fingers, like little blades of grass. "You are a good friend to him, Sylvan. You and I and the forest, we are his friends. Perhaps we can save him. Go back to Romulus now. Say that when Arcturus shines directly over the temple of Vesta, I will come to him in the woods below the city gate. Let him do nothing till I come, but have his men in readiness."

I pressed her hand; it was warm and small like a swallow. "Mellonia, I have not been kind to you."

"Nor I to you. But Remus has made us friends. You are his brother, Sylvan. Far more than Romulus, the Wolf. Trust me."

I turned to go and she called after me. "Sylvan, wait. In truth I am afraid for him. The forest is restless. The cranes have been flying all day, as they do before a storm. But there has been no storm. And all last night, owls cried in my tree. I have looked for vultures, birds of good omen. Especially for woodpeckers. There are none to be seen."

"Good omens?" I cried. "You are Remus's good omen!"

* * *

Tall above Alba Longa, the temple of Vesta burned in the moonlight, and orange Arcturus, the star of spring, climbed above the stone pediment. Fifty shepherds crouched in the forest below the gate: Romulus with his ancient spear consecrated to Mars; several with bows and arrows, the use of which Remus had taught them; but most armed only with knives, staves, or slingshots. The bodies of all were bare except for loin cloths—no greaves on their legs nor metal corselets to hide their chests and backs from the plunge of an arrow or the bite of a sword.

Their battering ram was an elm tree cut in the forest; their ladders looked as frail as saplings untested by storms. How many shepherds, I wondered, would survive the night? I was glad that the bent Faustulus, at Romulus's insistence, had remained on the Palatine. A momentary pity possessed me. Who could blame them, rough though they were, for wanting houses in town and women to tend their hearths?

"We can wait no longer," said Romulus. It fretted him following orders from a Dryad he had never seen. Nothing but concern for Remus, I think, and knowledge of his own inadequacy, could have made him listen at all.

"But Arcturus has just now risen above the temple," I protested. "Before, it was still climbing. I know she will come!"

"What can she do if she does? We are fools to try the gate, which seems to be her intention. We should scale the wall on the far side."

Then I heard the bees. "Hush," I said. "She is coming."

My ears quivered. The droning grew louder; curiously the men peered into the forest. I felt like a traveler approaching a waterfall. At first he hears just a murmur, faint and distant. Then the trees fall away and the murmur roars in his ears.

Now they surrounded us, bees beyond counting. Kindled by the moonlight, they curved like a Milky Way above our heads and wove a shield from the darkness. Mellonia led them. She seemed to be made out of leaves and mist and moonlight. She walked in a cloud of bees, and I had to look closely to see that her feet touched the ground. The men gaped at her; Romulus too, and that stupid Celer most of all.

"Is that your Dryad?" he whispered. "She looks like a goddess!"

I gaped too, but less at her beauty than at the dark stains on her face—were they blood?—and at her torn, disheveled robe.

"It is nothing," she whispered, passing me. "Part of my plan." She singled out Romulus. It was not hard for her to recognize him, the brawniest of all of the young men and the only one with a spear.

"Romulus," she said. "Brother of Remus, I salute you. When the gate is open, I will raise my arm. Enter with your men."

Before he could question her somewhat cryptic directions, she was gone, climbing the hill toward the gate. The bees swirled high above her; their droning died, their fires flickered out in the darkness.

"What does she mean to do?" Romulus gasped. "Sylvan, she is mad."

"Or a witch," cried Celer, staring after her.

The men shuddered and whispered among themselves. Something moved in the forest. Shapes inseparable from the trees, not to be seen, scarcely to be heard. Something breathed.

"Striges," went the whisper. "Vampires."

"Lemures. She sent to make us follow her!"

Now she was midway to the gate. "Guards," she called out, her voice broken as if with pain, yet strong enough to be heard in the towers that flanked the gate. "Help me. I am hurt." She fell to her knees. "Help me."

Silence. Then a voice, hesitant, testing. "Who are you?"

"I have come from Veii. Wolves attacked my escort in the forest."

Creaking, the gate swung inward on its massive stone pivot. A lamp flickered in one of the towers, vanished, reappeared on the ground. Its bearer paused in the gateway. Mellonia rose, staggered, fell again. "Help me." The guard walked toward her, sword in hand.

She raised her arm.

"They will shut the gate in our face," groaned Romulus. "We can never climb the hill in time!" But his hesitation was brief. Whatever his faults, he was not a coward. With a low cry to his men, he raced up the hill toward the gate. I ran beside him. The hill swelled above us, endless and black. I felt like a swimmer in the trough of a mountainous wave. Would we never make its crest?

Kneeling beside Mellonia, the guard raised his head and saw us. "Shut the gate!" he shouted. He scurried to safety; the gate swung inward, monstrous, implacable.

Then a shadow crossed the moon. I looked up; my ears stood on end. Mellonia's bees! In a deadly amber stream, they poured from the sky. A shout, a thrashing in the tower. The gate groaned slowly to silence, half open.

I dug my hooves in the turf, kicked aside stones, drove myself furiously forward. Romulus tripped and I heaved him back in the path. Through the half open gate, I saw the movement of men, the flash of a spear, the swirling of bees and bronze. Then we were in the city. The bees withdrew and left us to fight our battle.

A soldier charged me, leveling his spear and grinning like the demons of death in Etruscan tombs. I raised my sling and caught him in the teeth. He stopped, a round black hole where his teeth had been, and stared at me. Blood gushed out of the hole. Like a broken bow, he fell at my feet.

"We have them outnumbered," Romulus shouted. "They are falling back!" Spears wavered, shields swung aside. The street near the gate lay empty except for ourselves.

"Numitor! Numitor is king!" Romulus began the cry, and the rest of us took it up. "Numitor is king!" Dazed with too easy a victory, we surged toward the heart of town, the temple, the palace, and Remus.

But the street was barred. A row of spears glittered across our path, like the oars of a galley raised from the sea in sparkling unison. A wall of spears to bar our advance, and behind them another, another, and finally a row of archers, grim as Etruscan bronzes. The soldiers we had routed were few. Now we must meet an army. Already our limbs were streaked with blood. We had spent our wind in the climb and the fight at the gate. We had lost some men—six I counted with a hasty glance in the street. We were tired, outnumbered, and armorless. How could we shake those fixed, immovable spears?

"Where are the bees?" I cried. "Mellonia, where are your bees?"

Then I saw the wolves, thudding through the gate and into the street. Muffled as raindrops, their feet padded on the stones. My nostrils quivered with the scent of fur, grassy and wet from the forest. I felt hot breath and smelled decaying flesh. We crouched against the walls to let them pass. The wolves ignored us. Straight toward the soldiers they went, the leveled spears and the tightening bows. Mellonia and Luperca followed them.

Mellonia spoke so softly that I could not make out her words, or should I say incantation. It is said that the Etruscan princes, when they hunt, bewitch the animals with the piping of flutes and lure them into their nets. Mellonia's voice, it seemed, had such a power over wolves. Sometimes, it is true, an animal balked or threatened to turn from the pack. But Luperca, surprisingly agile, snapped at his heels and hurried him back into line. The venerable wolf who had suckled my friend in a cave and the aged, ageless Dryad: both were queens.

The line trembled, the spears wavered, like oars engulfed by a wave. The long taut bows swayed in the archers' arms. And the wolves attacked. High above the wavering spears, a body spun in the air. Spears shot up to ward off its deadly fall. The line was broken. The archers never fired. Men and animals rolled in the street; armor clattered on stones and weighed men down; animals sprang on their chests and tore at their naked faces. Spears were useless, arrows worse. A few had time to draw daggers. Most used their hands.

Some of the men broke free and began to run. Wolves loped after them. Wounded, in pain, the soldiers reeled against doorways and beat their fists for admittance. The doors remained shut.

The city had wakened. On the rooftops, torches flared, people crouched behind them and stared at the rout of the tyrants who, a few hours ago, had tyrannized Alba Longa. Now a weird procession formed: Mellonia and Luperca with the wolf pack, a cloud of returning bees above their heads: Romulus with his shepherds, raising their staves in token of victory.

But an army's march is slow, and Remus was still in the palace. Ignoring the wolves, I pushed to Mellonia's side.

"Come ahead with me," I urged.

She nodded. "Luperca can watch the wolves."

In a cloud of bees, we raced through the market of silent stalls, where tomorrow the vintner would hawk his wine and the farmer his gourds and grapes. A terrified soldier reeled from our path. A sheep dog snapped at our heels but, hearing the wolves, ducked in an alleyway.

The palace was almost dark. The temple of Vesta, across the road, lent a fitful light from its eternal hearth. The Etruscan lions growled in brazen impotence. They had no soldiers to guard them. The gate was unbarred. We entered the central corridor and, following a light, turned aside into a large hall.

"Amulius's audience room," Mellonia said. She pointed to a curule chair of gold and ivory raised on a stone platform. A tall candelabrum, hung with lamps, cast mournful flickerings on the tapestry behind the throne. Seeing that the room was empty, I turned to continue our search. Mellonia stopped me.

"We will lose minutes. Let my bees find him." She raised her arms and inscribed in the air a series of circles and lines, like the loopings of bees when they tell the location of flowers. The bees understood and swarmed from the room.

We looked at each other. Where was the powerful sorceress who had opened the gate of a city to admit the forest? Like a swallow after a storm, beaten and bruised, she sank to the floor. I motioned her to sit in the chair.

"No," she said. "Amulius sat there." She stared at the plum-colored hangings behind the chair. "Even his dye is false. Not Tyrian purple, the color of kings, but the dye of trumpet shells."

I sat beside her and rested her in my arms. "It will be all right," I said. "Soon we will have him back again."

"Now perhaps. But later? He will always be hurt, always be threatened."

"We will look after him."

"We are vulnerable too. Even now I am weary for my tall bark walls. I cannot leave them for long."

Abruptly the bees returned, circling in the doorway to catch our attention. In the dark corridor, we lost sight of them, but their droning guided us through several turnings and down a stairway redolent of rocks and moisture. We stepped into a cellar lit by a single torch, smoky and pungent with resin. The room opened through a barred door into a small cell. The door swung wide on its pivot and Amulius's body, clutching a dagger, hunched like a bloated toad across the sill. Remus stood in the cell beyond the body.

"He came to get me," he said, dazed.

"And you had to kill him?"

"No. They did." He pointed to the bees which had lit on the pallet in his cell. I knelt beside the body and saw the red welts, a hundred or more, and the closed swollen eyes.

"He unbolted the door and said that my friends were coming; he was going to make me his hostage. I stepped backward. He drew his dagger, and they hit him from the back like a hundred hundred slingshots. He scraped at his eyes, groaned, and fell to the floor. Then you came."

"The bees love you," Mellonia said proudly. "Some may have come from your own hive. They sensed your danger."

He buried his face in the fall of her hair and she held him with exquisite tenderness. For the first time, I loved him loving her. Two children they seemed, warm in each other's arms and forgetful that love, however strong, is also brief, because it is bound by the frailties of the flesh. I wanted to enfold them in the magic circle of my own love and blunt, like a ring of shields, all menacing arrows. But I was a Faun, briefer than men.

At last she drew apart from him. "How pale you have grown, shut up in the palace. In a single day, you wilt like a lotus."

"Come," I said. "We must find Romulus. He is much concerned." We climbed the stairs.

The palace thundered with men. Their shadows bristling on tapestried walls, they stalked through the rooms with torches and gasped at treasures which, to the eyes of a shepherd (and mine as well), rivaled the riches of Carthage. A fan made of peacock feathers. Pearls as big as acorns. A mirror whose handle was the neck of a graceful swan! Guards and servants were nowhere in evidence. They must have fled with our arrival, and the palace lay temptingly accessible. The shepherds seemed to forget that they had come to liberate and not to loot.

We found Romulus in Amulius's audience room, and I must say for him that he was not himself looting, but, torch in hand, trying to organize a search for Remus. He was having trouble; his men were more concerned with found treasures than with lost brothers. When he saw us, he whooped like a Gaul on the warpath. Throwing his torch to me, he lifted his twin from the floor and hugged him with brotherly ardor. Often he seemed the crudest of warriors, a brash young wolf who, in spite of his tender years, had somehow missed youthfulness. But with Remus he was youthful as well as young, and only with Remus could I like him.

"We have taken the city," he cried, while I steadied his torch and shielded my eyes from its sputtering resin. "Brother, Alba Longa is ours!"

"And Numitor's," Remus reminded us. "Has anyone seen the king?"

In a room at the back of the palace, we found him on a couch, his white beard overflowing a crimson coverlet. He had slept through the fall of the city, and he thought himself still asleep when Remus explained what had happened and said, "This is your grandson, Romulus."

At last the sleep had cleared from his eyes. He held out his arms to Romulus, though clearly he was ill at ease with this great muscular grandson, smelling of wolves and blood, who came to him from the forest.

Romulus and Remus supported the king between them and, with Mellonia and me, headed for the gate. Along the way, in corridors and sleeping chambers, Romulus gathered his men, and a sizable procession emerged from the palace. Beyond the Etruscan lions, twenty or more shepherds lounged or sat in the street, placed there by Romulus and awaiting his signal to enter the palace. They stared at Numitor with mild curiosity.

On the roofs of the houses, the townspeople waited too. But Mellonia's wolves still prowled the streets, and the timorous Alba Longans, though visibly moved at the presence of Numitor, were not yet ready to risk descent.

Romulus stepped forward with Numitor and raised the aged king's arm into the air. "People of Alba Longa, your king is restored to you!"

With a slight motion, Numitor released himself from Romulus's support and stood alone. He straightened his bowed shoulders and lifted his weathered face. Forgetting their timidity, the people cheered as if they themselves had restored him to his throne. The shepherds were silent; it was not Numitor they wanted but Romulus. Had they fought to restore an old man to a throne he had lost before they were born? I watched Romulus's face and saw his impatience for Numitor to address the people and abdicate in favor of his grandsons. The Wolf had done the honorable thing; he had proclaimed his grandfather king. The next move was Numitor's.

Meanwhile, Mellonia had left us. I saw her in the street with Luperca, gathering her wolves and bees as a shepherd gathers sheep. Remus saw her too, but she shook her head: he was not to follow.

"She is tired," I whispered. "She wants her tree."

"People of Alba Longa," Numitor was saying in a clear, resonant voice. "Amulius is dead. My grandsons have come back to me. A staff in my old age, they will help me to live out my years—to rule wisely if only for a little while. As king of Alba Longa, I hereby declare an amnesty to all who supported Amulius. I will end my reign with peace, even as I began it. The years between are forgotten." He paused, I should say posed, and lifted his arms with the studied flourish of a mime. A king, it seemed, even in exile, never forgot the gestures of royalty.

The applause was vehement.

"Long live Numitor!"

"King of Alba Longa!"

The people clambered from the rooftops and thrust their way through Romulus's men to the feet of their restored king. Remus tightened his hand on my shoulder. Romulus paled. A mutter, lost in the general cheering, ran among the shepherds. We had rescued Remus; for me, that was enough. But the shepherds wanted more, and rightly, while Romulus and Remus had dreamed of a throne since childhood.

At last the old man's strength was failing. "Help me to bed, will you, my grandsons? Tell your men the largess of the palace is theirs. The wines, the fruits, the venisons. Tomorrow I will rule—with your help. Now I will sleep."

When Numitor slept and Romulus's men roamed the palace, a sausage in one hand, a cluster of grapes in the other, Romulus, Remus, and I talked in the garden. The jonquils, beaten gold goblets by day, had paled with the moon into silver and seemed to be spilling moonlight into the pool.

For once, Celer was absent from our council. Romulus assured us that he had not been wounded, but no one had seen him since Numitor addressed his people.

"Chasing some wench," I muttered.

Our conversation turned to Numitor.

"Did you see his excitement?" Remus asked. "He will reign for years!"

"Then we will build our own city," Romulus announced. "Even if we reign with Numitor, we can't have our way in Alba Longa. What changes can we make while an old man holds the throne? His people will not accept changes as long as he lives. They have had a tyrant; now they want a venerable figurehead. Let them have what they want. We will build *our* city on the Palatine. Already we have a circle of huts. Next, add a wall, then a temple to Mars, then a place of government—"

"And a shrine to our mother," said Remus, kindling to the plan. "A temple to Rumina and a park for the birds and animals. I think, though, Romulus, that the Palatine is not the best hill. True, there are huts already. But some of the owners are thieves and cutthroats, as you well know. Let them keep their huts, but in our new city there will not be room for such men. Why not build on the Aventine? It is almost as high, and closer to the forest, to Mellonia and her friends, who won us our victory."

"Ask Father Mars who won our victory," Romulus snapped. "Mellonia helped, it is true. But my shepherds, Remus, took the city. The men you call thieves and cutthroats."

"Men like Celer make good warriors," Remus granted. "But not good citizens. I mean no disrespect to the man. But Romulus, can you see him worshiping in a temple or sitting in a senate house? Give him a woman and herds, but leave him on the Palatine. Build our city on the Aventine!"

"Ask for a sign from heaven," I interrupted. The gods, I thought, should favor Remus, who worshiped all of them and not the war god only. "Consult a sheep's liver, as the Etruscan augurs do, or watch for birds of good omen."

"Very well," said Romulus reluctantly. "We shall ask for a sign. Early one morning—the best time for omens—we shall climb our respective hills and watch the sky for vultures, the luckiest of birds. Whoever sees the most shall choose his hill for our city. Now, my brother, let us sleep before we quarrel."

The palace abounded in couches; I chose one with feet like an eagle's and fell asleep, dreaming of vultures.

5

WITH LESS reluctance than the brothers anticipated, Numitor received their declaration that they wished to build a city on the Tiber. Doubtless realizing that such a city would stand as a safeguard between Alba Longa and the Etruscans—now friendly, but expanding—Numitor had promised to send workmen and materials, and he had already purchased the herds of Tullius and given them to the twins who had long been their shepherds.

But first a site must be chosen. At sunrise three days after the capture of Alba Longa, Remus and I stood atop the Aventine, watching for vultures. The day had been chosen because it was sacred to the Pales, deities of shepherds who had given their name to the Palatine. Before sunrise, Remus had fumigated his herds with sulphur to drive out evil spirits and scattered the stalls with arbute boughs, beloved by the goats, and wreaths of myrtle and laurel. Later the shepherds on the Palatine would leap through bonfires and, facing the east, pray to the Pales. A lucky day, one would think, for omens. But for whom?

"I wonder why the gods favor vultures," I said, wrinkling my nose as I pictured the birds at a feast. "Such an ugly creature."

Remus laughed. "Ugly, yes. But helpful. They rid the forest of carcasses. And they never kill."

"Which way will they come?"

"They may not come at all. They are very rare in this country. Mellonia says to watch the river, where the animals go to drink and die."

He had visited her daily since the fall of Alba Longa. Her name had grown pleasant even to my long ears. Instead of his usual loin cloth, he was wearing a tunic, almost sleeveless and falling just below the thighs, which the Dryad had woven from rushes and leaves. Soon it would wilt, but Mellonia had promised him a leaf-colored garment of wool to take its place. "Now you are part of my tree," she had said. "Green leaves, green tunic. You carry the forest with you."

"But how will Romulus know if we *really* see the number we say?"

"He will take our word," said Remus, surprised.

"And you will take his?"

"Of course."

"It means a lot to him to build on the Palatine."

"I know. But he would never lie to us."

"Remus. Have you ever thought of building your own city—without Romulus. It won't be easy to rule with him. If you win your hill, it will be even harder. And men like Celer, how will you keep them out? Or make them behave if they enter?"

"I will build with Romulus or not at all. He is my brother. Do you realize, Sylvan, I shared the same womb with him? We have never been apart."

"You love him deeply, don't you?"

"He is one of three. You, Romulus, Mellonia. I love Mellonia as someone beyond me, a goddess or a queen. Green leaves in the uppermost branches of a tree. I love her with awe and a little sadness. I love you, Sylvan, as someone close and warm. A fire on a cold night. Barley loaves baking on the hearth. You never judge me. With you I am most myself. And Romulus? The stone pillars of a temple. The bronze of a shield. Hard things, yes. But strong and needed."

"You are very different from Romulus. He is not always a shield. He is"—I chose my words carefully, not wishing to offend him—"rash in some ways."

"I know," he said sadly. "And I try to temper his rashness. In return, he gives me courage."

"Courage, Remus? You have strength enough of your own. I never saw you hesitate when you knew what was right."

"You can't see my heart. It leaps like a grasshopper sometimes! Romulus, though, is fearless."

Then you are the braver, I thought. You conquer fear, while Romulus's courage is thoughtless, instinctive. But I said nothing; he would only make light of himself.

And then we saw them: High above the orange turbulence of the Tiber, six vultures glided to the north. Clumsy birds, ugly—I had not changed my mind—but oh, how welcome.

"Remus, you have won!" I cried. "Even if Romulus sees them, we saw them first. They are flying *toward* and not away from him."

We raced down the hill and scrambled up the Palatine, a few hundred yards to the north.

"Slow down, Woodpecker," I shouted. "Your tunic has given you wings."

He laughed and tore me a leaf from his waist. "Catch my feathers and fly!"

In a flurry of leaves and dust, we burst through the circle of huts and found Romulus, waiting with a small band of men, on the highest part of the hill.

"Six of them," Remus cried. "Romulus, we saw six at once!"

Romulus looked surprised, but he spoke blandly. "So did we. Just before you came." His face at last showed the start of a beard, a small black V below his chin. The ambitious boy, impatient but waiting, had hardened into a man who, no less ambitious, had ceased to wait.

"It must have been the same six. They were flying this way."

"No matter. They still count."

"Then we are tied."

"No," put in Celer. "We have seen *twelve.*" He twisted his mouth to the caricature of a smile, but his flat eyes were cold.

"Twelve? There have never been so many near these hills!"

Romulus started to speak, but Celer continued. "Today there were. The six that just passed, and before them, six more. Even larger—as big as eagles. They circled twice to be sure we saw them. Sent by the gods, eh, Romulus?"

"Is it true?" Remus asked his brother.

Romulus glowered. "Of course it is true. Celer has told you. And the city is mine to build where I choose."

Remus paled and spoke with an effort. "Build it then." It must have been clear to him that Celer had lied and that Romulus, though hesitant at first, had repeated the lie. "Sylvan," Remus said to me, "I am going to the cave."

We started down the hill. Behind us Romulus was giving orders. "Find me a bull and a heifer. We will plow the boundaries of our new city. But first we will celebrate the feast of the Pales. Celer, break out the wine. And the rest of you, build us some bonfires."

The men whooped approval and scuffled about their work. After the feast, Romulus would yoke the animals to a bronze-tipped plow and drive them around the base of the hill where he meant to build his walls, leaving a space for the gate. The area enclosed by the plow would be fortunate ground. Whoever crossed the furrow instead of entering by the designated gate would shatter the luck of the builders and allow the invasion of hostile spirits.

Remus was silent until we reached the cave. He threw himself on his pallet and Luperca, as if she sensed his trouble, crept beside him.

"You can build your own city," I suggested.

"No, I will help Romulus. But first I must understand him."

"I know how you feel. Your hill was the best."

He looked up at me. "The hill is not important. Romulus lied. That is important. He is building his city on a lie and the men know."

"No one objected. They like the Palatine."

"That is the harm. They knew and said nothing."

I left him alone all morning and waited under the fig tree. Once I looked in the cave. His eyes were open, but he did not appear to see me, nor to hear the merriment on top of the hill.

"Rumina," I said, more in conversation than in prayer. "You are the goddess of the suckling herds. But your tree stands right at our door. Neglect the lambs for awhile and help my friend."

In the afternoon, I climbed the fig tree and captured some honey in a round clay bowl. The bees, sensing perhaps for whom it was meant (or instructed by Rumina herself), made no objection. In the cave I knelt beside Remus.

"Eat it," I said crossly. "You have brooded enough."

He smiled, sat up, and took the bowl from my hands. He tilted it to his lips as if it were milk, for he relished the honey from his own bees, and drained the bowl.

"Now," he said, "I will help Romulus with his walls. But first I want to see Mellonia."

"I will wait for you here."

"No, come with me."

"You must have things to say in private. Who wants a Faun's big ears at such a time?"

"She has grown to love you. Besides—" His smile faded. "I want you with me. It is something I feel—a loneliness, a fear—I am not sure what. I want you with me."

In the woods beyond the Aventine, we encountered Celer and three of his friends, leaning on each other for support and thrashing through the undergrowth with such a racket that turquoise lizards flew in all directions. When they saw us they stopped, and Celer looked momentarily sobered. He forced a grin.

"Big Ears and Woodpecker," he said. "You missed our feast. The gods will be hurt."

"They are hurt already," said Remus, without slowing. "But not by Sylvan and me." The revelers made for the Palatine with surprising directness.

Suddenly I remembered that Celer had asked me the location of Mellonia's tree. I had not told him, but the night of the wolves he had vanished from Alba Longa. Had he followed her home, I wondered, and then today, emboldened with wine and friends, returned to invade her tree?

"Remus," I said. "Do you think he has found her tree?"

We began to run.

The branches of Mellonia's oak tree sprawled like a city which has grown without planning, its temples and archways mingled in artless beauty. From a distance, there was nothing to hint an invasion.

We approached the trunk.

"That lowermost branch," said Remus tensely. "I think it is starting to wilt."

"Too little sun," I said, but without conviction.

He began to call. "Mellonia! Mellonia!"

I searched the ground for traces of a fire or other means of assault, but the trunk was untouched. Around the altar, however, there were definite signs of Celer and his friends—jonquils in crushed profusion, rocks overturned, and, yes, they had entered the tunnel; it reeked of their wine.

Mellonia's room lay hushed and broken. We found her beside the couch, a white small body blackened with bruises and cradled, incongruously, in a bed of narcissus petals. Remus lifted her on to the couch and smoothed her tangled green hair, in which petals had caught as if to take root in its venture. She opened her eyes.

"Little bird," she said. "Who will look after you?" That was all.

He covered her body with petals and kissed her on the mouth which could no longer feel bruises. "I had never meant to outlive you," he said.

I turned my head but I heard his tears. Or was it the column of bees that swayed through the open window, the forest grieving for its queen, and for the king who had loved her? The shepherds say that bees speak only what is in our hearts—our grief, our joy, not theirs. That their murmur is always the same, and it is we who darken or lighten it to our mood. Perhaps, then, I heard my own tears.

We left her in the tree with the bees. "She would not want to be moved," Remus said. "The oak is dying. They will go to earth together."

We stared at the tree and already, it seemed, the wilt was stealing upward to the green and sunny towers.

"Did you hear what she said?" he asked.

I pressed his hand. "Yes. Yes, little bird."

* * *

When we reached the Palatine, Romulus had driven his team around the foot of the hill. For one short space, the gate, he had left the earth unbroken. Stripped completely in the hot April sun, he leaned on the plow, his massive thighs diamonded with sweat. Drops rolled down his beard. He looked very tired—and very royal.

With mattocks and shovels, the shepherds were setting to work inside the circle. Romulus had captured the *numen* or magic of the gods. Now they must build strong walls and enclose the magic securely. They sang as they dug, Celer and his friends the loudest:

> Romulus, son of the spear god Mars,
> Nursed by the long gray wolf. . .

Celer looked up from his work and saw us. He dropped his shovel.

Pausing outside the circle, Remus cried: "Romulus, your walls are useless, the luck is gone. A murderer stands inside!" He jumped the furrow. The shepherds stared at him in horror. I myself, midway to the gate, gasped at his daring. He sprang at Celer. Celer recovered his shovel but Remus parried, wrestled it from his hands, and felled him with a blow to his shoulder.

Romulus snatched a shovel from the shepherd nearest him. "Idiot!" he shouted to Remus. "It is you who have broken our luck. Fight me, not Celer."

"Keep away from me," Remus warned. But he made no move to defend himself from Romulus; he was waiting for Celer, dazed but conscious, to regain his feet.

Romulus struck him with the back of his shovel. I saw Remus's eyes. Surprise, that was all. Not fear, not anger. Then he fell. In the forest, once, I heard a she-wolf cry when a shepherd killed her cubs. All pain, all yearning. A cry from the vital organs of her body, as if their red swift pulsing could wrench her cubs from death. So Romulus cried and knelt beside his brother. In Remus's hair, the stains were of earth, not blood; the umber soil mingling with the sunflowers. But the stalk was broken.

I took Remus's shovel. "Stand up," I said to Romulus. "I am going to kill you."

He looked up at me through tears. "Sylvan, I wish you would."

I think it was Remus who held my hand. Born of one womb, he had said. Romulus, his brother, his pillar and shield of bronze. Instead of killing him, I knelt at his side.

Troubled and respectful, the shepherds surrounded us, and Faustulus laid his hand on Romulus's neck.

"My son, you meant him no harm. Let me prepare his body for burial."

Romulus shook his head. "I must make my peace with him first."

"And you, Sylvan?"

"I will stay with Remus."

The men climbed the hill. The sunlight thinned and shadows came to watch with us. Somewhere a cow lowed with quiet urgency. It is late, I thought. She is waiting for Remus to milk her.

"He must have a place for the night," I said. "He never liked the dark."

Romulus stirred. I think he had forgotten me. "The cave?"

"No. He would be alone there. We will take him to Mellonia's tree. Celer killed her, you know—he and his friends."

He looked at me with stunned comprehension. "Then that was why Remus attacked him. They will die for this, Sylvan."

I kindled a torch in the cave with pieces of flint and returned to Romulus. Luperca followed me. Romulus stroked her head.

"Old mother," he said, "you loved him too." He lifted his brother and held him lightly, with Remus's hair against his cheek. "His hair smells of clover."

"I know."

We walked slowly—Luperca was very weak—and came at last to the tree. Trembling but quiet, she waited outside the cave.

We placed him on the couch beside Mellonia. I pressed my cheek to the shoulder where, as a child, I had clung to be warmed and loved. I crossed his arms as if I were folding wings.

"Little bird," I said. "You reproached Mellonia because you had to outlive her. But I am the one you punished. All of your life was loving—except for this. Where is your city, my friend?"

"In me," Romulus answered.

I turned on him angrily. "In you?" Then I was sorry. Tears ran out of his eyes. He made no effort to hide them. I thought that he was going to fall and held out my hand. He grasped it and steadied himself.

"You think I want walls and armies," he said, "and nothing more? At first I did. This morning I did, when I lied about the birds. But then I had Remus; it seemed I would always have him. Whatever I did, he would love me. He was all I needed of gentleness. Now he is gone—unless I capture him in my city. A great city, Sylvan. Men will call her Rome after me, and her legions will conquer the world—Carthage and Sardis, Karnak, Sidon, and Babylon. But her highways will carry laws as well as armies, learning as well as conquest. Sylvan, don't you see?

Remus will live in us and the city we build. Come back with me, Little Faun!"

Where is the bird of fire? In the tall green flame of the cypress, I see his shadow, flickering with the swallows. In the city that crowds the Palatine, where Fauns walk with men and wolves are fed in temples, I hear the rush of his wings. But that is his shadow and sound. The bird himself is gone. Always his wings beat just beyond my hands, and the wind possesses his cry. Where is the bird of fire? Look up, he burns in the sky, with Saturn and the Golden Age. I will go to find him.

ACKNOWLEDGMENTS

I wish to express a particular debt to Alan Lake Chidsey's *Romulus: Builder of Rome* and Carlo Maria Franzero's *The Life and Times of Tarquin the Etruscan*. T.B.S.

JACK VANCE
Guyal of Sfere

GUYAL OF Sfere had been born one apart from his fellows and early proved a source of vexation for his sire. Normal in outward configuration, there existed within his mind a void which ached for nourishment. It was as if a spell had been cast upon his birth, a harassment visited on the child in a spirit of sardonic mockery, so that every occurrence, no matter how trifling, became a source of wonder and amazement. Even as young as four seasons he was expounding such inquiries as:

"Why do squares have more sides than triangles?"

"How will we see when the sun goes dark?"

"Do flowers grow under the ocean?"

"Do stars hiss and sizzle when rain comes by night?"

To which his impatient sire gave such answers as:

"So it was ordained by the Pragmatica; squares and triangles must obey the rote."

"We will be forced to grope and feel our way."

"I have never verified this matter; only the Curator would know."

"By no means, since the stars are high above the rain, higher even than the highest clouds, and swim in rarified air where rain will never breed."

As Guyal grew to youth, this void in his mind, instead of becoming limp and waxy, seemed to throb with a more violent ache. And so he asked:

"Why do people die when they are killed?"

"Where does beauty vanish when it goes?"

"How long have men lived on Earth?"

"What is beyond the sky?"

To which his sire, biting acerbity back from his lips, would respond:

"Death is the heritage of life; a man's vitality is like air in a bladder. Poinct this bubble and away, away, away, flees life, like the color of fading dream."

"Beauty is a luster which love bestows to guile the eye. Therefore it may be said that only when the brain is without love will the eye look and see no beauty.

"Some say men rose from the earth like grubs in a corpse; others aver that the first men desired residence and so created Earth by sorcery. The question is shrouded in technicality; only the Curator may answer with exactness."

"An endless waste."

And Guyal pondered and postulated, proposed and expounded, until he found himself the subject of surreptitious humor. The demesne was visited by a rumor that a gleft, coming upon Guyal's mother in labor, had stolen part of Guyal's brain, which deficiency he now industriously sought to restore.

Guyal therefore drew himself apart and roamed the grassy hills of Sfere in solitude. But ever was his mind acquisitive, ever did he seek to exhaust the lore of all around him, until at last his father in vexation refused to hear further inquiries, declaring that all knowledge had been known, that the trivial and useless had been discarded, leaving a residue which was all that was necessary to a sound man.

At this time Guyal was in his first manhood, a slight but well-knit youth with wide clear eyes, a penchant for severely elegant dress, and a hidden trouble which showed itself in the clamps at the corner of his mouth.

Hearing his father's angry statement Guyal said, "One more question, then I ask no more."

"Speak," declared his father. "One more question I grant you."

"You have often referred me to the Curator; who is he, and where may I find him, so as to allay my ache for knowledge?"

A moment the father scrutinized the son, whom he now considered past the verge of madness. Then he responded in a quiet voice, "The Curator guards the Museum of Man, which antique legend places in the Land of the Falling Wall—beyond the mountains of Fer Aquila and north of Ascolais. It is not certain that either Curator or Museum still exist; still it would seem that if the Curator knows all things, as is the legend, then surely he would know the wizardly foil to death."

Guyal said, "I would seek the Curator and the Museum of Man, that I likewise may know all things."

The father said with patience, "I will bestow on you my fine white horse, my Expansible Egg for your shelter, my Scintillant Dagger to illuminate the night. In addition, I lay a blessing along the trail, and danger will slide you by so long as you never wander from the trail."

Guyal quelled the hundred new questions at his tongue, including an inquisition as to where his father had learned these manifestations of sorcery, and accepted the gifts: the horse, the magic shelter, the dagger with the luminous pommel, and the blessing to guard him from the disadvantageous circumstances which plagued travelers along the dim trails of Ascolais.

He caparisoned the horse, honed the dagger, cast a last glance around the old manse at Sfere, and set forth to the north, with the void in his mind athrob for the soothing pressure of knowledge.

He ferried the River Scaum on an old barge. Aboard the barge and so off the trail, the blessing lost its puissance and the barge-tender, who coveted Guyal's rich accoutrements, sought to cudgel him with a knoblolly. Guyal fended off the blow and kicked the man into the murky deep, where he drowned.

Mounting the north bank of the Scaum he saw ahead the Porphiron Scar, the dark poplars and white columns of Kaiin, the dull gleam of Sanreale Bay.

Wandering the crumbled streets, he put the languid inhabitants such a spate of questions that one in wry jocularity commended him to a professional augur.

This one dwelled in a booth painted with the Signs of the Aumok-lopelastianic Cabal. He was a lank brownman with red-rimmed eyes and a stained white beard.

"What are your fees?" inquired Guyal cautiously.

"I respond to three questions," stated the augur. "For twenty terces I phrase the answer in clear and actionable language; for ten I use the language of cant, which occasionally admits of ambiguity; for five, I speak a parable which you must interpret as you will; and for one terce, I babble in an unknown tongue."

"First I must inquire, how profound is your knowledge?"

"I know all," responded the augur. "The secrets of red and the secrets of black, the lost spells of Grand Motholam, the way of the fish and the voice of the bird."

"And where have you learned all these things?"

"By pure induction," explained the augur. "I retire into my booth, I closet myself with never a glint of light, and, so sequestered, I resolve the profundities of the world."

"With all this precious knowledge at hand," ventured Guyal, "why do you live so meagerly, with not an ounce of fat to your frame and these miserable rags to your back?"

The augur stood back in fury. "Go along, go along! Already I have wasted fifty terces of wisdom on you, who have never a copper to your pouch. If you desire free enlightenment," and he cackled in mirth, "seek out the Curator." And he sheltered himself in his booth.

Guyal took lodging for the night, and in the morning continued north. The ravaged acres of the Old Town passed to his left, and the trail took to the fabulous forest.

For many a day Guyal rode north, and, heedful of danger, held to the trail. By night he surrounded himself and his horse in his magical habiliment, the Expansible Egg—a membrane impermeable to thew, claw, ensorcelment, pressure, sound and chill—and so rested at ease despite the efforts of the avid creatures of the dark.

The great dull globe of the sun fell behind him; the days became wan and the nights bitter, and at last the crags of Fer Aquila showed as a tracing on the north horizon.

The forest had become lower and less dense, and the characteristic tree was the daobado, a rounded massy construction of heavy gnarled branches, these a burnished russet bronze, clumped with dark balls of foliage. Beside a giant of the species Guyal came upon a village of turf huts. A gaggle of surly louts appeared and surrounded him with expressions of curiosity. Guyal, no less than the villagers, had questions to ask, but none would speak till the hetman strode up—a burly man who wore a shaggy fur hat, a cloak of brown fur and a bristling beard, so that it was hard to see where one ended and the other began. He exuded a rancid odor which displeased Guyal, who, from motives of courtesy, kept his distaste concealed.

"Where go you?" asked the hetman.

"I wish to cross the mountains to the Museum of Man," said Guyal. "Which way does the trail lead?"

The hetman pointed out a notch on the silhouette of the mountains. "There is Omona Gap, which is the shortest and best route, though there is no trail. None comes and none goes, since when you pass the Gap, you walk an unknown land. And with no traffic there manifestly need be no trail."

The news did not cheer Guyal.

"How then is it known that Omona Gap is on the way to the Museum?"

The hetman shrugged. "Such is our tradition."

Guyal turned his head at a hoarse snuffling and saw a pen of woven wattles. In a litter of filth and matted straw stood a number of hulking men eight or nine feet tall. They were naked, with shocks of dirty yellow hair and watery blue eyes. They had waxy faces and expressions of crass stupidity. As Guyal watched, one of them ambled to a trough and noisily began gulping gray mash.

Guyal said, "What manner of things are these?"

The hetman blinked in amusement at Guyal's naivete. "Those are our oasts, naturally." And he gestured in disapprobation at Guyal's white horse. "Never have I seen a stranger oast than the one you bestride. Ours carry us easier and appear to be less vicious; in addition no flesh is more delicious than oast properly braised and kettled."

Standing close, he fondled the metal of Guyal's saddle and the red and yellow embroidered quilt. "Your deckings however are rich and of superb quality. I will therefore bestow you my large and weighty oast in return for this creature with its accoutrements."

Guyal politely declared himself satisfied with his present mount, and the hetman shrugged his shoulders.

A horn sounded. The hetman looked about, then turned back to Guyal. "Food is prepared; will you eat?"

Guyal glanced toward the oast-pen. "I am not presently hungry, and I must hasten forward. However, I am grateful for your kindness."

He departed; as he passed under the arch of the great daobado, he turned a glance back toward the village. There seemed an unwonted activity among the huts. Remembering the hetman's covetous touch at his saddle, and aware that no longer did he ride the protected trail, Guyal urged his horse forward and pounded fast under the trees.

As he neared the foothills the forest dwindled to a savannah, floored with a dull, jointed grass that creaked under the horse's hooves. Guyal glanced up and down the plain. The sun, old and red as an autumn pomegranate, wallowed in the south-west; the light across the plain was dim and watery; the mountains presented a curiously artificial aspect, like a tableau planned for the effect of eery desolation.

Guyal glanced once again at the sun. Another hour of light, then the dark night of the latter-day Earth. Guyal twisted in the saddle, looked behind him, feeling lone, solitary, vulnerable. Four oasts, carrying men on their shoulders, came trotting from the forest. Sighting Guyal, they broke into a lumbering run. With a crawling skin Guyal wheeled his horse and eased the reins, and the white horse loped across the plain toward Omona Gap. Behind came the oasts, bestraddled by the fur-cloaked villagers.

As the sun touched the horizon, another forest ahead showed as an indistinct line of murk. Guyal looked back to his pursuers, bounding now a mile behind, turned his gaze back to the forest. An ill place to ride by night . . .

The darkling foilage loomed above him; he passed under the first gnarled boughs. If the oasts were unable to sniff out a trail, they might not be eluded. He changed directions, turned once, twice, a third time, then stood his horse to listen. Far away a crashing in the brake reached his ears. Guyal dismounted, led the horse into a deep hollow where a bank of foliage made a screen. Presently the four men on their hulking oasts passed in the afterglow above him, black double-shapes in attitudes suggestive of ill-temper and disappointment.

The thud and pad of feet dwindled and died.

The horse moved restlessly; the foliage rustled.

A damp air passed down the hollow and chilled the back of Guyal's neck. Darkness rose from old Earth like ink in a basin.

Guyal shivered: best to ride away through the forest, away from the dour villagers and their numb mounts. Away . . .

He turned his horse up to the height where the four had passed and sat listening. Far down the wind he heard a hoarse call. Turning in the opposite direction he let the horse choose its own path.

Branches and boughs knit patterns on the fading purple over him; the air smelt of moss and dank mold. The horse stopped short. Guyal, tensing in every muscle, leaned a little forward, head twisted, listening. There was a feel of danger on his cheek. The air was still, uncanny; his eyes could plumb not ten feet into the black. Somewhere near was death—grinding, roaring death, to come as a sudden shock.

Sweating cold, afraid to stir a muscle, he forced himself to dismount. Stiffly he slid from the saddle, brought forth the Expansible Egg, and flung it around his horse and himself. Ah, now . . . Guyal released the pressure of his breath. Safety.

Wan red light slanted through the branches from the east. Guyal's breath steamed in the air when he emerged from the Egg. After a handful of dried fruit for himself and a sack of meal for the horse, he mounted and set out toward the mountains.

The forest passed, and Guyal rode out on an upland. He scanned the line of mountains. Suffused with rose sunlight, the gray, sage green, dark green range rambled far to the west toward the Melantine, far to the east into the Falling Wall country. Where was Omona Gap?

Guyal of Sfere searched in vain for the notch which had been visible from the village of the fur-cloaked murderers.

He frowned and turned his eyes up the height of the mountains. Weathered by the rains of earth's duration, the slopes were easy and the crags rose like the stumps of rotten teeth. Guyal turned his horse uphill and rode the trackless slope into the mountains of Fer Aquila.

Guyal of Sfere had lost his way in a land of wind and naked crags. As night came he slouched numbly in the saddle while his horse took him where it would. Somewhere the ancient way through Omona Gap led to the northern tundra, but now, under a chilly overcast, north, east, south, and west were alike under the lavender-metal sky. Guyal reined his horse and, rising in the saddle, searched the landscape. The crags rose, tall, remote; the ground was barren of all but clumps of dry shrub. He slumped back in the saddle, and his white horse jogged forward.

Head bowed to the wind rode Guyal, and the mountains slanted along the twilight like the skeleton of a fossil god.

The horse halted, and Guyal found himself at the brink of a wide valley. The wind had died; the valley was quiet. Guyal leaned forward, staring. Below spread a dark and lifeless city. Mist blew along the streets and the afterglow fell dull on slate roofs.

The horse snorted and scraped the stony ground.

"A strange town," said Guyal, "with no lights, no sound, no smell of smoke . . . Doubtless an abandoned ruin from ancient times . . ."

He debated descending to the streets. At times the old ruins were haunted by peculiar distillations, but such a ruin might be joined to the tundra by a trail. With this thought in mind he started his horse down the slope.

He entered the town and the hooves rang loud and sharp on the cobbles. The buildings were framed of stone and dark mortar and seemed in uncommonly good preservation. A few lintels had cracked and sagged, a few walls gaped open, but for the most part the stone houses had successfully met the gnaw of time . . . Guyal scented smoke. Did people live here still? He would proceed with caution.

Before a building which seemed to be a hostelry flowers bloomed in an urn. Guyal reined his horse and reflected that flowers were rarely cherished by persons of hostile disposition.

"Hallo!" he called—once, twice.

No heads peered from the doors, no orange flicker brightened the windows. Guyal slowly turned and rode on.

The street widened and twisted toward a large hall, where Guyal saw a light. The building had a high facade, broken by four large windows, each of which had its two blinds of patined bronze filigree, and each overlooked a small balcony. A marble balustrade fronting the terrace shimmered bone-white and, behind, the hall's portal of massive wood stood slightly ajar; from here came the beam of light and also a strain of music.

Guyal of Sfere, halting, gazed not at the house nor at the light through the door. He dismounted and bowed to the young woman who sat pensively along the course of the balustrade. Though it was very cold, she wore but a simple gown, yellow-orange, a daffodil's color. Topaz hair fell loose to her shoulders and gave her face a cast of gravity and thoughtfulness.

As Guyal straightened from his greeting the woman nodded, smiled slightly, and absently fingered the hair by her cheek.

"A bitter night for travelers."

"A bitter night for musing on the stars," responded Guyal.

She smiled again. "I am not cold. I sit and dream . . . I listen to the music."

"What place is this?" inquired Guyal, looking up the street, down the street, and once more to the girl. "Are there any here but yourself?"

"This is Carchesel," said the girl, "abandoned by all ten thousand years ago. Only I and my aged uncle live here, finding this place a refuge from the Saponids of the tundra."

Guyal thought: this woman may or may not be a witch.

"You are cold and weary," said the girl, "and I keep you standing in the street." She rose to her feet. "Our hospitality is yours."

"Which I gladly accept," said Guyal, "but first I must stable my horse."

"He will be content in the house yonder. We have no stable." Guyal, following her finger, saw a low stone building with a door opening into blackness.

He took the white horse thither and removed the bridle and saddle; then, standing in the doorway, he listened to the music he had noted before, the piping of a weird and ancient air.

"Strange, strange," he muttered, stroking the horse's muzzle. "The uncle plays music, the girl stares alone at the stars of the night . . ." He considered a moment. "I may be oversuspicious. If witch she be, there is naught to be gained from me. If they be simple refugees as she says, and lovers of music, they may enjoy the airs from Ascolais; it will repay, in some measure, their hospitality." He reached into his saddle-bag, brought forth his flute, and tucked it inside his jerkin.

He ran back to where the girl awaited him.

"You have not told me your name," she reminded him, "that I may introduce you to my uncle."

"I am Guyal of Sfere, by the River Scaum in Ascolais. And you?"

She smiled, pushing the portal wider. Warm yellow light fell into the cobbled street.

"I have no name. I need none. There has never been any but my uncle; and when he speaks, there is no one to answer but I."

Guyal stared in astonishment; then, deeming his wonder too apparent for courtesy, he controlled his expression. Perhaps she suspected him of wizardry and feared to pronounce her name lest he make magic with it.

They entered a flagged hall, and the sound of piping grew louder.

"I will call you Ameth, if I may," said Guyal. "That is a flower of the south, as golden and kind and fragrant as you seem to be."

She nodded. "You may call me Ameth."

They entered a tapestry-hung chamber, large and warm. A great fire glowed at one wall, and here stood a table bearing food. On a bench sat the musician—an old man, untidy, unkempt. His white hair hung tangled down his back; his beard, in no better case, was dirty and yellow. He wore a ragged kirtle, by no means clean, and the leather of his sandals had broken into dry cracks. Strangely, he did not take the flute from his mouth, but kept up his piping; and the girl in yellow, so Guyal noted, seemed to move in rhythm to the tones.

"Uncle Ludowik," she cried in a gay voice, "I bring you a guest, Sir Guyal of Sfere."

Guyal looked into the man's face and wondered. The eyes, though somewhat rheumy with age, were gray and bright—feverishly bright and intelligent; and, so Guyal thought, awake with a strange joy. This joy further puzzled Guyal, for the lines of the face indicated nothing other than years of misery.

"Perhaps you play?" inquired Ameth. "My uncle is a great musician, and this is his time for music. He has kept the routine for many years . . ." She turned and smiled at Ludowik the musician. Guyal nodded politely.

Ameth motioned to the bounteous table. "Eat, Guyal, and I will pour you wine. Afterwards perhaps you will play the flute for us."

"Gladly," said Guyal, and he noticed how the joy on Ludowik's face grew more apparent, quivering around the corners of his mouth.

He ate and Ameth poured him golden wine until his head went to reeling. And never did Ludowik cease his piping—now a tender melody of running water, again a grave tune that told of the lost ocean to the west, another time a simple melody such as a child might sing at his games. Guyal noted with wonder how Ameth fitted her mood to the music—grave and gay as the music led her. Strange! thought Guyal. But then—people thus isolated were apt to develop peculiar mannerisms, and they seemed kindly withal.

He finished his meal and stood erect, steadying himself against the table. Ludowik was playing a lilting tune, a melody of glass birds swinging round and round on a red string in the sunlight. Ameth came dancing over to him and stood close—very close—and he smelled the warm perfume of her loose golden hair. Her face was happy and wild . . . Peculiar how Ludowik watched so grimly, and yet without a word. Perhaps he misdoubted a stranger's intent. Still . . .

"Now," breathed Ameth, "perhaps you will play the flute; you are so strong and young." Then she said quickly, as she saw Guyal's eyes widen. "I mean you will play on the flute for old uncle Ludowik, and he will be happy and go off to bed—and then we will sit and talk far into the night."

"Gladly will I play the flute," said Guyal. Curse the tongue of his, at once so fluent and yet so numb. It was the wine. "Gladly will I play. I am accounted quite skillful at my home manse at Sfere."

He glanced at Ludowik, then stared at the expression of crazy gladness he had surprised. Marvelous that a man should be so fond of music.

"Then—play!" breathed Ameth, urging him a little toward Ludowik and the flute.

"Perhaps," suggested Guyal, "I had better wait till your uncle pauses. I would seem discourteous—"

"No, as soon as you indicate that you wish to play, he will let off. Merely take the flute. You see," she confided, "he is rather deaf."

"Very well," said Guyal, "except that I have my own flute." And he brought it out from under his jerkin. "Why—what is the matter?" For a startling change had come over the girl and the old man. A quick light had risen in her eyes, and Ludowik's strange gladness had gone, and there was but dull hopelessness in his eyes, stupid resignation.

Guyal slowly stood back, bewildered. "Do you not wish me to play?"

There was a pause. "Of course," said Ameth, young and charming once more. "But I'm sure that Uncle Ludowik would enjoy hearing you play his flute. He is accustomed to the pitch—another scale might be unfamiliar . . ."

Ludowik nodded, and hope again shone in the rheumy old eyes. It was indeed a fine flute, Guyal saw, a rich piece of white metal, chased and set with gold, and Ludowik clutched this flute as if he would never let go.

"Take the flute," suggested Ameth. "He will not mind in the least." Ludowik shook his head, to signify the absence of his objections. But Guyal, noting with distaste the long stained beard, also shook his head. "I can play any scale, any tone on my flute. There is no need for me to use that of your uncle and possibly distress him. Listen," and he raised his instrument. "Here is a song of Kaiin, called 'The Opal, the Pearl and the Peacock'."

He put the pipe to his lips and began to play, very skillfully indeed, and Ludowik followed him, filling in gaps, making chords. Ameth, forgetting her vexation, listened with eyes half-closed, and moved her arm to the rhythm.

"Did you enjoy that?" asked Guyal, when he had finished.

"Very much. Perhaps you would try it on Uncle Ludowik's flute? It is a fine flute to play, very soft and easy to the breath."

"No," said Guyal, with sudden obstinacy. "I am able to play only my own instrument." He blew again, and it was a dance of the festival, a quirking carnival air. Ludowik, playing with supernal skill, ran merry phrases as might fit, and Ameth, carried away by the rhythm, danced a dance of her own, a merry step in time to the music.

Guyal played a wild tarantella of the peasant folk, and Ameth danced wilder and faster, flung her arms, wheeled, jerked her head in a fine display. And Ludowik's flute played a brilliant obbligato, hurtling over, now under, chording, veering, warping little silver strings of sound around Guyal's melody, adding urgent little grace-phrases.

Ludowik's eyes now clung to the whirling figure of the dancing girl. And suddenly he struck up a theme of his own, a tune of wildest abandon, of a frenzied beating rhythm; and Guyal, carried away by the force of the music, blew as he never had blown before, invented trills and runs, gyrating arpeggios, blew high and shrill, loud and fast and clear.

It was as nothing to Ludowik's music. His eyes were starting; sweat streamed from his seamed old forehead; his flute tore the air into quivering ecstatic shreds.

Ameth danced frenzy; she was no longer beautiful, she appeared grotesque and unfamiliar. The music became something more than the senses could bear. Guyal's own vision turned pink and gray; he saw Ameth fall in a faint, in a foaming fit; and Ludowik, fiery-eyed, staggered erect, hobbled to her body and began a terrible intense concord, slow measures of most solemn and frightening meaning.

Ludowik played death.

Guyal of Sfere turned and ran wide-eyed from the hall. Ludowik, never noticing, continued his terrible piping, played as if every note were a skewer through the twitching girl's shoulder-blades.

Guyal ran through the night, and cold air bit at him like sleet. He burst into the shed, and the white horse softly nickered at him. On with the saddle, on with the bridle, away down the streets of old Carchasel, past the gaping black windows, ringing down the starlit cobbles, away from the music of death!

Guyal of Sfere galloped up the mountain with the stars in his face, and not until he came to the shoulder did he turn in the saddle to look back.

The verging of dawn trembled into the stony valley. Where was Carchasel? There was no city—only a crumble of ruins . . .

Hark! A far sound? . . .

No. All was silence.

And yet . . .

No. Only crumbled stones in the floor of the valley.

Guyal, fixed of eye, turned and went his way, along the trail which stretched north before him.

The walls of the defile which led the trail were steep gray granite, stained scarlet and black by lichen, mildewed blue. The horse's hooves made a hollow clop-clop-clop on the stone, loud to Guyal's ears, hypnotic to his brain, and after the sleepless night he found his frame sagging. His eyes grew dim and warm with drowsiness, but the trail ahead led to unseen vistas, and the void in Guyal's brain drove him without surcease.

The lassitude became such that Guyal slipped halfway from his saddle. Rousing himself, he resolved to round one more bend in the trail and then take rest.

The rock beetled above and hid the sky where the sun had passed the zenith. The trail twisted around a shoulder of rock; ahead shone a patch of indigo heaven. One more turning, Guyal told himself. The defile fell open, the mountains were at his back and he looked out across a hundred miles of steppe. It was a land shaded with subtle colors, washed with delicate shadows, fading and melting into the lurid haze at the horizon. He saw a lone eminence cloaked by a dark company of trees, the glisten of a lake at its foot. To the other side a ranked mass of gray-white ruins was barely discernible. The Museum of Man? . . . After a moment of vacillation, Guyal dismounted and sought sleep within the Expansible Egg.

The sun rolled in sad sumptuous majesty behind the mountains; murk fell across the tundra. Guyal awoke and refreshed himself in a rill nearby. Giving meal to his horse, he ate dry fruit and bread; then he mounted and rode down the trail. The plain spread vastly north before him, into desolation; the mountains lowered black above and behind; a slow cold breeze blew in his face. Gloom deepened; the plain sank from sight like a drowned land. Hesitant before the murk, Guyal reined his horse. Better, he thought, to ride in the morning. If he lost the trail in the dark, who could tell what he might encounter?

A mournful sound. Guyal stiffened and turned his face to the sky. A sigh? A moan? A sob? . . . Another sound, closer, the rustle of cloth, a loose garment. Guyal cringed into his saddle. Floating slowly down through the darkness came a shape robed in white. Under the cowl and glowing with eer-light looked a drawn face with eyes like the holes in a skull.

It breathed its sad sound and drifted away on high . . . There was only the blow of the wind past Guyal's ears.

He drew a shuddering breath and slumped against the pommel. His shoulders felt exposed, naked. He slipped to the ground and established the shelter of the Egg about himself and his horse. Preparing his pallet, he lay himself down; presently, as he lay staring into the dark, sleep came on him and so the night passed.

He awoke before dawn and once more set forth. The trail was a ribbon of white sand between banks of gray furze and the miles passed swiftly.

The trail led toward the tree-clothed eminence Guyal had noted from above; now he thought to see roofs through the heavy foliage and smoke on the sharp air. And presently to right and left spread cultivated fields of spikenard, callow and mead-apple. Guyal continued with eyes watchful for men.

To one side appeared a fence of stone and black timber: the stone chiselled and hewn to the semblance of four globes beaded on a central pillar, the black timbers which served as rails fitted in sockets and carved in precise spirals. Behind this fence a region of bare earth lay churned, pitted, cratered, burnt and wrenched, as if visited at once by fire and the blow of a tremendous hammer. In wondering speculation Guyal gazed and so did not notice the three men who came quietly upon him.

The horse started nervously; Guyal, turning, saw the three. They barred his road and one held the bridle of his horse.

They were tall, well-formed men, wearing tight suits of somber leather bordered with black. Their headgear was heavy maroon cloth crumpled in precise creases, and leather flaps extended horizontally over each ear. Their faces were long and solemn, with clear golden-ivory skin, golden eyes and jet-black hair. Clearly they were not savages: they moved with a silky control, they eyed Guyal with critical appraisal, their garb implied the discipline of an ancient convention.

The leader stepped forward. His expression was neither threat nor welcome. "Greetings, stranger; whither bound?"

"Greetings," replied Guyal cautiously. "I go as my star directs . . . You are the Saponids?"

"That is our race, and before you is our town Saponce." He inspected Guyal with frank curiosity. "By the color of your custom I suspect your home to be in the south."

"I am Guyal of Sfere, by the River Scaum in Ascolais."

"The way is long," observed the Saponid. "Terrors beset the traveler. Your impulse must be most intense, and your star must draw with fervent allure."

"I come," said Guyal, "on a pilgrimage for the ease of my spirit; the road seems short when it attains its end."

The Saponid offered polite acquiescence. "Then you have crossed the Fer Aquilas?"

"Indeed; through cold wind and desolate stone." Guyal glanced back at the looming mass. "Only yesterday at nightfall did I leave the gap. And then a ghost hovered above till I thought the grave was marking me for its own."

He paused in surprise; his words seemed to have released a powerful emotion in the Saponids. Their features lengthened, their mouths grew white and clenched. The leader, his polite detachment a trifle diminished, searched the sky with ill-concealed apprehension. "A ghost . . . In a white garment, thus and so, floating on high?"

"Yes; is it a known familiar of the region?"

There was a pause.

"In a certain sense," said the Saponid. "It is a signal of woe . . . But I interrupt your tale."

"There is little to tell. I took shelter for the night, and this morning I fared down to the plain."

"Were you not molested further? By Koolbaw the Walking Serpent, who ranges the slopes like fate?"

"I saw neither walking serpent nor crawling lizard; further, a blessing protects my trail and I come to no harm so long as I keep my course."

"Interesting, interesting."

"Now," said Guyal, "permit me to inquire of you, since there is much I would learn; what is this ghost and what evil does he commemorate?"

"You ask beyond my certain knowledge," replied the Saponid cautiously. "Of this ghost it is well not to speak lest our attention reinforce his malignity."

"As you will," replied Guyal. "Perhaps you will instruct me . . ." He caught his tongue. Before inquiring for the Museum of Man, it would be wise to learn in what regard the Saponids held it, lest, learning his interest, they seek to prevent him from knowledge.

"Yes?" inquired the Saponid. "What is your lack?"

Guyal indicated the seared area behind the fence of stone and timber. "What is the portent of this devastation?"

The Saponid stared across the area with a blank expression and shrugged. "It is one of the ancient places; so much is known, no more. Death lingers here, and no creature may venture across the place without succumbing to a most malicious magic which raises virulence and angry sores. Here is where those whom we kill are sent . . . But away. You will desire to rest and refresh yourself at Saponce. Come; we will guide you."

He turned down the trail toward the town, and Guyal, finding neither words nor reasons to reject the idea, urged his horse forward.

As they approached the tree-shrouded hill the trail widened to a road. To the right hand the lake drew close, behind low banks of purple reeds. Here were docks built of heavy black baulks and boats rocked to the wind-feathered ripples. They were built in the shape of sickles, with bow and stern curving high from the water.

Up into the town, and the houses were hewn timber, ranging in tone from golden brown to weathered black. The construction was intricate and ornate, the walls rising three stories to steep gables overhanging front and back. Pillars and piers were carved with complex designs: meshing ribbons, tendrils, leaves, lizards, and the like. The screens which guarded the windows were likewise carved, with foliage patterns, animal faces, radiant stars: rich textures in the mellow wood. It was clear that much expressiveness had been expended on the carving.

Up the steep lane, under the gloom cast by the trees, past the houses half-hidden by the foliage, and the Saponids of Saponce came forth to stare. They moved quietly and spoke in low voices, and their garments were of an elegance Guyal had not expected to see on the northern steppe.

His guide halted and turned to Guyal. "Will you oblige me by waiting till I report to the Voyevode, that he may prepare a suitable reception?"

The request was framed in candid words and with guileless eyes. Guyal thought to perceive ambiguity in the phrasing, but since the hooves of his horse were planted in the center of the road, and since he did not propose leaving the road, Guyal assented with an open face. The Saponid disappeared and Guyal sat musing on the pleasant town perched so high above the plain.

A group of girls approached to glance at Guyal with curious eyes. Guyal returned the inspection, and now found a puzzling lack about their persons, a discrepancy which he could not instantly identify. They wore graceful garments of woven wool, striped and dyed various colors; they were supple and slender, and seemed not lacking in coquetry. And yet . . .

The Saponid returned. "Now, Sir Guyal, may we proceed?"

Guyal, endeavoring to remove any flavor of suspicion from his words, said, "You will understand, Sir Saponid, that by the very nature of my father's blessing I dare not leave the delineated course of the trail; for then, instantly, I would become liable to any curse, which, placed on me along the way, might be seeking just such occasion for leeching close on my soul."

The Saponid made an understanding gesture. "Naturally; you follow a sound principle. Let me reassure you. I but conduct you to a reception by the Voyevode who even now hastens to the plaza to greet a stranger from the far south."

Guyal bowed in gratification, and they continued up the road.

A hundred paces and the road levelled, crossing a common planted with small, fluttering, heart-shaped leaves, colored in all shades of purple, red, green and black.

The Saponid turned to Guyal. "As a stranger I must caution you never to set foot on the common. It is one of our sacred places, and tradition requires that a severe penalty be exacted for transgressions and sacrilege."

"I note your warning," said Guyal. "I will respectfully obey your law."

They passed a dense thicket; with hideous clamor a bestial shape sprang from concealment, a creature staring-eyed with tremendous fanged jaws. Guyal's horse shied, bolted, sprang out onto the sacred common and trampled the fluttering leaves.

A number of Saponid men rushed forth, grasped the horse, seized Guyal and dragged him from the saddle.

"Ho!" cried Guyal. "What means this? Release me!"

The Saponid who had been his guide advanced, shaking his head in reproach. "Indeed, and only had I just impressed upon you that gravity of such an offense!"

"But the monster frightened my horse!" said Guyal. "I am no wise responsible for this trespass; release me, let us proceed to the reception."

The Saponid said, "I fear that the penalties prescribed by tradition must come into effect. Your protests, though of superficial plausibility, will not bear serious examination. For instance, the creature you term a monster is in reality a harmless domesticated beast. Secondly, I observe the animal you bestride; he will not make a turn or twist without the twitch of the reins. Thirdly, even if your postulates were conceded, you thereby admit to guilt by virtue of negligence and omission. You should have secured a mount less apt to unpredictable action, or upon learning of the sanctitude of the common, you should have considered such a contingency as even now occurred, and therefore dismounted, leading your beast. Therefore, Sir Guyal, though loath, I am forced to believe you guilty of impertinence, impiety, disregard and impudicity. Therefore, as Castellan and Sergeant-Reader of the Litany, so responsible for the detention of law-breakers, I must order you secured, contained, pent, incarcerated and confined until such time as the penalties will be exacted."

"The entire episode is mockery!" raged Guyal. "Are you savages, then, thus to mistreat a lone wayfarer?"

"By no means," replied the Castellan. "We are a highly civilized people, with customs bequeathed us by the past. Since the past was more glorious than the present, what presumption we would show by questioning these laws!"

Guyal fell quiet. "And what are the usual penalties for my act?"

The Castellan made a reassuring motion. "The rote prescribes three acts of penance, which in your case, I am sure will be nominal. But—the forms must be observed, and it is necessary that you be constrained in the Felon's Caseboard." He motioned to the men who held Guyal's arm. "Away with him; cross neither track nor trail, for then your grasp will be nerveless and he will be delivered from justice."

Guyal was pent in a well-aired but poorly lighted cellar of stone. The floor he found dry, the ceiling free of crawling insects. He had not been searched, nor had his Scintillant Dagger been removed from his sash. With suspicions crowding his brain he lay on the rush bed and, after a period, slept.

Now ensued the passing of a day. He was given food and drink; and at last the Castellan came to visit him.

"You are indeed fortunate," said the Saponid, "in that, as a witness, I was able to suggest your delinquencies to be more the result of negligence than malice. The last penalties exacted for the crime were stringent; the felon was ordered to perform the following three acts: first, to cut off his toes and sew the severed members into the skin at his neck; second, to revile his forbears for three hours, commencing with a Common Bill of Anathema, including feigned madness and hereditary disease, and at last defiling the hearth of his clan with ordure; and third, walking a mile under the lake with leaded shoes in search of the Lost Book of Kells." And the Castellan regarded Guyal with complacency.

"What deeds must I perform?" inquired Guyal drily.

The Castellan joined the tips of his fingers together. "As I say, the penances are nominal, by decree of the Voyevode. First you must swear never again to repeat your crime."

"That I gladly do," said Guyal, and so bound himself.

"Second," said the Castellan with a slight smile, "you must adjudicate at a Grand Pageant of Pulchritude among the maids of the village and select her whom you deem the most beautiful."

"Scarcely an arduous task," commented Guyal. "Why does it fall to my lot?"

The Castellan looked vaguely to the ceiling. "There are a number of concomitants to victory in this contest . . . Every person in the town would find relations among the participants—a daughter, a sister, a niece—and so would hardly be considered unprejudiced. The charge of favoritism could never be levelled against you; therefore you make an ideal selection for this important post."

Guyal seemed to hear the ring of sincerity in the Saponid's voice; still he wondered why the selection of the town's loveliest was a matter of such import.

"And third?" he inquired.

"That will be revealed after the contest, which occurs this afternoon."

The Saponid departed the cell.

Guyal, who was not without vanity, spent several hours restoring himself and his costume from the ravages of travel. He bathed, trimmed his hair, shaved his face, and, when the Castellan came to unlock the door, he felt that he made no discreditable picture.

He was led out upon the road and directed up the hill toward the summit of the terraced town of Saponce. Turning to the Castellan he said, "How is it that you permit me to walk the trail once more? You must know that now I am safe from molestation . . ."

The Castellan shrugged. "True. But you would gain little by insisting upon your temporary immunity. Ahead the trail crosses a bridge, which we could demolish; behind we need but breach the dam to Peilvemchal Torrent; then, should you walk the trail, you would be swept to the side and so rendered vulnerable. No, Sir Guyal of Sfere, once the secret of your immunity is abroad then you are liable to a variety of stratagems. For instance, a large wall might be placed athwart the way, before and behind you. No doubt the spell would preserve you from thirst and hunger, but what then? So would you sit till the sun went out."

Guyal said no word. Across the lake he noticed a trio of the crescent boats approaching the docks, prows and sterns rocking and dipping into the shaded water with a graceful motion. The void in his mind made itself known. "Why are boats constructed in such fashion?"

The Castellan looked blankly at him. "It is the only practicable method. Do not the oe-pods grow thusly to the south?"

"Never have I seen oe-pods."

"They are the fruit of a great vine, and grow in scimitar-shape. When sufficiently large, we cut and clean them, slit the inner edge, grapple end to end with strong line and constrict till the pod opens as is desirable. Then when cured, dried, varnished, carved, burnished, and lacquered; fitted with deck, thwarts and gussets—then have we our boats."

They entered the plaza, a flat area at the summit surrounded on three sides by tall houses of carved dark wood. The fourth side was open to a vista across the lake and beyond to the loom of the mountains. Trees overhung all and the sun shining through made a scarlet pattern on the sandy floor.

To Guyal's surprise there seemed to be no preliminary ceremonies or formalities to the contest, and small spirit of festivity was manifest among the townspeople. Indeed they seemed beset by subdued despondency and eyed him without enthusiasm.

A hundred girls stood gathered in a disconsolate group in the center of the plaza. It seemed to Guyal that they had gone to few pains to embellish themselves for beauty. To the contrary, they wore shapeless rags, their hair seemed deliberately misarranged, their faces dirty and scowling.

Guyal stared and turned to his guide. "These girls seem not to relish the garland of pulchritude."

The Castellan nodded wryly. "As you see, they are by no means jealous for distinction; modesty has always been a Saponid trait."

Guyal hesitated. "What is the form of procedure? I do not desire in my ignorance to violate another of your arcane apochrypha."

The Castellan said with a blank face, "There are no formalities. We conduct these pageants with expedition and the least possible ceremony. You need but pass among these maidens and point out her whom you deem the most attractive."

Guyal advanced to his task, feeling more than half-foolish. Then he reflected: this is a penalty for contravening an absurd tradition; I will conduct myself with efficiency and so the quicker rid myself of the obligation.

He stood before the hundred girls, who eyed him with hostility and anxiety, and Guyal saw that his task would not be simple, since, on the whole, they were of a comeliness which even the dirt, grimacing and rags could not disguise.

"Range yourselves, if you please, into a line," said Guyal. "In this way, none will be at disadvantage."

Sullenly the girls formed a line.

Guyal surveyed the group. He saw at once that a number could be eliminated: the squat, the obese, the lean, the pocked and coarse-featured—perhaps a quarter of the group. He said suavely, "Never have I seen such unanimous loveliness; each of you might legitimately claim the cordon. My task is arduous; I must weigh fine imponderables; in the end my choice will undoubtedly be based on subjectivity and those of real charm will no doubt be the first discharged from the competition." He stepped forward. "Those whom I indicate may retire."

He walked down the line, pointing, and the ugliest, with expressions of unmistakable relief, hastened to the sidelines.

A second time Guyal made his inspection, and now, somewhat more familiar with those he judged, he was able to discharge those who, while suffering no whit from ugliness, were merely plain.

Roughly a third of the original group remained. These stared at Guyal with varying degrees of apprehension and truculence as he passed before them, studying each in turn . . . All at once his mind was determined, and his choice definite. Somehow the girls felt the change in him, and in their anxiety and tension left off the expressions they had been wearing to daunt and bemuse him.

Guyal made one last survey down the line. No, he had been accurate in his choice. There were girls here as comely as the senses could desire, girls with opal-glowing eyes and hyacinth features, girls as lissome as reeds, with hair silky and fine despite the dust which they seemed to have rubbed upon themselves.

The girl whom Guyal had selected was slighter than the others and possessed of a beauty not at once obvious. She had a small triangular face, great wistful eyes and thick black hair cut raggedly short at the ears. Her skin was of a transparent paleness, like the finest ivory; her form slender, graceful, and of a compelling magnetism, urgent of intimacy. She seemed to have sensed his decision and her eyes widened.

Guyal took her hand, led her forward, and turned to the Voyevode—an old man sitting stolidly in a heavy chair.

"This is she whom I find the loveliest among your maidens."

There was silence through the square. Then there came a hoarse sound, a cry of sadness from the Castellan and Sergeant-Reader. He came forward, sagging of face, limp of body. "Guyal of Sfere, you have wrought a great revenge for my tricking you. This is my beloved daughter, Shierl, whom you have designated for dread."

Guyal turned in wonderment from the Castellan to the girl Shierl, in whose eyes he now recognized a film of numbness, a gazing into a great depth.

Returning to the Castellan, Guyal stammered, "I meant but complete impersonality. This your daughter Shierl I find one of the loveliest creatures of my experience; I cannot understand where I have offended."

"No, Guyal," said the Castellan, "you have chosen fairly, for such indeed is my own thought."

"Well, then," said Guyal, "reveal to me now my third task that I may have done and continue my pilgrimage."

The Castellan said, "Three leagues to the north lies the ruin which tradition tells us to be the olden Museum of Man.

"Ah," said Guyal, "go on, I attend."

"You must, as your third charge, conduct this my daughter Shierl to the Museum of Man. At the portal you will strike on a copper gong and announce to whomever responds: 'We are those summoned from Saponce'."

Guyal started, frowned. "How is this? 'We'?"

"Such is your charge," said the Castellan in a voice like thunder.

Guyal looked to left, right, forward and behind. But he stood in the center of the plaza surrounded by the hardy men of Saponce.

"When must this charge be executed?" he inquired in a controlled voice.

The Castellan said in a voice bitter as oak-wort: "Even now Shierl goes to clothe herself in yellow. In one hour shall she appear, in one hour shall you set forth for the Museum of Man."

"And then?"

"And then—for good or for evil, it is not known. You fare as thirteen thousand have fared before you."

Down from the plaza, down the leafy lanes of Saponce came Guyal, indignant and clamped of mouth, though the pit of his stomach felt tender and heavy with trepidation. The ritual carried distasteful overtones: execution or sacrifice. Guyal's step faltered.

The Castellan seized his elbow with a hard hand. "Forward."

Execution or sacrifice . . . The faces along the lane swam with morbid curiosity, inner excitement; gloating eyes searched him deep to relish his fear and horror, and the mouths half-drooped, half-smiled in the inner hugging for joy not to be the one walking down the foliage streets, and forth to the Museum of Man.

The eminence, with the tall trees and carved dark houses, was at his back; they walked out into the claret sunlight of the tundra. Here were eighty women in white chlamys with ceremonial buckets of woven straw over their heads; around a tall tent of yellow silk they stood.

The Castellan halted Guyal and beckoned to the Ritual Matron. She flung back the hangings at the door of the tent; the girl within, Shierl, came slowly forth, eyes wide and dark with fright.

She wore a stiff gown of yellow brocade, and the wan of her body seemed pent and constrained within. The gown came snug under her chin, left her arms bare and raised past the back of her head in a stiff spear-headed cowl. She was frightened as a small animal trapped is frightened; she stared at Guyal, at her father, as if she had never seen them before.

The Ritual Matron put a gentle hand on her waist, propelled her forward. Shierl stepped once, twice, irresolutely halted. The Castellan brought Guyal forward and placed him at the girl's side; now two children, a boy and a girl, came hastening up with cups which they proffered to Guyal and Shierl. Dully she accepted the cup. Guyal took his and glanced suspiciously at the murky brew. He looked up to the Castellan. "What is the nature of this potion?"

"Drink," said the Castellan. "So will your way seem the shorter; so will terror leave you behind, and you will march to the Museum with a steadier step."

"No," said Guyal. "I will not drink. My senses must be my own when I meet the Curator. I have come far for the privilege; I would not stultify the occasion stumbling and staggering." And he handed the cup back to the boy.

Shierl stared dully at the cup she held. Said Guyal: "I advise you likewise to avoid the drug; so will we come to the Museum of Man with our dignity to us."

Hesitantly she returned the cup. The Castellan's brow clouded, but he made no protest.

An old man in a black costume brought forward a satin pillow on which rested a whip with a handle of carved steel. The Castellan now lifted this whip, and advancing, laid three light strokes across the shoulders of both Shierl and Guyal.

"Now, I charge thee, get hence and go from Saponce, outlawed forever; thou art waifs forlorn. Seek succor at the Museum of Man. I charge thee, never look back, leave all thoughts of past and future here at North Garden. Now and forever are you sundered from all bonds, claims, relations, and kinships, together with all pretenses to amity, love, fellowship and brotherhood with the Saponids of Saponce. Go, I exhort; go, I command; go, go, go!"

Shierl sunk her teeth into her lower lip; tears freely coursed her cheek though she made no sound. With hanging head she started across the lichen of the tundra, and Guyal, with a swift stride, joined her.

Now there was no looking back. For a space the murmurs, the nervous sounds followed their ears; then they were alone on the plain. The limitless north lay across the horizon; the tundra filled the foreground and background, an expanse dreary, dun and moribund. Alone marring the region, the white ruins—once the Museum of Man—rose a league before them, and along the faint trail they walked without words.

Guyal said in a tentative tone, "There is much I would understand."

"Speak," said Shierl. Her voice was low but composed.

"Why are we forced and exhorted to this mission?"

"It is thus because it has always been thus. Is not this reason enough?"

"Sufficient possibly for you," said Guyal, "but for me the causality is unconvincing. I must acquaint you with the void in my mind, which lusts for knowledge as a lecher yearns for carnality; so pray be patient if my inquisition seems unnecessarily thorough."

She glanced at him in astonishment. "Are all to the south so strong for knowing as you?"

"In no degree," said Guyal. "Everywhere normality of the mind may be observed. The habitants adroitly perform the motions which fed

them yesterday, last week, a year ago. I have been informed of my
aberration well and full. 'Why strive for a pedant's accumulation?' I
have been told. 'Why seek and search? Earth grows cold; man gasps his
last; why forego merriment, music, and revelry for the abstract and
abstruse?' "

"Indeed," said Shierl. "Well do they counsel; such is the consensus
at Saponce."

Guyal shrugged. "The rumor goes that I am demonbereft of my
senses. Such may be. In any event the effect remains, and the obsession
haunts me."

Shierl indicated understanding and acquiescence. "Ask on then; I
will endeavor to ease these yearnings."

He glanced at her sidelong, studied the charming triangle of her face,
the heavy black hair, the great lustrous eyes, dark as yu-sapphires. "In
happier circumstances, there would be other yearnings I would beseech
you likewise to ease."

"Ask," replied Shierl of Saponce. "The Museum of Man is close;
there is occasion for naught but words."

"Why are we thus dismissed and charged, with tacit acceptance of
our doom?"

"The immediate cause is the ghost you saw on the hill. When the
ghost appears, then we of Saponce know that the most beautiful maiden
and the most handsome youth of the town must be despatched to the
Museum. The prime behind the custom I do not know. So it is; so it
has been; so it will be till the sun gutters like a coal in the rain and
darkens Earth, and the winds blow snow over Saponce."

"But what is our mission? Who greets us, what is our fate?"

"Such details are unknown."

Guyal mused, "The likelihood of pleasure seems small . . . There are
discordants in the episode. You are beyond doubt the loveliest creature
of the Saponids, the loveliest creature of Earth—but I, I am a casual
stranger, and hardly the most well-favored youth of the town."

She smiled a trifle. "You are not uncomely."

Guyal said somberly, "Over-riding the condition of my person is the
fact that I am a stranger and so bring little loss to the town of Saponce."

"That aspect has no doubt been considered," the girl said.

Guyal searched the horizon. "Let us then avoid the Museum of Man,
let us circumvent this unknown fate and take to the mountains, and so
south to Ascolais. Lust for enlightenment will never fly me in the face
of destruction so clearly implicit."

She shook her head. "Do you suppose that we would gain by the ruse? The eyes of a hundred warriors follow us till we pass through the portals of the Museum; should we attempt to scamp our duty we should be bound to stakes, stripped of our skins by the inch, and at last be placed in bags with a thousand scorpions poured around our heads. Such is the traditional penalty; twelve times in history has it been invoked."

Guyal threw back his shoulders and spoke in a nervous voice. "Ah, well—the Museum of Man has been my goal for many years. On this motive I set forth from Sfere, so now I would seek the Curator and satisfy my obsession for brain-filling."

"You are blessed with great fortune," said Shierl, "for you are being granted your heart's desire."

Guyal could find nothing to say, so for a space they walked in silence. Then he spoke. "Shierl."

"Yes, Guyal of Sfere?"

"Do they separate us and take us apart?"

"I do not know."

"Shierl."

"Yes?"

"Had we met under a happier star . . ." He paused.

Shierl walked in silence.

He looked at her coolly. "You speak not."

"But you ask nothing," she said in surprise.

Guyal turned his face ahead, to the Museum of Man.

Presently she touched his arm. "Guyal, I am greatly frightened."

Guyal gazed at the ground beneath his feet, and a blossom of fire sprang alive in his brain. "See the marking through the lichen?"

"Yes; what then?"

"Is it a trail?"

Dubiously she responded, "It is a way worn by the passage of many feet. So then—it is a trail."

Guyal said in restrained jubilation, "Here is safety, if I never permit myself to be cozened from the way. But you—ah, I must guard you; you must never leave my side, you must swim in the charm which protects me; perhaps then we will survive."

Shierl said sadly, "Let us not delude our reason, Guyal of Sfere."

But as they walked, the trail grew plainer, and Guyal became correspondingly sanguine. And ever larger bulked the crumble which marked the Museum of Man, presently to occupy all their vision.

If a storehouse of knowledge had existed here, little sign of it remained. There was a great flat floor, flagged in white stone, now chalky, broken and inter-thrust by weeds. Around this floor rose a series of monoliths, pocked and worn, and toppled off at various heights. These at one time had supported a vast roof; now of roof there was none and the walls were but dreams of the far past.

So here was the flat floor bounded by the broken stumps of pillars, bare to the winds of time and the glare of cool red sun. The rains had washed the marble, the dust from the mountains had been laid on and swept off, laid on and swept off, and those who had built the Museum were less than a mote of this dust, so far and forgotten were they.

"Think," said Guyal, "think of the vastness of knowledge which once was gathered here and which is now one with the soil—unless, of course, the Curator has salvaged and preserved."

Shierl looked about apprehensively. "I think rather of the portal, and that which awaits us . . . Guyal," she whispered, "I fear, I fear greatly . . . Suppose they tear us apart? Suppose there is torture and death for us? I fear a tremendous impingement, the shock of horror . . ."

Guyal's own throat was hot and full. He looked about with challenge. "While I still breathe and hold power in my arms to fight, there will be none to harm us."

Shierl groaned softly. "Guyal, Guyal, Guyal of Sfere—why did you choose me?"

"Because," said Guyal, "my eye went to you like the nectar moth flits to the jacynth; because you were the loveliest and I thought nothing but good in store for you."

With a shuddering breath Shierl said, "I must be courageous; after all, if it were not I it would be some other maid equally fearful . . . And there is the portal."

Guyal inhaled deeply, inclined his head, and strode forward. "Let us be to it, and know . . ."

The portal opened into a nearby monolith, a door of flat black metal. Guyal followed the trail to the door, and rapped staunchly with his fist on the small copper gong to the side.

The door groaned wide on its hinges, and cool air, smelling of the under-earth, billowed forth. In the black gape their eyes could find nothing.

"Hola within!" cried Guyal.

A soft voice, full of catches and quavers, as if just after weeping, said, "Come ye, come ye forward. You are desired and awaited."

Guyal leaned his head forward, straining to see. "Give us light, that we may not wander from the trail and bottom ourselves."

The breathless quaver of a voice said, "Light is not needed; anywhere you step, that will be your trail, by an arrangement so agreed with the Way-Maker."

"No," said Guyal, "we would see the visage of our host. We come at his invitation; the minimum of his guest-offering is light; light there must be before we set foot inside the dungeon. Know we come as seekers after knowledge; we are visitors to be honored."

"Ah, knowledge, knowledge," came the sad breathlessness. "That shall be yours, in full plenitude—knowledge of many strange affairs; oh, you shall swim in a tide of knowledge—"

Guyal interrupted the sad, sighing voice. "Are you the Curator? Hundreds of leagues have I come to bespeak the Curator and put him my inquiries. Are you he?"

"By no means. I revile the name of the Curator as a treacherous non-essential."

"Who then may you be?"

"I am no one, nothing. I am an abstraction, an emotion, the ooze of terror, the sweat of horror, the shake in the air when a scream has departed."

"You speak the voice of man."

"Why not? Such things as I speak lie in the closest and dearest center of the human brain."

Guyal said in a subdued voice, "You do not make your invitation as enticing as might be hoped."

"No matter, no matter; enter you must, into the dark and on the instant, as my lord, who is myself, waxes warm and languorous."

"If light there be, we enter."

"No light, no insolent scorch is ever found in the Museum."

"In this case," said Guyal, drawing forth his Scintillant Dagger, "I innovate a welcome reform. For see, now there is light!"

From the under-pommel issued a searching glare; the ghost tall before them screeched and fell into twinkling ribbons like pulverized tinsel. There were a few vagrant motes in the air; he was gone.

Shierl, who had stood stark and stiff as one mesmerized, gasped a soft warm gasp and fell against Guyal. "How can you be so defiant?"

Guyal said in a voice half-laugh, half-quaver, "In truth I do not know . . . Perhaps I find it incredible that the Norns would direct me from pleasant Sfere, through forest and crag, into the northern waste, merely to play the role of cringing victim. Disbelieving so inconclusive a destiny, I am bold."

He moved the dagger to right and left, and they saw themselves to be at the portal of a keep, cut from concreted rock. At the back opened a black depth. Crossing the floor swiftly, Guyal kneeled and listened.

He heard no sound. Shierl, at his back, stared with eyes as black and deep as the pit itself, and Guyal, turning, received a sudden irrational impression of a sprite of the olden times—a creature small and delicate, heavy with the weight of her charm, pale, sweet, clean.

Leaning with his glowing dagger, he saw a crazy rack of stairs voyaging down into the dark, and his light showed them and their shadows in so confusing a guise that he blinked and drew back.

Shierl said, "What do you fear?"

Guyal rose, turned to her. "We are momentarily untended here in the Museum of Man, and we are impelled forward by various forces; you by the will of your people; I, by that which has driven me since I first tasted air . . . If we stay here we shall be once more arranged in harmony with the hostile pattern. If we go forward boldly, we may so come to a position of strategy and advantage. I propose that we set forth in all courage, descend these stairs and seek the Curator."

"But does he exist?"

"The ghost spoke fervently against him."

"Let us go then," said Shierl. "I am resigned."

Guyal said gravely, "We go in the mental frame of adventure, aggressiveness, zeal. Thus does fear vanish and the ghosts become creatures of mind-weft; thus does our elan burst the under-earth terror."

"We go."

They started down the stairs.

Back, forth, back, forth, down flights at varying angles, stages of varying heights, treads at varying widths, so that each step was a matter for concentration. Back, forth, down, down, down, and the black-barred shadows moved and jerked in bizarre modes on the walls.

The flight ended, they stood in a room similar to the entry above. Before them was another black portal, polished at one spot by use; on the walls to either side were inset brass plaques bearing messages in unfamiliar characters.

Guyal pushed the door open against a slight pressure of cold air, which, blowing through the aperture, made a slight rush, ceasing when Guyal opened the door farther.

"Listen."

It was a far sound, an intermittent clacking, and it held enough fell significance to raise the hairs at Guyal's neck. He felt Shierl's hand gripping his with clammy pressure.

Dimming the dagger's glow to a glimmer, Guyal passed through the door, with Shierl coming after. From afar came the evil sound, and by the echoes they knew they stood in a great hall.

Guyal directed the light to the floor: it was of a black resilient material. Next the wall: polished stone. He permitted the light to glow in the direction opposite to the sound, and a few paces distant they saw a bulky black case, studded with copper bosses, topped by a shallow glass tray in which could be seen an intricate concourse of metal devices.

With the purpose of the black cases not apparent, they followed the wall, and as they walked similar cases appeared, looming heavy and dull, at regular intervals. The clacking receded as they walked; then they came to a right angle, and, turning the corner, they seemed to approach the sound. Black case after black case passed; slowly, tense as foxes, they walked, eyes groping for sight through the darkness.

The wall made another angle, and here there was a door.

Guyal hesitated. To follow the new direction of the wall would mean approaching the source of the sound. Would it be better to discover the worst quickly or to reconnoitre as they went?

He propounded the dilemma to Shierl, who shrugged. "It is all one; sooner or later the ghosts will flit down to pluck at us; then we are lost."

"Not while I possess light to stare them away to wisps and shreds," said Guyal. "Now I would find the Curator, and possibly he is to be found behind this door. We will so discover."

He laid his shoulder to the door; it eased ajar with a crack of golden light. Guyal peered through. He sighed, a muffled sound of wonder.

Now he opened the door further; Shierl clutched at his arm.

"This is the Museum," said Guyal in rapt tone. "Here there is no danger . . . He who dwells in beauty of this sort may never be other than beneficent . . ." He flung wide the door.

The light came from an unknown source, from the air itself, as if leaking from the discrete atoms; every breath was luminous, the room floated full of invigorating glow. A great rug pelted the floor, a monster tabard woven of gold, brown, bronze, two tones of green, fuscous red and smalt blue. Beautiful works of human fashioning ranked the walls. In glorious array hung panels of rich woods, carved, chased, enameled; scenes of olden times painted on woven fiber; formulas of color, designed to convey emotion rather than reality. To one side hung plats of wood laid on with slabs of soapstone, malachite and jade in rectangular patterns, richly varied and subtle, with miniature flecks of cinnabar, rhodocrosite and coral for warmth. Beside was a section given to disks of luminous green, flickering and fluorescent with varying blue films

and moving dots of scarlet and black. Here were representations of
three hundred marvelous flowers, blooms of a forgotten age, no longer
extant on waning Earth; there were as many star-burst patterns, rigidly
conventionalized in form, but each of subtle distinction. All these and
a multitude of other creations, selected from the best of human fervor.

The door thudded softly behind them; staring, every inch of skin
a-tingle, the two from Earth's final time moved forward through the
hall.

"Somewhere near must be the Curator," whispered Guyal. "There
is a sense of careful tending and great effort here in the gallery."

"Look."

Opposite were two doors, laden with the sense of much use. Guyal
strode quickly across the room but was unable to discern the means for
opening the door, for it bore no latch, key, handle, knob or bar. He
rapped with his knuckles and waited; no sound returned.

Shierl tugged at his arm. "These are private regions. It is best not to
venture too rudely."

Guyal turned away and they continued down the gallery. Past the
real expression of man's brightest dreamings they walked, until the
concentration of so much fire and spirit and creativity put them into
awe. "What great minds lie in the dust," said Guyal in a low voice.
"What gorgeous souls have vanished into the buried ages; what marvelous creatures are lost past the remotest memory . . . Nevermore will
there be the like; now, in the last fleeting moments, humanity festers
rich as rotten fruit. Rather than master and overpower our world, our
highest aim is to cheat it through sorcery."

Shierl said, "But you, Guyal—you are apart. You are not like this
. . ."

"I would know," declared Guyal with fierce emphasis. "In all my
youth this ache has driven me, and I have journeyed from the old manse
at Sfere to learn from the Curator . . . I am dissatisfied with the mindless
accomplishments of the magicians, who have all their lore by rote."

Shierl gazed at him with a marveling expression, and Guyal's soul
throbbed with love. She felt him quiver and whispered recklessly,
"Guyal of Sfere, I am yours, I melt for you . . ."

"When we win to peace," said Guyal, "then our world will be of
gladness . . ."

The room turned a corner, widened. And now the clacking sound
they had noticed in the dark outer hall returned, louder, more suggestive of unpleasantness. It seemed to enter the gallery through an arched
doorway opposite.

Guyal moved quietly to this door, with Shierl at his heels, and so they peered into the next chamber.

A great face looked from the wall, a face taller than Guyal, as tall as Guyal might reach with hands on high. The chin rested on the floor, the scalp slanted back into the panel.

Guyal stared, taken aback. In this pageant of beautiful objects, the grotesque visage was the disparity and dissonance a lunatic might have created. Ugly and vile was the face, of a gut-wrenching silly obscenity. The skin shone a gun-metal sheen, the eyes gazed dully from slanting folds of greenish tissue. The nose was a small lump, the mouth a gross pulpy slash.

In sudden uncertainty Guyal turned to Shierl. "Does this not seem an odd work so to be honored here in the Museum of Man?"

Shierl was staring with eyes agonized and wide. Her mouth opened, quivered, wetness streaked her chin. With hands jerking, shaking, she grabbed his arm, staggered back into the gallery.

"Guyal," she cried, "Guyal, come away!" Her voice rose to a pitch. "Come away, come away!"

He faced her in surprise. "What are you saying?"

"That horrible thing in there—"

"It is but the diseased effort of an elder artist."

"It lives."

"How is this!"

"It lives!" she babbled. "It looked at me, then turned and looked at you. And it moved—and then I pulled you away . . ."

Guyal shrugged off her hand; in stark disbelief he faced through the doorway.

"Ahhhh . . ." breathed Guyal.

The face had changed. The torpor had evaporated; the glaze had departed the eye. The mouth squirmed; a hiss of escaping gas sounded. The mouth opened; a great gray tongue lolled forth. And from this tongue darted a tendril slimed with mucus. It terminated in a grasping hand, which groped for Guyal's ankle. He jumped aside; the hand missed its clutch, the tendril coiled.

Guyal, in an extremity, with his bowels clenched by sick fear, sprang back into the gallery. The hand seized Shierl, grasped her ankle. The eyes glistened; and now the flabby tongue swelled another wen, sprouted a new member . . . Shierl stumbled, fell limp, her eyes staring, foam at her lips. Guyal, shouting in a voice he could not hear, shouting high and crazy, ran forward slashing with his dagger. He cut at the gray wrist, but his knife sprang away as if the steel itself were horrified. His gorge at his teeth, he seized the tendril; with a mighty effort he broke it against his knee.

The face winced, the tendril jerked back. Guyal leapt forward, dragged Shierl into the gallery, lifted her, carried her back, out of reach.

Through the doorway now, Guyal glared in hate and fear. The mouth had closed; it sneered disappointment and frustrated lust. And now Guyal saw a strange thing: from the dank nostril oozed a wisp of white which swirled, writhed, formed a tall thing in a white robe—a thing with a drawn face and eyes like holes in a skull. Whimpering and mewing in distaste for the light, it wavered forward into the gallery, moving with curious little pauses and hesitancies.

Guyal stood still. Fear had exceeded its power; fear no longer had meaning. A brain could react only to the maximum of its intensity; how could this thing harm him now? He would smash it with his hands, beat it into sighing fog.

"Hold, hold, hold!" came a new voice. "Hold, hold, hold. My charms and tokens, an ill day for Thorsingol . . . But then, avaunt, you ghost, back to the orifice, back and avaunt, avaunt, I say! Go, else I loose the actinics; trespass is not allowed, by supreme command from the Lycurgat; aye, the Lycurgat of Thorsingol. Avaunt, so then."

The ghost wavered, paused, staring in fell passivity at the old man who had hobbled into the gallery.

Back to the snoring face wandered the ghost, and let itself be sucked up into the nostril.

The face rumbled behind its lips, then opened the great gray gape and belched a white fiery lick that was like flame but not flame. It sheeted, flapped at the old man, who moved not an inch. From a rod fixed high on the door frame came a whirling disk of golden sparks. It cut and dismembered the white sheet, destroyed it back to the mouth of the face, whence now issued a black bar. This bar edged into the whirling disk and absorbed the sparks. There was an instant of dead silence.

Then the old man crowed, "Ah, you evil episode; you seek to interrupt my tenure. But no, there is no validity in your purpose; my clever baton holds your unnatural sorcery in abeyance; you are as naught; why do you not disengage and retreat into Jeldred?"

The rumble behind the large lips continued. The mouth opened wide: a gray viscous cavern was so displayed. The eyes glittered in titantic emotion. The mouth yelled, a roaring wave of violence, a sound to buffet the head and drive shock like a nail into the mind.

The baton sprayed a mist of silver. The sound curved and centralized and sucked into the metal fog; the sound was captured and consumed;

it was never heard. The fog balled, lengthened to an arrow, plunged with intense speed at the nose, and buried itself in the pulp. There was a heavy sound, an explosion; the face seethed in pain and the nose was a blasted clutter of shredded gray plasms. They waved like starfish arms and grew together once more, and now the nose was pointed like a cone.

The old man said, "You are captious today, my demoniac visitant—a vicious trait. You would disturb poor old Kerlin in his duties? So. You are ingenuous and neglectful. So ho. Baton," and he turned and peered at the rod, "you have tasted that sound? Spew out a fitting penalty, smear the odious face with your infallible retort."

A flat sound, a black flail which curled, slapped the air and smote home to the face. A glowing weal sprang into being. The face sighed and the eyes twisted up into their folds of greenish tissue.

Kerlin the Curator laughed, a shrill yammer on a single tone. He stopped short and the laugh vanished as if it had never begun. He turned to Guyal and Shierl, who stood pressed together in the doorframe.

"How now, how now? You are after the gong; the study hours are long ended. Why do you linger?" He shook a stern finger. "The Museum is not the site for roguery; this I admonish. So now be off, home to Thorsingol; be more prompt the next time; you disturb the established order . . ." He paused and threw a fretful glance over his shoulder. "The day has gone ill; the Nocturnal Key-keeper is inexcusably late . . . Surely I have waited an hour on the sluggard; the Lycurgat shall be so informed. I would be home to couch and hearth; here is ill use for old Kerlin, thus to detain him for the careless retard of the nightwatch . . . And, further, the encroachment of you two laggards; away now, and be off; out into the twilight!" And he advanced, making directive motions with his hands.

Guyal said, "My lord Curator, I must speak words with you."

The old man halted, peered. "Eh? What now? At the end of a long day's effort? No, no, you are out of order; regulation must be observed. Attend my audiarium at the fourth circuit tomorrow morning; then we shall hear you. So go now, go."

Guyal fell back nonplussed. Shierl fell on her knees. "Sir Curator, we beg you for help; we have no place to go."

Kerlin the Curator looked at her blankly. "No place to go! What folly you utter! Go to your domicile, or to the Pubescentarium, or to the Temple, or to the Outward Inn. Forsooth, Thorsingol is free with lodging; the Museum is no casual tavern."

"My lord," cried Guyal desperately, "will you hear me? We speak from emergency."

"Say on then."

"Some malignancy has bewitched your brain. Will you credit this?"

"Ah, indeed?" ruminated the Curator.

"There is no Thorsingol. There is naught but dark waste. Your city is an eon gone."

The Curator smiled benevolently. "Ah, sad . . . A sad case. So it is with these younger minds. The frantic drive of life is the Prime Unhinger." He shook his head. "My duty is clear. Tired bones, you must wait your well-deserved rest. Fatigue—begone; duty and simple humanity make demands; here is madness to be countered and cleared. And in any event the Nocturnal Key-keeper is not here to relieve me of my tedium." He beckoned. "Come."

Hesitantly Guyal and Shierl followed him. He opened one of his doors, passed through muttering and expostulating with doubt and watchfulness, Guyal and Shierl came after.

The room was cubical, floored with dull black stuff, walled with myriad golden knobs on all sides. A hooded chair occupied the center of the room, and beside it was a chest-high lectern whose face displayed a number of toggles and knurled wheels.

"This is the Curator's own Chair of Knowledge," explained Kerlin. "As such it will, upon proper adjustment, impose the Pattern of Hynomeneural Clarity. So—I demand the correct sometsyndic arrangement—" he manipulated the manuals "—and now, if you will compose yourself, I will repair your hallucination. It is beyond my normal call of duty, but I am humane and would not be spoken of as mean or unwilling."

Guyal inquired anxiously, "Lord Curator, this Chair of Clarity, how will it affect me?"

Kerlin the Curator said grandly, "The fibers of your brain are twisted, snarled, frayed, and so make contact with unintentional areas. By the marvelous craft of our modern cerebrologists, this hood will compose your synapses with the correct readings from the library—those of normality, you must understand—and so repair the skein, and make you once more a whole man."

"Once I sit in the chair," Guyal inquired, "what will you do?"

"Merely close this contact, engage this arm, throw in this toggle—then you daze. In thirty seconds, this bulb glows, signaling the success and completion of the treatment. Then I reverse the manipulation, and you arise a creature of renewed sanity."

Guyal looked at Shierl. "Did you hear and comprehend?"

"Yes, Guyal," in a small voice.

"Remember." Then to the Curator: "Marvelous. But how must I sit?"

"Merely relax in the seat. Then I pull the hood slightly forward, to shield the eyes from distraction."

Guyal leaned forward, peered gingerly into the hood. "I fear I do not understand."

The Curator hopped forward impatiently. "It is an act of the utmost facility. Like this." He sat in the chair.

"And how will the hood be applied?"

"In this wise." Kerlin seized a handle, pulled the shield over his face.

"Quick," said Guyal to Shierl. She sprang to the lectern; Kerlin the Curator made a motion to release the hood; Guyal seized the spindly frame, held it. Shierl flung the switches; the Curator relaxed, sighed.

Shierl gazed at Guyal, dark eyes wide and liquid as the great water-flamerian of South Almery. "Is he—dead?"

"I hope not."

They gazed uncertainly at the relaxed form. Seconds passed.

A clanging noise sounded from afar—a crush, a wrench, an exultant bellow, lesser halloos of wild triumph.

Guyal rushed to the door. Prancing, wavering, sidling into the gallery came a multitude of ghosts; through the open door behind, Guyal could see the great head. It was shoving out, pushing into the room. Great ears appeared, part of a bull-neck, wreathed with purple wattles. The wall cracked, sagged, crumbled. A great hand thrust through, a fore-arm . . .

Shierl screamed. Guyal, pale and quivering, slammed the door in the face of the nearest ghost. It seeped in around the jamb, slowly, wisp by wisp.

Guyal sprang to the lectern. The bulb showed dullness. Guyal's hands twitched along the controls. "Only Kerlin's awareness controls the magic of the baton," he panted. "So much is clear." He stared into the bulb with agonized urgency. "Glow, bulb, glow . . ."

By the door the ghost seeped and billowed.

"Glow, bulb, glow . . ."

The bulb glowed. With a sharp cry Guyal returned the switches to neutrality, jumped down, flung up the hood.

Kerlin the Curator sat looking at him.

Behind the ghost formed itself—a tall white thing in white robes, and the dark eye-holes stared like outlets into nonimagination.

Kerlin the Curator sat looking.

The ghost moved under the robes. A hand like a bird's-foot appeared, holding a clod of dingy matter. The ghost cast the matter to the floor; it exploded into a puff of black dust. The motes of the cloud grew, became a myriad of wriggling insects. With one accord they darted across the floor, growing as they spread, and became scuttling creatures with monkey-heads.

Kerlin the Curator moved. "Baton," he said. He held up his hand. It held his baton. The baton spat an orange gout—red dust. It puffed before the rushing horde and each mote became a red scorpion. So ensued a ferocious battle, and little shrieks and chittering sounds rose from the floor.

The monkey-headed things were killed, routed. The ghost sighed, moved his claw-hand once more. But the baton spat forth a ray of purest light and the ghost sloughed into nothingness.

"Kerlin!" cried Guyal. "The demon is breaking into the gallery."

Kerlin flung open the door, stepped forth.

"Baton," said Kerlin, "perform thy utmost intent."

The demon said, "No, Kerlin, hold the magic; I thought you dazed. Now I retreat."

With a vast quaking and heaving he pulled back until once more only his face showed through the hole.

"Baton," said Kerlin, "be you on guard."

The baton disappeared from his hand.

Kerlin turned and faced Guyal and Shierl.

"There is need for many words, for now I die. I die, and the Museum shall lie alone. So let us speak quickly, quickly, quickly . . ."

Kerlin moved with feeble steps to a portal which snapped aside as he approached. Guyal and Shierl, speculating on the probable trends of Kerlin's disposition, stood hesitantly to the rear.

"Come, come," said Kerlin in sharp impatience. "My strength flags, I die. You have been my death."

Guyal moved slowly forward, with Shierl half a pace behind. Suitable response to the accusation escaped him; words seemed without conviction.

Kerlin surveyed them with a thin grin. "Halt your misgivings and hasten; the necessities to be accomplished in the time available thereto make the task like trying to write the Tomes of Kae in a minim of ink. I wane; my pulsing comes in shallow tides, my sight flickers . . ."

He waved a despairing hand, then, turning, led them into the inner chamber, where he slumped into a great chair. With many uneasy glances at the door, Guyal and Shierl settled upon a padded couch.

Kerlin jeered in a feeble voice, "You fear the white phantasms? Poh, they are pent from the gallery by the baton, which contains their every effort. Only when I am smitten out of mind—or dead—will the baton cease its function. You must know," he added with somewhat more vigor, "that the energies and dynamics do not channel from my brain but from the central potentium of the Museum, which is perpetual; I merely direct and order the rod."

"But this demon—who or what is he? Why does he come to look through the walls?"

Kerlin's face settled into a bleak mask. "He is Blikdak, Ruler-Divinity of the demon-world Jeldred. He wrenched the hole intent on gulfing the knowledge of the Museum into his mind, but I forestalled him; so he sits waiting in the hole till I die. Then he will glut himself with erudition to the great disadvantage of men."

"Why cannot this demon be exhorted hence and the hole abolished?"

Kerlin the Curator shook his head. "The fires and furious powers I control are not valid in the air of the demon-world, where substance and form are of different entity. So far as you see him, he has brought his environment with him; so far he is safe. When he ventures further into the Museum, the power of Earth dissolves the Jeldred mode; then may I spray him with prismatic fervor from the potentium . . . But stay, enough of Blikdak for the nonce; tell me, who are you, why are you ventured here, and what is the news of Thorsingol?"

Guyal said in a halting voice, "Thorsingol is passed beyond memory. There is naught above but arid tundra and the old town of the Saponids. I am of the southland; I have coursed many leagues so that I might speak to you and fill my mind with knowledge. This girl Shierl is of the Saponids, and victim of an ancient custom which sends beauty into the Museum at the behest of Blikdak's ghosts."

"Ah," breathed Kerlin, "have I been so aimless? I recall these youthful shapes which Blikdak employed to relieve the tedium of his vigil . . . They flit down my memory like may-flies along a panel of glass . . . I put them aside as creatures of his own conception, postulated by his own imagery . . ."

Shierl shrugged in bewilderment. "But why? What use to him are human creatures?"

Kerlin said dully, "Girl, you are all charm and freshness; the monstrous urges of the demon-lord Blikdak are past your conceiving. These youths, of both sexes, are his play, on whom he practices various junctures, joinings, coiti, perversions, sadisms, nauseas, antics and at last struggles to the death. Then he sends forth a ghost demanding further youth and beauty."

Shierl whispered, "This was to have been I . . ."

Guyal said in puzzlement, "I cannot understand. Such acts, in my understanding, are the characteristic derangements of humanity. They are anthropoid by the very nature of the functioning sacs, glands and organs. Since Blikdak is a demon . . ."

"Consider him!" spoke Kerlin. "His lineaments, his apparatus. He is nothing else but anthropoid, and such is his origin, together with all the demons, frits and winged glowing-eyed creatures that infest latter-day Earth. Blikdak, like the others, is from the mind of man. The sweaty condensation, the stench and vileness, the cloacal humors, the brutal delights, the rapes and sodomies, the scatophilac whims, the manifold tittering lubricities that have drained through humanity formed a vast tumor; so Blikdak assumed his being, so now this is he. You have seen how he molds his being, so he performs his enjoyments. But of Blikdak, enough. I die, I die!" He sank into the chair with heaving chest.

"See me! My eyes vary and waver. My breath is shallow as a bird's, my bones are the pith of an old vine. I have lived beyond knowledge; in my madness I knew no passage of time. Where there is no knowledge there are no somatic consequences. Now I remember the years and centuries, the millennia, the epochs—they are like quick glimpses through a shutter. So, curing my madness, you have killed me."

Shierl blinked, drew back. "But when you die? What then? Blikdak . . ."

Guyal asked, "In the Museum of Man is there no knowledge of the exorcisms necessary to dissolve this demon? He is clearly our first antagonist, our immediacy."

"Blikdak must be eradicated," said Kerlin. "Then will I die in ease; then must you assume the care of the Museum." He licked his white lips. "An ancient principle specifies that, in order to destroy a substance, the nature of the substance must be determined. In short, before Blikdak may be dissolved, we must discover his elemental nature." And his eyes moved glassily to Guyal.

"Your pronouncement is sound beyond argument," admitted Guyal, "but how may this be accomplished? Blikdak will never allow such an investigation."

"No; there must be subterfuge, some instrumentality . . ."

"The ghosts are part of Blikdak's stuff?"

"Indeed."

"Can the ghosts be stayed and prevented?"

"Indeed; in a box of light, the which I can effect by a thought. Yes, a ghost we must have." Kerlin raised his head. "Baton! one ghost; admit a ghost!"

A moment passed; Kerlin held up his hand. There was a faint scratch at the door, and a soft whine could be heard without. "Open," said a voice, full of sobs and catches and quavers. "Open and let forth the youthful creatures to Blikdak. He finds boredom and lassitude in his vigil; so let the two come forth to negate his unease."

Kerlin laboriously rose to his feet. "It is done."

From behind the door came a sad voice, "I am pent, I am snared in scorching brilliance!"

"Now we discover," said Guyal. "What dissolves the ghost dissolves Blikdak."

"True indeed," assented Kerlin.

"Why not light?" inquired Shierl. "Light parts the fabric of the ghosts like a gust of wind tatters the fog."

"But merely for their fragility; Blikdak is harsh and solid, and can withstand the fiercest radiance safe in his demonland alcove." And Kerlin mused. After a moment he gestured to the door. "We go to the image-expander; there we will explode the ghost to macroid dimension; so shall we find his basis. Guyal of Sfere, you must support my frailness; in truth my limbs are weak as wax."

On Guyal's arm he tottered forward, and with Shierl close at their heels they gained the gallery. Here the ghost wept in its cage of light, and searched constantly for a dark aperture to seep his essence through.

Paying him no heed Kerlin hobbled and limped across the gallery. In their wake followed the box of light and perforce the ghost.

"Open the great door," cried Kerlin in a voice beset with cracking and hoarseness. "The great door into the Cognative Repository!"

Shierl ran ahead and thrust her force against the door; it slid aside, and they looked into the great dark hall, and the golden light from the gallery dwindled into the shadows and was lost.

"Call for Lumen," Kerlin said.

"Lumen!" cried Guyal. "Lumen, attend!"

Light came to the great hall, and it proved so tall that the pilasters along the wall dwindled to threads, and so long and wide that a man might be winded to fatigue in running a dimension. Spaced in equal rows were the black cases with the copper bosses that Guyal and Shierl had noted on their entry. And above each hung five similar cases, precisely fixed, floating without support.

"What are these?" asked Guyal in wonder.

"Would my poor brain encompassed a hundredth part of what these banks know," panted Kerlin. "They are great brains crammed with all that known, experienced, achieved, or recorded by man. Here is all the lost lore, early and late, the fabulous imaginings, the history of ten million cities, the beginnings of time and the presumed finalities; the reason for human existence and the reason for the reason. Daily I have labored and toiled in these banks; my achievement has been a synopsis of the most superficial sort: a panorama across a wide and multifarious country."

Said Shierl, "Would not the craft to destroy Blikdak be contained here?"

"Indeed, indeed; our task would be merely to find the information. Under which casing would we search? Consider these categories: Demonlands; Killings and Mortefactions; Expositions and Dissolutions of Evil; History of Granvilunde (where such an entity was repelled); Attractive and Detractive Hyperordnets; Therapy for Hallucinants and Ghost-takers; Constructive Journal, item for regeneration of burst walls, sub-division for invasion by demons; Procedural Suggestions in Time of Risk . . . Aye, these and a thousand more. Somewhere is knowledge of how to smite Blikdak's abhorred face back into his quasi-place. But where to look? There is no Index Major; none except the poor synopsis of my compilation. He who seeks specific knowledge must often go on an extended search . . ." His voice trailed off. Then: "Forward! Forward through the banks to the Mechanismus."

So through the banks they went, like roaches in a maze, and behind drifted the cage of light with the wailing ghost. At last they entered a chamber smelling of metal; again Kerlin instructed Guyal and Guyal called, "Attend us, Lumen, attend!"

Through intricate devices walked the three, Guyal lost and rapt beyond inquiry, even though his brain ached with the want of knowing.

At a tall booth Kerlin halted the cage of light. A pane of vitrean dropped before the ghost. "Observe now," Kerlin said, and manipulated the activants.

They saw the ghost, depicted and projected: the flowing robe, the haggard visage. The face grew large, flattened; a segment under the vacant eye became a scabrous white place. It separated into pustules, and a single pustule swelled to fill the pane. The crater of the pustule was an intricate stippled surface, a mesh as of fabric, knit in a lacy pattern.

"Behold!" said Shierl. "He is a thing woven as if by thread."

Guyal turned eagerly to Kerlin; Kerlin raised a finger for silence. "Indeed, indeed, a goodly thought, especially since here beside us is a rotor of extreme swiftness, used in reeling the cognitive filaments of the cases . . . Now then observe: I reach to this panel, I select a mesh, I withdraw a thread, and note! The meshes ravel and loosen and part. And now to the bobbin on the rotor, and I wrap the thread, and now with a twist we have the cincture made . . ."

Shierl said dubiously, "Does not the ghost observe and note your doing?"

"By no means," asserted Kerlin. "The pane of vitrean shields our actions; he is too exercised to attend. And now I dissolve the cage and he is free."

The ghost wandered forth, cringing from the light.

"Go!" cried Kerlin. "Back to your genetrix; back, return and go!"

The ghost departed. Kerlin said to Guyal, "Follow; find when Blikdak snuffs him up."

Guyal at a cautious distance watched the ghost seep up into the black nostril, and returned to where Kerlin waited by the rotor. "The ghost has once more become part of Blikdak."

"Now then," said Kerlin, "we cause the rotor to twist, the bobbin to whirl, and we shall observe."

The rotor whirled to a blur; the bobbin (as long as Guyal's arm) became spun with ghost-thread, at first glowing pastel polychrome, then nacre, then fine milk-ivory.

The rotor spun, a million times a minute, and the thread drawn unseen and unknown from Blikdak thickened on the bobbin.

The rotor spun; the bobbin was full—a cylinder shining with glossy silken sheen. Kerlin slowed the rotor; Guyal snapped a new bobbin into place, and the unraveling of Blikdak continued.

Three bobbins—four—five—and Guyal, observing Blikdak from afar, found the giant face quiescent, the mouth working and sucking, creating the clacking sound which had first caused them apprehension.

Eight bobbins. Blikdak opened his eyes, stared in puzzlement around the chamber.

Twelve bobbins: a discolored spot appeared on the sagging cheek, and Blikdak quivered in uneasiness.

Twenty bobbins: the spot spread across Blikdak's visage, across the slanted fore-dome, and his mouth hung lax; he hissed and fretted.

Thirty bobbins: Blikdak's head seemed stale and putrid; the gunmetal sheen had become an angry maroon, the eyes bulged, the mouth hung open, the tongue lolled limp.

Fifty bobbins: Blikdak collapsed. His dome lowered against the febrile mouth; his eyes shone like feverish coals.

Sixty bobbins: Blikdak was no more.

And with the dissolution of Blikdak so dissolved Jeldred, the demonland created for the housing of evil. The breach in the wall gave on barren rock, unbroken and rigid.

And in the Mechanismus sixty shining bobbins lay stacked neat; the evil so disorganized glowed with purity and irridescence.

Kerlin fell back against the wall. "I expire; my time has come. I have guarded well the Museum; together we have won it away from Blikdak . . . Attend me now. Into your hands I pass the curacy; now the Museum is your charge to guard and preserve."

"For what end?" asked Shierl. "Earth expires, almost as you . . . Wherefore knowledge?"

"More now than ever," gasped Kerlin. "Attend: the stars are bright, the stars are fair; the banks know blessed magic to fleet you to youthful climes. Now—I go. I die."

"Wait!" cried Guyal. "Wait, I beseech!"

"Why wait?" whispered Kerlin. "The way to peace is on me; you call me back?"

"How do I extract from the banks?"

"The key to the index is in my chambers, the index of my life . . ." And Kerlin died.

Guyal and Shierl climbed to the upper ways and stood outside the portal on the ancient flagged floor. It was night; the marble shone faintly underfoot, the broken columns loomed on the sky.

Across the plain the yellow lights of Saponce shone warm through the trees; above in the sky shone the stars.

Guyal said to Shierl, "There is your home; there is Saponce. Do you wish to return?"

She shook her head. "Together we have looked through the eyes of knowledge. We have seen old Thorsingol, and the Sherrit Empire before it, and Golwan Andra before that and the Forty Kades even before. We have seen the warlike green-men, and the knowledgeable Pharials and the Clambs who departed Earth for the stars, as did the Merioneth before them and the Gray Sorcerers still earlier. We have seen oceans rise and fall, the mountains crust up, peak and melt in the beat of rain;

we have looked on the sun when it glowed hot and full and yellow
. . . No, Guyal, there is no place for me at Saponce . . ."

Guyal, leaning back on the weathered pillar, looked up to the stars.
"Knowledge is ours, Shierl—all of knowing to our call. And what shall
we do?"

Together they looked up to the white stars.

"What shall we do . . ."

ROGER ZELAZNY
Tower of Ice

THE DARK, horse-shaped beast paused on the icy trail. Head turned to the left and upward, it regarded the castle atop the glistening mountain, as did its rider.

"No," the man finally stated.

The black beast continued on, ice cracking beneath its cloven metal hooves, snow blowing about it.

"I'm beginning to suspect that there is no trail," the beast announced after a time. "We've come more than halfway around."

"I know," replied the muffled, green-booted rider. "I might be able to scale the thing, but that would mean leaving you behind."

"Risky," his mount replied. "You know my value in certain situations—especially the one you court."

"True. But if it should prove the only way . . ."

They moved on for some time, pausing periodically to study the prominence.

"Dilvish, there was a gentler part of the slope—some distance back," the beast announced. "If I'd a good start, I could bear you quite a distance up it. Not all of the way to the top, but near."

"If that should prove the only way, Black, we'll go that route," the rider replied, breath steaming before him to be whipped away by the wind. "We might as well check further first, though. Hello! What is—"

A dark form came hurtling down the side of the mountain. When it seemed that it was about to strike the ice before them, it spread pale-green, batlike wings and pulled itself aloft. It circled quickly, gaining altitude, then dove toward them.

Immediately his blade was in his hand, held vertically before him. Dilvish leaned back, eyes on the approaching creature. At the sight of his weapon, it veered off, to return immediately. He swung at it and missed. It darted away again.

"Obviously our presence is no longer a secret," Black commented, turning so as to face the flying thing.

The creature dove once more and Dilvish swung again. It turned at the last moment, to be struck by the side of his blade. It fell then, fluttered, rose into the air again, circled several times, climbed higher, turned away. It began to fly back up along the side of the Tower of Ice.

"Yes, it would seem we have lost the advantage of surprise," Dilvish observed. "Actually, I'd thought he would have noted us sooner."

He sheathed his blade.

"Let's go find that trail—if there is one."

They continued on their way about the base of the mountain.

Corpselike, the green and white face stared out of the mirror. No one stood before it to cast such an image. The high stone hall was reflected behind it, threadbare tapestries on its walls, several narrow windows, the long, heavy dining table, a candelabrum flickering at its farther end. The wind made moaning noises down a nearby chimney, alternately flattening and drawing the flames in the wide fireplace.

The face seemed to be regarding the diners: a thin, dark-haired, dark-eyed young man in a black doublet lined with green, who toyed with his food and whose nervous gestures carried his fingers time and again to the heavy, black metal ring with the pale pink stone that depended from a chain about his neck; and a girl, whose hair and eyes matched the man's, whose generous mouth quirked into occasional odd, quick smiles as she ate with better appetite. She had a brown and red cloak thrown about her shoulders, its ends folded across her lap. Her eyes were not so deep-set as the man's and they did not dart as his did.

The thing in the mirror moved its pale lips.

"The time is coming," it announced, in a deep, expressionless voice.

The man leaned forward and cut a piece of meat. The girl raised her wineglass. Something seemed to flutter against one of the windows for a moment.

From somewhere far up the long corridor to the girl's right, an agonized voice rang out:

"Release me! Oh, please don't do this! Please! It hurts so much!"

The girl sipped her wine.

"The time is coming," the thing in the mirror repeated.

"Ridley, would you pass the bread?" the girl asked.

"Here."

"Thank you."

She broke off a piece and dipped it into the gravy. The man watched her eat, as if fascinated by the act.

"The time is coming," the thing said again.

Suddenly Ridley slapped the table. His cutlery rattled. Beads of wine fell across his plate.

"Reena, can't you shut that damned thing off?" he asked.

"Why, you summoned it," she said sweetly. "Can't you just wave your wand or snap your fingers and give it the proper words?"

He slapped the table again, half rising from his seat.

"I will not be mocked!" he said. "Shut it off!"

She shook her head slowly.

"Not my sort of magic," she replied, less sweetly. "I don't fool with things like that."

From up the hall came more cries:

"It hurts! Oh, please! It hurts so . . ."

". . . Or that," she said more sternly. "Besides, you told me at the time that it was serving a useful purpose."

Ridley lowered himself into his seat.

"I was not—myself," he said softly, taking up his wineglass and draining it.

A mummy-faced individual in dark livery immediately rushed forward from the shadowy corner beside the fireplace to refill his glass.

Faintly, and from a great distance, there came a rattling, as of chains. A shadowy form fluttered against a different window. Ridley fingered his neck chain and drank again.

"The time is coming," announced the corpse-colored face under glass.

Ridley hurled his wineglass at it. It shattered, but the mirror remained intact. Perhaps the faintest of smiles touched the corners of that ghastly mouth. The servant hurried to bring him another glass.

There came more cries from up the hall.

"It's no good," Dilvish stated. "We've more than circled it. I don't see any easy way up."

"You know how sorcerers can be. Especially this one."

"True."

"You should have asked that werewolf you met a while back about it."

"Too late now. If we just keep going, we should come to that slope you mentioned pretty soon, shouldn't we?"

"Eventually," Black replied, trudging on. "I could use a bucket of demon juice. I'd even settle for wine."

"I wish I had some wine here myself. I haven't sighted that flying thing again." He looked up into the darkening sky, to where the snow- and ice-decked castle stood with a high window illuminated. "Unless I've glimpsed it darting about up there," he said. "Hard to tell, with the snow and shadows."

"Strange that he didn't send something a lot more deadly."

"I've thought of that."

They continued on for a long while. The lines of the slope softened as they advanced, the icy wall dipping toward a slightly gentler inclination. Dilvish recognized the area as one they had passed before, though Black's earlier hoof prints had been completely obliterated.

"You're pretty low on supplies, aren't you?" Black asked.

"Yes."

"Then I guess we'd better do something—soon."

Dilvish studied the slope as they moved along its foot.

"It gets a little better, farther ahead," Black remarked. Then: "That sorcerer we met—Strodd—had the right idea."

"What do you mean?"

"He headed south. I hate this cold."

"I didn't realize it bothered you, too."

"It's a lot hotter where I come from."

"Would you rather be back there?"

"Now that you mention it, no."

Several minutes later they rounded an icy mass. Black halted and turned his head.

"That's the route I'd choose—over there. You can judge it best from here."

Dilvish followed the slope upward with his eyes. It reached about three quarters of the way up to the castle. Above it the wall rose sheer and sharp.

"How far up do you think you can get me?" he asked.

"I'll have to stop when it goes vertical. Can you scale the rest?"

Dilvish shaded his eyes and squinted.

"I don't know. It looks bad. But then, so does the grade. Are you sure you can make it that far?"

Black was silent for a time, then: "No, I'm not," he said. "But we've been all the way around, and this is the only place where I think we've got a chance."

Dilvish lowered his eyes.

"What do you say?"

"Let's do it."

"I don't see how you can sit there eating like that!" Ridley declared, throwing down his knife. "It's disgusting!"

"One must keep up one's strength in the face of calamities," Reena replied, taking another mouthful. "Besides, the food is exceptionally good tonight. Which one prepared it?"

"I don't know. I can't tell the staff apart. I just give them orders."

"The time is coming," stated the mirror.

Something fluttered against the window again and stopped, hanging there, a dark outline. Reena sighed, lowered her utensils, rose. She rounded the table and crossed to the window.

"I am not going to open the window in weather like this!" she shouted. "I told you that before! If you want to come in, you can fly down one of the chimneys! Or not, as you please!"

She listened a moment to a rapid chittering noise from beyond the pane.

"No, not just this once!" she said then. "I told you that before you went out in it!"

She turned and stalked back to her seat, her shadow dancing on a tapestry as the candles flickered.

"Oh, don't. . . . Please, don't. . . . Oh!" came a cry from up the hall.

She settled into her chair once more, ate a final mouthful, took another sip of wine.

"We've got to do something," Ridley said, stroking the ring on the chain. "We can't just sit here."

"I'm quite comfortable," she answered.

"You're in this as much as I am."

"Hardly."

"He's not going to look at it that way."

"I wouldn't be too sure."

Ridley snorted.

"Your charms won't save you from the reckoning."

She protruded her lower lip in a mock pout.

"On top of everything else, you insult my femininity."

"You're pushing me, Reena!"

"You know what to do about it, don't you?"

"No!" He slammed his fist against the table. "I won't!"

"The time is coming," said the mirror.

He covered his face with his hands and lowered his head.

"I—I'm afraid . . ." he said softly.

Now out of his sight, a look of concern tightened her brow, narrowed her eyes.

"I'm afraid of—the other," he said.

"Can you think of any other course?"

"You do something! You've got powers!"

"Not on that level," she said. "The other is the only one I can think of who would have a chance."

"But he's untrustworthy! I can't anticipate him anymore!"

"But he gets stronger all the time. Soon he may be strong enough."

"I—I don't know. . . ."

"Who got us into this mess?"

"That's not fair!"

He lowered his hands and raised his head just as a rattling began within the chimney. Particles of soot and mortar fell upon the flames.

"Oh, really!" she said.

"That crazy old bat—" he began, turning his head.

"Now, that isn't nice either," Reena stated. "After all—"

Ashes were scattered as a small body crashed into the flaming logs, bounced away, hopped about the floor flapping long, green, membranous wings, beating sparks from its body fur. It was the size of a small ape, with a shriveled, nearly human face. It squeaked as it hopped, some of its noises sounding strangely like human curses. Finally it came to a stooped standstill, raised its head, turned burning eyes upon them.

"Try to set fire to me!" it chirped shrilly.

"Come on now! Nobody tried to set fire to you." Reena said.

". . . Said 'chimney'!" it cried.

"There are plenty of chimneys up there," Reena stated. "It's pretty stupid to choose a smoking one."

". . . Not stupid!"

"What else can you call it?"

The creature sniffed several times.

"I'm sorry," Reena said. "But you could have been more careful."

"The time is coming," said the mirror.

The creature turned its small head, stuck out its tongue.

". . . Lot you know," it said. "He . . . he beat me!"

"Who? Who beat you?" Ridley asked.

". . . The avenger." It made a sweeping, downward gesture with its right wing. "He's down there."

"Oh, my!" Ridley paled. "You're quite certain?"

". . . He beat me," the creature repeated. Then it began to bounce along the floor, beat at the air with its wings, and flew to the center of the table.

Somewhere, faintly, a chain was rattled.

"How—how do you know he is the avenger?" Ridley asked.

The creature hopped along the table, tore at the bread with its talons, stuffed a piece into its mouth, chewed noisily.

". . . My little ones, my pretty ones," it chanted after a time, glancing about the hall.

"Stop that!" Reena said. "Answer his question! How do you know who it is?"

It raised its wings to its ears.

"Don't shout! Don't shout!" it cried. ". . . I saw! I know! He beat me—poor side!—with a sword!" It paused to hug itself with its wings. ". . . I only went to look up close. My eyes are not so good. . . . He rides a demon beast! Circling, circling—the mountain! Coming, coming —here!"

Ridley shot a look at Reena. She compressed her lips, then shook her head.

"Unless it is airborne it will never make it up the tower," she said. "It wasn't a winged beast, was it?"

". . . No. A horse," the creature replied, tearing at the bread again.

"There was a slide near the south face," Ridley said. "But no. Even so. Not with a horse . . ."

". . . A demon horse."

"Even with a demon horse!"

"The pain! The pain! I can't stand it!" came a shrill cry.

Reena raised her wineglass, saw that it was empty, lowered it again. The mummy-faced man rushed from the shadows to fill it.

For several moments they watched the winged creature eat. Then: "I don't like this," Reena said. "You know how devious he can be."

"I know."

". . . And green boots," chirped the creature. ". . . Elfboots. Always to land on his feet. You burned me, he beat me. . . . Poor Meg! Poor Meg! He'll get you, too . . ."

It hopped down and skittered across the floor.

". . . My little ones, my pretty ones!" it called.

"Not here! Get out of here!" Ridley cried. "Change or go away! Keep them out of here!"

". . . Little ones! Pretties!" came the fading voice as Meg ran up the corridor in the direction of the screams.

Reena swirled the wine in her glass, took a drink, licked her lips.

"The time has come," the mirror suddenly announced.

"Now what are you going to do?" Reena asked.

"I don't feel well," Ridley said.

When they came to the foot of the slope, Black halted and stood like a statue for a long while, studying it. The snow continued to fall. The wind drove the flakes past them.

After several minutes, Black advanced and tested the grade, climbing several paces, standing with his full weight upon it, stamping and digging with his hooves, head lowered.

Finally he backed down the slope and turned away.

"What is the verdict?" Dilvish inquired.

"I am still willing to try. My estimate of our chances is unchanged. Have you given any thought to what you are going to do if—rather, when—you make it to the top?"

"Look for trouble," Dilvish said. "Defend myself at all times. Strike instantly if I see the enemy."

Black began to walk slowly away from the mountain.

"Almost all of your spells are of the offensive variety," Black stated, "and most are too terrible to be used, except in final extremes. You should really take the time to learn some lesser and intermediate ones, you know."

"I know. This is a fine time for a lecture on the state of the art."

"What I am trying to say is that if you get trapped up there, you know how to level the whole damned place and yourself with it. But you don't know how to charm the lock on a door—"

"That is *not* a simple spell!"

"No one said that it was. I am merely pointing out your deficiencies."

"It is a little late for that, isn't it?"

"I am afraid so," Black replied. "So, there are three good general spells of protection against magical attack. You know as well as I do that your enemy can break through any of them. The stronger ones, though, might slow him long enough for you to do something. I can't let you go up there without one of them holding you."

"Then lay the strongest upon me."

"It takes a full day to do it."

Dilvish shook his head.

"In this cold? Too long. What about the others?"

"The first one we may dismiss as insufficient against any decent operator in the arts. The second takes the better part of an hour to call into being. It will give you good protection for about half a day."

Dilvish was silent for a moment. Then: "Let's be about it," he said.

"All right. But even so, there must be servants, to keep the place running. You are probably going to find yourself outnumbered."

Dilvish shrugged.

"It may not be much of a staff," he said, "and there'd be no need to maintain a great guard in an inaccessible spot like this. I'll take my chances."

Black came to the place he deemed sufficiently distant from the slope. He turned and faced the tower.

"Get your rest now," he stated, "while I work your protection. It will probably be the last you have for a while."

Dilvish sighed and leaned forward. Black began speaking in a strange voice. His words seemed to crackle in the icy air.

The latest scream ceased on a weakened note. Ridley got to his feet and moved across the hall to a window. He rubbed at the frosted pane with the palm of his hand, a quick, circular motion. He placed his face near the area he had cleared, holding his breath.

Finally: "What do you see?" Reena asked him.

"Snow," he muttered, "ice . . ."

"Anything else?"

"My reflection," he answered angrily, turning away.

He began to pace. When he passed the face in the mirror, its lips moved.

"The time is come," it said.

He replied with an obscenity. He continued pacing, hands clasped behind his back.

"You think Meg really saw something down there?" he asked.

"Yes. Even the mirror has changed its tune."

"What do you think it is?"

"A man on a strange mount."

"Perhaps he's not actually coming here. Maybe he's on his way someplace else."

She laughed softly.

"Just on his way to the neighborhood tavern for a few drinks," she said.

"All right! All right! I'm not thinking clearly! I'm upset! Supposing—just supposing—he does make it up here. He's only one man."

"With a sword. When was the last time you had one in your hands?" Ridley licked his lips.

". . . And he must be fairly sturdy," she said, "to have come so far across these wastes."

"There are the servants. They obey me. Since they are already dead he'd have a hard time killing them."

"That would tend to follow. On the other hand, they're a bit slower and clumsier than ordinary folk—and they can be dismembered."

"You don't do much to cheer a man up, you know?"

"I am trying to be realistic. If there is a man out there wearing Elfboots, he has chance of making it up here. If he is of the hardy sort and a decent swordsman, then he has a chance of doing what he was sent to do."

". . . And you'll still be mocking and bitching while he lops off my head? Just remember that yours will roll, too!"

She smiled.

"I am in no way responsible for what happened."

"Do you really think he'll see it that way? Or care?"

She looked away.

"You had a chance," she said slowly, "to be one of the truly great ones. But you wouldn't follow the normal courses of development. You were greedy for power. You rushed things. You took risks. You created a doubly dangerous situation. You could have explained the sealing as an experiment that went bad. You could have apologized. He would have been irritated, but he would have accepted it. Now, though, when you can't undo what you did—or do much of anything else, for that matter—he is going to know what happened. He is going to know that you were trying to multiply your power to the point where you could even challenge him. You know what his response has to be under the circumstances. I can almost sympathize with him. If it were me, I would have to do the same thing—destroy you before you get control of the other. You've become an extremely dangerous man."

"But I am powerless! There isn't a damned thing I can do! Not even shut off that simple mirror!" he cried, gesturing toward the face that had just spoken again. "In this state I'm no threat to anybody!"

"Outside of his being inconvenienced by your having cut off his access to one of his strongholds," she said, "he would have to consider the possibility that you keep drawing back from—namely, that if you gain control of the other, you will be one of the most powerful sorcerers in the world. As his apprentice—pardon me, ex-apprentice—who has just apparently usurped a part of his domain, only one thing can follow —a sorcerous duel in which you will actually have a chance of destroying him. Since such a duel has not yet commenced, he must have guessed that you are not ready—or that you are playing some sort of waiting game. So he has sent a human avenger, rather than run the risk that you've turned this place into some sort of magical trap."

"The whole thing could simply have been an accident. He'd have to consider that possibility, too. . . ."

"Under the circumstances, would *you* take the risk of assuming that and waiting? You know the answer. You'd dispatch an assassin."

"I've been a good servant. I've taken care of this place for him. . . ."

"Be sure to petition him for mercy on that count the next time that you see him."

Ridley halted and wrung his hands.

"Perhaps you could seduce him. You're comely enough . . ."

Reena smiled again.

"I'd lay him on an iceberg and not complain," she said. "If it would get us off the hook, I'd give him the high ride of his long life. But a sorcerer like that—"

"Not him. The avenger."

"Oh."

She blushed suddenly. Then she shook her head.

"I can't believe that anyone who has come all this way could be dissuaded from his purposes by a bit of dalliance, even with someone of my admitted charms. Not to mention the thought of the penalty for his failure. No. You are skirting the real issue again. There is only one way out for you, and you know what that is."

He dropped his eyes, fingered the ring on the chain.

"The other . . ." he said. "If I had control of the other, all of our problems would be over . . ."

He stared at the ring as if hypnotized by it.

"That's right," she said. "It's the only real chance."

"But you know what I fear . . ."

"Yes. I fear it, too."

". . . That it may not work—that the other may gain control of *me!*"

"So, either way you are doomed. Just remember, one way it is certain. The other . . . That way there is still a chance."

"Yes," he said, still not looking at her. "But you don't know the horror of it!"

"I can guess."

"But you don't have to go through it!"

"I didn't create the situation either."

He glared at her.

"I'm sick of hearing you protest your innocence just because the other is not your creation! I went to you first and told you everything I proposed to do! Did you try to talk me out of it? No! You saw the gains in store for us! You went along with my doing it!"

She covered her mouth with her fingertips and yawned delicately.

"Brother," she said, "I suppose that you are right. It doesn't change anything, though, does it? Anything that has to be done . . . ?"

He gnashed his teeth and turned away.

"I won't do it. I can't!"

"You may feel differently about it when he comes knocking at your door."

"We have plenty of ways to deal with a single man—even a skilled swordsman!"

"But don't you see? Even if you succeed you are only postponing the decision, not solving the problem."

"I want the time. Maybe I can think of some way to gain an edge over the other."

Reena's features softened.

"Do you really believe that?"

"Anything is possible, I suppose. . . ."

She sighed and stood. She moved toward him.

"Ridley, you are deceiving yourself," she said. "You will never be any stronger than you are now."

"Not true!" he cried, beginning to pace again. "Not true!"

Another scream came from up the hall. The mirror repeated its message.

"Stop him! We have to stop him! *Then* I'll worry about the other!"

He turned and tore out of the room. Reena lowered the hand she had raised toward him and returned to the table to finish her wine. The fireplace continued to sigh.

Black completed the spell. They remained motionless for a brief while after that.

Then: "That's it?" Dilvish asked.

"It is. You are now protected through the second level."

"I don't feel any different."

"That's how you should feel."

"Is there anything special that I should do to invoke its defense, should the need arise?"

"No, it is entirely automatic. But do not let that dissuade you from exercising normal caution about things magical. Any system has its weak points. But that was the best I could do in the time that we had."

Dilvish nodded and looked toward the tower of ice. Black raised his head and faced it, also.

"Then I guess that all of the preliminaries are out of the way," Dilvish said.

"So it would seem. Are you ready?"

"Yes."

Black began to move forward. Glancing down, Dilvish noted that his hooves seemed larger now, flatter. He wanted to ask about it, but the wind came faster as they gained speed and he decided to save his breath. The snow stung his cheeks, his hands. He squinted and leaned farther forward.

Still running on a level surface, Black's pace increased steadily, one hoof giving an almost bell-like tone as it struck some pebble. Soon they were moving faster than any horse could run. Everything to both sides became a snowy blur. Dilvish tried not to look ahead, to protect his eyes, his face. He clung tightly and thought about the course he had come.

He had escaped from Hell itself, after two centuries' torment. Most of the humans he had known were long dead and the world somewhat changed. Yet the one who had banished him, damning him as he did, remained—the ancient sorcerer Jelerak. In the months since his return, he had sought that one, once the call of an ancient duty had been discharged before the walls of Portaroy. Now, he told himself, he lived but for vengeance. And this, this tower of ice, one of the seven strongholds of Jelerak, was the closest he had yet come to his enemy. From Hell he had brought a collection of Awful Sayings—spells of such deadly potency as to place the speaker in as great a jeopardy as the victim should their rendering be even slightly less than flawless. He had only used one since his return and had been successful in leveling an entire small city with it. His shudder was for the memory of that day on that hilltop, rather than for the icy blasts that now assailed him.

A shift in equilibrium told him that Black had reached the slope and commenced the ascent. The wind was making a roaring sound. His head was bowed and turned against the icy pelting. He could feel the rapid crunching of Black's hooves beneath him, steady, all of the movements extraordinarily powerful. If Black should slip, he knew that it

would be all over for him. . . . Good-bye again, world—and Jelerak still
unpunished . . .

As the gleaming surface fled by beneath him, he tried to push all
thoughts of Jelerak and death and vengeance from his mind. As he
listened to the wind and cracking ice, his thoughts came free of the
moment, drifting back over the unhappy years, past the days of his
campaigns, his wanderings, coming to rest on a misty morning in the
glades of far Elfland as he rode to the hunt near the Castle Mirata. The
sun was big and golden, the breezes cool, and everywhere—green. He
could almost smell the earth, feel the texture of tree bark. . . . Would
he ever know that again, the way he once had?

An inarticulate cry escaped him, hurled against the wind and destiny
and the task he had set himself. He cursed then and squeezed harder
with his legs as his equilibrium shifted again and he knew that the
course had steepened.

Black's hooves pounded perhaps a trifle more slowly. Dilvish's hands
and feet and face were growing numb. He wondered how far up they
were. He risked a glance forward but saw only rushing snow. We've
come a long way, he decided. Where will it end?

He called back his memory of the slope as seen from below, tried to
judge their position. Surely they were near the halfway point. Perhaps
they had even passed it. . . .

He counted his heartbeats, counted Black's hoof falls. Yes, it did
seem that the great beast was slowing. . . .

He chanced another look ahead.

This time he caught the barest glimpse of the towering rise above and
before him, sparkling through the evening, sheer, glassy. It obliterated
most of the sky now, so he knew that they must be close.

Black continued to slow. The roaring wind lowered its voice. The
snow came against him with slightly diminished force.

He looked back over his shoulder. He could see the great slope spread
out behind them, glistening like the mosaic tiles in the baths at Ankyra.
Down, down and back . . . They *had* come a great distance.

Black slowed even more. Now Dilvish could hear as well as feel the
crunching of crusted snow and ice beneath them. He eased his grip
slightly, leaned back a little, raised his head. There was the last stage
of the tower, glistening darkly, much nearer now.

Abruptly, the winds ceased. The monolith must be blocking them,
he decided. The snow drifted far more gently here. Black's pace had
become a canter, though he was laboring no less diligently than before.
The journey up the white-smeared tunnel was nearing its end.

Dilvish adjusted his position again, to better study the high escarpment. At this quarter, its surface had resolved itself into a thing of textures. From the play of shadow, he could make out prominences, crevices. Bare rock jutted in numerous places. Quickly he began tracing possible routes to the top.

Black slowed further, almost to a walk, but they now were near to the place where the greatest steepness began. Dilvish cast about for a stopping point.

"What do you think of that ledge off to the right, Black?" he asked.

"Not much" came the reply. "But that's where we're headed. The trickiest part will be making it up onto the shelf. Don't let go yet."

Dilvish clung tightly as Black negotiated a hundred paces, a hundred more.

"It looks wider from here than it did from back there," he observed.

"Yes. Higher, too. Hang on. If we slip here, it's a long way back down."

Black's pace increased slightly as he approached the ledge that stood at nearly the height of a man above the slope. It was indented several span into the cliff face.

Black leapt.

His hind hooves struck a waist-high prominence, a bare wrinkle of icy rock running horizontally below the ledge. His momentum bore him up past it. It cracked and fell away, but by then his forelegs were on the shelf and his rear ones had straightened with a tiny spring. He scrambled up over the ledge and found his footing.

"You all right?" he asked.

"Yes," said Dilvish.

Simultaneously they turned their heads, slowly, and looked back down to where the winds whipped billows of white, like clouds of smoke across the sparkling way. Dilvish reached out and patted Black's shoulder.

"Well done," he said. "Here and there, I was a little worried."

"Did you think you were the only one?"

"No. Can we make it back down again?"

Black nodded.

"We'll have to move a lot more slowly than we did coming up, though. You may even have to walk beside me, holding on. We'll see. This ledge seems to go back a little way. I'll explore it while you are about your business. There may be a slightly better route down. It should be easier to tell from up here."

"All right," Dilvish said, dismounting on the side nearest the cliff face.

He removed his gloves and massaged his hands, blew on them, tucked them into his armpits for a time.

"Have you decided upon the place for your ascent?"

"Off to the left." Dilvish gestured with his head. "That crevice runs most of the way up, and it is somewhat irregular on both sides."

"Looks to be a good choice. How will you get to it?"

"I'll begin climbing here. These handholds look good enough. I'll meet it at that first big break."

Dilvish unfastened his sword belt and slung it over his back. He chafed his hands again, then drew on his gloves.

"I might as well get started," he said. "Thanks, Black. I'll be seeing you."

"Good thing you're wearing those Elfboots," Black said. "If you slip you know that you'll land on your feet—eventually."

Dilvish snorted and reached for the first handhold.

Wearing a dark dress, wrapped in a green shawl, the crone sat upon a small stool in the corner of the long underground chamber. Torches flamed and smoked in two wall sockets, melting—above and behind them—portions of the ice glaze that covered the walls and the ceiling. An oil lamp burned near her feet on the straw-strewn stone of the floor. She hummed to herself, fondling one of the loaves she bore in her shawl.

Across from her were three heavy wooden doors, bound with straps of rusted metal, small, barred windows set high within them. A few faint sounds of movement emerged from the one in the middle, but she was oblivious to this. The water that dripped from the irregular stone ceiling above the torches had formed small pools that spread into the straw and lost their boundaries. The dripping sounds kept syncopated accompaniment to her crooning.

". . . My little ones, my pretty ones," she sang. ". . . Come to Meg. Come to Mommy Meg."

There was a scurrying noise in the straw, in the dim corner near to the left-hand door. Hastily she broke off a piece of bread and tossed it in that direction. There followed a fresh rustling and a small movement. She nodded, rocked back on her seat, and smiled.

From across the way—possibly from behind the middle door—there came a low moan. She cocked her head for a moment, but it was followed by silence.

She cast another piece of bread into the same corner. The sounds that followed were more rapid, more pronounced. The straw rose and fell. She threw another piece, puckered her lips, and made a small chirping noise.

She threw more.

". . . . My little ones," she sang again, as over a dozen rats moved nearer, springing upon the bread, tearing at it, swallowing it. More emerged from dark places to join them, to contest for the food. Isolated squeaks occurred, increased in frequency, gradually merged into a chorus.

She chuckled. She threw more bread, nearer. Thirty or forty rats now fought over it.

From behind the middle door came a clinking of chain links, followed by another moan. Her attention, though, was on her little ones.

She leaned forward and moved the lamp to a position near the wall to her right. She broke another loaf and scattered its pieces on the floor before her feet. Small bodies rustled over the straw, approaching. The squeaking grew louder.

There came a heavy rattling of chains, a much louder moan. Something moved within the cell and crashed against the door. It rattled, and another moan rose above the noises of the rats.

She turned her head in that direction, frowning slightly.

The next blow upon the door made a booming sound. For a moment, something like a massive eye seemed to peer out past the bars.

The moaning sound came again, almost seeming to shape itself into words.

". . . Meg! Meg . . ."

She half rose from her seat, staring at the cell door. The next crash— the loudest thus far—rattled it heavily. By then the rats were brushing against her legs, standing upon their hind paws, dancing. She reached out to stroke one, another . . . She fed them from her hands.

From within the cell the moaning rose again, this time working itself into strange patterns.

". . . Mmmmegg . . . Mmeg . . ." came the sound.

She raised her head once more and looked in that direction. She moved as if about to rise.

Just then, however, a rat jumped into her lap. Another ran up her back and perched upon her right shoulder.

"Pretty ones . . ." she said, rubbing her cheek against the one and stroking the other. "Pretty . . ."

There came a sound as of the snapping of a chain, followed by a terrific crash against the door across from her. She ignored it, however, for her pretty ones were dancing and playing for her. . . .

Reena drew garment after garment from her wardrobe. Her room was full of dresses and cloaks, muffles and hats, coats and boots, underthings and gloves. They lay across the bed and all of the chairs and two wall benches.

Shaking her head, she turned in a slow circle, surveying the lot. The second time around, she withdrew a dress from one of the heaps and draped it over her left arm. Then she took a heavy fur wrap down from a hook. She handed both to the tall, sallow, silent man who stood beside the door. His heavily wrinkled face resembled that of the man who had served her dinner—expressionless, vacant eyed.

He received the garments from her and began folding them. She passed him a second dress, a hat, hose, and underthings. Gloves . . . He accepted two heavy blankets she took down from a shelf. More hose . . . He placed everything within a duffellike sack.

"Bring it along—and one empty one," she said, and she moved toward the door.

She passed through and crossed the hallway to a stair, which she began to descend. The servant followed her, holding the sack by its neck with one hand, before him. He bore another one, folded, beneath his other arm, which hung stiffly at his side.

Reena made her way through corridors to a large, deserted kitchen, where a fire still smouldered beneath a grate. The wind made a whistling noise down the chimney.

She passed the large chopping block and turned left into the pantry. She checked shelves, bins, and cabinets, pausing only to munch a cookie as she looked.

"Give me the bag," she said. "No, not that one. The empty one."

She shook out the bag and began filling it—with dried meats, heads of cheese, wine bottles, loaves of bread. Pausing, she looked about again, then added a sack of tea and a sack of sugar. She also put in a small pot and some utensils.

"Bring this one, too," she said finally, turning and departing the pantry.

She moved more cautiously now, the servant treading silently at her heels, a bag in either hand. She paused and listened at corners and stairwells before moving on. The only things she heard, though, were the screams from far above.

At length she came to a long, narrow stair leading down, vanishing into the darkness.

"Wait," she said softly, and she raised her hands, cupping them before her face, blowing gently upon them, staring at them.

A faint spark occurred between her palms, faded, grew again as she whispered soft words over it.

She drew her hands apart, her lips still moving. The tiny light hung in the air before her, growing in size, increasing in brilliance. It was blue white, and it reached the intensity of several candles.

She uttered a final word and it began to move, drifting before her down the stairwell. She followed it. The servant followed her.

They descended for a long while. The stair spiraled down with no terminus in sight. The light seemed to lead them. The walls grew damp, cold, colder, coming to be covered with a fine patina of frost figures. She drew her cloak farther forward over her shoulders. The minutes passed.

Finally they reached a landing. Distant walls were barely visible in the blackness beyond her light. She turned to her left and the light moved to precede her.

They passed through a long corridor that sloped gently downward, coming after a time to another stair at a place where the walls widened on either hand and the rocky ceiling maintained its level, to vanish from sight as they descended.

The full dimensions of the chamber into which they came were not discernible. It seemed more a cavern than a room. The floor was less regular than any over which they had so far passed, and it was by far the coldest spot they had yet come to.

Holding her cloak fully closed before her now, hands beneath it, Reena proceeded into the chamber, moving diagonally to her right.

Finally a large, boxlike sled came into view, a waxy rag hanging from the point of its left runner. It stood near the wall at the mouth of a tunnel through which an icy wind roared. The light came to hover above it.

Reena halted and turned to the servant.

"Put them in there," she said, gesturing, "toward the front."

She sighed as this was done, then leaned forward and covered them over with a pelt of white fur that had lain folded upon the vehicle's seat.

"All right," she said, turning away, "we'd better be getting back now."

She pointed in the direction from which they had come and the floating light moved to follow her finger.

* * *

In the circular room at the top of the highest tower, Ridley turned the pages in one of the great books. The wind howled like a banshee above the pitched roof, which sometimes vibrated with the force of its passage. The entire tower even had a barely perceptible sway to it.

Ridley muttered softly to himself as he fingered the leather binding, casting his eyes down the creamy sheets. He no longer wore the chain with the ring on it. These now rested atop a small chest of drawers by the wall near the door, a high, narrow mirror above it catching their image, the stone glowing palely within it.

Still muttering, he turned a page, then another, and paused. He closed his eyes for a moment, then turned away, leaving the book on the reading stand. He moved to the exact center of the room and stood there for a long while, at the middle of a red diagram drawn upon the floor. He continued to mutter.

He turned abruptly and walked to the chest of drawers. He picked up the ring and chain. He unfastened the chain and removed it.

Holding the ring between the thumb and forefinger of his right hand, he extended his left forefinger and quickly slipped the ring over it. He withdrew it almost immediately and took a deep breath. He regarded his reflection in the mirror. Quickly he slipped the ring on again, paused several moments, withdrew it more slowly.

He turned the ring and studied it. Its stone seemed to shine a little more brightly now. He fitted it over his finger once more, withdrew it, paused, refitted it, withdrew it, refitted it, paused, withdrew it, replaced it, paused longer, slowly slid it partway off, then back again. . . .

Had he been looking ahead into the mirror, he might have noticed that each manipulation of the ring caused a change in expression to flit across his face. He cycled between bafflement and pleasure, fear and satisfaction as the ring came on and off.

He slipped it off again and placed it atop the chest. He massaged his finger. He glanced at himself in the mirror, looked back down, staring deep into the depths of the stone. He licked his lips.

He turned away, walked several paces across the pattern, halted. He turned and looked back at the ring. He returned and picked it up, weighing it in the palm of his right hand.

He placed it upon his finger again and stood there wearing it, still gripping it tightly with the fingers of his other hand. This time his teeth were clenched and his brow furrowed.

As he stood there, the mirror clouded and a new image began to take shape within it. Rock and snow . . . Some sort of movement across it . . . A man . . . The man was crawling through the snow. . . . No.

The man's hands grasped at holds. He drew himself upward, not forward! He was climbing, not crawling!

The picture came clearer.

As the man drew himself up and located a fresh foothold, Ridley saw that he had on green boots. Then . . .

He snapped an order. There was a distancing effect. The man grew smaller, the cliff face wider and higher. There, above the climbing man, stood the castle, this castle, his own light gleaming through this tower window!

With a curse, he tore the ring from his finger. The picture immediately faded, to be replaced by his own angry expression.

"No!" he cried, striding to the door and unfastening it. "No!"

He flung the door open and tore off down the winding stair.

Dilvish rested for a time, back and legs braced against the sides of the rock chimney, gloves in his lap, blowing on his hands, rubbing them. The chimney ended a small distance above his head. There would be no more resting after this until he reached the top, and then—who could tell?

A few flakes of snow drifted past him. He searched the dark sky, as he had been doing regularly, for a return of the flying creature, but saw nothing. The thought of it catching him in a vulnerable position had caused him considerable concern.

He continued to rub his hands until they tingled, until he felt some warmth returning. Then he donned his gloves again to preserve it. He leaned his head as far back as it would go and looked upward.

He had come over two thirds of the way up the vertical face. He sought and located his next handholds. He listened to his heartbeat, now returned to normal. Slowly, cautiously, he extended himself again, reaching.

He pushed himself upward. Leaving the chimney, he caught hold of a ledge and drew himself higher. His feet found purchase below him, and he reached again with one hand. He wondered whether Black had located a good way down. He thought of his last meal, cold and dry, almost freezing to his tongue. He recalled better fare from earlier days and felt his mouth begin to water.

He came to a slippery place, worked his way about it. He wondered at the strange feeling he had earlier, as if someone had been watching him. He had sought in the sky hurriedly, but the flying creature had been nowhere about.

Drawing himself over a thick, rocky projection, he smiled, seeing that the wall began to slant inward above it. He found his footing and leaned into the climb.

He advanced more rapidly now, and before very long a sharp edge that could be the top came into view. He scrambled toward it as the slope increased, giving thought now to his movements immediately upon reaching it.

He drew himself up faster and faster, finally rising into a low crouch as the grade grew more gentle. Nearing what he took to be the top, he slowed again, finally casting himself flat a little more than a body length below the rim. For a time, he listened, but there were no sounds other than those of the wind.

Carefully, gloves in his teeth, he drew his sword belt over an arm and shoulder, up over his head. He unfastened it and lowered it. He adjusted his garments, then fitted it in place about his waist once again.

He moved very slowly, approaching the rim. When he finally raised his head above it his eyes were filled with the gleaming white of the castle, standing like a sugary confection not too far in the distance.

Several minutes passed as he studied the scene. Nothing moved but the snow. He looked for a side door, a low window, any indirect entrance. . . .

When he thought that he had found what he was seeking, he drew himself up over the edge and began his advance.

Meg sang to the dancing rats. The torches flickered. The walls ran wet. She teased the creatures with bits of bread. She stroked them and scratched them and chuckled over them.

There came another heavy crash against the central door. This time the wood splintered somewhat about the hinges.

"Mmeg . . . Mmeg . . .!" came from beyond it, and again the large eye appeared behind the bars.

She looked up, meeting the moist blue gaze. A troubled expression came over her face.

"Yes . . . ?" she said softly.

"Meg!"

There followed another crash. The door shuddered. Cracks appeared along its edge.

"Meg!"

Another crash. The door creaked and protruded beyond its frame, the cracks widened.

She shook her head.

"Yes?" she said more loudly, a touch of excitement coming into her voice.

The rats jumped down from her lap, her shoulders, her knees, racing back and forth across the straw.

The next crash tore the door free of its hinges, pushing it a full foot outward. A large, clawed, dead-white hand appeared about its edge, chain dangling from a metal cuff about its wrist, rattling against the wall, the door. . . .

"Meg?"

She rose to her feet, dropping the remainder of the bread from within her shawl. A black whirlwind of furry bodies moved about it, the squeaking smothering her reply. She moved forward through it.

The door was thrust farther outward. A gigantic, hairless white head with a drooping carrot of a nose looked out around it. Its neck was so thick that it seemed to reach out to the points of its wide shoulders. Its arms were as big around as a man's thighs, its skin a grease-splotched albino. It shouldered the door aside and emerged, back bent at an unnatural angle, head thrust forward, moving on legs like pillars. It wore the tatters of a shirt and the rent remains of a pair of breeches that, like their owner, had lost all color. Its blue eyes, blinking and watering against the torchlight, fixed upon Meg.

"Mack . . .?" she said.

"Meg . . . ?"

"Mack!"

"Meg!"

She rushed to embrace the quarter ton of snowy muscle, her own eyes growing moist as he managed to hold her gently. They mumbled softly at one another.

Finally she took hold of his huge arm with her small hand.

"Come. Come, Mack," she said. "Food for you. Warm. Be free. Come."

She led him toward the chamber's exit, her pretty ones forgotten.

Ignored, the parchment-skinned servant moved about Reena's chambers on silent feet, gathering up strewn garments, restoring them to drawers and wardrobe. Reena sat at her dressing table, brushing her hair. When the servant had finished putting the room in order, he came and stood beside her. She glanced up, looked about.

"Very good," she said. "I have no further need of you. You may return to your coffin."

The dark-liveried figure turned and departed.

Reena rose and removed a basin from beneath the bed. Taking it to her nightstand, she added some water from a blue pitcher that stood there. Moving back to her dresser, she took up one of the candles from near the mirror and transferred it to a position to the left of the basin. Then she leaned forward and stared down at the moist surface.

Images darted there. . . . As she watched, they flowed together, fell apart, recombined. . . .

The man was nearing the top. She shuddered slightly as she watched him pause to unsling his blade and fasten it about his waist. She saw him rise further, to the very edge. She saw him survey the castle for a long while. Then he drew himself up, to move across the snow. . . . Where? Where would he seek entry?

. . . Toward the north and coming in closer, up toward the windows of that darkened storage room in back. Of course! The snow was banked highest there, and heavily crusted. He could reach the sill, draw himself up to climb upon it. It would only be the work of a few moments to knock a hole near the latch with the hilt of his weapon, reach through, and unfasten it. Then several long minutes with the blade to chip away all the ice that crusted the frame. More time to open it. Additional moments to locate the juncture of the shutters within, to slide the blade between them, lift upward, raise their latch . . . Then he would be disoriented in a dark room filled with clutter. It would take minutes more for him to negotiate that. . . .

She blew gently upon the surface of the water and the picture was gone among ripples. Taking up the candle, she bore it back to her dressing table, set it where it had been. She restored the basin to its former locale.

Seating herself before the mirror, she took up a tiny brush and a small metal box, to add a touch of color to her lips.

Ridley roused one of the servants and took him upstairs, to move along the corridor toward the room from which the screams still came. Halting before that door, he located the proper key upon a ring at his belt and unlocked it.

"At last!" came the voice from within. "Please! Now—"

"Shut up!" he said and turned away, taking the servant by the arm and turning him toward the open doorway immediately across the corridor.

He pushed the servant into the darkened room.

"Off to the side," he directed. "Stand there." He guided him further. "There—where you will be out of sight of anyone coming this way but can still keep an eye on him. Now take this key and listen carefully. Should anyone come along to investigate those screams, you must be ready. As soon as he begins to open that door, you are to emerge behind him quickly, strike him, and push him in through it—hard! Then close the door again quickly and lock it. After that you may return to your coffin."

Ridley left him, stepping out into the corridor where he hesitated a moment, then stalked off in the direction of the dining hall.

"The time is come," the face in the mirror announced, just as he entered.

He walked up to it, stared back at the grim visage. He took the ring into his hand and slipped it on.

"Silence!" he said. "You have served your purpose. Be gone now!"

The face vanished, just as its lips were beginning to form the familiar words anew, leaving Ridley to regard his own shadowy reflection surrounded by the ornate frame.

He smirked for an instant, then his face grew serious. His eyes narrowed, his image wavered. The mirror clouded and cleared again. He beheld the green-booted man standing upon a window ledge, chipping away at ice. . . .

He began to twist the ring. Slowly he turned it around and around, biting his lip the while. Then, with a jerk, he tore it from his finger and sighed deeply. The smirk returned to his reflected face.

He turned on his heel and crossed the room, where he passed through a sliding panel, a trapdoor, and down a ladder. Moving rapidly, down every shortcut he knew, he took his way once more to the servants' room.

Pushing the shutters aside, Dilvish stepped down into the room. A little light from the window at his back showed him something of the litter that resided there. He paused for several moments to memorize its disposition as best he could, then turned and drew the window shut, not closing it entirely. The heavily frosted panes blocked much of the light, but he did not want to risk betrayal by a telltale draft.

He moved silently along the map in his mind. He had sheathed his long blade and now held only a dagger in his hand. He stumbled once before he reached the door—against a jutting chair leg—but was moving so slowly that no noise ensued.

He inched the door open, looked to his right. A corridor, dark
. . .

He stepped out into it and looked to the left. There was some light
from that direction. He headed toward it. As he advanced, he saw that
it came from the right—either a side corridor or an open room.

The air grew warmer as he approached—the most welcome sensation
he had experienced in weeks. He halted, both to listen for telltale sounds
and to relish the feeling. After several moments there came the tiniest
clinking from around the corner. He edged nearer and waited again. It
was not repeated.

Knife held low, he stepped forward, saw that it was the entrance to
a room, saw a woman seated within it, reading a book, a glass of some
beverage on the small table to her right. He looked to both the right
and the left inside the doorway, saw that she was alone, stepped inside.

"You'd better not scream," he said.

She lowered her book and stared at him.

"I won't," she replied. "Who are you?"

He hesitated, then: "Call me Dilvish," he said.

"My name is Reena. What do you want?"

He lowered the blade slightly.

"I have come here to kill. Stay out of my way and you won't be
harmed. Get in it and you will. What is your place in this household?"

She paled. She studied his face.

"I am—a prisoner," she said.

"Why?"

"Our means of departure has been blocked, as has the normal means
of entrance here."

"How?"

"It was an accident—of sorts. But I don't suppose you'd believe
that."

"Why not? Accidents happen."

She looked at him strangely.

"That is what brought you, is it not?"

He shook his head slowly.

"I am afraid that I do not understand you."

"When he discovered that the mirror would no longer transport him
to this place, he sent you to slay the person responsible, did he not?"

"I was not sent," Dilvish said. "I have come here of my own will and
desire."

"Now it is I who do not understand you," said Reena. "You say that you have come here to kill, and Ridley has been expecting someone to come to kill him. Naturally—"

"Who is Ridley?"

"My brother, the apprentice sorcerer who holds this place for his master."

"Your brother is apprentice to Jelerak?"

"Please! That name!"

"I am tired of whispering it! Jelerak! Jelerak! Jelerak! If you can hear me, Jelerak, come around for a closer look! I'm ready! Let's have this out!" he called.

They were both silent for several moments, as if expecting a reply or some manifestation. Nothing happened.

Finally Reena cleared her throat.

"Your quarrel, then, is entirely with the master? Not with his servant?"

"That is correct. Your brother's doings are nothing to me, so long as they do not cross my own purposes. Inadvertently, perhaps, they have—if he has barred my enemy's way to this place. But I can't see that as a cause for vengeance. What is this transport mirror you spoke of? Has he broken it?"

"No," she replied, "it is physically intact. Though he might as well have broken it. He has somehow placed its transport spell in abeyance. It is a gateway used by the master. He employed it to bring himself here—and from here he could also use it to travel to any of his other strongholds, and probably to some other places as well. Ridley turned it off when he was—not himself."

"Perhaps he can be persuaded to turn it back on again. Then when Jelerak comes through to learn the cause of the trouble, I will be waiting for him."

She shook her head.

"It is not that simple," she said. Then: "You must be uncomfortable, standing there in a knife-fighter's crouch. I know that it makes me uncomfortable, just looking at you. Won't you sit down? Would you care for a glass of wine?"

Dilvish glanced over his shoulder.

"Nothing personal," he said, "but I prefer to remain on my feet."

He sheathed his dagger, however, and moved toward the sideboard, where an open wine bottle and several glasses stood.

"Is this what you are drinking?"

She smiled and rose to her feet. She crossed the room to stand beside him, where she took up the bottle and filled two glasses from it.

"Serve me one, sir."

He took up a glass and passed it to her, with a courtly nod. Her eyes met his as she accepted it, raised it, and drank.

He held the other glass, sniffed it, tasted it.

"Very good."

"My brother's stock," she said. "He likes the best."

"Tell me about your brother."

She turned partly and leaned back against the sideboard.

"He was chosen as apprentice from among many candidates," she said, "because he possessed great natural aptitudes for the work. Are you aware that in its higher workings, sorcery requires the assumption of an artificially constructed personality—carefully trained, disciplined, worn like a glove when doing the work?"

"Yes," Dilvish replied.

She gave him a sidelong look and continued:

"But Ridley was always different from most other people, in that he already possessed two personalities. Most of the time he is amiable, witty, interesting. Occasionally his other nature would come over him, though, and it was just the opposite—cruel, violent, cunning. After he began his work with the higher magics, this other side of himself somehow merged with his magical personality. When he would assume the necessary mental and emotional stances for his workings, it would somehow be present. He was well on his way to becoming a fine sorcerer, but whenever he worked at it he changed into something—quite unlikable. Still, this would be no great handicap, if he could put it off again as easily as he took it on—with the ring he had made for this purpose. But after a time, this—other—began to resist such a restoration. Ridley came to believe that *it* was attempting to control *him.*"

"I have heard of people like that, with more than one nature and character," Dilvish said. "What finally happened? Which side of him came to dominate?"

"The struggle goes on. He is his better self now. But he fears to face the other—which has become a personal demon to him."

Dilvish nodded and finished his wine. She gestured toward the bottle. He refilled his glass.

"So the other was in control," Dilvish said, "when he nullified the spell on the mirror."

"Yes. The other likes to leave him with bits of unfinished work, so that he will have to call him back. . . ."

"But when he was—this other—did he say why he had done what he did to the mirror? This would seem more than part of a mental struggle. He must have realized that he would be inviting trouble of the most dangerous sort—from elsewhere."

"He knew what he was doing," she said. "The other is an extraordinary egotist. He feels that he is ready to meet the master himself in a struggle for power. The denatured mirror was meant to be a challenge. Actually he told me at the time that it was meant to resolve two situations at once."

"I believe that I can guess at the second one," Dilvish said.

"Yes," she replied. "The other feels that in winning such a contest, he will also emerge as the dominant personality."

"What do you think?"

She paced slowly across the room and turned back toward him.

"Perhaps so," she said, "but I do not believe that he would win."

Dilvish drained his glass and set it aside. He folded his arms across his breast.

"Is there a possibility," he asked, "that Ridley may gain control of the other before any such conflict comes to pass?"

"I don't know. He has been trying—but he fears the other so."

"And if he should succeed? Do you feel that this might increase his chances?"

"Who can say? Not I, certainly. I'm sick of this whole business and I hate this place! I wish that I were someplace warm, like Tooma or Ankyra!"

"What would you do there?"

"I would like to be the highest-paid courtesan in town, and when I grew tired of that perhaps marry some nobleman. I'd like a life of indolence and luxury and warmth, far from the battles of adepts!"

She stared at Dilvish.

"You've some Elvish blood, haven't you?"

"Yes."

". . . And you seem to know something of these matters. So you must have come with more than a sword to face the master."

Dilvish smiled.

"I bring him a gift from Hell."

"Are you a sorcerer?"

"My knowledge of these matters is highly specialized. Why?"

"I was thinking that if you were sufficiently skilled to repair the mirror, I could use it to depart and get out of everyone's way."

Dilvish shook his head.

"Magic mirrors are not my specialty. Would that they were. It is somewhat distressing to have come all this distance in search of an enemy and then to discover that his way here is barred."

Reena laughed.

"Surely you do not believe that something like that will stop him?"

Dilvish looked up, dropped his arms, looked about him.

"What do you mean?"

"The one you seek will be inconvenienced by this state of affairs, true. But it would hardly represent an insuperable barrier. He will simply leave his body behind."

Dilvish began to pace.

"Then what's keeping him?" he asked.

"It will first be necessary for him to build his power. If he is to come here in a disembodied state, he would be at a slight disadvantage in whatever conflict ensues. It becomes necessary that he accumulate power to compensate for this."

Dilvish turned on his heel and faced her, his back to the wall.

"This is not at all to my liking," he said. "Ultimately I want something that I can cut. Not some disembodied wraith! How long will this power-building go on, do you think? When might he arrive here?"

"I cannot hear the vibrations on that plane. I do not know."

"Is there some way that we could get your brother to—"

A panel behind Dilvish slid open and a mummy-faced servant with a club struck him across the back of the head. Staggered, Dilvish began to turn. The club rose and fell again. He sank to his knees, then slumped forward onto the floor.

Ridley pushed his way past the servant and entered the room. The club wielder and a second servant came in behind him.

"Very good, sister. Very good," Ridley observed, "to detain him here until he could be dealt with."

Ridley knelt and drew the long blade from the sheath at Dilvish's side. He threw it across the room. Turning Dilvish over, he drew the dagger from the smaller sheath and raised it.

"Might as well finish things," he said.

"You're a fool!" she stated, moving to his side and taking hold of his wrist. "That man could have been an ally! He's not after you! It is the master he wants to slay! He has some personal grudge against him."

Ridley lowered the blade. She did not release his wrist.

"And you believed that?" he said. "You've been up here too long. The first man who comes along gets you to believe—"

She slapped him.

"You've no call to talk to me like that! He didn't even know who you were! He might have helped! Now he won't trust us!"

Ridley regarded Dilvish's face. Then he rose to his feet, his arm falling. He let go the dagger and kicked it across the floor. She released her grip on his wrist.

"You want his life?" he said. "All right. But if he can't trust us, we can't trust him either now." He turned to the servants, who stood motionless at his back. "Take him away," he told them, "and throw him down the hole to join Mack."

"You are compounding your mistakes," she said.

He met her gaze with a glare.

"And I am tired of your mocking," he said. "I have given you his life. Leave it at that, before I change my mind."

The servants bent and raised Dilvish's limp form between them. They bore him toward the door.

"Whether I was wrong or right about him," Ridley said, gesturing after them, "an attack will come. You know it. In one form or another. Probably soon. I have preparations to make, and I do not wish to be disturbed."

He turned as if to go.

Reena bit her lip, then said, "How close are you, to some sort of—accommodation?"

He halted, not looking back.

"Farther than I'd thought I might be," he replied, "at this point. I feel now that I do have a chance at dominating. This is why I can afford to take no risks here, and why I cannot brook any further interruptions or delays. I am returning to the tower now."

He moved toward the door, out of which Dilvish's form had just passed.

Reena lowered her head.

"Good luck," she said softly.

Ridley stalked out of the room.

The silent servants bore Dilvish along a dimly lit corridor. When they reached an indentation in the wall, they halted and lowered him to the floor. One of them entered the niche and raised a trapdoor. Returning to the still form, he helped to lift it then, and they lowered Dilvish, feet first, into the dark opening that had been revealed. They released him and he vanished from sight. One of them closed the trapdoor. They turned away and moved back along the corridor.

Dilvish was aware that he was sliding down an inclined surface. For a moment he had visions of Black's having slipped on the way up the mountain. Now he was sliding down the Tower of Ice, and when he hit the bottom . . .

He opened his eyes. He was seized by instant claustrophobia. He moved through darkness. He had felt the wall close beside him when he had taken a turn. If he reached out with his hands, he felt that the flesh would be rubbed away.

His gloves! He had tucked them behind his belt. . . .

He reached, drew them forth, began pulling them on. He leaned forward as he did so. There seemed to be a feeble patch of light ahead.

He reached out to his sides with both hands, spreading his legs as he did so.

His right heel touched the passing wall just as the palms of his hands did. Then his left . . .

Head throbbing, he increased the presure at all four points. The palms of his hands grew warm from the friction, but he slowed slightly. He pushed harder, he dug with his heels. He continued to slow.

He exerted his full strength now. The gloves were wearing through. The left one tore. His palm began to burn.

Ahead, the pale square grew larger. He realized that he was not going to be able to stop himself before he reached it. He pushed one more time. He smelled rotten straw, and then he was upon it.

He landed on his feet and immediately collapsed.

The stinging in his left hand kept him from passing out. He breathed deeply of the fetid air. He was still dazed. The back of his head was one big ache. He could not recall what had happened.

He lay there panting as his heartbeat slowed. The floor was cold beneath him. Piece by piece, the memories began to return. . . .

He recalled his climb to the castle, his entry. . . . The woman Reena . . . They had been talking. . . .

Anger flared within his breast. She had tricked him. Delayed him until help arrived for dealing with him—

But her story had been so elaborately constructed, full of unnecessary detail. . . . He wondered. Was there more to this than a simple betrayal?

He sighed.

He was not ready to think yet. Where was he?

Soft sounds came to him across the straw. Some sort of cell perhaps . . . Was there another inmate?

Something ran across his back.

He jerked partway upright, felt himself collapsing, turned to his side as he did. He saw the small, dark forms in the dim light. Rats. That was what it had been. He looked about the half of the cell that he faced. Nothing else . . .

Rolling over onto his other side, he saw the broken door.

He sat up, more carefully than before. He rubbed his head and blinked at the light. A rat drew back at the movement.

He climbed to his feet, brushed himself off. He felt after his weapons, was not surprised to find them missing.

A wave of dizziness came and went. He advanced upon the broken door, touched it.

Leaning against the frame, he peered out into the large room with frosty walls. Torches flickered in brackets at either end of it. There was an open doorway diagonally across from him, darkness beyond it.

He passed between the door and its frame, continuing to look about. There were no sounds other than the soft rat-noises behind him and the dripping of water.

He regarded the torches. The one to his left was slightly larger. He crossed to it and removed it from its bracket. Then he headed for the dark doorway.

A cold draft stirred the flames as he passed through. He was in another chamber, smaller than the one he had just quitted. Ahead he saw a stair. He advanced upon it and began to climb.

The stair took a single turn as he mounted it. At its top, he found a blank wall to his right, a wide, low-ceilinged corridor to his left. He followed the corridor.

After perhaps half a minute, he beheld what appeared to be a landing, a handrail jutting out of the wall above it. As he neared, he saw that there was an opening from which the railing emerged. Cautiously, he mounted the landing, listened for a time, peered around the corner.

Nothing. No one. Only a long, dark stair leading upward.

He transferred the torch, which was burning low, to his other hand and began to climb, quickly. This stair was much higher than the previous one, spiraling upward for a long while. He came to its ending suddenly, dropped the torch, and stepped upon its flame for a moment.

After listening at the top stair, he emerged into a hallway. This one had a long rug and wall decorations. Large tapers burned in standing holders along it. Off to his right, there was a wide stairway leading up. He moved to its foot, certain that he had come into a more frequented area of the castle.

He brushed his garments again, removed his gloves, and restored them to his belt. He ran his hand through his hair, while looking about for anything that might serve as a weapon. Seeing nothing suitable, he commenced climbing.

As he reached a landing, he heard a blood-chilling shriek from above. "Please! Oh, please! The pain!"

He froze, one hand on the railing, the other reaching for a blade that was not there.

A full minute passed. Another began. The cry was not repeated. There were no further sounds of any sort from that direction.

Alert, he began to move again, staying close to the wall, testing each step before placing his full weight upon it.

When he reached the head of the stair, he checked the corridor in both directions. It appeared to be empty. The cry had seemed to come from somewhere off to the right. He went that way.

As he advanced, a sudden soft sobbing began from some point to his left and ahead. He approached the slightly ajar door from behind which it seemed to be occurring. Stooping, he applied his eye to the large keyhole. There was illumination within, but nothing to view save for an undecorated section of wall and the edge of a small window.

Straightening, he turned to search again for some weapon.

The large servant's approach had been totally soundless, and he towered above him now, club already descending.

Dilvish blocked the blow with his left forearm. The other's rush carried him forward to collide with Dilvish, however, bearing him backward against the door, which flew wide, and through it into the room beyond.

Dilvish heard a cry from behind him as he strove to rise. At the same time the door was drawn shut, and he heard a key slipped into the lock.

"A victim! He sends me a victim when what I want is release!" There followed a sigh. "Very well . . ."

Dilvish turned as soon as he heard the voice, his memory instantly drawing him back to another place.

Bright red body, long, thin limbs, a claw upon each digit, it had pointed ears, backward-curving horns, and slitted yellow eyes. It crouched at the center of a pentacle, constantly shuffling its feet this way and that, reaching for him. . . .

"Stupid wight!" he snapped, lapsing into another tongue. "Would you destroy your deliverer?"

The demon drew back its arms, and the pupils of its eyes expanded.

"Brother! I did not know you in human form!" it answered in Mabrahoring, the language of demons. "Forgive me!"

Dilvish climbed slowly to his feet.

"I've a mind to let you rot there, for such a reception!" he replied, looking around the chamber.

The room was done up for such work, Dilvish now saw, everything still in its place. Upon the far wall there was a large mirror within an intricately worked metal frame. . . .

"Forgive!" the demon cried, bowing low. "See how I abase myself! Can you really free me? Will you?"

"First tell me how you came into this unhappy state," Dilvish said.

"Ah! It was the young sorcerer in this place. He is mad! Even now I see him in his tower, toying with his madness! He is two people in one! One day one must win over the other. But until then, he begins works and leaves them undone—such as summoning my poor self to this accursed place, forcing me upon this doubly accursed pentacle, and taking his thrice accursed self away without dismissing me! Oh! were I free to rend him! Please! The pain! Release me!"

"I, too, have known something of pain," said Dilvish, "and you will endure this for more questioning."

He gestured.

"Is that the mirror used for travel?"

"Yes! Yes, it is!"

"Could you repair the damage it has endured?"

"Not without the aid of the human operator who laid the counter-spell. It is too strong."

"Very well. Rehearse your oaths of dismissal now and I will do the things necessary to release you."

"Oaths? Between us? Ah! I see! You fear I envy you that body you wear! Perhaps you are wise. . . . As you would. My oaths . . ."

". . . To include everyone in this household," Dilvish said.

"Ah!" it howled. "You would deprive me of my vengeance on the crazy sorcerer!"

"They are all mine now," Dilvish said. "Do not try to bargain with me!"

A crafty look came over the demon's face.

"Oh . . . ?" it said. "Oh! I see! Yours . . . Well, at least there will be vengeance—with much good rending and shrieking, I trust. That will be sufficient. Knowing that makes it much easier to renounce all claims. My oaths . . ."

It began the grisly litany, and Dilvish listened carefully for deviations from the necessary format. There were none.

Dilvish commenced speaking the words of dismissal. The demon hugged itself and bowed its head.

When he had finished, Dilvish looked back at the pentacle. The demon was gone from that place, but it was still present in the room. It stood in a corner, smiling an ingratiating smile.

Dilvish cocked his head.

"You are free," he said. "Go!"

"A moment, great lord!" it said, cowering. "It is good to be free and I thank you. I know, too, that only one of the greater ones of Below could have worked this release in the absence of a human sorcerer. So I would grovel and curry your favor a moment longer in the way of warning you. The flesh may have dulled your normal senses, and I bid you know that I feel the vibrations on another plane now. Something terrible is coming this way—and unless you are a part of its workings, or it of yours—I felt that you must be warned, great one!"

"I knew of it," Dilvish said, "but I am pleased that you have told me. Blast the door's lock if you would do me a final service. Then you may go."

"Thank you! Remember Quennel in the days of your wrath—and that he served you here!"

The demon turned and seemed to blow apart like fog in a wind, to the accompaniment of a dull, roaring sound. A moment later there came a sharp, snapping noise from the direction of the door.

Dilvish crossed the room. The lock had been shattered.

He opened the door and looked out. The corridor was empty. He hesitated as he considered both directions. Then, with a slight shrugging movement, he turned to the right and headed that way.

He came, after a time, to a great, empty dining hall, a fire still smouldering upon its hearth, wind whistling down the chimney. He circled the entire room, moving along the walls, past the windows, the mirror, returning to the spot from which he had begun, none of the wall niches proving doorways to anywhere else.

He turned and headed back up the corridor. As he did, he heard his name spoken in a whisper. He halted. The door to his left was partly ajar. He turned his head in that direction. It had been a woman' voice.

"It's me, Reena."

The door opened farther. He saw her standing there holding a long blade. She extended her arm.

"Your sword. Take it!" she said.

He took the weapon into his hands, inspected it, sheathed it.

". . . And your dagger."

He repeated the process.

"I am sorry," she said, "about what happened. I was as surprised as you. It was my brother's doing, not mine."

"I think I am willing to believe you," he said. "How did you locate me?"

"I waited until I was certain that Ridley was back in his tower. Then I sought you in the cells below, but you had already gone. How did you get out?"

"Walked out."

"You mean you found the door that way?"

"Yes."

He heard her sharp intake of breath, almost a gasp.

"That is not at all good," she said. "It means that Mack is certainly abroad."

"Who is Mack?"

"Ridley's predecessor as apprentice here. I am not certain what happened to him—whether he tried some experiment that simply did not work out, or whether his transformation was a punishment of the master's for some indiscretion. Whichever, he was changed into a dull-witted beast and had to be imprisoned down there, because of his great strength and occasional recollection of some noxious spell. His woman went barmy after that. She's still about. A minor adept herself, at one time. We've got to get out of here."

"You may be right," he said, "but finish the story."

"Oh. I've been looking all over for you since then. As I was about it, I noticed that the demon had stopped screaming. I came and investigated. I saw that he had been freed. I was fairly certain that Ridley was still in the tower. It *was* you, wasn't it?"

"Yes, I released it."

"I thought then that you might still be near, and I heard someone moving in the dining hall. So I hid in here and waited to see who it was. I brought you your weapons to show that I meant you no ill."

"I appreciate it. I am only now deciding what to do. I am sure you have some suggestions."

"Yes. I've a feeling that the master will come here soon and slay every living thing under these roofs. I do not want to be around when that occurs."

"As a matter of fact, he should be here very soon. The demon told me."

"It is hard to tell what you know and what you do not know," she said, "what you can do and what you cannot do. Obviously you know something of the arts. Do you intend to stay and face him?"

"That was my purpose in traveling all this distance," he replied. "But I meant to face him in the flesh, and if I did not find him here I meant to use whatever means of magical transportation might be present to seek him in others of his strongholds. I do not know how my special presents will affect him in a disembodied state. I know that my blade will not."

"You would be wise," she said, taking his arm, "very wise, to live to fight another day."

"Especially if you need my help in getting away from here?" he asked.

She nodded.

"I do not know what your quarrel with him may be," she said, leaning against him, "and you are a strange man, but I do not think you can hope to win against him here. He will have amassed great power, fearing the worst. He will come in cautiously—so cautiously! I know a possible way away, if you will help. But we must hurry. He could even be here right now. He—"

"How very astute of you, dear girl" came a dry, throaty voice from back up the hall, whence Dilvish had come.

Recognizing it, he turned. A dark-cowled figure stood just beyond the entrance within the dining hall.

"And you," he stated, "Dilvish! You are a most difficult person to be rid of, bloodling of Selar, though it has been a long while between encounters."

Dilvish drew his blade. An Awful Saying rose to his lips but he refrained from speaking it, not certain that what he saw represented an actual physical presence.

"What new torment might I devise for you?" the other asked. "A transformation? A degeneration? A—"

Dilvish began to move toward him, ignoring his words. From behind him he heard Reena whisper, "Come back. . . ."

He continued on toward the form of his enemy.

"I was nothing to you . . ." Dilvish began.

"You disturbed an important rite."

". . . and you took my life and threw it away. You visited a terrible vengeance upon me as casually as another man might brush away a mosquito."

"I was annoyed, as another man might be at a mosquito."

"You treated me as if I were a thing, not a person. That I cannot forgive."

A soft chuckle emerged from within the cowl.

"And it would seem that in my own defense now I must treat you that way again."

The figure raised its hand, pointing two fingers at him.

Dilvish broke into a run, raising his blade, recalling Black's spell of protection and still loathe to commence his own.

The extended fingers seemed to glow for a moment and Dilvish felt something like a passing wind. That was all.

"Are you but an illusion of this place?" the other asked, beginning to back away, a tiny quavering note apparent in his voice for the first time.

Dilvish swung his blade but encountered nothing. The figure was no longer before him. Now it stood among shadows at the far end of the dining hall.

"Is this thing yours, Ridley?" he heard him ask suddenly. "If so, you are to be commended for dredging up something I'd no desire whatever to recall. It shan't distract me, though, from the business at hand. Show yourself, if you dare!"

Dilvish heard a sliding sound from off to his left, and a panel opened there. He saw the slim figure of a younger man emerge, a shining ring upon the left forefinger.

"Very well. We shall dispense with these theatrics," came Ridley's voice. He seemed slightly out of breath and striving to control it. "I am master of myself and this place," he continued. He turned toward Dilvish. "You, wight! You have served me well. There is absolutely nothing more for you to do here, for it is between the two of us now. I give you leave to depart and assume your natural form. You may take the girl back with you as payment."

Dilvish hesitated.

"Go, I say! Now!"

Dilvish backed from the room.

"I see that you have cast aside all remorse," he heard Jelerak say, "and learned the necessary hardness. This should prove interesting."

Dilvish saw a low wall of fire spring up between the two of them. He heard laughter from the hall—whose, he was not certain. Then came a crackling sound and a wave of peculiar odors. Suddenly the room was a blaze of light. Just as suddenly it was plunged into darkness again. The laughter continued. He heard pieces of tile falling from the walls.

He turned away. Reena was still standing where he had left her.

"He did it," she said softly. "He has control of the other. He really did it. . . ."

"We can do no good here," Dilvish stated. "It is, as he said, between them now."

"But his new strength may still not be sufficient!"

"I'd imagine he knows that, and that that is why he wants me to take you away."

The floor shook beneath them. A picture dropped from a nearby wall.

"I don't know that I can leave him like that, Dilvish."

"He may be giving his life for you, Reena. He might have used his new powers to repair the mirror, or to escape this place by some other means. You heard how he put things. Would you throw away his gift?"

Her eyes filled with tears.

"He may never know," she said, "how much I really wanted him to succeed."

"I've a feeling he might," Dilvish said. "Now, how are we to save you?"

"Come this way," she said, taking his arm, as a hideous scream came from the hall, followed by a thunderclap that seemed to shake the entire castle.

Colored lights glowed behind them as she led him along the corridor.

"I've a sled," she said, "in a cavern deep below here. It is filled with supplies."

"How—" Dilvish began, and he halted, raising the blade that he bore.

An old woman stood before them at the head of the stair, glaring at him. But his eyes had slid beyond her, to behold the great pale bulk that slowly mounted the last few stairs, head turned in their direction.

"There, Mack!" she screamed suddenly. "The man who hit me! Hurt my side! Crush him!"

Dilvish directed the point of his blade at the advancing creature's throat.

"If he attacks me, I will kill him," he said. "I do not want to, but the choice is not mine. It is yours. He may be big and strong, but he is not fast. I have seen him move. I will make a very big hole, and a lot of blood will come out of it. I heard that you once loved him, lady. What are you going to do?"

Forgotten emotions flickered across Meg's features.

"Mack! Stop!" she cried. "He's not the one. I was wrong!"

Mack halted.

"Not—the—one?" he said.

"No. I was—mistaken."

She turned her gaze up the hallway to where fountains of fires flashed and vanished and where multitudes of cries, as of two opposing armies, rang out.

"What," she said, gesturing, "is it?"

"The young master and the old master," Reena said, "are fighting."

"Why are you still afraid to say his name?" Dilvish asked. "He's just up the corridor. It's Jelerak."

"Jelerak?" A new light came into Mack's eyes as he gestured toward the awful room. "Jelerak?"

"Yes," Dilvish replied, and the pale one turned away from him and began shuffling in that direction.

Dilvish looked about for Meg, but she was gone. Then he heard a cry of "Jelerak! Kill!" from overhead.

He looked up and saw the green-winged creature that had attacked him—how long ago?—flapping off in the same direction.

"They are probably going to their deaths," Reena said.

"How long do you think they have waited for such an opportunity?" he said. "I am sure that they know that they lost a long time ago. But just to have the chance now is winning, for them."

"Better in there than on your blade."

Dilvish turned away.

"I am not at all sure that *he* wouldn't have killed *me,*" he said. "Where are we going?"

"This way."

She took him down the stair and up another corridor, heading toward the north end of the building. The entire place began shaking about them as they went. Furniture toppled, windows shattered, a beam fell. Then it was still again for a time. They hurried.

As they were nearing the kitchen, the place shook again with such violence that they were thrown to the floor. A fine dust was drifting everywhere now, and cracks had appeared in the walls. In the kitchen they saw that hot ashes had been thrown from the grate, to lay strewn about the floor, smoking.

"It sounds as if Ridley is still holding his own."

"Yes, it does," she said, smiling.

Pots and pans were rattling and banging together as they departed the kitchen, heading in the direction of the stairwell. The cutlery danced in its drawers.

They paused at the stair's entrance, just as a great, inhuman moan swept through the entire castle. An icy draft followed moments later. A rat flashed past them from the direction of the kitchen.

Reena signaled Dilvish to halt and, leaning against the wall, cupped
her hands before her face. She seemed to whisper within them, and a
moment after the small fire was born, to hover, growing, before her. She
moved her hands outward and it drifted toward the stairwell.

"Come," she said to Dilvish, and she led the way downward.

He moved behind her, and from time to time the walls creaked
ominously about them. When this happened, the light danced for a
moment, and occasionally it faded briefly. As they descended, the
sounds from above grew more muffled. Dilvish paused once, to place
his hand upon the wall.

"Is it far?" he asked.

"Yes. Why?"

"I can still feel the vibrations strongly," he said. "We must be well
below the level of the castle itself—down into the mountain by now."

"True," she replied, taking another turn.

"At first I feared that they might bring the castle down upon our
heads. . . ."

"They probably *will* destroy the place if this goes on much longer,"
she said. "I'm very proud of Ridley—despite the inconvenience."

"That wasn't exactly what I meant," Dilvish said, as they continued
their downward flight. "There! It's getting worse!" He put out a hand
to steady himself as the stair shuddered from a passing shockwave.
"Doesn't it seem to you that the entire mountain is shaking?"

"Yes, it does," she replied. "Then it must be true."

"What?"

"I'd heard it said that ages ago, at the height of his power, the
ma—Jelerak—actually raised this mountain by his conjuring."

"So?"

"If he is sufficiently taxed in this place, I suppose that he might have
to draw upon those ancient spells of his for more power. In which
case—"

"The mountain might collapse as well as the castle?"

"There is that possibility. Oh, Ridley! Good show!"

"It won't be so good if we're under it!"

"True," she said, suddenly moving even faster. "As he's not *your*
brother, I can see your point. Still, it must please you to see Jelerak so
hard pressed."

"It does that," Dilvish admitted, "but you should really prepare
yourself for any eventuality."

She was silent for a time.

Then: "Ridley's death?" she asked. "Yes. I've realized for some time now that there was a strong possibility of this, whatever the nature of their encounter. Still, to go out with such flare . . . That's something, too, you know."

"Yes," Dilvish replied. "I've thought of it many times myself."

Abruptly, they reached the landing. She turned immediately and led him toward a tunnel. The rocky floor trembled beneath them. The light danced again. From somewhere there came a slow, grinding sound, lasting for perhaps ten seconds. They rushed into the tunnel.

"And you?" she said, as they hurried along it. "If Jelerak survives, will you still seek him?"

"Yes," he said. "I know for certain that he has at least six other citadels. I know the approximate locations of several of them. I would seek them as I did this place."

"I have been in three of the others," she said. "If we survive this, I can tell you something about them. They would not be easy to storm either."

"It does not matter," Dilvish said. "I never thought that it would be easy. If he lives, I will go to them. If I cannot locate him, I will destroy them, one by one, until he must need come to me."

The grinding sound came again. Fragments of rocks fell about them. As this occurred, the floating light vanished before them.

"Remain still," she said. "I'll do another."

Several moments later another light glowed between her hands.

They continued on, the sounds within the rock ceasing for a time.

"What will you do if Jelerak is dead?" she asked him.

Dilvish was silent awhile. Then: "Visit my homeland," he said. "It has been a long while since I have been back. What will you do if we make it away from here?"

"Tooma, Ankyra, Blostra," she replied, "as I'd said, if I could find some willing gentleman to escort me to one of them."

"I believe that could be arranged," Dilvish said.

As they neared the end of the tunnel, an enormous shudder ran through the entire mountain. Reena stumbled; Dilvish caught her and was thrown back against the wall. With his shoulders, he felt the heavy vibrations within the stone. From behind them a steady crashing of falling rocks began.

"Hurry!" he said, propelling her forward.

The light darted drunkenly before them. They came into a cold cavern.

"This is the place," Reena said, pointing. "The sled is over there."

Dilvish saw the vehicle, took hold of her arm, and headed toward it.

"How high up the mountain are we?" he asked her.

"Two thirds of the way, perhaps," she said. "We are somewhat below the point where the rise steepens severely."

"That is still no gentle slope out there," he said, coming to a halt beside the vehicle and placing his hand upon its side. "How do you propose getting it down to ground level?"

"That will be the difficult part," she said, reaching within her bodice and withdrawing a folded piece of parchment. "I've removed this page from one of the books in the tower. When I had the servants build me this sled, I knew that I would need something strong to draw it. This is a fairly elaborate spell, but it will summon a demon beast to do our bidding."

"May I see it?"

She passed him the page. He unfolded it and held it near to the hovering light.

"This spell requires fairly lengthy preparations," he said a little later. "I don't believe we have that kind of time remaining, the way things are shaking and crumbling here."

"But it is the only chance we have," she said. "We'll need these supplies. I had no way of knowing that the whole damned mountain was going to start coming apart. We are simply going to have to risk the delay."

Dilvish shook his head and returned the page.

"Wait here," he said, "and don't start that spell yet!"

He turned and made his way along the tunnel down which icy blasts blew. Snow crystals lay upon the floor. After a single, brief turn, he saw the wide cave mouth, pale light beyond it. The floor there had a heavy coating of snow over ice.

He walked to the entrance and looked out, looked down. The sled could be edged over the lip of the ridge at his feet at a low place off to his left. But then it would simply take off, achieving a killing speed long before it reached the foot of the mountain.

He moved forward to the very edge, looked up. An overhang prevented his seeing anything above. He moved half a dozen paces to his left then, looked out, looked up, looked around. Then he crossed to the right-hand extremity of the ledge and looked up, shading his eyes against a blast of ice crystals.

There . . . ?

"Black!" he called, to a darker patch of shadow above and to the side. "Black!"

It seemed to stir. He cupped his hands and shouted again.

"Diiil . . . viish!" rolled down the slope toward him, after his own cry had died away.

"Down here!"

He waved both arms above his head.

"I . . . see . . . you!"

"Can you come to me?"

There was no answer, but the shadow moved. It came down from its ledge and began a slow, stiff-legged journey in his direction.

He remained in sight. He continued waving.

Soon Black's silhouette became clear through the swirling snow. He advanced steadily. He passed the halfway point, continued on.

As he came up beside him, Black pulsed heat for several moments and the snow melted upon him, trickling off down his sides.

"There are some amazing sorceries going on above," he stated, "well worth observing."

"Far better we do it from a distance," Dilvish said. "This whole mountain may be coming down."

"Yes, it will," Black said. "Something up there is drawing upon some very elemental, ancient spells woven all through here. It is most instructive. Get on my back and I'll take you down."

"It is not that simple."

"Oh?"

"There is a girl—and a sled—in the cave behind me."

Black placed his forefeet upon the ledge and heaved himself up to stand beside Dilvish.

"Then I had better have a look," he stated. "How did you fare up on top?"

Dilvish shrugged.

"All of that would most likely have happened without me," he said, "but at least I've the pleasure of seeing someone giving Jelerak a hard time."

"That's him up there?"

They started back into the cave.

"His body is elsewhere, but the part that bites has paid a visit."

"Who is he fighting?"

"The brother of the lady you are about to meet. This way."

They took the turn and headed back in the larger cave. Reena still stood beside the sled. She had wrapped herself in a fur. Black's metal hooves clicked upon the rock.

"You wanted a demon beast?" Dilvish said to her. "Black, this is Reena. Reena, meet Black."

Black bowed his head.

"I am pleased," he said. "Your brother has been providing me with considerable amusement while I waited without."

Reena smiled and reached out to touch his neck.

"Thank you," she said. "I am delighted to know you. Can you help us?"

Black turned and regarded the sled.

"Backward," he said after a time. Then: "If I were hitched facing it, I could draw back slightly and let it precede me down the mountain. You would both have to walk, though—beside me, holding on. I don't believe I could do it with you in the thing. Even this way it will be difficult, but I see it to be the only way."

"Then we'd better push it out and get started," Dilvish said, as the mountain shook again.

Reena and Dilvish each took hold of a side of the vehicle. Black leaned against its rear. It began to move.

Once they reached the snow on the cave floor, it proceeded more easily. Finally they turned it about at the cave mouth and hitched Black between its traces.

Carefully, gently then, they edged its rear end over the ledge at the low place to the left as Black advanced slowly, maintaining tension on the traces.

Its runners struck the snow of the slope, and Black eased it down until it rested full length upon it. Gingerly he followed it then, jerking stiffly upright to anchor it after he had jumped the last few feet.

"All right," he said. "Come down now and take hold of me on either side."

They followed him and took up their positions. Slowly he began to advance.

"Tricky," he said as they moved. "One day they will invent names for the properties of objects, such as the tendency of a thing to move once it is placed in motion."

"Of what use would that be?" Reena asked. "Everybody already knows that that's what happens."

"Ah! But one might put numbers to the amount of material involved and the amount of pushing required, and come up with wondrous and useful calculations."

"Sounds like a lot of trouble for a small return," she said. "Magic's a lot easier to figure."

"Perhaps you're right."

Steadily they descended, Black's hooves crunching through the icy crust. Later, when they finally reached a place from which they could view the castle, they saw that the highest tower and several low ones had fallen. Even as they watched, a section of wall collapsed. Fragments of it fell over the edge, fortunately descending the slope far to their right.

Beneath the snow the mountain itself was shaking steadily now, and had been for some time. Rocks and chunks of ice occasionally bounded past them.

They continued for what seemed an interminable time, Black edging the sled lower and lower with each step, Reena and Dilvish plodding numb-footed beside him.

As they neared the foot of the slope, a terrific crash echoed about them. Looking up, they saw the remains of the castle crumbling, shrinking, falling in upon itself.

Black increased his pace dangerously as small bits of debris began to rain about them.

"When we reach bottom," he said, "unhitch me immediately, but stay on the far side of the sled while you're doing it. I would be able to turn its side to the slope as we get there. Then, if you can hitch me properly in a hurry, do it. If the falling stuff becomes too severe, though, just crouch down on the far side and I will stand on the near one to help shield you. But if you can rehitch me, get in quickly and stay low."

They slid most of the final distance, and for a moment it seemed that the sled would turn over as Black maneuvered it. Picking himself up, Dilvish immediately set to work upon the harness.

Reena got behind the sled and looked upward.

"Dilvish! Look!" she cried.

Dilvish glanced upward as he finished the unfastening and Black backed out from between the traces. The castle had completely vanished and large fissures had appeared in the slope. Above the summit of the mountain, two columns of smoke now stood—a dark one and a light one—motionless despite the winds that must be lashing at them.

Black turned and backed in between the traces. Dilvish began harnessing him again. More debris was now descending the slope, off to their right.

"What is it?" Dilvish said.

"The dark column is Jelerak," Black replied.

Dilvish looked back periodically as he worked, seeing that the two columns had begun to move, slowly, toward one another. Soon they were intertwined, though not merging, twisting and knotting about one another like a pair of struggling serpents.

Dilvish completed the harnessing.

"Get in!" he cried to Reena, as another part of the mountain fell away.

"You, too!" said Black, and Dilvish climbed in with her.

Soon they were moving, gathering speed. The top of the ice mass came apart as they watched, and still the billowing combatants rolled above it.

"Oh, no! Ridley seems to be weakening!" she said, as they raced away.

Dilvish watched as the dark column seemed to bear the lighter one downward into the heart of the falling mountain.

Black's pace increased, though chunks of rubble still skidded and raced about them. Soon both smoky combatants were gone from sight, high above them. Black moved faster yet, heading south.

Perhaps a quarter of an hour passed with no change in the prospect behind them, save for its dwindling. But crouched beneath the furs, Dilvish and Reena still watched. An air of anticipation seemed to grow over the entire landscape.

When it came, it rocked the ground, bouncing the sled from side to side, and its tremors continued for a long while after.

The top of the mountain blew off, peppering the sky with an expanding, dark cloud. Then the dusky smear was streaked, spread by the winds, sections of it reaching like slowly extending fingers to the west. After a time a mighty shock wave rolled over them.

Much later, a single, attenuated, rough-edged cloud—the dark one—separated itself from the haze. Trailing ragged plumes, jounced by the winds, it moved like an old man stumbling, fleeing southward. It passed far to the right of them and did not pause.

"That's Jelerak," Black said. "He's hurt."

They watched the rough column until it jerked out of sight far to the south. Then they turned again toward the ruin in the north. They watched until it faded from view, but the white column did not rise again.

Finally Reena lowered her head. Dilvish put his arm about her shoulders. The runners of the sled sang softly on their way across the snow.